D0831034

select editions

Reader's Digest

The condensations in this volume
are published with the consent of the authors
and the publishers © 2010 Reader's Digest, Inc.

www.readersdigest.co.uk

Published in the United Kingdom by Vivat Direct Limited
(t/a Reader's Digest), 157 Edgware Road,
London W2 2HR

For information as to ownership of
copyright in the material of this book,
and acknowledgments, see last page.

Printed in Germany
ISBN 978 0 276 44443 2

select
editions

THE READER'S DIGEST ASSOCIATION, INC.

contents

the scarecrow
michael connelly

9

Veteran reporter Jack McEvoy has been fired from the *Los Angeles Times* and given one final task to accomplish: he must train his pretty, ambitious replacement. But Jack's chosen a different exit. He's going for the scoop of a lifetime, and heading into danger.

rainwater
sandra brown

173

Ella Barron is a single mother struggling through the Depression in a small town in Texas, so she's pleased when a courteous stranger requests a room in her boarding house. But Mr Rainwater is about to have a far greater impact on her life than she could ever imagine.

where the shadows lie
michael ridpath

305

Amid Iceland's wild, volcanic landscape, rumours abound concerning an 800-year-old manuscript inscribed with a long-lost saga about a ring of terrible power. A rediscovered saga alone would be worth a fortune, but this one holds a secret worth killing for.

the art of racing in the rain
garth stein

479

This is the moving story of a loving family, how they almost fell apart, and how they were brought back together by the wisest and most loyal member—Enzo. Have you ever looked at a dog and wondered if there might be more to him than meets the eye?

author in focus

One of the books in this collection is, well, a little unusual. The thing is, we don't often select stories that are told by dogs. As a matter of fact, you can count on one hand the number of books in Select Editions that have had dogs as their narrator. Come to think of it, there's just one—this one—*The Art of Racing in the Rain.* Garth Stein's extraordinary novel has captured hearts and minds and is a publishing phenomenon. We think you'll be enthralled by the 'fly on the wall' view of his marvellous canine narrator.

in the spotlight

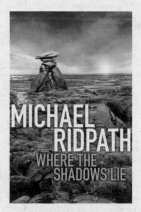

When Michael Ridpath was busy writing *Where the Shadows Lie*, he gave little thought to Eyjafjallajökull, the slumbering, glacier-topped volcano. It had erupted just twice since the Vikings settled in Iceland in the ninth century, but was about to erupt violently in March 2010. Strong winds whipped clouds of black, grey and white ash up into the North Atlantic jet-stream forcing closure of one of the world's busiest flight paths. 'My wife was in Beijing and my daughter was in America,' says Ridpath, 'and I wondered how were they going to get home. I think that with the eruption and the credit crunch, Iceland has been performing some attention-seeking tantrums.'

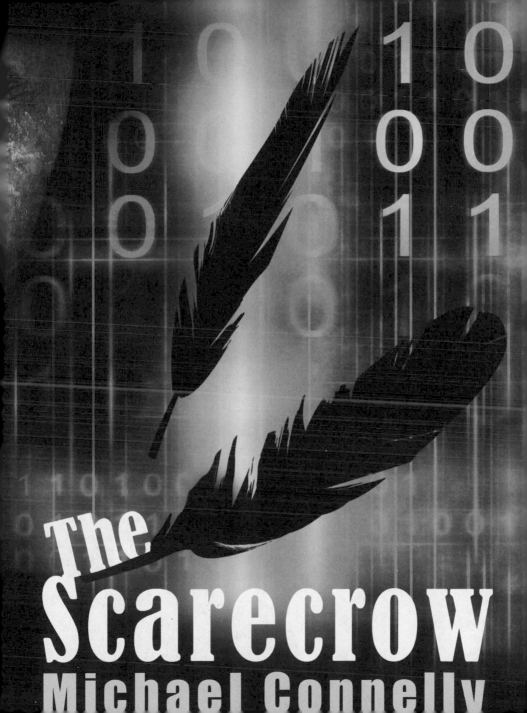

The Scarecrow

Michael Connelly

Recession has hit the *Los Angeles Times* and the editor has given Jack McEvoy a month's notice and one final assignment. But Jack's decided he's going to go out with a scoop. He's going to write a story that will win journalism's highest award—a Pulitzer prize. But he's unaware that the murder he's delving into is going to lead him into danger, bringing him up against an individual who exists beneath the police and FBI radar—the Scarecrow.

One: The Farm

arver paced in the control room, watching over the front forty. The towers were spread out before him in perfect neat rows. They hummed quietly and efficiently and, even with all he knew, he had to marvel at what technology had wrought. So much in so little space. Not a stream but a swift torrent of data flowing by him every day. Growing in front of him in tall steel stalks. All he need do was reach in to look and to choose. It was like panning for gold.

But it was easier.

He checked the overhead temperature gauges. All was perfect in the server room. He lowered his eyes to the screens on the work stations in front of him. His three engineers worked in concert on the current project. An attempted breach thwarted by Carver's skill and readiness. Now the reckoning.

The would-be intruder could not penetrate the walls of the farm, but he had left his fingerprints. Carver smiled as he watched his men retrieve the breadcrumbs, tracing the IP address through the traffic nodes, a high-speed chase back to the source. Soon Carver would know who his opponent was, what firm he was with, what he had been looking for, and the advantage he hoped to gain. And Carver would take a retaliatory action that would leave the hapless contender crumpled and destroyed. Carver showed no mercy. Ever.

The mantrap alert buzzed from overhead.

'Screens,' Carver said.

The three young men at the work stations typed commands that hid their work from the visitors. The control-room door opened and Declan

McGinnis stepped in with a man in a suit. Carver had never seen him before.

'This is our control room and through the windows there you see what we call the "front forty",' McGinnis said. 'All of our colocation services are centred here. This is primarily where your firm's material would be held. We have forty towers in here holding close to a thousand dedicated servers.'

The man in the suit nodded. 'Our main concern is security.'

'Yes, this is why we stepped in here. I wanted you to meet Wesley Carver. Wesley is our chief technology officer as well as our top threat engineer and the designer of the data centre. He can tell you all you need to know about colocation security.'

Carver shook the suit's hand. He was introduced as David Wyeth of the St Louis law firm, Mercer and Gissal. It sounded like crisp white shirts and tweed.

Carver gave Wyeth the show by rote, saying everything the lawyer wanted to hear. Wyeth would go back to St Louis and report on how impressed he had been. He would tell them that this was the way to go if the firm wanted to keep up with changing technologies and times. And McGinnis would get another contract.

All the while he spoke, Carver was thinking about the intruder they had been chasing. Out there somewhere, not expecting the comeuppance that was speeding towards him. Carver and his young disciples would loot his personal bank accounts, take his identity and hide photos of men having sex with eight-year-old boys on his work computer. Then he would crash it with a replicating virus. When the intruder couldn't fix it he would call in an expert. The photos would be found. The police would be called.

The intruder would no longer be a concern. Another threat kept away by the Scarecrow.

'Wesley?' McGinnis said.

Carver came out of the reverie. 'Excuse me?'

'Mr Wyeth asked if the colocation centre had ever been breached.'

McGinnis was smiling, already knowing the answer. 'No, sir, we've never been breached. There have been a few attempts. But they have failed, resulting in disastrous consequences for those who tried.'

The suit nodded sombrely. 'We represent the cream of the crop of St Louis,' he said. 'The integrity of our files and our client list is paramount to all we do. That's why I came here personally.'

Carver smiled but there was no warmth in it. 'Don't worry, Mr Wyeth,' he said. 'Your crops will be safe on this farm.'

Wyeth smiled back. 'That's what I wanted to hear,' he said.

Two: The Velvet Coffin

Every eye in the newsroom followed me as I left Kramer's office and walked back to my pod. The pink slips always came out on Fridays and they all knew I had just got *the word*. Except they weren't called pink slips any more. Now they called them RIF forms– –reduction in force.

I met no one's stare as I passed the Metro sign and headed back into pod-land. I moved into my cubicle and slipped into my seat, dropping from sight like a soldier diving into a foxhole.

Immediately my phone buzzed. On the read-out I saw that it was my friend Larry Bernard calling. He was only two cubicles away but knew if he had come to me in person it would have been a clear signal for others in the newsroom to crowd round me and ask the obvious. Reporters work best in packs like that.

I put on my headset and picked up the call.

'Hey, Jack,' he said.

'Hey, Larry,' I said.

'So? What did Kramer want?'

He pronounced the managing editor's name as *Crammer*, which was the nickname bestowed on Richard Kramer years earlier when he was an assignment editor more concerned with the quantity rather than the quality of news he got his reporters to produce.

'You know what he wanted. He gave me notice. I'm out of here.'

'Damn, you got pinked! Do you have to clear out right now?'

'No, I've got two weeks. May 22nd and I'm history.'

'Two weeks? Why two weeks?'

Most RIF victims had to clear out immediately.

'They gave me two weeks if I agreed to train my replacement.'

Larry was silent for a moment as he considered the humiliation of having to train one's own replacement. But to me two weeks' pay was two weeks' pay.

'So that's it? That's all he said? Two weeks and you're out?'

'He said I was a handsome guy, that I should try TV.'

'Oh, man. We gotta go out and get drunk tonight. This ain't right. Who's your replacement?'

'Angela Cook.'

'Figures. The cops are going to love her.'

Larry was a friend but I didn't want to be talking about all of this with him right now. I needed to be thinking about my options.

'What are you going to do?' Larry asked.

'I haven't thought about it but I'm about to now. Where do you want to go, Big Wang's or the Short Stop?'

'Short Stop. I was at Wang's last night.'

'See you there then.'

I was about to hang up when Larry blurted out a last question.

'One more thing. Did he say what number you were?'

Of course, he wanted to know what his own chances were of surviving this latest round of corporate bloodletting.

'He said I almost made it. I was ninety-nine.'

Two months earlier the newspaper announced that 100 employees would be eliminated from the editorial staff in order to cut costs and make our corporate gods happy.

'My tip is to keep your head down, Larry. The axeman's looking for number one hundred right now.'

I hit the disconnect button but kept the headset on. This would hopefully discourage anybody in the newsroom from approaching me. I had to concentrate on finishing a short on the arrest of a suspect in a murder-for-hire plot. Then I could disappear from the newsroom and head to the bar to toast the end of my career in daily journalism. Because that's what it was going to be. There was no newspaper out there in the market for a forty-four-year-old cop-shop reporter. Not when they had an endless supply of cheap labour—baby reporters like Angela Cook minted fresh every year at the

University of Southern California and Medill and Columbia. Like the paper-and-ink newspaper itself, my time was over. It was about the Internet now. It was about hourly uploads to online editions and blogs. The morning paper might as well be called the *Daily Afterthought*.

My phone buzzed in my ear and I was about to guess it would be my ex-wife, having already heard the news in the Washington bureau, but the caller ID said VELVET COFFIN. I had to admit I was shocked. Against my better judgment I took the call. As expected, the caller was Don Goodwin, self-appointed watchdog and chronicler of the inner workings of the LA *Times*.

'I just heard,' he said.

'How? I only found out myself less than five minutes ago.'

'Jack, you know I can't reveal. But I've got the place wired. You just walked out of Kramer's office. You made the thirty list.'

The 'thirty list' was a reference to those who had been lost over the years in the downsizing of the paper. 'Thirty' was old-time newspaper code for 'end of story'. Goodwin himself was on the list. He had worked at the *Times* and was on the fast track as an editor until a change of ownership brought a change in financial philosophy. He ended up taking one of the first buyouts offered.

Goodwin took his payout and set up a website covering everything that moved inside the *Times*. He called it thevelvetcoffin.com as a grim reminder of what the paper used to be; a place so pleasurable at which to work that you would easily stay till you died. The place was now more of a pine box.

But in another two weeks it wouldn't matter to me. I was moving on and already thinking about the half-started novel I had waiting in my computer. I was going to get on with that baby as soon as I got home. I could milk my savings for six months and after that I could live off the equity in my house.

'Are you out the door today?' Goodwin asked.

'No, I got a couple of weeks if I agreed to train my replacement. I agreed. It beats walking out with a cardboard box today.'

'But do you think that's fair? How long have you been there? Six, seven years, and they give you two weeks?'

He was trying to draw an angry quote from me. I was a reporter. I knew how it worked. But I wasn't biting. I told Goodwin I had no further comment for the Velvet Coffin.

'Look, Don, I need to go. I've got another call.'

I pushed the button before he could take another swing at getting me to discuss my employment situation.

'This is Jack McEvoy,' I said after switching over. I identified the person who replied as female, black and uneducated.

'McEvoy? When you goin' to tell the truth, McEvoy?'

'Who is this?'

'You tellin' lies, McEvoy, in your paper.'

I wished it *was* my paper.

'Ma'am, if you want to tell me who you are and what your complaint is about, I'll listen. Otherwise, I'm—'

'They now sayin' Zo is an adult and what kinda crap is that? He didn't kill no whore.'

Immediately I knew it was one of those calls. Those calls on behalf of the 'innocent'. The mother or girlfriend who had to tell me how wrong my story was. I got them all the time.

'Who is Zo?' I asked.

'Zo. My son, Alonzo. He ain't guilty a nothin'.'

I knew that was what she was going to say. They are never guilty. No one calls you up to say you got it right or the police got it right and their son or their husband or their boyfriend is guilty of the charges. The only thing I didn't understand about the call was the name. I hadn't written about anybody named Alonzo.

'Ma'am, I don't think I wrote about Alonzo.'

'Sure you did. You said he stuffed her in the trunk.'

Then it came together. The trunk murder from last week. It was a six-inch short because nobody on the desk was all that interested. Juvenile drug dealer strangles one of his customers and puts her body in the trunk of her own car. It was a black-on-white crime but still the desk didn't care, because the victim was a drug user.

I realised I didn't know the name Alonzo because I had never been given it in the first place. The suspect was sixteen years old and the cops didn't give out the names of arrested juveniles.

I flipped through the stack of newspapers on my desk until I found the Metro section from two Tuesdays back. I opened it and looked at the story.

It wasn't long enough to carry a by-line. But the desk had put my name as a tag line at the bottom. Otherwise I wouldn't have got the call. Lucky me.

'Alonzo is your son,' I said. 'And he was arrested for the murder of Denise Babbit, correct? That's what we're talking about?'

'That's right, and when are you goin' to write about the truth? You got it wrong and now they say he's goin' to be tried as an adult and he only sixteen. How can they do that to a boy?'

'What is Alonzo's last name?'

'Winslow.'

'Alonzo Winslow. And you are Mrs Winslow?'

'No, I am not,' she said indignantly. 'You goin' put my name in the paper now with a mess a lies?'

'No, ma'am. I just want to know who I am talking to, that's all.'

'Wanda Sessums. I don't want my name in no paper. I want you to write the truth is all. You ruin his reputation calling him a murderer.'

I almost laughed as I scanned the story I had written. 'I said he was arrested for the murder, Mrs Sessums. That is not a lie. That is accurate.'

'He arrested but he didn't do it. The boy wouldn't hurt a fly.'

'Police said he had an arrest record going back to twelve years old for selling drugs. Is that a lie, too?'

'He on the corners, yeah, but that don't mean he go an' kill nobody. They pinnin' a rap on him and you just along for the ride.'

'The police said that he confessed to killing the woman.'

'That's a lie! He did no such thing.'

I didn't know if she was referring to the murder or the confession but it didn't matter. I wanted to end this call and pass it and everything else off to Angela Cook. Let her deal with it.

'OK, Mrs Winslow, I'll—'

'It's Sessums, I told you! See how you gettin' things wrong?'

She had me there. I paused for a moment before speaking.

'I'm sorry, Mrs Sessums. I will look into this and if there is something I can write about, then I will call you. Best of luck—'

'No, you won't. You won't call me. You didn't even ask me for my number! You don't care. You just like the rest a' them and my boy goes to prison for somethin' he didn't do.'

She hung up on me. I sat motionless for a moment, thinking about what she had said about me.

I leaned back in my chair and studied the contents of my cubicle. A desk, a computer, a phone and two shelves stacked with files, notebooks and newspapers. A red leather-bound dictionary so old and well used that the *Webster's* had been worn off its spine. My mother had given it to me when I told her I wanted to be a writer.

It was all I had left after twenty years in journalism. All I would take with me at the end of the two weeks was that dictionary.

'Hi, Jack.'

I turned from my reverie to look up at the lovely face of Angela Cook. I didn't know her but I knew her: a fresh hire from a top-flight school. She was as green as can be but she was probably being paid $500 a week less than me and that made her a greater value to the company. Never mind the stories that would be missed because she had no sources. Never mind how many times she would be manipulated by the police brass.

She was probably a short-timer anyway. She'd get a few years' experience and move on to TV. But Larry Bernard was right. She was a beauty with blonde hair, green eyes and full lips. The cops were going to love seeing her around headquarters.

'Hi, Angela.'

'Mr Kramer said I should come over.'

I had got pinked fifteen minutes earlier and already my replacement had come knocking.

'Tell you what,' I said. 'It's Friday afternoon, Angela, and I just got laid off. So let's not start this now. Let's get together on Monday morning. We can meet for coffee and then I'll take you around Parker Center to meet some people. Will that be OK?'

'Yeah, sure. And, um, sorry, you know?'

'Thank you, Angela, but it's OK. I think it'll end up being the best thing for me anyway. I'll see you Monday morning?'

'Monday morning. And I'll buy the coffee.' She smiled and left.

I pulled my chair in close to my computer and opened a new document. I had to crank out a murder story before I could get out of the newsroom and go drown my sorrows in red wine.

ONLY THREE OTHER REPORTERS showed up for my wake. Larry Bernard and two guys from the sports desk who might have gone to the Short Stop regardless of my being there.

The Short Stop was on Sunset in Echo Park. That made it close to Dodger Stadium, so presumably it drew its name from the baseball position. It was also close to the Los Angeles Police Academy and that made it a cop bar in its early years. But those days were long past. The cops were crowded out by young professionals moving into the neighbourhood. The prices went up and the cops found other watering holes. Still, I liked the place.

It was early so we had our pick of the stools at the bar. We took the four in front of the TV. While we talked, I thought about the novel I was going to restart. I wanted to go home and start writing. I thought maybe it would help me get through the next two weeks.

My cellphone rang and I saw it was my ex-wife calling. I knew I had to get this one over with. I shoved off the bar stool and headed outside to the parking lot where it would be quieter.

It was three hours ahead in Washington but the number on the caller ID was her desk phone.

'Keisha, what are you still doing at work?' I checked my watch. It was almost seven here, almost ten there.

'I'm chasing the *Post* on a story, waiting for callbacks.'

The beauty and bane of working for a West Coast paper was that the last deadline didn't come up until well after the *Washington Post* and *New York Times* had gone to bed. The LA *Times* always had a shot at matching their scoops. As the newest reporter in the Washington bureau, Keisha was on the late shift. She was often tagged with chasing stories and pushing for the freshest developments.

'That stinks,' I said.

'Not as bad as what I heard happened to you today. I'm so sorry.'

I nodded. 'Yeah, I got downsized, Keish.'

A silence opened up between us and I tried to step on it.

'I'm going to pull out my novel and finish it,' I said. 'I've got some savings. I think I can go at least a year. It's now or never.'

'Yeah,' Keisha said with feigned enthusiasm. 'You can do it.'

I knew she had found the manuscript in one of my drawers when we were

still together and had read it, never admitting it because if she did she would
have to tell me what she thought.

'You going to be OK, Jack?'

'Yeah, sure. I just have to figure out what—'

'Jack, I'm sorry, I have one of my callbacks coming in.'

'Go!' I said quickly. 'I'll talk to you later.'

I clicked off the phone, thankful that some politician in Washington had
saved me from the embarrassment of further discussing my life with my ex-
wife, whose career was ascending day by day.

I went back into the bar and decided to get serious, ordering an Irish Car
Bomb. I grew morose, watching the Dodgers start a game against the hated
Giants and get shelled in the first inning.

The two sports guys were the first to bail and then by the third inning
even Larry Bernard had drunk enough and been reminded enough of the
dim future of the newspaper business. He slid off his stool and put his hand
on my shoulder.

'There but for the grace of God go I,' he said.

'What?' I said.

'It could've been me. It could've been anybody. But they tagged you
because you make the big bucks. You coming in here seven years ago, Mr
Best Seller and *Larry King* and all of that. They overpaid to get you then
and that made you a target now.'

'Whatever.'

'I'm going to go now. You staying?'

'I'm going to have one more.'

He slapped me on the back and sauntered out of the bar. I sat alone and
watched the game. For my next drink I skipped the Guinness and Baileys
and went straight to Jameson's over ice.

With the whiskey burning my scalp from underneath, another idea
burned through and seared an imprint on my brain. Elbow on the bar top,
I held the glass up in toast.

'Death is my beat,' I whispered to myself. 'I make my living from it.
I forge my professional reputation on it.'

Words spoken before but not as my own eulogy. I nodded to myself and
knew just how I was going to go out. I had written at least a thousand

murder stories in my time. I was going to write one more. A story that would stand as the tombstone on my career. A story that would make them remember me after I was gone.

THE WEEKEND was a blur of alcohol, anger and humiliation as I grappled with a new future that was no future. On Saturday morning I opened the file that held my novel in progress and began reading. I soon saw what my ex-wife had seen long ago. What I should have seen long ago. It wasn't there and I was kidding myself if I thought it was.

The conclusion was that I would have to start from scratch, and the thought of that was debilitating. I ended up going back to the Short Stop that night and closing the place out early Sunday morning. It took me all the way into Monday morning to get cleaned up. I rolled in forty-five minutes late to work and could still smell the alcohol coming out of my pores.

Angela Cook was already sitting at my desk in a chair she had borrowed from one of the empty cubicles.

'Sorry I'm late, Angela,' I said. 'It was kind of a lost weekend.'

She smiled demurely. 'I got you some coffee but it's probably cold by now,' she said.

'Thanks.' I touched the cup and it had indeed cooled. 'Tell you what. Let me go check in with the desk and if nothing's happening we can go get refills and talk about how you're going to take over.'

I left her there and walked towards the Metro desk. The city editor was a woman named Dorothy Fowler. Fowler had been a damn good government reporter and was eight months into commanding the crew of city-side reporters. I wished her well but knew it was impossible for her to succeed, given all the cutbacks.

Fowler had a little office in the line of glass but she preferred to be an editor of the people. She was usually at a desk at the head of the formation of desks where all the aces—assistant city editors—sat. This was known as the raft because all the desks were pushed together as if in some sort of flotilla.

All city-side reporters were assigned to an ace as the first level of management. My ace was Alan Prendergast, who handled all the cop and justice reporters. As such, he had a later shift, usually coming in around noon, because news that came off the law-enforcement beats most of the time developed late in the day. This meant my first check-in each day was usually with Dorothy Fowler.

Dorothy had her eyes glued to a screen and I had to say her name to get her attention. We hadn't talked since I'd been pink-slipped so she immediately looked up at me with a sympathetic frown.

'Come inside, Jack,' she said.

She left the raft and headed to her office. She sat behind her desk but I stayed standing because I knew this would be quick.

'I just want to say we are really going to miss you, Jack.'

I nodded my thanks.

'I'm sure Angela will pick up without a blip.'

'She's good and she's hungry, but she doesn't have the experience you have. In three or four years Angela will own that beat the way you own it now. But between now and then how many stories will she miss?'

I shrugged. These questions no longer mattered to me.

'Well,' she said. 'I'm sorry. I've enjoyed working with you.'

'I still have some time. Maybe I'll find something really good to go out on.'

She smiled brightly. 'That would be great!'

'Anything happening today that you know of?'

'Nothing big,' Dorothy said.

'I'm going to take Angela round Parker Center and I'll see if we can come up with something.'

'Good.'

A FEW MINUTES LATER Angela Cook and I refilled coffee cups and took a table in the cafeteria. It was on the ground floor in the space where the old presses had turned for decades before they started printing the paper offsite. The conversation with Angela was stiff. I had met her briefly six months earlier when she was a new hire. But since then I hadn't worked on a story with her.

'Where'd you come from, Angela?'

'Tampa. I went to the University of Florida.'

'Good school. Journalism?'

'I got my master's there, yeah.'

'Have you done any cop-shop reporting?'

'Before I went back for my master's I worked two years in St Pete. I spent a year on cops.'

I drank some coffee and I needed it. 'St Petersburg? What are you talking about there, a few dozen murders a year?'

'If we were lucky.' She smiled at the irony of it. A crime reporter always wants a good murder to write about.

'Well,' I said. 'If we go below four hundred here we're having a good year. LA is the place to be if you want to work crime.'

'This is what I want. I want to write murder stories. I want to write books about this stuff.'

She sounded sincere. She sounded like me—from a long time ago.

'Good,' I said. 'I'm going to take you over to Parker Center to meet some detectives. They'll help you but only if they trust you. If they don't trust you, all you'll get are the press releases.'

'How do I do that, Jack? Make them trust me?'

'Be fair, be accurate. Trust is built on performance. If you're fair, they'll know it. If you screw one of them over, they'll all shut you out. There's one other thing. The good ones have a hidden nobility. If you can get that into your stories you'll win them over. So look for the telling details, the little moments of nobility.'

'OK, Jack, I will.'

'Then you'll do all right.'

WHILE WE WERE MAKING the rounds at Parker Center we picked up a nice little murder story in the Open-Unsolved Unit. A twenty-year-old rape and murder of an elderly woman had been cleared when DNA collected from the victim in 1989 was unearthed in case archives and run through the state Department of Justice's sex crimes data bank. The match was called a cold hit. The DNA belonged to a man currently doing time at Pelican Bay for an attempted rape. It wasn't that flashy because the bad guy was already behind bars, but it was worth eight inches. When we got back to the news-room I asked Angela to write it up while I tried to run down Wanda Sessums, my angry caller from the Friday before.

I tried directory assistance with no luck. Then I called Detective Gilbert Walker at the Santa Monica Police Department. He was the lead investigator on the case that resulted in Alonzo Winslow's arrest in the murder of Denise Babbit. I had no relationship with Walker, as the Santa Monica Police Department investigated only a handful of homicides each year.

My call found Walker at his desk. His voice seemed friendly enough until I identified myself as a reporter with the *Times*. Then it went cold. That happened often. The media and the police have never been on comfortable terms.

'What can I do for you?' Walker said in a clipped tone.

'I'm trying to reach Alonzo Winslow's mother and I was wondering if you might be able to help.'

'And who is Alonzo Winslow?'

I was about to say, *Come on, Detective*, when I realised I wasn't supposed to know the suspect's name. There were laws about releasing the names of juveniles charged with crimes.

'Your suspect in the Babbit case.'

'How do you know that name? I'm not confirming that name.'

'I understand that, Detective. I'm not asking you to confirm the name. His mother called me on Friday and gave me the name. Trouble is, she didn't give me her phone number and—'

'Have a nice day,' Walker interrupted and hung up the phone.

I leaned back in my chair, noting that I needed to tell Angela that the nobility I mentioned earlier did not reside in all cops.

I then called a detective who was a source in the South Bureau of the Los Angeles Police Department and who I knew had been involved in the Winslow arrest. The case had originated in Santa Monica because the victim had been found in the trunk of her car near the pier. But the LAPD became involved when evidence from the murder scene led to Alonzo Winslow, a resident of South LA.

Following protocol, Santa Monica contacted Los Angeles, and a team of South Bureau detectives familiar with the turf located Winslow, took him into custody and then turned him over to Santa Monica. Napoleon Braselton was one of those South Bureau guys. I called him now and was honest with him. Well, almost.

'Remember the bust two weeks ago for the girl in the trunk?' I asked.

'Yeah, that's Santa Monica,' he said. 'We just helped out.'

'Yeah, I know, but I can't get hold of Walker over there and I don't know anybody else in that department. But I know you. I'm trying to find the kid's house. I want to go see where he was living, maybe talk to his mother.'

'He was living with his grandmother.'

'You sure?'

'The information we got in the briefing was that he was with the grandmother. There was no father in the picture and the mother was living on the street. Drugs.'

'OK, then I'll talk to the grandmother. Where's the place?'

'You're just cruising on down to say hello?' He said it in a disbelieving tone and I knew that was because I was white and would very likely be unwelcome in Alonzo Winslow's neighbourhood.

'Don't worry, I'll take somebody with me. Safety in numbers.'

'Good luck. Don't get shot until after I go off watch at four.'

'I'll do my best. What's the address, do you remember?'

'It's in Rodia Gardens. Hold on.'

He put the phone down while he looked up the exact address. Rodia Gardens was a huge public housing complex in Watts.

Braselton came back on and gave me the full address but said he had no phone number. I then asked if he had a name for the grandmother and he gave me the name I already had, Wanda Sessums.

Bingo. My caller. She had either lied about being the young suspect's mother or the police had their information wrong.

After ending the call with Braselton I wandered back into the photo department. I saw a photo editor named Bobby Azmitia at the assignment desk, and asked if he had any floaters currently out and about. He named two photographers and I knew one of them was black. I asked him if Sonny Lester could break free to take a ride with me and he agreed. We made arrangements for me to be picked up outside the globe lobby in fifteen minutes.

Back in the newsroom I checked with Angela on the DNA story and then went over to the raft to talk to my ace. Prendergast was typing up the day's first story budget. Before I could say anything he said, 'I already got a slug from Angela.'

A slug and budget line were a one-word title for a story and a line of description that was put on the overall story budget so when editors gathered in the daily news meeting they could discuss what was an important story, what wasn't, and how it should all be played in the paper.

'Yeah, she's got a handle on that,' I said. 'I wanted to let you know I'm going to take a ride down south with a photographer.'

'What's up?'

'Nothing yet. But I may have something to tell you later on.'

'OK.'

Prendo was always cool about giving me rope. I'd have to account for my time and what I was pursuing, but he gave me the chance to put it together before I had to bring him into the loop.

I headed away from the raft and over to the elevator alcove.

'Got dimes?' Prendergast called after me.

I waved a hand over my head without looking back. Prendergast always called that out to me when I left the city room to chase a story. It was a line from *Chinatown*. I didn't use payphones any more—no reporter did—but the sentiment was clear. Stay in touch.

The globe lobby was the formal entrance to the newspaper building at the corner of First and Spring. A brass globe the size of a Volkswagen rotated on a steel axis at the centre of the room, and had the many bureaus and outposts of the *Times* notched on the raised continents. The marble walls were adorned with photos and plaques denoting the many milestones in the history of the paper, the Pulitzer Prizes won and the staffs that won them. It was a proud museum, just as the whole paper would be before too long. The word was that the building was up for sale.

But I only cared about the next twelve days. I had one last deadline and one last murder story to write.

SONNY LESTER WAS WAITING in a company car when I pushed through the heavy front door. I got in and told him where we were going, and pretty soon we were on the 110 heading into South LA.

'I take it that it's no coincidence I'm on this assignment,' he said.

I looked over at him and shrugged. 'I don't know,' I said. 'Ask Azmitia. I told him I needed somebody and he told me it was you.'

Lester nodded like he didn't believe it and I didn't really care. Newspapers had a strong and proud tradition of standing up against segregation and racial profiling and things like that. But there was also a practical tradition of using newsroom diversity to its full advantage. Lester was black and his presence might provide me safety as I entered the projects. That's all I cared about.

Lester asked me questions about what we were doing. I told him that the woman we were going to see had complained about my story calling her grandson a murderer. I was hoping to tell her that I would look into disproving the charges against him if she and her grandson agreed to cooperate with me. I didn't tell him the real plan. I figured he was smart enough to put it together himself.

We rolled into Rodia Gardens at about one o'clock and it was quiet in the projects. School wasn't out yet and the drug trade didn't really get going until dusk. The complex was a maze of two-storey buildings painted brown and beige. The structures were unadorned by any bushes or trees, for these could be used to hide drugs and weapons.

We found the address Braselton gave me without difficulty. It was a corner apartment on the first floor with the stairway on the right side of the building. When we got upstairs I noticed that the front door to the apartment was open behind a screen door with bars on it. I knocked.

'Mrs Sessums?'

I heard a voice through the screen. 'Who that?'

'It's Jack McEvoy. We talked on Friday. From the *Times*?'

The screen was dirty and I could not see into the apartment.

'What you doin' here, boy?'

'I came to talk to you, ma'am. Over the weekend I did a lot of thinking about what you said on the phone.'

'How in hell you find me?'

I could tell by the closeness of her voice that she was on the other side of the screen now. I could only see her shape through the grit.

'Because I knew this is where Alonzo was arrested.'

'Who dat wit' you?'

'This is Sonny Lester, who works at the newspaper with me. Mrs Sessums, I'm here because I thought about what you said and I want to look into Alonzo's case. If he's innocent I want to help him get out.'

Accent on *if*.

'A course, he's innocent. He didn't do nothin'.'

'Can we come in and talk about it?' I said quickly.

'You can come in but don't be taking no pitchers.'

The screen door popped open. Alonzo Winslow's grandmother looked to be about sixty years old with dyed black corn rows showing grey at the roots. She was as skinny as a broom and wore a sweater over blue jeans. Her calling herself his mother on the phone was a curiosity but not a big deal. I had a feeling I was about to find out that she had been both mother and grandmother to the boy.

She pointed to a sitting area where there was a couch and a coffee table. There were stacks of folded clothes on most of the surfaces. Many had pieces of paper on top with names written on them. I could hear a dryer somewhere in the apartment and knew that she had a little business running.

'Move some a that laun'ry and have a seat and tell me what you goin' to do for my Zo,' she said.

I moved a folded stack of clothes off the couch onto a side table and sat down. Lester sat next to me. Wanda Sessums stayed standing in front of us. She lifted a laundry basket onto the coffee table and started folding clothes.

'Well, I want to look into Zo's case,' I said. 'If he's innocent like you said, then I'll be able to get him out.'

I kept that *if* working.

'Jus' like that you get him out, huh? When Mr Meyer can't even get him his day in court?'

'Is Mr Meyer his lawyer?'

'That's right. Public defender. He a Jew lawyer.'

She said it without a trace of enmity or bias. It was said as almost a point of pride that her grandson had a Jewish lawyer.

'Well, I'll be talking to Mr Meyer about all of this. Sometimes the news-paper can do what nobody else can do. If I tell the world that Alonzo Winslow is innocent, then the world pays attention. With lawyers that's not always the case, because they're always saying their clients are innocent—whether they really think it or not.'

She looked at me quizzically. I thought she either was confused or thought she was being conned. I tried to keep things moving.

'Mrs Sessums, I am going to need you to call Mr Meyer and ask him to cooperate with me. I'll need to look at all the discovery.'

'He ain't discovered nothin' so far.'

'By "discovery" I mean the legal term. The prosecutor has to turn all their paperwork and evidence over to the defence for viewing. I'll need to see it all if I'm goin' to work on getting Alonzo out.'

'But how you going to say my Zo's innocent when all yo facts come from the po-po and they lie like the serpent in the tree?'

It took me a moment to respond as I considered her juxtaposition of common street slang and religious reference.

'I'm going to gather all the facts for myself and make my own judgment,' I said. 'When I wrote that story I was saying what the police said. Now I am going to find out for myself. If your Zo's innocent I will know it. And I'll write it. When I write it, the story will get him out.'

'OK, then. Good. The Lord will help you bring my boy home.'

'But I'm going to need your help, too, Wanda.'

I dropped into first-name mode now. It was time to let her think she was going to be part of this.

'When it comes to my Zo, I'm always ready to help,' she said.

'Good,' I said. 'Let me tell you what I want you to do.'

Three: The Farm

Carver was in his office with the door closed. He was humming to himself and intently watching the cameras, his screens set in multiplex mode—thirty-two views on each. He was able to scan all the cameras, even the angles nobody knew about. With a flick of his finger on the heat pad he drew one camera angle into full screen.

Geneva was behind the counter, reading a paperback. Carver checked his watch. It was past time for her afternoon break. Yolanda Chavez from administration was due to walk through the door and let Geneva go for fifteen minutes. Carver planned to follow her with the cameras. Out for a smoke, to the rest room, it didn't matter. He had cameras everywhere.

Just as Yolanda walked into reception, there was a knock on Carver's door. He immediately hit the escape command and the screens returned to data-flow charts. He hadn't heard the mantrap buzzer out in the control room but he wasn't sure. Perhaps he had been concentrating so hard on Geneva that he had missed it.

'Yes?'

The door opened. It was only Stone. Carver became annoyed that he had killed his screens and that he was going to miss out on following Geneva.

'What is it, Freddy?' he asked impatiently.

'I wanted to ask you about vacation time,' Stone said loudly.

He entered and closed the door. He moved to the chair on the other side of the worktable from Carver and sat down.

'Actually, screw vacation time,' he said. 'That was for the benefit of the guys out there. I want to talk about iron maidens. Over the weekend I think I found our next girl.'

Freddy Stone was twenty years younger than Carver. Carver had first noticed him while lurking under a different identity in an iron maiden chat room. He tried to trail him but Stone was too good for that. He had disappeared into the digital mist.

Undaunted and intrigued, Carver had set up a capture site called www.motherinirons.com and, sure enough, Stone had eventually come through. That time Carver had made direct contact and the dance had begun. Carver had recruited him, changed his identity and mentored him.

Carver had saved him but, after four years, Stone was too close for comfort and at times Carver could not stand him. Freddy assumed too much. Like just coming in and sitting down without permission.

'Really,' Carver said, a note of disbelief placed intentionally in the word.

'You promised I could pick the next one, remember?'

Carver had made the promise, but it had come in the fervour of the moment. As they were on the I-10 freeway leaving Santa Monica, the windows open and the sea air blowing in their faces. He was still riding the high and he had foolishly told his young disciple that he could pick the next one.

Now he would have to change that. He wished he could just go back to watching Geneva, maybe catch her in the rest room.

'Don't you ever get tired of that song?' Stone asked.

'What?'

Carver realised he had started to hum again while thinking about Geneva. Embarrassed, he tried to move on.

'Who did you find?' he asked.

Stone smiled broadly. 'This girl who has her own porn site. I'll send you the link so you can check her out. You'll like her.'

'Where'd you find her?'

'Dewey and Bach, accountants. California. She got audited and they handled it. All her info is right there. Everything we need to set up. Then I went and checked her out on her website. Mandy For Ya dot com. She's a stone fox with long legs. Just our type.'

Carver could feel the slight thrill of anticipation. But he wasn't going to make a mistake.

'Where exactly in California?' he asked.

'Manhattan Beach,' Stone said.

Carver wanted to reach across the tabletop and whack Stone.

'Do you know where Manhattan Beach is?' he asked instead.

'Isn't it down by Lo Jolla and San Diego? Down there?'

Carver shook his head. 'First of all, it's *La* Jolla. And no, Manhattan Beach is not near it. It's by LA and not far from Santa Monica. So forget her. We're not going back there for a long time. You know the rules.'

'But, Dub, she's perfect! Plus, I already pulled files on her. LA's a big place. Nobody in Santa Monica is going to care about what happens in Manhattan Beach.'

Carver shook his head emphatically. 'You can put the files right back. We just burned LA for at least three years. I don't care who you find or how safe you think it is. I am not deviating from the protocol. And another thing. My name is Wesley, not Dub.'

Stone seemed crushed.

'Tell you what,' Carver said. 'I'll work on it and find us someone. Wait and see, you'll be very happy. I guarantee it.'

'But it was going to be my turn.' Now Stone was pouting.

'You had your turn and you blew it,' Carver said. 'So why don't you go back out there and get to work. You owe me status reports.'

'Whatever.'

'Go. And cheer up, Freddy. We'll be on the hunt again soon.'

Stone stood up and turned towards the door. Carver watched him go, wondering how long it would be before he had to get rid of him. Permanently. Working with a partner was always preferable. But eventually all partners got too close and assumed too much. They started thinking it was an equal partnership. That was unacceptable. One person called the shots. Himself.

'Close the door, please,' Carver said.

Stone did as instructed. Carver went back to the cameras. He quickly pulled up the camera over the reception area and saw Yolanda sitting behind the counter. Geneva was gone. Jumping from camera to camera he started searching for her.

Four: The Big Three-oh

By the time Sonny Lester and I left the apartment where Wanda Sessums lived, the projects were alive and busy. School was out and the drug dealers and their customers were up. The parking lots, playgrounds and burnt-out lawns between the apartment buildings were becoming crowded with children and adults.

As we crossed a lawn and approached Lester's company car we moved with a heads-down-minding-our-own-business purpose. We just wanted to get out of Dodge City. It wasn't until we were almost at the car that I saw the young man leaning against the driver's door. He was wearing untied work boots, blue jeans and a spotless white T-shirt. It was the uniform of the Crips set that ruled the projects.

'How y'all doin'?' he said.

'We're fine,' Lester said. 'Just going back to work.'

'You the po-po now?'

Lester laughed. 'Nah, man, we're with the paper.' He nonchalantly put his camera bag in the trunk and then came round to the door where the young man was leaning. He didn't move.

'Gotta go, bro. Can I get by you there?'

I was on the other side of the car by my door. I felt my insides tighten. I could see others in the same gang uniform standing on the shaded side of the parking lot, ready to be called in if needed.

The young man leaning on our car didn't move. He folded his arms and looked at Lester.

'What you talking to Moms about up there, *bro*?'

'Alonzo Winslow,' I said from my side. 'We don't think he killed anybody and we're looking into it.'

The young man pushed off the car so he could turn and look at me.

'That right?'

I nodded. 'We just started and that's why we came to talk to Mrs Sessums.'

'Then she tell you about the tax.'

'What tax?'

'The street tax, man. See, any newspaper people that come to talk about Zo has to pay the street tax. I can take it for you now.'

I nodded again. 'How much?'

'It be fifty dollah t'day'

I'd expense it and see if Dorothy Fowler raised hell. I reached into my pocket and quickly extracted two twenties and a ten.

'Here,' I said.

I moved to the back of the car and the man moved away from the driver's door. As I paid him Lester got in and started the car.

'We have to go,' I said as I handed over the money.

'Yeah, you do. You come back and the tax is double, Paperboy.'

'Fine.'

I got into the car and Lester backed out of the space. I turned round and saw the young man bend down and use the bills I had given him to pantomime a quick polish of his shoes. His fellow gangers in the shade whooped it up as he rejoined them.

I didn't feel the tension in my neck start to dissolve until we got back to the 110 and headed north. Then I put the fifty bucks out of my mind and started to feel good as I reviewed what had been accomplished during the trip. Wanda Sessums had agreed to cooperate fully in the investigation. Using my cellphone, she had called Winslow's public defender, Jacob Meyer, and told him that she was authorising my total access to all documents and evidence relating to the case. Meyer agreed to meet with me the next morning.

Wanda Sessums had also agreed to get me into Sylmar Juvenile Hall so that I could interview her grandson. My plan was to use the public defender's case file to become familiar with the case before I sat down to talk to Winslow.

I was thinking about how I was going to present my plan to Prendergast when Lester interrupted my thoughts.

'I know what you're doin',' he said. 'That washerwoman might be too dumb to see it but I'm not.'

'What are you talking about?'

'You're comin' on like you're the white knight that's gonna prove the kid innocent and set him free. But you're goin' to do the exact opposite. You're going to write a story about how a sixteen-year-old kid becomes a stone-cold killer. Hell, getting an innocent man free is a newspaper cliché nowadays. But gettin' inside the mind of a young killer like that? That's Pulitzer territory, bro.'

Lester had me cold. I put together a defence and then responded.

'All I promised her was that I would investigate the case. Where it goes it goes, that's all.'

'Bull,' Lester said. 'But, hey, it's OK.'

I turned and looked at him. 'What do you want, Sonny?'

'A piece, that's all. We work as a team. I do all the photo work.'

'Look,' I said, 'I haven't even told my editor about this yet. You are jumping way ahead. I don't even know if they'll—'

'They'll love it and you know it. Who knows, maybe we both get a prize. And they can't lay you off if you bring home a Pulitzer.'

'You're talking about the ultimate long shot, Sonny. Besides, I already got laid off. I've got twelve days and then I'm out of here.'

I saw his eyes register surprise at the news of my layoff. Then he nodded as he factored the new information into his ongoing scenario. 'Then this is the ultimate adios,' he said. 'I get it. You leave them with a story so good they gotta enter it in contests even though you're long out the door.'

I didn't respond. I hadn't thought I was so easy to read.

WITH COMPLETE ACCESS to Alonzo Winslow and his case now established, I was ready to discuss the story with my editor. When I got back to the newsroom I went directly over to the raft and found Prendergast at his desk. He was busily typing into his computer.

'Prendo, you got a minute?'

He didn't even look up. 'Not right now, Jack. I got tagged with putting together the budget for the four o'clock. You got something for tomorrow besides Angela's story?'

'No, I'm talking more long-range.'

He stopped typing and looked up at me and I realised he was confused. How long-range could a guy with twelve days left go?

'Not that long-range. We can talk later or tomorrow. Did Angela turn in the story?'

'Not yet. I think she was waiting for you to look it over. Can you go do that now and get it in?'

'I'm on it.'

'OK, Jack. We'll talk later or send me a quick email.'

I turned and my eyes swept the newsroom. Over the top edge of one of the nearby pods I saw Angela's blonde hair pulled back in a ponytail. I went over.

'How's it going?'

She jumped, startled.

'Sorry. Didn't mean to scare you.'

'That's OK. I was just so absorbed in reading this.'

I pointed to her computer screen. 'Is that the story?'

Her face coloured. 'No, it's from the archives. It's the story about you and that killer they called the Poet. That was creepy as hell.'

I checked the screen more closely. She had pulled out of the archives a story from twelve years before. From when I was with the *Rocky Mountain News* and in competition with the *Times* on a story that had stretched from Denver to the East Coast and then all the way back to LA. It was the biggest story I had ever chased. It had been the apex of my entire life.

'Yeah, it was pretty creepy. Are you finished with today's story?'

'What happened to that FBI agent you teamed up with? Rachel Walling. One of the stories said she was disciplined for crossing ethical lines with you.'

'She's still around. Here in LA. Can we look at today's story?'

'Sure. I have it done. I was just waiting for you to see it before I sent it to the desk.'

I pulled a chair away from an empty cubicle. Angela made room for me next to her and I read the twelve-inch story she had written. The first edit I made was to take my name off the by-line.

'Why, Jack?' Angela protested. 'We reported this together.'

'Yeah, but you wrote it. You get the by-line.'

She reached over and put her hand on top of my right hand. 'Please, I would like to have a by-line with you. It would mean a lot to me.'

I looked at her quizzically. 'Angela, this is just another murder story and it doesn't need a double by-line.'

'But it's my first murder story here and I want your name on it.'

She still had her hand on mine. I shrugged. 'Suit yourself.'

She let go of my hand and I typed my name back into the by-line. She then reached over again and held my right hand once more.

'Is this the one that got hurt? Can I see?'

I turned my hand over, exposing the starburst scar in the webbing between my thumb and forefinger. It was the place the bullet had passed through before hitting the killer they called the Poet.

'What's it feel like to kill somebody like that?' she asked.

The conversation was getting weird.

'Uh, I don't really like to talk about that, Angela.'

'I love serial-killer stories. I'm going to get the book you wrote. I heard it was a best seller.'

'Good luck. It's been out of print at least five years.'

'Well, I bet you have a copy I could borrow,' Angela said.

She gave me a pouting look. I studied her for a long moment before responding. In that moment I knew she was some sort of death freak. She wanted to write murder stories because she wanted the details they don't put in the articles and the TV reports.

'I'll see if I can find a copy. Let's get back to this story.'

'OK, Jack.' She raised her hands in mock surrender.

I went back to the story and got through the rest of it in ten minutes.

I stood up. 'You think you are OK to make the round of police checks in the morning and swing by Parker Center?'

She frowned. 'You mean without you?'

'Yeah, I'm going to be tied up in court on something I'm working on. You think you can handle it?'

'If you think so. What are you working on?'

I told her briefly about my visit to the Rodia Gardens projects and about the direction I was going. I then pointed at the story on her computer screen, made a fist and banged it lightly on her desk.

'Run that baby,' I said.

It was a line from *All the President's Men*, one of the greatest reporter stories ever told. I realised she didn't recognise it. Oh well, I thought, there's old school and there's new school. I headed back to my cubicle.

JACOB MEYER WAS LATE to our meeting on Tuesday morning. For half an hour I sat in the waiting room of the Public Defender's office. He came back from court carrying a leather briefcase fat with files. Meyer was a young man who I guessed was no more than five years out of law school. He asked the receptionist for messages and was pointed to me. We shook hands and I introduced myself.

'Come on back,' he said. 'I don't have a lot of time.'

'That's fine. I don't need a lot of your time at this point.'

We walked in a single file down a narrow hall.

'In here,' Meyer said.

I followed him into a communal office, a twenty-by-twelve room with desks in every corner and sound partitions between them.

'Home sweet home,' he said. 'Pull over one of those chairs.'

There was another lawyer at the desk diagonally from Meyer's. I pulled the chair over from the empty desk next to his and we sat down.

'Alonzo Winslow,' Meyer said. 'His grandmother's interesting, isn't she? Did she tell you how proud she was to have a Jew lawyer?'

'Yeah, actually she did.'

'Turns out I'm Irish, but I didn't want to spoil it for her. What are you looking to do for Alonzo?'

'Well, like I told you on the phone, Zo's grandmother is pretty convinced the cops picked up the wrong guy. I said I would look into it because I wrote the story in which the cops said he did it. Mrs Sessums, who is Zo's legal guardian, has given me full access to him and his case.'

'She might be his legal guardian, but her granting you full access means nothing in legal terms and therefore means nothing to me.'

This was not what he had said on the phone when I'd had Wanda Sessums speak to him. I was about to call him on that when I saw him throw a quick glance over his shoulder and realised he was talking for the benefit of the other lawyer in the room.

'Sure,' I said instead. 'And I know you have rules in regard to what you can tell me.'

'I can answer your questions to a point but I am not at liberty at this stage in the case to turn over any of the discovery to you.'

As he said this he swivelled in his seat to check that the other lawyer's back was still to us and then quickly handed me a flash drive, a data-storage stick with a USB-port connection.

'You have to get that stuff from the prosecutor or the police.'

'Who is the prosecutor assigned to the case?' I asked.

'Well, it has been Rosa Fernandez but she handles juvenile cases. They're saying they want to try this kid as an adult, so that will probably mean a change in prosecutors.'

'Are you objecting to them moving this out of juvenile court?'

'Of course. My client is sixteen. And his mental capacity and acuity is not even that of a sixteen-year-old.'

'But the police said this crime had a degree of sophistication and a sexual component. The victim had been raped and sodomised with foreign objects. Tortured.'

'You are assuming my client committed the crime.'

'The police said he confessed.'

Meyer pointed to the flash drive in my hand.

'Exactly,' he said. 'The *police* said he confessed. My experience is that if you put a sixteen-year-old kid in a closet for nine hours, lie to him about evidence that does not exist and refuse to let him talk to anybody, eventually he's going to give you what you want if he thinks it will get him out of the closet. Secondly, it's a question of what exactly he confessed to. The police point of view is definitely different from mine.'

I stared at him. The conversation was intriguing but too cryptic. I needed to get Meyer to a place where he could speak freely.

'Do you want to go get a cup of coffee?'

'No, I don't have time. And as I said, I can't get into specifics of the case. If you want a statement from me, I would say that I believe that my client is not guilty of this crime. I will be able to prove that once we get into court.'

It had been a statement nothing short of what I expected. But, still, it gave me pause. Meyer was crossing a line in giving me the flash drive and I had to ask myself why. Did he think Alonzo was actually innocent?

It dawned on me that I was wasting time. I had to get back to the office and see what was on the stick.

'Thanks for your help,' I said sarcastically, for the benefit of the other lawyer. I nodded and winked at Meyer, then I left.

WHEN I GOT to the newsroom I went to my cubicle without checking in at the raft or with Angela Cook. I plugged the data stick into my laptop and opened its contents. There were three files on it. They were labelled SUMMARY.DOC, ARREST.DOC, and CONFESS.DOC. The transcript of Alonzo Winslow's confession was 928 pages long. I closed it, saving it for last.

After loading the files onto my computer I emailed them to the in-house copy centre so that I would have hard copies of everything. I like hard copies of the materials I base my stories on.

I decided to take the documents in order. I opened the summary report on my screen. I assumed this would be a minimalist account of the investigation leading to the arrest of Winslow. The author of the document was my pal Gilbert Walker, who had hung up on me the day before. The summary was four pages long. Walker knew that his document would be studied for procedural mistakes by lawyers on both sides. The best defence against that was to put as little into the report as possible.

The surprise in the file, however, was not the short summary but the complete autopsy and crime scene reports as well as a set of crime scene photographs. These would be hugely helpful to me when I wrote the description of the crime in my story.

Before going to the words I went to the photos. There were forty-eight colour photographs taken at the crime scene that depicted the body of Denise Babbit as it had been found in the trunk of her 1999 Mazda Millennia. There were also photographs that showed the interior of the car and the trunk after the removal of the body.

One photo showed her face behind a clear plastic bag pulled over her head and tied tightly round her neck with what looked like clothes line. She had died with her eyes open in a look of fear.

I went back to the investigative summary and read it through, highlighting the paragraphs with information I thought was important and moving them into a new document I had created. I took each paragraph I moved from the stilted official report and rewrote it to make the story my own.

When I was finished I reviewed my work. I knew that when I finally wrote the story for publication, many of these paragraphs and nuggets of information would be included.

Denise Babbit was found in the trunk of her 1999 Mazda Millennia at 9.45 a.m. on Saturday, April 25, 2009, by SMPD patrol officers Richard Cleady and Roberto Jiminez. Detectives Gil Walker and William Grady responded as lead investigators of the crime.

The patrol officers had been called by Santa Monica parking enforcement, who found the car in the beach lot next to the Casa Del Mar hotel. When parking enforcement officer Willy Cortez approached the Mazda he found the car's windows open and the key in the ignition. A woman's bag was on the passenger seat and its contents were dumped beside it. Sensing that something wasn't right, he called the SMPD and officers Cleady and Jiminez arrived. They noticed that the trunk had been closed on what appeared to be part of a woman's silk-patterned dress. They reached into the car and popped the trunk.

The body of Denise Babbit was in the trunk. She was naked and her clothing was found on top of the body.

Denise Babbit was twenty-three years old. She worked as a dancer at a Hollywood strip bar called Club Snake Pit. She had an arrest record for possession of heroin dating back to a year before: the case was still pending, the conclusion delayed because of a pre-trial intervention programme that placed her in an out-patient drug treatment programme. She had been arrested during an LAPD sting operation in Rodia Gardens in which suspects were observed by undercover police making drug buys.

Hair and fibre evidence collected from inside the car included multiple exemplars of canine hair from an unknown but short-haired dog breed. Denise Babbit did not own a dog.

The victim had been asphyxiated with a length of clothes line used to tie the plastic bag round her neck. There were also ligature marks on her wrists and legs from when she had been bound. Autopsy would show that she had been repeatedly raped with a foreign object. Time of death was set at twelve to eighteen hours before the discovery of the body.

The victim had worked her scheduled night shift at the Snake Pit, leaving work at 2.15 a.m. on Friday, April 24. Her room-mate, also a dancer at the Snake Pit, told police that Babbit did not come home after work and never returned to their apartment. Her body was found the following morning.

Crime scene investigators found that the person who abandoned the victim's car with the body in the trunk had wiped down most surfaces in the car that potentially held fingerprints. The door handles, steering wheel and shift lever were all wiped clean. However, the investigators found a clear thumbprint on the interior rearview mirror, presumably left when someone driving the car adjusted it.

The thumbprint was matched to Alonzo Winslow, sixteen, who carried a juvenile arrest record for sale of narcotics in the same projects where Denise Babbit had bought heroin and been arrested the year before.

An investigative theory emerged. After leaving her job in the early-morning hours of April 24 the victim drove to the Rodia Gardens projects in order to buy heroin or other drugs. Despite her being white, Denise Babbit was familiar and comfortable going to the projects to make her purchase because she had purchased drugs there many times before.

However, this time she was forcefully abducted by Alonzo Winslow and possibly other unknown individuals. She was held in an unknown location and sexually tortured for six to eighteen hours. Because of the high levels of petechial haemorrhaging around the eyes, she also appeared to have been repeatedly choked into unconsciousness and then revived before final asphyxiation occurred. Her body was then stuffed in the trunk of her car and driven twenty miles to Santa Monica, where it was left in the ocean-side parking lot.

With the thumbprint as a solid piece of evidence supporting the theory, detectives Walker and Grady obtained an arrest warrant for Alonzo Winslow. He was taken into custody on Sunday morning, April 26, and after a lengthy interrogation confessed to the murder.

I closed the file and thought about how quickly the investigation had led to Winslow. Then my phone rang and I looked over to see Angela's name on the caller screen. I picked up. 'Angela, what's happening?'

'I'm over here at Parker and I think something is going on but nobody's telling me anything. There's all kinds of reporters and cameras coming in.'

'Um, I can make some calls. Stay there and I'll call you back.'

After hanging up with Angela I called Lieutenant Hardy in the Major Crimes Division to see what was shaking.

'We're lying low today, Jack,' Hardy said. 'Nothing to report.'

'You sure? I heard the building is crawling with TV people.'

'That's for that other thing. We've got nothing to do with that.'

'What other thing?' I asked.

'You need to talk to either Grossman or the chief's office. They're having the press conference.'

I started to get concerned. The chief of police didn't usually hold press conferences to discuss things already in the newspaper. He usually broke things out himself. The other reference Hardy had made was to Captain Art Grossman who was in charge of major narcotics investigations. Somehow we had missed an invitation to a press conference.

I quickly thanked Hardy for the help and told him I would check with him later. I called Angela back and she answered right away.

'Head up to the fifth floor. There is some sort of narcotics press conference with the chief and Art Grossman, who is the head narc.'

'OK, what time?'

'I don't know yet. Just get up there in case it's happening right now. I'll call you back.'

After hanging up I started multitasking. While putting in a call to Grossman's office I went online and checked the CNS wire. The City News Service operated a digital newswire that was updated by the minute with breaking news from the City of Angels. As a police reporter I checked it continuously through the day.

I had neglected to tell Angela she should too. And with her spending the morning at Parker Center and my spending it chasing the Babbit case, nobody had made the check.

My call to Grossman was answered by a secretary, but she told me the captain was already at the press conference.

Just as I hung up I found a short blurb on CNS announcing the press conference in the fifth-floor media room at Parker Center. There was little information other than to say it was to announce the results of a major drug sweep conducted through the night in Rodia Gardens. *Bang.* Just like that my long-term story was hooking nicely into a breaking story. I called Angela back.

'Are you on five?'

'Yeah, and they haven't started. What's this about? I don't want to ask any of these TV people, because then I'll come off as stupid.'

'Right. It's about a drug sweep overnight in Rodia Gardens. It's probably in response to the murder I told you about yesterday. The woman in the trunk was traced back to that place, remember?'

'Oh, right, right.'

'Angela, it connects with what I'm working on, so I want to try to sell it to Prendo. I want to write it because it will help set up my story.'

'Well, maybe we can work on it together.'

I paused but not too long. I had to be delicate but decisive.

'No, I'm going to come over for the conference. I want this story, Angela, because it's part of my larger story.'

'That's cool, Jack,' she said, without hesitation. 'It's still your beat. But if you need anything from me, just ask.'

I now thought I had overreacted and was embarrassed at having acted like a selfish jerk.

'Thanks, Angela. We'll figure it out. I'm going to give Prendo a heads-up on this for the daily budget and then I'll be over.'

PARKER CENTER was in its last year of life. The crumbling building had been the command centre for police operations for nearly five decades. A beautiful replacement was rising on Spring Street, right next to the *Times*. It would be state of the art and spacious and technologically savvy. But

I would not be there when it was time for everyone to move in.

The press conference was in full swing when I got to the big media room next to the chief's office. I pushed past a uniformed officer in the doorway, grabbing a copy of the handout from him, and took a seat. Angela was in the second row taking notes. I read the handout to get up to speed:

In the wake of the murder of Denise Babbit, presumed to have occurred somewhere in the Rodia Gardens Housing Project, the LAPD's South Bureau Narcotics Unit conducted one week of high-intensity surveillance of drug activities in the housing project and arrested sixteen suspected drug dealers in an early-morning sweep. The suspects included eleven adult gang members and five juveniles. Undisclosed amounts of heroin, crack cocaine and methamphetamine were seized during raids on twelve different apartments in the projects. Additionally, three search warrants that sought additional evidence against the sixteen-year-old charged with the murder were executed.

Having read thousands of press releases, I was pretty good at reading between the lines. I knew that when they didn't disclose the amounts of drugs seized it was because the amounts were so low as to be embarrassing. And I knew that when the press release said the warrants *sought* additional evidence, then the likelihood was that none had been found.

All of this was of mild interest to me. What had my adrenaline moving was the fact that the drug sweep was in response to the murder and it was an action that was sure to instigate racial controversy. That controversy would help me sell my long-term story to my own command staff.

Grossman stepped up to the microphone and started the narration that went along with a PowerPoint presentation of the sweep. He described how twelve teams of six officers each simultaneously raided twelve different apartments. The mugshot of the gang member who had extorted fifty dollars from me the day before flashed on the screen. Grossman identified him as twenty-year-old Darnell Hicks. I felt a small amount of joy knowing I would put his name first among the arrested when I wrote the story.

Grossman took another ten minutes to finish giving out the details the department was willing to part with, and then opened it up to questions. A couple of the television reporters threw him softballs. No one asked him the tough question until I raised my hand.

'Mr McEvoy, do you have a question?'

Grossman knew he wouldn't get a softball from me. 'Yes, Captain. I was wondering whether you can tell me if you are expecting any backlash from the community?'

'Backlash? No. Who complains about getting drug dealers off the street? Besides that, we had enormous support and cooperation from the community in regard to this operation.'

I put the line about support from the community into my back pocket for later and stayed on point with my response.

'Well, it's pretty well documented that the drug and gang problems in the Rodia projects have been there for a long time. But the department only mounted this operation after a white woman from Hollywood got abducted and murdered going down there.'

Grossman's face got pink. 'We don't . . . uh, view it that way,' he began. 'The murder of Denise Babbit only served to focus attention on the problems down there. Our actions today will help make that community a better place to live.'

I had no further questions, and Grossman ended the news conference. The uniformed officer who had given me the handout made his way to me and signalled me to the door on the other side of the room.

'Lieutenant Minter wants to show you something,' he said.

'Good,' I said. 'I wanted to ask him something.'

We went through the door and Minter was waiting for me, sitting on the corner of a desk. A handsome man with a ready smile, Minter was in charge of the Media Relations Office.

'Hey, Jack,' Minter said in a friendly manner as we shook hands.

'Hey, Lieutenant, thanks for seeing me. I was wondering if I could get a mugshot of the suspect named Hicks for my story.'

'No problem. It's funny that you want a photo of Hicks.'

'Why?'

He reached behind his back to the desk and handed me an eight-by-ten photo. It was a surveillance shot of me handing Darnell Hicks the fifty-dollar 'street tax'. I noted how grainy the shot was and knew it had to have been taken from inside one of the Rodia apartment buildings. I now knew what Grossman had meant by community support and cooperation. At least one resident had allowed them to use an apartment as a surveillance post.

I held the photo up.

'Are you giving me this for my scrapbook?'

'No, I was just wondering if you can tell me about it. If you have a problem, Jack, I can help.'

He had a phoney smile on his face. He was trying to squeeze me. A photo out of context like this could certainly send the wrong message if leaked to a boss or competitor. But I smiled right back.

'What do you want, Lieutenant?'

'We don't want to stir up controversy where there isn't any, Jack. Like with this photo. It could have several meanings.'

The point was clear. Lay off the community backlash angle.

'I guess you didn't get the memo,' I said. 'I'm out. I got a pink slip on Friday, Lieutenant, so there isn't anything you can do to me. Besides that, do the narcs down in South Bureau know you're showing their surveillance shots around like this? It says your drug teams had a set-up inside somebody's apartment in Rodia. If that gets out, those Crips down there will probably go on a witch hunt.'

Minter's smile froze.

'I gotta go write,' I said. 'I'll go down to media relations and pick up the mugshot on my way out. Thanks, Lieutenant.'

'OK, Jack,' he said routinely, as if the subterranean context of our conversation had not existed. 'Hope to see you again before you go.'

I stepped through the door back into the press conference room. I looked round for Angela Cook but she hadn't waited for me.

AFTER PICKING UP the mugshot of Darnell Hicks, I walked back to the *Times* building and up to the second-floor newsroom. I planned to make some calls and flesh out the drug sweep story.

The 928-page print-out of the Winslow confession as well as the other documents I'd asked to have printed were waiting on my desk.

I had just picked up the phone to make a call when I felt a presence hovering over me and looked up to see Alan Prendergast.

'Didn't you get my message?' he asked.

'No, I just got back. What's up?'

'I wanted to talk about your story.'

'Didn't you get the budget line I sent?'

'Not today's story. Cook's already putting it together. I want to hear about your long-term story. We have the futures meeting in ten minutes.'

'Wait a minute. What do you mean Cook's already putting today's story together?'

'She's writing it up. She came back from the press conference and said you were working together on it.'

I held back on telling him that Cook and I weren't supposed to be working together on it. It was my story and I'd told her so.

'So whadaya got, Jack? It's related to today's thing, right?'

'Sort of, yeah.' I was still stunned by Cook's move.

'Jack? I don't have much time.'

'Uh, right. Yeah, it's about the murder of Denise Babbit—but from the killer's angle. It's about how sixteen-year-old Alonzo Winslow came to be charged with murder.'

Prendo nodded. 'You have the goods?'

I knew he was asking if I had direct access. He wanted a crime feature, a story that went behind the basic news everybody already had and rocked the reader's world with gritty reality. He wanted breadth and depth, the hallmark features of any *Times* story.

'I have a direct line in. I've got the kid's grandmother and his lawyer, and I'm probably going to see the kid tomorrow.'

I pointed to the freshly printed stack of documents on my desk.

'And that's the pot of gold. His nine-hundred-page confession. I shouldn't have it but I do. And nobody else will get it.'

Prendo nodded with approval. He grabbed a nearby chair and pulled it over.

'I've got an idea, Jack,' he said as he sat down. He was using my name too much. I didn't like the way this was going.

'What is it, Alan?'

'What if it wasn't just about how a boy became a murderer? What if it was also about how a girl became a murder victim?'

I thought about it and slowly nodded. 'It's just going to take me more time when I split the focus of the story like that.'

'You won't have to split your focus. You stay with the kid. We'll put Cook on the victim and she'll cover that angle. We'll weave both strands together and create a column-one story.'

Column one on the front page was reserved each day for the signature story of the paper. The best-written piece, the one with the most impact. In seven years with the *Times* I had never had a column-one story.

'Did Cook give you this idea?'

'No, man, I just thought of it. Right now. What do you think?'

I didn't believe Prendergast for a moment, and was not swayed by his column-one overture. But I was smart enough to know that his suggestion—whether his or Angela's—could lead to a better story. And it had a better chance of doing what I wanted it to do.

'We could call it "The Collision",' I said. 'The point where these two— killer and victim—came together and how they got there.'

'Perfect!' Prendergast exclaimed. 'I'll wing it in the meeting, but why don't you and Cook put your heads together and give me something for the budget by the end of the day? I'm going to tell them you'll turn the story in by the end of the week.'

It was not a lot of time but it was doable. 'Fine,' I said.

'Good,' he said. 'I gotta go.' He headed on to his meeting.

In a carefully worded email I invited Angela to meet me in the cafeteria to get a cup of coffee. She responded immediately, saying she would meet me there in fifteen minutes.

Now that I was free of the daily story and had fifteen minutes to fill, I started reading the confession of Alonzo Winslow.

The interview had been conducted by the lead detectives Gilbert Walker and William Grady at the Santa Monica Police Department on Sunday, April 26. The transcript was in Q&A format.

They began by reading Winslow his rights. Then they went through a series of questions employed at the start of interviews with juveniles. These were designed to elicit his knowledge of right and wrong. Once that was established, Winslow became fair game.

For his part, Winslow fell victim to ego and the oldest flaw in the human book. He thought he could outsmart them. So he readily agreed to talk to them, and they played him like a three-string bass guitar. *Dum-de-dum-de-dumb*. Getting every implausible explanation and outright lie on record.

I breezed through the first 200 pages, skipping page after page of Winslow's denials of knowing anything or seeing anything pertaining to Denise Babbit's murder. Then the detectives turned the questions towards Winslow's whereabouts on the night in question. Winslow told them that he was at home sleeping and his 'moms'—Wanda Sessums—could vouch for him. He held up like a rock, but on page 205 the detectives started lying to him and setting traps.

WALKER: Alonzo, we know you know something.
WINSLOW: I ain't ever seen that girl you been talking about.
WALKER: Really? Then how come we got you on tape dropping her car in that parking lot by the beach? That puts this whole thing on you, man.
WINSLOW: Nah, it ain't me. I didn't do this.

I knew from the discovery documents Meyer had given me that there was no video that showed the victim's Mazda being left in the parking lot. But I also knew that the US Supreme Court had upheld the legality of the police lying to a suspect within certain guidelines.

I read on, until my cellphone rang. I looked at the screen and realised I had read right through my coffee meeting with Angela.

'Angela? Sorry, I got tied up. I'm coming right down.'

I hustled down the steps to the ground-floor cafeteria and joined her at a table without getting any coffee.

On the table was a stack of papers turned print-side down. I looked directly at her. 'I just wanted to tell you that I didn't appreciate you guzzling today's story. The beat is technically still mine.'

'I'm sorry. I got excited when you asked all the right questions in the press conference and I got back to the newsroom and sort of exaggerated things. I said we were working on it together. Prendo told me to start writing.'

'Is that when you suggested to Prendo that we work together on my other story, too?' I asked.

'I didn't. I don't know what you're talking about.'

'When I got back, Prendo told me we were on it together. I take the killer and you take the victim. He also told me it was your idea.'

Her face coloured. I had now outed two liars. Angela I could deal with because she was just boldly going for what she wanted. Prendo was the one that hurt. I guessed he was just choosing sides. The future was with Angela.

'Look, Angela, I don't like how you did this but I admire how you just go after what you want. The best reporters I have known are all that way. And your idea of doing the double-profile of both killer and victim is the better way to go.'

Now she looked at me. Her face brightened.

'Jack, I'm really looking forward to working with you on it.'

'I want to get straight that this started with me and it ends with me. When the reporting is all done, I'm the one who is going to write this. OK?'

'Oh, absolutely. It's your story, Jack. You get to write.'

I studied her closely for any sign that she was dissembling. 'All right. That's all I had to say. You need help with today's story?'

'No, I'm all set.'

'OK,' I said to Angela. 'I'll let you get back to it.'

'Here,' she said, and slid the stack of papers across the table to me.

'What's this?'

'Nothing, really, but it might save you some time. Last night I googled "trunk murder" and found there is a long history of people ending up in the trunks of cars. A lot of women. Mob guys, too.'

I turned the pages over and looked at the top sheet. It was a *Las Vegas Review-Journal* story from a year earlier, about the conviction of a man charged with murdering his ex-wife, putting her body into the trunk of his car, and then parking it in his own garage.

'That's just a story that sounded a little like yours,' she said. 'There's others in there about historical cases. I even found a website called trunk murder dot com, but it's still under construction.'

I nodded hesitantly. 'Uh, thanks.'

She pushed her chair back and picked up her empty cup.

'You want to walk up together?'

'Uh, no, I'm going to get a coffee and maybe look through all this stuff you came up with.'

'Suit yourself.'

She gave me a smile and walked away. I watched her dump her coffee cup into a trash can and head out of the cafeteria. My instinct told me that I might only have eleven days left on the job but I would have to watch my back with her during every one of them.

AFTER WRITING a budget line and emailing it to Prendergast, and then signing off on Angela's story for the morning edition, I concentrated on the Alonzo Winslow transcript.

The reading went fast. At one point the detectives scammed Winslow into a damaging admission. Grady apparently pulled out a tape measure. He explained to Winslow that they wanted to take a measurement of the line that ran from the tip of his thumb to the tip of his first index finger on each hand. Winslow cooperated and then the detectives announced that the measurements matched the strangulation marks left on Denise Babbit's neck. Winslow responded with a vigorous denial and then made a big mistake.

WINSLOW: Beside that, she wasn't even strangled with anybody's hands. Somebody tied a plastic bag over her head.
WALKER: And how do you know that, Alonzo?
WINSLOW: I don't know, man. It must've been on TV.
WALKER: No, son, we never put that out. The only person who knew that was the person who killed her.
WINSLOW: I'm telling you people, I didn't kill her like that.
GRADY: Then tell us what you did do to her.
WINSLOW: Nothing, man. Nothing!

The damage was done. By page 830 Winslow began to crack.

WINSLOW: I want to go home. I want to see my moms.
WALKER: If you want to finally start telling us the truth, then we can talk about getting you home.
WINSLOW: I didn't do this. I never met that girl.
GRADY: Then how did your fingerprints get all over that car, and how come you know how she was strangled?
WINSLOW: I don't know. That can't be true about my prints. You lying to me.
WALKER: You think we're lying because you wiped that car down, didn't you? But you forgot the rearview mirror!
GRADY: Hey, we can understand. Pretty white girl like that. Maybe she mouthed off to you. Something happened and she got killed. If you can tell us, then we can work with you.
WINSLOW: Nah, man, you got it all wrong.
WALKER: Alonzo, I'm tired. So you either come clean right now, son, or

you're going into a cell. I'll call your moms and tell her you ain't never coming back.

WINSLOW: OK, OK. I'll tell you what I know and then you let me go. I was walking my dog and I saw her car and when I look inside I saw the keys and I saw her bag. Just sitting there.

WALKER: Wait a minute. You have a dog? What kind?

WINSLOW: Yeah, for like protection. She a pit.

WALKER: OK, where was the girl?

WINSLOW: Nowhere, man. Like I told you, I never saw her—when she was alive, I mean.

WALKER: Uh-huh. Then what?

WINSLOW: So then I jump in the ride and take off.

WALKER: With the dog?

WINSLOW: Yeah, with my dog. Just for a ride, man.

WALKER: All right, that's it. I'm tired of your lies! This time we go.

WINSLOW: Wait. I drove it over by the Dumpsters, OK? Back in Rodia. I wanted to see what I got in the car, OK? So I pull in and I check out her bag and it's got like two hundred and fifty dollars and I check the glove box and everything and then I popped the trunk, and there she was. Plain as day and already dead, man. And that's the truth.

GRADY: You want us to believe that you stole the car and it already had the dead girl in the trunk.

WINSLOW: That's right, man. When I saw her in there, I closed that lid and drove that car outta there, thinking I'd just put it back where I found it, but then I knew it would bring all kinda pressure down on my boys, so I drove it on up to the beach. I figure she a white girl; I put her in the white 'hood. So that's what I did and that's all I did.

WALKER: When did you wipe the car down?

WINSLOW: Right there. Like you said, I missed the mirror.

WALKER: Who helped you dump the car?

WINSLOW: Nobody helped me. I was on my own.

GRADY: How'd you get back to the 'hood?

WINSLOW: Walked to Oakwood and got a bus.

WALKER: You still had your dog with you?

WINSLOW: No, man, I dropped her with my girlfriend. That's where she stay 'cause my moms don't want no dog in the house on account of all the people's laundry.

WALKER: So who killed the girl?

WINSLOW: How would I know? She dead when I found her.
WALKER: You just stole her car and robbed her money.
WINSLOW: That's it, man. That's all you got me on.
WALKER: Well, Alonzo, that doesn't add up to the evidence we've got. We
    got your DNA on her.
WINSLOW: No, you don't. That a lie! I didn't kill nobody!

And so it went for another 100 pages. The cops threw lies and accusations at Winslow and he denied them. But as I read those last pages, I quickly came to realise something. Alonzo Winslow never said he strangled Denise Babbit. The only confession was his acknowledgment that he had taken her money and then dumped the car with her body inside it. But that was a long way from murder.

I dug through the stack of papers in my outbox, looking for the press release distributed by the SMPD after Winslow was arrested for the murder. I finally found it and reread its four paragraphs. Knowing what I knew now, I realised the police had manipulated the media into reporting something that was not, indeed, true.

The Santa Monica Police announced today that a sixteen-year-old gang member from South Los Angeles has been taken into custody in the death of Denise Babbit. The youth, whose name will not be released because of his age, was being held by juvenile authorities at a detention centre in Sylmar.

Police spokesmen said identification of fingerprints collected from the victim's car after her body was found in the trunk on Saturday morning led detectives to the suspect. He was taken in for questioning on Sunday.

The suspect faces charges of murder, abduction, rape and robbery. During a confession to investigators, the suspect said he moved the car with the body in the trunk to a beach parking lot in Santa Monica so as to throw off suspicions that Babbit had been killed in Watts.

The press release was not inaccurate. But it had been carefully crafted to convey something that was not accurate. Winslow's lawyer was right. There was a chance that his client was innocent.

In the field of investigative journalism, the Holy Grail might be the taking down of a president, but when it came to the lowly crime beat, proving a guilty man innocent was as good as it gets. Alonzo Winslow may not have been judged guilty of anything yet, but in the media he had been condemned.

I had been part of that lynching and I now saw that I might have a shot at changing all of that and doing the right thing. I might be able to rescue him.

I thought of something and looked round on my desk for the print-outs Angela had produced from her research on trunk murders. I had scanned and dismissed them, thinking at the time that there was no way stories about other trunk murders could have any bearing on a story about the collision between a sixteen-year-old killer and his victim.

Now I wasn't so sure.

I found the print-outs. Angela had found several news stories about bodies being found in trunks. Most were old and seemed irrelevant. But a series of stories in the *Las Vegas Review-Journal* did not. They were reports on the trial of a man charged with killing his ex-wife and stuffing her body into the trunk of his car.

I quickly scanned the stories until I found the one I remembered.

Coroner: Ex-Wife Tortured for Hours
by Rick Heikes

Autopsy results showed that Sharon Oglevy was strangled more than twelve hours after her abduction, the Clark County coroner testified on Wednesday in the murder trial of the victim's ex-husband.

Coroner Gary Shaw testified for the prosecution and revealed new details of the abduction and murder. He said the time of death was determined to be approximately twelve to eighteen hours after a witness saw Oglevy forced into a van in a parking garage behind the Cleopatra Casino and Resort, where she worked as a dancer in the exotic Femmes Fatales show.

'For at least twelve hours she was with her abductor and many horrible things were done to her,' Shaw testified.

A day later her body was found in the trunk of her ex-husband's car by police officers who had gone to his home in Summerland to question him. He allowed the police to search the premises and the body was found in the car parked in the garage. The couple's marriage had dissolved eight months earlier in an acrimonious divorce. Sharon Oglevy had sought a restraining order prohibiting her ex-husband, a blackjack dealer, from coming within 100 feet of her. In her petition she said her husband had threatened to kill her and bury her in the desert.

Brian Oglevy was charged with first-degree murder, kidnapping and rape with a foreign object. He has denied killing his ex-wife and said he was set up as a fall guy for her murder. He has been held without bail.

Shaw said Sharon Oglevy was raped and sodomised with an unknown foreign object. He testified that she had been asphyxiated with a plastic bag that had been pulled over her head and tied closed round her neck. He said several cord markings on the victim's neck and a high level of haemorrhaging round her eyes indicated she had been asphyxiated slowly and may have been allowed to lose and regain consciousness several times.

Las Vegas Metro Police have never been able to determine where Brian Oglevy allegedly held and then murdered his ex-wife. Crime scene technicians determined that it was unlikely that the murder occurred at his home.

Brian Oglevy's attorney, William Schifino, is expected to mount his defence sometime next week.

I studied the *Review-Journal*'s trial stories that came before and after the one I had just read, and none gripped me like the report on the autopsy. The missing hours and the plastic bag and slow asphyxiation were descriptions that matched the murder of Denise Babbit. And, of course, the car trunk was the strongest match of all.

Could there be a connection here? I didn't know—yet. But there was one way to find out. I had to go to Las Vegas.

I stood up and headed towards the raft. I had to inform Prendo and get a travel authorisation. But when I got there his seat was empty.

'Anybody seen Prendo?' I asked the other aces on the raft.

'He took early dinner,' said one. 'He should be back in an hour.'

I checked my watch. It was after four and I needed to get moving, first home to pack a bag, and then to the airport.

Five: The Farm

Carver had been busy all day with a test run of data transmission from their new clients Mercer and Gissal in St Louis. He had not made his appointed rounds until it was almost time to go home. He checked his traps and a charge shot through him when he saw he had caught something in one of his cages. The screen avatar displayed it as a grey rat running on a wheel inside the cage labelled 'Trunk Murder'.

The animal wore a collar with a silver identity tag on it. Carver clicked on the tag and brought up the rat's information. The date and time of the visit had occurred the night before. A ten-digit Internet protocol address had been captured. The visit to his www.trunkmurder.com site had lasted twelve seconds. Now he would try to find out who had visited and why.

Two minutes later Carver's breath caught in his throat as he followed the IP—a basic computer address—back to an Internet service provider with the domain name of LATimes.com.

A reporter from the *Los Angeles Times* had gone to his trunk murder website. Carver thought about how he should approach this. He had the IP but no name to go with it.

He rolled his chair down to the next work station. He logged on as McGinnis, having broken his codes long ago. He went to the *Los Angeles Times* online archive and searched under *trunk murder.*

He got three hits on stories containing the phrase in the last three weeks, including one due to go into the next morning's paper.

Drug Crackdown Draws Community Fire
by Angela Cook and Jack McEvoy

A drug crackdown at a housing project has drawn fire from local activists who complained on Tuesday that the LAPD only paid attention to the problem in the minority-populated complex when a white woman was allegedly murdered there. Police announced the arrest of sixteen residents of Rodia Gardens on drug charges following a one-week investigation. Police spokesmen said the 'peep and sweep' operation was in response to the murder of Denise Babbit of Hollywood.

A sixteen-year-old alleged gang member who is a resident of Rodia Gardens was arrested for the slaying. Babbit's body was found two weeks ago in the trunk of her car in Santa Monica. The investigation traced the crime back to Rodia Gardens, where police believe Babbit went to buy drugs. Instead, she was abducted, held for several hours and repeatedly sexually assaulted before being strangled.

Several community activists questioned why efforts to stem the tide of drug dealing in the projects did not come before the murder. They were quick to point out that the victim of the trunk murder was white while the members of the community are almost 100 per cent African American.

Carver stopped reading the story. He didn't sense any threat to him. Still, it didn't explain why someone from the *Times*—presumably Cook or McEvoy—had put *trunk murder* into a search engine. The two previous stories in the archives that mentioned trunk murder had been written by McEvoy. They were straight news stories about the Denise Babbit case.

Carver plugged McEvoy into the archive search and soon found hundreds of stories, all related to crime in Los Angeles. He was the crime beat reporter. Carver then put Angela Cook into the search engine and got far fewer stories. She had been writing for the *Times* for less than six months and seemed to have no specific beat until this week, when she shared two by-lines with McEvoy.

'He's teaching her the ropes,' Carver said out loud.

He guessed that Cook was young and McEvoy was old. That would make her the easier mark. He logged on to Facebook, using a phony ID he had concocted long ago, and sure enough she had a page. She was a beauty with shoulder-length blonde hair. Green eyes and a trained pout to her lips. That pout, Carver thought. He could change that.

The photo was a portrait shot. He was disappointed that he could not see all of her. Especially the length and shape of her legs.

He started humming. It always calmed him. Songs he remembered from the sixties and seventies, when he was a boy. Hard rockers a woman could dance to and show her body off to.

He kept searching and found a professional profile on LinkedIn for Angela Cook. That led to the motherlode: a blog page called www.CityofAngela.com in which she kept an ongoing diary of her life and work in Los Angeles.

The latest entry in the blog brimmed with Cook's excitement over being assigned to the police and crime beat, and being trained for the position by the veteran Jack McEvoy.

It was always amazing to Carver how naive young people were. They believed that they could bare their souls on the Internet, post photos and information at will, and not expect any consequences. From her blog he was able to glean all the information he needed about Angela Cook. Her home town, her college sorority, even her dog's name. He knew pizza at a place called Mozza was her favourite food and that the restaurant was only two blocks from her apartment. He was circling her and she didn't even know it.

He paused when he found a blog post from nine months earlier with the heading 'My Top 10 Serial Killers'. Below it she listed ten killers that were household names because of their cross-country rampages of murder. Number one on her list was 'Ted Bundy—because I'm from Florida and that's where he ended up'.

Carver's lip twitched. He liked this girl.

The mantrap alert sounded and Carver immediately killed the Internet connection. He switched screens and on the camera saw McGinnis coming through. Carver swivelled round and was facing McGinnis as he opened the door to the control room.

'What are you doing out here?' McGinnis asked.

Carver stood up and rolled his chair carefully back into place at the empty work station. 'I'm running a program in my office and just wanted to check on something.'

McGinnis didn't seem to care. 'Anything else happening?'

'We have an issue in tower thirty-seven. I moved things off it until I can figure it out. It's temporary.'

McGinnis nodded. 'What about last week's intrusion?'

'Taken care of. The target was Guthrie, Jones. They're in tobacco litigation with a firm called Biggs, Barlow and Cowdry in Raleigh-Durham. Some genius at Biggs thought Guthrie was holding back on the discovery and tried to take a look for himself.'

'And?'

'The FBI has opened a child porn investigation and the genius is the target. I don't think he'll bother us much longer.'

McGinnis nodded his approval and smiled.

'That's my scarecrow,' he said. 'You're the best.'

Carver didn't need McGinnis to say it to know it. 'Thanks.'

McGinnis left the control room. His office was up on the surface in the front of the building. He stayed there most of the time. The web-hosting centre with all the designers and operators was on the surface as well. The high-security colocation farm was below surface in the so-called bunker. Few employees had subterranean access and Carver liked it that way.

Carver sat down again at the work station and went back online. It was now time to go to work on Jack McEvoy and to see if he had been smarter than Angela Cook in protecting himself.

He put the name into Google and soon a new thrill blasted through him. Jack McEvoy had no blog or profile on Facebook. But his name scored numerous hits. Carver had initially thought the name was familiar and now he knew why. A dozen years earlier McEvoy had written the definitive book on the killer known as the Poet. Carver had read that book—repeatedly. Check that, McEvoy had done more than simply write the book about the killer. He had been the journalist who had revealed the Poet to the world. He had got close enough to breathe in the Poet's last breath. Jack McEvoy was a giant slayer.

Carver slowly nodded as he studied McEvoy's book jacket photo on an old Amazon page.

'Well, Jack,' he said out loud. 'I'm honoured.'

ANGELA COOK'S DOG did her in. The dog's name was Arfy—according to an entry in her blog. From there it took Carver only two variations to come up with 'Arphie' and to successfully log on to her LATimes.com account.

His first stop was her email. There was only one unread message and a few others that had been read and saved. He saw none from Jack McEvoy. The new message seemed to be an international Times message that appeared to be a terse back-and-forth with a supervisor or an editor named Alan Prendergast.

From: Alan Prendergast<AlanPrendergast@LATimes.com>
Subject: collision
Date: May 12, 2009 2:11 PM PDT
To: AngelaCook@LATimes.com
Hold tight. A lot can happen in two weeks.

From: Angela Cook<AngelaCook@LATimes.com>
Subject: collision
Date: May 12, 2009 1:59 PM PDT
To: AlanPrendergast@LATimes.com
You told me I WOULD write it.

It looked like Angela was upset. Carver moved on, opening up her old mail folder. He scrolled through and found several messages from her colleague and cowriter Jack McEvoy. He began with the first one and started working his way forward to the most recent messages.

It was all innocuous enough. In the last message, sent just hours before, Jack had sent Angela an email with a summary of a story they were working on together, which he proposed to send to 'Prendo'. Their story seemed to focus on Alonzo Winslow as the suspect. He felt the muscles in his neck start to relax. McEvoy and Cook didn't know anything. Carver closed the email and went to the browser. He scrolled down, seeing all the websites Cook had visited in recent days. He saw trunkmurder.com as well as several visits to Google and the websites of other newspapers.

Carver tried Prendergast next since it appeared his password was so obvious. He went with 'Prendo' and was in on his first attempt. People were so stupid. He went to the mailbox and there was a message from McEvoy that had been sent only two minutes earlier:

From: Jack McEvoy <JackMcEvoy@LATimes.com>
Subject: collision
Date: May 12, 2009 4:33 PM PDT
To: AlanPrendergast@LATimes.com
Cc: AngelaCook@LATimes.com
Prendo, I was looking for you but you were at dinner. The story is changing. Alonzo DIDN'T confess to the killing and I don't even think he did it. I'm heading to Vegas tonight to pursue things further tomorrow. Will fill you in then. Angela can handle the beat. I've got dimes. Jack

Carver felt his gorge rise in his throat and he pushed back from the table in case he had to vomit. His vision momentarily darkened. Then it cleared and he leaned forward to study the message again.

McEvoy had made the connection to Vegas. Carver now knew that he had only himself to blame. He had repeated his modus operandi too soon. Now Jack the Giant Slayer was on his trail.

Carver closed his eyes and thought for a moment. The beginning tendrils of a plan were reaching to him and the first order of business was to delete the message on the screen in front of him, and then go back into Angela Cook's account and delete it from her mailbox as well. Carver deleted the message and uploaded a spyware program that would allow him to track all of Prendergast's and Cook's Internet activities in real time. McEvoy was next, but Carver decided that could come later—after Jack was in Vegas and operating alone. First things first. He got up and put his hand on the reader next to the glass door to the server room. Once the scan was completed, the door unlocked and he slid it open. He walked down the third row to the sixth tower, unlocked the front of the server, bent down and pulled two of the datablades out a quarter of an inch. He then closed and locked the door and headed back to his work station.

Within a few seconds a screen alarm buzzed from the work stations. Carver reached over to the phone. He pushed the intercom and typed in McGinnis's extension.

'Hey, boss, you still there? We've got a code-three problem. You'd better come and look.'

Three minutes later McGinnis came through the door.

'What's wrong?' he demanded.

'Dewey and Bach in LA just got data-bombed. The whole route collapsed.'

'Jesus, how?'

Carver shrugged. 'Can't tell from this end.'

McGinnis stood behind Carver, shifting his weight from foot to foot, looking through the glass at the servers.

'The problem's not here—I've checked everything. It's on their end. I think I need to go out there to fix it and reopen the traffic. I can leave now.'

'OK. I want Dewey and Bach to see that we don't mess around. We get thigns done. Just keep me informed.'

'Will do.'

McGinnis clapped him on the shoulder and went back out through the door. Carver sat there motionless for a few moments, feeling the residual compression on his shoulder. He hated to be touched.

Finally, he leaned towards his screen and entered the alarm disengagement code. He confirmed the protocol and then deleted it.

Carver pulled out his cellphone and hit a speed-dial number.

'What's up?' Freddy Stone said.

'Come back to the control room. We have a problem. Actually, two problems. And we need to take care of them.'

Six: The Loneliest Road in America

At 9 a.m. on Wednesday I was waiting outside the locked door of the third-floor offices of Schifino & Associates in downtown LA. After catching the last flight out of LA and checking into the Mandalay Bay at midnight, I found myself too keyed-up to sleep. I went down to the casino and turned the $200 I had brought with me into three times that amount at the blackjack tables.

The growth of my cash portfolio along with the free booze I'd drunk made sleep come easier when I returned to my room. Things took a dramatic downturn after the front desk called and woke me up to tell me my *Times*-issued American Express card had being rejected.

'That doesn't make sense,' I said. 'I bought an airline ticket with it last night, and got a car hire. And it was fine when I checked in here.'

'That was just an authorising process. The card is not charged until six o'clock on the morning of check-out. We ran the card and it was rejected. Could you please come and give us another card?'

'No problem.'

Only there *was* a problem, because my three other credit cards didn't work either. I was forced to chip back half of my winnings to get out of the hotel. Once I got to my rental car I pulled out my cellphone to start calling the credit-card companies. Only I couldn't make the calls because my phone service was disconnected.

Annoyed and confused but undaunted, I headed to the address I had looked up for William Schifino. I still had a story to pursue.

A few minutes after nine a woman stepped off the elevator and headed down the hallway towards me. I noticed the slight hesitation in her step when she saw me waiting outside Schifino's door. I nodded and smiled at her as she got closer.

'Do you work with William Schifino?' I asked.

'Yes, I'm his receptionist. What can I do for you?'

'I need to speak to Mr Schifino. I came from Los Angeles. I—'

'Do you have an appointment?'

'I don't have an appointment but I'm a reporter. I want to talk to Mr Schifino about Brian Oglevy.'

'You can come in and wait. I don't know when he'll be in.'

We went into the office and she directed me to a couch in a small waiting area. Twenty minutes later the office door opened and a man stepped in. He nodded to me and looked at the receptionist.

'Mr Schifino, this man says he's a reporter from Los Angeles—'

'Brian Oglevy is innocent.' I cut her off. 'And I think I can prove it.'

Schifino studied me for a long moment. He had dark hair and a handsome face with an uneven tan from wearing a baseball cap. His eyes were sharp and he quickly came to a decision about me.

'Then I guess you'd better come on back to the office,' he said.

I followed him to his office and he sat down behind a large desk while signalling me to the seat on the other side.

'So how did you come to the conclusion in LA that my guy over here is an innocent man?'

'Well, I've got a kid sitting in jail for a murder I'm thinking he didn't commit, and it seems that the details are a lot like the details in your Oglevy case. Only, my case happened two weeks ago.'

'So if they are the same, my client has an obvious alibi and there might be a third party here at work.'

'Exactly.'

'All right, well, let's see what you've got.'

'Well, I was hoping I could see what you've got, too.'

'Fair enough. My client is in prison and I don't think he's too worried about attorney-client privilege at this point.'

Schifino pulled his files and we began a show-me-yours-show-you-mine session. I maintained a reserved excitement as we went through the crime reports. But when we moved into comparisons of the crime scene photos the adrenaline kicked in. Not only did the Oglevy photos completely match those from the Babbit case, but the victims looked stunningly alike.

'This is amazing!' I said. 'It's almost like the same woman.'

Both were tall brunettes with brown eyes and long-legged bodies. Immediately I was hit with the sense that these women had been chosen.

They fitted some kind of mould that had made them targets.

Schifino was riding the same wave. He pointed from photo to photo, accenting the similarities in the crime scenes. Both women were suffocated with a plastic bag that was tied round the neck with a thin white cord. Each was placed naked and facing inwards in the trunk of the car, and their clothes were dropped on top of them.

'Look at this,' he said, gesturing to the photos we had laid out. 'These crimes are absolutely the same and it doesn't take an expert to see that. This is my client's freedom right here!'

'How did this happen?' I asked. 'How did this slip through?'

'Because they were solved quickly,' Schifino said. 'In each case the police were led to an obvious suspect and looked no further.'

'But how did the killer know to put Sharon Oglevy's body in her ex-husband's trunk? How would he know where to find the car?'

'I don't know, but that is off point. The point here is that these two killings are of such a strikingly similar pattern that there is no way that either Brian Oglevy or Alonzo Winslow could be responsible. There is no doubt in my mind that you're exposing something huge. I mean, there could be others.'

I nodded. Two cases make a pattern. There still could be more.

'What will you do now?' I asked.

'I'm going to file a petition for a writ of habeas corpus. This is new information that is exculpatory and we're going to put it into open court.'

'But I'm not supposed to have those files. You can't cite them.'

'Sure I can. What I don't have to do is say where I got them.'

I frowned. I would be the obvious source once my story was published.

'How long will it take for you to get this into court?'

'I'll file it by the end of the week.'

'That's going to blow this up. I don't know if I can be ready to publish my story by then.'

Schifino held his hands out wide and shook his head. 'My client's been up at Ely for more than a year.'

Schifino was right. I couldn't justify keeping Brian Oglevy in prison even a day longer just so I could have time to write the story.

'OK, then I want to talk to your client today. How do I do it?'

'He's in maximum security but I can get you in. I need to fax a letter up to the prison that says you are an investigator working for me and that you are entitled to access to Brian. I then give you a "To-whom-it-may-concern" letter that you carry with you, and that identifies you as working for me. You show that letter at the gate.'

'Technically, I don't work for you. My paper has rules about reporters misrepresenting themselves.'

Schifino reached into his pocket and handed me a dollar bill. 'There,' he said. 'I just paid you a dollar. You work for me.'

That didn't really cut it but I wasn't too worried about it, considering my employment situation. 'I guess that will work,' I said. 'How far is Ely?'

'It's three to four hours north. It's in the middle of nowhere and they call the road going up there The Loneliest Road in America.'

'OK, write the letters. And I'm going to need copies of everything in your files.'

'I'll work on the letters and get Agnes to start making copies. I'll need copies of what you have for the habeas petition. We can say that's what my dollar bought.'

AFTER STOPPING at a 7-Eleven to buy a throwaway phone with 100 minutes of call time on it, I headed towards Ely State Prison.

Highway 93 took me past Nellis Air Force Base and then connected with 50 North. It wasn't too long before I began to see why it was known as The Loneliest Road in America. The empty desert ruled the horizon in every direction.

The first calls I made with my new phone were to the credit-card companies, demanding to know why my cards were not working. With each call I got the same answer: I had reported the card stolen the night before, thereby temporarily cancelling use of the account. I had gone online, answered all security questions correctly and reported the card stolen.

It didn't matter that I told them I hadn't reported the cards stolen. Someone had, and that someone had known my account numbers, home address, birth date, mother's maiden name and Social Security number. I demanded that the accounts be reopened and the service reps gladly complied. The only catch was that new credit cards had to be sent to my home. That would take days.

I next called my bank in Los Angeles and found a variation on the same scheme, but with a deeper impact. The good news was that my debit card still worked. The bad news was that there was no money in my account. The night before, I had used the online banking service to make a debit transfer of the full amount to the Make-A-Wish Foundation. I was broke.

I disconnected the call and screamed as loud as I could in the car. What was happening to me? There were stories in the paper all the time about stolen identities. But this time the victim was me.

At eleven I called the city desk and learned that the intrusion and destruction had moved up yet another notch. I got hold of Alan Prendergast and his voice was tight with nervous energy.

'Where are you?'

'I told you, I'm in Vegas. Where's—'

'Vegas! Vegas? What are you doing in Vegas?'

'Didn't you get my message? I sent you an email before I left.'

'Didn't get it. Yesterday you just disappeared. I've got you in Vegas and I haven't heard from Cook. What are you doing there, Jack?'

'I told you in the email you haven't read. The story is—'

'I've got no email from you. No email,' he said curtly.

I was about to tell him he was wrong but thought about my credit cards. If somebody was able to crash my credit and wipe out my bank account, then maybe they crashed my email as well.

'Listen, Prendo, something is going on. My credit cards are dead, my phone's dead and now you're telling me my email never made it. Something is not right here. I—'

'For the last time, Jack. What are you doing in Nevada?'

I blew out my breath and looked out of the side window. 'The story on Alonzo Winslow has changed,' I said. 'I found out he didn't do it. He's innocent, Alan, and I can prove it.'

'He confessed, Jack. I read it in *your* story.'

'Yeah, because that's what the cops said. But I read the so-called confession and all he confessed to was stealing her car and her money. He didn't know her body was in the trunk.'

'Jack . . .'

'Listen, Prendo, I connected the murder to another murder in Vegas.

It was the same thing. A woman strangled and put in a trunk. She was a dancer, too. There's a guy in prison here for that one and he didn't do it either. I'm heading up to see him right now. I'm going to have to report and write this all by Thursday.'

'Jack, we need to talk about this.'

'I thought we were. Where is Angela? She's on the beat today.'

'She hasn't come in yet.'

'Did you call her?'

'Of course I called her. I've left messages.'

'Look, Prendo, this is huge. There's a killer out there who has flown below everyone's radar. A lawyer here in Vegas is going to file a motion by Friday that exposes the whole thing. We've got to beat him and everybody else to the punch. I'm going to go and talk to this guy in prison and then head back.'

I was met with silence.

'Prendo?'

'Listen, Jack,' he said, a calmness in his voice for the first time in the conversation. 'We both know the situation and what is going on here. If you think you can come up with a story that's going to save your job, I don't think that's going to work.'

Now I was silent as the anger welled up in my throat.

'Prendo, my only response is, "Screw you". I'm not concocting this story, man. This is happening! And I'm out here in the middle of nowhere and am not sure who is messing with me or why.'

'OK, Jack. Calm down, OK? I am not suggesting that you—'

'The hell you're not! You more than suggested it. You just said it. I've got other calls to make. If you don't want the story, then I'll find somebody who will print it, OK? I'll talk to you later.'

I hung up the phone and nearly threw it out of the window. But then I remembered I didn't have the replacement cash to spare. I drove in silence for a few minutes so I could compose myself. I had one more call to make and I wanted to sound calm when I made it.

I pulled my inoperable phone from my pocket and opened up the contacts list. I punched in the number for the FBI in Los Angeles and asked to speak to Agent Rachel Walling.

'Agent Walling.'

It was her. It had been a few years since I had heard her voice over the phone but there was no doubt.

'Hello? This is Walling, can I help you?'

'Rachel, it's me. Jack.'

She was momentarily caught in silence.

'Why are you calling me, Jack? We agreed it would be better not to talk.'

'I know . . . but I need your help. I'm in trouble, Rachel.'

'And you're expecting me to help you? What kind of trouble?'

A passing car blew past me going a hundred, at least.

'It's sort of a long story. I'm in Nevada. In the desert. I'm chasing a story and there's a killer out there nobody knows about. I need somebody to believe me and to help me.'

'Jack, I'm the wrong person. I can't help you. I have to go.'

'Rachel, please! Somebody's messing with me. My phone, my email, my bank accounts—I'm driving through the middle of the desert and I don't even have a credit card that works.'

'Where are you going?'

'To Ely, to the prison, to talk to somebody.'

'What, somebody called you up and said he was innocent and you come running, hoping to prove the real cops are wrong again?'

'No, nothing like that. Look, Rachel, this guy is strangling women and stuffing them into the trunks of cars.'

'Jack, I've read your stories about the girl in the trunk. It was a gang-kid and he confessed.'

I got an unexpected thrill from knowing she read my stories.

'Don't believe everything you read in the paper, Rachel. I'm getting to the truth now and I need somebody in authority—'

'But I'm not in Behavioural Science any more. Why call me?'

'Because I can trust you.'

That brought a long moment of silence. I refused to break first.

'How can you say that?' she finally said. 'We haven't seen each other in a long, long time.'

'Doesn't matter. After what we went through back then, I'll always trust you, Rachel. And I know you could help me now . . . and maybe make up for some things yourself.'

She scoffed at that. 'It doesn't matter. Please don't call me again, Jack. I can't help you. So good luck and be safe.' She hung up.

I felt like I'd been left alone on the surface of the moon.

AS WITH MOST PEOPLE who pass through the gates of Ely State Prison, my luck did not change for the better upon arrival. I showed the introduction letter William Schifino had written for me to the watch captain.

'Mr McEvoy,' the captain said, pronouncing my name wrong. 'I'm afraid we're not going to be able to do this today.'

'What do you mean? It was all set up. You saw the letter from the lawyer. He also faxed you a letter saying I was coming.'

'Yeah, we got the fax but the man you want to see is unavailable at this time. You can come back tomorrow.'

'Look, I just drove four hours from Vegas. I'm not go—'

'I'm not telling you to go back to Vegas. I'd just go into town and stay at the Hotel Nevada. It ain't bad. You come back here tomorrow morning and I'll have your man all ready for you.'

'Can you tell me why I can't see him today?'

'No, I can't. It's a security issue.'

I shook my head in frustration. 'I guess I'll see you tomorrow.'

'We'll be here.'

After getting back to my rental, I drove to the Nevada Hotel in Ely. I pulled into the parking lot and emptied my pockets. I had $248 in cash.

I took a forty-five-dollars-a-night room on the third floor. The room was neat and clean and the bed was reasonably comfortable. It was only 4 p.m., so I called Angela Cook, trying both her cellphone and desk line and getting no answer on either. I swallowed my pride and called Alan Prendergast back. I apologised for my outburst earlier.

He responded monosyllabically and said he had a meeting to go to. I told him I would get him a budget line for the revised story.

'Look, we want to move cautiously,' he said. 'We've got you running round in the desert. We haven't even heard from Angela and, frankly, we're getting worried. She should have checked in.'

'You've got no message from her all day?'

'Not a one. We don't know where she is.'

'Well, listen. If anybody hears from her, let me know, OK?'

'You got it, Jack.'

'OK, Prendo. We'll talk when I get back.'

I closed the phone and thought about Angela being missing in action. I started wondering if everything was connected. My credit cards, nobody hearing from Angela. It seemed like a stretch.

I booted up my laptop and used the hotel's WiFi to try to sign into my email account. My password was not accepted.

'This is crazy,' I said out loud.

Unable to make outside contact, I opened a file on the laptop and pulled out my hard-copy notes. I started writing a narrative summarising the moves of the day. It took me over an hour, but when I was done I had thirty solid inches of story. And it was good story.

After making some editing improvements, I realised that the work had made me hungry. I went downstairs to a bar by the dollar slots. I ordered a beer and a steak sandwich.

I checked my cash again and decided I had enough for a roll of quarters for the cheap slots. I set up in a row near the lobby entrance and started feeding money into an electronic poker machine. I lost my first seven hands before hitting on a full house. I followed that with a flush and a straight. Soon I was thinking about being able to afford a second beer.

Another gambler took a seat two machines over from me. I barely noticed him until he decided he liked the comfort of conversation while he lost his money.

'You here for the whores?' he asked cheerily.

I looked over at him. He was about thirty and had large mutton-chop side-burns. He wore a dusty cowboy hat over dirty blond hair, leather driving gloves and mirrored sunglasses, even though we were inside.

'Excuse me?'

'Supposed to be a couple of brothels outside of town. I was wondering which one's got the best-looking girls.'

'I wouldn't know, man.'

I went back to my machine and tried to concentrate on what to hold and what to drop. I had the ace, three, four and nine of spades along with the ace of hearts. I held my spades, dropped the ace of hearts and hit the draw button. I got the jack of spades and a seven-to-one payoff on the flush. I hit the cash-out button and a whopping fourteen dollars in quarters dropped into the tray. I got up and invested my winnings in two more beers to take back to my room.

While waiting for the elevator in the lobby I carried the bottles down by my side in case I was breaking some sort of house rule. I stepped in, pushed the button and moved to the back corner. The doors started to come together but then a gloved hand poked in and hit the infrared beam and the doors reopened.

My pal Sideburns stepped in. He raised a finger to push a button but then pulled it back. 'Hey, we've got the same floor,' he said.

'Wonderful,' I said.

I knew he was going to say something and there was no place for me to go. I just waited for it and I wasn't disappointed.

'Hey, buddy, I didn't mean to mess up your mojo down there. My ex-wife used to say I talked too much.'

'Don't worry about it,' I said. 'I have to get some work done anyway.'

'So you're here on work, huh? What kind of business would take you to this godforsaken part of the world?'

'I have an appointment tomorrow at the prison.'

'Gotcha. You a lawyer for one of them guys?'

'No. Journalist.'

'Hmm, a writer, huh? Well, good luck.'

When we reached the third floor, I said, 'Have a good night,' and stepped out of the elevator and to the left.

'You, too, partner,' Sideburns said.

As I stood in front of the door pulling my room key out of my pocket I saw him coming towards me. I got the key into the lock and pushed the door open. I looked back at Sideburns and gave him a final nod. His face broke into a strange smile as he got closer.

'Hi, Jack,' a voice said from inside my room.

I abruptly turned to see a woman getting up from the chair by the window in my room. And I immediately recognised her as Rachel Walling. She had an all-business look on her face. I felt Sideburns go by my back on his way to his room.

'Rachel?' I said. 'What are you doing here?'

'Why don't you come in and close the door?'

Stunned, I closed the door behind me. From out in the hallway I heard another door close loudly. Sideburns had entered his room.

'How'd you get in here?'

'Just sit down and I'll tell you all about it.'

TWELVE YEARS EARLIER I'd had a short, intense and, some would say, improper relationship with Rachel Walling. Not many days went by that I didn't think about her. She was the reason that I have always considered that time the high point of my life.

She showed little wear and tear from the years that had passed, even though I knew it had been a tough time. She had paid for her relationship with me with a five-year stint in a one-person office in South Dakota. She went from chasing serial killers to investigating bar stabbings on Indian reservations. But she had climbed out of that pit and had been posted in LA for the last five years, working for some sort of a secretive intelligence unit. I had called her when I'd found out, but had been rebuffed. Since then I had kept tabs on her from afar.

Now I couldn't stop staring and smiling at her. She maintained the professional front, but I could see her eyes holding on me.

'Who was that you were with?' she asked.

I turned and looked back at the doorway.

'I don't know. Just some guy who'd been talking to me downstairs in the gambling hall. He went to his room.'

She abruptly walked past me, opened the door and looked both ways in the hall before coming back inside and closing the door.

'Which room is he in?'

'I don't know. What's going on?'

I pointed to the bed. My laptop was open and my print-outs and notes were fanned across it. I hadn't left it all on the bed like that.

'Were you going through my stuff?'

'Look, just sit down, would you?'

I sat on the bed, closing my laptop sullenly and gathering the paperwork into one stack. She remained standing.

'OK, I showed my creds and asked the manager to let me in. I told him your safety might be in jeopardy.'

'What are you talking about? Nobody even knows I'm here.'

'I wouldn't be so sure about that. You told me you were going to the prison up here. Who else did you tell? Who else knows?'

'I told my editor and there's a lawyer in Vegas who knows.'

She nodded. 'William Schifino. Yes, I talked to him.'

'You talked to him? Why? What is going on here, Rachel?'

She pulled a chair to the middle of the room and sat down.

'OK, when you called me today you weren't making the most sense, Jack. But the part that stuck with me was what you said about your credit cards and bank account and your phone and Internet. I was concerned.'

'Why?'

'Because you were looking at all of that like it just happened to be going on while you were working on this story about this supposed killer.'

'Are you saying it could be related? The guy I am trying to chase down would have no idea that I'm even out here and onto him.'

'Don't be so sure about that, Jack. It is a classic hunting tactic. Separate and isolate your target and then move in for the kill. In today's society, separating and isolating someone would entail getting them away from their comfort zone and then eliminating their ability to connect. Cellphone, Internet, credit cards, money.' She ticked them off on her fingers.

'But how could he know about me? Look, Rachel, it's great to see you and I hope you stick around, but I'm not getting this. I mean, don't get me wrong. I appreciate the concern—in fact, how did you get here so quick?'

'I took an FBI jet to Nellis and had them jump me up here in a chopper.'

'Jesus! Why didn't you just call me back?'

'I couldn't. There's no caller ID on those throwaway lines.'

'So what's the Bureau brass going to say when they find out you dropped everything and hopped on a plane to save me?'

She waved the concern away with her hand. 'There's an inmate in Ely who has been on my interview list for months,' she said. 'Officially, I came to interview him. I can't talk to you about that part of my work. But I can tell you how easy it was to find you and why I know I wasn't the only one tracking you.'

She froze me with the word *tracking*. 'OK,' I said. 'Tell me.'

'You told me you were going to Ely to interview a prisoner. So I called Ely and was told that you had just left, and were staying here. They said your interview was postponed because your guy, Brian Oglevy, was in lockdown because there was a threat against him, sent by email. The email was sent by the warden's own secretary. Only she didn't write it. It was written anonymously by a hacker who had gained access to her state prison system account. So they took it seriously and put Oglevy in lockdown.'

'OK, what else? This is still a stretch.'

'The watch captain at the prison said that the lawyer, William Schifino, called to check on you and was told the same thing, that the interview was delayed and you were probably spending the night at the Nevada. Only I called William Schifino and he said he never made the call.'

I stared at her as a cold finger went down my spine.

'I asked Schifino if anyone else had called about you and he told me he had got one call from someone who said he was your editor—used the name Prendergast—and that he was worried about you. Schifino told him you were on your way up to the prison.'

I knew my editor couldn't have made that call because when I had called Prendergast he hadn't got my email and had no idea I had gone to Las Vegas. Rachel was right. Someone had been tracking me and doing it well.

My mind flashed on thoughts of Sideburns following me to my room. What if he hadn't heard Rachel's voice? Would he have walked on by or would he have pushed in behind me?

Rachel stood up and walked over to the room's phone. She dialled the operator and asked for the manager.

'It's Agent Walling. I'm still in room three-ten and I've located Mr McEvoy and he's safe. I am now wondering if you can tell me if there are any guests in the next three rooms going down the hall.'

She waited and listened. 'One last question,' she said. 'There is a door marked EXIT at the end of the hall. I'm assuming those are stairs. Where do they go?'

She listened, thanked him and then hung up.

'There's nobody registered in those rooms. The stairs go down to the parking lot.'

'You think that guy with the sideburns was him?'

She sat back down. 'Possibly. I'm sure he's long gone now.'

I thought about his sunglasses, the driving gloves and the cowboy hat. I realised that if I had to describe him I would only be able to remember the changeable features of a disguise.

'I can't believe how stupid I was. How did this guy find out about me and then actually find me?'

'That trick with the prison secretary's email shows he has a certain skill set. I think it would be wise to consider your email accounts to be breached at this point.'

I slapped the bed in annoyance and nodded my head.

'I did send emails last night. To both my editor and my partner on the story, telling them that I was following a lead to Vegas. I talked to my editor today and he said he never got it.'

Rachel nodded knowingly. 'Destroying outgoing communications. That would fall under isolation of the target. Did your partner get his?'

'It's a her and I don't know if she got it because she's not answering her phone or her email and she didn't—' I stopped and looked at Rachel.

'What?'

'She didn't show up for work today. She didn't call in and nobody could reach her.'

Rachel stood up abruptly.

'We've got to go back to LA, Jack. The chopper's waiting.'

'What about my interview?'

'What about your partner? The interview can wait till later.'

Embarrassed, I nodded and got off the bed. It was time to go.

I HAD NO IDEA where Angela Cook lived. I told Rachel what I did know about her, including her fixation with the Poet case, and that I'd heard she had a blog but had never read it. Rachel transmitted all the information to an agent in LA before we boarded the military chopper and headed south towards Nellis Air Force Base.

On the flight down we wore headsets that cut down on the engine noise but didn't allow for conversation. Rachel took my files and spent the hour with them. I watched her making comparisons between the crime scene and autopsy reports of Denise Babbit and Sharon Oglevy. She worked with a look of complete concentration.

For the most part I racked my brains, trying to put together an explanation for how all of this could have happened so fast. By the time we landed at Nellis I thought I had something.

We transferred to a waiting jet on which we were the only passengers. We sat across from each other, and the pilot informed Rachel that there was a call for her on the onboard telephone. She picked up the phone, listened, asked a few questions and hung up.

'Angela Cook was not at home,' she said. 'They can't find her.'

I didn't respond. Dread worked its way up under my ribs.

'Rachel, I think I know how this guy found us so quickly.'

'Tell me.'

'No, you first. Tell me what you found in the files.'

'Fine. But, first, let me commend you, Jack. There is no doubt in my mind that these cases are connected by a single killer. He escaped notice because in each case an alternate suspect came to light quickly and the local authorities proceeded with blinders on.'

I leaned forward, beaming with confidence after her compliment.

'What I was doing with the material you have here was profiling the two killings. Looking for a signature.'

'It's obvious. He likes strangling women with plastic bags.'

'Technically, they weren't strangled. They were asphyxiated. Suffocated. There's a difference. I was actually looking for something a little less obvious than the surface signature. I was also looking for connections or similarities between the women.'

'They were both strippers.'

'That's part of it but a little broad. They were very similar in physical make-up. Facial structure and hair were also alike. A victim's body type is a key component in terms of what makes them chosen. When you see two victims like this with exactly the same body types, it tells us this is a predator who is patient, who chooses.'

I waited but she didn't continue.

'What?' I said. 'You know more than you're saying.'

'There's something else,' she said. 'Both autopsies ascribe marks on the victims' legs to ligatures. That might be wrong.' She pulled several photos from the crime scenes and autopsies. 'You see the marks left above and below the knees—here and here?'

'Yeah, like they were tied up.'

'Not quite. The marks are too symmetrical to be from traditional bindings. Plus if these were ligature marks we would see them round the ankles. If you were going to tie someone up, you would tie their ankles. Yet we have no ligature marks in these areas.'

She was right. I just hadn't seen it until she explained it.

'So what made those marks on the legs?'

'Well, I can't say for sure, but when I was in Behavioural we came upon new paraphilias on almost every case.'

'You're talking about sexual perversions?'

'We didn't call them that. We call the behaviours paraphilias.'

'OK, and these marks, they're part of a paraphilia?'

'I think they are marks left by straps from leg braces.'

'You've got to be kidding. People get off on leg braces?'

Rachel nodded. 'It's called abasiophilia. A psychosexual fascination with leg braces. There are even websites dedicated to it. Women who wear braces are sometimes called iron maidens.'

I was reminded of how intoxicating Rachel's skill as a profiler had been when we were chasing the Poet. I had been captivated by her ability to take small pieces of information and draw telling conclusions.

'Where does an addiction like that come from?'

'Most paraphilias are embedded in early childhood.'

'They were both dancers. Do you think the killer made them dance or something?'

'It's all conjecture at this point, but that could be part of it. My guess is that it's about body type. Dancers by trade have thin, muscular legs. If that is what he wanted, then he would look at dancers.'

I was impressed. 'Will you put all of this through VICAP?'

'As soon as I get the chance.'

The FBI's Violent Criminal Apprehension Programme was a computer data bank of the details of thousands of crimes and could be used to find crimes of similar nature.

'You think if we ever capture this guy we'll be able to figure him out?'

'You never figure them out, Jack. You get hints, that's all.' She hesitated, then continued, 'There's something else to be noted about the killer's programme. In both cases he left the bag and neck ligature in place on the victims but the limb constraints—whether braces or not—were removed.'

'Right. What does that mean?'

'I don't know. The women are obviously constrained in some way during their captivity. Whether it is through braces or otherwise, those are removed but the bag stays in place. This could be part of a statement, part of his signature. It might have a meaning we are not aware of yet.' She sighed. 'There's got to be a link between these women somewhere.'

'We find it and we find him.'

'Right. Now it's your turn, Jack. What did you put together?'

I nodded. 'Well, there was something Angela found. She got the Vegas stories when she did an online search on the phrase *trunk murder*. She told me that she also got a hit on a website called trunk murder dot com, but that when she went to it there was a sign that said it was under construction. So I was thinking maybe—'

'Of course! It could have been an IP trap. He would be alert for anybody fishing around on the Internet for intel on trunk murders. He could then trace the IP back and find out who was looking. That would have led him to Angela and then to you. He probably got a big thrill when he saw your name,' Rachel added.

I looked at her.

'What are you talking about?'

'Your pedigree, Jack. You were the reporter who chased down the Poet. You wrote the book on it. Mr Big Best Seller. These serial guys pay attention to all of that. I'll make a bet with you. When we get this guy, we'll find your book in his possessions somewhere.'

'I hope not.'

'And I'll make you another bet. Before we get this guy he will make direct contact with you. He'll call or email.'

'Why? Why would he risk it?'

'Because once it's clear to him that we know about him, he will reach out for attention. They always do.'

WE LANDED at Van Nuys Airport and got into the car Rachel had left there.

'Where's your car?' she asked. 'At LAX?'

'No, I took a cab. It's at home. In the garage.'

I didn't think any line so basic could have sounded so ominous. *In the garage.* I gave Rachel my address and we headed off.

It was almost midnight and traffic was light. My house was on Curson, a block south of Sunset. It was a nice neighbourhood full of mostly small houses. I had a two-bedroom Craftsman with a single-car garage in the back. I had bought the place twelve years earlier with money from the sale of my book on the Poet.

Rachel pulled into the driveway and parked, but left the lights on. They shone brightly on the closed garage door. We got out and approached slowly.

'I never lock it,' I said.

I raised the garage door and we stepped in. An automatic light went on above and we stared at the trunk of my BMW. I already had the key ready. I pushed the button and we heard the *fump* of the trunk lock releasing. Rachel stepped forward without hesitation and raised the trunk lid.

Except for a bag of clothes I'd been meaning to drop at the Salvation Army, the trunk was empty.

Rachel had been holding her breath. I heard her slowly release it.

'Yeah,' I said. 'I thought for sure . . .'

She slammed the trunk closed angrily.

'What, you're upset that she's not in there?' I asked.

'No, Jack. I'm upset because I'm being manipulated. He had me thinking in a certain way and that was my mistake. It won't happen again. Come on, let's check the house to be sure.'

Rachel turned her headlights off and we went through the back door and into the kitchen. I led the way, turning lights on as we went. The living room looked unchanged from the way I had left it. Too many stacks of newspapers covering tables and the floor next to the couch.

'Nice place,' Rachel said.

We checked the guest room, which I used as an office, then moved on to the master bedroom. It was stuffy and I went to open a window while Rachel checked the closet and then stepped into the bathroom. I heard the shower curtain being slid open, then Rachel stepped back into the bedroom.

'Who are all the women?' She pointed to the chest of drawers where there was a row of framed photos.

I went down the line. 'Niece, sister-in-law, mother, ex-wife.'

Rachel raised her eyebrows.

'Ex-wife? You were able to get over me then.'

'It didn't last long. She's a reporter. When I first came to the *Times* we shared the cop beat. She works in the Washington bureau now. We're friends.'

I wanted to say more but something made me hold back. Rachel turned and headed back to the living room. I followed her.

'What now?' I asked.

'I'm not sure. Are you going to be all right here?'

'Sure. Why not? Besides, I've got a gun.'

'You have a gun? Jack, what are you doing with a gun?'

'I got it after the Poet, you know?'

She nodded. She understood. 'Well, then, if you're OK, I'll leave you here with your gun and call you in the morning.'

I nodded and knew that it was one of those moments. I could reach out for what I wanted or I could let it go like I had a long time before.

'What if I don't want you to leave?' I asked. 'What if I've never got over you?'

Her eyes dropped to the floor.

'Jack . . . ten years is a lifetime. We're different people now.'

'Are we?'

She looked back at me and we held each other's eyes. I stepped in close and pulled her into a long, hard kiss that she did not fight. Her phone dropped out of her hand and clunked to the floor. We grabbed at each other in some sort of emotional desperation. There was nothing gentle about it. It was about wanting, craving. Nothing loving, yet it was all about love and the reckless willingness to cross the line for the sake of intimacy with another human being.

'Let's go back to the bedroom,' I whispered against her cheek.

She smiled into my next kiss, then we somehow managed to get to my bedroom. We urgently pulled our clothes off and made love on the bed. It was over before I could think about what we were doing and what it might mean. We then lay side by side on our backs, both of us breathing in deep strides.

'Uh, oh,' she finally said.

I smiled. 'You are so fired,' I said.

And she smiled, too. 'What about you? The *Times* has to have some kind of rule about sleeping with the enemy, doesn't it?'

'What are you talking about, *the enemy*? Besides, they laid me off last week. I've got one more week there and then I'm history.'

'*What?*' Her voice was concerned.

'Yeah, I got downsized and they gave me two weeks to train Angela and clear out.'

'That's awful. Why you?'

'Because I have a big salary and Angela doesn't.'

'What are you going to do?'

'I don't know, probably write the novel I've been talking about. I think the bigger question is what are we going to do now, Rachel?' I said.

She opened her eyes and started rubbing my chest.

'I hope this wasn't a one-time thing. I don't want it to be.'

She didn't respond for a long time.

'Me neither,' she finally said. But that was all.

'What are you thinking?' I asked.

She looked at me with a half-smile. 'To be honest, I was thinking about something a man I was with a couple of years ago said. We'd, uh, had a relationship and it wasn't going to work. I had my own hang-ups and I knew he was still holding out for his ex-wife. When we talked about it, he told me about the "single-bullet theory". You know what that is?'

'You mean like with the assassination of Kennedy?'

She mock-punched me in the chest with a fist.

'No, I mean like with the love of your life. Everybody's got one person out there. One bullet. And if you're lucky in life, you get to meet that person. And once you do, once you're shot through the heart, then there's nobody else. No matter what happens—death, divorce, infidelity, whatever—nobody else can ever come close.'

She nodded. She believed it.

'What are you saying, that he was your bullet?'

'No, I'm saying he wasn't. He was too late. You see, I'd already been shot by someone else. Someone before him.'

I looked at her for a long moment, then pulled her down into a kiss. After a few moments she pulled back.

'But I should go. We should think about this.'

'Just stay here. Sleep with me. We'll get up early tomorrow.'

'No, I have to go home now or my husband will worry.'

I sat bolt upright. She started laughing and slipped off the bed. She began getting dressed.

'That wasn't funny,' I said.

'I think it was,' she insisted.

I climbed off the bed and started getting dressed, too. She kept laughing in a punch-drunk sort of way. Eventually, I was laughing too. I pulled on my trousers and shirt and then started hunting round the bed for my shoes and socks. I found them all except for one sock. I finally got down on my knees and looked for it under the bed.

And that was when the laughter stopped.

ANGELA COOK'S DEAD EYES stared at me from under the bed. I involuntarily propelled myself backwards, smashing my back into the chest of drawers.

'Jack?' Rachel yelled.

I pointed. 'Angela's under the bed!'

Rachel quickly came round to me. She was only wearing her black panties and white blouse. She got down to look.

'I thought you checked under the bed!' I said excitedly.

'I thought *you* did while I was checking out the closet.'

She got on her hands and knees and looked underneath the bed for a long moment before turning to look back at me.

'She's been dead about a day. Suffocation with a plastic bag. She's naked and wrapped in a plastic sheet. We need to call the LAPD. We'll say I brought you home, we searched the place and we found her. The rest we leave out. OK?'

'Fine. OK. Whatever you say.'

'I have to get dressed.'

She stood up and I realised the woman I had just made love to had completely disappeared. She was all Bureau now. She started pulling the sheets off the bed and gathering them into a ball.

'Can't we just tell them that we didn't find her until after we—'

'Think, Jack. I admit something like that and I am the butt of every joke in the squad room for the next ten years. We do it this way and they'll just think the killer took the sheets.'

She balled everything up together.

'Well, maybe there's evidence from the guy on the sheets.'

'He's too careful. If there was evidence he would have taken them. I doubt she was even killed on this bed. She was just wrapped up and hidden underneath it—for you to find.'

'What do you mean?'

She said it so matter-of-factly. There was probably nothing in this world that surprised her or horrified her any longer.

'Come on, Jack. We have to move.'

She left the room, carrying the sheets and pillows. I slowly got up then, found my missing sock behind a chair and carried my socks and shoes out to the living room. I was putting them on when I heard the back door close. Rachel came in empty-handed and I assumed she had stashed the pillows and sheets in the trunk of her car.

She picked her phone up off the floor and dialled. I listened to her speak briefly to someone who was probably an FBI supervisor. Next she called the LAPD, identified herself, gave my address and asked for a homicide team. She then ended the call.

She looked at me. 'What about you? If you need to call someone you'd better do it now.'

'Right.' I pulled out my throwaway and called the city desk at the *Times*. I checked my watch and saw it was almost midnight. The night editor was an old veteran named Esteban Samuel.

'Sam, it's Jack McEvoy.'

'Jack Mack! How you doing?'

'Not so well. I've got some bad news. Angela Cook has been murdered. An FBI agent and I just found her.'

'Oh my God! How terrible! That poor, poor girl. What happened?'

'It's related to the story we were working on.'

'Where are you? Where did this happen?'

'My house. I went to Vegas last night and Angela went missing today.

I came back tonight and an FBI agent escorted me home and we searched the house. We found her body under the bed.'

The whole thing sounded insane as I said it.

'Are you under arrest?' Samuel asked, confusion in his voice.

'No, no. The killer is trying to set me up. All of this will be in the story I write tomorrow. I'll be in as early as I can and I will write it for Friday's paper. OK? Make sure they know that.'

'Got it, Jack. I'll make some calls and you stay in touch.'

Rachel was pacing. 'That didn't sound very convincing.'

I shook my head. 'I know. I sounded like a nut job. I've got a bad feeling about this, Rachel. Nobody's going to believe me.'

'They will, Jack. And I think I know what he was trying to do.'

'Then tell me. The cops will be here any second.'

Rachel finally sat down. 'First of all, he's close. Our first two known victims were in LA and Las Vegas. So my guess is that he lives in or near to one of these places. He was able to react quickly and in a matter of hours get to both you and Angela.'

I nodded. It sounded right to me.

'Next, we know his tech skill is quite high. So if we assume that he was able to breach your email account, then we can also assume that he breached the entire LA *Times* data system. He would have been able to access home addresses for you and Angela, right?'

'Sure. That information has got to be in there.'

'What about you being laid off? Would there be any email or a data trail involving that?'

I nodded. 'I got a ton of emails about it. From friends, people at other papers, everywhere. But what would it have to do with this?'

She nodded as though she was way ahead of me and my answer fitted perfectly with what she already knew. 'OK. We know that somehow Angela or possibly you hit a tripwire and alerted him to your investigation.'

'Trunk murder dot com.'

'I will have it checked out as soon as I can. Somehow our guy was alerted. His response was to invade the *Los Angeles Times*. We know that you put your plan to go to Las Vegas last night into an email. I am betting that our guy read it and keyed his plan off of it.'

'You keep saying "our guy". We need a name for him.'

'In the Bureau we'd call him an unknown subject. An Unsub.'

'OK, Unsub then,' I said. 'What do you mean he keyed his plan off of my plan?'

'He knew that there was a good chance you had not confirmed your suspicions or talked to the authorities yet. Being a reporter, you would keep the story to yourself. This worked in his favour. But he still had to move quickly. He knew Angela was in LA and you were going to Vegas. I think he started in LA, somehow grabbed Angela, and then killed her and set you up for it.'

'Yeah, that's obvious.'

'He then focused on you. He went to Vegas and tracked you to Ely. I think he was the man who followed you in the hallway at the hotel. He was going to make his move against you in your room. He stopped when he heard my voice. That puzzled me until now.'

'Why?'

'Well, why did he abort the plan? This guy isn't shy about killing. What would it matter to him if he had to kill you and the woman he heard in your room?'

'So then why did he abort?'

'Because the plan was for you to kill yourself. If you end up murdered in a hotel room in Ely, there is going to be an investigation that would lead to all of this unravelling. But if you were a suicide in a hotel room in Ely, then the investigation would go in a completely different direction.'

I saw where she was going with this.

'Reporter gets laid off, has the indignity of having to train his own replacement, and has few prospects for another job,' I said, reciting a litany of true facts. 'He gets depressed and suicidal. Concocts a story about a serial killer, then abducts and murders his young replacement. He then gives all his money to charity, cancels his credit cards and runs off to the middle of nowhere, where he kills himself in a hotel room.'

She was nodding the whole time I was running it down.

'How was he going to kill me and make it look like suicide?'

'You gave the answer earlier, Jack. You said you had a gun.'

Bang. It all came together. I headed towards my bedroom. I'd bought a .45 calibre Colt Government Series 70 twelve years earlier, after my encounter with the Poet. I kept the weapon in a drawer next to my bed and only took it out once a year to go to the range.

Rachel followed me into the bedroom and watched me slide open the drawer. The gun was gone. I turned back to Rachel.

'How would he know I owned a gun?'

'Is it registered?'

'Yes, but this is getting far-fetched, don't you think?'

'Actually, no. If he tapped the prison computer, I don't see why he couldn't get into the gun registry.'

'But there was one big flaw in his plan. I flew to Vegas. All baggage is screened. I would have never got the gun there.'

'Maybe not. But I think it is a widely accepted fact that the scanning process is not perfect. It would probably bother the investigators in Ely but not enough to make them change their conclusion. There are always loose ends in any investigation.'

Rachel's phone rang and she answered immediately. 'It's just me and the homeowner,' she said. 'We're coming out now.'

She closed the phone and told me the police were out front.

'They'll feel more comfortable if we come out to meet them.'

We walked to the front door and Rachel opened it.

'Keep your hands in sight,' Rachel said to me.

She walked out, holding her credentials high. Four uniformed officers and two detectives were waiting on the driveway. The uniformed officers pointed their flashlights at us.

When we got closer I recognised the two detectives from Hollywood Division. They held their guns down at their sides and looked ready to use them if I gave them the right reason.

I didn't.

I DIDN'T GET TO THE *TIMES* until shortly before noon on Thursday. The place was bustling with activity. I knew it was all because of Angela and what had happened. Dorothy Fowler, the city editor, was the first to spot me as I came in from the stairwell. She jumped from her desk at the raft and came directly towards me.

'Jack, my office, please.'

She changed directions and headed to the wall of glass. I followed, knowing every eye was on me. We entered her small office and she told me to close the door. I did as instructed and then took the seat across from her.

'What happened with the police?' she asked.

No howyadoin'? Right down to business and I liked it that way.

'Well,' I said. 'I spent about eight hours being questioned by the LAPD, the FBI, Santa Monica detectives and the Las Vegas police, who flew in just to talk to me. After that they wouldn't let me go back to my house because it's an active crime scene. So I got a room at the Kyoto Grand, took a shower, and walked over here.'

The Kyoto was a block away and the *Times* used it to put up out-of-town reporters, new hires and job candidates when needed.

'What did you tell the police?' Fowler said.

'Basically, I told them what I tried to tell Prendo yesterday. I uncovered a killer out there who murdered Denise Babbit and a woman in Las Vegas named Sharon Oglevy. Somehow, either Angela or I hit a tripwire and alerted this guy that we were onto him. He then killed Angela and went to Nevada to try to get me. I convinced an FBI agent that all this was legit and she met me in Nevada. Her presence kept the killer away from me. If she hadn't believed me, you'd be putting together stories about how I killed Angela and went off to the desert to kill myself.'

Fowler shook her head in stunned disbelief.

'This is an amazing story, Jack.'

'Actually, the cops probably wouldn't have believed it if it was just coming from me. But I was with that FBI agent when I got home. She found Angela's body when we were searching the house. She backed me up on everything with the cops.'

'How are they handling the investigation now, do you know?'

'They were putting together a task force with LA, Las Vegas and Santa Monica contributing detectives and the FBI is taking part as well. I think they are going to run it out of Parker Center.'

'Can we get that confirmed so we can put it in the story?'

'Yeah. How many inches are you giving me for the story?'

'Uh, that was one of the things I wanted to talk to you about.'

I felt the bottom drop out of my stomach.

'We're going to go big with this. Main and sidebar on the front going to a double-truck inside. For once, we have a lot of space.'

'Double-truck' meant two full inside pages.

Dorothy continued the plan. 'Jerry Spencer is already in Las Vegas and Jill Meyerson is on her way up to Ely State Prison to try to talk to Brian Oglevy. In LA, we've got GoGo Gonzmart writing the sidebar, which will be on Angela, and Teri Sparks working on a piece on the kid charged with the Babbit murder.'

'Is Alonzo Winslow getting out of juvy jail today?'

'We're not sure yet. Hopefully, it will take another day and we'll have that to run with tomorrow.'

Even without Winslow getting out, they were going big. Sending Metro reporters out across the west and putting multiple writers on it locally was something I had not seen the *Times* do since fires last ravaged the state.

'All right,' I said. 'I have stuff to contribute to almost all of those stories and I'll still pull together and write the main story.'

Dorothy nodded, hesitated and then dropped the bomb.

'Larry Bernard is writing the main, Jack.'

I reacted swiftly and loudly. 'What the fuck are you talking about?'

'Jack, calm down. You can't write it and you know it. You *are* the story. I need to get you with Larry so he can interview *you* and then write the story. The switchboard's taken more than thirty messages from reporters wanting to interview you, including the *New York Times* and Katie Couric. You are the story, Jack. We can't let the subject of a major breaking story also write it.'

She paused to let me answer but I didn't. I leaned forward and put my face in my hands. I knew she was right. I'd known it before I even entered the newsroom.

'This was supposed to be my big exit. Get that kid out of jail and go out in a blaze of glory. Put the big three-oh on my career.'

'You're still going to get credit. Katie Couric, *The Late Show*—I'd say that's going out in a blaze of glory.'

I finally sat back up and looked at her. For the first time I noticed the photo taped to the wall behind her. It was a still shot from *The Wizard of Oz* that showed Dorothy skipping down the yellow brick road with the Tin Man, the Lion and the Scarecrow. Beneath the characters someone had printed in

Magic Marker: YOU'RE NOT IN KANSAS ANYMORE, DOROTHY. I had forgotten
that Dorothy Fowler had come to the paper from the *Wichita Eagle.*

'OK. I'll tell Larry what I know.' I still felt defeated.

AN HOUR LATER I was sitting with Larry Bernard in a conference room. We
had my files spread across the big table and were going step by step through
the moves I had made on the story. Bernard was diligent about understanding my decisions. I could tell he was excited about being the writer on a
story that would go out across the country, if not around the world.

It was important to Larry to get official confirmation from the police or
FBI on the things I was telling him. So to his side he had a legal pad on
which he wrote a series of questions he would later take to the authorities.
He was all business with me. There was very little small talk and I liked
that. I didn't have any small talk left.

My throwaway phone buzzed in my pocket. I pulled it out to check the
caller ID. It was Angela Cook's cell number.

'Larry, I'll be right back.'

I left the conference room and headed towards my cubicle.

'Hello?'

'Is this Jack?'

'Yes, who is this?'

'This is your friend, Jack. From Ely.'

I knew exactly who it was. Sideburns. I sat down at my desk and leaned
forward to help insulate the conversation from nearby ears.

'What do you want?' I asked.

'To see how you're doing,' he said.

'I'm doing fine, no thanks to you. In the hallway at the Nevada, why'd
you stop? Instead of sticking with the plan, you just walked on by.'

I thought I heard a low chuckle on the line.

'You had company. Who was she, your girlfriend?'

'Something like that. And she messed up your plan, right? You wanted to
make it look like suicide.'

Another chuckle.

'I can see you are very smart,' he said. 'Or are you just telling me what
they told you?'

'They?'

'Don't be silly, Jack. I know what's going on. The cat's out of the bag. There are a lot of stories being written for tomorrow's paper. But none of them with your name on it, Jack.'

That told me he was still floating around inside the *Times*'s data system.

'And I haven't seen a name for me yet. Aren't you all going to give me a name? We all get names, you know. The Yorkshire Ripper. The Hillside Strangler. The Poet. You know about that one, right?'

'Yeah, we're giving you a name. We're calling you the Iron Maiden. How do you like that?'

This time I heard no chuckle in the silence that followed.

'Are you still there, Iron Maiden?'

'You should be careful, Jack. I could always try again.'

I laughed at him. 'Hey, I'm not hiding. I'm right here. Try again, if you've got the guts.'

He was silent, so I laid it on thicker.

'Killing these defenceless women, that takes guts, doesn't it?'

The chuckle was back.

'You're very transparent, Jack. I know what you're doing. Baiting the trap. Hoping I'll come back to LA and go for you. Meantime, you have the FBI and the LAPD watching and ready to jump in and catch the monster just in the nick of time. Is that it, Jack?'

'If that's what you think.'

'Well, it won't work that way. I'm a patient man, Jack. Time will pass, maybe even years will go by, and then I promise we'll meet again face to face. No disguise. I'll return your gun then.'

His low chuckle came again and I got the impression that wherever he was calling from, he was trying to keep his voice down and not attract attention.

'Speaking of the gun, how was that going to be explained? You know, that I flew to Vegas but then somehow had my gun and killed myself with it? Seems like a flaw in the plan, doesn't it?'

He laughed out loud this time.

'Jack, you are not in possession of all the facts yet, are you? When you are, then you will understand how flawless the plan was. My one mistake was the girl in the room. I didn't see that coming.'

Neither did I but I wasn't saying so.

'Look, while I've got you on the line, can I ask you a few questions for the story we're putting together?'

'No, Jack. This is between you and me, not your readers.'

'You're right. I wouldn't give you the space. You think I'm going to let you try to explain your sick world in my newspaper?'

A dark silence followed. '*You*,' he finally said, his voice tight with anger, 'should respect me.'

Now I laughed. 'Respect you? How about "Screw you"? You took a young girl who had nothing but—'

He interrupted me by making a noise like a muffled cough.

'Did you hear that, Jack? Do you know what that was? That was her, saying your name through plastic when there was no air left.'

He laughed long and hard before abruptly hanging up. I sat there for a long time with the phone still pressed against my ear. Then I called Rachel. The call was answered after four rings.

'Jack, I can't talk,' she said by way of a greeting.

'You would've won the bet.'

'What bet?'

'He just called me. The Unsub. He has Angela's cellphone.'

'What did he say?'

'Not a lot. I think he was trying to find out who you are.'

'What do you mean? How would he know about me?'

'He doesn't. He was trying to find out who the woman in the room back in Ely was. You spoiled everything and he's curious.'

'Did you record it?' Rachel asked.

'No, because I wasn't expecting it.'

'We need to get your phone. We'll be able to ping the call and get the originating tower. It will get us close to where he is.'

'It sounded like he was someplace where he had to speak quietly. Like an office or something. He also made one slip.'

'What was that?'

'I tried to get him mad, and—'

'Jack, are you crazy? What are you doing?'

'I didn't want to be intimidated by him. So I went after him. He thought

I was intentionally baiting him into coming after me. That's when he slipped. He said I was baiting him into *coming back* to LA. That's how he said it. Coming back.'

'That's good, Jack. But he could have been playing you. Intentionally saying that because he actually is in LA.'

I hadn't thought of the reverse play.

'Well, there's one other thing. He's still hacking into the system here.'

'That's something we might be able to trace,' she said excitedly.

'Yeah, well, good luck getting the *Times* to cooperate.'

'It's worth a try. Can I send somebody over for your phone now?'

'Yes, but what about sending yourself?'

'I can't. I'm in the middle of something here. I told you.'

'Are you in trouble, Rachel?'

'I don't know yet, but I have to go.'

We made arrangements for me to meet the agent she would send for the phone outside the door of the globe lobby in half an hour. It was then time for both of us to go back to work.

'Hang in there, Rachel,' I said.

She was silent for a moment and then said, 'You too, Jack.'

We hung up then. And somehow, with all that had transpired in the last thirty-six hours, with what had happened to Angela and my having just been threatened by a serial killer, a part of me felt happy and hopeful.

I had a feeling, though, that it wasn't going to last.

Seven: The Farm

Carver intently watched the security screens. The two men at the front counter showed badges to Geneva. He couldn't tell what law enforcement agency they were from.

Carver tried to keep his anxiety in check. He was safe, he told himself. Freddy Stone was the only issue of concern, and Carver would have to take steps to make that potential problem go away.

On the screen he watched as Yolanda Chavez, McGinnis's second-in-command, shook hands with the men. One of them took a document from his pocket and presented it to her. She studied it for a moment and then handed it back. She then signalled for the men to follow her. By switching security screens Carver was able to follow them to the administration suite.

He picked up his phone and punched the button for Reception.

'Geneva, this is Mr Carver. I happen to be watching the cameras and am curious about those two men who just entered. Who are they?'

'They're FBI agents. They said they have a search warrant.'

'OK, thank you, Geneva.'

He hung up the phone and refocused on his screen. He typed in a command that opened a new set of camera angles, a multiplex screen that showed the four private offices of the top administrators. These cameras were hidden in ceiling-mounted smoke detectors and the occupants of the offices knew nothing about them. They came with audio feeds as well.

Carver saw the two FBI agents enter McGinnis's office and shake hands with the company CEO. One was black and one was white. They identified themselves as Bantam and Richmond.

'So I am told you have a search warrant?' McGinnis asked.

'Yes, sir, we do,' Bantam said, and passed it across the table. 'You are hosting a website called trunk murder dot com and we need to know every piece of information you have about it.'

McGinnis read the document. Carver ran his hands through his hair. He needed to know what was in that warrant.

He killed the feed and then the screen. He opened a desk drawer and pulled out the stack of monthly server volume reports his staff had prepared earlier in the week. Usually, he sent them up to McGinnis with one of his server engineers. This time he would make the delivery himself. He left and locked his office.

In the control room he told Mizzou and Kurt, the engineers on duty, where he was going. Thankfully, Freddy Stone was not on shift until the evening, because he could never come back to Western Data Consultants. Carver knew the FBI would take every employee name and run it through their computers. They would learn that Freddy Stone was not Freddy Stone and they would come back for him.

Carver wasn't going to allow that. He had other plans for Freddy.

He took the elevator up and entered the administration suite with his head down, reading the top page of the stack of reports. He nonchalantly looked up and saw through the open door of McGinnis's office that he had company.

'Wesley?'

It was McGinnis, waving him into the office.

Carver entered. He nodded to the two men.

'Wesley Carver, meet Agents Bantam and Richmond from the FBI's Phoenix office. I was just about to call you.'

Carver shook hands with the men.

'Wesley wears a number of hats round here,' McGinnis said. 'He's our chief technology officer and our chief threat officer—'

'Do we have a problem?' Carver cut in.

'We may,' McGinnis said. 'The agents have been telling me that we're hosting a website here that is of interest to them and they've got a warrant that allows them to see all our records pertaining to it.'

Carver put his hands into the pockets of his white lab coat because he knew it gave him the posture of a deep-thinking man. He then addressed the agents.

'What is the website?'

'Trunk murder dot com,' McGinnis answered. 'I just checked and it's part of a larger bundle. An account out of Seattle.'

Carver nodded and kept a calm demeanour. He had a plan for this.

'May I see the warrant?'

'Sure.' The agent handed it to Carver, who unfolded it and scanned it. He checked himself to make sure he wasn't humming.

In general terms the search warrant described an investigation of an unknown subject using the Internet to conduct a criminal conspiracy involving data theft and fraud. The warrant sought all records relating to the website's origin, operation and financing.

Carver knew the Bureau would be unhappily surprised by what they got. 'Well, we can get you all of this,' he said. 'What is the account in Seattle?'

'See Jane Run,' McGinnis said. 'That's the company's name.'

Carver turned to the agents. 'OK, we'll get this done,' he said. 'Should we head down to the bunker, then?'

'Absolutely.' The two agents stood up.

'Good luck, gentlemen,' McGinnis offered. 'I hope you catch the bad guys. We're willing to help in any way we can.'

Eight: Home Sweet Home

On Saturday morning I was in my room at the Kyoto reading Larry Bernard's front-page story about the release of Alonzo Winslow from custody when one of the detectives from Hollywood Division called me. Her name was Bynum. She told me my house had been cleared as a crime scene and returned to my custody.

'Detective, can I ask you about Angela?'

'What about her?'

'I was wondering if she had been . . . tortured or anything.'

There was a pause while the detective decided how much to tell me. 'I'm sorry but the answer is yes. There was evidence of rape with a foreign object and the same pattern of slow suffocation as in the other cases. Multiple ligature marks on the neck. He repeatedly choked her out and revived her. Whether this was a means of getting her to talk about the story you two were working on, or just his way of getting off, is unclear at this time. I guess we will have to ask the man himself when we get him.'

I was silent as I thought about the horror Angela had faced.

'Anything else, Jack?'

'Uh, no.'

'Well, you can go home now. Have a nice day.'

Bynum hung up. I sat there, thinking. Calling it home seemed wrong. I wasn't sure I wanted the house back. To now live and try to sleep in that place seemed impossible to me. I spread the curtains and looked out of the window of my small room. I had a view of the civic centre. The sidewalks and green lawns were empty. It was Saturday and nobody came downtown on the weekend. I pulled the curtains closed.

I decided I would keep the room as long as the paper was paying. I would go to the house but only to get fresh clothes and things I needed.

My cellphone rang. My real cellphone. I had finally got it turned back on the day before.

It was Rachel.

'Hey,' I said.

'You sound down. What's wrong?'

What a profiler. She had read me with one word.

'Nothing. I'm just . . . nothing. Are you working?'

'Yeah.'

'Want to take a break and get some coffee? I'm downtown.'

'No, I can't.'

I had not seen her since we had been split apart by the detectives after finding and reporting Angela's body.

'Well, when will I get to see you?' I asked.

'I don't know, Jack. Have patience. I'm under the gun here.'

I felt embarrassed and changed the subject.

'Why did you call?'

There was a silence before she answered. 'To check in and to update you on a few things. If you wanted to hear them.'

'Down to business. Sure, go ahead.'

I sat down on the bed and opened a notebook to write in.

'Yesterday they confirmed that the trunk murder website Angela visited was indeed the tripwire she stepped on,' Rachel said. 'But it's a dead end.'

'A dead end? I thought everything can be traced on the Internet.'

'The physical location of the site is a web-hosting facility in Mesa, Arizona, called Western Data Consultants. Agents went there and pulled the details. It was registered through a company in Seattle called See Jane Run, which builds and maintains websites for clients and pays Western Data to host them.'

'So did they go to Seattle?'

'Agents from Seattle are handling it. The trunk murder site was paid for entirely over the Internet. No one at See Jane Run ever met the man who paid for it. The physical address given when the sites were set up was a mail drop that is no longer valid.'

'You just said sites—plural. Did he set up more than one?'

'Yes. Trunk murder dot com was the first site and the second is Denslow Data. That was the name he used in setting these up. Bill Denslow. He set up both sites on a five-year plan, paid for in advance. He used a money order—untraceable. Another dead end.'

I took a couple of moments to write some notes down.

'OK,' I finally said. 'So is Denslow the Unsub?'

'The man posing as Denslow is the Unsub but we're not dumb enough to think he would put his real name on a website.'

'So why the two websites?'

'One was the capture site and one was the OP site. Observation point. The trunk murder site was set up to collect the IP—the computer address—of anybody who visited the site. This is what happened with Angela. You understand?'

'Right. She did a search and it brought her to the site.'

'Right. The site collected IPs but then those addresses were automatically forwarded to another dot com site. This one was called Denslow Data.'

I nodded. 'I see. So he has the captured IP address forwarded to another site where there is no capture mechanism and he can check it without fear of being tracked and having his own ID captured.'

'Exactly.'

'So after Angela hit on the trunk murder site he went to the Denslow site and got her IP. He traced it back to the *Times* and figured this might be more than a morbid curiosity about trunk murders. He breaches the *Times* system and that leads him to me and Angela and our stories. He reads my emails and he knows that I'm onto something and heading to Vegas.'

'That's right. So he concocted the scheme to take you both out in a murder-suicide.'

I was silent for a moment. It added up.

'Jack, you there?'

'I'm just thinking. So this is all completely untraceable?'

'From this angle. Once we get this guy and his computer, we'll be able to trace his visits to Denslow. That will be solid evidence.'

'Seems unlikely that he would use his own computer, given the skill he's already shown.'

'Maybe. It appears he was onto Angela less than twenty-four hours after her visit to the trunk murder site. That would indicate a daily trap check, and that might indicate he was using his own computer or one in close proximity.'

I closed my eyes. What I knew about the world was depressing.

'There's something else I want to tell you,' Rachel said. 'We figured out how he drew Angela to your house.'

'How?' I opened my eyes.

'You did it. Or that is how it was meant to look. In her home email account is an email from you, sent Tuesday night. You said you had picked up some very important information on the Winslow case. You invited her over to show it to her.'

'Hell!'

'She returned the email, saying she was on her way. She came to your house and he was waiting. It was after you'd left for Vegas.'

'He must've been watching my house. He watched me leave.'

'You leave, he gets in and uses your home computer to send the message. Then he waits for her. And once he is through with her, he follows you out to Vegas to complete the set-up by killing you and making it look like a suicide.'

'But what about my gun? He gets in the house and finds it easily enough. He could then drive it to Vegas to follow me. But it still doesn't explain how I supposedly got it there. I flew and I didn't check a bag. It's a big hole, isn't it?'

'We think we've got that filled in, too. After he baited Angela he used your computer to print out a GO! cargo shipping form.'

'Go? I never heard of Go.'

'It's airport-to-airport shipping. You can download shipping forms off the Internet, and someone did just that on your computer. It was for a package sent overnight to yourself. It was held for pick-up at McCarran International. No signature required. Just show your copy of the shipping form.'

I could only shake my head.

'This is how we think he did it,' Rachel said. 'He emails Angela and then goes to work on the shipment. Angela shows up and he does his thing with her. He then goes to the airport and drops the package with the gun. He then either drives to Vegas or flies. Once he's there, he picks up the package and has the gun. He then follows you to Ely to complete the plan.'

'It seems so tight. Are you sure he could have pulled this off?'

'It is tight and we're not sure, but the scenario works.'

'What happened with the trace from Angela's phone?'

'We traced it to a cell tower at McCarran. The US Airways terminal. Within two hours of the call to you, there were flights from that terminal to twenty-four different American cities. He could have been going just about anywhere.'

'What else is the Bureau doing?'

'Well, we're profiling Babbit and Oglevy. We know they fit into his programme and we need to figure out where they intersect. We're also still looking for his signature.'

'You're talking about the secret signature, right?'

'Yes, Jack. The program is what he does with the victim. The signature is something he leaves behind to mark his turf. It's the difference between a painting and the artist's signature marking it as his work. Only with these killers the signature is not so obvious. Most times we don't see it until after. But if we could decipher the signature now, it might help lead us to him.'

'Is that what they have you doing? Working on that?'

'Yes.' But she had hesitated before answering.

'Using your notes off my files?'

'That's right.'

Now I hesitated, but not too long.

'That's a lie, Rachel. What is going on?'

'What are you talking about?'

'Because I have your notes right here. When they finally cut me loose on Thursday they gave me your notes, thinking they were mine. So why are you lying to me?'

'Jack, I'm not lying. So what if you have my notes, you think—'

'Where are you? Right now. Tell me the truth.'

She hesitated. 'I'm in Washington DC. I have an OPR hearing on Monday morning.'

I knew that the OPR was the Office of Professional Responsibility, the Bureau's version of Internal Affairs.

'You told them about us? They're going after you for it?'

'No, Jack. It's about the jet I took to Nellis on Wednesday. After you called me.'

I jumped off the bed and started pacing round the room.

'You have to be kidding me. Doesn't it matter that you saved one life—mine—and brought this killer to law enforcement attention? They should be giving you a medal, not a hearing.'

There was silence and then she spoke.

'Look, I appreciate what you are saying, but the reality is, I made some bad judgments and they seem more concerned about that and the money it cost than anything else.'

'If they do one thing to you, Rachel, it's going to be all over the front page. What time is the hearing on Monday?'

'It's at nine.'

I was going to alert Keisha, my ex-wife. I knew they wouldn't let her into a closed-door personnel hearing, but if they knew a *Times* reporter was hovering outside, waiting on the results, they might think twice about what they did inside.

'Jack, I know what you're thinking. But I want you to cool your jets and let me deal with this. It's my job and my hearing. OK?'

'I don't know. It's hard to just sit back when they are messing with somebody . . . somebody I care about.'

'Thank you, Jack, but I need you to stand down on this one. I'll let you know what happens as soon as I know. I promise.'

I yanked open the curtains and sunlight entered the room. 'OK.'

We ended the call after that. I stood at the window, looking out but not seeing what was there. I was thinking about Rachel, fighting for her job and the one thing that seemed to keep her tethered to the world. I realised she wasn't that much different from me.

CARVER WATCHED the home in Scottsdale from the darkness of his car. It was too early to make his move. He would wait and watch until he was sure it was safe. This didn't bother him. He enjoyed being alone and in the dark. It was his place. He had his music on the iPod and the Lizard King had kept him company his whole life.

I'm a changeling, see me change. I'm a changelin', see me change.

It had always been his anthem, a song to set his life by. He turned the volume up and closed his eyes. The music transported him back. Past all the memories and nightmares. Back to the dressing room with Alma. She was supposed to be watching him but she had had her hands full with the thread and needlework. She couldn't watch him all the time. The mother was ultimately responsible, even while onstage.

Young Wesley had made his move, slipping through the beaded curtains as quiet as a mouse. He then went down the hall to where the flashing lights emanated from. The music had been loud, but not so loud that Wesley didn't hear the cheers. He had crept up further and looked out. The stage was splashed with harsh white light. He saw her then. Naked in front of all the men. The music pulsing through him. She moved perfectly with the music. As if it had been written and recorded just for her. He had watched and felt entranced. He didn't want the music to stop.

He was suddenly grabbed from behind by his T-shirt and yanked backwards down the hall. He looked up and saw it was Alma.

'You are a very bad little boy!' she had scolded. She had dragged him back to the dressing room. 'You are in big troub—What is that?'

She was pointing at him, her finger aimed low. At the place where he felt strange feelings begin from.

'Let's see what you've got in there.' She had started to pull his trousers down. 'You little pervert,' Alma said. 'I'm going to show you what we do with perverts round here.'

Wesley had been frozen in terror. He didn't know what that word meant. He didn't know what to do.

A sharp knock on the car window cut through the music and the dream. Carver jumped up in his seat. Disorientated, he looked round, realised where he was, and pulled the buds out of his ears.

He looked out of the window, and there was McGinnis, standing in the street. He was holding a leash that led to a pipsqueak dog.

Carver lowered the window. At the same time, he used his foot to make sure the gun he'd placed on the floor was out of sight.

'Wesley, what are you doing here?'

'I wanted to talk to you.'

'Why didn't you come up to the house?'

'Because I also have to show you something. It has to do with that visit from the FBI. I think I know who they're looking for.'

McGinnis took a step forward to look in closely at Carver.

'Wesley, it's almost midnight. What's going on?'

'Get in and I'll explain it on the way. You can bring the dog.'

McGinnis looked annoyed but walked round to get into the car. As he did so, Carver hid the gun in the rear waistband of his trousers.

McGinnis put the dog in the back seat and then got into the front.

'Where are we going?'

'To where Freddy Stone lives.'

'Have you talked to Stone? Did you ask him where he's been?'

Carver shook his head. 'No, that's why I went to his place tonight, to find him. He wasn't there but I found something else. The website the FBI was asking about. He's the guy behind it.'

'Then we need to call the FBI, Wesley.'

'But it could hurt the business if it blows up in the media.'

McGinnis shook his head. 'We'll just have to take our punishment.'

'All right. We go to his place first and then we call the FBI.'

The lights of downtown Phoenix spread out before them on both sides of the freeway. Carver stopped talking and McGinnis did likewise. The dog was sleeping on the back seat of the car.

Carver's mind wandered back to the memory the music had conjured earlier. He wondered what had made him go down the hallway to look. He knew the answer was tangled down deep in his darkest roots. In a place no one could go.

I NEVER LEFT my hotel room on Saturday, even when some of the reporters on the weekend shift invited me for cocktails after work. They were celebrating another day on the front page with the story. The latest report being on Alonzo Winslow's first day of freedom and an update on the search for the trunk murder suspect. I didn't feel much like celebrating a story that was no longer mine.

Instead I stayed in on Saturday night and started working my way through the files, using Rachel's notes as a blueprint. I worked late into the night, pulling together the details of two dead women's lives, looking for the commonality Rachel was sure was there.

They were women from two different home towns who had migrated to two different cities in two different states. As far as I could tell, they had never crossed paths, except on the outside chance that Denise Babbit had gone to Las Vegas and happened to catch the Femmes Fatales show at the Cleopatra.

Could that really be the connection between their murders? It seemed far-fetched.

I finally exhausted that pursuit and decided to approach things from a different angle. The killer's angle. On a fresh sheet of Rachel's notebook paper, I started listing all the things the Unsub would have needed to know in order to accomplish each murder in terms of method, timing and location. This proved to be a daunting task and by midnight I was spent. I fell asleep in my clothes on top of the bedspread, the files and my notes all around me.

IT WAS ALMOST SUNRISE. Carver could see the light just beginning to etch the silhouette of the mountain chain. It was beautiful. He sat on a large rock and watched as Stone laboured in front of him. His young acolyte was working hard with the shovel and was down to the hard earth that lies beneath the soft top of loose soil and sand.

'Freddy,' Carver said calmly. 'I want you to tell me again.'

'I've already told you!'

'Then tell me again. I need to know exactly what was said because I need to know exactly the extent of the damage.'

'There is no damage.' He drove the shovel angrily into the hole.

Carver looked round again to make sure they were alone. He reached behind his back and gripped the gun. He thought about it, then decided to wait. Freddy could still be useful. Carver would just teach him a lesson this time instead.

'Tell me again,' Carver repeated.

'I just tried to find out who the bitch was that was waiting in his room,' Stone said. 'And I told him that someday I would get his gun back to him, that I would personally deliver it.'

Carver nodded. So far Stone had said the same thing each time he had recounted the conversation with McEvoy.

'OK, and what did he say to you?'

'He didn't say much of anything. I think he was scared—oh, there is one thing he said.'

Carver tried to remain calm. 'What?'

'He knows about our thing. About the irons.'

Carver tried to keep the urgency out of his voice.

'How does he know? You told him?'

'No, I didn't tell him. He just knew somehow. He said the name he was going to give us was the—'

'He said "us"? He knows there are two of us?'

'No, no, I don't mean that. He doesn't know that. He said the name he was going to put in the paper for me, because he thought it was only me, was "Iron Maiden". That was what they were going to call us—I mean, me. He was just trying to get me mad, I think.'

Carver thought for a moment. McEvoy knew more than he should know. He must have had help. He had insight and knowledge, and that made Carver think about the woman who had been in the room, waiting. He now thought he might know who she was.

'Is this deep enough or not?' Stone said.

Carver stepped over to the grave and pointed his flashlight down.

'Yes, Freddy, that will be fine. Put the dog in first.'

Carver turned his back while Stone reached over to pick up the little dog's body. He hated having had to kill the dog. She had done nothing wrong. She was just collateral damage.

'OK.'

Carver turned. 'Now him.'

McGinnis's body was on the ground by the end of the grave. Stone reached forward and grabbed the ankles and started backing up in the grave, pulling the body into it. The shovel was leaning against the far wall of the excavation. Carver grabbed the handle and pulled it out as Stone moved back.

Stone walked the body in. McGinnis's shoulders and head dropped down the three feet with a dull thud. While Stone was still stooped forward, Carver swung the shovel and slammed the heel of it down between the younger man's shoulder blades.

The air blasted out of Stone's lungs and he fell forward in the grave, landing face to face with McGinnis. Carver pushed the point of the tool into the back of Stone's neck.

'Take a good look, Freddy,' he said. 'I had you dig this one deeper so I could put you in it on top of him.'

'Please . . .'

'You broke the rules. I did *not* tell you to call McEvoy.'

'I know, I'm sorry. It'll never happen again. Please.'

'I could make sure it doesn't happen again right now.'

'No, please. I'll make up for it. I won't—'

'Shut up and listen!'

Stone nodded, his face just inches from the dull, lifeless eyes of Declan McGinnis.

'Do you remember where you were when I found you?'

Stone dutifully nodded.

'You were going to that dark place to face endless days of torment. But I saved you. I gave you a new name. I gave you a new life. I gave you the opportunity to escape from that and to join me in embracing the desires we share. I taught you the way and I only asked one thing in return. Do you remember what that was?'

'You said I was the student and you were the teacher. I must do as you say.'

Carver pushed the steel point deeper into Stone's neck.

'And yet here we are. And you have failed me.'

'I won't let it happen again. Please. Let me make it up.'

Carver pulled the shovel back and stepped away.

'Bury them now.'

Stone turned and looked up tentatively, fear still in his eyes. Carver held the shovel out to him. Stone got up and took it.

Carver reached behind his back and pulled out the gun. With great delight he watch Stone's eyes go wide. But then he pulled the handkerchief from his front pocket and started wiping the weapon clean of all fingerprints. When he was finished he dropped it into the grave by McGinnis's feet. He wasn't worried about Stone making a grab for it. Freddy was totally under his command and control.

'I am sorry, Freddy, but whatever we do about McEvoy, we will not be returning his gun to him. It's much too risky to keep it around.'

'Whatever you say.'

Exactly, Carver thought.

'Hurry now,' he said. 'We're losing the dark.'

Stone quickly started shovelling dirt and sand back into the hole.

CARVER WORKED HIS HUNCH on the computer while Stone gathered the things he wanted to take with him. Between searches, Carver printed out and shredded the pages in Stone's recycle box. He wanted to leave the FBI something that would keep its agents busy.

He stopped everything when the photo and story appeared on the screen. He scanned it, then looked across the warehouse at Stone. He was throwing clothing into a trash bag. He had no suitcase.

'I was right,' Carver said. 'She's in LA.'

Stone dropped the bag he was filling and crossed the concrete floor. He looked over Carver's shoulder at the middle screen.

'Is that her?' Carver asked.

'All I got was a quick glance when I went by the room. It could be her.'

'I think it was her. Rachel and Jack, together again.'

Carver got excited by the prospect of McEvoy and Walling being on his trail. It raised the stakes to have two such opponents.

'What's that story about?' Stone asked.

'It's about her and an LA cop getting the guy they called the Bagman. He cut up women and put them in trash bags. This picture was taken at the press conference they had.'

Carver could hear Stone breathing through his mouth.

'Finish gathering your things now, Freddy. I think we'll sit back and wait. She'll come to us and when she does, she'll be a prize.'

Carver cut the Internet link and stood up. He reached down behind the computer tower and detached the keyboard cable. He knew that the Bureau could gather DNA from the microscopic bits of skin that fell between the letters on a keyboard. He would not leave this board behind.

'Let's hurry up and finish now,' Carver said. 'I'm going to need you at full strength when Agent Walling shows up.'

'Don't worry. I'll be ready.'

ON MONDAY MORNING I got up early and cruised into the newsroom at 5 a.m. to continue my work with the files.

The place was dead, not a reporter or editor in sight. I sat down in my cubicle and checked email. My account had been reopened by newsroom techs with a new password the Friday before. Over the weekend I had accumulated almost forty emails, mostly from strangers in reaction to the stories about the trunk murders.

After that I got down to work. I had completed my study of the records relating to the murder of Denise Babbit and had composed a comprehensive list of the things about the victim that the killer would have had to know in order to commit the crime. I was halfway through my study of Sharon Oglevy's murder and was still compiling the same sort of information.

I worked undisturbed as the newsroom came to life, editors and reporters trudging in, coffee cups in hand, to start another week of work. At eight o'clock my first email of the day chimed on my computer. It was from the axeman, Richard Kramer.

Date: May 18, 2009 9:11 AM PDT
To: JackMcEvoy@LATimes.com
Jack, swing on by when you get a chance. RK

I decided to get it over with and made my way to Kramer's office. The door was open but I knocked on it before entering. Kramer turned from his computer screen and beckoned me in.

'Jack, have a seat. How are we doing this morning?'

I took one of the two chairs in front of his desk and sat down.

'I'm doing OK, I guess. Considering.'

Kramer nodded thoughtfully. 'Yes, it's been an amazing ten days since you last sat in that chair.'

I remained silent, waiting for whatever he was going to say.

'I've got some good news for you here,' he said.

He smiled and moved a thick document from the side of his desk to front and centre. He looked down at it as he spoke.

'You see, Jack, we think this trunk murder case is a story we're going to ride with for a while. And so, we're going to need you.'

I looked at him blankly. 'You mean, I'm not being laid off?'

Kramer continued as if I had not asked a question.

'What we're offering here is a six-month contract extension.' Kramer slid the document across the desk so I could read it.

'I don't have a contract. How can it be extended?'

'They call it that because you are currently an employee and there is an implied contract. It's just legal mumbo jumbo, Jack.'

I was speed-reading the front page of the document until I bottomed out on a big, fat speed bump.

'This pays me thirty thousand dollars for six months,' I said.

'Yes, that is the standard extension rate.'

I did the quick maths. 'Let's see, that would be about eighteen thousand less than I make for six months now. So you want me to take less to help you stay out front with this story. And I'm betting I no longer get any medical, dental or pension benefits, right?'

'Jack,' Kramer said in a calming tone. 'There is some negotiation I can do financially, but you would have to pick up the benefits yourself. It's simply the wave of the future.'

I dropped the contract back on his desk and looked up at him.

'I'm not signing this. I'd rather take my chances on unemployment. But someday they're going to come for you and ask you to sign one of these things and then you'll have to wonder how you'll pay for your kids' teeth and their doctors and their school and everything else. And I hope it's OK with you because it's simply the wave of the future.'

I got up and walked out of the office and straight back to my pod. Along the way I pulled out my cellphone to check whether I had somehow missed a call. I hadn't. It was nearing 1 p.m. in Washington, DC, and I had heard nothing yet from Rachel.

I had avoided intruding on her till now. But I needed to know what was happening. I called her cell and it went right to voicemail without a ring. I told her to call me as soon as she could.

I put the phone down, shoved my laptop and files into my backpack and headed out of the newsroom to the stairwell. The newsroom might have at one time been the best place in the world to work. But it wasn't now. People like the axeman and the unseen forces behind him had made it forbidding and claustrophobic.

I had to get away. I felt like I was a man without home or office to go to. But I still had a car, and in LA, the car was king.

I HEADED WEST, jumping onto the 10 freeway and taking it towards the beach and the clean ocean air. I didn't know exactly where I was going but I drove with subconscious purpose, as though the hands on the wheel and the foot on the pedal knew what my brain didn't.

In Santa Monica I exited on Fourth Street and then took Pico down to the beach. I pulled into the parking lot where Denise Babbit's car had been abandoned by Alonzo Winslow. The lot was almost empty and I parked in the same row where she had been left.

Now what? I thought. I opened my backpack and pulled out Rachel's legal pad. I flipped to the last page and studied the notes I had put down.

WHAT HE NEEDED TO KNOW
   Denise Babbit
   1. Details of prior arrest
   2. Car: trunk space
   3. Work location
   4. Work schedule: abducted after work
   5. Visual: body type—tall, long legs

   Sharon Oglevy
   1. Husband's threat
   2. His car: trunk space
   3. Work location
   4. Work schedule: abducted after work
   5. Visual: body type—tall, long legs
   6. Husband's home location

The two lists were short and almost identical. I thought about the Unsub and how he had come to choose these two women from these two different places. The simple answer was that he had seen them. They both displayed their bodies publicly. If he was looking for a specific set of physical attributes he could have seen both Denise Babbitt and Sharon Oglevy on stage.

Or on computer. The night before, I had checked and found that both the Femmes Fatales exotic review and Club Snake Pit had websites that featured photographs of their dancers. If the Unsub's paraphilia included leg braces and the need for a tall body type, then the website would have allowed him to research his prey.

Once a victim was chosen, the killer would need to go to work identifying the woman and filling in the other details on the lists. It could be done that way but I had a hunch that it wasn't. I felt sure that there was something else at play here.

I zeroed in on the first item on both lists. It seemed clear to me that at some point the killer had acquainted himself with the details of each of his victims' legal affairs.

With Denise Babbit he had to have known of her arrest last year for buying drugs, and that the arrest took place around the Rodia Gardens housing project. With Sharon Oglevy, the killer had to have known the details of her divorce. In particular, he had to have known of her husband's alleged threat to kill her and bury her out in the desert.

In both cases the legal details could have been obtained from court documents that were open to the public.

Then it hit me. The thing I had missed. Denise Babbit had been arrested a year before her death but at the time of her murder the prosecution was ongoing. Her attorney had got her into a pre-trial intervention programme. As part of her outpatient drug-abuse treatment, her urine was tested once a month for indications of drug use and the courts were ostensibly waiting to see if she straightened out her life. If she did, the charges against her would go away.

All of that was just legal detail but now I saw something I had overlooked. If her case was still active, it would not yet have been entered into the public record. And if it was not part of the public record, then how did the Unsub get the details he needed?

I decided that the only way he would have been able to get the information was from someone directly associated with her case—the prosecutor or the defence attorney. I leafed through the Babbit file until I found the name of her attorney and then I made the call.

'Daly and Mills, how can I help you?'

'May I speak to Tom Fox?'

'Mr Fox is in court this morning. Can I take a message?'

I gave my name and number and said I was a reporter with the *Times* and to tell Fox that the call was important.

After closing the phone I booted up my laptop and put the Internet slot card in place. I decided I would test my theory and see if I could access Denise Babbit's court records online.

I spent twenty minutes on the project but could glean very little information about Babbit's arrest. I did, however, pick up a reference to her attorney's email address and composed a quick message.

I sent the message and knew that all I could do was wait. It was now after 2 p.m. in Washington, DC. There seemed no way that Rachel's hearing could have lasted this long.

My computer dinged and I looked down and saw I had already received a return email from Fox.

To: JackMcEvoy@LATimes.com

Hi, I cannot respond to your email in a timely manner because I am in trial this week. You will hear from me or my assistant, Madison, as soon as possible. Thank you.

Tom Fox

Senior Partner, Daly & Mills, Counsellors at Law

It was an automatically generated response, which meant Fox had not yet seen my message.

I noticed the law firm's website listed at the bottom of the message and clicked on the link. It brought me to a site that boldly trumpeted the services the firm provided its prospective clients. At the bottom of the page was a listing of the firm's partners by name. I was about to click on Tom Fox's bio when I saw the line and link that ran along the very bottom of the page:

Site Design and Optimisation by Western Data Consultants.

It felt to me like atoms crashing together. I knew I had the connection. The law firm's website was hosted in the same location as the Unsub's tripwire site. That was too coincidental to be coincidence. I quickly clicked on the link and I was taken to the home page of Western Data Consultants.

The site offered a guided tour of the facility in Mesa, Arizona, which offered state-of-the-art security and service in the areas of data storage, managed hosting and web-based grid solutions—whatever that meant. The company offered businesses an economical means of storing and securing data. Every keystroke made on a computer at a law firm in Los Angeles could be instantly recorded and stored in Mesa.

I went back to my files and pulled out the documents William Schifino had given me. Included in these was the Oglevy divorce file. I put the name of Sharon Oglevy's attorney into the search window and got an address, phone number and website.

I went to the website for Allmand, Bradshaw and Ward and scrolled to the bottom of the home page. There it was.

Site Design and Optimisation by Western Data Consultants.

I felt that I had nailed the connection. Both of the law firms that had represented the Unsub's two victims stored their case files at Western Data Consultants in Mesa. That had to be the place where Denise Babbit and Sharon Oglevy crossed paths. That was where the Unsub had found and chosen them.

I shoved all the files back into my backpack and started the car.

On the way to the airport I called Southwest Airlines and bought a round-trip ticket from LAX that would get me into Phoenix at 2 p.m. I just booked a rental car when my phone started buzzing.

The screen said PRIVATE CALLER and I knew it was Rachel.

'Rachel, it's about time,' I said. 'Where are you?'

'At the airport. I'm coming back.'

'Switch your flight. Meet me in Phoenix. I found the connection. It's Western Data. I'm going there now.'

'Jack, what are you talking about?'

'I'll tell you when I see you. Will you come?'

There was a long delay. 'Yes, Jack, I'll come.'

'Good. I have a car booked. Make the switch and then call me back with your arrival time. I'll pick you up at Sky Harbor.'

'OK.'

'How did the OPR hearing go? It seemed like it went on a long time.'

Again, a hesitation. 'I quit, Jack. I'm not an agent any more.'

WHEN RACHEL CAME through the terminal exit at Sky Harbor International she was pulling a roller bag with one hand and carrying a laptop briefcase with the other. I stepped into her path and pulled her into a tight hug.

I didn't kiss her, I just held her. She bowed her head into the crook of my neck and said nothing.

'Hi,' I finally said.

'Hi,' she said back.

'Long day, huh? You OK?'

'I will be.'

I reached down and took the handle of the roller bag out of her grasp. Then I turned her towards the exit to the parking garage.

'This way. I already got the car and the hotel.'

'Great.'

We walked silently and I kept my arm round her. Rachel had not told me a lot on the phone, only that she had been forced to quit to avoid prosecution for misuse of government funds—the FBI jet she had taken to Nellis in order to save me.

'The hotel's pretty nice,' I said. 'But I've only got one room.'

'One room is perfect. I don't have to worry about that any more.'

'So are you hungry? Do you want to get something to eat?'

'What about Western Data?' she said.

'I called and set up an appointment tomorrow at ten. They said it had to be tomorrow because the CEO is out today. Guy named McGinnis. He runs the place.'

'And they fell for the charade you're going to pull?'

'It's not a charade. I have the letter from Schifino and that makes me legit.'

'Doesn't your paper have some kind of code of ethics that prevents you from misrepresenting yourself?'

I shrugged as if to say, *No big deal.* We got to my rental car and I loaded her bag in the trunk.

'Jack, I want to go there now,' Rachel said as we got in the car. 'To Western Data.'

'It will be after six by the time we get there. They'll be closed.'

'Fine, we don't go in. But we can still case the joint. I need something to take my mind off what happened today. OK?'

'Got it. We're going.'

I looked up Western Data's address in my notebook and plugged it into the car's GPS system. After twenty minutes of driving, Western Data

Consultants loomed small on the horizon on McKellips Road on the east side of Mesa. It was in a sparsely developed area of warehouses and small businesses surrounded by scrub brush and cacti. It was a one-storey building with two windows located on either side of the front door. The address number was painted on the top right corner.

'It's smaller than I thought it would be,' Rachel said.

'You have to remember, most of it is underground.'

A few blocks past the target there was a coffee shop called Hightower Grounds. I pulled in to turn round and then we took another pass at Western Data. This time the property was on Rachel's side and she turned all the way in her seat to view it.

'They've got cameras all over the place,' she said. 'I count one, two, three—six cameras on the outside.'

'Cameras inside and out, according to the website,' I responded. 'Do you want me to turn round and go by again?'

'No, I've seen enough. I'm hungry now, Jack. Let's go to the hotel and get room service and raid the minibar.'

I detected a smile on her face. 'That sounds like a plan to me.'

I had already set the address for the Mesa Verde Inn into the car's GPS device and it took us only ten minutes to get there. I parked in the garage behind the hotel and we went in.

Once we got to the room, we both kicked off our shoes and drank dark rum out of water glasses while sitting side by side, propped against the bed's multiple pillows. I watched Rachel in the mirror across from the bed. After a few minutes she shook her head.

'I was an FBI agent! What am I going to do now? What are we going to do now?'

I liked that she had thrown the 'we' in there at the end.

'Maybe we pool our skills and become private eyes. Walling and McEvoy, Discreet Investigations. We'll use your picture on the billboards. That'll bring in the business.'

She laughed. 'Well, thanks for putting my name first.'

I put my glass down on the bedside table and turned to her. Our eyes were only inches apart.

'I'll always put you first, Rachel. Always.'

She put her hand behind my neck and pulled me into a kiss.

After we had made love, Rachel seemed invigorated while I felt completely spent. She jumped up from the bed and went to her roller bag. She opened it and started looking through her belongings.

'Don't get dressed,' I said. 'Can't we stay in bed for a while?'

'No, I'm not getting dressed. I got you a present—here it is.'

She came back to the bed and handed me a little black felt pouch. I opened it and out came a silver neck chain with a pendant. The pendant was a silver-plated bullet.

'A silver bullet? What, are we going after a werewolf?'

'No, a *single* bullet. Remember the single-bullet theory?'

'Oh, yeah.' I felt embarrassed by my inappropriate attempt at humour. This was something important to her.

'Where'd you get this?'

'I had a lot of time to kill yesterday, so I went into this jewellery store near FBI headquarters. I guess they know their neighbourhood clientele because they were selling bullets as jewellery.'

I nodded as I turned the bullet in my fingers.

'There's no name on it. You said the theory was that everybody's got a bullet out there with someone's name on it.'

Rachel shrugged. 'They said I'd have to come back today if I wanted to put anything on it. I obviously didn't get the chance.'

I opened the clasp and reached up to put it round her neck. 'Why don't you give it to me when it's got your name on it?'

She thought about that and looked at me with a smile.

'You know what?' she asked. 'I'm really starving now.'

I almost laughed at the abrupt change in direction.

'OK, then let's order room service. I want a steak. And more rum.'

We ordered and both of us were able to get showers in before the food arrived. We ate in our hotel bathrobes while sitting across from each other at the table the room-service waiter had rolled into the room. I could see the silver chain on Rachel's neck but the bullet had been tucked inside her thick, white robe.

'Want to tell me about what happened in DC today?' I asked.

She finished a bite of steak before answering.

'There is nothing really to talk about,' she said. 'They had me. I had misled my supervisor about the interview at Ely, and he authorised the flight. They said fourteen thousand dollars' worth of jet fuel constitutes misuse of government funds on a felony level. They had a prosecutor in the hallway ready to go with it if I wanted to push it. I would've been booked right there and then.'

'That's incredible.'

'The thing is, I really was planning to do the interview at Ely and that would have made everything fine. But things changed when you told me about Angela being missing. I never got to Ely.'

'This is bureaucracy at its worst. I have to write about this.'

'You can't, Jack. I signed a confidentiality agreement, which I've already violated by telling you what I just told you. But if it makes its way into print, they will probably end up charging me after all.'

She poured another round of rum. I watched her take down her whole snifter of rum. She then poured herself another shot.

'Better be careful,' I said. 'This stuff is easy to get blasted on.'

'I want to get blasted.'

'Yeah, well, we'll have to leave here by about nine thirty tomorrow morning if you want to make our appointment on time.'

She put her glass down heavily and drunkenly on the table.

'Yeah, what about that? What are we doing tomorrow, Jack? You know I have no badge or gun any more. You want to just waltz into this place?'

'I want to see it. I want to figure out if he's in there. After that, we can call in the Bureau or the police or whoever you want. But it's my lead and I want to get in there first.'

'And then write about it in the paper.'

'Maybe, if they let me. But one way or another I'm going to write about this whole thing. So I want to be there first.' I paused. 'We can go in there and act like prospective clients. We take a tour of the place and meet as many people as we can. We ask questions about security and who has access to the sensitive legal files our firm will be backing up in storage. Things like that.'

'And?'

'And we hope that somebody gives themselves away or maybe I see the guy from Ely with the sideburns.'

'This doesn't sound like a plan, Jack. It sounds like you're making it up as you go along.'

'Maybe I am and maybe that's why I need you to be there.'

'I have no idea what you mean by that.'

I got up and came round to her side and got down on one knee. I put my hand on her forearm.

'Look, I don't need your gun or your badge, Rachel. I want you there because if somebody in that place makes a false move, even a small one, you're going to read it and then we've got him.'

She pushed my hand off her arm. 'If you think I'm some sort of mind-reader who can—'

'Not a mind-reader, Rachel, but you've got instincts. After a short phone conversation with me you stole an FBI plane and flew to Nevada because you knew. You *knew*, Rachel. And it saved my life. That's instinct, and that's why I want you there tomorrow.'

She looked at me for a long moment and then nodded.

'OK, Jack,' she said. 'I'll be there.'

THE RUM DIDN'T DO us any favours in the morning. Rachel and I were both moving pretty slowly but still managed to get out of the hotel with more than enough time to make our appointment.

The front gate of the complex was open and I pulled into a parking space. We got out and I grabbed my sports jacket out of the back seat. I was wearing a new shirt and tie. Rachel was wearing her agent outfit—a navy suit—and she looked impressive.

We had to push a button at the door and identify ourselves through a speaker before being buzzed in. There was a small entrance area and a woman sitting behind a reception counter.

'We have a ten o'clock appointment with Mr McGinnis,' I said.

'Yes, Ms Chavez will be showing you the plant,' the receptionist said cheerfully. 'Let's see if she's ready.'

I shook my head. 'No, our appointment was with Mr McGinnis, the company CEO. We came down from Las Vegas to see him.'

'I'm sorry, but Mr McGinnis has unexpectedly been detained.'

'Well, we wanted to speak to him about our particular needs.'

'Let me see if I can get Ms Chavez. I'm sure she will be able to see to your needs.'

The receptionist made a call. I looked at Rachel, who raised an eyebrow. Something was off about this.

The receptionist looked up and smiled at us. 'Ms Chavez will be right out.'

A door opened behind the reception counter and a young woman with dark hair stepped out. She held her hand out to me.

'Mr McEvoy, I'm Yolanda Chavez, Mr McGinnis's executive assistant. I hope you don't mind my taking you around today.'

I shook her hand and introduced Rachel.

'Our appointment was with Declan McGinnis,' Rachel said.

'Mr McGinnis is home ill today. I hope you understand.'

I looked at Rachel and shrugged. 'If we could still get the tour, we could talk to Mr McGinnis when he's feeling better,' I said.

'Of course,' Chavez said. She handed us two clipboards. 'We first have to get a security clearance,' she said. 'If each of you could sign this waiver, I will make copies of your driver's licences.'

Rachel and I handed over our licences and Chavez studied them.

'You're both from California? I thought you—'

'We're both new hires. I'm doing mostly investigative work and Rachel will be the firm's IT person—once we reconfigure our IT.'

Chavez looked at me, adjusted her horn-rimmed glasses and said she would be back to collect us for the tour in ten minutes.

Rachel and I sat down on the couch beneath one of the windows and signed the waiver forms.

'What do you think about McGinnis not being here?' I whispered. 'First he's unexpectedly detained, next he's home sick. I mean, which is it?'

The receptionist looked up from her computer screen.

'I think we should talk about it after,' Rachel whispered.

We sat silently until Chavez returned to the reception area. She handed back our driver's licences and we gave her the clipboards.

'If you follow me, we'll get the show on the road,' Chavez said.

She used a keycard to open the door between the reception area and the rest of the facility. We stepped into a hallway and she turned to face us.

'Let me tell you a little about what we do here,' she said. 'We opened four years ago. Answering the growing demand for secure data management and storage, Western Data is the brainchild of Declan McGinnis, our CEO. We have almost one thousand clients, ranging from small firms to major corporations.

'Our most common type of client has become the American law firm. We provide a full raft of services specifically aimed at satisfying the needs of the law firm of any size in any location. From web hosting to colocation, we are the one-stop shop for your firm.'

She made a full turn with her arms outstretched, as if to take in the whole building, although we were still standing in a hallway.

'Mr McGinnis designed and built a facility with the highest level of security. We operate in a hardened structure able to withstand a seven-point-oh earthquake. All visitors are recorded while on site twenty-four-seven with the camera recordings archived for forty-five days.'

She pointed to the casino-style camera ball located on the ceiling above. 'All secure areas of the facility are protected by keycards and biometric hand scanners. Security and monitoring is done from the network operations centre, which is located in the underground bunker adjacent to the colocation centre, or "farm", as we call it.'

She went on to describe the plant's cooling, power and network systems and their back-up subsystems, but I was losing interest. We had moved into a vast lab where about a dozen techs were building and operating websites for Western Data's massive client base.

Chavez introduced us to a graphic designer named Danny O'Connor, who was a supervisor in the lab. I studied him as he spoke and decided he was too chunky to have been Sideburns.

I looked past him at the techs working in cubicles. Half of them were women and easy to dismiss. With the men, I saw nobody I thought might have been the man who had gone to Ely to kill me.

After we were finished in the design lab, Chavez took us through a door with her keycard and into another hallway, which led to an elevator. She needed her keycard again to summon the elevator.

'I am going to take you down now to what we call the "bunker",' she said. 'Our network operations centre is there, along with the server farm dedicated to colocation services. It's the heart of our enterprise, really.'

As we entered the elevator, Chavez explained that we were going down only one level structurally but that it totalled a twenty-foot descent beneath the surface. Once we reached the bottom, the elevator opened onto a space Chavez called the octagon, an eight-walled waiting room with four other doors in addition to the elevator. Chavez pointed to each one.

'Our network operations centre; our core network equipment room; plant facilities; and our colocation control room, which leads to the server farm. Only employees with full-access clearance can enter the core.'

Chavez slid her keycard through the locking device of the network operations centre door and we entered a narrow room.

'Each of the locations in the bunker is entered through a mantrap. When I carded the outside door I set off a tone inside. The techs in there now have the opportunity to view us and hit an emergency stop if we are determined to be intruders.'

She waved to an overhead camera and then slid her card through the lock on the next door. We entered the network operations centre, which was slightly underwhelming. I was expecting a NASA launch centre but we got two rows of computer stations with three technicians monitoring multiple screens. Chavez explained that the techs were monitoring power, temperature, bandwidth and every other measurable aspect of Western Data's operations, as well as the 200 cameras located throughout the facility.

Nothing here struck me as sinister or relating to the Unsub. I saw no one that I thought could be Sideburns. No one did a double take when they looked up and saw me. I waited impatiently while Chavez continued her sales pitch.

'We're going to head over to the farm now,' Chavez finally said. 'I'm going to turn you over to Mr Carver, who runs the data centre. I need to step out and make a phone call, but you'll be in good hands with Mr Carver. He's also our CTE.'

'Chief threat engineer,' Rachel answered before I could ask.

'Yes,' Chavez said. 'He's our scarecrow.'

WE WENT THROUGH another mantrap and then entered the data centre. We stepped into a dimly lit room with three work stations that had multiple computer screens at each. Two young men sat at stations, while the other was empty. To the left was an open door to a private office that appeared empty. The work stations faced two big windows and a glass door that looked out on a large space where there were several rows of server towers under bright overhead lighting. I had seen this room on the website. The farm.

The two men swivelled in their chairs to look up at us when we came through the door but then almost immediately turned back to their work. It was just another dog and pony show to them. They wore shirts and ties but with their scruffy hair and cheeks they looked like they should be in T-shirts and blue jeans.

'Kurt, I thought Mr Carver was in the centre,' Chavez said.

One of the men turned to us again. He was a pimply-faced kid of no more than twenty-five. He was about as suspicious as flowers at a wedding.

'He went into the farm to check server seventy-seven.'

Chavez stepped up to the unused work station and raised a microphone that was built into the desk.

'Mr Carver, can you break away for a few minutes to tell our guests about the data centre?'

Chavez turned to Rachel and me and then looked at her watch.

'OK, then. He will handle this part of your journey and I will collect you in about twenty minutes.'

She turned to leave and I saw her eyes hold for a moment on a cardboard box sitting on the chair in front of the empty desk.

'Are these Freddy's things?' she asked.

'Yup,' Kurt said. 'He didn't get a chance to get it all. We boxed it up and were thinking about taking it to him.'

Chavez turned towards the door without responding. Through the glass I saw a man in a lab coat walking down one of the aisles created by the rows of server towers. He was tall and thin and at least fifteen years older than Sideburns. Rachel subtly gave me a questioning look. I surreptitiously shook my head. Not him.

'Here comes our scarecrow,' Kurt said.

I looked at the kid.

'Why do you call him that? Because he's skinny?'

'He's in charge of keepin' all the nasty birds off the crops.'

Rachel filled in the blanks. 'Hackers, trolls, virus carriers,' she said.

'He's in charge of security on the data farm.'

I nodded. The man in the lab coat made his way to the glass door and reached for an unseen locking mechanism to his right. I heard a metallic click and then he slid the door open. I noticed that next to the door was an electronic hand-reader—it took more than a simple keycard to access the actual farm. Mounted above the reader was a case with a glass door that contained what looked like a pair of gas masks.

'Hello, I'm Wesley Carver. How do you do?'

He extended his hand first to Rachel, who shook it and told him her name. He then turned to me and I did the same.

'Have you met today's crew? This is Kurt and Mizzou, our server support engineers. They keep things running while I chase down the people who think they can have a go at the palace walls.'

'The hackers?' Rachel asked.

'Yes, well, places like this are a bit of a challenge to the people out there with nothing better to do. We have to constantly be alert.'

Carver turned so he was looking into the server room.

'This is the heart and brains of the beast,' he said. 'As I'm sure Yolanda told you, data storage, colocation, dry-docking, whatever you want to call it, is the main service we provide. O'Connor and his boys up on the design and hosting floor talk a good game, but this down here is what we have that nobody else has.'

I noticed Kurt and Mizzou give each other a fist bump.

'No other aspect of the digital business world has grown so exponentially fast as this segment,' Carver said. 'Safe, clean storage and access to vital company records and archives. We offer the advantage of our own direct, high-speed, Internet backbone. Why build it in the back room of your firm when you can have it here and have the same sort of access?'

'We're already sold on that, Mr Carver,' Rachel said. 'We don't need to be convinced of the product. We need to be convinced of the people we are entrusting our data to.'

I liked how she was moving it in the direction of people.

'Exactly,' Carver said. 'It always comes down to people, doesn't it? Let me give you a quick overview of what we have here and then perhaps we could retire to my office and discuss personnel issues.'

He walked to the big windows that looked into the server room. We followed him and he continued the tour.

'What you see here is our server room. The farm. With Western Data, you get your own managed server with one-hundred-mega-bit service. That gives you instant access to the information you store here. If needed, every keystroke made on your computers could be instantaneously backed up and stored here. But what good is it to back everything up here if it is not safe?'

'Exactly,' Rachel said.

'Security means two different things,' Carver said. 'Plant security and data security. Let's talk about the facility first. This room is completely impregnable. The walls, floor and ceiling are two-foot-thick cast concrete. These windows are impact resistant and ballistic proof. And the door is controlled by biometric hand scan.'

He pointed to the device next to the glass door.

'Access to the server room is limited to key personnel. The biometric scanner unlocks the door after reading and confirming three distinct hand groups: palm print, vein pattern and hand geometry. It also checks for a pulse. Nobody can get away with chopping my hand off and using it to get into the server farm.'

Carver smiled but Rachel and I didn't join in.

'What about if there's an emergency?' I asked. 'Could people be stuck in there?'

'No, of course not. From the inside you simply push a release button that opens the lock and then slide open the door. The system is designed to keep intruders out. As far as fire protection goes, we employ a three-stage protection scheme. We have a standard VESDA system with a—'

'VESDA?' I asked.

'Very Early Smoke Detection Alarm, which relies on laser-based smoke detectors. In the event of a fire the VESDA will activate a series of alarms followed by the waterless fire-suppression system.'

Carver pointed to red pressure tanks lined on the back wall.

'There you see our carbon dioxide tanks, which are part of this system. If there is a fire, the gas floods the room, extinguishing the fire without harming any of the electronics or the client data.'

'What about people?' I asked.

Carver looked at me. 'Good question, Mr McEvoy. The three-stage alarm allows sixty seconds for any personnel in the server room to escape. Additionally, anyone entering the server room is required to carry a respirator as a redundancy.'

From the pocket of his lab coat he withdrew a breathing mask similar to the two hanging in the case by the door.

'Do either of you have any questions?'

I had nothing to ask because I was pretty much at sea on the technology. But Rachel looked like she understood everything.

'So again it's about people,' she said. 'No matter how well you build the mousetrap, it comes down to the people who operate it.'

Carver brought his hand to his chin and nodded. 'Why don't we step into my office so we can discuss that aspect of our operation.'

We followed him to his office. Along the way I looked down into the cardboard box that was on the chair of the empty station. It was full of personal belongings. Magazines, cigarettes, a *Star Trek* coffee mug. I also saw flash drives, a set of keys and an iPod.

Carver closed the door of his office after we entered. We took the two seats in front of the glass table he used as a desk.

'Where are you staying?' Carver asked as he moved behind his worktable.

'The Mesa Verde,' I said.

'Nice place,' Carver said, and sat down. 'Now then, you want to talk about people,' he said, looking directly at Rachel.

'Yes, we do. We appreciate the tour of the facility but we really came to get a feel for the people we would entrust our data to. We're disappointed we were unable to meet Declan McGinnis and, frankly, a little put off by it. We haven't received a credible explanation for why he stood us up.'

Carver raised his hands in a gesture of surrender.

'Yolanda is not at liberty to discuss personnel matters,' Carver said. 'But as a director of the company I can assure you that Declan's situation in no way affects our operation here. He simply took a few days off.'

'Well, that is troubling, because that's the third different explanation we've received. It doesn't leave us with a good impression.'

Carver nodded and exhaled heavily.

'If I could tell you more I would,' he said. 'But you have to realise that what we sell here is confidentiality. And that starts with our own personnel.'

He had drawn a line. Rachel capitulated.

'Very well, Mr Carver. Then tell us about the people who work for you. I look at your two server engineers and I have to say they look to me like the type of people you are protecting this facility from.'

Carver smiled broadly and nodded.

'Those young men are the best and the brightest when it comes to this work. Yes, there is no doubt that some of our employees have done their share of hacking and mischief before coming to work here. And that's because sometimes it takes a sly fox to catch a sly fox. But every employee here is thoroughly vetted for criminal records, as well as the content of their character and psychological make-up. We have never had an employee make an unauthorised intrusion into client data.'

Rachel and I nodded. But we knew something Carver either didn't know or was covering up. Someone here *had* dipped into client data. A killer had stalked his prey in the digital fields of the farm.

'What happened to the guy who worked out there?' I asked, jerking a thumb towards the outer room. 'They said his name was Freddy. Why did he leave without taking his things? Was he fired?'

'No, he was not fired. He quit for unknown reasons. He failed to show up for his shift on Friday night and instead sent me an email saying he resigned to pursue other things. These young kids, they are in high demand. I'm assuming Freddy was lured away by a competitor. We pay well but somebody else can always pay better.'

I nodded as if I agreed but I was thinking about the box out there and putting other things with it: the FBI visits and asks questions about the trunk murder website on Thursday, and Freddy splits without so much as coming back in for his iPod.

And what about McGinnis? I was about to ask if his disappearance could be related to Freddy's abrupt departure, but was interrupted by the mantrap buzzer. I noticed a screen on a pivoting arm beneath Carver's glass desk switch to the camera in the mantrap. Yolanda Chavez was coming back in to collect us.

Rachel leaned forward, inadvertently putting an urgent spin on her question. 'What is Freddy's last name?' She was still acting like an agent, asking direct questions and expecting answers.

'Why would you want his name? He no longer works here.'

'I don't know. I just . . .'

Rachel was cornered. There was no good answer to the question, at least from Carver's point of view. But we got lucky and were saved by Chavez, who poked her head in through the door.

'So how are we doing in here?' she asked.

Carver kept his eyes on Rachel. 'We're doing fine,' he said. 'Are there any other questions I can answer?'

Still back-pedalling, Rachel looked at me and I shook my head.

'I've seen all I need to see,' I said. 'I appreciate the tour.'

'Yes, thank you,' Rachel said. 'Your facility is impressive.'

'Then I'll take you back up to the surface now.'

Rachel got up and turned towards the door. I stood up, thanked Carver again and reached across the table to shake his hand.

'Nice to meet you, Jack,' he said. 'I hope to see you again.'

THE CAR WAS AS HOT as an oven when we got back into it. I quickly cranked the air to high, lowered my window, then backed out. As we headed towards the exit, I caught a glimpse of the rear of the building. There was an exit door and a bench beneath a small awning. Sitting on the bench was the server engineer named Mizzou. He was smoking a cigarette.

'The smokers' porch,' Rachel said. 'When addiction calls . . .'

I closed my window after I drove onto the main road. When we were no longer in view of Western Data I turned to Rachel.

'So what do you think?'

'I think I almost blew it. Maybe I did.'

'You mean at the end? I think we're fine. You just have to remember you no longer carry that badge that opens all doors and makes people answer your questions.'

I suddenly realised how callous I must have sounded.

'Sorry, Rachel. I didn't mean—' I decided to change the subject. 'What was your vibe back there? What do you think of Carver and everybody else?'

'I'm more interested in who I didn't see than who I did see.'

'You mean Freddy?' I said.

'And McGinnis. I think we have to find out who this Freddy who quit is, and what the deal is with McGinnis.'

I nodded. We were on the same page. 'You think they're connected, Freddy quitting and McGinnis not showing up?'

'We won't know until we talk to them both.'

'How do we find them? We don't know Freddy's last name.'

She hesitated before answering.

'I could try to make some calls, see if anybody is still talking to me. I am sure that when they went in there last week with a warrant, they got a list of names of all employees.'

I thought that was wishful thinking on her part. In law enforcement bureaucracies, once you were out, you were out.

'What if that doesn't work?'

'Then I don't know,' she said curtly. 'I guess we do it the old-fashioned way. We go back and wait for Freddy's slacker buddies to punch out and go home. Maybe they'll lead us to him.'

I liked the plan. Though I wasn't sure we'd find Freddy himself.

'I think it's a good plan, but my vibe is that Freddy's long gone.'

'Why?'

The timing of it. The FBI shows up one day and he's gone the same night. I don't think we're going to find him here in Mesa, Arizona.'

Rachel furrowed her brow. 'You're probably right. It makes me think we have to call in the pros. Like I said, they probably already have his name and they can run him down quickly.'

'Not yet, Rachel. Let's at least see what we can find out today.'

'Look, Jack, you made the connection. No matter what happens it will be because you made the break. You'll get the credit.'

'I'm not worried about the credit.'

'Then why are you doing this? Don't tell me it's still about the story. Aren't you over that yet?' Rachel said.

'Are you over being an agent yet?'

She didn't answer and looked out of the window.

'Same as me,' I said. 'This is my last story and it's important. Besides, this could be your ticket back inside.'

She shook her head. 'Jack, you don't know the Bureau. I resigned under threat of prosecution. I could find Osama bin Laden hiding in a cave in Griffith Park and they wouldn't take me back.'

'OK, OK. Sorry.'

We drove in silence and soon I saw a barbecue restaurant called Rosie's come up on the right. It was early for lunch but I was famished.

'Let's get something to eat, make some calls and then go back and wait for Kurt and Mizzou to punch out,' I said.

'You got it, partner,' Rachel said.

Nine: The Farm

C arver sat in his office, studying the camera angles. Over 100 views of the building and its surroundings, all at his command. At the moment, he was manipulating an exterior camera at the front of the building. It didn't take long to spot them. He knew they'd come back. He knew about thought processes.

McEvoy and Walling were parked outside the self-storage centre. They were watching Western Data at the same time as he was watching them.

Carver toyed with the idea of letting them bake out there. But then he decided to get things moving. He picked up his phone.

'Mizzou, come in here, please. It's unlocked.'

He waited until Mizzou opened the door and stepped in.

'Close the door,' Carver said.

The young computer genius did as instructed. 'What's up, boss?'

'I want you to deliver Freddy's belongings to him. Those people that were in here earlier saw that box on his chair and realised we either had to fire somebody or we have a turnover problem. It doesn't instil confidence in the prospective customer.'

'I understand.'

'Good. Then take that box, strap it to the back of your motorcycle and take it to his warehouse.'

'And then come all the way back?'

Carver knew Mizzou was angling for the rest of the day off.

'Fine,' he said. 'Take the rest of the day. Just go.'

Mizzou left the office. Carver watched the cameras, waiting to track him once he got on his motorcycle in the parking lot. Carver started humming. He went to the song that had pervaded all corners of his life for as long as he could remember. Soon he quietly sang his two favourite lines and found himself repeating them faster and faster instead of continuing the song:

> *There's a killer on the road; his brain is squirming like a toad*
> *There's a killer on the road; his brain is squirming like a toad*
> *There's a killer on the road; his brain is squirming like a toad*
> *If you give this man a ride . . .*

Finally, Mizzou entered the camera frame and started securing the cardboard box to the cargo rack behind the seat of his motorcycle. When the box was secured, Mizzou started the engine and rode out of the front gate. Carver then turned the camera towards the self-storage centre down the street. He saw that McEvoy and Walling had seen the box and taken the bait. McEvoy was pulling out to follow.

Ten: The Dark of Dreams

We had found a shaded spot next to a self-storage centre and had just settled in for a long, hot wait, when we got lucky. A motorcyclist pulled out of Western Data and headed west. Rachel and I both recognised the box that was lashed to a rear rack.

'Follow the box,' Rachel said.

I managed to stay with the box for the next ten minutes through stop-and-go traffic. Then the motorcycle got on the 202 freeway heading towards Phoenix. For fifteen minutes we followed him in clear traffic as he transitioned onto 110 and then north on I-17 through the heart of Phoenix.

'What do you think he's doing?' I asked.

'Taking Freddy his box.'

'I know that. But I mean, why now?'

'Maybe he's finished for the day. Could be a lot of reasons.'

Something about that explanation bothered me but I didn't have time to think about it. The motorcycle started heading towards the next exit. I fell in behind him with a car between us. Soon we were in an old warehouse district.

Mizzou stopped in front of a one-storey brick building and dismounted. I pulled to the kerb half a block away. He took the box off the bike rack and carried it towards a large sliding door at the side of the building.

Mizzou pounded on the door, but nobody came. He then walked over to a large window and looked in. He went back to the door, grabbed the door handle and tried to slide it open. To his surprise and ours, the door easily moved on its rollers. It was unlocked.

Mizzou hesitated and for the first time looked round. His eyes didn't hold on my car. They quickly returned to the open door. It looked like he called out Freddy's name and after a few seconds he went in.

'What do you think?' I asked.

'I think we need to get in there,' Rachel said.

I dropped the car into gear, and drove the remaining half block to the building. Rachel was out and moving towards the sliding door before I had it back in park. I jumped out and followed.

Rachel pulled the door open just enough for us to slip in. It was dark inside and it took a few moments for my eyes to adjust. The place was wide open with steel roof supports going up every twenty feet. Plasterboard partitions had been erected to divide it into living, working and exercise space. Further down was a dresser and an unmade bed. Against one of the partitions was a refrigerator and a table with a microwave. I saw the box Mizzou had carried on the table next to the microwave, but I saw no sign of Mizzou.

I caught up with Rachel and saw a work station set up against the wall. There were three screens and a PC underneath. The keyboard, however, was missing.

Rachel seemed to study the spot where the keyboard should have been.

'He took the keyboard,' she whispered. 'He knows we can—'

She stopped at the sound of a toilet flushing. It came from the corner of the warehouse. Rachel reached up to one of the shelves and grabbed a cable tie used for bunching computer wires, then pulled me into the sleeping area. We stood against the wall and waited. The moment Mizzou passed, Rachel grabbed him by the wrist and neck, spinning him onto the bed. She planted him face-first on the mattress and jumped on his back.

'Don't move!' she yelled. She yanked his hands behind his back and used the cable tie to quickly bind them.

'What is this? What did I do?'

'What are you doing here?'

'I came to drop off Freddy's stuff and decided to use the can.'

'Where is Freddy?'

'I don't know. Who are you anyway?'

'Never mind who I am. Who is Freddy?'

'What? He lives here. He's Freddy Stone. I work with him. I mean—hey, you! You're that lady that was on the tour today.'

Rachel climbed off him. Mizzou turned round on the bed and propped himself up. Wide-eyed, he looked from Rachel to me.

'You can't do this! I don't even think you're cops. I want a lawyer.'

Rachel took a threatening step closer to the bed. She spoke in a low, calm voice. 'If we're not cops, what makes you think we'd get you a lawyer?'

Mizzou's eyes became scared. 'Look,' he said. 'I'll tell you everything I know. Just let me go.'

'Is Freddy a hacker?' Rachel asked.

'More like a troller. He likes doin' pranks and stuff.'

'What's your name?'

'Matthew Mardsen.'

'OK, Matthew, what about Declan McGinnis? Where is he?'

'I don't know. I heard he emailed that he was home sick,' he offered desperately. 'I told you everything I know.'

Rachel came up close and spoke directly into his ear.

'If I find out differently, I'm going to come back for you.'

Holding him by the cable-tie she pulled him round the wall into the work station. She found a pair of scissors and cut the binding from his wrists.

'Get out of here and don't tell anybody what happened,' she said. 'If you do, we'll know.'

'I won't. I promise I won't.'

'Go!'

He almost slipped on the polished concrete when he turned to run towards the door. Within five seconds we heard the motorcycle.

'I don't know if he's going to go running to the cops or not, but let's not take too much more time here.'

'Let's get the hell out now.'

'No, not yet. Look round, see what you can find. Ten minutes and then we're out of here. Don't leave fingerprints.'

But we didn't need ten minutes. It quickly became clear that the place had been stripped of anything personal. The refrigerator was almost empty. The freezer contained a couple of frozen pizzas. I checked in the dresser. Empty. Even the trash cans were empty.

'Let's go,' Rachel said.

I looked up from checking under the bed and saw she was already to the door. Under her arm she was carrying the box that Mizzou had just dropped off. I hurried after her. She rounded the corner of the building and entered the alley.

I realised she was heading towards the first of two industrial-sized Dumpsters that were pushed into alcoves on opposite sides of the alley. Just as I caught up with her she handed me Freddy Stone's box.

'Hold this.'

She flung the heavy steel lid up and it banged against the wall.

'You checked the kitchen cabinets, right?' Rachel asked. 'Were there any trash-can liners?'

It took me a moment to understand. 'Uh, yeah, under the sink. Black with the red drawstring.'

'Good. That narrows it down.'

She was reaching into the Dumpster, moving things around. It was half full and smelt awful. At first I thought we had found Freddy Stone. I stepped back and turned away.

'Don't worry, it's not him,' Rachel said. 'I know what a rotting body smells like, and it's worse.'

I moved back to the Dumpster and pulled out every black bag and dropped them on the ground. Rachel started opening them by tearing the plastic in such a way that the contents stayed in place inside. Like performing an autopsy on a garbage bag.

'Do it like this, and don't mix contents from different bags,' she said.

'Got it.'

The first bag I opened mostly contained shredded documents.

'I've got shreddings here.'

Rachel looked over. 'That could be his. There was a shredder by the work station. Put that one aside.'

I did as I was told and opened the next bag. This one contained basic household trash. I recognised one of the empty food boxes.

'This is him. He had the same brand of pizza in the freezer.'

Rachel looked over.

'Good. Look for anything of a personal nature.'

I carefully moved my hands through the refuse in the torn bag. It had all come from the kitchen area. Food boxes, cans, rotting banana peels. At the bottom of the bag was a newspaper. I carefully pulled it out. It was the previous Wednesday's edition of the *Las Vegas Review-Journal*. That was the day I had been in Vegas.

I unfolded it. There was a coffee ring that partially obscured a name written with a marker pen.

'I've got a Vegas paper with a name written here.'

Rachel looked up. 'What name?'

'It's blurred by a coffee ring. It's Georgette something. Begins with a B and ends M-A-N.'

I held the paper up. She studied it for a second and I saw recognition fire in her eyes.

'This is it. He's our guy. Remember, I told you about the email to the prison in Ely that got Oglevy put in lockdown? It was from the warden's secretary. Her name is Georgette Brockman.'

Still crouched on my haunches next to the open bag, I stared up at Rachel as I put it all together. Freddy Stone was Sideburns.

Rachel's conclusions were the same as mine.

'He was in Nevada trailing you. He got her name and wrote it down while he was hacking the prison system's database. This is the link, Jack. You did it!'

I got up and approached her.

'*We* did it, Rachel. But what do we do now?'

I saw a sad realisation play on her face.

'I don't think we should be touching anything else. We need to back off and call in the Bureau. They have to take it from here.'

EQUIPMENT-WISE, THE FBI always seemed ready for anything. Within an hour of Rachel's calling the local field office, we were placed in separate interrogation rooms in a nondescript vehicle the size of a bus. It was parked outside the warehouse where Freddy Stone had lived. We were being questioned by agents inside while other agents were in the warehouse and the nearby alley looking for further signs of Stone's involvement in the trunk murders.

My interrogator was an agent named John Bantam. This was a misnomer because Bantam was so big he seemed to fill the room. He regularly paced in front of me, slapping his leg with a legal pad in a way I think was designed to make me think that my head could be its next destination.

Bantam grilled me for an hour about how I had made the connection to Western Data and all the moves Rachel and I had made after that. I told the truth, but not the whole truth. I only answered the questions put to me and offered no detail that was not specifically asked for. The session went from a cordial interview to a tense interrogation.

Finally, I hit my limit and stood up from my chair.

'Look, I told you all I know. I have a story to go write.'

'Sit down. We're not finished,' Bantam said.

'This is a voluntary interview. I've answered every question and now you're just repeating yourself, trying to see if I get crossed up. It's not going to happen because I told you the truth. Now, can I go?'

'I could arrest you right now for breaking and entering.'

'I didn't break and enter. I followed someone into the warehouse when we thought he might be committing a crime.'

Bantam slapped the pad against his leg and turned his back to me. He walked to the door and then turned back and sat down.

'We need you to hold your story,' he said.

I nodded. Now we were finally down to it.

'I can't hold the story. It's a major break. Besides, splashing Stone's face across the media might help you catch him.'

Bantam shook his head.

'Not yet. We need twenty-four hours to assess what we've got here and at the other locations. We want to do that before he knows we're onto him.'

I thought about the possibilities.

'This is what I am willing to do,' I said. 'Today is Tuesday. I write the story for Thursday's paper. That would give you a solid thirty-six hours, at least.'

Bantam nodded. 'OK. I think that will work.'

He made a move to get up.

'Wait a minute, that's not all. I want access. I want to be in the loop. I want to know what is going on. I want to be embedded.'

He smirked and shook his head.

'We don't do embedded. We don't take reporters inside investigations. Legally, it could compromise a prosecution.'

'Then we don't have a deal and I need to call my editor right now.'

I reached into my pocket for my cellphone.

'All right, wait,' Bantam said. 'I can't make this call. Sit tight and I'll get back to you.'

He stood up and left the room, closing the door. I got up and checked the knob. The door was locked. I pulled my phone and checked the screen. It said NO SERVICE. So much for my dramatic move.

I spent another hour sitting on a hard folding chair. Finally, the door opened. But it wasn't Bantam who entered. It was Rachel. My eyes probably showed my surprise but my tongue held in check.

Rachel sat down in front of me. I looked at her and pointed to the ceiling, raising my eyebrows in question.

'We're being recorded,' she said. 'But you can speak freely.'

I shrugged. 'Something tells me you've put on weight since I last saw you. Like maybe a badge and a gun?'

She nodded. 'I actually don't have the badge or gun yet but they're on their way.'

'Don't tell me, you found Osama bin Laden in Griffith Park?'

'Not exactly.'

'But you were reinstated.'

'My resignation had not been signed off on yet. The slow pace of bureaucracy, you know? I was allowed to withdraw it.'

I leaned forward and whispered. 'What about the jet?'

'You don't have to whisper. The jet is no longer an issue.'

'Let me guess, they want it to read that an agent identified Stone as the Unsub, not someone they had just run out of the Bureau.'

She nodded. 'I'm now assigned to dealing with you. They're not going to let you inside, Jack. It's a recipe for disaster.'

'Look, can we get out of this cube? Can we just take a walk where there are no hidden cameras or microphones?'

'Sure, let's walk.'

She went to the door and knocked with a two-and-one pattern. The door was opened immediately. I followed Rachel out of the bus.

Outside I could see that several agents and technicians were still moving about the alley, collecting evidence.

'All these people, have they found anything we didn't find?'

She smiled slyly. 'Not so far.'

'Bantam said the Bureau was swarming other locations—plural. What other locations?'

'Look, Jack, before we talk we need to be straight on something. This isn't a ride-along and you're not embedded. I am your contact as long as you hold the story for a day the way you offered.'

'The offer was based on full access.'

'Jack, that's not going to happen. But you can trust me. Go back to LA. Tomorrow you can call me every hour on the hour if you want and I'll tell you what we've got. I promise. Do we have a deal?'

'Yes, we have a deal.'

'Thank you.'

I turned away from the alley to face her. 'So what's happening right now? What about the other locations Bantam mentioned?'

'We also have agents at Western Data and at the home of Declan McGinnis in Scottsdale.'

'And what's McGinnis have to say for himself?'

'Nothing so far. We haven't found him. He's gone, and so has his dog. He might have got too close to Stone, and Stone reacted. There's another possibility, too.'

'That they were in it together?'

She nodded. 'Yes, a team. McGinnis and Stone.'

It was not without precedent. The Hillside Strangler turned out to be two cousins. And there were other serial killer teams.

'This is why we need time before the media firestorm. Both men had laptops and they took those with them. But they also had computers at Western Data and we have them. We've got an EER team coming in from Quantico. They'll be on the ground by—'

'EER?'

'Electronic Evidence Retrieval team. They're in the air now. We'll put them on the system at Western Data and see what we can learn. And remember, that place is wired for sight and sound. The archived recordings should be able to help us as well.'

'You think it's one Unsub or two?' I asked Rachel.

'I think we're talking about a team.'

'Why?'

'You know the scenario we spun the other night? Where the Unsub comes to LA, lures Angela to your house, then kills her and flies to Vegas to follow you?'

'Yeah.'

'Well, the Bureau checked every airline flying out of LAX and Burbank to Vegas that night. Only four passengers on the late flights bought tickets that night. Everybody else had reservations. Agents cleared three of them. The fourth, of course, was you.'

'OK, then he could have driven.'

'But why send the GO! package overnight if you were driving to Vegas? Sending the package overnight only works if he was flying and was going to pick it up, or if he was sending it to somebody.'

'His partner.'

I nodded and started pacing. It all seemed to make sense.

'So Angela goes to the trap site and alerts them. They read her email.

They read my email. And their response is that one goes to LA to take care of her and one goes to Vegas to take care of me.'

'That's how I'm seeing it.'

It made sense to me.

'There's another thing that indicates a team,' Rachel said. 'Denise Babbit was put in the trunk of her car and it was abandoned in South LA where Alonzo Winslow happened upon it. If the killer worked alone, how did he get out of South LA after he dropped off the car? Did he wait on the kerb for a bus? Did he walk, a white man in a black neighbourhood at night? I don't think so.'

'So whoever dropped her car off had a ride out of there.'

'You got it.'

I went silent for a long moment while I thought of all the new information. Rachel finally interrupted.

'I have to get to work, Jack. And you need to get on a plane.'

'What is your assignment? I mean, besides me.'

'I'm going to work with the EER team at Western Data. I need to get over there now to get things ready.'

'Did they shut that place down?'

'More or less. They sent everybody home except for a skeleton crew to help with the EER team.'

I nodded. 'OK. I'm going back to the hotel to get my stuff. You want me to leave the room for you?'

'No, the Bureau's paying my way now. When you check out, can you just leave my bag with the front desk?'

'OK, Rachel. You be careful.'

As I turned to head to my car I slyly reached out and squeezed her wrist.

THE THREE AGENTS comprising the FBI Electronic Evidence Retrieval team had commandeered the three work stations in the control room. Carver was left pacing behind them. He knew they would find only what he wanted them to find. But he had to act like he was worried.

'Mr Carver, you need to relax,' Agent George Torres said.

'Sorry,' Carver said. 'I'm just worried.'

'Yes, sir, we understand,' Torres said. 'Why don't you—'

The agent was interrupted by the sound of 'Riders on the Storm' coming from the pocket of Carver's lab coat.

'Excuse me,' Carver said. He answered the cellphone.

'It's me,' Freddy Stone said.

'Hi, there,' Carver said cheerily for the benefit of the agents.

'Have they found it yet?'

'No. It's going to be a while. You'll have to play without me.'

'This is my test, isn't it? I have to prove myself to you.'

He said it with a slight note of indignation.

'After what happened last week, I'm happy to sit this one out.'

There was a pause and then Stone changed directions.

'Do those agents know who I am yet?'

'I don't know but there's nothing I can do about it right now.'

'I'll meet you later at the place?' Stone asked.

'Yes, my place. You bring the chips and beer. See you then.'

He ended the call and dropped the phone back into his pocket. Stone's hedging and indignation were beginning to concern Carver. He probably should have ended it in the desert and put Stone in the hole with McGinnis and the dog. End of story. End of threat.

He could still do it. Later tonight maybe. It would be the end of the line for Stone and a lot of other things. Western Data would not be able to withstand the scandal. It would close and Carver would move on. By himself. Like before. He would take the lessons he had learned and begin again somewhere else. He was the Changeling. He knew he could do it.

I'm a changeling, see me change. I'm a changelin', see me change.

Torres turned from his screen and looked at Carver. Carver checked himself. Had he been humming?

'Poker night?' Torres asked.

'Yeah.'

'Sorry you're missing your game.'

'That's OK. You guys are probably saving me fifty bucks.'

'The Bureau is always happy to help out,' said Torres. He smiled and the other agent, a woman named Sarah Mowry, smiled too.

Carver tried to smile but it felt phoney and he stopped. The truth was, he had nothing to smile about.

Eleven: A Call To Action

I stayed in my hotel room the whole evening, writing the next day's story and repeatedly calling Rachel. I already had the main components of the story well in hand. Beginning the following morning I would gather the latest details and stick them in.

That is, if I was given any new details. My mild dose of paranoia bloomed into something larger when my hourly calls to Rachel's cell went unanswered and the messages unreturned. My plans for the evening—and the future—hit the rocks of doubt.

Finally, just before eleven o'clock, my cellphone rang. The caller ID said Mesa Verde Inn. It was Rachel.

'How's LA?' she asked.

'LA's fine,' I lied. 'I've been trying to call,' I said. 'Didn't you get my messages?'

'My phone died. I was on it so much earlier. I'm at the hotel now and just checked in. Thanks for leaving my bag with the desk.'

The dead phone explanation sounded plausible. I started to relax.

'No problem,' I said. 'What room did they put you in?'

'Six seventeen. What about you, did you go back to your house?'

'No, I'm still at the hotel.'

'Really? I just called the Kyoto and they put me through to your room but I got no answer.'

'Oh. It must have been when I went down the hall to get ice.'

I stared at the bottle of Grand Embrace chardonnay I had cooling in the room service ice bucket.

'So,' I said, to change the subject, 'are you in for the night?'

'I hope so. I just ordered room service. I suppose I'll get called back out if they find something at Western Data. The EER team is still there with Carver. But I had to get some food and sleep.'

'And Carver's just going to let them work through the night?'

'Turns out the scarecrow is a night owl. He takes several midnight shifts every week. Says he gets his best work done then.'

'So what's the latest update on McGinnis and Stone?'

'There's good news and bad news. The good news is that we know who Freddy Stone really is and he's not Freddy Stone. Knowing his real identity will help us run him down.'

'Freddy Stone's an alias? How'd he get by the supposedly vaunted security screening at Western Data?'

'The company records show Declan McGinnis signed off on hiring him. So he could have greased it.'

I nodded. 'OK, so who is Freddy Stone?' I opened my backpack on the bed and took out a notebook and pen.

'His real name is Marc Courier. That's Marc with a *c*. Same age, twenty-six, with two felony arrests in Illinois for fraud. He skipped three years ago before trial. They were identity theft cases. He's a gifted hacker and he was right there in the bunker.'

'When did he come to work for Western Data?'

'Also three years ago.'

'So McGinnis already knew him?'

'We think he recruited him.'

'How'd you make Courier's ID?'

'The handprint stored on the biometric reader on the entrance to the server farm.'

'Will I be able to get a mugshot of Courier?'

'Check your email. I sent one before I left.'

I pulled my laptop across the bed and logged on to my email. I opened the photo and stared at a mugshot of Marc Courier from his arrest three years before. He had long dark hair and a scraggly goatee and moustache.

'Could it be the man from the hotel in Ely?' Rachel asked.

'I don't know. It could be.'

I studied the photo for a few more seconds and then moved on.

'So you said you had good and bad news. What's the bad news?'

'Before he split, Courier planted replicating viruses in his own computer in the lab at Western Data and in the company archives. The camera archives are gone. So is a lot of the company data.'

'What's that mean?'

'It means we're not going to be able to track his movements as easily as we had hoped.'

'How did that go unnoticed by Carver?'

'The easiest thing to pull off is an inside job. Courier knew the defence systems. He built a virus that navigated round them.'

'What about McGinnis and his computer?'

'Better luck there, I am told. A search team was at his house all night as well. He lives alone, no family. I heard they found some interesting stuff but the search is ongoing.'

'How interesting?'

'Well, they found a copy of your book on the Poet on his bookshelf. I told you we'd find it.'

I felt heat on my face as I considered the idea that I had written a book that might somehow have been a primer for another killer.

I needed to change the subject. 'What else did they find?'

'I'm told they found a set of leg braces designed for a woman. There was also pornography dealing with the subject.'

'Man, this is one sick son of a bitch.'

I wrote a few notes about the findings. I would have a hell of a story for the next day.

'What about Carver? You checked him out, right?'

'Yes, he's clean, all the way back to MIT.'

I was silent as I wrote a few final notes. I had more than enough to write the story the next day. I was sure it would lead the paper.

'Jack, you there?'

'Yeah, I'm just writing. Anything else?'

'That's about it.'

I heard the knock on her door and the muffled voice of someone calling out, 'Room service.'

'My dinner's here,' Rachel said. 'I gotta go.'

'OK. I'll see you later, Rachel.'

'OK, Jack. Good night.'

I smiled as I disconnected the call. Later was going to be sooner than she thought.

AFTER BRUSHING MY TEETH, I pulled the bottle of Grand Embrace out of the bucket and slipped the folding corkscrew that room service had provided into my pocket. I made sure I had my keycard and left the room.

The stairwell was right outside my door, and Rachel was only one floor up, so I decided not to waste any time. I started up the stairs, thinking about what her first words were going to be when she saw me. I was smiling when I crested the next flight. And that's when I saw a man lying in the stairwell, next to the door to the sixth floor hallway. He was wearing black trousers and a white shirt with a bow tie.

All in a moment I realised he was the room-service waiter who had earlier brought me my dinner. As I got to the top step, I saw blood beneath him. I dropped to my knees and put the bottle down.

I pushed his shoulder to see if I could get a response. There was nothing and I thought he was dead. I made another quick leap.

Rachel!

I jumped up and yanked the door open. As I entered the sixth floor hallway, I pulled out my phone and punched in 911. When I got to Rachel's room I saw the door was ajar.

The room was empty but there were obvious signs of a struggle. The bed covers were gone and there was a pillow smeared with blood on the floor. I realised I was holding my phone down at my side and there was a tinny voice calling to me.

I headed back out into the hall as I raised the phone. 'Hello?'

'Nine-one-one, what is your emergency?'

I started running down the hall, panic engulfing me. 'I need help! Mesa Verde Inn, sixth floor! Now!'

I made the turn into the central hallway and caught a glimpse of a man with bleached-blond hair and wearing a red waiter's jacket. He was pushing a large laundry cart through a pair of double doors on the far side of the guest elevators.

'Hey!' I increased my speed and hit the double doors just seconds after I saw them close. I came into a small housekeeping vestibule and saw the door of a service elevator closing. I was too late. It was gone. I ran to the guest elevators.

I quickly pushed the down button. I thought about the laundry cart and the forward leaning angle of the man who was pushing it. There was something heavier than laundry in it. He had Rachel.

There were four guest elevators and I got lucky. As soon as I hit the button the door chimed and an elevator opened. I leapt through the opening doors and machine-gunned the close-door button. As I waited impatiently for the doors to close, I remembered the phone in my hand.

'Hello? Are you still there?'

There was static on the line but I still had a connection.

'Yes, sir. I've dispatched the police. Can you tell me—'

'Listen to me, there's a guy dressed like a waiter and he's trying to abduct a federal agent. Call the FBI. Send every—Hello?'

Nothing. I'd lost the call. I felt the elevator come to a hard stop as we reached the lobby. I stepped up to the door and moved through them before they had barely opened. Adjusting my bearings I took a left and went through a door marked EMPLOYEES ONLY and entered a rear hallway. I heard kitchen noises and smelled food. I saw the service elevator but there was no sign of the man in the red jacket or the laundry cart.

Had I beat the service elevator down? Or had he gone up?

I pushed the elevator call button.

'Hey, you're not supposed to be back here.'

I turned quickly to see a man in kitchen whites and a dirty apron walking towards me in the hall.

'Did you see a guy pushing a laundry cart?' I asked quickly.

'Not in the kitchen, I didn't.' He gestured with a hand holding a cigarette and I realised he was going outside for a smoke break. There was an exit somewhere close.

'Is there a way out from here to the parking garage?'

He pointed past me. 'The loading dock is—Hey, look out!'

I started to turn back to the elevator just as the laundry cart came crashing into me. It hit me thigh-high. I put my hands out to break my fall into the pile of linens and the bedspread in it. I could feel something soft but solid under the covers and knew it was Rachel.

I looked up and saw the elevator closing again on the man in the red jacket. I recognised his face from the mugshot I had seen earlier. It was Marc Courier. I looked back at the elevator control panel. He was going back up.

I reached into the cart and yanked back the bedspread. There was Rachel. She was face down with her arms and legs behind her back. Her nose and mouth were bleeding profusely. Her eyes were glassy and distant.

'Rachel? Are you all right? Can you hear me?'

She didn't respond. The kitchen man stepped over and looked down into the cart. 'What the hell is going on?'

She was bound with plastic cable-ties. I pulled the folding corkscrew out of my pocket and used the small blade designed for cap cutting to slice through the plastic.

'Help me get her out!'

We carefully put her on the floor. I looked up at the kitchen man.

'Go call security. And nine-one-one. Now! GO!'

He started running down the hall for a phone. I looked back down at Rachel and saw she was becoming alert.

'Jack?'

'It's all right, Rachel. You're safe. Help is on the way.'

She nodded and I saw more life returning to her eyes. She coughed and tried to sit up. I pulled her into a hug.

'I thought you were in LA,' she whispered.

I smiled and shook my head. 'I was too paranoid about going away from the story. And from you. I was going to surprise you with a good bottle of wine. That's when I saw him. It was Courier.'

'You saved me, Jack. I didn't recognise him through the peephole. When I opened the door, it was too late. He hit me. I tried to fight but he had a knife.'

I shushed her. No explanation was necessary.

'Listen, was he by himself? Was McGinnis there?'

She shook her head. 'I only saw Courier.'

I leaned down and put my face into the crook of Rachel's neck. I hugged her tightly, breathed in her scent and whispered in her ear.

'He went in the elevator. I'm going to go get him.'

'No, Jack, you wait here. Stay with me.'

I looked into her eyes. I then looked up at the kitchen man who had returned after calling security. 'I want you to wait here with her. Don't leave her. When security gets here you tell them there's another victim on the sixth floor stairwell and that I went up to the top to look for the guy. Tell security to cover all the exits and elevators.'

Rachel started to get up. 'I'm going with you,' she said.

'No, you're hurt. You stay here. I'll be right back. I promise.'

THE SERVICE ELEVATOR moved slowly upwards and I came to realise that so much of Rachel's rescue had relied on pure luck—a slow elevator, my staying in Mesa to surprise her, my taking the stairs with the bottle of wine. But I didn't want to dwell on what could have been. I concentrated on the moment and when the elevator finally reached the top of the building, I stood ready with the one-inch corkscrew blade as the door opened.

The housekeeping vestibule on eleven was empty except for the red waiter's jacket I saw dropped on the floor. I pushed through the doors and into the hallway. I could hear sirens outside.

Looking both ways I saw nothing and I realised that a one-man search of a large hotel was going to be a waste of time. I decided to go back down to Rachel and leave the search for hotel security and the police.

But I knew that on the way down I could cover at least one exit route. Maybe my luck would hold. I chose the north stairwell because it was closest to the hotel's parking garage.

I went down the hallway and pushed through the stairwell exit door. I saw nothing and heard only the echo of the sirens. I was just about to head down the steps when I noticed that even though I was on the top floor of the hotel, the stairs continued up.

If there was access to the roof, I needed to check it. I headed up.

The stairwell was dimly lit. When I reached the mid-level landing and turned to take the next set of stairs to what would be the twelfth floor, I saw the upper and final landing was crowded with stored hotel room furnishings.

I came all the way up to where the stairs ended in a large storage area and started to work my way round a group of lamps towards a door with a small window and the word ROOF stencilled on it. The door was locked. I leaned in closer to the window so I could get a wider view of the roof. Courier could be out there. Just as I did this, I saw a reflection of movement in the glass.

Someone was behind me.

Instinctively, I jumped sideways and turned at the same time. Courier's arm swung down with a knife and barely missed me.

I planted my feet and then drove my body into his. Courier took a round-house swing at me. I managed to duck underneath it but got a good look at his blade. It was at least four inches long.

I grabbed one of the lamps, ready to deflect his next assault. He had a desperate sort of smile on his face and was breathing heavily.

'Where are you going to go, Courier? Hear those sirens? There's going to be cops and FBI all over this place in two minutes.'

He didn't say anything and I took a swing at him with the lamp. He grabbed the base and we momentarily struggled, but I pushed him into a stack of mini-refrigerators and they crashed to the floor.

My instincts told me to keep talking. If I distracted Courier, then I would lessen the threat from the knife.

'Where's your partner? Where's McGinnis? What did he do, send you to do the dirty work by yourself? Just like Nevada, huh? You missed your chance again.'

Courier grinned at me but didn't take the bait.

'The master's not going to be very happy with you tonight. You've screwed up, man.'

This time he couldn't control it.

'McGinnis is dead, you dumbass! I buried him in the desert. Just like I was going to bury your bitch after I was through with her.'

I feigned another jab at him and tried to keep him talking.

'I don't get it, Courier. If he's dead, why didn't you just run? Why risk everything to go for her?'

At the same moment he opened his mouth to reply, I brought the lamp base up into his face, catching him flush on the jaw. Courier staggered backwards and I quickly went for the knife with both hands. I finally man-aged to bend his wrist at a painful angle. He cried out and the knife clat-tered to the floor. With an elbow I shoved it towards the stairwell shaft but it stopped just shy of the mark, balancing on the edge below the blue guardrail. It was six feet away.

I went after him like an animal then, punching and kicking, fuelled by a primal rage I had never felt before. I grabbed an ear and tried to rip it off.

I swung an elbow into his teeth. But he brought a knee up into my crotch and paralysing pain shot through me. He broke free and went for the knife.

Calling on my last reserve of strength, I half crawled, half lunged after him as I struggled to my feet. I was hurt and spent but I knew that if he got to the knife I would be dead.

I threw my weight into him from behind. He lurched forward into the blue guardrail of the stairwell shaft, his upper body pivoting over it. Without thinking, I reached down, grabbed one of his legs and flipped him over the rail. He tried to grab the steel piping but his grip slipped and he fell.

His scream lasted only two seconds. His head hit either a railing or the concrete siding of the shaft, and after that, he fell silently, his body caroming from side to side on its way down twelve floors.

I wish I could say I felt guilt or even a sense of remorse. But I felt like cheering every moment of his fall.

THE NEXT MORNING I went back to Los Angeles for real. I had spent most of the night in the now-familiar surroundings of the FBI. Agent Bantam and I faced off again in the mobile interview room for several hours, during which I told and retold the story of what I had done that evening. I told him what Courier had said about McGinnis and the desert and the plan for Rachel Walling.

During the interview Bantam never dropped the mask of detached federal agent. When it was finally over, he informed me that the details regarding the death of Marc Courier would be submitted to a state grand jury to determine if my actions constituted self-defence. It was only then that he spoke to me like a human being.

'I have mixed feelings about you, McEvoy. You no doubt saved Agent Walling's life, but going after Courier was the wrong move. If you had waited he might be alive and we might have answers. As it is, most of the secrets went down that shaft with Courier. It's a big desert out there, if you know what I mean.'

'Yeah, well, I'm sorry about that, Agent Bantam. I kind of looked at it like if I hadn't gone after him he might have got away.'

'Maybe. But we'll never know.'

'So what happens now with the investigation?'

He paused as if to consider whether he should tell me anything.

'We're not done at Western Data. We'll continue there and we'll try to put together a picture of what these men did. And we'll keep looking for McGinnis. Dead or alive.'

I shrugged. 'Can I go back to LA now?'

'You're free to go. But if anything else comes to mind, call us.'

He didn't shake my hand. He just opened the door. When I stepped out of the FBI bus, Rachel was waiting for me. We were in the front parking lot of the Mesa Verde Inn. It was close to five in the morning, but neither of us seemed very tired. The paramedics had checked her out. Her nose had stopped bleeding but she had a badly cut and bruised lip.

'How are you feeling?' I asked.

'I'm OK,' she said. 'How are you?'

'I'm fine. Bantam said I'm clear to take off. I think I'll catch the first flight back to LA. How long do you think you'll be here?'

'I don't know. I guess until they wrap things up.'

I nodded and checked my watch.

'You want to get breakfast somewhere?' I asked.

'I'm not that hungry. I just wanted to say goodbye. I need to get back to Western Data. They found the mother lode.'

'Which is what?'

'An unaccounted-for server that both McGinnis and Courier had been accessing. It's got archived videos. They filmed their crimes.'

'And both of them are in the videos?'

'I haven't seem them but I am told they are not readily identifiable. They wear masks and shoot at angles that mostly show their victims, not them.'

'Is Angela on film?'

'No, she was too recent. But there are others. They have at least six victims. McGinnis and Courier were doing this for a long time.'

Now I wasn't so sure I wanted to leave.

'What about the braces? Were you right about that?'

She nodded. 'Yeah, they made the victims wear leg braces.'

I shook my head to ward off the thought of it. I checked my pockets. I had no pen and my notebook was back up in my room.

'You have a pen?' I asked Rachel. 'I need to write this down.'

'No, Jack, I don't have a pen to give you. And I've told you more than

I should have. Wait till I have a better handle on everything and then I'll call you. Your deadline isn't for another twelve hours, at least.'

She was right. I had a full day to put the story together, and the information would develop through the day. Besides that, I knew I was part of the story again. I had killed one of the two men the story was about. Conflict of interest dictated that I wouldn't be writing it. I was going to sit with Larry Bernard once again and feed him a front-page story that would echo round the world.

'All right, Rachel. I guess I'll go pack and head to the airport.'

'OK, Jack. I'll call you. I promise.'

I liked that she promised before I had to ask. I looked at her for a moment, and she pulled me into a tight embrace.

'You saved my life tonight, Jack.'

I kissed her lightly on the cheek, avoiding her bruised lips. If Agent Bantam or anybody else behind the smoked windows of the FBI mobile command centre was watching, neither one of us cared.

It was almost a minute before Rachel and I separated. She looked into my eyes and nodded. 'Go write your story, Jack.'

'I will . . . if they let me.'

I turned and walked towards the hotel.

ALL EYES WERE ON ME as I walked through the newsroom. It had spread as quickly as a Santa Ana wind through the newsroom that I had killed a man the night before.

As I approached my cubicle the phone was buzzing and the message light was on. I decided I would deal with the calls later. It was almost eleven o'clock, so I walked over to the raft to see if Prendo was in. I wanted to get this part over with. If I was going to give my information to another reporter, I wanted to start giving it up now.

Prendo wasn't in but Dorothy Fowler was sitting at the head of the raft. She saw me and did a double take.

'Jack, how are you?'

I shrugged. 'OK, I guess. When's Prendo coming in?'

'Probably not till one. Are you up to working today?'

'You mean, do I feel bad about the guy who fell down the stairwell last night? No, Dorothy, I'm actually OK with that. The guy was a killer who liked to torture women while he raped and suffocated them. I don't feel too bad about what happened to him.'

'OK. I think I understand that.'

'The only thing I don't feel good about right now is that I'm guessing I don't get to write the story, right?'

She frowned and nodded. 'I'm afraid not, Jack.'

'Who do you want me to give my stuff to? The FBI has confirmed to me that there were two killers and they have found videos of them with at least six victims. They'll be announcing this at a press conference but I have lots of stuff they won't be putting out.'

'Just what I want to hear. I'm going to put you with Larry Bernard again for continuity. Are you ready to go?'

'Ready when he is.'

'OK, let me call and book the conference room.'

I spent the next two hours giving Larry Bernard everything I had. Larry then interviewed me for a sidebar story on my hand-to-hand battle with the serial killer.

'Too bad you didn't let him answer that last question,' he said.

'What are you talking about?'

'At the end, when you asked him why he didn't just take off instead of going after Walling. That's the essential question, isn't it?'

I didn't like Larry's question. It was as if he was suspicious of my veracity or what I had done.

'Look, it was a knife fight and I didn't have a knife. When I saw my chance I took it. That's why I'm alive and he's not.'

Larry leaned forward and checked his tape recorder.

'That's a good quote,' he said.

I'd been a reporter for twenty-plus years and I had just been baited by my own friend and colleague.

'I want to take a break. How much more do you need?'

'I actually think I'm good,' Larry said. 'Let's take a break and I'll go through my notes and make sure.'

I went back to my cubicle and checked my phone messages. I had nine of them, most from other news outlets wanting me to comment for their own reports. I would deal with all such requests the next day, after the story had run exclusively in the *Times*. I was being loyal to the end, even though I didn't know why I should be.

The last message was from my long-lost literary agent. I hadn't heard from him in more than a year. His message told me that he was already fielding offers for a book about the trunk murders case. Any frustration I was feeling about not getting to write the day's story was beginning to drain away.

I went to my screen and looked into the city basket to see if Larry's stories were on the daily budget. As expected, the top of the budget was weighted with a three-story package on the case. It would lead the paper and be the authoritative report on the case. All other media outlets would have to credit the *Times*. It would be a good day for the paper. The editors could already smell a Pulitzer.

I closed the screen and thought about the sidebar story Larry was going to write. He was right. It came down to that last question—why didn't Courier just run? Why did he risk everything by going after Rachel? I sure wished I had an answer.

THE NEXT MORNING the *Times* basked in the glow of national news exposure. My phone never stopped buzzing and my email box overflowed. But I didn't answer my calls or emails. I was brooding. I had spent the night with the unanswered question I had posed to Marc Courier. No matter which way I considered it, things didn't add up. The attempt to abduct Rachel did not fit.

I started to look at it from another angle. I thought about what would have happened if I had gone to Los Angeles and Courier had been successful in grabbing Rachel and getting her out of the hotel.

It seemed likely that the abduction would have been discovered shortly after it occurred, when the room-service waiter did not report back to the kitchen. I estimated that within an hour the hotel would have been a hive of FBI activity. But by then Courier would have been long gone.

'Jack?'

I looked over the wall of my cubicle and saw Molly Robards, the executive assistant to the managing editor.

'Yes?'

'Mr Kramer would like to see you.'

'Oh, OK.' I pushed my chair back and got up.

Kramer was waiting for me with a big, phoney smile on his face.

'Jack, sit down.'

I did. He straightened things on his desk before proceeding.

'Well, I've got some good news for you. We've decided to withdraw your termination plan.'

'What's that mean? I'm not laid off?'

'Exactly.'

'What about my pay and benefits?'

'Nothing's changed. Same old same old.'

It was just like Rachel getting her badge back. I felt a thrill of excitement but then reality hit home.

'So what's that mean, you lay somebody else off instead of me?'

Kramer cleared his throat. 'Jack, I'm not going to lie to you. Our objective was to drop one hundred slots in editorial by June 1st. You were number ninety-nine—it was that close.'

'But somebody else will get the hook because I got to stay. What happens after this story winds down? Will you call me back in here and can me all over again?'

'We're not expecting another involuntary reduction in force.'

I looked out at the newsroom. I wouldn't miss the place. I would only miss some of the people. I gave Kramer my answer.

'This morning my literary agent in New York woke me up at six. He said he had got me an offer for a two-book deal. A quarter of a million dollars. It would take me almost three years to make that here. So thanks for the offer but after tomorrow, I'm gone.'

'Then I want you to clear your desk out right now,' he sputtered. 'I'll call security and have you escorted out.'

I smiled down at him as he picked up the phone.

'Fine by me.'

I found an empty cardboard box in the printer room and ten minutes later was filling it with the things I wanted to keep from my desk. The first to go in was the worn red dictionary my mother had given me. After that, there wasn't much else worth keeping.

A guy from security watched me as I packed. Soon my box was as full as it was going to get. It looked pitiful. I stood up, slung my backpack over my shoulder and picked up the box, ready to go.

I headed for the elevator alcove, the security man trailing behind me. I didn't want any goodbyes. I walked along the row of glass offices and didn't look in at any of the editors I had worked for.

'Jack?'

I stopped and turned round. Dorothy Fowler had stepped out of the glass office I had just passed. She beckoned me back.

'Can you come in for a minute before you go?'

I hesitated and shrugged. Then I handed the box to the security man. 'Be right back.'

I stepped into the city editor's office and sat down in front of her desk.

'I told Richard that you wouldn't take the job back.'

'You shouldn't have been so sure. I almost took it.'

'I doubt that, Jack. Very much.'

I thought that was a compliment. I nodded and looked behind her at the wall covered with photos and cards and newspaper clips. She had a classic headline from one of the New York tabs on the wall: 'Headless Body in Topless Bar.' You couldn't beat that one.

'What will you do now?'

I told her I planned to write a book about my part in the Courier-McGinnis story.

'That sounds great,' she said. 'We're really going to miss you round here. You are one of the best.'

I don't take compliments like that well. If I was that good, why did I get put on the thirty list in the first place? I looked away from her, and back at the images taped to the wall.

That's when I saw it. Something that had eluded me before. I bent forward so I could see it better. I pointed to the wall.

'Can I see that? The card from *The Wizard of Oz*.'

She looked up at the wall, at the still shot that showed the movie's main characters. Below the photo someone had printed YOU'RE NOT IN KANSAS ANY MORE, DOROTHY. Fowler pulled the card off the wall and handed it to me.

'It's a joke from a friend,' she said. 'I'm from Kansas.'

'I get that,' I said. I studied the photo, zeroing in on the Scarecrow.

The photo was too small for me to be completely sure.

'Can I run a search on your computer real quick?' I asked.

I was coming round her desk before she answered.

'Uh, sure, what is it that—'

'I'm not sure yet.'

I took her seat, looked at her screen and opened up Google image search. I typed *Scarecrow* into the search block and let it fly.

The screen soon filled with sixteen small images of scarecrows. There were photos of the character from *The Wizard of Oz* and colour sketches from Batman comics of a villain called the Scarecrow. There were several other photos and drawings of scarecrows.

They all had one thing in common. Each scarecrow included a burlap bag pulled over the head to form a face. Each bag was cinched round the neck with a cord. Sometimes it was a thick rope and sometimes it was clothes line. But it didn't matter. The image matched what I had seen in the files I had accumulated, as well as the lasting image I had of Angela Cook.

I could see now that in the murders a clear plastic bag had been used to create the face of the scarecrow.

I clicked to the next screen of images. Again the same construction. This time the images were older, going back through a century to the original illustrations in the book *The Wonderful Wizard of Oz*. And then I saw it. The illustrations were credited to William Wallace Denslow. William Denslow as in Bill Denslow, as in Denslow Data.

I felt no doubt that I had just found the signature. The secret signature that Rachel had told me would be there.

I killed the screen and stood up.

'I have to go.'

I went round her desk and grabbed my backpack off the floor.

'Jack?' Fowler asked.

I headed towards the door.

'It was nice working with you, Dorothy.'

THE PLANE LANDED hard on the tarmac at Sky Harbor but I barely noticed. I had not called Rachel yet. I wanted to get to Arizona first so that whatever happened with my information included my involvement.

I was no longer a reporter, but I was still protecting my story.

After picking up a rental and getting to Mesa, I pulled into the lot of a convenience store and went in to buy a throwaway phone. I knew Rachel was working in the bunker at Western Data. When I called her, I didn't want her seeing my name on the ID screen and then answering with it in front of Carver.

Back in the car, I made the call. She answered after five rings.

'Hello, this is Agent Walling.'

'It's me. Don't say my name.'

There was a pause before she continued. 'How can I help you?'

'Are you with Carver?'

'Yes.'

'OK, I'm in Mesa and about ten minutes away. I need to meet you without anybody else in there knowing.'

'I'm sorry, that's not going to be possible. What is this about?'

At least she was playing along.

'I can't tell you. I have to show you. Tell them you need a latte or something. Meet me at Hightower Grounds in ten minutes. It's about Carver. Don't tell anyone what you're really doing.'

'That will be fine,' she said. 'I'll talk to you then.'

She clicked off the call.

In another five minutes I was at Hightower Grounds. I went in and found the place almost empty. I set my computer up on a corner table then went to the counter and ordered two cups of coffee, which I carried back to the table. Through the window I checked the parking lot and saw no sign of Rachel.

I sat down and took a sip of steaming coffee. The receipt for the coffee said *Free WiFi with every purchase! Check us out on the net. WWW. Hightowergrounds.com* so I connected to the Internet.

Fifteen minutes went by. I was about to call Rachel again when I finally saw her pull into the lot. She came directly to my table. She was holding a piece of paper with coffee orders written down on it.

'The last time I went out for coffee I was a rookie agent at a hostage negotiation in Baltimore,' she said. 'This had better be good.'

'Don't worry, it is. I think. Why don't you just sit down?'

She did. I had been wondering if I should kiss her but took the hint from her all-business demeanour and kept my distance.

'OK, Jack, I'm here. What are you doing here?'

'I think I found the signature. McGinnis was just a cover. The other killer is the Scarecrow. It's Carver.'

She stared at me for a long moment. Finally, she spoke.

'So you jumped on a plane to tell me the man I'm working beside is also the killer I've been chasing.'

'That's right. Who's back in the bunker with Carver?'

'Two agents from the EER team, Torres and Mowry. But never mind them. Tell me what's going on.'

I tried to set the stage for what I would show her on the laptop.

'First of all, I was bothered by a question. What was the plan in abducting you? Why take so big a risk to go after you? The easy answer is that it would create a large distraction from the central investigation. But at best it would be a temporary diversion.'

Rachel followed the logic and nodded in agreement.

'OK, but what if there was another reason?' I asked. 'You have two killers out there. A mentor and a student. The student tries to abduct you on his own. Why?'

'Because McGinnis was dead. There was only the student.'

'OK, then if that is true, why even make the move? Why not get the hell out of Dodge? But what if McGinnis wasn't the mentor? What if he was just a fall guy and abducting you was part of a plan to secure the real mentor? To help him get away?'

'What about the evidence we recovered?'

'You mean McGinnis having my book on his bookshelf and the leg braces and porno in the house? Isn't that kind of convenient?'

'That stuff was hidden and only found after an hours-long search. But never mind all that. Yes, it could have been planted. I'm thinking more about the server in Western Data we found that was full of video evidence.'

'You said he isn't identifiable on the videos. And who is to say McGinnis and Courier were the only ones with access to that server.'

She didn't respond right away and I knew I had her thinking.

'It still doesn't make sense if you're claiming the mentor is Carver. He didn't try to get away. When Courier was trying to grab me, Carver was in the bunker with Torres and . . .'

She didn't finish. I did.

'Mowry? Yes, he was with two FBI agents.'

I watched the realisation come to her.

'He would have a perfect alibi because two agents would vouch for him,' she finally said. 'If I disappeared while he was with the EER team, he would have an alibi and the Bureau would be almost certain that it was McGinnis and Courier who had grabbed me.'

I nodded.

'Think about it. How did Courier know what hotel you were in? We told Carver when he asked us during the tour. Remember? Then he told Courier. He *sent* Courier.'

She shook her head.

'But it isn't enough, Jack. It doesn't add up to Carver being—'

'I know. But this does.'

I turned the computer so she could see the screen. I had the page of scarecrow images up on Google. She leaned over and looked at the images, one by one. I didn't need to say anything.

'Denslow!' she suddenly said. 'Did you see this? The original illustrator of *The Wonderful Wizard of Oz* was named William Denslow.'

'Yeah, I saw that. That's why I'm here.'

'I can't believe this,' she said after a while. 'We checked him out! He was clean. He's some sort of genius out of MIT.'

'Clean how? You mean no arrest record? It wouldn't be the first time one of these guys operated completely beneath law enforcement radar.'

'But I have a vibe for these guys and I didn't pick up a thing. I had lunch with him today.'

I could see self-doubt in her eyes. She hadn't seen this coming.

'Let's go get him,' I said. 'We confront him and make him talk. Most of these serials are proud of their work. My bet is he'll talk.'

She looked at me. 'Go get him? Jack, you're not an agent and you're not a cop. You're a reporter.'

'Not any more. It's a long story that I'll tell you later—but what are we going to do about Carver?'

'I don't know, Jack. We need to move carefully. I'll call Bantam and we'll go to the US Attorney's office. Your Google pictures are convincing me, but they don't qualify as direct evidence.'

'Look, you can't sit on this. This guy might split.'

'We're not going to sit on anything.'

I noticed one of the customers sitting a few tables behind Rachel turn from his laptop and look up towards the open-beamed ceiling and smile. He then raised a fist and offered up his middle finger. I followed his gaze to one of the crossbeams. There was a small camera mounted on the beam, its lens trained on sitting area of the coffee shop.

I jumped up, leaving Rachel and moving towards him.

'Hey,' I said, pointing up at the camera. 'What is that?'

The kid crinkled his nose at my stupidity and shrugged.

'It's a live cam, man. It goes everywhere. I just got a shout from a buddy in Amsterdam who saw me.'

It suddenly dawned on me. The receipt. *Free WiFi with every purchase! Check us out on the net.* I looked at Rachel. The laptop, with a full-screen photo of a scarecrow on it, was facing the camera. I turned back and looked up at the lens. Call it a premonition or call it certain knowledge, but I knew I was looking at Carver.

'Rachel?' I said, not looking away. 'Did you tell him where you were going to get coffee?'

'Yes, I said I was just going down the street.'

I walked back to the table. I picked up the laptop and closed it.

'He's been watching us,' I said. 'We gotta go.'

I headed out of the coffee shop and she came out right behind me.

'I'll drive,' she said.

RACHEL TURNED her rental car through the main gate and went charging up to the front door of Western Data. She was driving one-handed, working her phone with the other. She threw the car into park and we got out.

'Something's wrong,' she said. 'Neither of them is answering.'

Rachel used a Western Data keycard to enter the front door. The reception desk was empty and we quickly moved to the next door. As we entered the internal hallway, she pulled out her gun.

We took the stairs down to the octagon room and approached the mantrap leading to the bunker. Rachel hesitated before opening the door.

'Stay behind me.'

She raised the gun and we squeezed in together, then quickly moved to the second door. When we came through the other side, the control room was empty.

'This isn't right,' Rachel said. 'Where is everybody? And that's supposed to be open.'

She pointed to the glass door that led to the server room. It was closed. I scanned the control room and saw the door to Carver's private office was ajar. I pushed it all the way open.

The room was empty. I went to Carver's worktable. I put one finger down on the touch pad and the two screens came alive. On the main screen I was looking at a view of the coffee shop.

'Rachel?'

She came in and I pointed at the screen.

'He was watching us.'

She hurried back into the control room and I followed. She moved to the centre work station and started working the keyboard. The two monitors came alive and soon she had pulled up multiplex screens divided into thirty-two interior camera views of the facility. All of the squares were blank.

'He's killed all of the cameras,' Rachel said. 'What is—'

'Wait. There!'

I pointed to one camera angle surrounded by several black squares. Rachel brought the image up to full screen.

The camera view captured a passageway between two rows of server towers in the farm. Lying face down were two bodies, their wrists cuffed behind their backs and their ankles bound.

Rachel grabbed the stem microphone attached to the desk, depressed the button and almost shrieked into it. 'George! Sarah! Can you hear me?'

At the sound of Rachel's voice the figures on the screen stirred and the male raised his head. There was blood on his white shirt.

'Rachel?' he said, his voice weak. 'I can hear you.'

'Where is he? Where's Carver, George?'

'I don't know. He was just here. He just brought us in here.'

'What happened?'

'After you left he went into his office. When he came out, he got the drop on us. He grabbed my gun out of my briefcase. He herded us in here and put us on the floor.'

'Sarah, where's your weapon?'

'He got that, too,' Mowry called out. 'I'm sorry, Rachel.'

'Not your fault. It's mine. We're going to get you out of there.'

Rachel quickly went to the biometric reader and put her hand on the scanner. The device completed the scan and she grabbed the handle to open the door. It didn't move. Her scan had been rejected.

'That makes no sense. My profile was put in yesterday.'

'Who put it in?' I asked.

She looked back at me and didn't need to answer for me to know it had been Carver.

'Who else can open that door?' I asked. 'What about other employees?'

'They're on a skeleton staff upstairs and there's nobody with authorisation for the farm. We're screwed! We can't get—'

'Rachel!'

I pointed at the screen. Carver had suddenly stepped into the view of the one working camera in the server room. He stood in front of the two agents on the floor, hands in the pockets of his lab coat, and looking directly up at the camera.

'What's he doing?' Rachel asked.

I didn't need to answer because it became clear that Carver was pulling a box of cigarettes and a lighter from his pockets. He calmly drew a cigarette from the box and put it in his mouth.

Rachel quickly pulled over the microphone.

'Wesley? What's going on?'

Carver looked up at the camera.

'You know what I'm doing, Agent Walling,' Carver said. 'I'm ending it. I'd rather not spend the rest of my days in a cage, being trotted out for interviews with shrinks and profilers hoping to learn all the dark secrets in the universe.' He raised the lighter.

'Don't, Wesley! At least let Mowry and Torres go. They did nothing to hurt you.'

'That's not the point, though, is it? The world hurt me, Rachel, and that's enough. I'm sure you've studied the psychology before.'

Rachel took her hand off the transmit button and turned to me.

'Get on the computer. Shut down the VESDA system.'

'No, you do it! I don't know the first thing about—'

'Is Jack there with you?' Carver asked.

I hand-signalled Rachel to trade places with me. I moved to the microphone while she went to work on the computer.

'I'm here, Carver,' I said. 'This is not how this should end. I want to tell your story. Let me explain it to the world.'

Carver shook his head. 'Some things can't be explained. Some stories are too dark to be told.' He flicked the lighter and the flame came up. He lit the cigarette.

'Carver, no! Those are innocent people in there!'

Carver inhaled deeply, held it, and then tilted his head back and exhaled a stream of smoke towards the ceiling. I was sure he had positioned himself under one of the infrared smoke detectors.

'No one is innocent, Jack,' he said. 'You should know that.' He drew in more smoke and spoke almost casually. 'I know, Agent Walling, that you are trying to shut down the system but that isn't going to work. I took the liberty of resetting it. Only I have access now. And the exhaust component that takes the carbon dioxide out of the room one minute after dispersal has been checked off for maintenance.'

Carver exhaled again, sending smoke towards the ceiling. Rachel's fingers raced across the keyboard but she shook her head.

'I can't do it,' she said.

The blast of an alarm filled the control room. An electronic voice said, '*Attention, the VESDA fire-suppression system has been activated. All personnel must exit the server room. The VESDA fire-suppression system will engage in one minute.*'

Rachel stared helplessly at the screen in front of her. Carver was blowing another round of smoke towards the ceiling. There was a look of calm resignation on his face.

'Rachel!' Mowry called from behind him. 'Get us out of here!'

Carver looked back at his captives and shook his head.

'It's over,' he said. 'This is the end.'

I was jolted by a second blast of the warning horn.

'*Attention, all personnel must exit the server room. The VESDA fire-suppression system will engage in forty-five seconds.*'

Rachel stood up and grabbed her gun off the desk.

'Get down, Jack.'

'Rachel, no, it's bulletproof!'

'According to him.'

She fired three quick rounds at the window directly in front of her. The bullets barely impacted the glass. One of the ricocheting slugs took out one of the screens in front of me, the image of Carver disappearing as it went black. Rachel lowered her gun.

'*Attention, all personnel must exit the server room. The VESDA fire-suppression system will engage in thirty seconds.*'

I looked out through the windows into the server room. Black pipes ran along the ceiling in a grid pattern and then down the back wall to the row of red carbon dioxide canisters. The system was about to go. It would extinguish three lives.

'Rachel, you have to keep trying! There's gotta be a back door to the system. These guys always put in a back—'

I stopped and looked out into the server room as I realised something. Carver was nowhere to be seen through the windows. He had chosen an aisle between two rows of towers out of view from the control room. Was this because of the location of the smoke detector or for some other reason?

I looked over at the undamaged screen in front of Rachel. It showed a multiplex cut of thirty-two cameras that had been turned dark by Carver. All in a moment I had an idea.

'Rachel—'

The horn blast came loud and long this time. Rachel stood up and stared at the glass as the carbon dioxide system engaged. A white gas exploded out of the pipes crossing the ceiling of the server room. Within seconds the windows were fogged and useless.

'Rachel!' I yelled. 'Give me your key. Carver's not killing himself! He's got that breather and there's got to be a back door!'

The whistling stopped and we both turned back to the windows. It was a complete whiteout in the server room but the carbon dioxide delivery had at least ended.

'Give me the key, Rachel.'

She looked at me. 'I should go.'

'No, you need to call for back-up and medical emergency. Then work the computer. Find the back door.'

There wasn't time to think and consider things. People were dying. She pulled the keycard out of her pocket and gave it to me.

'Wait! Take this.'

She handed me her gun. I took it and headed into the mantrap.

RACHEL'S GUN felt heavier in my hand than I remembered my own gun ever feeling. I went through the mantrap and entered the octagon with the muzzle up. There was no one there.

I quickly crossed the room to the door on the opposite side. I knew from my tour that this led to the large rooms that housed the power and cooling systems for the facility. The workshop where Carver and his techs built the server towers was back here, too. I remembered seeing a second stairwell on the tour.

I moved into the plant facilities room first. It was a wide space with large equipment. I ran to a door on the far left side and used Rachel's keycard to open it.

I stepped into a narrow equipment room that we had not been shown on the tour. There was a second door at the other end. I saw that there was another biometric hand scanner mounted to the left of the door. Above it was a case holding the emergency-breathing devices. It had to be the back door to the server room.

There was no way to tell whether Carver had already made his escape. I turned and headed back. I quickly moved through the plant facilities room again until I reached a set of double doors on the far side.

Holding the gun up and ready, I opened one of the doors with the key-card and stepped into the workshop. This was another large room with tool benches lining the walls and a workspace in the centre, where one of the server towers was in mid-construction.

Beyond the server tower I saw a circular stairway leading up to the surface. This had to be the way up to the back door and the smokers' bench. I quickly headed for the stairs.

'Hello, Jack.'

Just as I heard my name, I felt the muzzle of the gun on the back of my neck. I hadn't even seen Carver. He had stepped out from behind the server tower as I had passed.

'A cynical reporter. I should've known that you wouldn't buy my suicide.'

His free hand grabbed a hold of my collar from the back and the gun remained pressed against my skin.

'You can drop the gun now.'

I dropped the weapon and it made a loud clatter on the floor.

'I take it that was Agent Walling's, yes? So why don't we go back and pay her a visit? And we'll end this thing right now. Or who knows, maybe I'll just end it for you and take her with me. I think I'd like to spend some time with Agent—'

I heard an impact of heavy object on flesh and bone and Carver fell into my back and then dropped to the floor. I turned and there was Rachel, holding an industrial-size wrench she had taken off the workbench.

'Rachel! What are—'

'He left Mowry's keycard on her work station. I followed you out. Come on. Let's get him back to the control room. His hand can open the server room.'

We bent down to Carver, who was moaning on the concrete floor. Rachel took her weapon and the one Carver was holding. I saw a second gun in his waistband and grabbed it. I secured it in my own waistband and then helped Rachel drag Carver to his feet.

'The back door is closer,' I said. 'And there are breathers there.'

'Lead the way. Hurry!'

We half carried Carver through the facilities room and into the narrow equipment room beyond. The whole way he moaned and uttered words I couldn't understand.

'Jack, that was good, figuring out the back door. I just hope we're not too late.'

I didn't respond to Rachel but believed we had a good chance to get to her fellow agents in time. When we got to the back door of the server room, I took on Carver's weight and started to turn him so Rachel would be able to put his hand up on the scanner.

At that moment, I felt Carver's body stiffen. He grabbed my hand and pivoted. My shoulder slammed into the door as Carver dropped one hand and went for the gun in my waistband. I grabbed at his wrist but was too late. His right hand closed around the gun.

'*Gun!*' I yelled.

There was a sudden sharp explosion next to my ear and Carver's hands fell away from me and he slumped to the floor. A spray of blood hit me as he fell.

I stepped back and doubled over, holding my ear. The ringing was as loud as a passing train. I looked up to see Rachel holding her gun in firing position.

'Jack, you OK?'

'Yeah, fine!'

'Quick, grab him! Before we lose the pulse.'

I moved behind Carver so I could get my arms underneath his shoulders and lift him up. I held him while she extended his right hand onto the reader. There was a metal snap as the door's lock disengaged and Rachel pushed it open.

I dropped Carver in the threshold, keeping the door open to let air in. I opened the case and grabbed the breathing masks. There were only two. I gave one to Rachel. We put them on and entered the farm. The mist was dissipating. Visibility was about six feet.

We moved down a central corridor between two lines of servers and were lucky as we came upon Torres and Mowry almost right away. Carver had put them near the back door so he would be able to escape quickly.

Rachel crouched down next to the agents and tried to shake them awake. Neither was responsive.

'You take him, I'll take her!' she yelled.

She tore off her breather and put it into Mowry's mouth. I took mine off and put it in Torres's. Then we each grabbed one of the agents under the arms and dragged them back towards the door.

When I reached the door I dragged Torres over Carver's body and into the equipment room. The bumpy landing seemed to jump-start Torres. He started coughing and coming to.

Rachel came in behind me with Mowry.

'I don't think she's breathing!' Rachel started CPR procedures. 'How is

Torres?' she asked without taking her focus off Mowry.

'He's good. He's breathing.'

I moved to Rachel's side as she conducted mouth-to-mouth. I wasn't sure how I could help but a few moments later Mowry convulsed and started coughing.

'Its OK, Sarah. You're all right. You're safe.' Rachel gently patted Mowry's shoulder and I heard the agent cough out her thanks.

I moved to the nearby wall and sat with my back against it. I was spent. My eyes drifted to the body of Carver sprawled on the floor near the door. The bullet had strafed across his frontal lobes. He had not moved since he had fallen but after a while I thought I could see the slight tic of a pulse on his neck just below the ear.

Exhausted, Rachel moved over and slid down the wall next to me.

'Back-up's coming. I should probably go up and wait for them.'

'Catch your breath first. Are you OK?'

She nodded yes but she was still breathing heavily. So was I. I watched her eyes and saw them focus on Carver.

'It's too bad, you know?'

'What is?'

'That with both Courier and Carver gone, the secrets died with them. Everybody's dead and we've got no clue to what made them do what they did.'

I shook my head slowly.

'I got news for you. I think the Scarecrow's still alive.'

Twelve: The Scarecrow

It has been six weeks since the events that took place in Mesa. Still, those events remain vivid in my memory and imagination.

I am writing now. Every day. I reserve the mornings for research on my subject. Wesley Carver remains an enigma but I am getting closer to who he is. As he lies in the twilight world of a coma in the hospital ward of the Metropolitan Correction Center in Los Angeles, I close in on him.

Some of what I know has come from the FBI, which continues to work the case in Arizona, Nevada and California. But most of it I have discovered on my own and from several sources.

Carver was a killer of high intelligence. He manipulated people by tapping into their darkest desires. He lurked on websites, identified potential disciples and victims and then traced them through the labyrinthine portals of the digital world. He then made contact in the real world. He used them or killed them or both.

He had been doing it for years, well before Western Data and the trunk murders had caught anyone's eye.

Still, the grim deeds Carver committed cannot overshadow the motivations behind them. That is what my editor in New York tells me. I must be able to tell more than what happened. I must tell why. It's breadth and depth again, and I am used to that.

I have learned so far that Carver grew up an only child without ever knowing his father. His mother worked the strip-club circuit, which kept the two of them on the road during his younger years. He was a dressing-room baby, held backstage in the arms of costumiers or other dancers while his mother worked in the spotlights out front. She was a featured act, performing under the stage name 'LA Woman' and dancing exclusively to the music of the signature Los Angeles rock band of the era, The Doors.

There are hints that Carver was abused sexually by more than one of the people he was left with in the dressing rooms and that on many nights he slept in the same hotel room where his mother entertained men who had paid to be with her.

Most notable in all of this was that his mother had developed a degenerative bone disease that threatened her livelihood. When not onstage, she wore leg braces prescribed to provide support for weakening ligaments and joints. Young Wesley often helped secure the leather straps round his mother's legs.

It is a depressing portrait, but not one that adds up to multiple murders. What made the horrors of Carver's upbringing metastasise into the cancer of his adulthood remains to be learned.

I am in Bakersfield today. For the fourth day in a row I will spend the morning with Karen Carver and she will tell me her memories of her son. She has not talked to him since the day he left as an eighteen-year-old for MIT, but her knowledge of his early life brings me closer to answering the question of why.

Tomorrow I will drive home, my conversations with the now wheelchair-bound mother of the killer completed for the time being. I have other research to complete and a looming deadline for my book. More importantly, it has been five days since I have seen Rachel and the separation has grown difficult to take. I have become a believer in the single-bullet theory and need to return home.

Meantime, the prognosis for Wesley Carver is not good. His physicians believe he will never regain consciousness, and that the damage from Rachel's bullet has left him in permanent darkness. He mumbles and sometimes hums in his prison bed but that is all.

There are some who have called for his prosecution, conviction and execution in such a state. And others have called this idea barbaric, no matter how heinous his crimes.

I wonder what Carver would think.

All I know is that I can't erase the image of Angela Cook slipping into darkness, eyes open and afraid. I believe that Wesley Carver has already been convicted in some sort of court of higher reason. And he is serving a life sentence without the possibility of parole.

CARVER WAITED IN DARKNESS. His mind was a jumble of thoughts. So many he was not sure which were true memories and which were made up.

They filtered through his mind like smoke. Nothing that stayed. Nothing that he could grab on to.

He heard the voices on occasion but could not make them out. They were like muffled conversations all round him. Nobody was talking to him. They were talking round him. When he asked questions, nobody answered.

He still had his music and it was the only thing that saved him. He heard it and tried to sing along but often he had no voice and had to just hum. He kept falling behind.

This is the end . . . beautiful friend, the end . . .

He felt a terrible amount of pain. Like an axe embedded in the centre of his forehead. Unrelenting pain. He waited for someone to stop it. To save him from it. But no one came. No one heard him.

He waited in darkness.

michael **connelly**

Michael Connelly was studying building construction at the University of Florida when he began reading the books of Raymond Chandler. Within a short space of time, he had made up his mind to become a crime writer, had changed his degree to journalism, and had signed up for a course in creative writing.

The trouble was, he knew next to nothing about crime. He had considered joining the police in order to experience the various aspects of the criminal world, but says that he quickly realised he did not have 'the temperament or the guts'. Following a suggestion from his father, Connelly concluded that going into journalism would allow him to observe police work without having to participate in it. After graduating in 1980 he began his chosen career, working as a crime journalist for small newspapers around Daytona Beach and Fort Lauderdale, before co-authoring a magazine story that was short-listed for the Pulitzer Prize. This led to a job at the *Los Angeles Times*, where he was on the cop beat, just like Jack McEvoy.

Three years later he embarked on his first novel, *The Black Echo*, which was published in 1992. It was met with instant acclaim, winning Connelly the Edgar Allan Poe Award for Best First Novel by the Mystery Writers of America, and introducing readers to Connelly's now well-known character, LAPD Detective Hieronymous Bosch. Connelly approached the creation of his character with a desire for, 'all aspects of his character to be meaningful, if possible. This, of course, would include his name. Hieronymus Bosch was a fifteenth-century painter who created richly detailed landscapes of debauchery, violence and human defilement. There is a "world gone mad" feel to many of his works, and I saw the metaphoric possibilities of juxtaposing contemporary Los Angeles with some of the Bosch paintings.'

Connelly wrote his first few novels while still a reporter at the *Los Angeles Times*. Finally believing that he could actually make a living as a novelist, he left his job. He recalls that, at first, the transition to full-time author felt strange. He missed the background noise of the newsroom so much that he would open the window of his home office just to hear the rush of the freeway outside.

Since those early days, Connelly has been the winner of every major prize in the genre and was elected President of the Mystery Writers of America in 2003 and 2004. He credits his reporting experience as being an integral part of his success, saying it gave him countless ideas for novels and also taught him to write fast, well and often. However, he says he does not regret leaving the profession. He had observed himself becoming hardened, and still describes himself as a 'recovering cynic'.

Partly because he understands the life of a crime reporter so well, he found that *The Scarecrow* was accomplished without effort. 'McEvoy was an easy character to write,' he says, 'because I was writing about myself!'

Vital Statistics

Birthday:
July 21, 1956.
Birthplace:
Philadelphia, Pennsylvania.
Residence:
Tampa, Florida.
Most important hobby:
Golf, 'because it is so hard'.
Series characters:
Harry Bosch, Mickey Haller, Jack McEvoy, Terry McCaleb.

Awards won:
Among others: the Edgar Allan Poe Award; the Anthony Award; the Macavity Award.
Languages into which his books have been translated:
Thirty-five.
A best-selling author in the UK:
In 2009, the Nielsen survey charting the top 100 authors of the decade, placed Connelly 39th, with sales of 3,785,330.

Sandra Brown

Rainwater

When Mr Rainwater comes to stay in Ella

Barron's boarding house in the little Texan

town of Gilead, Ella is careful to stay aloof. Her

situation seems clear: she's a widow struggling

to rear her young son, Solly, in the Depression.

Why should she discuss her life with a lodger?

But David Rainwater can see that Solly needs

support, there are things to put right in Gilead,

and time is running out . . .

Prologue

'By any chance, is your pocket watch for sale?'

The old man raised his head. The woman asking about his watch was leaning across the glass display case that separated them. Inside the case were snuffboxes, hatpins, razors with bone handles, salt cellars with their dainty sterling-silver spoons, and various pieces of jewellery recently acquired at an estate sale.

But the woman's focus was on his watch.

He guessed the woman and her husband to be in their mid-forties. To them the gold timepiece probably looked dapper and quaint. The couple were dressed in the preppy fashion of country-club members. Both were trim and tanned, and they looked good together, the man as handsome as his wife was attractive. In the half-hour they'd been there, several items had attracted their interest. The things they had decided to purchase were of good quality.

The old man had been listing the items on a sales receipt when his customer posed the question about his pocket watch. He laid a protective hand over it where it rested against his waistcoat and smiled. 'No, ma'am. I couldn't part with my watch.'

'Not for any price? You don't see pocket watches like that these days.'

Her husband leaned across the display case to better inspect the watch's workmanship. 'Twenty-four-carat gold?'

'I would imagine so, although I've never had it appraised.'

'I'd take it without having it appraised,' the man said.

'I wouldn't consider selling it. Sorry.' The shopkeeper continued to painstakingly write up their purchases. Some days the arthritis in his knuckles made handwriting difficult, but what place did a computer have in an antiques store? Besides, he distrusted computers.

He did the arithmetic the old-fashioned way. 'With tax, it comes to three hundred and sixty-seven dollars and forty-one cents.'

'Sounds fair enough.' The man pinched a credit card out of a small alligator wallet. 'Add two bottles of Evian, please.' He went to the sleek refrigerated cabinet with the glass door. It had no place in an antiques store, either, but thirsty browsers stayed to browse longer if drinks were available.

'On the house,' he told his customer. 'Help yourself.'

'That's awfully nice of you.'

'I can afford it,' he told them with a smile. 'This is my biggest single sale of the weekend.'

The man took two bottles of water from the refrigerator and passed one to his wife, then signed the credit-card receipt. 'Do you get a lot of traffic off the interstate?'

The store owner nodded. 'People who're in no particular hurry to get where they're going.'

'We noticed your billboard,' the woman said. 'On the spur of the moment, we decided to take the exit.'

'The rental on that billboard is expensive so I'm glad it's working.' He began carefully wrapping their purchases.

The man took a look round the shop. 'Do you do a good business?'

'Fair to middling. The store's more a hobby than anything. It keeps my mind sharp. Gives me something to do in my retirement.'

'What line of work were you in?'

'Textiles.'

'Were antiques always an interest?' the woman asked.

'No,' he admitted. 'Like most things in life, this'—he raised his hands to indicate the shop—'came about unexpectedly.'

The lady pulled forward a tall stool and sat down. 'It sounds like there's a story.'

The old man smiled, welcoming her interest and the opportunity to chat. 'The furnishings from my mother's house had been in storage for years. When I retired and had time to sort through everything, I realised I didn't have any use for most of the stuff, but I thought other people might. So I started selling off the china and doodads at weekend flea markets and such. I wasn't all that ambitious but, as it turned out, I was a good merchant, and I began to get some regular customers.

'Pretty soon, friends and acquaintances began bringing me items to sell on consignment. Almost before I knew it, I'd run out of space in the garage and had to rent this building.' He shook his head, chuckling. 'I just sort of fell into becoming an antiques dealer. But I like it.' He grinned at them. 'Keeps me occupied, keeps me in spending money, and I get to meet nice folks like y'all. Where's your home?'

They told him they were from Tulsa and had been to San Antonio for a long golf weekend with friends. 'We're not on a deadline to get home, so when we saw your sign, we decided to stop and take a look. We're furnishing our lake house with antiques and rustics.'

'I'm glad you stopped.' He passed the woman a business card with the shop's logo on it. 'If you change your mind about that Spode tureen you spent so much time considering, call me. I ship.'

'I just might.' She read the name embossed on the card aloud. '*Solly's*. That's an unusual name. First or last?'

'First. Short for Solomon, after the wise king in the Old Testament.' He smiled ruefully. 'I've often wondered if my mother had second thoughts about that choice.'

'That's twice you've mentioned your mother.' The woman's smile was even warmer. 'You must have been very close to her. I mean, I assume she's no longer living.'

'She died in the late sixties.' He reflected on how long ago that must have sounded to this couple. 'I miss her to this day.'

'Is Gilead your home?'

'I was born here, in a big yellow house that had belonged to my maternal grandparents.'

'Do you have a family?'

'My wife passed on eight years ago. I have two children, a boy and a girl. Between them, they've given me six grandchildren.'

'We have two sons,' the woman said.

'Children are a joy.'

The woman laughed. 'As well as a challenge.'

Her husband had been following their conversation while examining the selections in the bookcase. 'These are first editions.'

'All signed and in excellent condition,' the shopkeeper said. 'I picked them up at an estate sale not long ago.'

'Impressive collection.' The man ran his finger along the row of book spines and grinned. 'I should have left my credit card out.'

'I also take cash.'

The customer laughed. 'I'll bet you do.'

His wife added, 'For everything except your pocket watch.'

The old man slipped the fob through the buttonhole on his waistcoat and cupped the watch in his palm. It hadn't lost a second since he'd last wound it. Time had yellowed the white face, but the discolouration gave it a richer look. 'I wouldn't take anything for it.'

Softly she said, 'It's invaluable to you.'

'In the strictest sense.'

'How old is it?' the man asked.

'I don't know for certain,' replied the shopkeeper, 'but its age isn't what makes it meaningful to me.' He turned it facedown so they could read the inscription on the back of the gold case.

'*August 11th, 1934,*' the woman read aloud. Then looking back at him, she asked, 'What does it commemorate? An anniversary? Birthday? Something exceptional?'

'Exceptional?' The old man smiled. 'Not particularly. Just very special.'

One

When Ella Barron woke up that morning, she didn't expect it to be a momentous day.

As on most mornings, sleep released her gradually half an hour before daylight. She yawned and stretched, but catching another forty winks was out of the question. She had responsibilities, chores that couldn't be shirked or even postponed. She lay in bed only long enough to remember what day of the week it was. Wash day.

She quickly made her bed, then checked on Solly, who was still deep in slumber. She dressed with customary efficiency. With no time for vanity, she hastily twisted her long hair into a bun and secured it with pins, then made her way to the kitchen, moving quietly so as not to awaken the others in the house.

This was the only time of day when the kitchen was quiet and cool. As the day progressed, heat was produced by the stove and seeped in from outside through the screened door, and the window above the sink. Even Ella's own energy acted as a generator. Proportionately with the thermometer, the noise level would rise, so that by suppertime, the kitchen, which was the heart of the house, would have taken on a pulsating life of its own and didn't settle into cool repose again until Ella extinguished the overhead light for the final time, most often hours after her boarders had retired.

This morning she didn't pause to enjoy either the relative coolness or the silence. Having put on her apron, she lit the oven, put the coffee on to brew, then mixed the biscuit dough. Margaret arrived right on time, and after removing her hat and hanging it on the peg inside the door, and gratefully taking a tin cup of sweetened coffee from Ella, she went back outside to fill the washing machine with water for the first load of laundry. The prospect of buying an electric washing machine was so remote that Ella didn't even dream about it. For her foreseeable future, she must continue using the one with the hand-crank wringer that had been her mother's.

On a summer day like today, the washing shed became stifling by midmorning. But wet laundry seemed heavier when one's hands were numb from cold during the winter. In any season, laundry days were dreaded. By nightfall her back would be aching.

Solly, still in his pyjamas, wandered into the kitchen while she was frying bacon.

Breakfast was served at eight. By nine everyone had been fed, the dishes washed and put away. Ella set a pot of mustard greens on the stove to simmer, cooked a pan of Faultless starch, then, taking Solly with her, went outside to hang up the first basket of laundry that Margaret had washed.

It was almost eleven when she went inside to check on things in the kitchen. While she was adding more salt to the greens, someone pulled the bell at her front door. As she walked along the dim hallway, she glanced at herself in the wall mirror. Her face was flushed from the heat, and her heavy bun had slipped down onto her nape, but she continued to the door without stopping to primp.

On the other side of the screened door was Dr Kincaid. ''Morning, Mrs Barron.' He removed his white straw hat and held it against his chest in a rather courtly manner.

She was surprised to see the doctor on her porch. Dr Kincaid's office was in town, but he also made house calls, usually to deliver a baby, sometimes to keep a contagious patient from spreading his infection through Gilead, their town of 2,000 inhabitants.

Had one of her boarders sent for the doctor today? She'd been outside most of the morning, so it was possible that one of the sisters had used the telephone without her knowledge.

'Good morning, Dr Kincaid. Did the Dunnes send for you?'

'No. I'm not here on a sick call. Is this a bad time?'

She thought of the clothes piled into baskets and ready to be starched, but the starch needed a while longer to cool. 'Not at all. Come in.' She reached up to unlatch the screened door and pushed it open.

Dr Kincaid turned to his right and made a come-forward motion with his hat. Ella was unaware of the other man's presence until he stepped round the large fern to the side of the front door and into her range of vision.

Her first impression of him was how tall and lean he was. One could almost say he looked underfed. He was dressed in a black suit with a white shirt and black tie and was holding a black felt fedora. She thought his clothes looked severe and out of season for such a hot morning, especially compared to Dr Kincaid's seersucker suit and white hat with the red band.

The doctor made the introduction. 'Mrs Barron, this is Mr Rainwater.'

He inclined his head. 'Ma'am.'

'Mr Rainwater.'

She moved aside and indicated for them to come in. Dr Kincaid allowed the other man to go ahead of him.

Ella motioned them into the formal parlour. 'Please, have a seat.'

'We thought we heard the doorbell.'

The chirping voice brought Ella round. The Misses Dunne, Violet and Pearl, were standing on the bottom stair. In their pastel print dresses and old-fashioned shoes, they were virtually interchangeable. Each had a nimbus of white hair. Their veined, spotted hands clutched matching handkerchiefs.

With unabashed curiosity, the two were looking beyond Ella to catch a glimpse of the visitors. Having callers was an event. 'Is that Dr Kincaid?' asked Pearl. 'Hello, Dr Kincaid,' she called.

'Good morning, Miss Pearl.'

'Who's that with you?'

Miss Violet frowned at her sister. 'We were coming down to play rummy until lunch. Will we disturb?'

'Not at all.'

Ella asked them to use the informal parlour and led them to it. When they were situated at the card table, she said, 'Please excuse us, ladies,' and pulled together the heavy oak pocket doors that divided the large room in half. She rejoined the two men on the formal side, which overlooked the front porch.

Ella switched on the fan on the table in the corner, then motioned the men towards a pair of wingback chairs. 'Please.'

They sat when she did.

This being summer, she hadn't put on stockings that morning. Embarrassed by her bare legs, she crossed her ankles and pulled her feet beneath the chair. 'Would you like some lemonade? Or tea?'

'That sounds awfully good, Mrs Barron, but I'm afraid I have to pass,' the doctor said. 'I've got patients to see at the clinic.'

She looked at Mr Rainwater.

'No, thank you,' he said.

Dr Kincaid cleared his throat and said, 'I heard you lost a boarder.'

'That's right. Mrs Morton went to live with an ailing sister.'

'Have you had anyone speak for her room?'

'She only left yesterday. I haven't had time to advertise.'

'Well then, that's good,' the doctor said.

Discerning the purpose for their call, she looked at Mr Rainwater. He sat leaning slightly forward. His black shoes were shined, she noticed. His thick, dark hair was smoothed back off his face, but one strand had defiantly flopped over his broad forehead. His cheekbones were pronounced, his eyebrows as black as crows' wings. He had startling blue eyes, and they were steady on her.

'Are you interested in lodging, Mr Rainwater?'

'Yes. I need a place to stay.'

'I haven't had a chance to give the vacant room a thorough cleaning, but as soon as it's ready, I'd be happy to show it to you.'

'I'm not particular.' He smiled, showing teeth that were very white although slightly crooked on top. 'I'll take the room as is.'

'Oh, I'm afraid I couldn't let you have it now,' she said quickly. 'Not until I've scrubbed everything. I have very high standards.'

'For boarders or cleanliness?'

'For both.'

'Which is why I've brought him to you,' the doctor said. 'I told Mr Rainwater that you keep an immaculate house and run a tight ship. To say nothing of the excellent meals your boarders enjoy. He desires a place that's well maintained. A peaceful and quiet house.'

Just then, from the direction of the kitchen, came a terrible racket followed by a bloodcurdling scream.

Ella was out of her chair like a shot. 'Excuse me.'

She ran down the hallway and burst into the kitchen, where Solly was screeching and holding his left arm away from his body.

Hot starch had spattered his arm from wrist to shoulder. Some had splashed onto his chest, plastering his cotton shirt to his skin. The pan that had been on the stove was lying overturned on the floor. The sticky blue stuff was oozing out of it, forming a puddle.

Heedless of the mess, Ella lifted her son and hugged him to her. 'Oh, no, oh God. Solly, Solly, oh, sweetheart. Oh Lord.'

'Cold water.' Dr Kincaid had rushed into the kitchen practically on her heels. He pushed her towards the sink and turned on the cold water spout, forcing Solly's arm beneath the stream.

'Do you have ice?' Mr Rainwater addressed the question to Margaret, who'd come rushing in from the back yard.

Ella shouted above Solly's screams. 'There's ice in the box.'

She and Dr Kincaid continued to struggle with the boy to keep his burnt arm under the cold water. None of this was easily done. They had to battle Solly, whose right arm was flailing about, often connecting painfully with either Ella or the doctor. The boy was also trying to butt heads with them. Several pieces of crockery were knocked off the draining board and onto the floor.

'This will help.' Mr Rainwater moved up beside Ella with a chunk of freshly chipped ice. While she and Dr Kincaid held Solly's arm as still as possible, Mr Rainwater rubbed the ice up and down her child's arm, which now bore ugly red splotches.

The ice cooled the burns, and eventually Solly stopped screaming, but he continued to bob his head rhythmically. The doctor turned off the tap. Ella realised that her dress was drenched.

'Thank you.' She took the ice from Mr Rainwater and continued to rub it up and down Solly's arm as she carried him to a chair and sat down with him on her lap. She hugged him and kissed the top of his head as she cradled him against her chest. Even then it took several minutes before he stopped bobbing his head.

From the open doorway, the two Dunne spinsters cooed commiseration and encouragement. Margaret was holding the hem of her apron to her lips with one hand; the other palm was raised beseechingly towards the ceiling. She was crying loudly and praying plaintively, 'Jesus, he'p this poor baby. Lord Jesus, he'p this child.'

Ella was grateful for Margaret's prayers and hoped the Lord was listening, but the loud praying was adding to the confusion. 'Margaret, please bring me one of his candy sticks,' she said.

Her quiet tone cut through Margaret's fervent litany. She ceased praying and went into the pantry, where Ella kept a jar of candy sticks hidden behind canisters of flour and sugar. The candy sticks were reserved for times of crisis. Like now.

Margaret was choking back sobs. 'It's my fault. He was playin' there in the dirt. You know how he likes to dig with that big wood spoon? I turned my back, couldn't've been more'n a minute. Next I know, he's in the house a-screamin'. I'm sorry, Miss Ella. I—'

'It wasn't your fault. I know how quickly he can disappear.'

Margaret muttered on about how she was to blame as she brought the candy jar from the pantry, lifted off the metal lid, and extended it to Solly. 'What flavour you want, baby doll?'

Solly remained unaware of Margaret, so Ella selected for him, a white stick with orange stripes. She didn't hand it to him directly but laid it on the table. He picked it up and began to lick. Everyone in the kitchen sighed with relief.

'Let me take a look at the burns.'

'No.' Ella held up her hand to prevent the doctor from setting Solly off again. 'The spots aren't blistering, and the starch had been cooling for over two hours. It wasn't that hot. When he pulled the pan off the stove, I think it frightened him more than anything.' Ella smoothed her hand over her son's head, but he dodged the caress. The rejection pierced her heart, but she smiled bravely.

'I have some salve at the clinic,' the doctor said. 'Even though the skin's not blistered, it wouldn't hurt to keep it lubricated.'

Ella nodded and looked over at Mr Rainwater, who was hovering near the stove. 'The ice helped. Thank you.'

He nodded.

She said, 'About the room—'

'See, I told you he was to be a new boarder.' Miss Pearl spoke to her sister in a whisper that everyone heard.

'We'll excuse ourselves until lunch.' Miss Violet grasped her sister's arm with enough pressure to make her wince and practically dragged her towards the staircase. Miss Pearl was still whispering excitedly as they made their way up. 'He seems awfully nice, don't you think, sister? Very clean fingernails. I wonder who his people are.'

Ella eased Solly off her lap and into the chair in which she was seated. She made a futile attempt to smooth back strands of hair that had shaken loose from her bun.

'As I was saying, Mr Rainwater, I simply haven't had time to give the room a proper cleaning. If you're wanting to move in immediately—'

'I am.'

'You can't.'

'Then when?'

'When the room meets my standards.'

The statement seemed to amuse him, and she wondered if his quick grin was mocking her standards or her pride in them.

In either case, she resented it. 'In light of what the last quarter of an hour has been like, I'm surprised you're still interested in securing a room in my house. You haven't even seen the room yet.'

'Then let's take a look,' Dr Kincaid said. 'But I really must get back to the clinic soon.'

Mr Rainwater said, 'You don't have to stay, Murdy.'

Dr Kincaid's first name was Murdock, but Ella had never heard him addressed as Murdy, not even by close acquaintances.

'No, no. I want to help in any way I can.' The doctor turned to her. 'Mrs Barron?'

She glanced down at Solly, who had eaten half his candy stick. Margaret, sensing her hesitation, said, 'You go on with the gentlemen. I'll keep an eagle eye on this boy. I swear I won't take my eyes off him.'

Reluctantly Ella led the two men from the kitchen and up the stairs, then to the room at the end of the hallway. Opening the door, she said, 'It's got a southern exposure. You can catch the breeze.'

The sheer curtains, now catching the breeze, were ruffled. The wallpaper had a yellow cabbage-rose pattern, and the iron bed looked too short for Mr Rainwater. In fact, even though he was slender, the room looked smaller with him standing in its centre.

But he seemed either not to notice or not to care about the feminine decor or the limited size of the bed, the room or the narrow closet. He looked out of the window, nodded, then turned back to her. 'This will do.'

'You would share a bathroom with Mr Hastings.'

'Chester Hastings,' Dr Kincaid supplied. 'Extremely nice man. He's not in town much. Haberdashery salesman. Travels all over.'

'I don't have a problem with sharing a bathroom.'

On the way downstairs, Ella told Mr Rainwater the cost for room and board, and he agreed to it.

'Splendid,' Dr Kincaid said. 'I'll let the two of you work out the particulars about moving in and so forth.'

Ella led the way to the front door, but when she got there, she discovered that only Dr Kincaid had followed her. Behind them the hallway was empty. Presumably Mr Rainwater had ducked into the parlour, waiting there to discuss the details of his occupancy.

'Can I have a word, Mrs Barron?' the doctor asked.

She looked at him curiously as he ushered her out onto the porch.

The doctor dabbed his bald head with his handkerchief. 'I wanted to speak to you in private.'

'About Solly?'

'Well, that, yes.'

They'd had this discussion many times before. Bracing for an argument, she clasped her hands at her waist. 'I refuse to place him in an institution, Dr Kincaid. I also refuse to keep him medicated.'

'So you've told me. Many times.'

'Then please stop trying to persuade me otherwise.'

'What happened just now—'

'Could have happened to any child,' she said. 'Remember when the Hinnegar boy turned that kerosene lamp over on himself?'

'That boy was two years old, Mrs Barron. Solly is ten.'

'His birthday is still months away.'

'Close enough.' Softening his tone, the doctor continued. 'I'm well aware of the perils inherent to childhood. Based on what I've seen, it's amazing to me that any of us reaches adulthood.'

He paused, then looked at her kindly. 'But your boy is particularly susceptible to mishaps. Even at his age, Solly can't understand the dangers associated with something like pulling a pan of hot starch off the stove. Please don't think I'm being insensitive or cruel. It's your situation that's cruel. The fact is, without medication to suppress your son's . . . impulses, he could harm himself, and others, especially when he's in the throes of one of his fits.'

'I keep careful watch over him to prevent that.'

'I don't question how dutiful—'

'It's not my duty; it's my privilege. Only the running of this house prevents me from devoting every waking moment to Solly. This morning was an exception. I was unexpectedly called away.'

That was a subtle reminder that he was responsible for her distraction, but the doctor ignored the rebuke.

'You bring me to the next point, Mrs Barron. This constant vigilance is detrimental to *your* health. How long can you keep it up?'

'For as long as Solly needs supervision.'

'What happens when you can no longer physically restrain him?'

In a deliberate voice, she said, 'The medications you're suggesting - would also inhibit his ability to learn.'

Her saying that caused the doctor's eyes to become even sadder.

She took umbrage. 'I know you doubt Solly's capacity to learn, Dr Kincaid. I do not. I won't have him drugged into a stupor. What kind of life would he have?'

'What kind of life do *you* have?' he asked gently.

Her face was hot with indignation. 'I appreciate your professional opinion, Dr Kincaid. But that's all it is, an *opinion*. No one really knows what Solly is or isn't capable of understanding and retaining. But as his mother, I have a better perception of his abilities than anyone. So I must do what I think is best for him.'

Yielding the battle if not the war, the doctor glanced away from her. 'Send Margaret round for that salve,' he finally said.

'Thank you.'

The street was deserted except for a dog that was trotting alongside a wagon being driven by an elderly black man, and pulled by a pair of mules. The man tipped his hat to them as the wagon rolled past. They waved back at him. Ella didn't know him, but the doctor addressed him by name and called out a greeting.

'If that's all, Dr Kincaid, I need to set out lunch.'

He turned back to her. 'Actually, there is something else, Mrs Barron. About Mr Rainwater.'

Other than his name and his willingness to pay for room and board, she knew nothing about the man. 'Is he of good character?'

'Impeccable character.'

'You've known him for a long time?'

'He's my wife's late cousin's boy. I guess that makes him some sort of a second or third cousin by marriage.'

'I guessed he might be a family member. He called you Murdy.'

Absently he nodded. 'Family nickname.'

'Is he in the medical profession, too?'

'No. He was a cotton broker.'

'*Was?*' Was Mr Rainwater a victim of the Depression, one of the thousands of men in the nation who were out of work? 'If he's unemployed, how does he plan to pay his rent? I can't afford—'

'He's not without funds. He's . . .' The doctor looked towards the retreating wagon. Coming back to her, he said, 'The fact is, he won't be needing the room in your house for long.' She stared at him, waiting. Softly he said, 'He's dying.'

Two

'Please, Mr Rainwater. Leave that.'

He was crouched, picking pieces of broken china off the kitchen linoleum. He glanced up at her but continued what he was doing. 'I'm afraid the boy will hurt himself again.'

'Margaret and I will tend to the mess, and to Solly.'

Margaret was at the stove drizzling bacon grease from that morning's breakfast into the greens. Solly was sitting in his customary chair at the kitchen table, rocking back and forth, fiddling with a yo-yo. His concentration was fixed on the winding and rewinding.

The crisis had passed, and he didn't appear to be suffering any lasting effects. Looking at his blond head bowed over the yo-yo, she felt the familiar pinching sensation deep within her heart, a mix of unqualified love and the fear that even that might not be sufficient to protect him.

Mr Rainwater came to his feet and held out his filled hands. Ella took the dustpan off the nail on the wall and extended it to him. He carefully placed the chips of broken dishware into it. 'Those are the larger pieces. There are some slivers I couldn't pick out of the starch.'

'We'll watch for them when we clean up.'

He turned to the sink and washed the starch off his hands.

She set the dustpan on the floor in the corner. 'Margaret, could you get out the lunch things while I speak with Mr Rainwater?' She turned and gestured towards the hallway. 'Mr Rainwater?'

'We can talk here,' he said.

Ella preferred not to discuss business in the kitchen, where, as anticipated, the temperature had climbed. She was also afraid that Margaret would gossip. On several occasions, Ella had been forced to chide her for sharing personal information about their boarders and about Ella herself.

The accident with the starch had left Ella frazzled and distracted. She'd been further shaken by what Dr Kincaid had told her about Mr Rainwater. Although her livelihood depended on keeping her house filled, to take in a dying man was an unappealing prospect on numerous levels. She already had her hands full, what with keeping her other boarders happy and dealing with Solly.

However, Mr Rainwater's unfortunate circumstance was the only hindrance to his being a suitable boarder. On that basis alone, how could she live with her conscience if she refused to rent the room to him?

Dr Kincaid should have informed her of his condition first, before she'd agreed to let him the room. The omission had left her at a distinct disadvantage, and Mr Rainwater was placing her at one now by discussing business in the presence of her talkative maid.

Trying to keep the resentment from her voice, she said, 'There's a collection box for your rent on a table under the stairs. I collect the rent each Monday, but you'll pay me the first week in advance before you move in. Is that satisfactory?'

'Yes. Fine.'

'About meals,' Ella said. 'A full breakfast is served each morning at eight o'clock. Dinner is at six thirty. So as not to waste food, I would appreciate being notified if you plan to have a meal out.'

'I doubt I'll have any meals out.'

'For lunch, I put out cold meats, cheese, fruit. Sometimes leftovers.' She motioned towards Margaret, who was unwrapping slices of ham from butcher paper. 'It's on the dining table between noon and one, and it's first come, first served.' She glanced at the wall clock. 'I'm running a bit late today, but the Dunnes rarely eat more than a piece of fruit, and Mr Hastings is out of town.'

'Are they your only boarders, besides myself?'

She nodded. 'The sisters share the largest room. Mr Hastings has the room at the top of the stairs.'

'And you and Solly?'

'Here on the ground floor. On Sunday,' she continued briskly, 'I serve the main meal at two. That gives me time to return from church. Everyone is on their own for Sunday night supper, but the kitchen is open for your use. I only ask that you clean up after yourself.'

'Of course.'

'Is there anything you shouldn't eat?' She asked that of all her new boarders, although it might appear to him that she had singled him out because of his illness.

As though following her thoughts, he gave a faint smile. 'I can eat anything, and I'm not a picky eater.'

She pressed on. 'Bed linens are changed once a week. I don't allow liquor in the house. If you have visitors, you can receive them in the formal parlour, but please give me notice. For a nominal charge, you can have a guest for dinner if I'm informed ahead of time.'

'I won't have any visitors; no guests for dinner.'

His eyes burned intensely blue. They arrested her for a moment; then she looked away. 'Does all of this sound acceptable, Mr Rainwater?'

Having waited patiently for her to go over the rules of the house, he asked, 'When may I move in?'

'Tuesday.'

'This is Thursday.'

'As I explained, the room needs to be cleaned. Can you continue to stay with Dr and Mrs Kincaid until the room is ready?'

'I've been with them for two nights already. They've been very hospitable and have given me the use of their boys' bedroom. But the boys are having to sleep on pallets in the living room, inconveniencing everyone. I'd like to move in tomorrow at the latest.'

'The room won't be ready by then. The furniture must be removed so the floor can be scrubbed. The mattress and pillows need to be aired. I can't get everything done by tomorrow.'

'My new preacher's looking for work.'

Ella looked towards Margaret. 'What?'

'Brother Calvin,' she said. 'He just come to town to take over the pulpit. But our congregation can't pay him nothing. He's sleeping on a member's porch, and they's feeding him, but he's wanting to earn some money so he can get a place of his own and move his wife here. She's down in South Texas with her folks. For a little bit of nothing he'd do them chores, Miz Barron. Why'n't you let me fetch Brother Calvin?'

Mr Rainwater was following this conversation with interest. He said, 'I'd be willing to pay Brother Calvin's fee.'

Margaret smiled at him as though the matter had been settled. She headed towards the hallway, where the telephone was. 'I'll call over to the store right now.' To Mr Rainwater she said, 'Randall's Dry Goods and Grocery is where my boy, Jimmy, works. While he's on a delivery, he can run right over to where the preacher's stayin' and tell him to get hisself over here.'

When Margaret was out of earshot, Mr Rainwater said to Ella, 'I hope that's all right with you.'

It wasn't. This was her house. All decisions regarding it were hers to make. But it seemed that nothing was normal this morning. She was being swept along by an unusual series of events, and that alarmed her. Routine wasn't just a preference; it was a necessity.

But in the grand scheme of things, retaining the services of Brother Calvin was a small matter, and she would look peevish to object to so workable a plan.

However, she wasn't quite ready to concede. 'I would prefer to do the work myself, Mr Rainwater.'

'Because your standards are so high.'

'But since time is a factor . . .'

She hadn't intended to mention his limited time. Embarrassment made her face feel even hotter than it already did.

He said, 'This is a good plan.'

She sighed defeat. 'All right. But if you would give me tomorrow morning, I would appreciate it.'

'How about four o'clock tomorrow afternoon?'

'Four? Yes, good. By then I'll have the room ready.'

'I'll be sure to come with cash in hand. To cover Brother Calvin's charges and the first week's rent.'

He grinned, but she didn't return it. Instead, she motioned him towards the hall, indicating that their business was concluded.

'I can go out the back way.'

Nodding, she walked him to the screened back door. As he went down the steps, he put on his hat. At the bottom of the steps, he turned back and touched its brim with one finger. 'Mrs Barron.'

'Mr Rainwater. I hope you'll be comfortable here.'

She had other duties to attend to, but for some reason, she didn't turn away. She maintained eye contact with the man who would share her address for the last weeks of his life. Did her pity show?

He said, 'He told you, didn't he? Murdy told you about me.'

Being coy wasn't in Ella's nature. 'He thought I should know.'

He nodded in approval of her straightforwardness. 'I'd thank you not to tell the others. Knowing makes people uncomfortable. I don't want to be treated differently from anyone else.'

'I won't say anything to anyone.'

'Thank you.'

'There's no need to thank me, Mr Rainwater.'

'See what I mean?' he said, grinning. 'You're already making concessions for me.'

She had the grace to look abashed.

His grin held; then he turned serious again. 'Does he talk?'

'What?'

'Your son.'

He motioned with his head. She turned. Behind her, Solly was still at the table. He was winding the yo-yo string round and round his finger, unwinding it, winding it again as he rocked forward and back to a beat that only he could hear.

She shook her head. 'No, he doesn't talk.'

'Well,' he said pleasantly, 'I find that most people who do often have nothing worthwhile to say.'

His easy dismissal of Solly's limitations was almost more difficult to withstand than the rude, curious stares of strangers, and she reacted with an unexpected rush of tears. Perhaps he saw them and wanted to spare her embarrassment, because he said no more, only touched the brim of his hat again, turned and walked away.

BROTHER CALVIN TAYLOR turned out to be a godsend, and not just to the African Methodist Episcopal church. The preacher was a tall and robust man in his late twenties, with an engaging manner and a wide smile, made even more brilliant by a gold front tooth. His speaking voice was the voice of a prophet, the bass tones rolling like thunder off a hillside. She imagined it reverberating inside the church, filling the faithful with renewed devotion.

He had indeed made a favourable impact on the congregation. When Margaret introduced Brother Calvin to Ella, she boasted that the church's attendance had increased threefold since he'd taken over.

'Any given Sunday, there ain't an empty pew.'

The preacher reacted to her praise with humility, crediting God with his success. 'The Lord is blessing us in tremendous ways.'

Ella liked him immediately and put him straight to work, even though the Dunne sisters might very well swoon when they saw a coloured man inside the house. Ella didn't share their prejudices.

The preacher soon proved he wasn't all talk. By the end of the day, he had scrubbed and polished the floor of the vacant room. 'May as well do the hallway while I'm at it,' he'd said. It, too, was hand-buffed to a shine.

At suppertime, Ella gave him a plate of food to eat in the kitchen while she served the Dunne sisters in the dining room. When he'd finished his meal, he carried the bedding in from the back yard, where it had been airing all afternoon, and replaced it in the room that was to be Mr Rainwater's.

Before Brother Calvin left, he told Ella he would be back early in the morning to help Margaret with any other chores that needed to be done. 'By four o'clock, that room will be sparkling, I promise.'

He kept his promise. All the work was done to Ella's satisfaction.

MR RAINWATER ARRIVED at the appointed time. The Dunnes had gone to the lending library. Margaret was ironing in the kitchen while keeping an eye on Solly. Mr Hastings was still out of town.

Except for the grandfather clock in the formal parlour chiming the hour of four, the house was hushed when Ella unlatched the door for him. They exchanged pleasantries; then she led him upstairs.

He paused in the open doorway of the bedroom and looked it over. Then he turned to Ella. 'You were right to hold to your standards, Mrs Barron. The room is much nicer now. Thank you.'

'You're welcome.'

He passed her a white envelope with his name printed on it. 'The first week's rent. Let me know what I owe Brother Calvin.' Then he carried two suitcases into the room and gently closed the door.

'NORTHEAST TEXAS. Halfway between Dallas and Texarkana.'

Throughout the evening meal, the Dunnes had peppered Mr Rainwater with questions. Ella was stacking their empty dinner plates on a tray when Miss Violet enquired where he was from.

Miss Pearl said, 'That's good cotton-growing country up there.'

'He knows that,' Violet said. 'He's a cotton broker, after all.'

'I realise that,' Pearl returned. 'I'm just remarking.'

To prevent a sibling quarrel, Ella tactfully intervened. 'Should I bring out cream with the berry cobbler, Miss Pearl?'

'Oh, cream, yes, please. Don't you think cobbler is best served with cream, Mr Rainwater?'

'I certainly do.' He glanced up at Ella, the corners of his lips twitching to contain a smile. 'Cream for me, too, please.'

She lifted the tray.

Mr Rainwater stood up. 'Can I help you with that?'

'No.'

The word came out more emphatically than Ella had intended, and everyone, even Ella herself, was taken aback by her tone. The sisters were gaping not only at her but also at the new boarder. They were as surprised as Ella by his unprecedented offer to help.

To hide her embarrassment, Ella ducked her head and murmured, 'No, thank you, Mr Rainwater,' then headed for the kitchen.

As she left the room, she overheard Miss Violet clear her throat before enquiring, 'What about your family, Mr Rainwater?'

'My mother and father are deceased, and I'm an only child.'

'Oh, that's unfortunate,' Pearl said. 'Violet and I have only each other. The rest of our family has died out.'

The kitchen door swung shut, preventing Ella from hearing Mr Rainwater's comment on that.

'Them ol' ladies is goin' drive that man plumb crazy with all them questions about hisself,' Margaret said, shaking her head.

'I heard you asking him some questions earlier.'

'I's just being polite,' she grumbled.

'Have you spooned up the cobbler yet?'

'Ain't I always got dessert ready before I start washing up?' The maid used her shoulder to point out the dishes of cobbler on the counter, waiting to be placed on a serving tray. 'What about them shutters on the front windows?'

'What about them?'

'I tol' you. Brother Calvin offered to paint them.'

'I know they *need* painting, Margaret, but—'

'Brother Calvin said he'd do it for cheap. It was nice of him to bring us those dewberries. Picked 'em hisself.'

Ella sighed. 'Have him come and talk to me about the shutters. We'll see.' She checked Solly's dinner plate. He had eaten enough to sustain him. 'Solly can have cobbler now,' she told Margaret.

The maid smiled down at the boy as she removed her hands from the sink. 'I'll feed it to that baby myself.'

Ella carried the tray to the door, put her back to it and gave it a push.

'David,' Margaret said.

'What?'

'Mr Rainwater's first name. I figure you wanted to know.'

Ella looked at her with annoyance as she backed through the door between the kitchen and the dining room. When she turned, her eyes went to Mr Rainwater. His gaze held hers before he directed his attention back to Miss Violet, who was telling him about her and Pearl's days as schoolteachers.

'It's so nice to have pleasant conversation with a new acquaintance, isn't it, sister?' Violet said.

'It is indeed,' Pearl simpered, patting her lace collar. 'I hope you're with us for a very long time, Mr Rainwater.'

Ella kept her expression impassive as she served the dewberry cobbler.

SHE WAS SITTING at the kitchen table eating her own meal when he poked his head round the door. Immediately she came to her feet, blotting her mouth. 'Mr Rainwater. Can I get you something?'

He stepped into the kitchen.

Margaret gave him a wide smile. 'Coffee's still on.'

'No more for me, thank you.'

Solly, sitting across from Ella and tapping his spoon against the edge of the table, didn't react.

The new boarder nodded down at Ella's plate. 'I wondered when you got to eat. Forgive me for interrupting. I was wondering if it's all right for me to turn on the porch light so I can read out there.'

'Oh, of course. The switch is—'

'I've located the switch. I wanted to ask before I turned it on.'

'Just be sure to turn it off when you come back inside.'

He gave Margaret and Ella a nod and backed out of the door.

'Nice of him to ax,' Margaret said. 'I hope Mr Rainwater plans to be with us for a long spell.'

Ella sat down and resumed eating.

AFTER MARGARET LEFT for home, Ella put Solly to bed, and he fell asleep quickly. She remained kneeling beside his bed, gazing into his sweet face, listening to his soft breathing. When her knees began to ache, she kissed the air just above his cheek and slipped from the room. She listened for any signs of him stirring as she sat at the kitchen table shelling black-eyed peas for tomorrow's dinner. It was well after ten when she made her last inspection of the kitchen and turned out the light.

Her neck and shoulders burned with fatigue as she moved down the darkened hallway. The front porch light was off. Mr Rainwater hadn't forgotten. But she went to see that he'd also locked the screened door. He hadn't. She reached for the latch.

'If you hook that, I won't be able to get back in.'

She jumped at the sound of his voice.

'I'm sorry,' he said. 'I didn't mean to startle you.'

She pushed open the door and stepped out onto the porch. He was sitting in the darkness in one of the wicker chairs. 'I'm the one who's sorry,' Ella said. 'I thought you had come inside. I hate that I disturbed your solitude.'

'You didn't. I turned out the light because the bugs were a nuisance.' He stood up and indicated the other chairs. 'Join me.'

She hesitated, then sat down in one of the chairs.

'The air feels so good I couldn't bring myself to go to my room.' He smiled at her. 'Even as comfortable as it is.'

'I'm glad you like it.'

They lapsed into a silence broken by the night song of cicadas. He stretched his long legs far out in front of him. Ella wasn't sure that such a loose-limbed posture was appropriate when a man and woman, strangers, were alone in the darkness.

'Where was the food going?'

She looked over at him.

'The food that Margaret was packing up when I came into the kitchen,' he said. 'Where did you send it?'

'To the shantytown. It's on the far east side of town.'

He continued to look at her, his eyebrow arched with interest.

'It started out with just a few hoboes who got off the freight trains to camp by the creek. The law ran them off, but more kept coming, until finally the sheriff gave up trying to keep them away. For the most part, they're left alone now. I understand a few hundred are over there at any given time. Whole families. So every few days I send leftovers, stale bread, overripe fruit. Like that.'

'That's very benevolent of you.'

She lowered her head and smoothed her hands over her skirt. 'It's food I'd have to throw out otherwise.'

'I doubt the people in shantytown mind if an apple is bruised.'

'In exchange for these scraps, I ask them not to come begging here at the house. Word gets round to the newcomers and drifters: don't go to the Barron's Boarding House for a handout. You won't get one.'

'Still, you're charitable.'

She didn't want him giving her more credit than she deserved. 'I don't take it to those poor people myself, Mr Rainwater. That would be charitable. I send it by Margaret.'

'A lot of people wouldn't send it at all,' he countered quietly.

She was about to protest further but changed her mind, feeling it would be better to let the subject drop. Another silence fell between them. She sensed that he was more comfortable with it than she was. She was about to excuse herself and return indoors when he said, 'Have you lived here all your life?'

'In this house. My father built it after he and my mother married. Years later he added on the rooms that Solly and I now share.'

'Your parents are dead?'

'Yes.'

'Brothers and sisters?'

'Twin brothers born three years after me. Both died in infancy.'

'I'm sorry.'

'I can't really remember them. Mother and Father never talked about them.'

It had been a sorrow that was unbearable to her parents. Neither recovered from it. Overnight, her mother had turned into a bitter woman. She had no longer smiled, no longer found joy in her healthy daughter, who from then on she had kept at arm's length. Ella's father, losing his wife's affection as well as his twin sons, had found his only consolation in whiskey. He'd died of cirrhosis at forty-five.

Upon his death, her mother had been forced to take in boarders. When she finally succumbed to her sadness—with relief, it seemed to Ella—Ella had taken over management of the house. She'd been eighteen. Despite her youth, as prideful as it sounded, she was much better at running the household than her mother had been.

'Murdy told me you're a widow.'

She looked at Mr Rainwater sharply. then almost immediately dropped her gaze. 'That's right.'

'Unfortunate for you.'

She nodded.

'You were left with sole responsibility for Solly.'

She raised her head. 'He's not a responsibility, Mr Rainwater. He's a child. *My* child. A gift.'

He retracted his long legs. 'Of course. I didn't mean to imply—'

'I'd better go inside.' She stood up quickly.

He did likewise.

'Please stop doing that.'

'I'm sorry?'

'Stop popping up whenever I stand or enter a room. I'm your landlady, not your . . . not a . . .' She couldn't think of what she *wasn't* to him, only what she *was*. 'You don't have to stand for me.'

'I was taught to stand up for ladies. Habits die hard. But I wouldn't have done it if I'd known it would make you angry.'

'I'm not angry.'

But her sharp tone indicated otherwise. His eyes penetrated the darkness between them, making her feel uncomfortable.

'Good night, Mr Rainwater.' She turned and walked to the door, but when she reached for the handle, his hand was there first, reaching round her to pull it open. Rather than raise another ruckus about his manners, she went inside. He followed her in, then stood there watching as she went up on tiptoe to latch the door.

'Isn't that hook placed inconveniently high for you?'

'Yes, it's inconvenient.' She hooked the latch. 'But it has to be where Solly can't reach it. He wandered off once and was missing for hours before we found him walking on the railroad tracks.'

He expelled a long breath, looking regretful. 'This is my first night in your house. I've failed to make a good impression.'

'You shouldn't be concerned about impressing me.'

'I want you to think well of me.'

'I thought well enough of you to rent you the room. Beyond that—'

'You have no opinion of me,' he said, finishing for her and further fomenting her irritation with him and the entire conversation.

'That's right, Mr Rainwater. I don't think too much about you or about any of my boarders, because, in return, I don't want you thinking too much about me, or Solly, or our circumstances.'

He studied her a moment, then said, 'You should allow yourself to get angry more often. I think it would do you good.'

His candour robbed her of words. Taking umbrage, she just stood there and stared at him.

'Good night, Mrs Barron.' He stepped round her and went upstairs.

Three

A week passed. Ella saw little of David Rainwater other than at break-fast and dinner. During meals, he showed remarkable forbearance for the Dunne sisters' chatter and ill-disguised curiosity.

The spinsters began 'dressing' for dinner, each night coming downstairs arrayed in their Sunday best, wearing pieces of jewellery and explaining this sudden affectation by asking, rhetorically, what good was having nice things if one never used them?

Mr Hastings returned one afternoon, barely having time to wash before dinner. As Ella served the salad course, the sisters made the introductions.

'Pleased to meet you, Mr Rainwater,' the salesman said. 'It'll be nice to have another man in the house. Do you play chess?'

'Not too well, I'm afraid.'

'Excellent! Maybe I can win a game for a change. Ah, Mrs Barron, I've missed your cooking. Nothing like it where I've been.'

'Thank you, Mr Hastings. Did you have a productive trip?'

'Nothing to boast of, sorry to say. Nobody can afford new furnishings these days. Times seem to be getting worse, not better.'

'Which should make us all the more grateful for our blessings,' Miss Violet intoned.

After dinner that night, the two men played chess in the formal parlour while the sisters listened to the radio in the informal parlour. Ella could hear strains of music as she worked in the kitchen. Occasionally she detected a male voice coming from the front room.

Mr Hastings stayed for two days, then doggedly carried his sample cases down the stairs and out to his car. 'I should be back next Tuesday,' he informed Ella. 'I'll call you if I'm delayed.'

He tipped his hat to her and set off. That evening, Mr Rainwater excused himself immediately after dinner and went up to his room. He hadn't spent any more evenings sitting on the porch.

Their encounters were polite, but brief and stilted. As she'd requested, he no longer stood up when she entered a room. It felt as though they had quarrelled. They hadn't, exactly. But she avoided being alone with him, and he made no attempt to seek her out.

He'd been in residence for two weeks when they had their next private conversation. She'd been cleaning upstairs while Margaret was in the front parlour mending a drapery and watching Solly as he played with spools of thread, one of his favourite pastimes.

Ella was toting her cleaning supplies down the stairs when she heard a scraping sound. She followed it out of the back door.

Mr Rainwater was using a garden hoe to chop the dry soil between rows of tomato plants. With his coat draped over a fence post, he was in shirt-sleeves. Sweat plastered his shirt to his skin.

'Mr Rainwater! What are you doing?' she asked.

He looked at her with amusement. 'I'm hoeing the garden.'

His calm statement of the obvious made her even angrier. The weeds were evidence that the garden needed attention, but his presumption was unten-able. 'I was going to weed it tomorrow.' She glanced up at the blister-ing sun. 'Early. Before it got too hot.'

He chuckled. 'It *is* hot. Almost too hot to breathe.'

'Which is my point, Mr Rainwater. Besides doing my work for me, which you shouldn't be, strenuous work like hoeing a garden can't be good for a man in your condition.'

His amusement evaporated, and his face became taut. 'I promise not to drop dead on your tomato plants.'

His tone struck her like a slap to the face. She may even have flinched, because immediately he let the hoe drop and took a step towards her. 'I'm sorry. Please forgive me. That was uncalled for.'

She was still too taken aback to speak.

'You think because I took it upon myself to hoe the garden that I'm suggesting you're not competent to do it?' he asked. 'Nothing of the sort, Mrs Barron. I didn't do it for you. I did it for me.'

She tilted her head up and looked into his face.

'I dislike inactivity. It makes the days pass slowly.' He flashed a rueful smile. 'You'd think I'd welcome the slow passage of time, but I deplore being idle. I want to keep active as long as I can.'

He stared at her for several beats. Then his shoulders sagged slightly. He picked up the hoe and retrieved his coat from the fence post. 'I'll replace this in the shed.'

As he walked past, she said, 'I didn't mean to sound so cross.'

He stopped and faced her. She was on eye level with his exposed neck, where he'd loosened his tie and unbuttoned his collar button. He smelled of sun and summer heat, of freshly turned loam.

'My boarders shouldn't do my chores.'

In a soft voice, he asked, 'Not even if doing a chore makes one happy? What's the harm in it, Mrs Barron?'

'The harm in it is, I don't want any upset of my routine.' Sounding desperate, she took a deep breath. 'If I allowed every boarder to do what he pleased, the house would be in chaos. I can't let—'

She was shocked into silence when he placed his hand on her shoulder. But before she had fully registered that he was touching her, she realised he was looking beyond her. Gently, he pushed her aside and rushed past. 'Brother Calvin?'

Ella turned to see the preacher sitting astride a mule. Legs dangling, Brother Calvin was slumped forward. As she watched, he let go of the rope serving as reins and slid to the ground.

When Mr Rainwater reached him, he turned the young preacher onto his back. Ella gasped. The preacher's face was bloody and swollen. She ran to the kitchen door and shouted for Margaret, then hurried back and dropped to her knees beside the two men.

'What happened to him?'

'Looks to me like he's been beaten,' Mr Rainwater replied.

Brother Calvin was bleeding from several cuts on his face and scalp. His clothing was torn. He was wearing only one shoe. He was conscious, but he was moaning, and his head lolled when Mr Rainwater gently levered him into a sitting position.

'Help me get him inside,' he said to Ella.

The man's size made it an effort. Mr Rainwater and Ella half carried, half dragged him to the back steps.

Margaret pushed open the screened door and upon seeing her beloved minister in that condition, began to shriek.

'Stop that!' Ella ordered. 'We need your help. Get his feet.'

The maid was struck silent. She tucked one of the preacher's feet under each arm, then backed up the steps. All three staggered under his weight, but they got him through the doorway.

Mr Rainwater said, 'Lower him to the floor.'

Brother Calvin continued to moan. 'Get towels and water,' Ella told Margaret. 'And fetch the Mercurochrome. Where's Solly?'

'Right behind you. I brought him with me when you called.'

Solly was sitting on the floor against the pantry door, tapping his shoes together, seemingly unaware of what was taking place.

Ella turned back to Brother Calvin, who groaned when Mr Rainwater's fingers probed a large lump on his temple. 'Should I call Dr Kincaid?'

'And the sheriff.'

'No!' Brother Calvin's eyes sprang open. In his right one, the brown iris floated in a pool of solid red. 'No. No doctor. No sheriff.'

He squeezed his eyes closed and groaned again. Margaret brought the basin of water. Ella bathed his wounds, then dabbed them with the antiseptic.

Eventually his groans subsided. They helped him into a chair at the table. 'Do you hurt anywhere inside?' Ella asked him.

'Ribs. A few may be cracked.'

Margaret slid a glass of tea within the preacher's reach. He picked it up and sipped from it. Ella noted that his knuckles were scraped and bloody. He must have landed some punches of his own.

'Who did this?' Mr Rainwater asked.

'They were shootin' cows.'

'Government men? From the Drought Relief Service?'

The preacher nodded.

'Whose herd was it?' Ella asked.

'Pritchett, his name is.'

She looked at Mr Rainwater. 'George Pritchett. His family has been operating that dairy farm for at least three generations.'

The federal government programme had been formulated earlier that year to protect farmers, dairymen and cattlemen from ruin. The worst drought in a hundred years had earned the Plains States the nickname of Dust Bowl. Land once farmed or used to graze cattle was now a vast wasteland, ravaged by wind and hordes of insects. Responding to the worsening emergency, Congress had allocated millions of dollars with which to buy animals from dairy farmers and cattlemen whose herds were starving to death. Agents were authorised to pay up to twenty dollars a head, which was far below market value during normal times but better than nothing in the crisis situation.

It seemed a viable programme. Livestock deemed healthy enough for consumption was shipped to the Federal Surplus Relief Corporation for slaughtering and processing. The canned meat was then distributed to transient communities, soup kitchens and breadlines. Farmers and ranchers earned something; hungry people were fed.

But there was also a disquieting aspect to the programme. The cattle that weren't culled from herds for meatpacking were destroyed and buried in pits at the point of purchase. It might be a rancher's whole herd or a farmer's single milk cow. While the programme had been designed to rescue families suffering the dual effects of the drought and the economic depression, seeing one's lifework destroyed in such a brutal fashion was heart-wrenching.

Brother Calvin continued, 'They picked out the fattest ones from the herd—weren't many—and loaded them on a truck. Hauled them off. The ones left, they herded into the bottom of a big hole that'd been dug. Six of them marksmen lined up along the rim of it. Mr Pritchett went inside the house with his wife and kids and closed the door. He couldn't bear to watch those cows get shot.'

In the telling of it, the preacher's rolling voice gained strength.

'Then they opened fire. First shots spooked the cows. They's bawling as they dropped. Cows, calves, ever' last one.'

It made Ella ill to think of such carnage. She said, 'I know it's necessary. It's intended to help. But it just seems so cruel.'

'Especially to the man who's toiled day and night building a herd,' Mr Rainwater said. 'Who beat you up, Brother Calvin?'

The man wiped his eyes with his scratched fist. 'Those folks in the shantytown heard about what was going to happen out at Mr Pritchett's place. They came. Coloureds and whites together. Joined up on account of they's all hungry. They came with knives and hatchets. Brought cooking pots, thinking they could butcher those cows, get what meat was to be had. But soon as those government men left, some locals moved in to see that the dead cows didn't get butchered. They's led by a rifle-toting white man with a purple birthmark on his face.'

'Conrad Ellis,' Ella said. 'He has a birthmark that covers most of his face. A port-wine stain, I think they call it. He's a bully; always has been.'

'He be meaner than sin,' said Margaret.

Ella went on, 'Mr Ellis, Conrad's father, owns a meatpacking plant. He buys from most of the local ranchers.'

'People getting free meat would be bad for his business,' Mr Rainwater remarked. 'So he sent his son out there to make sure those folks didn't get any.'

Ella frowned. 'Conrad wouldn't need an excuse. He enjoys beating up people. He's always spoiling for a fight.'

'Especially since—'

'Margaret.'

Ella's implied reprimand stopped the maid from saying more, but she looked madder than a hornet, mumbling, 'I'll put coffee on.'

Mr Rainwater caught a look passing between the two. Then Ella returned her attention to Brother Calvin, who was saying, 'That white boy was sure spoiling for a fight today. Soon as those government shooters cleared out, those shantytown people, me with them, ran down into that hole and started butchering those cows. Long as they were dead anyway, they could feed folks. That was my thinking. And Mr Pritchett's, too, 'cause he come back outside and was passing out knives to anybody who didn't have one.

'Then those boys roared up in a pick-up truck. They spilled out the back of it waving baseball bats and rifles and yelling for those folks to scatter. When nobody paid them any mind, they began knocking heads with the bats and the butts of their rifles.'

'Where was the law?'

'The sheriff and a carload of deputies were there. Watching, but doing nothing till Mr Pritchett took up a shotgun. He was shouting at those boys to leave those poor shantytown folks alone. Sheriff told him to put down that fool shotgun before he killed somebody.'

The preacher began weeping. 'That mean one with the birthmark went up on the porch and yanked a little boy out of Mrs Pritchett's arms. He threatened to bash that child's skull in if Mr Pritchett didn't lay down his shotgun and let him get on with making sure the government programme went off like it was s'pposed to. It was an awful sight.' He wiped his tears. 'Anyhow, seeing his wife goin' all hysterical and his baby boy's life threatened, Mr Pritchett give up. He dropped down on the steps of his porch and watched as those mean boys chased hungry folks back to the shantytown. All he could do was sit there and cry over that bloody mess left in his pasture.'

Ella asked, 'What happens now?'

'They'll be buried.'

Brother Calvin agreed to Mr Rainwater's explanation with a nod. 'There were front loaders parked down the road, ready to fill up the hole they'd dug.' He shook his head sorrowfully.

Mr Rainwater leaned across the table towards him. 'You were trying to help the shantytown people and got caught in the fray?'

'That's right. I go down there sometimes and hold services for those folks,' he explained. 'I encouraged them to be ready when those shooters went out to the Pritchett farm. I promised them meat. I didn't count on men threatening to brain little boys with baseball bats. I feel responsible for ever' blow struck.'

Ella laid a comforting hand on his forearm. 'You're not to blame, Brother Calvin. You were trying to help.' She looked across at Mr Rainwater. 'You know Dr Kincaid better than I do. Do you think he would go to the shantytown, treat people with the worst injuries?'

He stood up. 'I'll go now.'

'Stop back here before you leave for the shantytown. Margaret and I will gather some things.'

He nodded as he left through the back door.

ELLA WAS WAITING for them when Mr Rainwater returned half an hour later with Dr Kincaid. 'I need some help,' she called from the front porch.

The two men carried boxes of food, clothing and household items from the house and loaded them into Mr Rainwater's car. 'You did all this in the brief time I was gone?' he asked as he lifted a flour sack filled with clothing that Solly had outgrown.

'I've been collecting it for a while, waiting for the right time to give it away.'

While the men were stowing the things in the car, Ella rushed back into the kitchen, asking Margaret to keep an eye on Solly and promising to return in time to serve dinner. Then she grabbed her hat and went running out of the front door. 'Wait, I'm coming.'

'That isn't necessary, Mrs Barron,' the doctor said.

'I know it isn't necessary, but I can help.'

'Maybe Margaret would be better suited—'

'Margaret is a Negro, Dr Kincaid. I don't want to put her in danger of reprisal from a group of bigoted hoodlums.'

The doctor looked towards Mr Rainwater for reinforcement, but Mr Rainwater took her side. 'You can't argue with that, Murdy.'

The doctor clapped his hat on his head. 'Let's go, then. Mrs Kincaid is having a hissy fit as it is. She swore to send the law out looking for me if I wasn't back in an hour.'

But an hour wasn't nearly enough time to see everyone who had sustained an injury in the melee at the Pritchetts' farm.

Ella and Mr Rainwater doled out aspirin tablets to those with minor injuries, while the doctor treated the worst of them. He set the bones of grim-faced men. He bound bleeding wounds. He stitched what gashes he could with his limited supplies.

When all the wounded were treated, Ella and Mr Rainwater circulated among the patched tents, pasteboard boxes and rusty cars serving as shelters. They passed out clothing, cast-off household items and food they'd brought. The eyes of the people looking at Ella were either apathetic towards her generosity or pathetically grateful for it. She found both reactions equally disturbing.

When she'd given away everything she was carrying with her, she picked her way through the encampment back to Dr Kincaid. His shirt was dirty and damp with perspiration.

'We've done a little good, I think,' he remarked.

'Not enough.'

'No, never enough.' He smiled at Ella grimly.

'Will there be any pain?' Ella asked him.

He realised then that Ella was looking at Mr Rainwater. He was shaking hands with a man dressed in grimy overalls. At each of the man's legs was a grubby barefoot child clinging to the dirty denim of his daddy's trousers. The man was holding a third child in his arms. Ella had heard him telling Mr Rainwater that his wife had died of tuberculosis a week ago and that he didn't know how he was going to look for work and take care of his children at the same time.

She turned to Dr Kincaid, her question hovering between them.

'Yes,' he said.

A shudder passed through her. 'Can you give him something?'

'When he asks for it, yes.'

'Will he? Ask.'

The doctor watched his kinsman winding his way round huddles of people. 'Yes,' the doctor replied bleakly. 'He will.'

THE SUNDAY FOLLOWING the incident at the Pritchetts' farm, someone driving a pick-up truck threw a bottle through a window of the African Methodist Episcopal church during the evening worship service. Beyond shattering a large pane of glass, it did no other harm. Leaving a wake of shouted racial slurs and a cloud of dust, the pick-up sped away.

Brother Calvin's melodious voice kept his congregation under control. None of the women panicked; none of the men went after the pick-up. Brother Calvin continued his sermon and, by the conclusion of the service, had added ten converts to his flock.

It was first believed that the attack on the church was racially motivated. That opinion changed when, the next night, two tents in the shantytown went up in flames and a bag of manure was dumped into the creek from which the people there drew their water. It seemed the bigotry extended to poor whites and hoboes, too.

But after those incidents, Conrad Ellis and his crowd apparently lost interest in organised terrorism. They reverted to their customary forms of mischief making—reckless driving, public intoxication and behaving obnoxiously at every opportunity.

The mass grave at the Pritchett farm was barely noticeable from the road, but the incident was still fresh on everyone's mind. Other dairy farmers in the region were selling their herds to the Federal Surplus Relief Corporation's agents, but none of those transactions had sparked incidents.

No one blamed a man for trying to make the most of a dire situation. Many townsfolk admired Mr Pritchett, who had denounced Sheriff Anderson for standing by and doing nothing when the ruffians turned a terrible situation into a life-threatening melee. Others were outspoken in their contempt for Mr Ellis and his ilk, who would actually profit from the programme, while cattlemen and farmers were left with nothing with which to rebuild.

Rumours spread rampantly. Tempers were short and tension was high. Everyone seemed to be waiting for something bad to happen. Dread was as oppressive as the unrelenting heat.

ONE EVENING as he studied the chessboard, waiting for Mr Rainwater to make his move, Mr Hastings remarked, 'Sticky today.'

Mr Rainwater limited his response to an absentminded nod.

Ella had been baking all day, so even after the sun went down, the kitchen remained a hotbox. She had asked the gentlemen if they minded her and Solly sharing the front parlour with them, where the small electric fan at least stirred the sultry air.

Mr Hastings had answered for both of them. 'Of course not.'

She'd settled into a chair and situated Solly on the floor beside her, where he played with spools of thread while she mended.

Mr Hastings took a sip from his glass of iced tea and, continuing his one-sided conversation, said, 'Humid as it is, it could storm before daybreak. Dare I think we might actually see rain?'

Mr Rainwater thoughtfully moved a chess piece. 'If I didn't know better,' he said slowly, 'I'd think you were trying to distract me with all this talk of the weather.'

'Guilty,' Hastings chuckled. 'You improve with each game.'

'But you still outplay me.'

'Not for long, is my guess.'

Mr Rainwater smiled at him, but Ella also caught his gaze shifting to Solly. She had become aware that Mr Rainwater spent as much time studying Solly as he did the chessboard. Solly had been playing quietly, but it suddenly occurred to her that he might be a distraction, preventing her boarders from fully enjoying their game.

Hastily she replaced her thread and scissors in the sewing basket.

Mr Rainwater, noticing, asked, 'Are you finished?'

'For tonight.'

Mr Hastings turned round in his seat. 'Are you leaving us, Mrs Barron? I was enjoying your company.'

She smiled wanly, grateful to him for the polite lie. 'It's time I put Solly to bed.'

She bent down to gather up the spools of thread that he'd been playing with. He protested when she wrested one from his hand and dropped it into the basket. 'Time for bed, Solly,' she said, praying he would go without creating a scene. Her prayer was in vain.

Solly began the high-pitched whine that signalled he was distressed. He raised his hands and began flapping them against his ears as the whine intensified into a full-blown screech.

Ella picked him up and wrapped her arms round him in an effort to pin his waving hands and kicking feet to her body.

'I apologise for the interruption, gentlemen. Good night.'

Carrying Solly, she rushed to her bedroom and closed the door, hoping the heavy oak would block the terrible sound issuing from her boy. She clutched him to her, shushing him, whispering a litany of comforting words, yet knowing the uselessness of them. He was tortured by demons against which she was powerless.

Each time something like this happened, it increased her fear that she wouldn't be able to protect Solly from being institutionalised. What if Mr Rainwater reported this episode to Dr Kincaid? What if the doctor took matters into his own hands and notified authorities of the dangers Solly's fits posed?

Short of that, if this continued to happen, she might lose boarders. Kind as they were, there was a limit to their tolerance for these outbursts. She couldn't afford to lose good, permanent boarders.

After catching her breath, she carried Solly into the small room in which he slept. Closing the door made the room even hotter, but the door would remain closed until she got him calmed down.

But nothing she did stopped his hand-flapping or his squeal. In the end, she left him long enough to rush back into the formal parlour and, ignoring the anxious eyes of the two men, retrieve her sewing basket. When she returned to Solly's bedroom, she upturned the basket onto his bed, spilling the contents onto it.

He stopped screeching instantly. Picking out two spools, he set them carefully on the floor. Then, one by one, he replaced the items scattered across his bed in the basket. When he was done, he set the basket on the floor, climbed up onto his bed, lay his head on the pillow and closed his eyes. He was asleep within seconds.

Ella fell back against the wall and slid down it until she was sitting on the floor. She was exhausted. Bending her head low, she picked the pins from her hair, relieving her neck from the weight of the tight bun. She looked into the sleeping face of her son, and her heart constricted with love and a twinge of pity. She wondered if perhaps sleep was the only state in which he found his own peace.

Gently, she touched Solly's hand. Barely making contact, she ran her finger across his eyelashes, then along the rim of his ear.

He didn't stir. These were the moments of her life most precious to her, when she could luxuriate in touching her child without being rebuffed. During the hours that others slept in her house, she often spent time in this tiny cell of a room that had bars on its only window to prevent escape. She passed many dark nights caressing Solly, imagining a day when he would look at her and smile with recognition and reciprocated love.

It was a ridiculous hope. But she clung to it nonetheless.

ONLY ONE CLAP OF THUNDER preceded the rain. It didn't start with a few sprinkles. It fell suddenly and violently, an instant downpour.

In a heartbeat, Ella was up. She grabbed her robe and left her room. The hallway was dark, but flashes of lightning provided intermittent illumination as she rushed towards the formal parlour.

Carefully she felt her way across the room to the west wall, where the tall windows remained open. Rain had already doused the sills. Quickly she closed the corner window and moved to the next.

She made her way down the row, shutting out the pelting rain. Jagged bolts of lightning opened up cracks in the black sky. When the last window had been closed, she left the twin parlours and went to the front door. It was protected by the first-floor balcony but rain had been wind-driven across the porch and through the screen. The wind was so strong she felt resistance when she closed the solid door against it. She flipped the lock to secure it, rested against it for a moment, then turned.

He was standing on the bottom tread of the staircase, his right hand on the newel post. Only one button in the centre of his shirt was done up. He hadn't taken time to tuck in his shirt-tail. His braces formed loops against his thighs. His feet were bare.

Ella knew she must look as dishevelled as he, maybe more so. Her hair was wildly curling round her face, a tangled mane down her back. Her robe was damp from rain. The wet hem of it clung to her ankles, reminding her she was barefoot.

All this registered with her in a matter of seconds, during which it seemed that her breath had been snatched from her body. A lightning bolt struck dangerously close. The thunder that followed shook the house. The back door slammed shut, echoing the thunderclap.

Even then, neither of them moved. Their eyes stayed locked. Ella's heart felt on the verge of bursting.

She said hoarsely, 'The storm finally broke.'

He held her stare for several moments longer, slowly shaking his head. 'No, it didn't.'

She drew in a tremulous breath and forced her feet to move.

As she went past him towards her room, he added quietly, 'Not yet.'

AS SOON AS BREAKFAST had been served, Ella and Margaret went outside to clear up the debris left by the storm. Ella was surprised to find Brother Calvin gathering tree limbs and heaping them into the ditch that ran along her property line.

She looked at Margaret accusingly, but her maid shrugged. 'I didn't send for him.'

'That's true, Mrs Barron. I came on my own, hoping to help.'

She had relented and let him paint the shutters. He'd also been paid to do other chores that required more strength and time than she had. 'I can't afford another employee,' she told him now, even as he sawed a broken limb from the pecan tree.

'No charge. I owe you.'

When the damaged limb fell free from the tree trunk, he turned and looked at her. She saw that the white of one of his eyes still had a spot of red in it. Realising that this was a matter of honour to him, she assented with a nod. 'I appreciate your help, Brother Calvin.'

'That storm was all bluster. Ground's hardly damp.'

Ella had heard on the radio that morning that rainfall amounts were barely measurable. It hadn't put an end to the drought.

The preacher motioned towards the ditch. 'Later today I'll burn this brush for you. There's more to add to the pile.'

'Come to the kitchen at lunchtime. Margaret will feed you.'

'I thank you, ma'am.'

Ella was busy the rest of the morning, seeing to it that the windowsills and floors that had been rained on the night before were mopped and dried.

The noon meal was served; then she sent Margaret to the store with a shopping list. By mid-afternoon, Ella had pork chops braising on the stove and was putting finishing touches on a banana pudding when she realised that Solly was no longer in the kitchen with her.

'Solly!' She burst out of the kitchen and raced towards the front door, through which he'd ventured once before.

'In here.'

She retraced her steps, stopping when she reached the arched opening into the informal parlour. Mr Rainwater was sitting on the floor, a set of dominoes scattered in front of him. Beside him was Solly, watching intently as Mr Rainwater picked up a domino and stood it on end in perfect alignment with the previous one.

'What—'

'Shh. He's OK. Watch.'

Any other time, she would resent being shushed, but she was so intrigued by Solly's apparent concentration, she stepped into the room and lowered herself onto the nearest chair.

Mr Rainwater continued to add dominoes to the snaking line he had formed. Solly's eyes followed every motion of his hands.

'I noticed last night how he was playing with the spools. Stacking them, placing them in perfect juxtaposition.' Although Mr Rainwater was speaking to Ella, he didn't look up at her. His concentration on placing the dominoes was as intense as Solly's. 'Seeing that gave me this idea.'

To prevent any false impressions, she said, 'He does that with other things, Mr Rainwater. Toothpicks. Buttons. Bottle caps. Anything uniform in shape.'

Rather than dim his enthusiasm, her statement seemed to validate his optimism. 'Really?' Smiling, he continued to add to the column of dominoes. Solly remained transfixed. He seemed not to notice that his knee was touching Mr Rainwater's.

When all the dominoes had been placed, Mr Rainwater withdrew his hands and then sat motionless.

Solly stared at the line of dominoes for the better part of a minute before he extended his index finger to the last one in the line and nudged it. It toppled, creating a contagion until all were down.

Ella stood up. 'Thank you for watching him.'

Mr Rainwater raised his hand. 'Wait.' Moving slowly, he began to turn the dominoes over so that they lay with the dots down. Then he shuffled them as though he was about to start a game. When they were spread out, he sat back again. 'Your turn, Solly.'

The boy sat, staring at the dominoes for a long time before he reached for one and stood it on its end.

Ella knew that her son had responded not to his name but to his mysterious inner urging to line up the dominoes. It was that trait, his insistence on uniformity and order, and his violent outbursts if things weren't in that particular order, that had first signalled to her that he was different from other children. Normal children left their playthings helter-skelter.

'He wasn't always like he is now.'

Mr Rainwater looked up at her.

'He was a perfectly normal baby,' she continued. 'He reacted normally to voices and sounds. He recognised me and his father; Margaret; the boarders who were living here then. He laughed. He walked at thirteen months. He was just like every other baby.'

She looked down and realised that she was clutching her apron.

'But during his twos, when most children are asserting their independence, Solly seemed to retreat. He stopped responding when we played games. Once his attention was focused on something, we couldn't draw it away, and he became distressed when we tried.

'His awareness of what was going on around him decreased. His fits became more frequent. The rocking, the hand-flapping became constant. Each day, my sweet, smart baby boy slipped further away from me, until he disappeared entirely.' She looked at Mr Rainwater and raised her shoulder. 'I never got him back.'

He'd listened without moving. Now he looked down at Solly. 'Murdy thinks he should be placed in a facility.'

She went on the defensive. 'The two of you discussed my child?'

'I asked him why Solly is the way he is.'

'Why? Mr Rainwater, your curiosity is—'

'Not curiosity, concern.'

'Why should you be concerned about a boy who, up till a few weeks ago, you didn't even know existed?'

'Because the first time I saw him, he had pulled a pan of hot starch onto himself.'

Would she have preferred that he not be concerned about a child who'd burned himself? No. Nevertheless, his interest offended her. She'd thought he was different from gawking strangers. He wasn't. He was merely too well mannered to ask rude questions and stare. But discussing Solly with the doctor was equally contemptible.

'If you wanted to know about Solly, why didn't you ask me?'

'Because I sensed that you would react exactly as you are.'

His reasonable tone only emphasised how uneven hers was. She couldn't help but wonder what else the doctor had told him about her. It was infuriating, the two of them talking about her.

As though reading her mind, he said, 'We weren't gossiping, Mrs Barron. I asked Murdy a few questions, and he explained.'

'Did he enlist you to persuade me to put Solly away?'

'No.'

'I will never have Solly locked up in an institution.'

He nodded. 'That's a very courageous decision.'

She stood. 'It will be dinnertime soon. I have work to do.' She knelt down beside Solly, ready to pick him up.

To her consternation, her boarder laid a hand on her arm. 'Please. Look. Tell me what you notice.'

Solly had finished lining up all the dominoes and was staring at the serpentine row. As she watched, he gently poked the one at the end. It took only seconds for them to topple just as they had before.

Missing Mr Rainwater's point, she looked at him inquisitively.

He said, 'Notice the dots.'

It took only a few seconds for her to see what he wanted her to, and when she did, gooseflesh broke out on her arms. Her heart hitched. She made a small, involuntary sound of astonishment.

The dominoes had been scattered on the floor, facedown. Yet Solly had selected them one by one and lined them up in numerical order, from the double blank to the double six.

Her breath coming quickly, she turned to Mr Rainwater. 'How did you teach him to do that?'

His smile widened. 'I didn't.'

Four

'They're called idiot savants.'

It was the day following the discovery of Solly's remarkable ability. Last evening Ella and Mr Rainwater had tested him several times. He had never failed to place the dominoes in ascending order.

That morning, Ella had dispatched Margaret to the doctor's office with a note briefly describing what had taken place the night before and asking if she could bring Solly in for a consultation as soon as possible.

She purposely didn't use the telephone to communicate with the doctor, mistrusting the operator, who was notorious for listening in on conversations. Until she had an explanation for Solly's rare talent, she didn't want town gossips whispering about it.

Dr Kincaid had sent back a message with Margaret that he would see them at three o'clock, which was after regular office hours. Mr Rainwater had asked if he could accompany them, and Ella had consented. They rode to town in his car.

They'd been shown into a cramped office by Mrs Kincaid, who told them that the doctor would be with them soon. They'd been waiting only a minute or two when the doctor came in, bringing a box of dominoes with him.

Ella felt her pulse rise when Mr Rainwater went through the ritual of shuffling and placing the dominoes on the doctor's scarred desktop, then turning them facedown. But Solly performed as he had the day before. Dr Kincaid shook his head in wonderment, then leaned back in his squeaky chair and made his startling and offensive statement.

'Idiot savant?' Ella repeated.

'It's a disagreeable term. But until the medical community comes up with a better one, that's the name for this particular anomaly.'

'Anomaly,' she said, testing the word. 'What is it, precisely?'

'*Precisely*, no one knows.' Dr Kincaid motioned to the medical book on his desk, which was open. 'Are you familiar with the term IQ—intelligence quotient? It's a relatively new term referring to the measurement of one's mental capacity.'

She and Mr Rainwater said they'd heard of it.

'Today we would deem a person with an IQ of twenty or below uneducably mentally retarded. But for centuries, someone with that limited a capacity was known as an idiot.' The doctor slid on a pair of reading glasses and consulted the text. 'Late in the nineteenth century, a German doctor studied individuals with classic mental retardation, either from birth or resulting from injury, who also possessed uncanny skills. Usually they were mathematical, musical or memory-related talents. He combined the term for people with extremely low intelligence with the French word for an extremely learned individual and derived the term idiot savant.'

'And that's what Solly is?' Ella was eager to know more.

Dr Kincaid removed his eyeglasses. 'I don't know that for certain, Mrs Barron. I've heard about idiot savants, but until your note described to me what Solly did with the dominoes, I had little knowledge of the classification. I looked it up for this visit.

'And frankly,' he continued, 'I'm still in the dark. Information on the subject is scarce. No one has provided a definitive explanation of how this anomaly occurs, or why. Does something happen in the womb, or is it post-natal in origin?' He shrugged.

Ella hesitated, then said, 'Rarely a day goes by that I don't ask myself if Solly is this way because of something I did or didn't do.' It was a hard admission to make.

Dr Kincaid gave her a smile. 'I can almost assure you no, Mrs Barron. If it happened in the womb, it was an unavoidable accident of nature. I assisted you with his birth, and nothing out of the ordinary happened. If, when he was an infant, Solly had suffered an injury or illness severe enough to cause brain damage, you would have known it. The theories concerning the causes of his condition are so widely varied that none have substance. At least, not in my opinion.'

'Solly was developing as other children do.'

Dr Kincaid laid his hand on the open text. 'It's a matter of record that symptoms generally begin showing up around the age Solly was when you started noticing them.'

Ella looked at her son where he sat, rocking back and forth from his waist up, locked inside a realm she couldn't breach. Mr Rainwater asked the question forming in her mind.

'Do these people ever recover, Murdy?'

Dr Kincaid consulted the open textbook again, but Ella thought he was buying time, not really seeking an answer to the question.

'The documented cases wouldn't fill a thimble. The only thing they have in common is that there's little commonality. Each individual is different. Their symptoms and the severity of them vary. Some do learn language skills, but they rarely apply their superior knowledge to any practical use.'

Mr Rainwater asked him to elaborate.

The doctor thought for a moment. 'For instance, an individual who has demonstrated amazing powers of recall might read one of Shakespeare's plays once and be able to quote it verbatim. He doesn't do that for any reason other than because he can. He has no interest in the material whatso-ever. The words would mean no more to him than the listings in the phone book. If he reads it, he knows it. However, it's not something he seeks to do for enlightenment.'

'But he *can* read Shakespeare,' Ella said.

The doctor must have detected her hopeful inflection. 'Some do read. Others don't read, speak or communicate, while, miraculously, they can play difficult compositions on the piano after hearing them only once. Some can solve complicated mathematical problems quickly.' He raised his hands, palms up.

'The truth is, I'm delighted that you've discovered Solly's special gift. But I can't explain it or speculate on how beneficial it will be to him. I wouldn't dare give you false hope that he'll eventually acquire language skills. I simply don't know, Mrs Barron. And I fear that no one else does, either.'

DR KINCAID'S SUMMARY of Solly's condition should have dampened Ella's excitement over his incredible skill, but she didn't let it. She considered this a tremendous milestone in her attempts to reach her son. It represented to her a small crack in the wall behind which his mind and personality were barricaded.

Having found that small chink, she set her mind to prying it wider. Her heart's desire was to have some channel of communication between them, no matter how narrow.

Each day, she stole time away from her chores to spend with him. Replicating the dots on dominoes, she drew sets of dots on paper, then handed the pencil to Solly, hoping he would draw his own groups of dots and from there learn that a set of dots represented a particular number and that numbers could be added and subtracted.

But he never took hold of the pencil. When she covered his hand with hers and tried to guide the pencil, he threw a tantrum. Banging his head against hers, he caused a bruise on her chin that was visible for days. For the time being, she went back to the dominoes.

One evening Solly was seated on the kitchen floor lining up the dominoes while she folded towels and washcloths. Mr Rainwater came in to return a used coffee cup.

He remarked, 'I see Solly hasn't lost interest.'

'No. But he hasn't advanced, either.' She explained her frustration over her son's failure to understand that he could draw domino dots on paper. 'I was hoping he would come to understand that the dots represent a number and that numbers mean something.'

'Maybe he does understand. If he didn't, why would he always put the dominoes in order? Would you mind if I worked with him?'

'Doing what?'

He raised a shoulder. 'I don't know. I'll have to think about it.'

The vagueness of his reply made her uneasy. She was about to say no when she remembered the many kindnesses he had extended to Solly. He seemed to have a genuine and unselfish interest in him. She also was thinking about the day he was hoeing up weeds for lack of something better to do. Mr Rainwater needed to feel useful.

She consented, but with a condition. 'If he becomes anxious—'

'I'll stop whatever we're doing. I promise.'

THREE DAYS LATER Ella came in from outside, her apron full of tomatoes and yellow squash she'd picked in the garden. Margaret was peeling potatoes. 'We can't eat all these tomatoes.' Ella carefully spilled them onto the kitchen table. 'And I've got plenty canned already. Put these with the stuff going to the shantytown tonight.'

'Yes, ma'am.'

Ella pushed back strands of hair that had escaped her bun.

'Is Solly still with Mr Rainwater?'

'In the back parlour doing they's lessons.'

Ella opened the icebox. 'One of us will need to go to the store tomorrow. Remind me to add a pound of butter to the grocery list.'

'Mr Rainwater sure is nice to be taking such notice of our Solly. Why do you reckon that is?'

'We need mayonnaise, too. And some bologna. If you're the one who goes, ask Mr Randall to slice it more thinly this time, please.'

'He sure be different.'

Ella knew Margaret wasn't referring to the grocer. She headed for the door, pretending not to hear her maid's remark. 'I'm going to check on Solly; then I'll get that squash ready to bake.'

Ella continued on to the parlour. Solly and Mr Rainwater were seated in adjacent chairs at the card table. When she walked in, Mr Rainwater looked up at her and smiled. 'I think you're wrong.'

'About what?'

'I think Solly does grasp the concept of numbers. Watch.'

She moved closer. A deck of playing cards had been scattered facedown over the table. The twos of each suit were neatly stacked; so were the threes and fours. As she watched, Solly picked all the fives from the scattered cards, starting with the club, then the spade, the heart and the diamond last. He lined up the edges evenly and placed the group beside the stack of fours. He did the same with the sixes and sevens, choosing them unseen from the scattered deck, picking them out in the same sequence.

Ella wasn't all that encouraged. 'He remembers where each card is on the table. It's a miracle, but he's not really learning. He's only matching the pattern of clubs on a card with the pattern of spades on another and so on. What he's doing really has nothing to do with the quantities and how they relate.'

'I'm not so sure. Cards, unlike dominoes, have the numbers printed on them. Keep watching.'

Solly continued until he had stacked the tens beside the nines. Then he sat back and began to rock.

Ella looked at Mr Rainwater, then at the cards still lying facedown on the table. 'He didn't pick face cards or aces.'

'They don't have numerals.'

She sat down in the chair adjacent to Solly. Gathering the stacks Solly had made, along with the cards still on the table, she shuffled the deck, then spread the cards out, first faceup, then turned them over until all fifty-two were facedown.

Solly watched intently. As soon as all the cards were turned over, he actually pushed her hands aside so he could begin. He collected all the twos and proceeded until his stack of tens was placed neatly beside the stack of nines. He left the face cards and the aces.

Mr Rainwater looked at Ella, his eyebrow cocked. 'He knows the numerals represent the amount of symbols on each card, and he knows the sequence of the numbers. Four is greater than three.'

Still doubtful, she murmured, 'Possibly.'

'He does.'

'How do you know?'

'Before you came in, I removed the fours from the deck. He stopped at three and didn't proceed until I'd returned the fours to the cards scattered on the table. I did it again with the eights. He stopped at seven, and that time, he reached into my coat pocket and took out the eights, arranged them in his sequence—clubs, spades, hearts, diamonds—and went from there.'

Almost more miraculous to her was that Solly had voluntarily touched someone. 'He reached into your pocket?'

Mr Rainwater smiled. 'With no guidance from me.'

Her gaze shifted back to Solly. Reflexively, she stroked his cheek and said, 'Good job, Solly.' He batted her hand away, but she hoped that, in some recess of his brain, her love registered.

Looking back at the man across the table, she said, 'Thank you for spending so much time with him.'

'My pleasure.'

'If he can learn to recognise numbers, he might be able to learn letters. He could learn simple arithmetic; he could learn to read.'

'That's my thinking.'

'At least there's hope. There's always hope, right?'

His smile slipped a fraction. 'Not always. But sometimes.'

THE FOLLOWING MORNING, Ella was in the dining room clearing the breakfast dishes when Margaret burst through the door of the kitchen. Her hat was askew, and she was trying to catch her breath.

'What in the world!' Ella exclaimed.

Mr Rainwater surged to his feet. 'What's wrong?'

'I heard it at the store,' Margaret gasped. 'There may be trouble out the Thompsons' place.'

'Ollie and Lola's?' Ella asked.

'That's right. Your friends.'

'I must go.' Her heart in her throat, Ella gave her apron strings a yank, and when the apron came off, she ran through the door connecting the dining room and kitchen.

She put on her hat, then knelt down and lifted Solly out of the chair where he sat tapping his cereal spoon against the table. 'Finish up breakfast, Margaret. Put the groceries away. If I'm not back by lunchtime—'

'You go on,' Margaret said. 'I'll take care of things here.'

'I'll drive you.' Mr Rainwater had followed them into the kitchen.

'No. I'll take my car.'

'Your car ain't been started since—' Margaret began.

'I can drive myself, Margaret,' Ella snapped.

'But my car is parked out front.'

Ella caught a look between her maid and her boarder, who'd extended the commonsense offer of taking his car, which was newer, more reliable and easily accessible. 'Thank you, Mr Rainwater.' She preceded him down the hallway, carrying Solly, who was now tapping his spoon against her shoulder.

'THEY'RE YOUR FRIENDS?'

Ella had tucked Solly between her and Mr Rainwater in the front seat of his car. She'd given him directions out of town. He was driving fast.

'We went through school in the same class, although they dropped out in tenth grade. Ollie's daddy died, leaving him to take over the management of the dairy. He was the youngest child and the only boy. All his sisters were married and long gone.

'There was never any doubt that he and Lola would get married. They'd always been crazy about each other. They've got four children now. They're good people. Take a right at the crossroads.'

The road onto which Mr Rainwater turned was unpaved.

Tall weeds grew in the ditches on both sides. Beyond the ditches, barbed-wire fences separated rows of corn struggling for survival in the arid soil.

It wasn't yet ten o'clock, but Ella guessed that already the temperature was topping ninety. The wind was hot. It had whipped off Ella's hat and was tearing at her hair, but she barely noticed.

Her thoughts were on her friends and their misfortune. With each baby, Lola had grown a little chubbier, and the gap between her front teeth seemed to widen, but she was one of the happiest individuals Ella had ever known. She loved her husband, loved her children, loved her life.

Ollie was a salt-of-the-earth type, big-eared and big-hearted. He'd struggled to pass from one school grade to the next because of all the days he had to miss in order to help his father work their farm. But Ollie had given up school willingly. Know-how had been more valuable to him than book learning, and his hands-on experience had paid off. He took pride in how much the farm had prospered.

At least, until the past few years, when he'd been forced to borrow money to sustain his herd and his family until the drought ended. What milk he could get from his underfed cows, he'd had to sell cheap, creating a need for another loan. That vicious cycle had put him and Lola deeply in debt and in danger of losing their farm. They would benefit greatly from the programme to buy their herd for pennies on the dollar, but at what cost emotionally?

Mr Rainwater said, 'I'm afraid we're too late.'

Ella spotted the cloud of dust rising out of the roadbed almost at the same time he spoke. 'What is it?'

'A convoy, I suspect.'

The distance between them and the on-coming column of swirling dust closed rapidly. In the lead was a cattle truck with dairy cows crammed inside. Following it were three black cars, all with insignias painted on the sides. One man in the first car was standing on the running board, holding on to a rifle propped on his shoulder.

'Are they the—'

'Shooters,' Mr Rainwater said, finishing for her.

Over the roar of the passing cars, she heard another sound, which at first she thought was one of the cars backfiring. But when Mr Rainwater said a swear word under his breath, she noticed how tightly he was gripping the steering wheel.

'What's that popping noise?'

'Gunfire.'

She watched as the government cars disappeared behind a swell in the road. The gunshots weren't coming from them. So who was shooting? A cold knot of fear formed in her chest.

'Hurry,' she urged. 'It's the next left.'

Just before they reached the turnoff to the Thompsons' farm, a pick-up spun out onto the road, made a sharp turn and headed straight towards them. It stayed in their lane until the last moment, then, with a blast of the horn, it swerved to cross the yellow stripe.

The truck buffeted Mr Rainwater's coupé as it zoomed past. Ella recognised the man at the wheel—Conrad Ellis. There were a dozen men in the truck bed, laughing, whooping, firing pistols into the air.

Mr Rainwater took the left turn virtually on two wheels. It was a quarter of a mile between the main road and the farmhouse. Mr Rainwater kept the accelerator on the floorboard until they were even with a pasture where a large pit had been dug. He braked suddenly. The car skidded several yards before it came to a stop.

Mr Rainwater got out and walked round the bonnet of the car. He surveyed the mass grave. Solly seemed content to be tapping the toes of his shoes together, so Ella got out, too.

When Brother Calvin had recounted the incident at the Pritchetts' farm, he'd described the scene vividly. But the preacher's graphic depiction hadn't adequately prepared Ella for what she saw. Several dozen scrawny cows and calves had been herded into the pit and shot through their heads. It was a sickening sight.

'This is the damnedest thing.'

She realised that Mr Rainwater was speaking mostly to himself, and anyway, what could she possibly add? Shading her eyes against the sun, she looked towards the willow trees where two tractors with front loaders were parked. The men operating them were waiting in the shade before finishing their job of burial. One was smoking a cigarette. The other had pulled his hat low over his face, dozing.

Ella had to remind herself that they, and the marksmen, too, were just men, doing a tough job during tough times. Nevertheless, she felt as though they were the enemy.

Turning away, she checked on Solly, who was still fixated on tapping his shoes together, then started walking up the incline towards the house. A white picket fence enclosed the yard. The house was also white, but it was now pockmarked with black dots. Ella realised with shock that these were fresh bullet holes. When she reached the fence, she saw that the gate had been torn off.

Lola was sitting on the porch swing, her hands to her face, crying into her apron. Two solemn-faced children sat, one on either side of her. The boy, obviously the older, was dry-eyed but much too young for the embittered expression on his smooth face.

The little girl was resting one hand on her mother's knee. Tear tracks were on her cheeks. She stopped crying as she watched Ella cross the yard and climb the steps onto the porch.

'Ollie.'

He was sitting on the top step, his beefy shoulders hunched, his work boots planted on the step below. He was holding a Colt pistol in his right hand, but the gun seemed on the verge of slipping from his grasp. He was staring into space, seemingly unaware of Ella's approach, but when she spoke his name, he looked at her with haunted eyes.

'Ella. What are you doing out here?'

'I came . . . I came to lend whatever support I can.'

His gaze shifted to the car parked in the lane, still a distance from the house. He spotted Mr Rainwater where he stood staring forlornly at the crater in the pasture. 'Who's that?'

Mr Rainwater couldn't have heard them from that distance, but just as Ollie asked about him, he turned away from the gruesome sight and started walking towards the house.

'A distant cousin of Dr Kincaid's. He's staying in town for a while. He's boarding with me.'

They watched Mr Rainwater as he walked up the lane and through the damaged gate. As he entered the yard, Ella was struck by how thin he was compared to Ollie.

'Mr Thompson?' he said as he approached. 'David Rainwater.'

Ollie stared at the right hand extended to him as though unsure what to do with it. Then he shifted the revolver to his left hand and shook hands. 'Ollie Thompson.'

'I hate that we're meeting under these circumstances.'

'Yeah, me too.' With an effort, Ollie pulled himself up.

'We saw the cattle truck. Did they pay you fairly?' Mr Rainwater asked.

'Going rate. Sixteen a head, plus a three-dollar bonus on each. I'm glad to get it. I applied for the relief. But hell, it was awful.'

Ella left the men to their solemn conversation and moved to the swing. Lola blotted her eyes and gave Ella a weak version of her gap-toothed smile. She patted her son on the back. 'Scoot,' she said to him. 'Let Mrs Barron sit down.'

The boy jumped off the porch and disappeared round the house.

'He's upset,' Lola said as Ella sat down on the swing beside her. 'I hope he'll get over it.'

Ella smiled at the little girl, who gave her a shy smile back. 'Where are your other children?'

'I called my mama and told her to come and get them and keep them until the cows are buried. These two are having a hard enough time with it. I didn't want the younger two seeing something they can't understand.'

'What happened?'

Tears welled up in the woman's eyes. 'The men with the tractors got here just after daylight. It didn't take them long to dig the hole. Then the men in the government cars arrived and sorted the herd. Loaded the healthier ones onto the truck. The rest . . .' She nodded towards the pit as Ollie and Mr Rainwater joined them.

'Forty head,' Ollie said. There were tears standing in his eyes now. 'I had no choice,' he said, his voice cracking. 'I gotta make a loan payment or lose this place. This is my daddy's place. I had to save it.'

He was unable to go on, so Lola continued for him. 'Soon's the government men got them into the pit, they started shootin'. Those poor mama cows and their babies.' She began crying in earnest.

'What about the truckload of rabble-rousers?'

'We saw Conrad on the road,' Ella said, clarifying Mr Rainwater's question.

Ollie spat into the dirt off the porch. 'White trash son'bitch.'

'Ollie,' Lola said, nodding towards their daughter.

'Well, he is. For all the money he and his daddy have, they're trash. That whole branch of Ellises is rotten to the core.'

'What were they doing here?' Mr Rainwater asked.

'What I think is, those government cowards brung them along, just in case.' Ollie spat again.

'In case of what?' Mr Rainwater asked.

'I tried bargaining with the head guy,' Ollie said angrily. 'Told him he didn't have to turn his shooters loose, that I'd get rid of those cows myself. Told him I'd take the best of the lot to the shantytown. Let those folks have at least one good meal for their kids.

'But no. He said he had orders to shoot and bury those that were culled and I couldn't stop him. "Fine," I said. "You go ahead and be the goverment's whore."' He wiped tears from his eyes. ''Course, I'm a whore, too, I reckon, for taking his damn cheque.'

'Hush that talk right now, Ollie! You did what you had to.'

He looked at his wife remorsefully. 'Don't make it right, Lola.' He paused before continuing, 'I guess the man didn't take me at my word, because while they were shooting the cows, Conrad and his bunch had their guns trained on us, like we was going to try and stop them. When it was over, the government men left. But before Conrad peeled out, he and his cronies shot up my house.'

Mr Rainwater's eyes picked out several splintered bullet holes in the wood. 'Why?'

'Meanness, I guess.' Ollie ran his sleeve under his nose. 'Or else to scare me into doing nothin', which is what I did.' He glanced in the direction of where his son had rounded the corner of the house. 'Made my boy ashamed of me, I think.'

'What could you have done, Ollie?' Lola asked, her staunch loyalty showing. 'Picked a fight with Conrad and got us all shot?'

'She's right,' Mr Rainwater said.

Ella told them what had happened when Mr Pritchett tried to face him down. 'We had an eyewitness tell us how he grabbed the child right out of Mrs Pritchett's arms.'

'If he'd laid a hand on Lola or one of my kids, I'd've killed him,' Ollie said.

Speaking to Mr Rainwater, Lola said, 'One of the calves didn't die right away. Conrad and his friends heard it bawling. They stood at the rim of the pit, laughing and chucking rocks down at it.'

'Like I said,' Ollie muttered. 'Trash.'

'Ollie went inside the house to get his pistol and put the poor thing outta its misery. But those boys wouldn't let Ollie go near that pit. Finally the calf died, I guess. He stopped bawling. Conrad and his friends piled into that pick-up of his and left.'

'Party over.'

Ella noticed that whenever Mr Rainwater was extremely angry, his lips barely moved when he spoke. He caught her looking at him now. She quickly diverted her gaze to Ollie.

He said, 'Them cows would have died soon anyway. They were starving. But seeing them shot like that was terrible.'

Ella laid her hand on Lola's arm. 'Is there anything I can do?'

To everyone's surprise, she chuckled. 'You can get on your knees and thank the Lord that Ollie didn't shoot Conrad Ellis right between the eyes.'

Ella appreciated the other woman's irrepressible humour.

'I'm glad Ollie didn't have to shoot that calf, either,' Lola added. 'Butchering an animal for food is one thing. Killing one for any other reason, well, that's somethin' else. He had to put down an old horse once and he cried hisself to sleep three nights in a row.'

She spoke with an affection produced by long-standing love for Ollie Thompson. The look the two exchanged was so personal that Ella felt like an intruder. She also felt a pang of envy.

The swing rocked gently as she stood up. 'I ran out on Margaret, so I'd better get back to the house.'

'Thank you for coming,' Lola said.

'I didn't do anything.'

'Just coming was something.' Lola looked at Mr Rainwater. 'I ain't actually made your acquaintance. I'm Lola. Thank you for driving Ella out here.'

'You're welcome, Mrs Thompson. I wish better times for you.'

Five

Little was said on the drive back into town. Ella didn't know where Mr Rainwater's thoughts were, but hers were on Solly. She worried about how much he'd seen. He seemed unaffected, but there was no way of knowing for certain what kind of impact the incident had made. As for her, it had left deep impressions: the pit of bony carcasses, Lola and Ollie in such despair. She feared it would be a long time before those disturbing memories receded.

They plagued her as she slogged through her chores that afternoon. The heat was blistering, so that even the most routine task seemed insurmountable. By late afternoon, Ella's stamina and patience were spent. She wanted only to get through the dinner hour and the clean-up, then retreat with Solly to their rooms.

With that in mind, Ella set the dining-room table while Margaret was shredding cabbage for coleslaw and mixing corn-bread batter. When Ella returned to the kitchen, she discovered Mr Rainwater sitting at the table with Solly, who was lining up toothpicks.

Mr Rainwater smiled at her. 'He's making real progress. He's forming groups of ten after watching me do it only once. Each time he reaches into the box for the toothpicks, he takes out an even ten.'

Ella took a pitcher of tea from the icebox and placed it on a serving tray. 'That's not progress. That's a worthless trick.'

Margaret gave Ella a disapproving glance over her shoulder.

Several moments of tense silence elapsed; then Mr Rainwater asked quietly, 'Why do you say that?'

Keeping her back to him, Ella added a sugar bowl and a dish of sliced lemons to the tray. 'You heard what Dr Kincaid said. Solly's talent, for lack of a better word, has no practical application.'

'I'm stunned to hear you say that.'

She turned round quickly. 'Why?'

'This could be a breakthrough. A start. The initial step towards—'

'What, Mr Rainwater?' She motioned at Solly, who was placing the toothpicks equidistantly apart. 'What is this moving him towards? A parlour act? Something to entertain Houston socialites?' In a carnival barker's voice, she said, 'Come and see Solomon Barron. He screeches and flaps his hands and throws tantrums every time his mother touches him, but he's a whiz at card tricks.'

'Miss Ella?' Margaret turned from the counter. 'What's come over you?'

'Nothing!' Ella said, her voice cracking. 'I'm just trying to explain to Mr Rainwater how futile his lessons are.' She took a step towards the table. 'I don't want my son to be a freak. I want him to read and write and *talk* to me, not . . . not . . .' Furiously she raked her hand across the table, sending Solly's carefully arranged rows of toothpicks to the linoleum.

Solly immediately emitted an ear-piercing shriek and began striking the sides of his head with his fists.

Ella, suddenly immobilised by her behaviour, gaped at the toothpicks scattered across the floor. She wouldn't have thought herself capable of losing control so quickly and completely.

Mr Rainwater calmly stood and went for the broom to sweep up the toothpicks. Ella, mortified, pulled Solly from his chair. She finally got him, kicking and screaming, into his room. She closed the door so that only she had to withstand his tantrum.

It was violent and went on for half an hour. She dodged his fists and feet as best she could but knew that tomorrow she would have bruises. Eventually he exhausted himself enough to fall asleep.

Ella sat on his bed and wept. The frustration and sorrow that had been building inside her all day erupted in great gulping sobs. She cried over her friends Ollie and Lola, who could now stave off foreclosure but only by paying a tremendous emotional price. She cried over their children, who'd experienced such a horrible thing. And in a rare moment of self-pity, she cried over herself and Solly.

When Solly grew larger, how *would* she control his tantrums? What would happen to him if something happened to her? Adults in their prime contracted terminal illnesses. Like Mr Rainwater. What if she got a cancer and died? Where would Solly live? Or what if he injured someone during one of his tantrums? He would be taken from her and placed in an asylum.

Eventually she cried herself out. She tidied her hair, checked Solly one more time, and left her room.

The house was quiet. Dinner was over, and the dining room had been cleared. Margaret was finishing up the dishes in the kitchen. 'I saved you a plate, Miss Ella.' It was in the centre of the table.

'Thank you, Margaret,' she said, 'but I'm not very hungry. You go on home.' Seeing Margaret's hesitation, she added, 'Solly's sleeping. I'll see you in the morning.'

Margaret removed her apron and put on her hat, then gave Ella a hug. 'Today's troubles is past now. Tomorrow will be better.'

That turned out not to be true.

MR RAINWATER DIDN'T come down for breakfast. Ella figured he was disinclined to leave his room out of pique over her harsh words to him yesterday. Unfairly she had unleashed her frustration on him. In her heart of hearts, she knew that Mr Rainwater's wanting to plumb the depths of Solly's abilities was honourable and kind.

She planned to apologise for her rudeness, but the morning passed without his coming downstairs. She didn't become concerned until he failed to appear at lunch. Margaret confirmed that she hadn't seen him all day. Neither had the Dunne sisters.

'Nothing's wrong, I hope,' Miss Violet said tremulously.

'He's probably just trying to evade the heat.'

But Ella doubted her own explanation and decided to check on him. Leaving Solly in Margaret's care, she went upstairs.

She paused outside his door and listened but heard no sounds. 'Mr Rainwater?' She tapped on the door, waiting for a reply. None came. She knocked softly again. 'Mr Rainwater, are you all right?'

When he didn't answer, her mouth went dry. Dr Kincaid had said six to twelve weeks. Possibly more if he was fortunate. He said Mr Rainwater would have good days and bad, but the steady decline as the cancer spread was inevitable. There would be pain.

With her heart in her throat, she opened the door to his room.

He was lying on the bed outside the covers, dressed in shirt, trousers and socks, but by the look of the twisted bedding beneath him, he'd been there for a while. He'd placed one forearm over his eyes; the other hand was clutching his stomach. She was relieved to see he was breathing. The sour smell of sweat permeated the room.

'Mr Rainwater?'

He made a feeble motion. 'Please go, Mrs Barron.'

Instead, she approached the bed. 'Do you need Dr Kincaid?'

'I—' Before he could finish, he was gripped by what appeared to be an excruciating pain. He strained a groan through gritted teeth.

Ella spun round and ran from the room, shouting for Margaret as she raced down the hallway. By the time she had clattered down the stairs, Margaret was standing at the bottom of them, her eyes wide with alarm. 'Is somethin' the matter with Mr Rainwater?'

'He's sick. Call Dr Kincaid. Tell him to come immediately.'

Ella went into the formal parlour and unplugged the fan. On her way back to the staircase, she could hear Margaret speaking to the telephone operator. Quickly she went back upstairs with the fan.

Mr Rainwater was as she'd left him, but the spasm that had seized him seemed to have abated. He lowered his arm from his eyes when she came in. 'Please, Mrs Barron, don't fret. Bad spells like this are to be expected. I'll get through it.'

'In the meantime, this should make you more comfortable.' She set the fan on the table in front of the window and plugged it in. 'How long have you been suffering like this?'

'Since last night.'

'Last night! Why didn't you let me know so I could call Dr Kincaid?'

'I thought it would pass. I'm sure it will.'

She didn't share his optimism. His lips were rimmed white with agony, and his eyes were sunk into their sockets. 'Dr Kincaid will be here shortly. Do you want me to get you something to drink?'

'Water, maybe.'

She made her way hastily to the kitchen. Margaret looked at her expectantly when she barged through the kitchen door.

'Is it a stomach flu, Miss Ella?'

'I suppose, yes. Is Dr Kincaid coming?'

'Right away, he said.'

'Good. Get the water pitcher from the icebox. And a drinking glass. Where's that porcelain basin we wash vegetables in?'

'Same place it's always at.'

Ella found the basin on its customary shelf in the pantry. She put the basin, the pitcher of cooled water and the glass on a tray. 'Stay with Solly.' He was sitting on the floor underneath the table, playing with empty spools. 'Send the doctor up the moment he arrives.'

Upstairs in Mr Rainwater's room, she moved aside a book and his gold pocket watch in order to place the tray on his nightstand. She poured water into the glass, then slid her hand beneath his head and lifted it. He drank thirstily and signalled to her when he'd had enough.

'I'll be right back.'

She left again, taking the basin. She filled it with cold water from the bathroom and took a washcloth from the cabinet. Being careful not to slosh the water, she returned it to the nightstand, dipped the cloth in it and bathed his face. He closed his eyes. 'Thank you.'

'You're welcome.'

'Did you tend your husband?'

'Pardon?'

'I assumed Mr Barron died of an illness. Did you tend to him? Is that how you acquired your nurse's touch?'

'He died suddenly.'

'Oh. Then your nursing skills come to you naturally.'

'I think it's part of the maternal instinct.'

He smiled faintly. 'A feminine skill, unique to your sex.'

She wet the cloth again and, after wringing it out, laid it on his forehead. Then she withdrew and sat down in the chair near the window. He said nothing more, and she would have thought that he was asleep except for the occasional tightening of his jaw, indications that he was experiencing gripping pains.

Through the open window, she heard Dr Kincaid's car. Moments later he appeared in the doorway, looking anxious. 'David?'

With barely a glance towards Ella, he set his black medical bag on the foot of the bed and bent over his patient with obvious concern.

Mr Rainwater opened his eyes. 'Hello, Murdy.'

Ella stood. 'I'll leave you. If you need anything . . .'

'Of course, Mrs Barron. Thank you,' the doctor said absently.

She went out, pulling the door closed behind her.

IT WAS ALMOST half an hour before Dr Kincaid came downstairs. The Dunne sisters had gone to visit a friend. Margaret was cooking dinner while keeping an eye on Solly. The doctor found Ella in the informal parlour, where she was dusting.

'How is he?'

Dr Kincaid removed a handkerchief from his pocket and wiped his face. Ella wondered if this habit was merely to blot up perspiration, or if he used it to delay imparting bad news. 'I gave him something. The crisis is past.'

'He was in terrible pain.'

'The worst he's experienced so far.'

His inflection implied that that day's pain was only a harbinger of what was to come.

'I've left him something to give himself. He says he won't use it unless the pain becomes unbearable. He's stubborn on that point. For now,' he added grimly. 'He'll change his mind.'

Ella looked away. 'Isn't there a treatment of some kind?'

'If there was, he'd already have had it. Believe me, I've written to specialists. They all arrive at the same sad prognosis. It started in his bones and went undetected until it metastasised to vital organs.'

Ella brushed a stray curl off her forehead. 'Do you have any instructions?'

'He's not your patient.'

'But he lives under my roof. I can't ignore him if he's in agony.'

'Call me at the first sign of discomfort. Any time of the day or night, no matter how loudly David protests.'

'I will.'

She walked the doctor to the front door and unlatched the screen. He hesitated on the threshold and looked at her remorsefully. 'You didn't need this additional strain, Mrs Barron. I shouldn't have brought David to you. I regret now that I did.'

The doctor's house was overcrowded with his two active sons. His patients called on him at all hours of the night. She believed he'd brought Mr Rainwater to her not to shirk his responsibility but so Mr Rainwater would have a peaceful place in which to live.

Hoping to alleviate his guilt, she told him that Mr Rainwater was an ideal boarder. 'He's considerate and well liked by the others. He's patient with Solly. He goes out of his way not to be a burden.'

'I hope he doesn't become one.' The doctor started down the steps, then halted and turned back. 'On the other hand, Mrs Barron, I wouldn't trust anyone else to take such good care of him.'

SHE TAPPED on his door. 'May I come in?'

'Please.'

He was seated in the chair at the window. Through it, he watched the doctor drive away. 'What did Murdy tell you?'

'He suggested I come up and change your bedding.'

He turned his head and saw that she was carrying fresh folded bedsheets. 'I doubt that's what you two talked about.'

'I noticed you could use fresh linens.'

'Murdy helped me change into a clean shirt, but I should have known my sickbed wouldn't comply with your standards.'

She was about to smile at the gentle gibe when she spotted the syringe. It was lying on the top of the bureau alongside a black leather pouch, which she assumed contained vials of medication.

He followed her gaze. 'Murdy's trying to turn me into a dope fiend.'

'He doesn't want you to suffer needlessly.'

He looked at the syringe with distaste. Ella moved to the bed and began stripping off the damp, wrinkled sheets.

'I'll be quick, and then you can return to bed.'

'Take your time. I'm not anxious to return to it. I enjoy the view from here.' After a moment, he said, 'I've been looking out of the window at the cottonwood tree across the street. When I was a boy, I climbed one that was as tall. One day I was about a third of the way up when I came across a raccoon that was foaming at the mouth. I had to drop to the ground or get bit. I broke my arm.'

'Better than getting rabies.'

He gave a soft laugh. 'It wasn't quick thinking on my part. The thing was hissing—scared the daylights out of me. I was so frightened I actually fell out of the tree.'

She smiled across at him. 'Did you ever climb that tree again?'

'Soon as my arm healed. I had to in order to restore my pride.'

She spread the bottom sheet over the mattress. 'Mr Rainwater?'

'Hmm?'

'I must apologise for yesterday.' She could feel his gaze on her back as she unfurled the sheet. 'The incident with the toothpicks. The things I said. I didn't mean them. I don't know what came over me.'

'You were upset about what happened to your friends.'

She finished tucking the sheet into the foot of the bed, then straightened up and turned to face him. 'Yes. But it wasn't only that.' She bowed her head briefly, then raised it to look directly at him. 'I was jealous.'

'Jealous?'

'Of the progress you're making with Solly. And despite what I said yesterday, it *is* progress.' Feeling the heat in her cheeks and knowing it must show, she turned her back to him again and picked up a pillow. She pulled on a pillowcase and placed the pillow at the base of the headboard. 'Your progress with him underscores my failure to reach him on any level.'

She smoothed the bedspread over the bed. After making one last adjustment, she turned. Astonishingly, he was standing directly in front of her. He was still in stockinged feet, so she hadn't known he'd left the chair. Now they were face to face. And close.

'You have no reason to feel jealous. If I've made progress with Solly, it's because I have idle time to devote to him. You don't. You're too busy doing what you must to provide for him.' He paused, then added, 'At tremendous sacrifice to yourself.'

That was a presumptuous statement. She could have taken issue with it, but she was afraid to have him expand upon what aspects of life he thought she was sacrificing. It seemed like a dangerous conversation to enter into, especially in this room at this moment.

She swallowed. 'It's very generous of you to think so.'

'I'm not being generous. I'm stating the way things are.'

Averting her gaze, she asked, 'Do you accept my apology?'

'Even though it's unnecessary, yes.'

'Thank you.'

She was about to pick up the dirty sheets when he shocked her further by reaching for her hand. She was so startled by the unexpected contact that she looked at their hands to confirm it, noting the difference in size. She tilted her head and looked into his face.

He said, 'I hate that you saw me like that today.'

'You were in pain.'

'You bathed my face.'

'It was the least I could do.'

'It helped. Thank you.'

'You're welcome.'

For several seconds more, they remained connected; then she pulled her hand from his and hastily gathered up the sheets. At the door, she said, 'I'll have Margaret bring up your dinner on a tray.'

'I'll be down for dinner.'

'You should rest, Mr Rainwater.'

'I'll be down.'

HE SEEMED TO SUFFER no lasting ill effects from the bad spell. Whether or not he was injecting the painkiller—Ella presumed it was morphine—she didn't know. But he definitely took a turn for the better. The very next day, he resumed working with Solly, but only after he had cleared it with her first.

'I don't want you flying off the handle again.'

She didn't take offence, because he said it with a teasing smile.

'I promise not to sling any more toothpicks. You can work with Solly anytime you like.'

He set aside time each day.

And he began going out often. He would tell her the approximate time he would be back. He never said where he was going.

Sometimes he was gone for only a short while in the afternoons. Other times he left after dinner and didn't return until hours later.

'What do you figure is going on?' Margaret asked one afternoon.

They were in the front parlour moving pieces of furniture so they could wash the baseboards behind them. Mr Rainwater had paused on his way out to tell them that he would be back by suppertime.

Ella responded with feigned disinterest. 'Going on?'

'With Mr Rainwater. Where's he off to here lately?'

'I don't know, Margaret. He doesn't tell me, and it's none of my business. Or yours,' she added pointedly.

A few days later Ella ran into Lola Thompson in the post office. Lola's youngest child was riding on her hip. She had another by the hand, and she was juggling a handful of mail.

When Ella greeted her, she was as ready as ever with a wide grin. 'You've been on my mind,' Ella told her. 'How have you been?'

'Oh, fine.'

'Ollie?'

'He's mending fences. Plugging up holes in the roof. Working towards the day he can start another herd. We're not making anything, but we're not spending much, either.'

'I admire your resilience.'

Lola chuckled. 'I've had my dark hours. Wouldn't be human if I didn't. But I try not to let on in front of Ollie and the kids.'

'Anytime you'd like to talk, call me or come by.'

Lola snorted. 'Like you need my big self crying on your shoulder, what with your backward boy, and you running that house by yourself. If anybody should be admired, Ella, it's you, not me.'

She didn't take exception to Lola's description of Solly, knowing there was no malice intended. 'I would welcome a visit. Anytime.'

'I appreciate that. Sometimes talking to another woman is just the thing. We females understand each other, don't we?'

Ella nodded.

Lola reflected a moment, then said, 'I guess it's the same with men, though. I'm glad Ollie's come to know Mr Rainwater right good. He came along just when Ollie needed a friend. Their talks have helped Ollie, I think.'

Ella's heart gave a little bump. 'Mr Rainwater has been having talks with Ollie?'

'Before and after their meetings. Sometimes he stays over after everybody else has left, or he comes early.'

Ella stared at her. 'What are you talking about? What meetings?'

'You know.' Lola glanced round to see if anyone was close enough to overhear. She whispered, 'The *meetings*.'

HIS HEADLIGHTS CUT through the darkness even before he turned his car onto the street. Nearby houses were dark. It was past bedtime for most folks. The town was quiet.

Mr Rainwater had left the house while Ella was working in the kitchen after dinner. The spinsters had played cards for a while, then retired, while Mr Hastings, tired from another trip, had gone upstairs directly after dinner. Ella put Solly to bed, saw Margaret off, then went out onto the porch to wait for her boarder's return.

Now Mr Rainwater parked his car behind Mr Hastings's, turned off the headlights and cut the engine. He had come up the walk and climbed the steps when she said, 'Good evening, Mr Rainwater.'

He turned towards her and whipped off his hat. 'Mrs Barron. I didn't see you.' He walked towards the rocking chair where she sat. 'I hope you weren't waiting up for me so you could lock the door.'

'I was waiting for you, but not so I could lock the door. In fact, I may wish I had locked you out.'

His head went back an inch or two. 'I beg your pardon?'

'Where have you been?'

He paused for several beats, then said, 'May I sit down?'

She gave a curt nod. He took the chair nearest hers.

In response to that, she moved her knees, directing them away from him. 'Before you say anything, Mr Rainwater, you should know that I saw Lola today. She mentioned secret meetings taking place at their house, assuming that I knew the purpose of them.'

'They're not always at the Thompsons' house.'

His composure was infuriating.

'Where these meetings are conducted isn't the point. What *kind* of meetings are they? What's the purpose of them?'

Her voice had gone up in volume. He glanced over his shoulder towards the hedge that separated her property from her neighbour's.

His caution only heightened her misgivings, but she lowered her voice. 'Please don't think I care about your comings and goings for any reason other than that you're living in my house. That entitles me to know if you're into something dangerous or criminal.'

'I assure you it's not criminal.'

'But dangerous?'

'I hope it won't become so.'

Ella swallowed, and then said, 'But you still haven't answered my question. What is the purpose of the meetings?'

He leaned towards her. 'This drought-relief programme to buy livestock was designed to help people in dire straits, not cause them more grief. People shouldn't have their houses riddled with bullets and their children threatened. We want to stop it.'

'We? Who?'

'Me, Ollie, Brother Calvin. He's rallied men in the shantytown— Negroes and whites, those who were beaten. Remember the man with the three children whose wife had just died?'

She nodded.

'His name's Emmett Sprule. He's been in the shantytown for a long time, so he knows a lot of people. Mr Pritchett signed on. He's brought in all his lodge friends, even deacons in his church.'

'Brought them in to do what?'

'We've got a network in place, a relay system. When it comes time for a farmer's herd to be bought and culled, he sends word. It's spread through the system we've worked out. We all drop what we're doing and converge on the place. We can't change the rules of the programme'—he flashed a grin—'but we can stop Conrad Ellis and his cronies from doing their meanness.'

'Conrad's wild. He and his gang are armed and reckless.'

'We're armed, too. But we're not wild or reckless. We're organised, and there are more of us than there are of them. If we make a stand, I think those thugs will back down.'

The idea behind their organisation was noble, but she feared men from the shantytown armed with sticks, and church deacons with Christian decency, as their armour wouldn't pose much of a threat to Conrad and his heavily armed, drunken, violent friends.

'It's the law's job to protect people and property,' she argued. 'Why don't you send a committee to appeal to the sheriff?'

'Anderson is scared of the Ellises. He won't cross Conrad's father, who bankrolled his election.'

It was true, but she wondered how Mr Rainwater, an outsider, had come by that information. When she asked him, he said, 'Ollie told me Sheriff Anderson was on the take, and everyone confirmed it. Brother Calvin said Anderson and his deputies stood by and watched Conrad and his friends beat up those people at Pritchett's place.'

'Which only proves my point. Please don't get involved.'

'I already am.'

'This isn't your town. You've only just met these people. I'm surprised they'd even have the nerve to invite you to join them.' She stopped suddenly. 'Who organised these men? Who devised this system of communication, this relay?'

His steady gaze didn't falter.

'You did.'

He said nothing.

Ella's breath caught in her throat. '*Why?*'

'It needed to be done.'

'Not by you! It's not your fight. You're not a rancher or dairy farmer. You don't live in the shantytown. You're not involved.'

'I involved myself.'

'Well, you shouldn't have. It's a dangerous situation. Sheriff Anderson could arrest you.'

He looked amused. 'For what? Meeting with friends?'

'For anything. For spitting on the sidewalk. If the Ellises tell him to put you behind bars, he will. Or worse, they may leave him out of it and come after you themselves.'

'Come after me?' he repeated, again looking amused. 'And do what?'

'Whatever they have a mind to! Do not underestimate Conrad, Mr Rainwater. He could hurt you, and he would.'

'It's too late to back out even if I wanted to, and I don't want to.'

'I don't understand you. Truly, I don't. Why risk your life—' She bit back her words, stopping before finishing the thought.

Mr Rainwater smiled wanly and gave a small shrug. 'Exactly.'

Six

They said no more about it that night. At breakfast the following morning, they exchanged polite nods but didn't speak. At mid-morning, he came out into the back yard, where she was hanging towels on the clothesline. Solly was sitting in the dirt, drumming a wooden spoon against a metal bucket.

As Mr Rainwater approached, he touched the brim of his hat. 'Good morning, Mrs Barron.'

'Good morning.'

'We didn't finish our conversation last night.'

'I can't tell you how to live your life. But I won't allow you to bring any trouble into my house.'

'That's the last thing I want to do.'

'That may not be your intention, but that doesn't mean it won't happen.

People know you live here. Your involvement in this business puts Solly and me—everyone in this house—at risk.'

'I would leave before I let anything bad happen to you.'

'I'll hold you to that.'

'If you ask me to move out, I will.'

'Do you have a firearm? I don't want guns in my house.'

'No, I don't have one.'

'And I don't want any meetings conducted on my property.'

'I would never suggest it.'

She gave him a long look, then took another wet towel from the basket. 'I still think it's foolhardy for you to become involved in this when you don't even have a stake in it.'

'But I do have a stake in it, Mrs Barron. A big stake.'

She looked at him inquisitively.

'I'd like the time I have left to count for something.' He backed away and headed towards the front of the house.

'Mr Rainwater?' She called out to him without thinking and was embarrassed by her spontaneity. But it was too late; he had turned back and was looking at her expectantly. 'Take care,' she said.

He smiled. 'Thank you. I will.'

HOLDING SOLLY by the hand, Ella entered the sanctuary and found them seats on one of the back pews. Each Sunday, she timed her arrival to be a few minutes late, during the singing of a hymn or when heads were bowed in prayer, in order to avoid the other church-goers, who stared at Solly with compassion that bordered on pity.

He looked like an angel today. She'd dressed him in a white linen shirt and matching shorts, which she'd bought at a rummage sale last summer. His knee socks were spotless; she'd polished his shoes last night. This morning, she'd managed to rake a comb through his pale hair several times before he began squealing.

She went to great pains every Sunday to dress him up, knowing the effort was wasted. No one ever noticed how well he was turned out, only that he was different.

She'd brought along a small bag of empty spools to keep Solly occupied during the service. Prayers were said; hymns were sung; the offering plates were passed. The pastor began his sermon.

This morning's message wasn't all that inspiring. Ella's attention began to drift, and so did her gaze. As it moved across the congregation, she spotted Mr Rainwater. He was seated with Dr and Mrs Kincaid and their restless sons, on the outside aisle, about midway between where she sat and the altar. She was surprised to see him. To her knowledge, this was the first time he'd attended a service.

The Ellises were occupying their customary pew, the second on the right side of the centre aisle. No one else dared sit in their pew. If a visitor did so unknowingly, another seat was suggested to him.

Even from the back, Conrad looked pugnacious. His large head sat upon his wide shoulders with barely an inch of neck supporting it. His hair was as curly and dense as wool, covering his head like a tightly fitted cap. It added to his belligerent look.

Mr Ellis sat beside him. He was a smaller man than his son, much less brawny, but he led with his chin, his head jutting slightly forward of his shoulders, in a way that looked aggressive and combatant.

Although Mrs Ellis, decked out this morning in pink voile, was the best-dressed woman in town, she was not well liked. The consensus was that she put on airs. She hosted social events in her home, but only for her fancy Waco friends, never for local women.

It seemed to Ella that everyone in the church heaved a sigh of relief when the pastor finally closed the sermon with a prayer. At the end of it, he beseeched God to give direction to the misguided. It seemed an odd note on which to conclude the service, but it was explained when Mr Ellis said a resounding 'Amen' from his pew.

'I THINK ELLIS wrote the closing prayer.'

Recognising the voice, Ella turned. Mr Rainwater was beside her, but his gaze was on the family talking to the pastor. As they watched, Mr Ellis enthusiastically pumped the minister's right hand. Mrs Ellis fanned her face with a lace hanky. Conrad, looking bored, walked away and lit a cigarette.

'I wouldn't put it past him,' Ella said. 'Mr Ellis is a very influential member of the church.'

Mr Rainwater looked down at Solly, who was standing docilely at her side, staring at the stained-glass window. 'I didn't hear a peep out of this young man. Can't say the same for Murdy's boys.'

Ella laughed. 'They're a handful. But today Solly was very good.' She was aware of eyes on them, especially when Mr Rainwater politely cupped her elbow as they started down the steep front steps. When they reached ground level, she slipped her arm free but covered the move by saying, 'I haven't seen you here before.'

'First time.'

'What did you think?'

'Boring sermon.'

'Even the diehards were snoozing this morning.' They smiled at each other; then she ducked her head. 'Margaret's made a pork roast and two pies for Sunday dinner. I'll see you then.' Pulling Solly along behind her, she turned and headed down the sidewalk.

'I'll walk you to your car.'

'We came on foot this morning.'

'Then I'll drive you home.'

'Thank you, Mr Rainwater, but we have a . . . an errand.'

'I'll drive you wherever you need to go.'

'Our errand is here, actually.'

He looked towards where she indicated: the cemetery that was adjacent to the church.

'I brought some flowers from the yard for my parents' . . . For my parents.' Because of his prognosis, she felt too uncomfortable with the subject of burial to say the word *graves*.

'Where are the flowers?' he said.

'I put them in the shade so they would stay fresh.'

He made a motion with his head for her to lead on.

'You don't have to stay with us,' she said.

'Do you mind if I do?'

'Not at all.' Without further argument, she led him round the corner of the building to the deep shade, where the bouquet was where she'd left it. Still in the mason jar of water were colourful zinnias, a pair of creamy gardenias and yellow roses.

Mr Rainwater picked up the jar. 'Very fragrant.'

'I thought it was nice.'

Together they covered the distance to the cemetery and went through the iron picket gate. He didn't seem upset to be in a place so remindful of death. He read with interest the names and dates on the headstones as they moved to the plot shared by her parents.

She knelt down and set the jar of flowers in the centre of the headstone on which were engraved their names, their dates of birth and death, and a simple inscription: UNITED IN HEAVEN FOR ETERNITY.

Flanking their graves were two smaller ones, with only brass plaques. Ella removed two roses from the jar and laid one on each.

'Your twin brothers?'

She nodded, pulled up several weeds, rearranged the flowers in the jar, then brushed off her hands and stood up.

'Do you come here every Sunday?' he asked.

'Once a month, maybe.'

'Is your husband also buried here?'

The question was unexpected. 'No, he isn't,' she said as she reached for Solly's hand and started retracing their path to the gate. 'He wasn't from Gilead. He grew up in a small town in the Panhandle. He liked the wide-open spaces of the plains. He told me on more than one occasion that he wished to be buried out there.'

They walked on, but when they reached the gate, Ella stopped. Mr Rainwater did likewise. By now, even the stragglers had left. Only Mr Rainwater's car remained parked in front of the church.

'My husband didn't die, Mr Rainwater.' He remained silent and unmoving at her side. Eventually she turned to him. 'I don't know why Dr Kincaid told you that I was a widow. To spare me embarrassment, I suppose.'

She glanced down at Solly. He seemed fascinated by the even placement of the pickets in the fence. Ella lightly stroked his hair with her fingertip. He jerked his head away from her touch.

'The truth is, my husband abandoned us six years ago. One day while I was out, he packed his belongings and left. I have no idea where he went. I never heard from him again.'

She turned her gaze back to the man beside her. 'You've been kind to

Solly and to me. In good conscience, I couldn't continue lying to you.'
Before he could say anything, she ushered Solly through the gate, having
every intention of walking home.

But Mr Rainwater went ahead of her and opened the passenger door of
his car, motioning her in. She hesitated but saw no reason to refuse his offer
of a lift. Placing Solly in the middle of the seat, she climbed in after him.
Mr Rainwater closed her door, walked round the bonnet and got in. He
started the motor, then let it idle. Finally he turned his head. She braced herself for the dreaded questions.

'What kind of pies?'

'What?'

'You said Margaret made two pies for dinner. What kind?'

For six years, she had withstood the gossip, speculation, insinuation,
blatant nosiness and sympathy of everyone who knew her. To newcomers in
town, she was identified as the woman with the retarded boy whose husband had deserted them. She had borne the humiliation and pity with as
much fortitude as she could muster.

Mr Rainwater had subjected her to neither.

With emotion in her throat, she replied, 'It's a surprise.'

'IT WASN'T JUST a stomach flu, was it?'

Ella and Margaret were in the kitchen pickling cucumbers, okra pods
and watermelon rind. It was hot work, and there were no shortcuts to the
process. The vegetables and rinds had to be thoroughly washed, sliced and
blanched. The mason jars and their lids had to be boiled. The spices and
vinegar were simmered together to achieve the best flavours. Everything in
the kitchen was steaming. Including Ella, who pushed back coils of hair
that had escaped her bun. She looked at Margaret, who was ladling a hot
vinegar mixture redolent with dill over the cucumber spears she had
packed tightly into a jar. Ella was prepared to fib, but when her loyal maid
looked back at her, she knew that duplicity was pointless.

Margaret sensed that Mr Rainwater suffered from an ailment, and she
hadn't been fooled by the explanation they'd provided the day Dr Kincaid
had been summoned to the house to treat him.

'No, Margaret, it wasn't just a stomach flu.'

'He don't eat much. I thought it was just the heat.' Margaret set the seal on the jar, then twisted on the ring. 'Is he bad sick?'

'Very bad.'

Tears filled Margaret's eyes. 'Poor, poor soul. How long?'

'No one knows that for sure.'

'A year?'

Ella shook her head. 'Not that long.'

Margaret raised her apron to catch a sob in the hem of it.

'But please don't say anything about it to anyone. Promise me.'

'I won't,' Margaret mumbled as she blotted her eyes. 'But it ain't gonna be easy, 'cause I think a lot of him. He's a gentleman, about the most decent white man I know.'

'If you feel that way about him, the nicest thing you can do for him is to treat him normally. Don't let on like you know.'

'Yes, ma'am.'

Ella began slicing cucumbers for her bread and butter pickles.

'Miss Ella, did you know? Before that day we called the doctor?'

'I knew before he moved in.'

'You a good woman.'

AFTER THAT CONVERSATION, Ella began taking particular notice of Mr Rainwater's appetite, or lack thereof. She monitored how much food he left on his plate after each meal. One night as she was clearing the table, she asked if the meat loaf hadn't been to his liking.

'It was delicious, Mrs Barron. But I took too large a portion.'

From then on, however, he did better towards finishing his plate. Ella was heartened, until one evening she saw how little he served himself.

She didn't mention it to him in front of the Dunne sisters or Mr Hastings, who was disappointed when Mr Rainwater declined a game of chess and, saying he preferred to read that night, excused himself and went upstairs.

Before going to bed, Ella decided she should check on him. Rarely did she go upstairs once her boarders had retired, feeling they deserved their privacy. But knowing that Mr Rainwater had suffered in silence before, she felt justified in breaking her rule. Keeping her footsteps light, she made her way down the dark hallway to his room, where she tapped on the door.

'Yes?'

'It's me, Mr Rainwater,' she whispered. 'Are you all right?'

'Yes.'

When he didn't say more, she asked if she could come in.

'Yes.'

She pushed open the door. He was sitting on the side of the bed, but it was apparent that he'd been lying on it seconds earlier. The pillow bore the imprint of his head, and his hair was tousled. He was dressed, although he had removed his jacket and tie. His shoes were on the floor, but he was still wearing his socks.

His skin looked pale and waxy, but that could have been attributed to the harsh glow of the reading lamp on his nightstand. It also turned his eye sockets into dark caverns.

She stepped into the room. 'I hope I'm not disturbing you.'

'Not at all.'

'I wanted to ask if you thought I should write to one of those schools for special children that Dr Kincaid has mentioned.'

He looked at her and then stood up. 'You didn't believe me when I told you that I was all right. That's why you came in.'

She smiled self-consciously. 'I confess.'

'You're a terrible liar.'

'I'm aware of that.'

'It's not a bad quality, being so honest you can't conceal a lie.'

They smiled across at each other. She asked, 'Are you?'

'Am I a good liar?'

'Are you all right?'

'Yes.'

She nodded towards the book he held in one hand. 'You really did come up early so you could read your book.'

'*A Farewell to Arms.* Have you read it?'

'I've wanted to. I don't have much time for reading.'

'It's excellent.'

'Doesn't it have a sad ending?'

'Sad but beautiful, they say. I'll let you know.'

Feeling awkward now, she backed away and reached for the doorknob. 'I apologise for the intrusion. I noticed you didn't eat well tonight. I wanted to make sure that . . . you were resting well.'

'I appreciate your concern, but I'm fine.'

'Then good night, Mr Rainwater.'

'Good night, Mrs Barron.'

She pulled the door closed, but then huddled in the dark hallway, wondering if she'd been right to pretend that she hadn't seen on the bedside table, along with his gold pocket watch, the syringe and vial of pain medication.

THE FOLLOWING MORNING, Ella was still wrestling with uncertainty. Should she, or should she not, notify Dr Kincaid, whom she had promised to send for at the least sign of discomfort from Mr Rainwater? She was on the verge of making the call when he joined the Dunne sisters at the dining table.

'What's for breakfast this morning, ladies?'

'Pancakes,' Miss Violet informed him.

'My favourite.'

Not to be outdone by her sister, Miss Pearl said, 'And the most delicious honeydew melon we've had all season.'

'That must be it, then.'

'Must be what, Mr Rainwater?'

'The source of that special glow you both have this morning,' he said, teasing them with a wink. 'Honeydew melon!'

They tittered. He met Ella's eyes as she poured coffee into his cup. 'Good morning, Mrs Barron.'

'I hope you had a restful night, Mr Rainwater.'

'Slept like a baby.'

But the deep shadows beneath his eyes made her wonder if he were, in jhgfdsafact, a better liar than she. He did justice to his breakfast, reassuring her somewhat. After the meal, he took a box of dominoes, a deck of cards and Solly out onto the front porch. They stayed an hour. When he brought Solly back to her, he smiled down at the boy. 'Good job, Solly.'

'Did he do something special?'

'Everything he does is special, Mrs Barron.'

'Yes, it is.' After a beat, she said, 'What I asked you last night wasn't just a ruse to check on you. I'd like your opinion.'

'About the special schools?'

'Should I write to them and ask about their curriculums?'

'What would it hurt?'

'Nothing, I suppose, although I don't think I could ever bring myself to send Solly away.'

'Until you know more, you can't make an informed decision. By his own admission, Murdy knows very little about children like Solly. But these schools may be able to provide guidance.'

Making up her mind, she said, 'I'll send out some enquiries.'

'Good.' Looking happy about her decision, he excused himself and continued towards the staircase. When he was about halfway up, she called after him, 'Can I get you anything, Mr Rainwater?'

He stopped, turned. 'Like what?'

'A glass of iced tea?'

'No, thank you.'

'Are you sure you're feeling all right? You look—'

He spun round again, continuing up the stairs. 'I'm *fine*.'

It was the first time she'd ever heard him raise his voice, and it came as a shock. She took Solly by the hand and led him into the kitchen, letting the door swing closed behind them.

AFTER LUNCH, Ella decided that she and Solly would walk to town. She believed that time away from the house would do them good.

The heat was unrelenting, however. Her dress was damp with perspiration by the time they reached the store. Its comparatively cool interior brought relief, and Solly was content to watch the circulating ceiling fan, so she dawdled among the shelves as she checked items off her shopping list. Too soon she was done.

'Is that it for today, Mrs Barron?'

'Yes, Mr Randall. Oh, wait. Two cold Dr Peppers, please.'

The grocer glanced at Solly, who was standing at her side, bobbing his head. 'Sure thing.'

A large hand came into view and slapped two nickels onto the counter. 'My treat.' When Ella turned, she was looking into Conrad Ellis's face. His leer was more disfiguring than the birthmark.

'Long time no see, Ella.'

'Hello, Conrad.'

He assessed her appearance in a way that made her skin crawl. 'You're lookin' good. Staying trim.' She didn't say anything to that. His grin only widened over her apparent embarrassment. Turning to Mr Randall, he said, 'The Dr Peppers are on me.'

'Thank you, Conrad,' she said crisply, 'but Mr Randall will add them to my account.'

Conrad socked the grocer on the arm. 'Mr Randall will let me buy you a soda, won't you, Mr Randall?'

The grocer gave Ella a weak smile. 'I've already closed out your tab, Mrs Barron.' He hadn't, but he obviously didn't want to haggle with Conrad. He swept the nickels off the counter then quickly turned and took two soft drinks from the metal chest. He uncapped them, then set them on the counter. 'I'll have your purchases boxed and sent over by Margaret's boy.'

'Thank you.'

After looking askance at Conrad, he disappeared into his storeroom.

Conrad was a bulky presence she tried to ignore as she took Solly's hand and headed for the door. There was no one else in the store. She was alone with Conrad, which made her uncomfortable.

As she stepped past him, he said, 'Hey, you forgot your drinks.'

'I've changed my mind.'

'Aw, now, don't be like that, Ella.' He hooked her arm, which she yanked back immediately. He laughed. 'What's the matter? No time to chat with an old friend?'

'Not today. I need to get home.'

'You still cooking and cleaning for other people?'

'I'm running a business.'

'Is that what they call making beds and mopping floors these days? Running a business?' He snorted. 'You're too good for that, Ella. Don't you ever get a hankering for something better?'

'No.' She tried to go round him, but he executed a quick sidestep and blocked her. 'Let me by, Conrad.'

'You ever hear from that sorry husband of yours?'

Again she tried to go round him, but he was too quick for her.

'He just upped and ran off, didn't he? On account of your boy here. I guess he couldn't take his kid being the town idiot.'

Ella seethed as he bent at the waist and put himself on an eye level with Solly, who stared through him.

'What's the matter with him, anyway?' He waved his hand in front of Solly's face and said, 'Yoo-hoo! Anybody home?'

'Stop that!' Ella tried to push Conrad aside, but it was like trying to shove a railroad car. He pressed his hand over hers, trapping it against his chest. She struggled to pull it free. 'Let me go!'

Chuckling over her efforts, he said, 'You always did have sass, Ella. I liked that about you. Even your husband running off hasn't got the best of you, has it? Shame about your kid, though. Now that I've seen him up close, it goes to show you can't believe everything you hear. What I heard was that he duh . . . duh . . . drools.'

'You really should try to correct that stutter, Mr Ellis.'

Mr Rainwater pulled open the store's screened door and strolled in. Ella almost cried out in relief upon seeing him. Conrad released her hand and spun round to see who'd interrupted his bullying.

'Afternoon, Mrs Barron.' Mr Rainwater doffed his hat as he approached, deftly manoeuvring himself between her and Conrad.

Their eyes locked. With effort, she brought her breathing under control. 'Mr Rainwater.'

'Margaret told me you'd come to town. I had an errand to run, so I thought I'd intercept you and offer you and Solly a ride home.'

'That's very kind of you. Thank you.'

He motioned her towards the door and away from Conrad, but Conrad placed his hand on Mr Rainwater's shoulder and brought him round to face him. 'Hey, I've heard of you.'

'I've heard of you, too.'

'What I've heard, I don't particularly like.'

Mr Rainwater smiled pleasantly. 'Then we also have that in common.'

It took Conrad several seconds to process his meaning, and when he did, his eyes narrowed to slits. 'You're Ella's new boarder.'

'I'm leasing a room in her house, yes.'

Conrad snickered and asked, 'What else are you doing there?'

Mr Rainwater remained stonily silent, although Ella recognised the familiar tightening of his jaw. 'Please stand aside, Mr Ellis. We're leaving now.'

Conrad raised both hands in surrender. 'All I was doing was trying to do something nice for her. But I think it's *you* who's doing something nice for her. Every night? In that big ol' house of hers?' He gave Ella an obscene wink.

Mr Rainwater gave her a gentle push towards the door. They had almost reached it when Conrad again clamped his hand on Mr Rainwater's shoulder.

'You think 'cause you're kin to Doc Kincaid you can go poking your nose into business where it doesn't belong? Around here we don't like meddlesome outsiders. You want to make trouble, you go someplace else and spare me the trouble of whipping your ass.'

Seven

As soon as they were in Mr Rainwater's car, he said, 'It would tickle him to know he'd upset you.'

'I'm not upset.'

'You're shaking.'

Ella looked down at her hands and realised that he was right. To keep her hands from trembling, she clasped them in her lap.

Solly started screeching.

Just like that he took a sudden and violent objection to his shoes. When she was finally able to hold his feet still, she saw that the toe of one had been scuffed. The smudge was barely discernible, but the mark was enough to bring on a fit. He bucked, kicked, flapped his hands and all the while emitted an ear-shattering squeal.

She removed the offending shoes. He stopped screeching and began to rock back and forth so vigorously that his head thumped into the upholstered seat. It seemed not to bother him, so she didn't try to stop it.

When the crisis was over, Mr Rainwater politely asked if she had any other stops to make in town. She made it plain to him that she did not. She only wanted to get home and, with the help of routine chores, put Conrad out of her mind.

Mr Rainwater appeared unfazed both by Solly's fit and by the confrontation in the grocery market. His hands were steady on the steering wheel as he drove them through town. He even touched the brim of his hat to several people they passed. Ella wished he wouldn't. Anyone seeing her and Solly with him might give credence to gossip that there was something illicit going on under her roof.

To her knowledge, Conrad had been the only one who'd implied such a thing, but the mere idea that she and a male boarder were the subjects of lewd speculation made her feel ill.

'He's not worth fretting over,' Mr Rainwater said quietly.

'His fits are getting worse, not better. More intense.'

'Not Solly. Conrad Ellis.'

'I disagree. Conrad is very much worth fretting over.'

'The man is a bully and a moron. Your best defence against him is to ignore him.'

'As you did.' The words came out sharply, almost like a reproof.

He looked at her but replied in his typically calm manner. 'I couldn't ignore the things he said; I simply declined to take issue with them, knowing that's exactly what he wanted me to do. If I'd challenged what he suggested about us, it would have given him an opportunity to lay into me.'

'He could break you in half.'

He smiled. 'Yes. In a fistfight, I would most definitely lose. But he didn't fight me, did he?'

She thought of the steely resolve she'd seen in Mr Rainwater's eyes as he had stared down Conrad. Apparently, Conrad had seen it, too. He had removed his hand from Mr Rainwater's shoulder and had even taken a hasty step back.

Could it be that Conrad had been afraid of a quality he'd detected in Mr Rainwater's eyes? Perhaps the strength of a man who had nothing to lose? Whatever the reason, Conrad's brute strength and belligerence had tucked tail and retreated from it.

As soon as Mr Rainwater brought the car to a stop in front of the house, she scrambled out, pulling Solly along with her. She entered through the front door and didn't stop her steady march until she reached the kitchen, where Margaret and her son, Jimmy, were unloading the grocery items he'd delivered.

As soon as Margaret saw her, she planted a fist on her hip and smacked the back of Jimmy's head with her other hand. 'I done yell at him good for leaving you in the store alone with that white trash. And I can tell by your face that somethin' bad happened.'

'We're fine, Margaret.'

'Well, it's a wonder,' she huffed. 'That Ellis boy was born mean and just got meaner when he had to give you up. He ain't got over you turnin' him down flat.'

Hearing motion behind her, Ella turned. Mr Rainwater had followed her into the kitchen, Solly's shoes in his hand. 'You left these in the car, Mrs Barron.'

She snatched the shoes from him. 'Thank you, Mr Rainwater.'

He looked at her more closely, but she turned away.

Margaret said, 'This is my boy, Jimmy. Jimmy, Mr Rainwater.'

The two acknowledged the introduction; then Jimmy scuttled out of the back door, grateful to have escaped his mother's wrath.

'Margaret,' Mr Rainwater said, 'if I pick the peaches myself, could I bribe you into making a cobbler for dessert tonight?'

'Shoot! You don't have to bribe me. I'd be pleasured to do it.'

He picked peaches from the tree in Ella's yard and Margaret baked the cobbler. But Mr Rainwater wasn't there for dessert to eat it.

THE PHONE RANG during the dinner hour. Ella answered.

'Ella, it's Ollie. Let me speak to David, please.'

So it was *David* now. But sensing urgency, she asked if something was wrong.

'If he's there, just put him on, please.'

'Hold on.' Ella returned to the dining room. 'Mr Rainwater, you have a telephone call.'

He stood immediately. Excusing himself to the others, he stepped past Ella and into the hallway, walking quickly to the telephone.

'Who is it?' he asked her over his shoulder.

'Ollie Thompson.'

He picked up the telephone. 'Ollie?' He listened for what seemed like an eternity. 'I'll be right there,' he said.

He replaced the earpiece and returned the telephone to the table. Stepping round Ella again, he headed for the front door.

'What is it? Where are you going? What's happening?'

'I'll fill you in when I get back.' He yanked his hat from the hall tree on his way out. He didn't look back.

TIME PLODDED BY.

When she had returned to the dining room without him, the Dunne sisters had been all a-flutter. 'Is something wrong?' Miss Violet asked.

'Mr Rainwater has been called to the home of a friend.' Her calmness was faked, of course, but it had allayed the sisters' concern.

'It's like him, isn't it, to rush to the aid of a friend at a moment's notice,' Miss Pearl said. 'He's such a nice young man.'

As soon as dinner was over, Ella left Margaret to deal with the clean-up and took Solly to their rooms. His fit in the car that afternoon seemed to have sapped him of energy. He was docile when she gave him a sponge bath and dressed him in pyjamas.

She was relieved to discover that her boarders had retired early, too. The parlours were empty by the time she returned to the kitchen, where Margaret was wrapping a rag round her index finger.

'Oh dear, what happened?'

'I cut myself with that blamed ol' butcher knife. I'll bandage it soon as I get home.'

'Go on now.'

Margaret put up token protests, but Ella entreated her to leave and see to her injury. Eventually she did, apologising for leaving Ella with so much work still to be done. Actually, Ella didn't mind the seclusion. She didn't want to field any questions about the run-in with Conrad or Mr Rainwater's abrupt departure.

She ate her own dinner at the kitchen table, but nervousness robbed her of appetite. According to the kitchen clock, Mr Rainwater had been gone for over two hours. Where was he?

She was washing dishes when she heard his car coming down the street. Quickly drying her hands, she ran down the hallway and unlatched the screened door just as he reached it.

He stepped inside, pulled the door closed, and locked it again, then switched out the porch light. Sensing his tension, Ella stayed still and silent as he looked out across the yard and into the street.

After several minutes, he visibly relaxed. In a low voice, he asked, 'Is any of the cobbler left?'

She led him into the kitchen. They didn't speak until the door had closed behind them. 'There's food left. I can fix you a plate.'

He shook his head. 'Just the cobbler. After Margaret went to the trouble of making it, I should eat some. I expected her to be here.'

She told him about the cut finger. 'I sent her home. Coffee?'

'Definitely.'

She served him a mug of coffee and a dish of cobbler with a liberal helping of cream, then sat down at the table across from him. 'Where did you go? Why did Ollie call?'

'It seemed worse than it turned out to be.'

'What happened?'

'They attacked his house. When he called me, it was surrounded by several vehicles. Pick-ups, mostly. They were driving round and round the house, knocking down fence posts and Lola's clothes line. One flattened the hog pen. The hog got out. It's still missing.'

'Who was it?'

'I think we can guess.'

'Conrad?'

He blew on his coffee and took a sip. 'It was a warning, I think. They must've got wind of our organisation and the reason for it.'

'Or else this is retaliation over our encounter in the store today.'

Mr Rainwater dismissed her concern with a shake of his head. 'This had nothing to do with you. Recently we've had indications that they're on to us. Several times this week a rancher or farmer got a call that the cattle buyers would be there to evaluate their herd. They were given a day and time. The word was passed, as planned. We assembled. The buyers never showed up.'

'The calls were phony.'

'But effective.' He took another sip of coffee. 'Because now, when someone gets a call that the government is ready to do business with him, he doesn't know if it's false or the real thing.'

'Why not call the government office for verification?'

'We tried that, but nothing happens fast in a bureaucracy. By the time we'd get word that it was a false alarm, men had already wasted hours. My guess is that Conrad and his friends hope to wear us down. They think we'll give up our plan to protect each other.'

'Will you?'

'No.' He scraped up the last bit of cream. 'And if anyone's resolve was wavering, it was reinforced by what those thugs did tonight. When I got there, the pick-ups were still circling the house, throwing bottles. I could hear Ollie's kids screaming in fear.'

'They must have been terrified.'

'Which was the point. But our communication system worked. Angry men began to converge. When Conrad's gang saw they were about to become outnumbered, they struck out across the pasture and turned off their headlights. They got away.'

'What about Lola and the children? Was anyone hurt?'

'No. They were just scared. Ollie's father-in-law came and got Lola and the kids. Lola begged Ollie to leave with them, but he stayed. He was afraid those guys might come back, set fire to his barn. Something. A couple of men volunteered to stay with him.'

'Where will it end? How?'

Holding her eyes, he said earnestly, 'I don't know. But I'm afraid it might get worse before it gets better.'

She was afraid of that, too. 'Why do you think that?'

'The line has been drawn in the sand. There are two opposing sides. These things have a way of coming to a head. Especially when the law-enforcement agency is inept or flat-out corrupt.'

She left the table and went to the sink. She curved her hands over the edge of the draining board, bracing herself against it.

He brought his dish and coffee mug and added them to the stack of dishes to be washed. She turned towards him. 'I'm afraid.'

'I know. I'm sorry.'

'It's not your fault.'

'It is. You tried to talk me out of becoming involved. You said—'

'I remember clearly what I said, Mr Rainwater. But my quarrel with Conrad didn't start with you. I've always been afraid of him.'

He held her gaze until she could bear it no longer. Turning to the sink, she began washing the dishes. 'He pursued me through high school. My mother was thrilled. Conrad was the richest boy around. She thought he would make an ideal husband. I didn't.'

In a separate basin, she rinsed the dishes she had washed.

Out of the corner of her eye, she saw Mr Rainwater take off his suit jacket and drape it over a chair. He rolled up his shirtsleeves. Then he picked up a towel and reached for one of the rinsed dishes.

She put out a hand. 'Don't do this.'

Gently he moved her hand aside. 'Wash.'

How could she argue with him without admitting that the mundane chore had suddenly taken on an intimacy that panicked her?

'You weren't swayed by the Ellises' affluence?' he asked.

She resumed washing dishes. 'Hardly. I'd known Conrad since grade school. He was a terror in the classroom but got away with all his antics. He was spoiled and ornery. I don't believe his parents ever said no to him. They gave him everything he wanted.'

'He wanted you.'

She shrugged self-consciously. 'At Mother's urging, I attended a few dances and parties with him. In that smart-alecky way of his, he made it understood to everyone that we were a pair. But I didn't like him and was always uneasy whenever we were alone. I think he knew that. I think he enjoyed my unease.'

'He still does.'

'I'm sure,' she murmured. 'Anyway, when he failed to woo me, he turned his charm on my mother formally asked her for my hand. She had dollar signs in her eyes and couldn't see through him. When I rejected his proposal, Mother told me I was a fool and that I would regret my decision.'

She rinsed the meat platter and passed it to Mr Rainwater. Reading the silent question in his expression, she added, 'The only thing I regret is that when she died, she still hadn't forgiven me.'

'When did you marry Mr Barron?'

'Shortly after Mother died. I was running the house then. I'd placed an ad in the train depot. He worked for the railroad. He saw the ad and came to look at the room. He didn't rent it.'

Mr Rainwater thought that through, then said, 'He saw something here he liked better than the room.'

'If he'd been living in the house, he couldn't have courted me.'

'Did he court you?'

'Quite effectively. He was soft-spoken and polite, which was so different from Conrad's boasting and bullying.' Softly she added, 'But we both made vows we were unable to keep.'

They worked in silence until the last pan was dried and put away. She drained the sink and the rinse basin. He rolled down his shirtsleeves and fastened his cuff links. She removed her apron and hung it on a hook. And then both went still.

'Long day,' he said.

'Yes. Exhausting.'

Reluctant to look at him, she leaned across the table and repositioned the salt and pepper shakers in the centre of it.

'Ella?'

Hearing him speak her given name made her breath catch. She slowly raised her head and looked at him.

He lowered his gaze. 'I owe you an apology for speaking to you so brusquely this morning.'

This morning seemed like a very long time ago. Several moments passed before she recalled the harsh words to which he was referring: *I'm fine.* Spoken in anger from the staircase. 'It was nothing.'

'I was abrupt and rude. I'm sorry.'

'I made a pest of myself.'

'You were asking about my health out of genuine concern. That's why I got angry.'

She gave her head a slight shake of incomprehension.

'Why would my concern make you angry?'

His eyes took on a deeper intensity. 'Because you're the last beautiful woman I'll know. When you look at me, I don't want you seeing an invalid.'

ELLA SPENT a restless night.

Mr Rainwater didn't come down for breakfast, sending word by Margaret, who'd been upstairs gathering laundry, that he wanted only coffee. Ella sent Margaret back to his room with a tray. When she came downstairs, Ella expected a report on his condition. But Margaret said nothing until she asked.

'He seemed all right to me, Miss Ella.'

Ella didn't fish for more, and she resisted the impulse to check on him herself. She hoped that if his pain became unbearable, he wouldn't let his masculine pride prevent him from alerting her to it.

After lunch, a soft rain began to fall. It made the air even heavier with humidity. But the summer shower was a rare blessing that Ella wanted to enjoy, so she took a sack of string beans with her onto the front porch. She sat in the rocker with the sack of beans and a ceramic bowl in her lap. Solly was beside her on the floor with his bag of empty spools and the box of dominoes.

It was mindless work. She would cook the beans tomorrow. Maybe she'd toss in some new potatoes with the red jackets still on.

Her mind wandered from tomorrow's menu to yesterday's unsettling confrontation with Conrad, to the menace he'd wreaked at the Thompsons' farm last night, and then to the late interlude in the kitchen, where she had barely avoided breaking dishes she'd been washing for watching Mr Rainwater's hands as he'd dried them.

Ella, he'd said.

She hadn't acknowledged his addressing her by her first name, because it had been inappropriate. After his saying what he had about her being beautiful, she'd asked him to excuse her and had beaten a hasty retreat to her room.

Still, she had the memory of his speaking her name. Secretly she was glad to have heard the special resonance his voice had lent those two ordinary syllables. Somehow she knew it was a memory she would hold on to for a long time. Possibly for ever.

She was so lost in thought that at first she didn't realise Solly had got up and moved to the railing.

'Solly?'

He didn't respond, of course. He was intent on standing a domino on its end, squarely in the centre of the board that formed the rail. While she'd been wool-gathering, he'd been lining up the dominoes, so that now a dozen formed a straight line along the railing.

She left the beans in the seat of her chair and moved closer to the railing. After watching him for several moments, she saw that he was lining up the dominoes in ascending order. But, more importantly, he wasn't picking them out of a scattered pile, as he'd done before. He was searching in the box for the next one in sequence.

This wasn't the talent that idiot savants displayed, as explained to her by Dr Kincaid. Apparently, Solly possessed that extraordinary trait, too, but today he was reasoning. He was thinking it through before choosing the next domino. Essentially, he was counting!

She pressed her fingers to her lips to contain a sob of joy.

'Margaret said you didn't have the good sense to come in out of the rain.'

She whirled round as Mr Rainwater stepped onto the porch.

'Look.' She pointed at the dominoes. 'He took it upon himself to do this. I didn't begin the project for him. And watch.'

Mr Rainwater came and stood by her side. Solly had added only two dominoes to the row before Mr Rainwater realised what had caused her excitement. 'He's sorting through those in the box until he finds the next one in sequence.'

'Don't you think that's significant?'

'Absolutely.'

'Sunday, in the cemetery, I remember him gazing at the iron pickets of the gate. Obviously he's intrigued by the ordered and precise placement of things. Couldn't that fascination be fed and nurtured? It could even be developed into a skill, don't you think?'

'I certainly do. He could be building bridges one of these days.'

She smiled at his optimism. 'I'd be satisfied with less than that.'

Mr Rainwater touched Solly's shoulder. The boy flinched, but he didn't stop what he was doing. 'Good job, Solly.'

'Very good job, Solly,' she repeated.

Mr Rainwater said, 'I think this calls for a celebration. An ice-cream cone. Would you let me treat you and Solly?'

'Before dinner?'

'Celebrations should be spontaneous. Rules can be broken—'

'Mr Rainwater!' Margaret burst through the door, breathless with alarm. 'My boy, Jimmy, just called from the store, said there's gonna be trouble out the Hatchers' place. Conrad Ellis and his bunch were in the store talkin' 'bout what they was gonna do to any riffraff that showed up to interfere with gov'ment business.'

'I'm leaving now.' He went inside only long enough to snatch his hat from the hall tree. 'Where is the Hatcher place?'

'I'll go with you.' Ella tossed her apron onto the chair.

'Absolutely not,' he said. 'It could be dangerous.'

'It's easier for me to show you to their place than to give directions.' Sensing his hesitation, she added, 'We're wasting time.'

He nodded and charged down the front steps, Ella following.

'Watch Solly, Margaret,' she called over her shoulder.

'Don't you worry 'bout him. You take care of your own selves. Jimmy said they was drunk and actin' wild.'

BY THE TIME they arrived at the beef-cattle ranch located several miles west of Gilead, the situation was already tense. Assembled there were Ollie Thompson, Mr Pritchett, the postmaster, a minister and many others whom Ella recognised.

They nodded sombrely when Mr Rainwater parked his car and joined them just outside the barbed-wire fence that delineated the pasture. He was the only one of them unarmed.

Standing apart from them was another group, mostly Negroes, but some whites, too. By their gaunt faces and shabby clothing, Ella knew they must have come from the shantytown. Standing a full head taller than the others was Brother Calvin, looking grim but calm.

Mr Rainwater had advised Ella to remain in the car, when actually she had no intention of getting out. The only other woman in sight was Mrs Hatcher, who was standing in the hardscrabble patch of yard in front of her house, holding on to her husband's arm.

The rain shower had been short-lived, but the cloud cover was thick and oppressive. The air seemed too dense to inhale, made no easier to breathe by the stench of manure from the loaded cattle truck that rumbled out through the pasture gate and then down the dirt road in the direction of the main highway.

A wide, deep pit had been gouged out of the pasture. Possibly a hundred head of bawling cattle had been herded into it. Around it, men with rifles stood waiting the signal to start firing.

When they did, Ella jumped. The racket was deafening. She felt the concussion of each shot against her chest and closed her eyes.

The first gunshots had alarmed the cattle. Their lowing of discontent escalated into bellows of terror, heard even above the gunfire, which seemed to go on for ever. The silence that followed was as thick as the gunsmoke that wafted above the carnage.

Ella opened her eyes. None of the men, either in Mr Rainwater's group or with Brother Calvin, had moved a muscle.

The shooters lowered their rifles and began a slow progress towards the row of black cars parked along the road. A few of them lit cigarettes. All avoided eye contact with the silent spectators.

The leader stopped to say something to Mr Hatcher. Mr Hatcher gave a brusque motion of his hand. The man moved on and joined the others, who were climbing into the government cars.

No one moved as they drove away.

The convoy had gone several hundred yards but was still in sight when Mr Hatcher called, 'Y'all help yourselves if you like.'

Still no one moved. It was Mr Pritchett who called out, 'What did he say to you, Alton?'

'He said they'd be buried sometime today before dark. But not to let y'all butcher any meat off those carcasses or there'd be trouble and weren't nothin' he would do to stop it.'

Then Mr Hatcher turned and crossed his yard to a chopping block that was used for splitting firewood. He grabbed the axe and walked towards the pit. 'He can go to hell. For myself, I ain't gonna deny hungry folks some scraps of beef.'

A cheer went up. Brother Calvin gave a signal that seemed to unleash the men. They ran towards the pit carrying knives, hatchets and containers for whatever meat they could carve off the bony carcasses. Without a moment's hesitation, they plunged down into the mass grave. Ella realised what a motivator hunger was.

It wasn't until they had begun hacking at the dead cattle that anyone noticed the roar of engines. Mr Rainwater was the first to turn towards the sound, and his expression immediately registered alarm.

Across the road, speeding out from the dense woods, were several pick-up trucks and cars, overflowing with men brandishing firearms. They must have been hiding there, waiting for this moment.

Their vehicles crossed the road and braked at the ditch. Men spilled from the vehicles and swarmed round Mr Rainwater's car.

Ella saw Mr Hatcher scramble out of the cattle pit. He ran back to his petrified wife, shooed her into the house, and locked the door. Then he ran back to the pit, the bloody axe still in his hand.

Brother Calvin cautioned the men with him to remain calm. Men from town spread out, forming a human barricade against the onslaught of the new arrivals.

Ella watched Conrad as he stayed behind his vanguard until they were toe to toe with the townsmen. Then two of them moved aside and let him saunter between them. He walked up to Mr Rainwater.

Without thinking, Ella opened the car door and got out.

Conrad looked Mr Rainwater up and down, then made a scoffing sound. His friends laughed. He said, 'Are you their ringleader?'

'No.'

'Well, whoever your leader is better tell those niggers and ne'er-do-wells to get out of that pit or they're liable to get buried along with those dead cows.'

'Would you shoot unarmed men?'

'They're armed with knives.'

'Nobody with a knife has threatened anyone.'

'They're breaking the law.'

Mr Rainwater made a show of looking round. 'There isn't a lawman here to arrest them.'

'The government men put me in charge of making sure that no cattle were butchered.'

'Do you have documentation of that?'

Conrad hesitated. 'I don't need documentation. I'm in charge.'

'So you said,' Mr Rainwater said drily. 'Mr Ellis, if the government was against these men getting some free beef, Mr Hatcher's property would be crawling with agents wearing badges. Why would you want to do something so distasteful that even law-enforcement agencies avoid it? Why don't you let these men take what meat they can get and carry it back to their hungry families?'

'Why don't you kiss my ass?' That won Conrad another round of laughter from his friends, but even that ceased when he drove his fist into Mr Rainwater's face.

Mr Rainwater had seen the blow coming and dodged, but not fast enough. Conrad's knuckles grazed his cheekbone, drawing blood. Mr Rainwater reeled backwards, but Tad Wallace, owner of the salvage yard, put out an arm to catch him.

As soon as he'd steadied Mr Rainwater, Mr Wallace lunged at Conrad. But Mr Rainwater grabbed him and pulled him back. 'That's what he's asking for. An excuse to attack.'

Others murmured agreement. Mr Wallace backed down.

With the back of his hand, Mr Rainwater swiped the blood trickling down his face. 'You got what you came for, which was a swipe at me. You hit me, and now you've got bragging rights. So clear out and leave these folks alone.'

Looking amused, Conrad glanced over his shoulder at his buddies, and they all chuckled on cue. 'No. We're not ready to clear out just yet. And don't think you and these other yahoos can scare us off with a few shotguns and some rusty knives.'

'What about the promise of damnation? Would that scare you?'

As if from nowhere, Brother Calvin was suddenly standing behind some of Conrad's gang. His rumbling voice startled them. He walked forward until he stood only a foot away from Conrad. Even Conrad was diminished by Brother Calvin's imposing height and the breadth of his shoulders.

But Conrad wasn't intimidated. 'Aren't you the nigger preacher who's been keeping the others agitated?'

'You know who I am. You broke a window of my church, which didn't offend me nearly as much as it offended God. I know you're a bigot, and that doesn't make any difference to me. You'll have to answer for your hatred to the Almighty. What matters to me is that people are hungry, and here's a chance for them to get some meat.'

Conrad sneered at Brother Calvin. 'I'm giving you one minute to get away from here or we're going to start shooting.'

Mr Rainwater stepped forward. 'You'll have to shoot past us.'

Conrad extended his hand behind him, and one of his friends slapped a pistol into his palm. He brought it round and aimed it at Mr Rainwater's middle. 'Fine by me. I'll start with you.'

Ella froze, and there was a nervous shifting among Mr Rainwater's allies.

In contrast to them, Mr Rainwater remained unflappable. 'I didn't think you were that stupid, Mr Ellis.'

Conrad made a jabbing motion with the pistol.

Mr Rainwater didn't flinch. 'I didn't think you would be stupid enough to gun down men when there are so many witnesses.'

'I'll take my chances.'

'Yes, I'm sure you would. Since you've got Sheriff Anderson in your pocket.' Mr Rainwater angled his head to one side. 'Who do you know at the FBI?'

Conrad blinked. 'This isn't their business.'

'It will be. You said the government men put you in charge. Which I doubt. But if that's true and people wind up dead, who do you think is going to be left holding the bag?' He shook his head. 'If this turns into a bloodbath, they—from President Roosevelt on down—are going to blame you for shedding a bad light on a government programme that's meant to help people. But I guess you want a fight so bad none of that matters to you.'

One of Conrad's cronies whispered something in his ear. Ella couldn't hear what he said, but Conrad barked, 'Shut up.' To Mr Rainwater, he said, 'You think you're smart, don't you?'

'I think you are, Mr Ellis. I think you're too smart to continue this.'

'Come on, Conrad,' one of his friends whined. 'Let 'em have the damn cows. Who cares? Let's get outta here. Let's go get drunk.'

Muttering among themselves, Conrad's men began returning to their pick-ups. Eventually, Conrad was the only one left facing the townsmen.

He took a few steps backwards; then he pointed his pistol at all the men in turn, wagging it like a shaking finger 'Y'all know me, and you know I mean what I say. This isn't over. Not by a long shot.' Then he fired the revolver into the air until all six chambers were empty. Only then did he turn and stalk away.

Ella still stood in the wedge of the open car door. Fury blazed from Conrad's eyes as he passed her, snarling, 'You chose wrong again, Ella.'

Eight

'Isn't Mr Rainwater joining us tonight?' Miss Violet asked as Ella served the sisters their salads.

'He's out with friends.'

'Oh.' Miss Pearl couldn't mask her disappointment. She was wearing a fresh flower in her hair.

Miss Violet sighed. 'And Mr Hastings is gone again, so it's just the two of us tonight, sister.'

They ate their meal as mechanically as Ella served it. Her mind was elsewhere, with Mr Rainwater and the others who'd stayed behind to carve what edible meat they could from the slaughtered cattle and distribute it among those living in the shantytown.

'It's nasty work,' Mr Rainwater had told her after insisting he drive her back to town.

'I'm not afraid of raw meat. I could help.'

'You have other responsibilities.'

He was right, but she felt a bit let down to be returning to the mundane chore of preparing dinner for her elderly boarders.

'And I don't trust Conrad's surrender,' Mr Rainwater had said, adding it as a footnote. 'There may still be trouble.'

Ella feared Mr Rainwater was right about that, too. After being humiliated, the Conrad she knew would be plotting a harsh reprisal.

Mr Rainwater had then asked, 'What did he say to you as he left?'

'Something about me being on the wrong side.' She had remembered word for word Conrad's parting shot, but the paraphrase omitted the personal connotation, which she'd rather not share with Mr Rainwater.

He had dropped her at home, apologising for not walking her to the door. 'I need to get back to Hatcher's place right away. I probably won't be back by dinnertime.'

'Take care.'

He'd touched the brim of his hat and driven away.

After the sisters finished their dinner and went into the parlour to play cards, Ella coaxed Solly into eating. Margaret looked on, bragging on each bite he took. The maid was in good spirits tonight, having heard from Ella the outcome of the showdown. While Margaret finished the dishes, Ella put Solly down for the night and said good night to the spinsters as they made their way upstairs.

Margaret intended to stop in the shantytown before going home. Ella sent her off with two baskets of leftovers, then ate her own dinner alone at the kitchen table. Just as she was finishing, she heard a car. She made her way to the front door and tried not to reveal her disappointment when she saw Dr Kincaid huffing up the steps.

'Good evening, Mrs Barron,' he said when he saw her through the screen. 'I hoped to catch you before you went to bed.'

'My bedtime will be a while yet. Come in.' She motioned him towards the formal parlour. 'Would you like a glass of tea?'

'No, thank you. I just finished dinner. Is David here?'

'He's out tonight.'

'Hmm.' He removed his hat and took a seat. 'I received this today and wanted to share it with you as soon as possible.'

He extended to her a large envelope. It had been opened.

Ella sat down and withdrew several typewritten sheets. She scanned the top sheet, then looked at the doctor expectantly.

'He's a well-respected specialist,' he explained. 'I told you I'd written to doctors around the country asking for information about idiot savants. One of them sent this to me. The article was published in a medical journal. I thought you'd find it interesting.'

'Thank you.' She flipped through the pages.

'Some of the children with developmental impairments similar to Solly's are being taught to speak and read,' Dr Kincaid said. 'Of course, no one can boast one hundred per cent success, but any improvement is a stupendous step forward, wouldn't you say?'

She clutched the sheets against her chest. 'Thank you, Dr Kincaid. You can't know how grateful I am for your interest.'

'I believe I do,' he said, smiling.

She told him about Solly's achievement that day. 'He's only putting dominoes in a line and in numerical order, but I doubt most children his age would have the concentration to be that . . .'

'Meticulous?'

'Yes.'

'So says the doctor in his paper,' he said. 'That preciseness is a common trait among children with Solly's symptoms. After reading about this study, I believe I was wrong to urge you to keep him medicated. Solly can't communicate the level of his intelligence, so we have no way of knowing what his capabilities are. He may be limited to lining up dominoes, or he may harbour a brilliant mind. You owe it to him to make that determination if it's possible.'

She told him she'd written to several schools. 'I haven't received any replies yet. These particular institutions may have no experience with children like Solly. If they do have suitable curriculums, the expense of enrolling him would probably be prohibitive.' She paused, then added, 'Besides, I can't imagine sending him away.'

'Even if it was the best thing you could do for him?'

Unprepared to commit, she murmured, 'We'll see.'

After a moment, he stood up. 'I should run along.'

Ella showed him to the door and profusely thanked him again for bringing her the research paper. 'I can't wait to read it thoroughly.'

'After you've had time to digest the information, let's talk.' His gaze moved to the upper floor. 'How's he doing?'

She knew he was no longer speaking of Solly. 'He got snippy with me yesterday. He'd told me repeatedly that he was feeling fine, but I continued to badger him. He finally had enough.' That was essentially the truth. 'Ordinarily, he's so even-tempered.'

'He can also be bull-headed. He was the most stubborn child I've ever run across. Not bratty, just persistent. He would wear you down until he got his way.' He chuckled. 'I also remember him pitching a temper tantrum or two when he didn't.'

She couldn't envision Mr Rainwater throwing a tantrum, but she could imagine him being mulish. Twice his steely resolve had forced Conrad to stand down.

Dr Kincaid frowned. 'You said he was out. I suppose he was at Alton Hatcher's ranch today. And in the shantytown tonight.'

She nodded.

'I tried to discourage his involvement in this business. You don't want Conrad Ellis and his gang as enemies.'

'I tried to tell him that, too, Dr Kincaid. It did no good.'

The doctor sighed. 'It wouldn't.'

'Has he always been committed to causes like this?'

'Lost causes, you mean?'

'Why do you say it's a lost cause?'

'Because throughout history, there have been bullies, and I don't think that's likely to change. During this economic depression, there are going to be those who suffer and vultures who take advantage of their suffering. But just so I don't sound like an old codger, let me add that hard times can also bring out the best in people.'

'Like Mr Rainwater.'

'Yes. David typically takes up for the underdog. I think he grew up feeling guilty for the advantages he was born with. David's father inherited thousands of acres of good land, and he was a savvy cotton grower. He made a lot of money during the Great War. By the time David was an adolescent, he knew more about cotton growing than most men who'd been in the business for decades.

'He went to college and learned even more about business. On graduation, he became a successful broker in his own right. He still owns the acreage that made his daddy rich. The market is so low now, he only cultivates a fraction of it, but he hasn't cast off a single tenant. The income from it is less than it's been in years past, but when this depression is over . . . well, the land isn't going anywhere, and there will always be a market for cotton.'

What he was telling her was that David Rainwater had significant money. 'He could live anywhere. Why here?' she asked.

'For one thing, he wanted me to treat him. Mrs Kincaid and I are his only family.'

'He never married?'

'No, but not for lack of opportunity,' he said, laughing softly. 'Every single lady in north Texas tried to nab him. I asked him once why he remained a bachelor when he had lovely ladies throwing themselves at him. He told me he was holding out for a woman who wanted him for himself, not for his means.'

Ella was still curious as to why Mr Rainwater, who could obviously afford better, would live in a boarding house. 'He could be in a house of his own,' she mused aloud. 'And one much grander than mine.'

'He had a house of his own. He left it and came here. I suppose he'd rather not be alone while going through this.' He put on his hat. 'I really must say good night. Let me know what you think of the research paper. And it goes without saying to call me if David takes a downturn.'

'Of course. Good night. Thank you again.'

After seeing him off, she began to read the medical report. She was going through it a second time when Mr Rainwater returned.

She was at the door before he reached it. When she saw him, her heart surged to her throat and she gasped.

'It's all right,' he said quickly. 'It isn't my blood. I told you it would be messy business. Do you mind if I use the tap in the laundry shed to wash?'

'I'll bring a bar of soap and a towel to the back door.'

'Could I also trouble you to fetch me some clean clothes?'

'I'll bring them right down.'

He disappeared round the corner of the house, making for the back. Ella hurried upstairs to his room. She found shirts and slacks hanging neatly in the closet and hesitated only a moment before opening his bureau drawer and taking out a pair of undershorts and socks.

She had touched his undergarments before, when she did laundry, but she always left her boarders' clothes folded on the bed. It was different to take such personal items from his bureau drawer.

From the bathroom, she took a cloth, towel and bar of soap, then hastened downstairs, through the kitchen, to the back door, where he was waiting. She pushed open the screened door. He reached out for the items, but she withheld them. 'If you touch the clothes, they'll only get blood on them. I'll carry them out for you.'

'Thank you.'

She picked her way across the dark back yard to the shed and set his clothes on the worktable. 'There's no light out here.'

'I'll manage.'

'Are you hungry?'

'Not for red meat.'

She smiled. 'I made chicken salad for tomorrow's lunch. I'll fix you a sandwich.' She left him. Before she entered the house, she heard the tap being turned on and the splash of water.

She made the sandwich, then put it on a plate along with sliced tomatoes and a wedge of cantaloupe. She also cut a piece of pound cake and put it on a separate plate. She fixed a pot of coffee. Then she sat down, her back to the door, and waited.

When she heard him pull open the screened door, she turned. He was standing on one leg, pulling on his sock. 'My shoes are filthy. I'll have to clean them in the morning, when I can see better.' He pulled on his other sock, then walked into the kitchen.

He smelled of soap. His hair was wet, finger-combed off his face. 'I left my clothes soaking in a washtub. I hope that's all right.'

'Margaret will see to them in the morning.'

'I can't ask her to do that.'

She motioned him towards the table, where his supper was waiting. 'She'll do it gladly. You're her hero.'

He looked at the food. 'This looks awfully good. Thanks.' He pulled the chair from beneath the table and sat down.

'What would you like to drink?'

'Milk, please.'

She filled a glass, but after replacing the milk bottle in the icebox, she was unsure what to do next. Join him at the table?

He looked up. 'What's the matter?'

'Do you want company?'

He stood up and indicated the chair across the table. 'Please.'

She sat down. 'I thought you might be tired of talking about it.'

'I'm tired, but in a good way.'

'So it went well? No more trouble?'

'No more trouble. We managed to butcher several head before the front loaders showed up to bury them. The rest of the time was spent distributing the meat so it could be cooked before it spoiled.'

'Dr Kincaid said these times bring out the best in people.'

'When did you see him?'

She told him about the doctor's visit and the article on the study that he'd left with her. His eyes shone with interest. 'When you're finished, I'd like to read it if I may.'

'I'll welcome your opinion.'

He finished his meal and stood up. 'I'll be right back.'

He was out of the kitchen before she could ask where he was going. When he reappeared, he brought with him a book.

He grinned as he extended it to her. 'Seems everyone is bringing you reading material today.'

Ella read the title. *A Farewell to Arms.* 'You finished it?'

'This morning. That's why I didn't come down for breakfast. I didn't want to stop until I'd read it through. I was going to give it to you immediately, but then the day got away from us.'

She ran her fingertips over the title. 'I'll read it quickly and get it back to you. In the meantime, I'll take excellent care of it.'

'It's a gift, Ella.'

Quickly she looked up at him. 'I can't accept it.'

'Please do. Please. I want you to have it.'

She held his gaze, then lowered her head. 'Is the ending sad?'

'Very.' In a low voice, he said, 'Even knowing the ending was sad, I wouldn't have deprived myself the beauty of the story. Would you?'

She glanced up but dropped her gaze back to the book. She didn't *know* her answer. She sought it in the words on the cover, but they began to blur. She was looking at them through tears.

THE FOLLOWING DAY, she avoided him.

He came down for breakfast and chatted cheerfully with the Dunne sisters. Each time he tried to catch Ella's eye, she avoided looking at him. Two nights in a row he'd been the last person to whom she'd said good night, and that was unsettling. Nothing improper had happened between them, but she would be less than honest with herself if she didn't admit that their relationship had shifted to something beyond that of landlady and boarder. There had been an air of intimacy during those moments.

With him, she felt uncertain and flustered. His mere presence caused an unaccountable tension in her chest. Last night, being close enough to feel his breath on her face and hearing the bittersweet sadness in his voice had provoked tears. When they spilled onto her cheeks, she had wished him a good night and fled, just as she had the night before. But last night he had seen her tears and would have wondered what had caused them. *She* had wondered.

Something about his insisting that she accept the sentimental novel as a gift had caused an outpouring of emotions. She was skilled at containing fear, anger, heartache, even joy. She was adept at holding back tears. But her rigid control had deserted her.

It frightened her, this loss of restraint. She didn't want to feel any emotion that keenly, believing that if she ever allowed any slippage in the wall of protection she'd built round her heart, she wouldn't be able to prevent its total collapse. And then where would she be?

Exactly where she was now. Her circumstances wouldn't have changed. She would still be living as a widow without benefit of the official status. Her child would still be locked inside a realm she couldn't trespass. Day would follow day, each exactly the same, all with their endless, thankless chores, without any respite.

But if she ever gave way to self-pity, she would be reduced by it and left even more susceptible to disappointment and despair.

That's what she'd tried to explain to Mr Rainwater when she stopped him from weeding the garden. She had her life in careful balance, and she couldn't allow anything or anyone to upset it. But what she feared most, what had kept her tossing and turning last night, was the fear that the scales already had been tipped.

Today her fear manifested itself in a cross mood that Margaret remarked upon as she prepared the string beans to simmer. After Ella admonished her twice to go easy on the bacon grease, she muttered, 'Somebody's got they's jaw out of joint this mornin'.'

Ignoring her, Ella went about doing her routine tasks, even invented extra ones, to more easily avoid Mr Rainwater. Which she did successfully until after dinner, when he came out onto the porch, where she was watching Solly as he lined up the dominoes.

Mr Rainwater closed the screened door gently. 'He's at it again?'

'Of his own accord. I brought the dominoes out. He took the box from me and went to work.' Even her determination to keep her distance from Mr Rainwater couldn't dampen her pride in this.

'Thank you for leaving the medical report in my room. I read it this afternoon. I understand why you're excited about this study.'

'I wish there were a way for that specialist to see Solly. There isn't, of course, but I'm thinking of asking Dr Kincaid to write to him, describing Solly's characteristics. He may be more inclined to reply to another physician than to an anxious mother.'

'I'm sure Murdy would do that for you.'

In silence, they watched until Solly had lined up all the dominoes; then Mr Rainwater said, 'Good job, Solly.'

Ella said, 'Yes, Solly. Good job.'

'We were stopped from celebrating yesterday.' Mr Rainwater took out his pocket watch and checked the time. 'The drugstore is open until nine thirty. Let's go to town and get an ice-cream cone.'

'The last time I tried feeding Solly an ice-cream cone, he got upset when it began to melt over his hand. He didn't like the mess.'

'Then we'll get his in a cup.'

'Thank you, Mr Rainwater, but it's time I put him to bed.'

'Miss Ella?'

'Out here, Margaret.'

Margaret came onto the porch, her handbag on her arm. 'I's leavin' 'less you need me to do something else before I go.'

'Thank you, no. I'll see you in the morning.'

Mr Rainwater said, 'I'm trying to talk Mrs Barron into letting me take her and Solly to the drugstore for some ice cream. Maybe she'll agree to it if you come with us. I'll drive you home after.'

'I can't sit at the soda fountain, Mr Rainwater. You know that.'

'I don't want to sit at the soda fountain,' he said. 'I was thinking of taking a stroll around the square while I was eating my cone.'

'It's too late,' Ella said, but neither of them paid her attention.

Margaret was beaming. 'I'm partial to plain ol' vanilla.'

'My favourite is strawberry. How about you, Mrs Barron?'

'Chocolate. But it's too late—'

'Come on, Miss Ella,' Margaret wheedled. 'It's pleasant out. How come you won't let Mr Rainwater buy Solly an ice cream?'

He had outfoxed her. There was no way she could refuse without denying Margaret a treat, because he couldn't be seen strolling round the square alone with a coloured lady without inviting censure from both whites and Negroes.

Defeated and not unhappy about it, Ella said, 'I'll get my hat.'

ELLA HAD RESOLVED not to be seen riding with him again. If people saw them often together in his car, they would begin to talk. But the square was deserted when he parked in front of the drugstore.

The only person she had to worry about gossiping was Doralee, who was tending the fountain that night. She was bucktoothed and compensated for it with a sour disposition.

Doralee was squinting at them curiously through the store's windows as they climbed out of Mr Rainwater's car and approached the door. Ella said, 'Solly and I will wait out here with Margaret.'

'What flavour will Solly want?'

'Vanilla.'

'Chocolate for you?'

'Please.'

'Looks like Brother Calvin is working late,' Margaret remarked as she sat down beside Ella on the bench outside the store.

Ella followed her gaze toward the African Methodist Episcopal church. It was two blocks off the town square, on Elm Street, which was the racial demarcation of town. Because the lights were on inside, the church was visible through the trees.

'I guess he's fixin' that broke window,' Margaret mused.

Mr Rainwater paused on his way into the drugstore. 'Go and invite him to join us.'

Margaret smiled. 'That's very kindly of you, Mr Rainwater.'

Margaret crossed the street, then walked along the sidewalk to the nearest corner, where she turned out of sight.

Ella could hear Mr Rainwater ordering their ice creams. 'And put one of those vanillas in a cup, please.'

Beside her on the bench, Solly was staring straight ahead, rocking back and forth. In the next block, she noticed a light going off in an office building. Moments later the town's only lawyer came out of the office, got into his car, and drove away.

'Here we are.' Mr Rainwater pushed his way through the door, carrying a dish of ice cream for Solly and a chocolate cone for her. 'Miss Doralee is dishing up—'

He was interrupted by a scream so piercing that even Solly reacted. He stopped rocking. Ella shot to her feet.

Mr Rainwater dropped the dish and the cone onto the sidewalk and bolted across the street, running in the direction of the church, from where the scream seemed to have come. He didn't go to the corner but plunged into the alley between the grocery store and the post office.

Another scream rent the night air.

Ella grabbed Solly's hand and followed Mr Rainwater. She was practically dragging her son as she ran into the alley into which Mr Rainwater had disappeared. It opened into a wider alley, which ran the length of the block behind the commercial buildings.

The lane was littered with debris and Ella paused, unwilling to take Solly down it. In the fence that bordered the alley, Ella noticed that several boards were missing, creating an opening. Gripping Solly's hand, she squeezed him with her between the slats. On the other side was the back yard of an abandoned house. Without decreasing her speed, she forged a path through the weeds and across the uneven ground, her heart in her throat and her lungs burning.

She had gained on Mr Rainwater. He was still running, but he seemed to have a stitch in his side. He had a hand to it as he crossed Elm Street and entered the churchyard. Ella was only steps behind him by the time he climbed the stairs to the door of the church. Inside, the screams had been reduced to keening.

Before going in, he glanced back at Ella. 'Don't look.'

His warning came too late. Through the open door, she saw Brother Calvin hanging by his neck from a ceiling beam.

MARGARET WAS INCONSOLABLE. Mr Rainwater drew her up from her huddled position and guided her onto the stairs. Ella sat down beside her and embraced her, murmuring words of comfort.

Mr Rainwater and she had been the first to reach the church, but others, alerted by Margaret's screams, converged from every direction of the coloured community. Mr Rainwater had closed the church door, but the hanging body could easily be seen through the windows. Cries of horror punctuated the buzz of voices. There was weeping. Children were standing wide-eyed and subdued.

A car stopped at the kerb, and the lawyer Ella had seen leaving his office minutes before got out. He spied Ella and threaded his way through the crowd. Approaching the church stairs, he removed his hat. 'Mrs Barron? I heard screams.'

'The pastor has been lynched, Mr Whitehead.'

'Oh.' He released the word on a sigh of regret and sympathy.

'Could you notify the sheriff, please?' Mr Rainwater asked.

The lawyer looked beyond Ella at him and must have sensed his trait of calm command. 'Right away, sir.' He ran back to his car.

Mr Rainwater knelt down beside Ella. He looked pale. She remembered him holding his side. 'Are you in pain?'

He shook his head. 'Just winded. Here is the key to my car.' He pressed the key into her hand. 'I'll wait for the sheriff. Take Margaret home. You can come back by here and pick me up.'

'Won't she need to tell him what she saw? For his investigation.'

His lips formed a thin line. 'There won't be an investigation.'

ELLA ARRIVED at Margaret's house, surprised to find a gathering of friends and relatives. Although she shouldn't have been surprised. Word of something this tragic had a way of spreading quickly.

Men stood in the yard, smoking and talking. Women were waiting inside the house for Margaret's return. Ella left Solly in the front seat of the car, where he seemed content, and helped Margaret up onto the porch.

Margaret's son, Jimmy, was waiting just inside the door. Margaret let out a wail and collapsed into his arms.

Knowing that Margaret would be well taken care of, Ella turned to go. As she stepped out onto the porch, Jimmy followed her. 'Thank you, Miz Barron,' he said.

'This is terrible for her, Jimmy. She thought so highly of Brother Calvin. We all did.'

'Yes, ma'am.' He looked across the yard for a moment; then his eyes came back to her. 'We all know who did it.'

The young man's anger made Ella afraid for him. She looked at him with appeal. 'Don't make trouble for yourself, Jimmy. Your mother would never recover if something happened to you.'

'I'll be careful.'

That wasn't exactly a promise not to seek reprisal for the lynching, but Ella knew it wasn't her place to admonish him. 'Tell Margaret not to come back to work until she feels up to it.'

'I will.'

'And let me know when the funeral is.'

'Thank you again for bringing her home.' Then he looked at her with puzzlement. 'How come y'all were in town tonight?'

She told him about Mr Rainwater taking them to get ice cream and sending Margaret to invite Brother Calvin to join them. Jimmy lowered his head. When, after a moment, he raised it, she saw tears in his eyes. He thanked her again, then went back into the house.

'HE SEEMED very touched by your kindness to his mother,' Ella told Mr Rainwater, concluding her account to him of what had happened when she took Margaret home.

Only a few people had still been at the church when she returned to pick him up. The sheriff's car had been parked in front. He was talking to the justice of the peace, who'd been summoned to pronounce Brother Calvin dead. A few onlookers were milling about.

Mr Rainwater was standing near the street. He got into the car as soon as Ella brought it to a stop. Now he glanced down at Solly, who was sitting between them docilely. 'He looks almost asleep.'

'He ran along beside me all the way from the drugstore to the church. Through it all, he's been a real trouper.'

'Maybe he sensed you needed him to.'

'Maybe.'

SOLLY WAS ASLEEP by the time they arrived at the house. Ella welcomed the sweet pressure of his head against her arm and almost hated having to get out. 'I'll get him,' Mr Rainwater said.

Gently he lifted Solly into his arms, careful not to awaken him.

Both Dunne sisters rushed to the front door to let them in. They were dressed in nightclothes, slippers and hairnets. They were twittering, speaking over each other.

'We've been scared out of our wits!' Miss Violet exclaimed.

'What's going on in town? We heard sirens.' Miss Pearl clutched her sister's arm, managing to look both alarmed and excited at the same time.

'Mr Rainwater, you look peaked.' Miss Violet's concerned voice cut through Pearl's chatter.

Ella looked at him. He did look peaked.

'What's the matter with the boy?'

'Nothing, Miss Pearl. He's sleeping. And I'm fine, just winded.' Mr Rainwater carried Solly in the direction of Ella's room.

She followed him, saying over her shoulder, 'You can go to bed. There was a . . . a situation on the other side of town. Sheriff Anderson was summoned. Everything is fine now.' Soon enough they would learn of the lynching, but Ella didn't want to go into it tonight. She left them at the staircase and continued towards her room.

Mr Rainwater was standing in the centre of it, holding Solly in his arms.

'Through there. Thank you.' Ella pointed him towards the small room in which Solly slept.

He squeezed through the narrow doorway and laid Solly carefully on the bed. She slipped off Solly's shoes but decided to let him sleep in his clothes. 'Thank you again, Mr Rainwater.'

'Will you join me on the porch?'

'I don't think so. It's late.'

'Please? There's something I need to tell you.'

Nine

'Conrad Ellis has been deputised.'

Mr Rainwater broke that to her the moment she joined him on the porch, before she had even sat down.

'*What?*'

'The sheriff made him a deputy. At his request, I'm sure.'

Stunned, she moved to the railing where Solly's dominoes had been left standing in their precise row. 'How do you know?'

'He arrived with the sheriff, sporting a badge, carrying a shotgun. He made certain I saw both. He had the honour of being appointed to cut down Brother Calvin.'

'From the beam on which he'd hanged him.'

'Almost certainly.'

The enormous inequity of the situation had left Ella speechless. Apparently, Mr Rainwater had nothing to say, either. He looked dispirited and tired. His face was gaunt. She noticed that when he stood up, he was holding his side. He walked to the door, pulled open the screened door, then looked back at her.

'I don't need to tell you what this means.'

'Conrad has been given authority to run roughshod over anyone he chooses and get away with it.'

'You must take care.'

'And so must you.'

Mr Rainwater nodded, then went inside.

Ella picked the dominoes off the railing and stacked them neatly inside their box. An unheralded sob escaped her. Tears formed, then flowed. She covered her mouth with one hand in an effort to suppress the sobs, but they wouldn't be contained. She cried for Margaret, who'd had the misfortune of making that ghastly discovery. She cried for Brother Calvin, who'd been kind, generous and courageous. For Ollie and Lola. For the Hatchers and the Pritchetts, for all those who'd had to destroy their herds in order to hang on to their farms. She wept over the cruel and bizarre irony of that.

Eventually she brought the sobs under control. She went inside and locked the door, then went through the house turning out lights. In her room, she undressed down to her slip and pulled on her summer-weight wrapper. Ashamed of her red eyes, she bathed them with cold water until they looked normal, then cleaned her teeth and finally pulled the pins from her hair and uncoiled the heavy bun.

She was turning down her bed when the knock on her door came.

Making certain that her wrapper was securely belted, she went to the door and opened it a crack. 'Mr Rainwater.' Instantly concerned, she opened the door wider. 'Are you ill?'

'I heard you crying. My room is just above the porch.'

'Oh. Yes. I didn't think. I'm sorry if I disturbed you.'

'You didn't.' He paused, then asked her why she'd been crying.

'It was silly.'

He said nothing, just stood there looking down into her face, patiently— or stubbornly—waiting for her to explain.

She made a helpless gesture. 'There just seems to be . . .'

'What?'

'So much cruelty, and pain and sadness in life. And I was just wondering why that is.' Of course the ultimate unfairness was his circumstance. The reminder of that brought fresh tears to her eyes. 'Thank you for your concern, but I'm fine.'

'Are you?'

She looked into his eyes, but her nod of affirmation must not have been convincing, because he didn't move. Nor did she. They continued to stare at each other until she began to feel the same tightness in her chest that she'd felt last night when she'd held the gift of his book in her hands.

He took a step nearer. She saw her name, *Ella*, form on his lips, but she couldn't hear it for the sound of her pulse drumming in her ears.

Slowly he placed one hand on each side of her face, curving them to fit her cheeks. He lowered his head. Feeling his breath warm on her face, she made a weak mewling sound. He touched his lips to the corner of her mouth. Her breath caught.

Then he kissed the other corner of her lips. She closed her eyes, squeezing out tears that felt very wet, very hot on her cheeks.

'Don't cry,' he whispered.

The brush of his lips across hers sparked a longing deep within. It didn't unfurl gradually. It erupted. So that when he kissed her mouth fully, she began making such hungry sounds he backed her gently into the room and softly closed the door with his foot.

With the door at his back for support, he pulled her to him, and they clung to each other. She revelled in the feel of his arms round her, his breath quick against her neck. She leaned into him, feeling the solidness of his form in thrilling contrast to the softness of hers.

She touched his throat with her lips. His skin was warm. She breathed deeply of his smell, so familiar to her now but so very forbidden until this moment, when she didn't deny herself indulging in it, drinking it in, committing it to memory for life.

He eased her away and combed his hands through her hair. Then his eyes settled on hers. His remarkable eyes. Blue and pure, the most beautiful eyes she had ever seen. 'I love you, Ella.'

She closed her eyes for a brief few seconds, and when she opened them again, she whispered shakily, 'I know.'

'I would never do anything to damage you.'

'No, you wouldn't.'

'So if you tell me to leave, I will.'

She laid her cheek against his chest. 'If you left me now, I wouldn't survive my regret.'

He tilted her face up and slanted his lips across hers.

SHE DIDN'T HAVE a mirror, but she knew that, as she gazed into his face, her eyes must have been full of wonder. 'I had no idea.'

He was equally intent on his study of her face. 'What?'

'That I could feel, that *anyone* could feel, something that extraordinary and live through it.' She smiled and laid her head on his shoulder. 'It was nothing like that with my husband. I didn't love him. Perhaps that's why.'

'If you didn't love him, why did you marry him?'

'I'd already rejected Conrad. I suppose I was afraid that if I continued turning down suitors, I soon wouldn't have any. I didn't want to wind up the old-maid landlady of a boarding house.' Pensively, she added, 'Of course, that's what happened. Essentially.'

Mr Rainwater took a strand of her hair. 'Your husband must not have loved you, either, Ella. If he had, he wouldn't have left you.'

'He loved me, I think. But he just couldn't handle what was happening to Solly. Maybe he was frustrated because he couldn't fix it. Or perhaps he saw what having a child like Solly would mean to our lives, and he simply had to escape. But I don't suppose I'll ever know what drove him to leave.'

'You don't know if he's dead or alive?'

She shook her head, then lifted it from his shoulder and, looking down on him, smiled wanly. 'It's likely that I'm an adulteress. Willfully and gladly I've committed that sin tonight.' Her eyes began to fill. 'Is loving you God's way of punishing me?'

He drew her to him, saying, 'No, Ella, no. It's His blessing.'

IT WAS INEVITABLE—morning came.

As the eastern sky began to turn grey, Ella woke up. She lay perfectly still, revelling in the feel of him against her.

Begrudgingly, she woke him. He groaned a protest but knew he had to leave her room before they were discovered. They got the giggles as he searched in the dark for his clothes.

'Hurry,' she said, stifling her laughter. 'You don't want the Dunne sisters to catch you sneaking out of my bedroom.'

'How do you know I haven't been sneaking out of theirs since I moved in?'

That set her off again, and she had to cover her mouth to trap the giggles inside. He removed her hand and tried to kiss her, but she dodged it. 'Go! If you want biscuits for breakfast—'

'I'm going.'

HE WAS THE FIRST to come downstairs. He had washed, shaved and changed clothes. Her eyes gobbled him up.

She missed Margaret's helping hands, but despite the reason for her absence, Ella was glad she wasn't there this morning. Surely Margaret would have sensed the change in her.

The atmosphere crackled each time she and Mr Rainwater made eye contact. When she was near him, only the strongest act of will kept her from touching him. She knew he was feeling similarly.

The spinster sisters seemed oblivious to the dramatic differences between yesterday and today, which Ella found incredible. She swore she could feel her blood coursing through her veins as though dams that had been holding it back all her life had been opened, unlocked by Mr Rainwater's touch. Her body tingled deliciously.

Were these overpowering physical sensations what the preachers called lust? If so, she now realised why they were warned against from pulpits around the world. They were more powerful than the sweetest narcotic, more intoxicating than the strongest liquor. She now understood how easily and happily one would relinquish control to them until they governed one's whole being. Little had she known, or ever even imagined, that what men and women did together could be so breathtakingly beautiful.

She finished her chores quickly. After lunch, he invented an errand for himself and invited her and Solly to go along. It was a contrivance to get the three of them out of the house and alone.

They drove into the countryside and found a shady, pleasant spot in a grove of pecan trees that grew alongside a creek. There they spread a quilt. For a time, Mr Rainwater engaged Solly in card games, and they marvelled at the progress he'd made.

'He's grasping concepts, Ella,' he said excitedly when Solly responded successfully to a challenge. 'I'm sure of it.'

'So am I.' She was equally sure that Solly wouldn't have come this far if not for Mr Rainwater. She was immensely thankful.

They could not, however, coax Solly to wade into the creek with them. He got visibly upset when they tried to remove his shoes, so they returned to the quilt and gave him the deck of cards. He played with them while Mr Rainwater laid his head in Ella's lap and read aloud to her from the Hemingway novel.

At one point, he stopped, tilted his head back, and seeing the tears in her eyes, said, 'This isn't even the sad part.'

'I'm not crying because I'm sad. I don't remember a moment of my life when I've been this happy. And it's because of you.'

He sat up and placed his arms round her. They kissed, chastely. But for the remainder of the time, they sat with their arms wrapped round each other, basking in the love they'd found.

ELLA HAD TO RUSH to get dinner on the table by six thirty and guiltily used Margaret's absence as an excuse for it being a cold supper of sliced ham and various salads. The Dunnes didn't seem to mind, probably because Mr Rainwater paid them extra attention.

As Ella was finishing the dishes, Jimmy came to the back door with a message. 'Brother Calvin's funeral is tomorrow at five o'clock.'

'Why so late in the day?'

'So they can have dinner on the grounds after.'

It was a term used for picnics usually held after Sunday services when people tended the graves of loved ones in the adjacent cemetery. Food was brought and shared in the churchyard.

'The funeral is at the church?'

'Seemed fittin'.'

Ella supposed it did, although she didn't know how anyone could enter that sanctuary without thinking of the young minister's body hanging from the beam. Maybe the funeral was an attempt to purify it, rid it of that stigma. 'How is your mother?'

'She's heartbroke.'

'All of us are.'

'Meanin' no disrespect, Miss Ella. But not all.'

Later she recounted the conversation to Mr Rainwater. 'I'm worried about Jimmy and other young men. I hope they won't try and get revenge.'

'I hope they won't, either, because that would create more trouble. But one could hardly blame them if they wanted vengeance.'

Ella's concerns were justified later that evening.

She and Mr Rainwater were sitting apart in the parlour, waiting in an agony of anticipation for the Dunne sisters to retire, when he went to the front window. 'Something's burning.'

Ella joined him at the window. The flames could be seen against the night sky. 'Something near the highway.'

Just then the telephone rang. As Ella walked towards the back of the staircase to answer it, Miss Pearl appeared in the arched opening of the informal parlour. 'Mrs Barron, we smell smoke.'

'Something in town is on fire.'

'Oh dear,' whimpered Miss Violet.

Ella answered the phone. It was Ollie Thompson. He was calling to pass along information. She thanked him and hung up, turning to find her three boarders in the hallway, waiting to hear the news.

'That was Ollie. He knew we had probably smelled the smoke. He called to tell us that the fire is at Packy Simpson's auto garage.'

'Oh, what a shame,' Miss Pearl said. 'He's such a nice Nigra. Always tips his hat to us, doesn't he, sister?'

Ignoring them, Ella looked at Mr Rainwater, who asked, 'How did it start?'

'The sheriff accused him of leaving a cigarette burning in an ashtray when he closed up shop. Mr Simpson dips snuff. He doesn't smoke.' She let that sink in, then said, 'His business is a total loss, but he's glad the fire didn't spread to his house. The two buildings are separated by only twenty yards.'

The sisters drifted back into the informal parlour. Ella motioned Mr Rainwater back into the front room. Solly was where she'd left him, sitting on the rug stacking spools. 'Mr Simpson is a deacon at Brother Calvin's church,' she said in a voice that the spinsters couldn't overhear. 'He's a pall-bearer for the funeral tomorrow.'

Mr Rainwater asked, 'Where was Ollie calling from?'

'The drugstore. People had congregated there to watch the fire.'

He headed to the door. Ella rushed after him. 'You're going?'

'I want to see what I can learn. It can't be a coincidence that a Negro's business burns down the night after another was lynched.'

She agreed, but her heart constricted with anxiety. 'Don't go.'

'I won't be long.' He put on his hat.

'You're favouring your side. I didn't want to make you angry by asking about it. It's hurting you, isn't it? Let me call Dr Kincaid.'

'I'm fine.' He smiled at her attempt to keep him there. 'I won't be long.'

As he stepped through the door, she grabbed his arm. 'Promise me you'll be careful.'

'I promise.' He glanced behind her to see that the coast was clear, then whispered, 'I'll see you later.'

Ten

It was much later when she heard his car. By that time she had put Solly down for the night, finished preparations for tomorrow's meals and whipped herself into a full-blown panic, which he dispelled the instant she unlocked the screened door to let him in.

'I'm all right. When the drugstore closed, some of us hung around, making ourselves visible in the hope there wouldn't be any more incidents tonight. There weren't.'

'Thank heaven for that.'

'Yes, but the general consensus is that the fire was set as a warning to anyone who might be plotting revenge for Brother Calvin. As you might guess, Mr Simpson had been rather outspoken about the lynching. There was a prayer meeting held at noon. He prayed that God's wrath would rain down on those guilty of his pastor's murder. Which, by the way, Sheriff Anderson ruled a suicide.'

'That's ludicrous.'

'Everyone knows better. That's why tension is so high.'

While Ella was worried about the volatile situation, she was selfishly relieved to have Mr Rainwater back safe and sound. She wanted to throw her arms round him and tell him so, but a wavering voice came from the top of the stairs.

'Is everything all right in town, Mrs Barron?'

She turned to see both the Dunne sisters peering at them over the banister. 'Yes, fine,' she said, struggling to keep the disappointment out of her voice. She'd been hoping that Mr Rainwater could come directly to her room. Now that was impossible. She was being cheated of time with him and she wanted to rant over it. Instead, she said calmly, 'Mr Rainwater has just come back.'

He headed for the staircase. 'Ladies, I'm pleased to report that the fire is out and that it was contained to one structure. It's a sad loss for Mr Simpson, but at least there were no casualties.'

The sisters murmured their agreement.

He was halfway up the staircase before he glanced down at Ella. 'I apologise for making you wait up to let me in, Mrs Barron.'

'I would have been up anyway, Mr Rainwater. Good night.'

IT WAS THE LONGEST HOUR of Ella's life, because each minute that passed was one that she didn't have with him. She despaired that once he reached his room, he'd fallen asleep. The thought of having to forfeit a night with him almost brought her to tears.

She didn't recognise this hysteria in herself. Twenty-four hours ago she had been uneasy with his using her given name. Now she was afraid that he wouldn't share her bed again.

When he knocked, she practically flew across the room. She opened the door; he slipped in. 'Did they hear you?' she asked.

'I don't think so.'

She was seized by a sudden shyness, barely breathing, trying to make out his shape in the darkness. But then he reached for her and pulled her to him. When their lips met, her timidity dissolved.

Afterwards she enfolded his head in her arms and held him fast, wishing that she could heal him.

Grief overcame her. She began to sob. 'Don't leave me.'

He raised his head and touched her cheeks. 'Shh, Ella.'

'I can't bear it if you leave me. Swear you won't.'

'Shh, shh.' He held her against him, rocking her in his arms like a child. 'Don't ask me for the one thing I can't give you, Ella.'

He continued to hold her until she quieted. When he eventually pulled back so he could look at her, he brushed strands of hair off her face. 'This is the first time, as well as the last time, I've loved. And it's perfect, Ella. Perfect.'

Her heart was full to bursting, so full she couldn't speak, but he understood what she felt without her having to say a word.

He understood everything.

IN THE MORNING, she was ashamed of that outburst. She had asked the impossible of him and knew that it broke his heart as much as it did hers that he couldn't grant her fervent wish. But she pushed it from her mind and thought instead of the miracle of making love with him. Loving him was the dearest of gifts.

Following breakfast, he offered to assist her with the clean-up, and she accepted. Not because she needed the help in Margaret's absence, but so they could share a room. He kept an eye on Solly while she did general housekeeping. She did only what was necessary to keep the house tidy, not wanting to spend her time scrubbing when she could be looking at Mr Rainwater instead. She wanted to record for memory his smile, the disobedient lock of hair, each eyelash and every line in the palms of his hands.

After lunch, she fried two chickens, made potato salad and baked a cake to contribute to the meal following Brother Calvin's funeral service. Mr Rainwater stayed in the kitchen with her while she worked, helping with the chopping. Solly played at the table.

Ella pretended . . . well, she pretended lots of things.

When the food was ready, Mr Rainwater went to his room to change clothes. Ella dressed herself and Solly in their Sunday best.

'Well, don't you look nice, Solly!' Miss Pearl exclaimed when Ella walked with him into the parlour.

Again, Ella marvelled that the sisters detected nothing out of the ordinary. The changes that loving Mr Rainwater had wrought were so vital she couldn't believe they were undetectable.

'The table is set, and a platter of fried chicken is on the kitchen table,' she told them. 'Potato salad, cucumber salad and tea are in the icebox. If I've forgotten something, please help yourselves.'

'I still question if it's appropriate for you to attend this funeral.' Miss Violet's expression was one of a reproving schoolteacher.

'It might not be safe,' Miss Pearl added.

'We'll be perfectly safe.'

Miss Violet sighed. 'Well, if you're determined to go, I'm glad Mr Rainwater will be by your side.'

'I'm glad of that, too,' Ella said.

He appeared then, carrying the picnic hamper and a cake box. Ella took the box from him.

'You ladies enjoy your evening,' he said, tipping his hat. Then he escorted Ella and Solly to his car.

THEY WERE EARLY, but the church was already packed when they arrived. Every pew was filled. A spillover crowd stood in the churchyard looking in through the windows. Many of the people Ella recognised from the shanty-town had chosen to remain outside. Some whites, too, apparently shared the Dunne sisters' reservations about attending. They were there, but they stayed clumped together for the most part. Her heart warmed to see Lola and Ollie Thompson and Mr and Mrs Pritchett.

Because of the circumstances of the preacher's death, Ella was sure there would be plenty of law-enforcement officers nearby, but she saw no one in uniform.

Mr Rainwater found the absence of lawmen unusual, too, and remarked on it. 'Since the sheriff is in cahoots with the criminals, I had hoped he would keep his distance. But I'm surprised that he did. I would have thought he and his deputies would be camped nearby, if for no other reason than to intimidate. Or even to gloat.'

Jimmy appeared in the open doorway and waved them inside, where Margaret had saved them seats. Ella feared that Solly might panic when he was jammed in between her and Mr Rainwater, but Mr Rainwater took several nickels from his trouser pocket and scattered them upon the worn cover of a hymnal. Solly focused on them immediately and began rearranging the coins to his liking.

Ella smiled at Mr Rainwater. He smiled back.

Ella had attended the funeral service for Margaret's husband, so she wasn't surprised by the vocal outpourings of grief. Brother Calvin's young widow was inconsolable. The choir sang long and loud. The visiting preacher's homily escalated into a lengthy sermon.

Miraculously, Solly remained quiet and docile. Ella grew damp with per-spiration. The heat inside the church became intense.

However, her own discomfort was nothing compared to Mr Rainwater's. She noticed him frequently reaching inside his suit coat to rub his side. His face grew pale and bathed with sweat.

He caught her watching him and smiled reassuringly. 'Just a twinge,' he mouthed. But she knew it was more than that. As much as she'd admired Brother Calvin, she wished for a swift conclusion to the service so she could take Mr Rainwater home.

As soon as the last 'Amen' was said, Ella manoeuvred Solly into the aisle. 'I'll leave the food we brought,' she said to Mr Rainwater when they were at the door. 'But let's go home.'

'I'm fine.' He surreptitiously squeezed her hand. 'And it would hurt Margaret's feelings if we didn't stay.'

So they stayed. There was no graveside service, because Brother Calvin was being transported to Houston for burial. Tables were set up beneath the trees shading the churchyard. While Mr Rainwater minded Solly, Ella added their food to what others had brought.

'Not as good as yours,' Mr Rainwater said as he bit into a fried chicken drumstick. 'But word must have got round. The platter you brought was empty within minutes.'

They'd gone through the line to get their food; then Ella spread a quilt on a spot at the edge of the churchyard. Mr Rainwater appeared to be feeling somewhat better. He wasn't sweating as profusely, but his complexion looked waxy and his lips were rimmed with white.

'You're not hungry?' he asked. She'd barely nibbled at the food.

'It's the heat, I think.' But it wasn't the temperature. It was him. She was worried sick about him.

He saw through her fib. 'Don't fret over me, Ella.'

'I can't help it.'

'I love you for your concern, but I don't want to cause you one moment of heartache. Ever.'

Peering deeply into his eyes, she said hoarsely, 'You will.'

He returned the drumstick to his plate. Staring into near space, he said, 'Then I should never have come to you.'

She shook her head furiously. 'No. Oh, no. It would have been like not reading the book because of the sad ending. I had a choice.' Not caring who saw, she reached out and stroked his cheek. 'I wouldn't have missed loving you. Not for anything in the world.'

They gazed at each other, communicating without words. The spell was broken when they became aware of Solly's restlessness. 'He needs the bathroom.' She stood up and took her son's hand.

'Where's the nearest one?'

'It's an outhouse behind the church. I'll be right back.'

'I'll clean up here and meet you at the car.'

It was deep twilight by now. A large, yellow moon and the stars were out, and the crowd had thinned considerably. She had been so wrapped up with Mr Rainwater, she hadn't noticed.

Hurrying Solly along, Ella led him over smooth turf towards the rear of the church. The two outhouses were a distance from the sanctuary. One was for men, the other for women. She dreaded taking Solly into either.

The stench assailed her when she opened the door to the women's outhouse. Holding her breath, she guided Solly inside. He did his business without mishap.

Hastily she buttoned up his shorts. 'Good job, Solly. Good job.' She must remember to scrub both their hands with soap and hot water as soon as they got home. She pushed Solly through the outhouse door and quickly closed it behind her.

'Hey, Ella.'

Startled, she spun round. Conrad Ellis was there, his shoulder casually propped against the exterior wall of the building. The deputy's badge was pinned to a uniform shirt, and he was wearing a leather holster with a pistol in it. A cigarette dangled from his lips.

'What are you doing here?' she asked.

'Official duty,' he said, tapping the grip of the pistol with his index finger. 'Keeping the niggers from running amok.'

Ella realised the worst thing she could do was to show fear. She took Solly firmly by the hand and started walking quickly away.

But Conrad wasn't having it. He stepped in front of her, blocking her path. 'You're too good to say a polite hello to old friends?'

'If I say a polite hello, will you get out of my way?'

He threw his cigarette in the grass and took a step closer to her. 'Well, that depends.'

'On what?'

He leered. 'On how polite you're willing to get.'

Instantly she understood his intention. She opened her mouth to scream, but he lunged and slammed her into the wall of the outhouse, clamping one of his hands over her mouth.

Something landed on the ground beside her, and she realised Conrad had knocked Solly aside. The way Conrad had her pinned made it impossible for her to move her arms. She struggled to free her mouth from his hand. If she could scream, someone would hear.

'You should be nicer to me, Ella.' He was panting like an animal. 'Like you're nice to that boarder you've got. How come you're giving him what you never gave me, huh?' His damp breath smelled of whiskey, but she was powerless to turn her face away. A sound of outrage issued from her throat when he squeezed her breast with his free hand. 'How come you like that pale pantywaist instead of me? If you wanted a man, why didn't you call on me?'

He managed to work his hand between their bodies and push it between her legs. She tried to evade his crude thrusting motions, but he was pressed against her so solidly she couldn't move.

And Solly, was he hurt? Had he been knocked unconscious? She tried to see him, but her entire field of vision was filled with Conrad's face, congested with rage, resentment and cruelty.

Grunting with the effort, he pushed her feet apart with his, making it impossible for her to close her legs. To her horror, she realised that he was fumbling with his fly.

Her mind was screaming, *This cannot be happening to me.* But it was, it *would*, if she didn't stop it.

Suddenly she ceased struggling and went limp. Confused, Conrad staggered back. He relaxed his hold on her only marginally, but Ella used that split second to cram her knee into his crotch.

He opened his mouth to scream, but only a gasp of agony came out. He toppled onto the ground. Ella covered her face with her hands, partially to block out the sight of him as he writhed in pain, partially to slow down her pounding heart and pull herself together.

She heard the rumble of racing motors coming near, the squeal of tyres, men laughing and whooping drunkenly. Conrad's crowd closing in. She had to get away from him before his friends arrived. But she needed a few more seconds to collect her wits.

'Ella?'

Her name. Shouted in Mr Rainwater's voice. His dear voice. It was a blessed sound reaching her despite Conrad's choked sobs.

'Ella?'

Conrad's groans intensified.

And then there was another sound. An abrupt cracking sound that was wet-sounding, like the splat of a ripe melon being busted open.

Conrad's moaning abruptly ceased.

Ella lowered her hands from her face.

Conrad still lay on the ground at her feet. But he was no longer moving. The back of his head had been split right down the centre of his skull. It was too dark now to distinguish colour, but the liquid pooling on the ground appeared as black as motor oil.

Over him stood Solly, a large bloodstained stone in his hands.

Ella clapped her hand over her mouth. She sank to her knees, looking in turn at Conrad's skull and her son's placid, angelic face.

'Ella!'

She saw Mr Rainwater's shoes skid to a stop beside Conrad's still form. His breath left his body in an audible gush. He knelt beside Solly, and Ella watched as he removed from her son's small hands the stone with which Conrad Ellis had been brained. Only then did she raise her eyes to meet Mr Rainwater's and saw in them the disbelief and alarm that matched hers.

'Good job, Solly.'

They turned and stared aghast at the boy, who'd spoken the words. He was staring down at the damage he'd wreaked, having no comprehension of what it signified except an end to suffering, and speaking the words of commendation that had so often been repeated to him. They had penetrated his mind, and now he called them forth. 'Good job, Solly. Good job, Solly.'

'Oh *God*!' Ella clasped him against her, muffling his incriminating litany. Having lived for the day she would hear him speak, now she wanted to shush his sweet voice. 'Shh, Solly. Shh.'

On the street in front of the church, they heard shouts and laughter, the slamming of car doors, breaking glass, running footsteps. Lantern light flickered through the trees.

Someone called in a singsong voice, 'Conrad? Where are you?'

'Come out, come out, wherever you are.'

'Let's go nigger knockin'!'

Solly was now screeching and trying to escape Ella's grasp. His hands were flapping. Above his head, she frantically looked at Mr Rainwater.

Their gazes locked. And then Mr Rainwater did the oddest thing.

He dipped his hands in the blood that had collected under Conrad's head.

Ella gaped at him with bafflement as he came to his feet, the stone in his hands, and turned towards the on-rushing group of men who were rounding the corner of the church, led by the sheriff.

One of the men drew up short. 'What the hell? Conrad?'

One by one, the others saw what had brought their friend to a standstill. They stared at Ella, Solly and Mr Rainwater, trying to register what their minds refused to accept.

Then the pack surged forward as one, yelling and cursing. Two of them tackled Mr Rainwater, following him down when he fell and pummelling him with their fists.

'Stop! No!' Ella screamed. 'Leave him alone.'

But nobody was listening to her. They were like rabid dogs.

'Hold off, hold off!' Sheriff Anderson elbowed his way through them, until he hauled the last man off Mr Rainwater. Gripping him beneath his arms, the sheriff pulled him to his feet. But Mr Rainwater couldn't stand on his own, so two of the men held him upright while the sheriff jerked his bloody hands behind his back and cuffed them. His head was bowed low over his chest. He swayed on his feet.

Ella made a low keening sound, then croaked, 'No.'

The sheriff turned to her. 'One of these men will see you and your boy home, Mrs Barron. They'll stay with you till I get this character locked up. Then I'll come round to question you.'

'No! Mr Rainwater didn't do anything.'

'Ella.'

Wildly her eyes swung to him who spoke her name as no one else ever had. His head was raised. He was looking directly at her. Quietly he said, 'Do as the sheriff says. This is the way it's to be.'

Realisation of what he meant to do came to her slowly as she stood there breathing hard. She shook her head. 'No!'

He was perfectly composed. 'It's all right.'

She looked down at Solly, who, since she had released him, had calmed down and was no longer screeching but was still flapping his hands and chanting in a whisper, 'Good job, Solly.'

Then she looked back at the man who'd touched her son, reached him, when no one else had, even she.

She looked at the man who had touched her.

His image began to waver as her eyes filled. Again she shook her head, saying feebly, 'No, no.'

His eyes had never looked more serene or more loving. Slowly he nodded. His lips moved, and she read the word on them. *Yes.*

Epilogue

'**H**e died before they could execute him.'

The couple hadn't moved for the past hour. The afternoon was leaning towards dusk, but the passage of time had gone unnoticed. The woman was sniffing. Her husband passed her his handkerchief.

'That's his pocket watch?' she asked. 'Mr Rainwater's?'

The antiques dealer nodded. 'He asked Dr Kincaid to have it engraved with the date on which the doctor brought him to my mother's house and introduced them.'

He fingered the characters etched into the gold. 'After the sheriff took him away that night, they never saw each other again.'

'Surely she attended his trial,' the woman said.

'There wasn't a trial. He confessed. He refused to see her in prison. He didn't want to leave her with that memory of him. Dr Kincaid carried messages back and forth between them.'

'How long did he live?' the man asked.

'Five weeks. He didn't have to suffer for long.'

The lady reached for her husband's hand and clasped it tightly. 'Your mother probably suffered more than he did.'

'She desperately wanted to see him, but later she came to understand that, as usual, he knew what was best.'

'How did she ever recover?'

'After he died, she was shocked to learn he'd bequeathed everything to her.' The old man smiled. 'Mother was well ahead of her time and put the legacy to good use. As soon as it was practical, she closed the boarding-house and moved to north Texas, where she started replanting cotton on Mr Rainwater's land. Harvested it, ginned it, sold it. Brokered for other planters, too, just like he had.

'A few years later she used the profits to build a textile plant. She became quite wealthy and well respected. She received, oh, I can't even remember all the citations and awards. Outstanding businesswoman, citizen of the year, commendations like that.'

'Remarkable,' the woman said with awe.

'She was, actually.' Again the old man fingered the watch wistfully. 'She told me once it had taken a dying man to teach her how to live. Before Mr Rainwater, she'd been resigned to a life of virtual imprisonment.'

'He was remarkable in his own right,' the man observed. 'He died a con-demned man when he was blameless. I realise he would have died soon anyway. Still, he made a huge sacrifice for you.'

The old man noticed a puzzled look between them, then realised it was they who were confused. 'He made the sacrifice for *Solly.*'

'But . . . aren't you . . .?'

He shook his head.

The woman glanced at the business card he'd given her. 'I assumed . . . The name of your shop—'

'Is in honour of my brother, Solly. My name is David Rainwater Barron.'

They looked at him. 'You're his son?' the woman whispered.

'I am.'

She began crying again, this time with joy. Her husband placed his arm round her. He asked, 'What happened to Solly?'

'After moving to north Texas, Mother looked into a school in Dallas. It had a wonderful reputation, and they accepted Solly. It broke her heart to leave him there, but she knew it was for the best. The language barrier had been broken the night Conrad Ellis was killed. Solly eventually spoke almost normally.'

'Did he remember or ever know—'

'What he'd done? No. Mother never burdened him with that.'

'Did he ever learn to read, as she'd hoped he would?'

'He did, yes. He grasped mathematical concepts that boggled most minds, and he could construct complicated models of buildings and bridges, but he was never able to direct those skills towards any vocation. Perhaps now, with advanced knowledge and understanding of autism, he could have. But the condition wasn't even given a name until the mid-forties.

'When he was too old to stay at school, Mother brought him home. He had an aide who looked after him while she worked. He was content until the day he died, suddenly and unexpectedly at the age of thirty-two, of a heart abnormality that no one knew he had.

'We grieved, naturally. But when I couldn't be consoled, Mother reminded me that Solly had a much better life than she could have dreamed he would, and he owed it to Mr Rainwater. He knew what would have happened to Solly if anyone suspected him of killing Conrad Ellis. He would have been locked in an institution for the criminally insane. In that last shared moment, my father made Mother realise that the only way Solly could have a life was to let him make the sacrifice.'

The couple was quiet for a time; then the man glanced at his watch. 'We should go.' He extended his hand to the old man. 'It's been a fascinating afternoon. We got much more than we bargained for when we decided to stop.'

The antiques dealer walked them to the door, where the woman spontaneously hugged him, which pleased him greatly.

'Goodbye,' she said. 'It's been a true pleasure.'

'Likewise. Goodbye.'

They had almost reached their SUV when she turned back. 'Did Mr Rainwater know about you?'

He smiled. 'Dr Kincaid was able to tell him only hours before he died. Weakened as he was, he wrote my mother a letter.'

Reading the question in their eyes, he shook his head. 'She told me everything I've told you, but she never shared the contents of that letter. I'm sure the message was far too dear to her to be shared. She was buried with it, along with the copy of *A Farewell to Arms* that he'd given her.'

He looked down at the timepiece lying in his palm, then folded his fingers round it tightly. 'His watch she gave to me.'

sandra **brown**

When *People* magazine reviewed *Rainwater*, it was described as 'a warm, nostalgic detour from the suspense queen's comfort zone'. It is indeed a detour. Sandra Brown is the author of more than seventy books, most of them best sellers, most of them fast-paced, racy mysteries. Some of the more recent ones include *Smash Cut*, *Smoke Screen* and *Play Dirty*. *Rainwater* is without doubt quite a departure for this prolific writer.

'These characters insisted that their story be told,' Brown explains in a video on her publisher's website. 'I almost didn't have a choice.'

The genesis of the story goes back to Brown's father's vivid memory of living on a farm as a child. In 1934, the Federal Surplus Relief Corporation tried to remove surplus commodities from the market. As part of this plan, Brown's grandfather was ordered by federal agents to pour out his surplus milk. But he refused, knowing that there were large numbers of people who had lost their homes and livelihoods during a long period of drought and devastating dust storms, who had need of that milk for their families. With the aid of gun-toting friends and relatives, he continued to give away the milk until the federal agents finally backed down.

Brown wrote *Rainwater* in her own time, without a contract, in between two other books for her publisher. Starting with this germ of an idea, she was not exactly sure where it would go. Solly's autism, for instance, came as a surprise to her. 'I didn't know Solly was autistic until he pulled the pan of hot starch onto himself,' she explained to an interviewer. 'I didn't know he was going to be a special child in any way.'

When questioned about how she researches her novels, Brown says: 'It depends on the subject matter. I write about things or places that interest me, so the research doesn't become too tedious. I do enough to make it believable without telling so much it bores the reader. I use the internet, atlases, maps, personal visits and interviews.'

One thing that does connect this story to Brown's other books is that they all have an underlying secret that is not revealed until the end. We won't reveal *Rainwater*'s secret here, but it is true that you won't know the whole story until you've finished reading it.

Sandra Brown was born in Waco, Texas, and raised in Forth Worth. After leaving school, she attended Texas Christian University, majoring in English. Before she began her writing career in 1981, as a result of a dare from her husband, Brown worked as a model in Dallas; as a television weather forecaster for WFAA-TV in Dallas; and also as a feature reporter on an evening news programme, *PM Magazine*.

Since 1990, when *Mirru or Image* made the *New York Times* best-seller list, all Brown's novels have been *NY Times* best sellers. There are now seventy million copies of her books in print worldwide. The author is also much in demand as a speaker and has appeared at the National Book Festival in Washington, DC, and the Texas Book Festival in Austin, Texas, as well as speaking at charity functions throughout the year. In 2008 Sandra realised her dream of a college degree when she was presented with an Honorary Doctorate of Humane Letters from Texas Christian University.

Depression era in the Dust Bowl

Although few farmers in the Southern and Central Plains of America were directly affected by the 1929 stock-market crash, this large rural population, all dependant on the harvest and sale of their crops, suffered devastating unemployment, bankruptcy and destitution, as a result of the Great Depression that followed.

The Dust Bowl or the 'Dirty Thirties' was a period of severe dust storms causing major ecological and agricultural damage to American and Canadian prairie lands in the 1930s. The phenomenon was caused by severe drought coupled with decades of extensive farming without crop rotation, fallow fields, or other techniques to prevent erosion.

The era also served as a seminal ground for some of America's most memorable literature, including John Steinbeck's classic, *The Grapes of Wrath*, which defined those hard times in American popular culture.

eyjamk ꝥkeys Olaff ꝧ tua
ur kom skipi siɲm̄ t Jsland
huaf ꝑad er ꝥ nedan t h
pa kona tu t son er Hrut
vatra gamall mutuen̄ ok
t Bu saman vm̄ vetur̄
Arnfridur giet
tun vm̄ nout fard
di i gierde Bu ꝥ sem h
mdc hn̄ ad m̄ kam ad
dur t hilltur ovart
tur ꝑma Lafa t h
n̄ tien Ok ꝥer buset
ad heit n̄ Hall

Magnus Jonson of the Boston Police Department grew up in Iceland but he's spent little time there since. Now he's been given a two-year assignment as a detective with the Reykjavik police, who need his help in unravelling the murder of a local professor, an expert in the Icelandic sagas.

As Magnus searches for clues, he is soon drawn into an even deeper mystery. One that is as beguiling and ancient as Iceland itself, with its shadowy landscapes and simmering volcanoes . . .

CHAPTER ONE

Professor Agnar Haraldsson folded the letter and slipped it back into its small, yellowing envelope. He glanced again at the address inscribed in an upright, ornamental hand: Högni Ísildarson, Laugavegur 64, Reykjavík, Iceland. The stamp bore the profile of a beardless British king, an Edward or a George, Agnar wasn't certain which.

His heart thumped, the envelope performing a tiny dance in his shaking hand. The letter had arrived that morning enclosed within a larger envelope bearing a modern Icelandic stamp and a Reykjavík postmark. It was all that Agnar could have hoped for. It was more than that; it was perfect.

As a professor of Icelandic at the University of Iceland, Agnar had been privileged to handle some of the oldest manuscripts of his country's sagas, copied out by monks onto sheaves of calf skins using black bearberry juice for ink, and feathers from the wings of swans for pens. Those magnificent documents were Iceland's heritage, Iceland's soul. But none would cause as great a stir in the outside world as this single sheet of paper.

He looked up from his desk over the serene lake in front of him. It glittered a rare deep blue in the April sunshine. A perfect location for a summerhouse. Agnar had escaped there for the weekend to work with no distractions. His wife had just given birth to their second child, and Agnar had a tight deadline to get through the pile of translation in front of him.

'Aggi, come back to bed.'

He turned to see the breathtakingly beautiful figure of Andrea, ballet dancer and third-year literature student, naked as she glided across the bare wooden floor towards him, her blonde hair a tangled mess.

'I'm sorry, darling, I can't,' he said, nodding towards the mess of papers.

'Are you sure?' She bent down to kiss him and ran her fingers under his shirt and through the hair on his chest. 'Are you really sure?'

He smiled and removed his spectacles.

Well, perhaps he would allow himself one distraction.

SERGEANT DETECTIVE Magnus Jonson trudged along the street in Roxbury towards his car. He was tired: he hadn't slept properly for a week, but he had a load of typing to do back at the station before he could go home.

Maria Campanelli, white female, twenty-seven. She had been dead thirty-six hours, stabbed by her boyfriend after an argument and her body left to decompose in her apartment. The officers of the Boston Police Department's Homicide Unit were out looking for him now, and Magnus was confident he would be found. But to be certain of a conviction they needed to make sure they got the paperwork 100 per cent accurate.

Magnus was good at the paperwork, which was one of the reasons he had recently been promoted to sergeant. Perhaps Colby was right, perhaps he should go to law school.

Colby. For the twelve months they had been living together she had gradually turned up the pressure: why didn't he quit the department and go to law school, why didn't they get married? And then, six days ago, when they were walking arm in arm back from their favourite Italian restaurant in the North End, a Jeep had driven past with its rear window wound down. Magnus had thrown Colby to the sidewalk just as a rapid succession of shots rang out from a semiautomatic rifle. Maybe the shooters thought they had hit their target, maybe there were too many people around, but the Jeep had driven off without finishing the job.

That was why she had kicked him out of her apartment. That was why he had spent sleepless nights at his brother's house in Medford.

Magnus felt a touch on his elbow. It was a guy of about fifty, Latin, bald, short and overweight, unshaven.

'Detective?'

Magnus stopped. 'Yeah?'

'I think I saw something. The night the girl was stabbed.'

Magnus was tempted to tell the guy to beat it. They had a witness who had seen the boyfriend come, another who had seen him leave six hours later, three who had heard a loud argument, one who had heard a scream. But you could never have enough witnesses.

Magnus sighed as he reached for his notebook. Another statement to type up when he got back to the station.

The man looked nervously up and down the street. 'Not here, I don't want nobody to see us talking.'

Magnus was about to protest—the victim's boyfriend was a cook, hardly someone to be scared of—but then he shrugged and followed the man down a small side street. Little more than an alley with a high wire fence at the end. A heavily tattooed kid with a yellow T-shirt stood at the street corner. He smoked a cigarette, his back to Magnus.

As they entered the alleyway, the bald guy seemed to speed up. Magnus was about to yell to the guy to slow down, when he stopped himself. He had been asleep. Now he was awake.

Among the forest of tattoos on the kid's arms, Magnus had noticed a small dot above one elbow, and a pattern of five dots above the other, the tattoo of the Cobra-15 gang. They didn't operate in Roxbury. This kid was way outside his territory, by at least three miles. But the Cobra-15 were customers of Soto's operation, local distribution agents. The guys in the Jeep in the North End had been working for Soto, Magnus was sure.

His instinct was to straighten up and turn, but he forced himself not to break his stride and alert the kid. Think. Think fast. He could hear footsteps behind him. Gun or knife? The kid knew Magnus was armed and no one brings a knife to a gunfight. Which meant gun. Which meant the kid was probably pulling it out of his waistband right then.

Magnus dived to the left, grabbed a garbage can and toppled it over. As he hit the ground he rolled once, reached for his gun and pointed it towards the kid, who was raising his own weapon. Magnus's finger curled round the trigger, and then his training kicked in. He hesitated. The rule was clear: don't fire if there is a chance of hitting a civilian.

In the mouth of the alleyway stood a young woman, grocery bags in both arms, staring at Magnus, her mouth open. She was wide, real wide, and directly behind the kid in the yellow T-shirt in Magnus's line of fire.

The hesitation gave the kid time to raise his own gun. Magnus was looking straight down the barrel. A stand-off.

'Police! Drop your weapon!' Magnus shouted.

What would happen next? If the kid fired first, he might miss Magnus, and then Magnus could get away his own shot. Although he was six foot four and weighed over 200 pounds, Magnus was lying prone on the street, partially hidden by the trash can, a smallish target for a panicked kid.

If only the woman would move. She was still rooted to the spot, her mouth open, trying to scream.

Then Magnus saw the kid's eyes flick upwards and behind Magnus. The bald guy. The kid wouldn't have taken his eyes off Magnus's gun if the bald guy wasn't relevant to the situation. Hold off for a couple of seconds until the bald guy shot Magnus in the back, that was the kid's plan.

Magnus pulled his trigger. The kid was hit in the chest; he jerked and fired his own gun, missing Magnus. Magnus reached out to the trash can and flung it behind him. He turned to see it hitting the bald guy in the shins. The man was reaching for his own gun, but doubled over as he tripped on the can. Magnus fired twice, hitting the guy each time, once in the shoulder and once in the crown of his head. He pulled himself to his feet. The fat woman had dropped her groceries and was screaming now, loud, very loud. It turned out there was nothing wrong with her lungs. A police siren started up somewhere close. There was the sound of shouting and running feet.

The bald guy was still, but the kid was sprawled on his back on the ground, his chest heaving, his yellow T-shirt now stained red. His fingers were curled round his gun as he tried to summon up the strength to point it towards Magnus. Magnus kicked the gun out of the way and stood panting over the boy who had tried to kill him. Seventeen or eighteen, Hispanic, taut muscles under swirls of ink on his arms and chest, intricate gang tattoos. A tough kid. A kid his age in Cobra-15 could already have several dead bodies to his name.

But not Magnus's. At least not today.

'I'M TAKING YOU off the street.' Deputy Superintendent Williams, the chief of the Homicide Unit, was firm. He was always firm; that was one of the things Magnus appreciated about him.

'I don't think that's necessary,' Magnus said.

'I do. This is the second time someone has tried to kill you in a week.'

'I was tired. I let my guard down. It won't happen again.'

Williams raised his eyebrows. His black face was deeply lined. He was small, compact, determined, a good boss, and honest. That was why Magnus had gone to him six months before when he had overheard his partner, Detective Lenahan, talking on his cellphone to another cop about tampering with evidence in a homicide investigation.

They were on a stake-out. Magnus had gone for a walk and was returning to the car when he stopped in the fall sunshine just behind the passenger window. The window was open a crack. Magnus could hear Lenahan clearly, threatening a Detective O'Driscoll to do the right thing and smudge the fingerprint evidence on a gun.

Magnus and Lenahan had not been partners for long. At fifty-three, Lenahan was twenty years older than Magnus. He was experienced, smart, popular. But he was lazy. He used his three decades of experience and knowledge of police methods to do as little work as possible.

Magnus saw things differently. As soon as he had closed one case he was eager to move on to the next; his determination to nail the perp was legendary within the department. Lenahan thought there were good guys and there were bad guys; there always were and there always would be. There was not very much that he or Magnus or the whole Boston police force could do about that. Magnus thought that every victim, and every victim's family, deserved justice, and Magnus would do his very best to get it for them. So the Jonson–Lenahan partnership was hardly made in heaven.

But until then, Magnus had not imagined that Lenahan was crooked.

There are two things that a cop hates more than anything else. One is a crooked cop. Another is a cop who rats on one of his colleagues. For Magnus the choice was easy—if people like Lenahan were allowed to get away with destroying evidence of a homicide, then everything he had devoted his career towards was worthless.

Magnus knew that most of his colleagues would agree with him. But some would turn a blind eye, convince themselves that Magnus had misheard, that good old Sean Lenahan could not be one of the bad guys. Which was why Magnus had gone straight to Williams, who had understood the situation. A couple of weeks later Magnus's promotion came through and he and Lenahan were split up. An undercover team from the FBI was brought in from out of state. A major investigation was launched and Lenahan was linked with two other detectives, O'Driscoll and Montoya.

The Feds discovered the gang that was paying them off; it was Dominican, led by a man named Pedro Soto. Soto supplied cocaine and heroin wholesale to street gangs all over New England. The three crooked detectives were arrested and charged. Magnus was billed as the star witness when the case eventually came to trial. But the FBI hadn't yet amassed enough evidence to charge Soto. He was still out there.

'Your guard slips once, it can slip again,' said Williams. 'If we don't do something you'll be dead within two weeks.'

'But I don't see why they want to kill me,' Magnus said. 'Sure, my testimony will nail Lenahan, but I can't point to Soto or the Dominicans. And you said Lenahan isn't cooperating.'

'The FBI thinks it's figured out Lenahan's angle. The last thing he wants is to wind up in a maximum-security prison with a bunch of convicted killers; no cop would want that, he'd be better off dead. But without your testimony, he'll walk. Our guess is that he has given the Dominicans an ultimatum: they get rid of you or he'll give them to us. And if he doesn't, his buddy Montoya will. If you die, Lenahan and the other two go free, and Soto's operation continues as if nothing has happened.' Williams looked Magnus right in the eye. 'Which is why we have to figure out what to do with you.'

Magnus saw Williams's point. But full witness protection would mean starting up a new life with a new identity on the other side of the country. He didn't want that. 'Got any ideas?' he asked Williams.

'Matter of fact, I do.' He smiled. 'You're an Icelandic citizen, right?'

'Yes. As well as US. I have dual.'

'Do you speak the language?'

'Some. I spoke it as a child. I moved here when I was twelve. Why?'

'An old buddy in the NYPD called me a while ago. Said he'd heard I had someone who spoke Icelandic in my unit. He'd just had a visit from the National Police Commissioner of Iceland. He was looking to the NYPD to loan him a detective as an advisor. Apparently, they don't get many homicides in Iceland, or at least they didn't until recently. Obviously, if that detective happened to speak Icelandic, it would be a bonus. So I called the Icelandic Police Commissioner an hour ago. He sounded very excited by the idea of a detective who speaks the language. So, what do you think?'

There really was no choice.

'I'll do it,' Magnus said. 'On one condition.'

Williams frowned. 'Which is?'

'I take my girlfriend with me.'

MAGNUS HAD SEEN Colby angry before, but never this angry.

'What do you think you are doing, getting your goons to kidnap me? Is this some kind of joke? Some kind of weird romantic gesture where you think I'm going to take you back? Because if it is, I can tell you right now it's not going to work. So tell these men to take me back to my office!'

They were sitting in the back seat of an FBI van in the parking lot of a restaurant. The agents who had whisked her there were gathered around their car fifty feet away, with the two agents who had driven Magnus.

'They tried to kill me again,' Magnus said. 'Almost succeeded this time.'

He still couldn't believe how stupid he had been, how he had let himself be led off the main street down an alley. Since the shooting he had been interviewed at great length by two detectives from the Firearm Discharge Investigative team. He had told them that he had traded the near certainty of his own death for a small probability that the innocent woman at the end of the alley would be harmed. And if the gangsters had shot him, they would probably have shot the woman next, as a witness. They were careful not to ask him whether he had thought of that before or after he had pulled the trigger. They were going to do things by the book, but they were on his side.

This was the second time he had shot and killed someone while on duty.

After the first, when he was a rookie patrol officer in uniform two months into the job, he had suffered weeks of guilt-filled, sleepless nights. This time he was just glad to be alive.

'But it's got nothing to do with me,' Colby said.

'It does have something to do with you, Colby.'

'What do you mean?'

'The chief wants me to go. Leave Boston. He doesn't think the Dominicans will stop until they've killed me.'

'Leaving sounds like a good idea.'

Magnus took a deep breath. 'And I want you to come with me.'

'Are you serious?'

'It's for your own safety. If I'm gone they might go after you.'

'What about my work? What about my job, dammit?'

'You'll have to leave that. It'll only be for a few months. Until the trial.'

Colby bit her lip. A tear ran down her cheek. Magnus reached out and touched her arm. 'Where would we go?'

'I'm sorry, I can't tell you until I know you will say yes.'

She stared him right in the eye. 'Do you want to get married?'

Magnus returned her stare. He couldn't believe she was serious.

'I don't know,' Magnus hesitated. 'We could talk about it.'

'No! I don't want to talk about it, we've talked about it for months. I want to decide right now. You want me to decide to drop everything and go away with you. Fine. I'll do it. If we get married.'

'But this is totally the wrong way to make a decision like that.'

'What do you mean? Do you love me?'

'Of course I love you,' Magnus replied.

'Then let's get married. You've asked me to commit to going away with you, and I'll do it if you commit to me. Come on, Magnus, decision time.'

Magnus took a deep breath. 'I want you to come with me for your own safety,' he said.

'So that's a no, then?' Her eyes bored into his.

Magnus nodded. 'No.'

Colby pursed her lips and reached for the door handle. 'OK. We're done here. I'm going back to work.'

Magnus grabbed her arm. 'Colby, please!'

'Get your hands off me!' Colby shouted and threw open the door. She walked rapidly over to the agents standing around the other car and muttered something to them. Within a minute the car was gone.

Two of the agents returned to the van and climbed in.

'I guess she's not going with you,' said the driver.

'I guess she's not,' said Magnus.

CHAPTER TWO

Magnus looked up from his book and out of the airplane window. It had been a long flight, but at last the plane was descending. Beneath him was a blanket of coarse grey clouds, torn in only a couple of places. As the aircraft approached one of these Magnus craned his neck to try to get a glimpse of land, but all he could see was a patch of crumpled grey sea, flecked with white caps. Then it was gone.

He was worried about Colby. If he had agreed to marry her, she would be in the seat next to him on her way to safety, instead of in her apartment, waiting for the wrong guy to knock at the door. And if the Dominicans came after her it would unequivocally be his fault. But Magnus had had to do what was right. He always had and he always would. It was right to go to Williams about Lenahan. It would have been wrong to marry Colby because she forced him to. He had never been sure why his parents had got married but he had lived with the consequences of that mistake.

Williams had agreed to organise some police protection for her. But if the Dominicans did catch her, would he be able to live with the consequences of that? Perhaps he should just have said yes, agreed to whatever she wanted if only to get her out of the country.

Colby hadn't cared that he was a tough cop when they had first met. It was at a party given by an old friend of his from college. The mutual attraction had been instantaneous. She was pretty, vivacious, smart, strong-willed, determined. She liked the idea of an Ivy League graduate walking the streets of South Boston with a gun. Until she started to view him not as a lover but as a potential husband.

She was thirty, she wanted to get married and she wanted to marry Magnus. Or a modified Magnus: a successful lawyer pulling in a good salary, living in a big house in Brookline? Who did she want him to be? Who did *he* want to be? It was a question Magnus often asked himself.

He pulled out his electric-blue Icelandic passport. The photograph was similar to the one in his US passport: red hair, square jaw, blue eyes, traces of freckles on his nose. But the name was different. His *real* name, Magnús Ragnarsson. His name was Magnús, his father's name was Ragnar, and his grandfather's name was Jón. So his father was Ragnar Jónsson and he was Magnús Ragnarsson. Simple.

But the US bureaucracy could not cope with this logic. A son could not have a different last name from his father *and* his mother, whose name was Margrét Hallgrímsdóttir. It didn't really like the nonstandard spelling of Jónsson either. Ragnar had fought this for a few months after his son arrived in the country and then thrown in the towel. The twelve-year-old Icelandic boy Magnús Ragnarsson became the American kid Magnus Jonson.

He turned back to the book on his lap. *Njáls Saga*, one of his favourites. Although Magus had spoken very little Icelandic over the past few years, he had read a lot. His father had read the Icelandic sagas to him when Magnus had moved to Boston and the sagas had become a source of comfort to him in the new, confusing world of America. They still were. The word *saga* meant literally *what is said* in Icelandic.

The sagas were the archetypal family histories, most of them dealing with the three or four generations of Vikings who had settled Iceland around A.D. 900 until the coming of Christianity to that country in 1000. Their heroes were brave adventurers with a clear moral code, a sense of honour and a respect for the laws. For a lone Icelander in a huge junior high school in the United States, they were a source of inspiration. If one of their kinsmen was killed, they knew what to do: they demanded money in compensation and if that was not forthcoming they demanded blood, all strictly according to the law. So when his father was murdered when Magnus was twenty, *he* knew what to do. Search for justice.

The police never found his father's killer and, despite Magnus's efforts, neither did he, but he decided after leaving college to become a policeman. He was still searching for justice, but even with all the murderers he had arrested over the past decade, he still hadn't found it.

The plane descended. Another gap in the clouds; this time he could see the waves breaking against the brown lava field of the Reykjanes Peninsula.

He had the feeling, as Iceland came nearer and nearer, that somehow he was moving towards solving his father's murder, or at least *re*solving it. Perhaps in Iceland he could finally place it in some kind of perspective. But the airplane that was turning for its final approach was also bringing him closer to his childhood, closer to pain and confusion.

There was a golden period in Magnus's life before the age of eight, when his family all lived together in a little house, close to the centre of Reykjavík. It had a tiny garden with a white picket fence and a stunted tree, an old whitebeam, in which to clamber. His father went off to the university every morning, and his mother, who was beautiful and always smiling then, taught at the local secondary school.

Then it all changed. His father left home to go and teach mathematics at a university in America. His mother became angry and sleepy—she slept all the time. Her face became puffy, she got fat; she yelled at Magnús and his little brother, Óli.

They moved to the farm on the Snaefellsnes Peninsula where his mother had been brought up. That's where the misery started. Magnús realised that his mother wasn't sleepy all the time, she was drunk. Unable to hold down her job as a teacher, she took a series of jobs in the nearest town, first teaching and then working cash registers. Worst of all, Magnús and Óli were left for long periods in the care of their grandparents.

Their grandfather was a strict, scary, angry man, who liked a drink himself. Their grandmother was small and mean.

One day, when Magnús and Óli were at school, their mother had drunk half a bottle of vodka, climbed into a car and steered it straight into a rock, killing herself instantly. Within a week, amid acrimony of nuclear proportions, Ragnar had arrived to take them both away to Boston with him.

Magnus returned to Iceland with his father and Óli for camping trips in the back country and to see his grandmother and his father's friends. They had never gone near his mother's family. Until a month after his father died, when Magnus made the trip to try to effect a reconciliation. The visit had been a disaster. Magnus was stunned by the strength of the hostility from his grandparents. They didn't just hate his father, they hated him too. And that hurt. Since then he had never been back.

THIRTY MINUTES after landing, Magnus was sitting in the back of a white car hurtling along the highway between Keflavík and Reykjavík through a curtain of rain. It was April 24, the day after Iceland's official first day of summer. The lavascape, undulating mounds of stones, boulders and moss, stretched towards a line of squat mountains in the distance, without a tree in sight. Thousands of years after the event, this patch of Iceland hadn't recovered from the devastation of a massive volcanic eruption. The thin layers of mosses nibbling at the rocks were only just beginning a process of restoration that would take millennia.

But Magnus wasn't looking at the scenery. He was concentrating hard on the man sitting next to him, Snorri Gudmundsson, the National Police Commissioner. He was a small man with shrewd blue eyes and thick grey hair. He was speaking rapidly in Icelandic, and it took all Magnus's powers of concentration to follow him.

'As I am sure you must know, Iceland has a low per-capita homicide rate and low levels of serious crime,' he was saying. 'Until the *kreppa* and the demonstrations over last winter, most policing involved clearing up the mess on Saturday and Sunday mornings once the partygoers had had their fun.'

Kreppa was the Icelandic word for the credit crunch, which had hit the country particularly badly. The banks, the government and many of the people were bankrupt, drowning under debt incurred in the boom times.

'The trend is worrying,' the Commissioner went on. 'There are more drugs, more drug gangs. The press here exaggerates the problem, but it would be a foolish police commissioner who ignored the threat.'

He paused to check if Magnus was following. Magnus nodded to indicate he was, just.

'I am proud of our police; they work hard and they have a good clear-up rate, but they are not used to the kind of crimes that occur in big cities with large populations. The greater Reykjavík area has a population of only a hundred and eighty thousand. The entire country has only three hundred thousand people, but I want us to be prepared in case the kinds of things that happen in Amsterdam, or Manchester, or Boston for that matter, happen here. Which is why I asked for you.' He paused. 'I've read your file and spoken to Deputy Superintendent Williams. He was very complimentary.'

Magnus raised his eyebrows. He didn't know Williams did compliments. And he knew there were some serious black marks in his record from times when he hadn't always done exactly what he had been told.

'The idea is that you will go through a crash course at the National Police

College. In the meantime, you will be available for training seminars and for advice should something crop up that you can help us with.'

'A crash course?' said Magnus. 'How long would that take?'

'We would hope to get you through in less than six months. It's unavoidable. You can't arrest someone unless you know Icelandic law.'

'No, I see that, but how long did you see me being here?'

'I specified a minimum of two years. DS Williams assured me that would be acceptable.'

'He never mentioned that kind of time frame to me,' said Magnus.

Snorri's eyes bored into Magnus's. 'Williams did, of course, mention the reason why you were so eager to leave Boston on a temporary basis. I admire your courage.' His eyes flickered towards the uniformed police driver in the front seat. 'No one here knows about it apart from me.'

Magnus was about to protest, but he let it drop. As yet, he had no idea how many months it would be until the trial of Lenahan and the others. He would go along with the Police Commissioner until he was called to testify, then he would return to Boston and stay there, no matter what plans the Commissioner had for him.

Snorri smiled. 'As luck would have it, we have something to get your teeth into right away. A body was discovered this morning, in a summerhouse by Lake Thingvellir. And I am told that one of the initial suspects is an American. I am taking you straight there now.'

Keflavík Airport was at the tip of the peninsula that stuck out to the west of Reykjavík into the Atlantic Ocean. As they drove, Magnus could see the multicoloured metal roofs of houses that marked the centre of Reykjavík, dominated by the rocket spire of the Hallgrímskirkja, Iceland's largest church, rising up from the top of a small hill. Beyond that was the foot of Mount Esja, an imposing ridge of stone that reached up into the low cloud.

They passed through bleak suburbs of square, squat blocks of flats to the east of the city, then turned away from the bay and climbed up Mosfell Heath, a heath land of yellow grass and green moss, bulky rounded hills and cloud—low, dark, swirling cloud.

After twenty minutes or so they descended and Magnus saw the black waters of Lake Thingvellir ahead of him. He had been there several times as a boy, visiting Thingvellir itself, a grass plain that ran along the floor of a rift valley at the northern edge of the lake. It was the spot where the American and European continental plates split Iceland in two. More importantly for Magnus and his father, it was the dramatic site of the Althing, Iceland's annual outdoor parliament during the age of the sagas.

They turned off the main road, past a large farm, down to the lake itself. They followed a stone track to a row of half a dozen summerhouses, protected by a stand of scrappy birch trees, not yet in leaf. Magnus saw the familiar signs of a newly established crime scene: badly parked police cars, flashing lights, yellow tape fluttering in the breeze and figures milling about in a mixture of dark police uniforms and white forensic overalls.

The focus of attention was the fifth house, at the end of the row. Magnus checked the other summerhouses. It was still early in the season, so only one, the second, showed signs of habitation, a Range Rover parked outside.

The police car pulled up next to an ambulance and the Commissioner and Magnus got out. He could hear the rustle of the wind and a haunting bird call that he recognised from his childhood. A curlew?

A tall, balding man wearing forensic overalls approached them.

'Let me introduce Inspector Baldur Jakobsson of the Reykjavík CID,' the Commissioner said. 'He is in charge of the investigation. Baldur, this is Sergeant Detective Magnús Jonson from the Boston Police Department . . .' He paused and looked at Magnus quizzically. 'Jonson?'

'Ragnarsson,' Magnus corrected him.

The Commissioner smiled, pleased that Magnus was reverting to his Icelandic name. 'Ragnarsson.'

'*Good afternoon*,' said Baldur stiffly, in halting English.

'*G'dan daginn*,' replied Magnus.

'Baldur, can you explain to Magnús what's happened here?'

'Certainly,' Baldur said. 'The victim was Agnar Haraldsson. He is a professor at the University of Iceland. This is his summerhouse. He was murdered last night, hit over the head in the house, we think, and then dragged down into the lake. He was found by two children from the house just back there at ten o'clock this morning.'

'The house with the Range Rover out front?' asked Magnus.

Baldur nodded. 'They fetched their father and he dialled 112.'

'When was he last seen alive?' Magnus asked.

'The neighbours saw Agnar arrive at about eleven o'clock yesterday morning. They saw him park his car outside his house and go in. They waved to him, he waved back, but they didn't speak. He did receive a visitor, or visitors, that evening.'

'Description?'

'None. They just saw the car, small, bright blue, something like a Toyota Yaris, although they are not precisely sure. The car arrived about seven thirty, eight o'clock. Left at nine thirty. They didn't see it, but the woman remembered what she was watching on TV when she heard it drive past.'

'Any other visitors?'

'None that the neighbours know of. But they were out all afternoon at Thingvellir, so there could have been.'

Baldur answered Magnus's questions simply and directly, his long face giving an air of serious intensity to his responses. The Commissioner was listening closely, but let Magnus do the talking.

'Can I see the body?'

Baldur nodded and led Magnus and the Commissioner down a narrow pathway to a blue tent, erected on the edge of the lake. Baldur called for overalls, boots and gloves. Magnus and the Commissioner put them on and ducked into the tent. Inside, a body was stretched out on the boggy grass.

'The paramedics from Selfoss who responded to the call dragged him out of the lake when they found him,' Baldur said. 'They thought he had drowned, but the doctor who examined the body was suspicious.'

'Why?'

'There was a blow on the back of his head. There are some rocks on the bottom of the lake and there was a chance that he might have struck one of them if he had fallen in, but the doctor thought the blow was too hard.'

'Can I take a look?'

Agnar was, or had been, a man of about forty, with longish dark hair with flecks of grey at the temples, sharp features, stubble of the designer variety. The body was still stiff, suggesting he had been dead for more than eight and less than twenty-four hours. Magnus doubted whether the pathologist would be able to come up with anything very precise about the time of death.

Gently Magnus parted the professor's hair and examined the wound at the back of his skull.

He turned to Baldur. 'The doctor is right. He was clearly hit by a rock,' Magnus said. 'Something with jagged edges. There are still flecks of stone in the wound. My guess is the killer threw it into the lake afterwards. It's the perfect place to lose a rock. Can I see inside the house?'

Baldur nodded. They walked back to the summerhouse. The place was getting the full forensics treatment, powerful lamps, a vacuum cleaner, and technicians crawling round with tweezers and fingerprint powder.

Magnus looked around. The door opened directly into a large living area, with big windows overlooking the lake. The furniture was modern but not expensive. Lots of book shelves, an impressive collection of CDs, no television. A desk covered with papers occupied one corner of the room, and in the middle were chairs and a sofa around a low table, on which was a glass half filled with red wine, and a tumbler containing the dregs of what looked like Coke. Both were covered in a thin film of smudged fingerprint powder. Through one open door Magnus could see a kitchen.

'It looks as if Agnar was hit on the back of the head, then dragged out of the house and dumped in the lake,' Baldur said.

'Sounds plausible,' said Magnus.

'Except . . .' Baldur hesitated. 'Come and look at this.' He led Magnus through to the kitchen. It was tidy, except for an open bottle of wine and the makings of a ham and cheese sandwich on the counter.

'We found some specks of blood here,' Baldur said, pointing to the counter. 'They look like high-velocity blood spatter, but that makes no sense. Perhaps Agnar somehow staggered in here, but there are no other signs of a struggle in here at all.'

Magnus glanced around the room. Three flies were battering the window in a never-ending attempt to get out.

'Don't worry about it,' he said. 'It's the flies.'

'Flies?'

'Sure. They land on the body, gorge themselves, then fly into the kitchen where it's warm. There they regurgitate the blood—it helps them to digest it. Maybe they wanted some of the sandwich for dessert.' Magnus bent down to examine the plate. 'Yes. There's some more there. Of course, it means that the body must have been lying around long enough for the flies to have their feast. But that's only fifteen, twenty minutes.'

Baldur wasn't smiling, but the Commissioner was. 'Thank you,' was all the inspector could manage.

'Footprints?' asked Magnus, looking at the floor. Footprints should show up well on the polished wood.

'Yes,' said Baldur. 'One set, a man's size forty-five. Which is odd.'

It was Magnus's turn to look puzzled. 'How so?'

'Icelanders usually take their shoes off when they enter a house. Except perhaps if they are a foreign visitor and don't know the customs.'

'Ah, of course,' said Magnus. 'Anything in the papers on the desk?'

'It's mostly academic stuff, essays from students, draft articles on Icelandic literature, that kind of thing. We need to go through it more thoroughly. The forensics team have taken his laptop away to analyse. And there is a diary with an entry; it tells us who was here last night.'

'The Commissioner mentioned an American,' Magnus said. 'With size forty-five feet, no doubt?'

'American. Or British. The name is Steve Jubb and the time in the diary is seven thirty yesterday evening. And a phone number. The number is for the Hótel Borg, the best hotel in Reykjavík. We're picking him up now. In fact, if you'll excuse me, Snorri, I have to go back to interview him.'

Magnus was struck by the informality of Icelanders. No 'Sir', or 'Commissioner Gudmundsson'. It would take getting used to, but he liked it.

'Be sure to include Magnús in the interviews,' the Commissioner said.

Baldur's face remained impassive, but Magnus could tell that he was seething inside. And Magnus couldn't blame him. This was probably one of Baldur's biggest cases of the year, and he would not appreciate doing it under the eyes of a young foreigner of junior rank.

'Certainly,' he said. 'I'll get Árni to look after you. He'll drive you back to Headquarters and get you settled in. And by all means come and chat to me about Steve Jubb later on.'

'Thank you, Inspector,' Magnus said, before he could stop himself.

Baldur called over a detective to escort Magnus, and then left with the Commissioner back to Reykjavík.

'Hi, how are you doing?' said the detective in fluent, American-accented English. 'My name's Árni. Árni Holm. You know, like the Terminator.'

He was tall, painfully thin, with short, dark hair and an Adam's apple that bobbed furiously as he spoke. He had a wide, friendly grin.

'*Komdu saell*,' said Magnus. 'I appreciate you speaking my language, but I really need to practise my Icelandic.'

'All right,' said Árni, in Icelandic. He looked disappointed not to be showing off his English skills.

'Although I have no idea what "Terminator" is in Icelandic.'

'*Tortimandinn*,' said Árni. 'Some people call me that.' Magnus couldn't resist a smile. Árni was on the weedy side of wiry. 'OK, not many, I admit,' said Árni.

'Your English is very good.'

'I studied Criminology in the States,' Árni replied proudly. 'Kunzelberg College, Indiana. It's a small school, but it has a very good reputation. You might not have heard of it.'

'Uh, I can't say I have,' said Magnus. 'So where to next? I'd like to join Baldur for the interview of this Steve Jubb.'

THE FIRST THING Magnus noticed was that Steve Jubb wasn't American. He had some kind of British accent, from Yorkshire, it transpired; Jubb was a truck driver from a town called Wetherby in that county. He was unmarried, living alone. His passport confirmed he was fifty-one.

Magnus and Árni were watching the interview on a computer screen in a room down the hall. There were four men in the interview room: Baldur, another detective, a young Icelandic interpreter and a big, broad-shouldered man with a beer belly. He was wearing a denim shirt open over a white T-shirt, black jeans and a baseball cap, from under which peeked thin, greying hair. A neat little grey beard on his chin. Magnus could just make out the green and red swirls of a tattoo on his forearm. Steve Jubb.

Baldur was a good interviewer, confident and more approachable than he had been with Magnus earlier. He even smiled occasionally, an upward twitch of the corners of his lips. But the interview was slow and stilted, as everything had to be translated back and forth by the interpreter. Árni explained that this wasn't because Baldur didn't speak good English—it was a requirement if anything said in the interview was to be admitted in court.

Jubb's story was that he had met Agnar on a holiday to Iceland the previous year and had arranged to look him up on this trip. He had hired a car, the blue Toyota Yaris, and driven out to Lake Thingvellir. Agnar and he had chatted for a little over an hour and then Jubb had driven straight back to the hotel. The receptionist corroborated the timing of his return. Agnar and Jubb had discussed places in Iceland that Jubb should visit.

Jubb confirmed that he had drunk Coca-Cola and his host red wine. He had kept his shoes on in the summerhouse: his shoe size was ten and a half under the UK measurement system.

After half an hour of this Baldur left the room and found Magnus. 'What do you think?' he asked.

'His story holds up,' Magnus replied.

'But he's hiding something.' It was a statement, not a question.

'I think so, too, but it's tough to tell from in here. Can I speak to him face to face? Without the interpreter? I know anything he tells me won't be admissible, but I might loosen him up.'

Baldur thought for a moment and then nodded.

Magnus wandered into the interview room and sat down.

'Hey, Steve, how's it going?' he said. 'You holding up OK?'

Jubb frowned. 'Who are you?'

'Magnus Jonson,' Magnus said. It seemed natural to slip back into his American name when he was speaking English.

'You're a bloody Yank.' Jubb's Yorkshire accent was strong and direct.

'Sure am. I'm helping these guys out for a spell.'

Jubb grunted.

'So, tell me. What did you and Agnar talk about?'

'This and that. Places to visit. He knows the country pretty well.'

'No, I mean what did you talk about that made you want to see him again? He was a university professor, you're a truck driver.'

Jubb hesitated, then answered. 'Sagas. He was an expert, I'd always been interested in them. It was one of the reasons I came to Iceland.'

'Sagas!' Magnus snorted. 'Give me a break.'

Jubb shrugged his broad shoulders. 'You asked.'

Magnus paused, assessing him. 'I'm sorry. Which is your favourite?'

'The *Saga of the Volsungs*.'

Magnus raised his eyebrows. 'Unusual choice.' The most popular sagas were about the Viking settlers in Iceland during the tenth century, but the *Saga of the Volsungs* was set in a much earlier period. It was a myth about an early Germanic family of kings, the Volsungs, who eventually became the Burgundians: Attila the Hun had a role in the story. It wasn't one of Magnus's favourites but he had read it a few times.

'OK. So what was the name of the dwarf who was forced to give his gold to Odin and Loki?' he asked.

Jubb smiled. 'Andvari.'

'And Sigurd's sword?'

'Gram. And his horse was called Grani.'

Jubb knew his stuff. He might be a truck driver, but he was well read. Not to be underestimated.'I like the sagas,' Magnus said with a smile. 'My dad used to read them to me. But he was Icelandic. How did you get into them?'

'My grandfather,' Jubb said. 'He studied them at university. He used to tell me the stories when I was a lad. I was hooked.'

'In English?'

'Obviously.'

'They are better in Icelandic.'

'That's what Agnar said. But it's too late for me to learn another language now.' Jubb paused. 'I'm sorry he's dead. He was an interesting bloke.'

'Did you kill him?' Magnus didn't expect an honest answer, but the reaction the question provoked might be useful.

'No,' said Jubb. 'Of course I bloody didn't!'

Magnus studied Steve Jubb. The denial was convincing, and yet . . . The lorry driver was hiding something.

At that moment the door opened and Baldur burst in, clutching some sheets of paper, followed by the interpreter. He leaned over and flicked a switch on a small console by the computer. 'Interview recommences at eighteen twenty-two,' he said, sitting down. And then, in English, staring at Jubb, 'Who is Isildur?'

Jubb tensed. 'I've no idea. Who is Isildur?'

Magnus asked himself the same question, although he thought the name sounded familiar from somewhere.

'Take a look at these,' Baldur said, returning to Icelandic. He pushed three sheets of paper towards Jubb and handed another three to Magnus. 'These are print-outs of emails taken from Agnar's computer.'

Jubb picked up the sheets of paper and read them, as did Magnus. Two were simple, businesslike messages confirming the visit Steve had suggested on the phone and arranging a date, time and place to meet. The tone was more businesslike than an informal arrangement to meet for a chat with an acquaintance.

The third email was the most interesting:

From: Agnar Haraldsson
To: Steve Jubb
Subject: Meeting 23 April
Dear Steve ,

I'm looking forward to seeing you on Thursday. I have made a discovery that I think you will find very exciting. It is a shame that Isildur can't be there as well. I have a proposal for him that it would be good to discuss in person. Is it too late to persuade him to come?

Kind regards,
Agnar

'So—who is Isildur?' Baldur asked again.

Jubb sighed heavily, tossed the papers onto the desk and crossed his arms. He said nothing.

'What was the proposal Agnar wanted to discuss with you?'

'I'm not answering any more questions,' said Jubb. 'I want to go back to my hotel.'

'You can't,' said Baldur. 'You're staying here. You are under arrest.'

Jubb frowned. 'In that case, I want to speak to someone from the British Embassy.'

'You are a suspect in a murder inquiry. We can inform the British Embassy that we are holding you, but you don't have the right to see them. We can get you a lawyer if you wish.'

'I do wish. And until I've seen him, I'm not saying anything.' And Steve Jubb sat in his chair, a big man, arms folded tightly across his chest, lower jaw jutting out, immovable.

CHAPTER THREE

Baldur ran a brisk and efficient morning meeting. Half a dozen detectives were present, plus Magnus, the assistant prosecutor—a young red-haired woman called Rannveig—and Chief Superintendent Thorkell Holm, the head of the Reykjavík Metropolitan Police CID. Thorkell was a jovial man in his early sixties who seemed at ease with his detectives, happy to blend into the background.

At least he, like Árni, seemed friendly. Magnus couldn't see any physical similarity between them, but they shared the same last name, Holm, and so they were probably related. A small minority of Icelanders used the same family naming system as the rest of the world. They were often from wealthier families who had travelled abroad to Denmark to study, and had given themselves family names while they were there.

There was an air of expectancy around the table, and Magnus felt himself caught up in the excitement. Árni had driven him back to his hotel the night before. He had grabbed something to eat and gone to bed—it had been a long day, and he slept well for once. It was good to be out of reach of Soto's gang. He was eager to get a message to Colby somehow, but in the meantime the investigation into the professor's murder intrigued him.

And he intrigued the detectives around him. They stared at him when he entered the room. Magnus didn't know if this was the typical initial reserve of Icelanders, a reserve that was usually replaced by warmth within ten minutes, or if it was something more hostile. He decided to ignore it.

'Our suspect is still saying nothing,' Baldur said. 'We've heard from the British police: his record is clean apart from two convictions for possession of cannabis in the 1970s. Rannveig will take him before the judge this morning to get an order to keep him in custody for the next few weeks.'

'Do we have enough evidence for that?' Magnus asked.

Baldur frowned at the interruption. 'Steve Jubb was at the scene of the crime at about the time the murder was committed. We know he was discussing some kind of deal with Agnar but he won't tell us what he was doing there. He's hiding something, and until he tells us otherwise, we'll assume it's a murder. I'd say we have enough to hold him. So will the judge.'

'Sounds good to me,' said Magnus. And it did. In the US it would not be nearly enough to hold a suspect.

Baldur nodded curtly. 'Now, what have we got?'

Two detectives had interviewed Agnar's wife, Linda, at their house in Reykjavík. She was devastated. They had been married seven years and had two small children. It was Agnar's second marriage: he was divorced when they met—Linda had been one of his students.

He had gone to the summerhouse to catch up on work—he had had a deadline looming for a translation. He had spent the previous two weekends there. His wife, stuck alone with the children, had not been too happy with that.

Agnar's laptop had not revealed any more interesting emails. There was a jumble of Word files and internet sites visited, all of which would be analysed, as well as piles of papers in his university office and at the summerhouse.

Forensics had found four sets of fingerprints in the summerhouse: Agnar's, Steve Jubb's and two others as yet unidentified. None from Agnar's wife, who had stated that she had not yet visited the summerhouse that year. There were no prints on the passenger door of Jubb's rented Toyota, confirming his claim that he had visited Agnar alone. They had also found traces of cocaine use in the bedroom, and a small bag of the drug hidden in a wardrobe.

'Vigdís. Any luck with the name Isildur?' Baldur asked.

He turned to a tall, elegant black woman of about thirty, who was wearing a black sweater and jeans. Magnus had noticed her as soon as he had walked into the room. She was the first black person Magnus had seen in Iceland.

'It seems that Ísildur is a legitimate Icelandic name. Although it is very rare indeed. I have searched the National Registry database, and only come up with one entry for that name in the past eighty years, a boy named Ísildur Ásgrímsson. Born 1974, died 1977 in Flúdir.' Flúdir was a village in the south-west of Iceland, Magnus dimly remembered. 'His father, Ásgrímur Högnason, was a doctor. He died in 1992.'

'But no sign of anyone alive today with that name?'

Vigdís shook her head. 'I suppose he might be a *vestur-íslenskur*.' She meant a Western Icelander, one of those Icelanders, predecessors of Magnus himself, who had crossed over the Atlantic to North America a century before. 'If he was born overseas he won't be on our database.'

'Anyone heard of an Ísildur?' Baldur asked the room. 'It does sound Icelandic.' No one said anything, although Árni, who was sitting next to Magnus, seemed about to open his mouth and then had thought better of it.

'All right,' said Baldur, staring round the room. 'We need to find out what it is that Agnar had discovered, and what deal he and Jubb were negotiating. We need to find out a lot more about Agnar. And most of all we need to find out who the hell this Ísildur is. Let's hope Steve Jubb will begin to talk once he realises that he is going to spend the next few weeks in jail.'

ÁRNI LED MAGNUS to an office stuffed with small, screened-in cubicles, with a '*Violent Crimes*' sign on the door. His desk was opposite Árni's. Two or three of the detectives that Magnus has seen at the meeting were on the phones or their computers. The others were already out interviewing people.

The phone worked, and Árni assured him someone from the IT department would set him up with a computer password that morning. Árni disappeared to the coffee machine and returned with two cups.

Magnus sipped his coffee and considered Agnar. He didn't yet know much about the professor, but he did know that he was someone's husband, and the father of two children. Magnus thought of the devastated wife and those kids growing up with the knowledge that their father had been murdered. They needed to know who had killed Agnar and why, and they needed to know that the murderer had been punished. Otherwise—well, otherwise they would end up like Magnus.

The familiar urge returned. Even though Magnus might never meet them, he could promise them one thing: he would find Agnar's killer.

'Have you decided where you are going to stay in Reykjavík?' Árni asked, sipping from his own cup.

'No, not really,' Magnus replied. 'The hotel's OK, I guess.'

'My sister has a spare room in her apartment. It's a nice place, very central, in Thingholt. You could rent that. She wouldn't charge much.'

Magnus hadn't begun to think about money, accommodation, clothes; he was just pleased to be alive. But Árni's sister might provide a quick and easy solution to a problem he hadn't even begun to address yet. And cheap. That might be important. 'Sure, I'll take a look at it.'

'Great. I'll show you around this evening, if you like.'

The coffee wasn't bad. Icelanders lived on many cups of coffee a day—the whole society was fuelled by caffeine.

'I'm sure I've heard this name Ísildur somewhere,' Magnus said.

'Probably just the movie,' Árni said.

'The movie? What movie?'

'*The Fellowship of the Ring.* Haven't you seen it? It's the first of *The Lord of the Rings* trilogy.'

'No, but I did read the book. So Ísildur's one of the characters, right?'

'Yes,' said Árni. 'He wins the ring at the beginning of the movie and then loses it in a river somewhere.'

'Árni! Why didn't you mention this at the meeting?'

'I was going to, but I thought everyone would laugh at me. They do that sometimes. And it obviously doesn't have anything to do with the case.'

'Of course it does!' Magnus just stopped himself from adding the words, *you idiot!* 'Have you read the *Saga of the Volsungs*?'

'I think I did at school. It's about Sigurd and Brynhild, isn't it?'

'And a magic ring. It's an Icelandic take on the *Nibelungenlied,* which Wagner based his *Ring Cycle* on. I bet J. R. R. Tolkien read it, too. And it's Steve Jubb's favourite saga. He's probably a *Lord of the Rings* nut and has a friend who is another *Lord of the Rings* nut whose nickname is Ísildur.'

'So Isildur isn't Icelandic at all?'

Magnus shook his head. 'No, he's probably another truck driver from Yorkshire. Come on, Árni. We need to talk to Baldur.'

THEY HAD TO WAIT an hour for Baldur to return from the courthouse on the Laekjargata, but he looked happy. 'We can detain Steve Jubb for three weeks,' he said when he saw them.

'Didn't he make bail?' Magnus asked.

'There's no chance of bail in Iceland for a murder suspect. We usually get three weeks to pursue our investigation before we have to hand over evidence to the defence.'

'I like it,' Magnus said.

'Strange thing is, he has a new lawyer. He's already fired the one we gave him and hired Kristján Gylfason, who is about the most experienced criminal lawyer in Iceland. Someone must be helping him; Kristján doesn't come cheap. And for that matter, neither does the Hótel Borg.'

'Isildur?' Magnus asked.

Baldur shrugged. 'Maybe. Whoever he is.'

'We think we have an idea about that.'

Baldur listened to Magnus's theory, a frown crossing his forehead. 'I think we need to have another word with Mr Jubb.'

STEVE JUBB'S new lawyer, Kristján Gylfason, had an air of calm competence and wealth. There were now five men in the interview room: Jubb, his lawyer, Baldur, Magnus and the interpreter.

Baldur flung an English copy of *The Lord of the Rings* onto the desk. Jubb's eyes flicked down to it. Árni had rushed out and bought it from Eymundsson's Bookshop in the middle of town.

Baldur tapped the book. 'Ever read this before?'

Jubb nodded.

Baldur slowly and deliberately opened the book at chapter two and passed it over to Jubb. 'Now tell me you don't know who Isildur is.'

'It's a character in a book,' Jubb said. 'That's all.'

'How many times have you read this book?' Baldur asked.

'Once or twice.'

'Once or twice?' Baldur snorted. 'Isildur is a nickname, isn't it? He's a friend of yours. A fellow *Lord of the Rings* fan.'

Steve Jubb shrugged.

Magnus glanced at the lower extremity of a tattoo peeking out from beneath Jubb's sleeve. 'Take off your shirt.'

Steve Jubb shrugged and removed his shirt. On his forearm was a tattoo of a helmeted man, or perhaps a dwarf, with a beard, wielding an axe.

'Let me guess,' said Magnus. 'Your nickname is Gimli.' He remembered that Gimli was the name of the dwarf in *The Lord of the Rings*.

Jubb shrugged again.

'Is Isildur a buddy from Yorkshire?' Magnus asked. 'You meet in a pub every Friday, have a few beers and talk about old Icelandic sagas?'

No answer.

'You get cop shows in England?' Magnus asked. '*CSI, Law and Order*?'

Jubb frowned.

'In those shows the bad guy gets to remain silent while the good guys ask all the questions. But it doesn't work that way in Iceland.' Magnus leaned forward. 'In Iceland if you keep quiet we think you've got something to hide.'

'That's right. And we *will* find out what you are hiding,' Baldur said. 'And your failure to cooperate will be remembered when it comes to trial.'

The lawyer was about to say something, but Jubb put a hand on his arm. 'Look, if you two are so bloody clever, you'll eventually figure out that I had bugger all to do with Agnar's death. Until then, I'm saying nowt.'

The arms folded, the jaw jutted out. Steve Jubb didn't utter another word.

VIGDÍS WAS WAITING for them outside the interview room. 'Agnar had a lover,' she said, with a small smile of triumph.

Baldur raised his eyebrows. 'Did he indeed?'

'Andrea Fridriksdóttir. She is one of Agnar's students. She came forward as soon as she heard he had been killed. She's downstairs now.'

'Excellent. Let's go and talk to her.'

Realising that he was not invited, Magnus returned to his desk, where a woman from the National Police Commissioner's office was waiting for him. Cellphone, bank account, daily allowance, payment of salary, cash advance, even the promise of a car in a few days, she had it all prepared. But no gun. No one in Iceland was allowed to carry a gun, apart from a few firearms officers, known as the Viking Squad.

She was followed by a man from the IT Department, who gave Magnus his password, and showed him how to use the computer system. Magnus was impressed.

Once the man had gone, Magnus stared at the screen in front of him. The time had come. Magnus could put it off no longer.

It had turned out that the FBI agents who had escorted Magnus in his last days in Massachusetts were from the Cleveland Field Office. One, Agent Hendricks, had been designated his contact man. Magnus had agreed never to use the phone to the United States. The fear, which was never articulated, was that the three police officers who had been arrested were not alone. That they had accomplices, or perhaps just friends in the Boston PD, for whom tracing Magnus's whereabouts would all be in a day's work.

So the idea was that the only form of communication would be emails. Even those Magnus could not send directly, but via Agent Hendricks.

He stared at the screen for several minutes more. He couldn't take the risk that Colby would be attacked or killed on his account. She had out-manoeuvred him, and he had to accept that. In the end he kept it simple.

The answer to your question is yes. Now please come with me. I am very worried about you.

With all my love,

Magnus

Not very romantic—hardly the right way to start a life together. Although he was attracted to Colby, loved her even, the more he got to know her the more sure he was that they shouldn't get married. It wasn't only his fear of commitment; he just knew that if there was a woman out there somewhere that he could spend the rest of his life with, it wasn't Colby. Her latest high-stakes ploy was an example of why. But he had no choice. She had given him no choice.

He composed a brief report to Williams, telling him he was safe and in email contact should Williams learn anything about the trial date.

He thought of writing to Ollie, as his brother now called himself, but decided against it. The FBI had informed him that Magnus was disappearing, and an agent had taken his stuff from the guest room in Ollie's house. That would have to be enough—the less Magnus had to do with Ollie the better. It wasn't just Colby who was at risk from Soto's gang.

Magnus closed his eyes. Maybe he should just have pretended that he hadn't heard Lenahan's conversation. Of course, in his beloved sagas, the heroes always did their duty. But then most of their relatives came to a bloody end. It was easy to be brave with your own skin, much harder with other people's. Then the ancient Icelandic reaction kicked in. If they touched a hair of Colby's or Ollie's head, he would make the bastards pay. All of them.

BALDUR HELD ANOTHER CONFERENCE at two o'clock that afternoon. The team were still fresh and enthusiastic.

He began with the findings from the autopsy. It looked likely that Agnar had drowned; there was some mud found in his lungs, which suggested that he was still breathing when he hit the water. The fragments of stone in the victim's head wound were from the nearby dirt road rather than the lake floor. There were traces of cocaine in the victim's blood, and some alcohol, but not enough to cause intoxication. The pathologist's conclusion was that the victim was struck on the back of the head with a stone, fell unconscious and was dragged into the lake where he drowned. No surprises there.

Baldur and Vigdís had interviewed Andrea. She had admitted that her affair with Agnar had been going on for about a month. She had spent one weekend with him at the summerhouse. Her fingerprints were indeed one of the two unidentified sets. Andrea said that Agnar had seemed terrified of his wife, terrified that she would discover what had happened. He had promised her after she had caught him with a student four years before that he would remain faithful, and until Andrea he had kept his word.

Magnus outlined the theory that Isildur was a nickname for a *Lord of the Rings* fan, and that Steve Jubb was one himself.

Baldur handed round the list of entries from Agnar's appointments diary. Dates, times and the names of people he had met. One afternoon the previous week was blocked out with the word 'Hruni'.

'Hruni is near Flúdir, isn't it?' Baldur said.

'Just a couple of kilometres away,' Rannveig said. 'I've been there. There's nothing but the church and a farm.'

'Perhaps the entry refers to the dance rather than the place,' Baldur said. 'Something collapsing that afternoon? A disaster?'

Magnus had heard of Hruni. Back in the seventeenth century, the pastor of Hruni was notorious for the wild parties he held in his church at Christmas. One Christmas Eve the devil was seen hanging around outside, and the following morning the whole church and its congregation had been swallowed up by the earth. Since then the phrase 'Hruni dance' had slipped into the language to mean something that was falling apart.

'The little boy who died young came from Flúdir,' said Vigdís. 'Ísildur Ásgrímsson. And here's his sister.' She pointed to a name on the list of appointments. 'Ingileif Ásgrímsdóttir, sixth of April, two thirty. At least, I'm pretty sure that she was the boy's sister. I can check.'

'Do that,' said Baldur. 'And if you are right, interview her. We're assuming that Isildur is a foreigner but we need to keep an open mind.'

He picked up a sheet of paper from the table in front of him. 'We have searched Steve Jubb's hotel room and the forensics people are examining his clothes. We found a couple of interesting text messages that had been sent on his cellphone. Take a look at the transcriptions.'

He passed round the sheet, on which two short sentences had been typed. They were in a language that Magnus didn't recognise, didn't even begin to recognise. 'Does anyone know what this is?' Baldur asked.

There were frowns and slowly shaking heads around the table.

Magnus noticed that Árni was shifting uncomfortably again.

'Árni?' Magnus said.

Árni glared at Magnus, and then swallowed, his Adam's apple bobbing. 'Elvish,' he said, very quietly. 'I think Tolkien created some Elvish languages. This might be one of them.'

Baldur put his head in his hands and then glared at his subordinate. 'You're not going to tell me the *huldufólk* did this, are you now, Árni?'

Árni shrank. The *huldufólk*, or hidden people, were elflike creatures who were supposed to live all over Iceland in rocks and stones. In everyday conversation Icelanders were proud of their belief in these beings, but Baldur did not want his murder investigation to be derailed by the most troublesome of all Iceland's many superstitions.

'Árni could be right,' said Magnus. 'We know Steve Jubb and Isildur, whoever he is, were doing a deal with Agnar. If they needed to communicate with each other about it they could have used a code. They are both *Lord of the Rings* fans: what better than Elvish?'

Baldur pursed his lips. 'All right, Árni. See if you can find someone who speaks Elvish, get them to translate it.'

He glanced round the table. 'If Steve Jubb won't tell us, we need to find out who this Isildur is ourselves. We need to get in touch with the British police in Yorkshire to see if they can help us with Jubb's friends. And we need to check all the bars and restaurants in Reykjavík to find out if Jubb met anyone else apart from Agnar. Perhaps Isildur is here in town; we won't know until we ask around.' He doled out specific tasks for everyone at the table, asking Magnus to join Vigdís in tracking down Ásgrímsson's sister, and the meeting was over.

INGILEIF ÁSGRÍMSDÓTTIR owned an art gallery on Skólavördustígur. New York had Fifth Avenue, London had Bond Street and Reykjavík had Skólavördustígur. Small stores lined the road, part concrete, part brightly painted corrugated metal, selling art supplies, jewellery, designer clothes and fancy foods. But the credit crunch had made its mark: some premises were discreetly empty, displaying small signs showing the words *Til Leigu*, meaning *For Rent*.

Vigdís parked her car a few metres away from the gallery. She pushed open the door to the gallery and Magnus followed her in. A woman, presumably Ingileif Ásgrímsdóttir, was speaking to a tourist couple in English.

Magnus and Vigdís examined the objects on sale in the gallery, as well as Ingileif herself, while they waited for her to finish. She was slim with blonde hair that came down in a fringe over her eyes and was tied back in a ponytail. A quick, broad smile beneath high cheekbones, a smile that she was using to maximum effect on her customers, who ended up buying a large glass vase and an abstract painting that hinted of Reykjavík, Mount Esja and horizontal layers of pale grey cloud.

After they had left the store, the owner turned to Magnus and Vigdís. 'Sorry to keep you waiting,' she said in English. 'Can I help you?'

Magnus hadn't appreciated that he looked so obviously American; then he realised it was Vigdís who had prompted the choice of language. In Reykjavík, black meant foreigner.

Vigdís herself was all business. 'Are you Ingileif Ásgrímsdóttir?' she asked in Icelandic.

The woman nodded.

Vigdís pulled out her badge. 'My name is Detective Vigdís Audarsdóttir, and this is my colleague, Magnús Ragnarsson. We have some questions for you relating to the murder of Agnar Haraldsson.'

The smile disappeared. 'You'd better sit down.' The woman led them to a cramped desk at the back of the gallery and they sat on two small chairs. 'I saw something about Agnar on the news. He taught me Icelandic literature when I was at the university.'

'You saw him recently,' Vigdís said, checking her notebook. 'On the sixth of April, at two thirty?'

'Yes, that's right,' said Ingileif, her voice suddenly hoarse. She cleared her throat. 'Yes, I bumped into him in the street, and he asked me to drop in on him some time at the university. So I did.'

'What did you discuss?'

'Oh, nothing, really. My design career, mostly. This gallery. He was very attentive, very charming.'

'Did he say anything about himself?'

'Not much had changed really. He said he had two children now.' She smiled. 'Difficult to imagine Agnar with kids, but there you are.'

'You come from Flúdir, don't you?'

'That's right,' said Ingileif. 'Best farmland in the country, biggest courgettes, reddest tomatoes. Can't think why I ever left.'

'Sounds like quite a place. It's near Hruni, isn't it?'

'Yes. Hruni is the parish church. It's three kilometres away.'

'Did you meet Agnar at Hruni on the twentieth of April?'

Ingileif frowned. 'No, I didn't. I was in this shop all day.'

'He met someone in Hruni that day. Doesn't it strike you that it's a bit of a coincidence that he should go to Flúdir, the village where you grew up?'

Ingileif shrugged. 'Not really.' She forced a smile. 'This is a small country. Coincidences happen all the time.'

Vigdís looked at her doubtfully. 'Is there anyone who could confirm that you were in the shop that afternoon?'

She thought a moment. 'That was Monday, wasn't it? Dísa in the boutique next door borrowed some tea bags. I'm pretty sure that was Monday.'

Vigdís glanced at Magnus. He realised that she was holding off on pushing Ingileif directly on her relationship with Agnar, and so he decided on a different tack. 'You had a brother, named Ísildur, who died young?'

'Yes,' said Ingileif. 'It was several years before I was born. Meningitis, I think. He was my parents' first child, and it hit them badly.'

'Do you know why they called him Ísildur? It's an unusual name.'

Ingileif shook her head. 'No idea.' She seemed nervous and was frowning slightly. Magnus noticed a V-shaped nick above one of her eyebrows, partly hidden by her fringe. 'Except that Ísildur was my great-grandfather's name, I think. On my father's side. Maybe my dad wanted to honour him.'

'We'd like to ask your mother,' Magnus asked. 'Can you give us her address?'

Ingileif sighed. 'I'm afraid she died last year. And my father died in 1992.'

'I'm sorry,' Magnus said, and he meant it. Ingileif appeared to be in her late twenties, which would mean she had lost her father at about the same age Magnus was when he had lost his mother.

'Were either of them fans of *The Lord of the Rings*?'

'I don't think so,' said Ingileif. 'I mean, we had a copy in the house so one of them must have read it, but they never mentioned it.'

'And you? Have you read it? Or seen the movies?'

'I saw the first one. Not the other two. I didn't really like it. When you've seen one orc you've seen them all. But I read the book when I was a kid.'

Magnus paused, waiting for more. Ingileif's pale cheeks blushed red.

'Have you ever heard of an Englishman named Steve Jubb?'

Ingileif shook her head firmly. 'No.'

Magnus glanced at Vigdís. Time to get back to Ingileif and Agnar. 'Ingileif, were you having an affair with Agnar?' she asked.

'No,' Ingileif replied angrily. 'No, absolutely not.'

'But you found him charming?'

'Yes, I suppose so. He always was charming, and that hasn't changed.'

'Have you ever had an affair with him?' Magnus asked.

'No,' said Ingileif, her voice hoarse again.

'Ingileif, this is a murder investigation,' Vigdís said slowly and firmly. 'If you lie to us we can arrest you. It will be a serious matter, I can assure you. Now, once more, did you ever have an affair with Agnar?'

Ingileif bit her lip, her cheeks reddening again. She took a deep breath. 'OK. All right. I did have an affair with Agnar when I was his student. But it was hardly an affair, we slept together a few times, that was all.'

'Did he finish it, or did you?'

'I suppose it was me. He did have a real magnetism; in fact, he still had it when I last saw him. But he was sleazy, basically. He wanted to sleep with as many girls as he could just to prove to himself what a good-looking guy he was. When I saw him the other day he tried to flirt with me again, but I saw through it this time. I don't mess around with married men.'

'One last question,' said Vigdís. 'Where were you on Friday evening?'

'I went to a party for a friend who was launching an exhibition of her paintings. I was there from about eight until, maybe, eleven thirty.

Her name is Frída Jósefsdóttir. I can give you her details if you want.'

'Please,' said Vigdís, passing her her notebook. Ingileif scribbled something on a blank page and handed it back.

'And after you left the gallery?' asked Vigdís.

Ingileif smiled shyly. 'I went home. With Lárus Thorvaldsson.'

'Is he a regular boyfriend?'

'Not really,' said Ingileif. 'He's a painter: we've known each other for years. We just spend the night together sometimes. You know how it is.'

For once in the conversation, Ingileif seemed completely unembarrassed. So did Vigdís for that matter. She obviously knew how it was.

Vigdís passed the notebook across again and Ingileif scribbled down Lárus's details.

'SHE'S NOT a very good liar,' Magnus said when they were out on the street.

'I knew there was something going on between her and Agnar.'

'But she was convincing that that was all in the past.'

'Possibly,' said Vigdís. 'I'll check her alibi, but I expect it will hold up.'

'There must be some connection with Steve Jubb,' Magnus said. 'The name Isildur is significant, I know it. Did you notice she didn't seem surprised we were asking about her long-dead brother? And if she saw *The Lord of the Rings* movie the name Isildur would have jumped out at her. She didn't mention that connection at all.'

'You mean she was trying to downplay the Isildur name?'

'Exactly. There's a connection there she's not talking about.'

'Shall we bring her in to the station for questioning?' Vigdís suggested. 'Perhaps Baldur should see her.'

'Let's leave it. She has my number, and we'll come back and interview her again in a day or two. It's easier to find the hole in a story second time round.'

They checked with the woman who owned the boutique next door. She confirmed she had dropped into Ingileif's gallery to borrow some tea bags, although she wasn't sure whether it was the Monday or the Tuesday.

Vigdís drove past the Hallgrímskirkja, Iceland's largest church.

'Where are you from originally?' Magnus asked.

'I'm an Icelander,' Vigdís said. 'I was born here, I live here, I have never lived anywhere else.'

'Right,' Magnus said. A touchy subject, clearly. But he had to admit that Vigdís was an incontrovertibly Icelandic name.

Vigdís sighed. 'My father was an American serviceman at the Keflavík air base. I don't know his name, I've never met him and, according to my mother, he doesn't even know I exist. Does that satisfy you?'

'I'm sorry,' said Magnus. 'I know how difficult it can be to figure out your identity. I still don't know whether I am an Icelander or an American, and I just get more confused the older I get.'

'Hey, I don't have a problem with my identity,' said Vigdís. 'I know exactly who I am. It's just other people never believe it.'

'Ah,' said Magnus. A couple of raindrops fell on the windscreen. 'Do you think it will rain all day?'

Vigdís laughed. 'There you are, you are an Icelander. When in doubt discuss the weather. No, Magnús, I do not think it will rain for more than five minutes.' She drove on towards police headquarters. 'Look, I'm sorry, I just find it easier to straighten out those kind of questions up front. Icelandic women are a bit like that. We say what we think.'

'It must be tough being the only black detective in the country.'

'You're damn right. I'm pretty sure that Baldur didn't want me to join the department. And I don't exactly blend in when I'm out on the streets, you know. But I did well in the exams and Snorri gave me the job.'

'The Commissioner?'

'He told me my appointment was an important symbol for Reykjavík's police force to be seen as modern and outward looking.' She sighed. 'The problem is I feel like I have to prove myself every day.'

'Well, you seem like a good cop to me,' Magnus said.

Vigdís smiled. 'Thanks.'

They reached police headquarters, an ugly concrete office block opposite the bus station. Vigdís drove her car into a compound around the back and parked. The rain began to fall hard, thundering down on the car roof. Vigdís peered out at the water leaping about the parking lot and hesitated.

Magnus decided to take advantage of Vigdís's direct honesty to find out a bit more about what he had got himself into. 'Is Árni Holm related to Thorkell Holm in some way?'

'Nephew. And yes, that is probably why he is in the department. He's not exactly our top detective, but he's harmless. I think Baldur might be trying to get rid of him.'

'Baldur isn't very happy with me being here either, is he?'

'No, he isn't. We Icelanders don't like being shown what to do by the Americans, or anyone else for that matter.'

Magnus sighed. He could understand Baldur's position, but it wasn't going to make his life in Reykjavík easy. 'And what do you think?'

Vigdís smiled. 'I think I might learn something from you, and that's always good. Come on. The rain is easing off, just like I said it would. I don't know about you, but I've got work to do.'

CHAPTER FOUR

Ingileif was shaken by the visit of the two detectives. An odd couple: the black woman had an Icelandic accent, whereas the tall, red-haired man spoke with an American lilt. Neither of them had believed her, though.

As soon as she had read about Agnar's death in the newspaper, she had expected the police. She thought she had perfected her story, but in the end she didn't think she had done very well. She just wasn't a good liar.

The shop was empty so she returned to her desk, and pulled out some sheets of paper and a calculator. She stared at all the minus signs. If she delayed the electricity bill, she might just be able to pay Svala, the woman who made the glass pieces in the gallery. Something in her stomach flipped, and an all-too familiar feeling of nausea flowed through her.

This couldn't go on much longer.

She loved the gallery. They all did, all seven women who owned it and whose pieces were sold there. At first they had been equal partners: her own skill was making handbags and shoes out of fish skin tanned to a beautiful luminescent sheen. But it emerged that she had a natural talent for promoting and organising the others, and sales had increased.

Her breakthrough had been the relationship she had developed with Nordidea. The company was based in Copenhagen, but had shops all over

Germany. Orders had grown so fast that Ingileif had had to recruit more designers. The only problem was that Nordidea were slow payers. Then, as the credit crunch bit, they became even slower. Then they just stopped paying at all.

There were repayments on a big loan from the bank to be made. On the advice of their bank manager the partners had borrowed in low-interest euros. The rate may well have been low for a year or two, but as the króna devalued, the size of the loan had ballooned to the point where the women had no chance of meeting their original repayment schedule.

More importantly for Ingileif, the gallery still owed its designers millions of krónur, and these were debts that she was determined to meet. Her fellow partners had no inkling of how serious the problem was, and Ingileif didn't want them to find out. These designers weren't just her friends: Reykjavík was a small place and everyone in the design world knew her.

She picked up the phone to call Anders Bohr at the firm of accountants in Copenhagen that was trying to salvage something from Nordidea's chaotic finances. She telephoned him once a day, using a mixture of charm and chastisement in the hope of badgering him into giving her something. He hadn't cracked yet. She could only keep trying.

A HUNDRED KILOMETRES to the east, a red Suzuki four-wheel-drive pulled up outside a church. A big man climbed out of the car—he was well over six feet tall, with dark hair greying at the temples, a strong jaw hidden by a beard, and dark eyes glittering under bushy eyebrows. He looked more like forty-five than his real age, which was sixty-one.

He was the pastor of Hruni. He stretched and took a deep gulp of cool, clear air. White puffs of clouds skittered through a pale blue sky. The sun was low—it never rose very high at this latitude—but it emanated a clear light that picked out in shadow the lines of the hills and mountains surrounding Hruni. Low hills, meadows and rock surrounded the hamlet.

The pastor turned to look at his beloved church. It was a small building with white-painted corrugated sides and a red-painted corrugated roof, standing in the lee of a rocky ridge. The church was about eighty years old, but the gravestones around it were weather-beaten grey stone. Like everywhere in Iceland, the structures were new, but the places were old.

The pastor had just come back from ministering to one of his flock, an eighty-year-old farmer's wife who was terminally ill with cancer. For all his forbidding presence the pastor was good with his congregation. Some of his colleagues in the Church of Iceland might have a better understanding of God, but the pastor understood the devil, and in a land that lay under constant threat of earthquakes and volcanoes, and where trolls and ghosts roamed the countryside, an understanding of the devil was important.

Every one of the congregation of Hruni was aware of the awful fate of their predecessors who had danced with Satan and been swallowed up into the ground for their sins. So at the old farmer's wife's request, the pastor had used a blessing from the old pre-1982 liturgy to ward off evil spirits from her house. It had worked. Colour had returned to the old lady's cheeks and she had asked for some food, the first time she had done so for a week.

In years gone by, the pastor used to perform an effective double act with his old friend Dr Ásgrímur, who had understood how important it was to give his patients the will to heal themselves. But the doctor had been dead nearly seventeen years, and his replacement, a young woman, put all her faith in medicine and did her best to keep the pastor away from her patients.

He missed Ásgrímur. The doctor had been the second-best chess player in the area, after the pastor himself. The pastor needed the stimulation of a fellow intellectual, especially during the long winter evenings. He didn't miss his wife, who had walked out on him after Ásgrímur's death, unable to understand or sympathise with her husband's increasing eccentricity.

Thoughts of Ásgrímur reminded the pastor of the news he had read the previous day about the professor who had been found murdered in Lake Thingvellir. He frowned and turned towards his house.

To work. The pastor was writing a major study of the medieval scholar Saemundur the Learned. He wondered whether his own reputation would ever match that of Saemundur's. Perhaps one day he would be called upon to do something that the whole world would notice. One day.

ÁRNI WAS HAVING TROUBLE locating Elvish speakers in Iceland, so Magnus suggested that he dive into the internet and see what he came up with.

Magnus himself decided to make use of the internet to try to track down Isildur. The more he thought about it, the more likely it seemed to him that

Isildur was an online nickname. Isildur was clearly the senior partner in the relationship with Steve Jubb and probably the one putting up the money. If Steve Jubb wouldn't tell them anything about the deal he was discussing with Agnar, maybe Isildur would. If they could find him.

But before he got to work, there was an email waiting for him, forwarded by Agent Hendricks. It was from Colby. He took a deep breath and opened it.

Magnus,
    The answer must be no. I can tell you don't really mean it, so don't pretend you do. Don't bother sending me any more emails, I won't reply.
    C.

She was right, of course, he didn't really want to marry her, and there was no chance that he would be able to persuade her that he did. But he was worried about her safety. He typed rapidly.

Hi Colby,
    I am very worried about you. I need to get you to safety. Now. If you don't want to come with me then I will try to arrange something else. So please get in touch with me, or with DS Williams at Schroeder Plaza. Speak to him directly and only him. Please do this one thing for me,
    Love,
    Magnus

It probably wouldn't work, but it was worth a try.

Magnus spent the rest of the afternoon in the murky waters of the internet, feeling his way around forums and chat rooms. There were an awful lot of *Lord of the Rings* fans out there. They ranged from thirteen-year-old girls who had seen the movies and thought that Orlando Bloom was really hot, to obsessives who wrote thousands of words on whether Balrogs had real wings or metaphysical ones.

Magnus hadn't read *The Lord of the Rings* since he was thirteen, and he had only a vague recollection of all these characters. But it wasn't just the obscurity of the arguments that surprised him; it was the passion and occasionally vitriol that accompanied them. To a great many people, *The Lord of the Rings* was clearly very, very important.

After two hours he found a posting from a man named Isildur. One of the obsessives. It consisted of several paragraphs commenting on a long academic article by someone called John Minshall on the nature of the power of the One Ring in *The Lord of the Rings*.

The One Ring was the greatest of all the rings in Tolkien's books and was made by Sauron, the Dark Lord. Long before the events of the book took place, a desperate battle was fought between the evil Sauron and an alliance of men and elves, a battle that was won by the alliance. The ring was cut off the Dark Lord's hand by a man named Isildur. On their march home, Isildur and his men were waylaid by orcs. As Isildur tried to escape he jumped into a river, where the ring slipped off his finger and was lost.

The ring was discovered by a hobbit named Déagol, who was fishing there with his friend, Sméagol. Sméagol was overwhelmed with desire for the ring, and stole it from his friend. Over time Sméagol was consumed by it, becoming a slithering, obsessive creature called Gollum, until eventually, centuries later, the ring was taken from him by Bilbo Baggins.

The ring had all kinds of powers. The keeper of the ring did not grow old, and if he wore the ring, he became invisible to normal mortals. Over time, the ring exerted a power over its keeper, causing him to lie, cheat or even kill to maintain possession of it. But most importantly, Sauron, the Dark Lord, searched for the ring. When he found it, he would gain total domination of Middle Earth. The only way the Ring could be destroyed was if it was taken to Mount Doom, a volcano, and thrown into the 'Crack of Doom'. This became the quest for Bilbo's nephew, Frodo.

Minshall argued that Tolkien had been inspired by Wagner's *Ring Cycle* of operas, in which the gods competed to take control of the Ring and dominate the world. This idea seriously upset the present-day Isildur, who claimed that Tolkien had read the Volsung saga when he was still a schoolboy and that it had inspired him for the rest of his life.

This saga describes how three gods, Odin, Hoenir and the trickster god Loki, were travelling when they came upon a waterfall where a dwarf named Andvari was fishing. Loki caught him, and stole some gold from him. Andvari tried to keep back a magic ring, but Loki spotted it, and threatened to send the dwarf to Hel, the goddess of death, unless he gave the ring to Loki. Andvari laid a curse on the ring and disappeared into a rock. During the rest of the saga, the ring passed from person to person, creating mayhem wherever it went. Isildur seemed to believe that both Tolkien and Wagner had read the Volsung saga, which explained the similarity between the two.

Magnus strongly suspected that this was the same Isildur who was Steve Jubb's partner. Fortunately the web page included a link to the email address of the people posting the commentaries. Isildur's address indicated an Internet Service Provider from the US. If he could provoke an email response from Isildur that included a 'header' divulging the IP address of Isildur's computer, he might be able to track him down.

He thought for a minute and then tapped something out.

Hi Isildur,
I found your comment about the *Saga of the Volsungs* very interesting. Where can I get a copy?
Matt Johnson

A simple, if slightly dumb question that would take Isildur only a few seconds to respond to, with luck not enough time to worry about the email address from which it was sent. Worth a try.

While he was waiting for a reply, Magnus went to check how Árni was doing. He had made some progress: he had found a lecturer at the University of New South Wales who claimed to be an expert on Tolkien's invented languages. Like Magnus, he was waiting for a response to his enquiry.

Magnus went back to his own computer. He was in luck. There was a brief email from Isildur.

Hi Matt,
You should be able to get a copy from Amazon. There is a good Penguin Classics edition. It's well worth reading. Enjoy.
Isildur

Magnus hit a few keys on his computer, and a string of codes and numerals was revealed, the email header. Pay dirt.

'Árni. Do you know anyone in your Computer Forensics department who could check out an email header for me?'

Árni looked doubtful. 'It's Saturday. They'll be at home. I could try to get hold of someone, but we might have to wait until Monday.'

Monday was no good. Magnus checked his watch. It was about lunchtime in Boston. There was a young technician he'd worked with before called Johnny Yeoh who was the kind of geek who'd drop everything to be helpful if he was interested.

Magnus tapped out a quick email, cutting and pasting the header from Isildur's message. He made sure that there was nothing in the text of the email that might suggest that he was anywhere but some city in the heart of America. He considered sending it to Johnny's Boston PD address via Agent Hendricks. The problem was Johnny wouldn't get it till Monday. Magnus needed a result more quickly than that.

Magnus could remember Johnny's home email address—he had used it enough times before. He weighed the risks. There was no way that anyone would be monitoring Johnny Yeoh for a contact with Magnus. He was a civilian, not a police officer, and about the least likely person to be one of Lenahan's buddies. He tapped out Johnny's address and pressed send.

With any luck, by morning they would know who Isildur was.

THINGHOLT WAS A JUMBLE of brightly coloured little houses in the central 101 postal district of Reykjavík, clinging to the side of the hill below the big church. It was where the artists lived, the designers, the writers, the poets, the actors, the cool and the fashionable.

It wasn't really a cop's neighbourhood, but Magnus liked it.

Árni drove him along a quiet street and stopped outside a tiny house. The walls were cream, and the roof lime-green corrugated metal. It reminded Magnus of the house he had grown up in as a child.

Árni rang the doorbell. Waited. 'She's probably asleep.'

Magnus checked his watch. It was only 7 p.m. 'She's in bed early.'

'No, I mean she hasn't got up yet.'

Just then the door opened, and there stood a very tall, black-haired girl, with a pale face, wearing a skimpy T-shirt and shorts. 'Árni!' she said. 'What are you doing waking me up at this hour?'

'What's wrong with this hour?' Árni said. 'Can we come in?'

The woman nodded, a slow droop of her head, and stood back to let them in. They went through the hallway into a small living room, in which was a long blue sofa, a big TV, a couple of beanbags on the polished wooden floor and a bookcase heaving with books.

'This is my sister, Katrín,' Árni said. 'This is Magnús. He's an American friend of mine. He was looking for a place to stay and so I suggested here.'

Katrín rubbed her eyes and tried to focus on Magnus. She looked quite a lot like Árni, tall, thin and dark, but where Árni's features were weak, hers were strong: angled cheekbones and jaw, short black hair, big dark eyes.

'Hi,' she said speaking in English. 'How are you?'

'I'm doing good,' Magnus replied. 'And you?'

'Yeah. Cool,' she mumbled.

'Shall we sit down and have a chat?' Árni asked.

Katrín focused on Magnus, staring at him. 'No. He's cool. I'm going back to bed.' With that she disappeared into a room off the hallway.

'Looks like you passed,' said Árni. 'Let me show you the room.' He led Magnus up some narrow stairs. 'Our grandparents used to live here. It belongs to both of us now, and we rent out the room on the first floor.'

They emerged into a small room with basic furniture: bed, table, a chair and so on. There were two windows; pale evening light streamed in through one, and through the other Magnus could see the spire of the Hallgrímskirkja high above the multicoloured patchwork of metal roofs.

'Do you like the room?'

'Nice view,' he said. 'What happened to the previous tenant?'

Árni looked pained. 'We arrested him last week. Narcotics.'

'I see.'

Árni coughed. 'I would appreciate it if you could keep an eye on Katrín while you're here. In a low-key way, of course.'

'Will she mind that? I mean, is she happy sharing a place with a cop?'

'There's no need to tell her what you do, is there, do you think? And I wouldn't let Chief Superintendent Thorkell know you are staying here.'

'Uncle Thorkell wouldn't approve?'

'Let's just say that Katrín isn't his favourite niece.'

'How much is the rent?'

Árni mentioned a figure that seemed very reasonable. 'It would have been twice that a year ago,' he assured Magnus.

'I believe you.' Magnus smiled. He liked the little room, he liked the view, and he even liked the look of the weird sister. 'I'll take it.'

'Excellent,' said Árni. 'Now let's go and get your stuff from your hotel.'

IT DIDN'T TAKE LONG to ferry Magnus's bag back to the house, and once Árni had made sure that Magnus was installed, he left him. There was no sound from Katrín.

Magnus stepped out onto the street, and made his way down the hill towards the centre of town. The sky had cleared, apart from a single thin slab of cloud that covered the top of Mount Esja. The air was clear and crisp. At eight thirty it was still light.

He stopped at Eymundsson's bookstore on Austurstraeti, a short shopping street in the centre of town, where he picked up an English copy of *The Lord of the Rings*, and a copy of the *Saga of the Volsungs*, in Icelandic.

He headed over towards the Old Harbour and was suddenly confronted by a memory from his childhood; a small red kiosk, *Baejarins beztu pylsur*. He and his father used to go there every Wednesday night, after hand-ball practice, for a hot dog. He joined the line. Unlike the rest of Reykjavík, *Baejarins beztu* hadn't changed over the years, except there was now a picture outside of a grinning Bill Clinton tucking into a large sausage.

Munching his hot dog, he strolled through the harbour area and along the pier. It was a working harbour, but at this time of the evening it was peaceful. On one side were trawlers, on the other, sleek whale-watching vessels and inshore fishing boats. He paused at the end, a respectful distance from a fisherman fiddling with his bait, and surveyed the stillness.

Iceland had changed so much since the disruptions of his childhood, but what he recognised of Reykjavík brought back the early years, the happy years. There was no reason to visit his mother's family; they need never even find out he was in the country. He was pleased with the way his Icelandic seemed to be coming back so well, although he was aware that he needed to work on rolling his 'r's.

But he would be glad when the trial date came up and he could go back. Although the Agnar case was an interesting one, he missed the violent edge of the streets of Boston. At some point over the past ten years, finding the bad guys and bringing them to justice had become more than a job. It had become a need, a habit, a drug. Reykjavík just wasn't the same. Toytown.

He turned back to the city. As he walked back up the hill along Laugavegur he looked out for a bar for a quick beer. Down a side street he spied a place called Grand Rokk. There was a tent covering tables at which a dozen people were smoking as they drank. Magnus eased his way past a group of regulars and ordered himself a large Thule from the shaven-headed barman. He found a stool in the corner and sipped his beer. The other drinkers looked as if they had been there a while. Quite a few had shot glasses containing a brown liquid next to their beers. A line of tables along one wall were inlaid with chessboards, and there was a game in progress.

He smiled when he remembered challenging his father, a formidable player, night after night. The only way Magnus could ever beat him was by aggressive assaults on his king. They nearly always failed, but sometimes, just sometimes he would break through and win, to the pleasure of both father and son. Magnus knew that although his father would never dream of giving him a break, he was always rooting for Magnus.

Too often, Magnus saw his father only through the dreadful prism of his murder, and forgot the simpler times. Simpler, but not simple.

Ragnar had been a very clever man, a mathematician with an international reputation, which was why he had been offered the position at MIT. Magnus had many fond memories of his father, not only playing chess and reading the sagas together, but also as the saviour who had whisked Magnus and his little brother away from misery in Iceland when they had feared that he had abandoned them.

But there was one aspect of his father's life that Magnus had never understood: his relationships with women. He didn't understand why Ragnar had married his mother, or why he left her. He certainly didn't understand why he had then gone on to marry that awful woman Kathleen. She was the young wife of one of the other professors at MIT. Although outwardly charming and beautiful, she was a controlling woman who resented Magnus and Ollie. Within a few months of their marriage she seemed to resent Ragnar, too. Why his father hadn't seen that coming, he had no idea.

Eighteen months after that, Ragnar was dead, found stabbed in the house they were renting for the summer, on Boston's South Shore.

Magnus had had no doubt who was the chief suspect. The detectives investigating the case listened to his theories about his stepmother with sympathy at first. After an initial couple of days where they seemed to pursue her vigorously, they let her drop. This made no sense to Magnus, since they didn't have another suspect. It was only the following year, when Magnus devoted his summer vacation to making his own enquiries, that he discovered that his stepmother had had a cast-iron alibi: she was in bed with an air-conditioning engineer in town at the time of the killing. A fact that his stepmother and the police had conspired to keep from Magnus and his brother.

The bar was filling up with a younger crowd now. A band set up, and within a few minutes began to play. The music was too loud for a contemplative beer, so Magnus left.

Outside, the streets, so quiet earlier, were full, teeming with the young and not-so-young dolled up for a night on the town.

Time for bed, Magnus thought. As he opened the door of his new lodgings, he passed Katrín on her way out, dressed in black gothic finery, her face powdered white and studded with metal.

'Hi,' she said, with a half-smile.

'Have a good evening,' said Magnus.

She paused. 'You're some kind of cop, aren't you?'

Magnus nodded. 'Kind of.'

'Árni's such an arsehole,' she muttered, and disappeared into the darkness.

REYKJAVÍK METROPOLITAN Police Headquarters was a busy place early on Sunday morning, as exhausted uniformed police led pale and shaky citizens through the later stages of the Saturday-night arrest cycle.

As soon as Magnus arrived at his desk, he turned on his computer and smiled. Johnny Yeoh had come up with the goods.

At the morning meeting, Baldur began with the latest reports from forensics. With Agnar, Steve Jubb and Andrea, three of the four sets of fingerprints in the house were accounted for. The footprints were confirmed as Steve Jubb's. But there were no bloodstains on any of Jubb's clothes, not even the tiniest spatter.

Magnus knew it would be difficult to smash someone over the head and then drag them the twenty metres to the lake without getting any blood on their clothes. Difficult, but not impossible.

'I spoke to Agnar's wife yesterday,' Baldur said. 'She's an angry woman. She had no idea of the existence of Andrea. Also, she has been through Agnar's papers and discovered that he was in a much deeper financial hole than she had realised. Debts, big debts. Cocaine. And he gambled. She estimates he owed about thirty million krónur. But now he's dead, a life insurance policy will take care of that.'

Magnus did a quick mental calculation. Thirty million krónur was over two hundred thousand dollars. Even by the standards of Iceland's debt-addicted citizens, Agnar owed a lot of money.

'All in all, Linda had a motive to kill her husband,' Baldur continued. 'She says she was alone with her young children on the Thursday night. But she could easily have slung them in the back of the car and driven to Thingvellir. We need to keep her in the frame. Now, Vigdís. Did you speak to the woman from Flúdir?'

Vigdís ran through the interview with Ingileif. She had checked out Ingileif's alibi: she had indeed been at her friend's party until eleven thirty on the evening of the murder. And with her 'old friend' afterwards.

'She might have been telling the truth about that, but we think she was lying about other stuff,' said Magnus.

'She was very coy about Agnar,' Vigdís explained. 'My hunch is there was more going on there than she let on. We'll go back and talk to her in a couple of days and see if her story sticks.'

'Any progress on Isildur?' Baldur asked.

'Yes,' said Magnus. 'I found someone calling himself Isildur on a *Lord of the Rings* forum on the internet. I got hold of his email details and asked a buddy of mine in the States to check him out. His name is Lawrence Feldman and he's obsessed with Icelandic sagas, just like Steve Jubb. He has two houses in California, one in Palo Alto and one in Trinity County, north of San Francisco. That's where the email message came from.'

Baldur grunted. 'Two houses? Do we know if he is wealthy?'

'He's loaded.' Although Johnny Yeoh hadn't been able to pull the police files on Feldman, he had found plenty of stuff on the internet about him. 'He was one of the founders of a software company in Silicon Valley, 4Portal. The company was sold last year, and each of the founders walked away with forty million bucks. Not bad going.'

'So he could easily afford an expensive lawyer,' said Baldur. 'OK. We need to request this guy's police record, if he has one.'

'I could go and see him,' Magnus said.

'In California?' Baldur looked doubtful. 'We don't know for sure that this is the same Isildur that Steve Jubb is working for. And anyway, he won't talk. Why should he? Jubb isn't saying anything, and we have him in custody.'

'Depends how I ask him.'

Baldur shook his head. 'I'm not sure I can get authorisation for a trip that will probably be a waste of time. Haven't you heard of the *kreppa*?'

It was impossible to spend more than a few hours in Iceland without hearing about the *kreppa*.

'Just an economy fare and one night in a motel,' Magnus said.

Baldur glared at Magnus. 'I'll think about it,' he said, giving Magnus the distinct impression that he wouldn't. 'OK,' Baldur continued, addressing the group. 'It looks like someone calling himself Isildur was behind the negotiations with Agnar. If this Feldman was that man, he had the cash to back a significant deal.'

'But what could they have been negotiating over?' said Vigdís.

'Something to do with *The Lord of the Rings*?' Magnus said. 'Or the Volsung saga. There's a theory that Tolkien was inspired by the saga.'

'All the old copies of the saga will be in the Árni Magnússon Collection at the University of Iceland,' said Baldur. Árni Magnússon was an antiquarian who had travelled around Iceland in the seventeenth century gathering up all the sagas he could find. An institute bearing the great collector's name now housed those sagas. 'Are you saying Agnar had stolen a copy?'

'He might have switched it for a facsimile,' suggested Vigdís.

'Perhaps,' said Magnus. 'Was there anything in Agnar's papers that suggests what this deal could be?'

'No, I checked most of them myself,' Baldur said. 'Apart from those emails on his computer, there is nothing about a deal with Steve Jubb. And the files on his laptop are all work related.'

'What was he working on when he died?'

'I'm not sure he was researching anything. He was marking exam papers. And translating a couple of sagas into English and French.'

Magnus leaned forward. 'Which sagas?'

'I don't know,' Baldur said, defensively. He clearly didn't appreciate being interrogated in his own meeting. 'I haven't read through all his working papers yet. There are piles of them.'

Magnus restrained himself from pushing the point. He didn't want to put Baldur's back up. 'Can I take a look? At his working papers.'

Baldur stared at Magnus, making no attempt to hide his irritation. 'Of course,' he said drily. 'That would be a good use of your time.'

THERE WERE TWO PLACES to look: Agnar's room at the university, or the summerhouse. There would be more papers at the university, but if Agnar had been working on something relevant to Steve Jubb it was likely to be at the summerhouse where it would have been available for his meeting.

Árni drove Magnus out to Lake Thingvellir. 'Do you think Baldur will let you go to California?' he asked.

'I don't know. He didn't seem excited by the idea.'

'If you do go, can you take me with you?' Árni asked. 'I did my degree in the States so I am familiar with US police procedures. Plus, California is my spiritual home.'

'What do you mean?'

'You know. The Gubernator?'

Magnus shook his head. Árni would be demanding a personal interview with Arnold Schwarzenegger next. 'We'll see,' he said.

Deflated, Árni drove over the pass beyond Mosfell Heath and down towards the lake. A boy and a girl were playing by the shore—the boy was about eight, the girl much smaller. Again, only the one summerhouse with the Range Rover was occupied. Agnar's property was still a crime scene, with a police car parked outside, in which sat a solitary constable.

The policeman was glad of the company and let Magnus and Árni into the house. It was cold and still. Magnus examined the desk: drawers full of papers, most of them print-outs from a computer. There was also a low cupboard just to the left of the desk, in which more reams of paper lay.

'OK, you check out the cabinet, I'll check out the desk,' Magnus said.

The first bundle he examined was a French translation of the Laxdaela saga, on which were scribbled comments in French.

'What have you got, Árni?'

'*Gaukur's Saga*,' he said. 'Have you ever heard of it?'

'No,' said Magnus. That wasn't necessarily a surprise. There were dozens of sagas, some well known, some much less so. 'Wait a minute. Wasn't Gaukur the guy who lived at Stöng?'

'That's right,' said Árni. 'I went there as a kid. I was scared out of my wits.'

'I know what you mean,' said Magnus.'My father took me there when I was sixteen. There was something really creepy about that place.'

Stöng was an abandoned farm about twenty kilometres north of Mount Hekla volcano. It had been smothered in ash after a massive eruption in the Middle Ages, and had only been rediscovered in the past century.

'Let me take a look.'

Árni handed the manuscript to Magnus. It was 120 crisp, newly printed pages, in English.

Magnus scanned the text. On the second page he came upon a word that brought his eyes to an abrupt halt. *Ísildur*.

'Árni, look at this!' He flicked rapidly through more pages. Ísildur. Ísildur. Ísildur. The name cropped up several times on each page.

'Wow,' said Árni. 'Shall we get Forensics to look at it?'

'I'm going to read it,' Magnus said. 'Then Forensics can take a look.'

So he sat down in a comfortable armchair, and began to read, passing each page carefully to Árni as he finished with it.

ÍSILDUR AND GAUKUR were two brothers who lived at a farm called Stöng. Ísildur was strong and brave with dark hair, but Gaukur, though two years younger, was even stronger. He had fair hair and was very handsome, but he was vain. Both brothers were honest and popular in the region.

Their father, Trandill, wanted to pay a visit to his uncle, Earl Gandalf, in Norway. Their mother had died when the boys were small, so Trandill asked a friend, Ellida-Grímur, to foster them. Ellida-Grímur agreed to manage the farm at Stöng in Trandill's absence. She had a son, Ásgrímur, who was the same age as Ísildur. The three boys became firm friends.

Trandill was away for three years. Then one day a traveller from Norway arrived at Stöng with a message. Trandill had been killed in a fight with Erlendur, Earl Gandalf's son. Gandalf was willing to pay the compensation that was due to Trandill's sons if they would come to Norway to collect it.

When Ísildur was nineteen, he decided to travel to Norway to claim his inheritance. Gandalf and his son Erlendur welcomed him warmly. Gandalf said that Erlendur had killed Trandill in self-defence when Trandill had attacked him in a drunken rage.

Ísildur decided to spend the summer on Viking raids with Erlendur. Ísildur was a brave warrior and won much booty, but after many adventures, he told Gandalf that he wanted to return to Iceland. Gandalf gave Ísildur the compensation he was owed for his father's death. But the night before Ísildur was due to set sail, Gandalf said he had something else to give him. It was locked in a small chest. Inside was an ancient ring.

Gandalf explained that Trandill had won the ring on a raid in Frisia when he had fought the chieftain, Ulf Leg Lopper. Trandill felled the fearsome old fighter. He saw the ring on his finger and chopped the finger off.

Despite the fact that he was dying, Ulf Leg Lopper had smiled. 'I give you thanks for relieving me of my burden. I found this ring in the River Rhine seventy years ago. I have worn it every day since then. During that time I have won great victories and wealth in battle. The ring will bring you great power, but then it will bring you death. And now I can die, in peace at last.'

Gandalf told Ísildur that the ring had belonged to a dwarf named Andvari. The ring was seized from Andvari, together with a hoard of gold, by Odin and Loki, two ancient gods. Andvari laid a curse on the ring, saying it would take possession of its bearer and use the bearer's power to destroy him, until it was taken home to Hel (Hel was the domain of Hel, the goddess of death, and Loki's daughter).

Odin had reluctantly given the ring to a man named Hreidmar as compensation for killing his son. In the following years it had fallen into the possession of a number of keepers, including the hero Sigurd, the Valkyrie Brynhild, and Sigurd's sons Gunnar and Högni. Everywhere it went it left a trail of treachery and murder in its wake, until finally Gunnar threw it in the Rhine where it lay for centuries, until it was found by Ulf Leg Lopper.

When Trandill returned to Norway from Frisia he was a changed man: secretive, cunning and selfish. One evening, in a drunken rage, he attacked Erlendur, who killed him with a lucky blow. Erlendur was going to take the ring, but Gandalf laid claim to it. That evening he put it on. At once he felt different: stronger, powerful, and also greedy.

Later that evening a Sami sorceress from the North knocked at the door of Gandalf's house seeking shelter. When she saw Gandalf wearing the ring she was overcome with terror and told him it would consume all who owned it, until a man so powerful wore it that he would rule the world and destroy everything good in it. The world would be plunged into eternal darkness. She said that the only way the ring could be destroyed was as Andvari had prophesied; it must be thrown into the mouth of Hel.

'I know where she means,' said Erlendur. 'Trandill told me of it. It is Hekla, a great volcano near his farm at Stöng.'

So Gandalf decided never to wear the ring again. He told Ísildur to take the ring to Hekla and throw it into the volcano.

Ísildur returned home to Iceland with the ring in its box and his treasure. Gaukur had taken over the management of the farm at Stöng, and was betrothed to a woman named Ingileif. When Ásgrímur heard that Ísildur had returned he travelled to Stöng to meet his foster-brother. Ísildur told Gaukur and Ásgrímur about Andvari's ring, and Earl Gandalf's instruction that he toss it into Hekla. He said that he intended to take the ring up the mountain the very next day and he asked Gaukur and Ásgrímur to accompany him to make sure that he wasn't tempted to try on the ring.

The next morning the three men set off for the volcano. On the second day, Ásgrímur slipped down a gully and broke his leg. He could not continue further, but he agreed to wait until the brothers returned from the summit.

He waited until nearly midnight before he heard the sound of footsteps scrambling down the mountain. But there was only one man, Gaukur. He told Ásgrímur that when Ísildur tried to toss the ring into the crater, he was unable to do so. He said that the ring was very heavy. Gaukur urged him to throw it, but Ísildur had become angry and put the ring on his finger. Then, before Gaukur could grab him, he had leaped into the crater.

'At least the ring is destroyed,' said Ásgrímur. 'But at a very high price.'

In the years afterwards, Gaukur changed, and though he became quarrelsome, his foster-brother Ásgrímur remained steadfast in his loyalty.

Gaukur married Ingileif. She was a wise woman and beautiful. She noticed the change in her husband and did not like it. She also noticed that he spent much time at the farm of his neighbour, Ketil the Pale.

Ketil the Pale was popular with everyone, except perhaps his wife, Helga. She was contemptuous of her husband for being weak.

One day, after midsummer, when Gaukur was passing by Ketil the Pale's farm, he came across a slave of Ketil the Pale who was slow to get out of his way. Gaukur chopped off his head. Ketil the Pale protested, but when

Gaukur brushed him off, he did nothing. Helga vowed never to share her husband's bed again until he had demanded compensation from Gaukur.

So Ketil the Pale rode over to Stöng to speak to Gaukur.

Gaukur had laughed at him. 'You understand little, Ketil. Everyone knows that every ninth night you are the woman to the troll of Búrfell.'

'And they know that you could not sire anyone because you were gelded by the troll's daughters,' Ketil had replied, for at that time Gaukur and Ingileif had no children.

Whereupon Gaukur picked up his axe and, after a brief struggle, chopped off Ketil the Pale's leg. Ketil dropped down dead.

Afterwards Gaukur made even more visits to Ketil the Pale's farm, where Helga was now the mistress. Ketil's brothers demanded compensation from Gaukur, but he refused to pay.

Ingileif was jealous, and determined to stop Gaukur. She spoke to Thórdís, Ásgrímur's wife, and told her a secret: Ísildur had not jumped into the crater of Hekla while wearing the ring. He had been killed by Gaukur, who had taken the ring, and then pushed his brother's body into the crater. Gaukur had hidden the ring in a small cave watched over by a troll's hound.

Thórdís told her husband what Ingileif had said. Ásgrímur did not believe her. But that night he had a dream. In his dream he was with a group of men in a great hall and an old Sami sorceress pointed to him. 'Ísildur tried and failed to destroy the ring and was killed in the process. Now it is up to you to find the ring and to take it to the mouth of Hel.'

Ásgrímur was convinced by his dream, but he had no proof with which to accuse Gaukur. Ásgrímur went to his neighbour Njáll, a great and clever lawyer, to help him. Njáll suggested a trap.

Ásgrímur told Thórdís, who told Ingileif, that Ísildur had given him a helm, or helmet, in secret when he returned from Norway. This helm had belonged to Fafnir and was famous in legend. Ásgrímur had hidden it in an old barn.

Then Ásgrímur stood watch, hiding in the roof of the barn to ambush Gaukur, if he should come looking for the helm. Sure enough, on the third night, he caught Gaukur entering the barn, looking for the helm.

Ásgrímur confronted Gaukur, who drew his sword.

'Would you kill me in order to steal what is not yours, just as you killed your brother?' Ásgrímur asked.

In answer Gaukur swung his sword at Ásgrímur. They fought. Although Gaukur was the better warrior, Ásgrímur was fired with anger at the betrayal by his foster-brother. He ran Gaukur through with a spear.

Ásgrímur searched for the ring but never found it, and Ingileif would not tell him where it was hidden, saying that the ring had already caused enough evil and should be left to rest.

Six months after Gaukur's death, Ingileif gave birth to a son, Högni.

But the ring did not lie quietly. A century later, there was an enormous volcanic eruption and Hekla smothered Gaukur's farm in ash.

The ring was still hidden somewhere in the hills near Stöng. One day it would emerge, just as it emerged out of the Rhine before. When it did, it had to be tossed into the mouth of Mount Hekla, as the Sami sorceress decreed. Until that time, the saga was to be kept secret by the heirs of Högni.

MAGNUS HANDED the last page to Árni, who was still reading. He tried to control his excitement. Could the saga be real? If it was, it would be one of the greatest finds in Icelandic literature. He was quite certain that it was previously unknown. The Ring of Andvari, and the fact that the main character was Gaukur, the owner of Stöng, would have ensured that the story would have become widely known within Iceland and beyond.

But was it genuine? It was difficult to be sure in translation, but it looked authentic. Icelandic sagas had none of the poetic flourishes of medieval tales from the rest of Europe. At best they were terse and down-to-earth, to be read by farmers and their households during the long winter nights.

Magnus had no doubt that this was what Agnar wanted to sell to Steve Jubb and the modern-day Isildur. He was not surprised they were prepared to pay so much, because Ísildur's quest to throw the ring into Mount Hekla had obvious parallels with Frodo's quest to fling Sauron's Ring into Mount Doom in *The Lord of the Rings*. But this was an English translation. There must be an Icelandic original, from which Agnar had made his translation.

Magnus searched through Agnar's other papers. Nothing.

'Perhaps it's in Agnar's office at the university?' Árni suggested.

'Or maybe someone else has it,' said Magnus, thinking. He looked out of the window towards the snow-topped mountains in the distance. Then it came to him. 'Come on, Árni. Let's get back to Reykjavík.'

CHAPTER FIVE

The gallery on Skólavördustígur was open for only a couple of hours on Sundays and by the time Magnus and Árni got there it was closed. But they could see a figure at the desk at the back of the shop.

Magnus rapped on the glass door. Ingileif appeared, looking irritated. The irritation increased when she saw who it was. 'We're closed.'

'We want to ask you some questions,' Magnus said.

Ingileif saw the grim expression on his face and let them in. She led them back to her desk. They sat facing her.

'You said your great-grandfather's name was Ísildur?' Magnus began.

'I did.'

'And your father's name was Ásgrímur?'

Ingileif frowned. 'Obviously. You know my name.'

'Interesting names.'

'Not especially,' said Ingileif.

Magnus said nothing, let silence do its work. Ingileif began to blush.

'Anyone in your family named Gaukur?' he asked.

Ingileif closed her eyes, exhaled and leaned backwards. Magnus waited.

'You found the saga, then?' she said.

'Just Agnar's translation. You should have known we would. Eventually.'

'Actually, Gaukur is a name we tend to avoid in our family.'

'I'm not surprised. Why didn't you tell us about it?'

Ingileif put her head in her hands. Magnus waited.

'I was stupid not to. But if you have read the saga, you might understand why I didn't. My family has kept it secret for generations.'

'Until you tried to sell it.'

Ingileif nodded. 'Until I tried to sell it. Which I deeply regret now.'

'You mean now that someone is dead?'

Ingileif took a deep breath. 'Yes.'

'And this saga was really kept a secret for all those years?'

Ingileif nodded. 'Until my father, knowledge of the saga had been passed on only from father to eldest son, or in a couple of instances, eldest daughter. My father decided to read it to all us children. But we were sworn to secrecy.'

'Do you still have the original?'

'Unfortunately, it wore out. We have only scraps left, but an excellent copy was made in the seventeenth century. I made a copy of that myself for Agnar to translate; it will be in his papers somewhere.'

'So, after all those centuries, why did you decide to sell it?'

Ingileif sighed. 'My father was obsessed by the saga. He was convinced that the ring mentioned in it still existed and he used to go on expeditions all round the valley of the River Thjórsá, which is where Gaukur's farm was, to look for it. He never found it, of course, but that's how he died. He fell off a cliff in bad weather.'

'I'm sorry,' said Magnus. And although she had lied to him, he was sorry.

'That put the rest of us off *Gaukur's Saga*. My brother, whose obsession until then had matched Dad's, wanted nothing more to do with it. My sister was never very interested. And my mother held it responsible for Dad's death. So when I found I needed money desperately, it seemed to me that I was the only one who would really care if we sold it.

'The gallery is going bust. It is bust really. I need money badly—a lot of money. So when my mother died last year I spoke to my brother and my sister about selling the saga. Birna, my sister, couldn't give a damn, but at first my brother Pétur argued against it. Eventually he relented as I think he might have money problems of his own. Everyone does these days.'

'What does he do?'

'He owns bars and clubs.'

'So why did you approach Agnar?' Magnus asked.

'He taught me at university,' Ingileif said. 'And, as I told you, I knew him quite well. He was sleazy enough to agree to sell the saga on the quiet. And it turned out he knew just the right buyer. A wealthy American *Lord of the Rings* fan, who was willing to keep the purchase private.'

'Lawrence Feldman? Steve Jubb?'

'I didn't know his name. You mentioned the name Steve Jubb before, didn't you? But you said he was English.'

'That's why you said you had never heard of him?'

'I admit I wasn't very helpful. I was desperately trying to keep the saga secret. As soon as I had told Agnar about it, I had second thoughts. I even told him that I wanted to take it off the market and keep it in the family.' She pursed her lips. 'He told me that it was too late. He knew all about it, and unless I went through with the sale, he would tell.'

'He blackmailed you?' Magnus said.

'I suppose you could call it that. I deserved it.'

'How much did he say it would bring?'

'He said it would be millions. Of dollars.'

Magnus took a deep breath. 'And where is this saga now?'

'In the gallery safe.' She hesitated. 'Do you want to see it?'

Magnus and Árni followed her through to a store cupboard at the back of the shop. On the floor was a combination safe. Ingileif twiddled the knobs. She pulled out a leather-bound volume, and placed it on the desk.

'This is the seventeenth-century copy, the earliest complete copy.' She opened up the book at a random page. The pages were paper, covered in a neat black handwriting, clear and easy to read.

She turned back to the safe. 'And then there is this. The original, or what's left of it.' She carefully extracted a large old envelope, laid it on the desk, and slipped out two layers of stiff card, between which, separated by tissue paper, were perhaps half a dozen sheets of brown vellum. She pulled back the tissue so that they could see one of the sheets closely.

It was faded, torn at the edges, and covered in clear black writing.

'Amazing,' Magnus said.

And indeed it was. Any doubts he had had about the authenticity of the translation he had read were dispelled. He couldn't resist reaching out with his fingertip to touch it.

'It is, isn't it?' Ingileif said, a note of pride in her voice.

'But if this was such a great family secret, how did Tolkien ever see it?' Magnus asked. 'I mean, the links to *The Lord of the Rings* are so strong, it can't just be coincidence. He must have read it.'

Ingileif hesitated. 'Wait a minute.' She went to the safe, and returned a moment later. She placed a small, yellowing envelope in front of Magnus.

'May I look?' Ingileif nodded. Magnus carefully pulled out a single sheet of paper, folded once. He unfolded it and read:

20 Northmoor Road
Oxford
March 9, 1938

My dear Ísildarson,
    Thank you so much for sending me the copy of Gaukur's Saga, *which
I have read with great pleasure. It is almost fifteen years now, but
I remember very clearly that meeting of the Viking Club in the college
bar at Leeds when you told me something of the saga.*
    *I am very glad you enjoyed the book I sent you. I have recently
begun a second story about Hobbits set in Middle Earth, a much
darker work than the first, and I have written the first chapter, entitled
'A long-expected party', with which I am very pleased. I have been
searching for a means of linking the two stories. I think perhaps you
might have given me that link.*
    *Please forgive me if I borrow some of the ideas from your saga.
I can promise absolutely to respect your family's wish that the saga
itself should remain secret, but if you do object, please let me know.*
    With best wishes,
    J. R. R. Tolkien

Magnus's heart was pounding. The letter would double the value of the
saga, treble it. It was an astounding discovery. A wealthy *Lord of the Rings*
fan would pay a fortune for the two documents. Or kill for them. Magnus
had read the first two chapters of *The Lord of the Rings* only the night
before. The first was indeed 'A Long-Expected Party', which celebrated
Bilbo Baggins's eleventy-first birthday, at the end of which Bilbo put on his
magic ring and disappeared. In the second, 'The Shadow of the Past', the
wizard Gandalf lectured Bilbo's nephew Frodo on the evil powers of the
ring, and gave him the task of destroying it in the Crack of Doom.

It was clear that between the first and the second chapters lay *Gaukur's
Saga.* 'You showed this to Agnar?' Magnus asked.

Ingileif nodded. 'I let him have it for a few days. He was convinced it
would help us get a better price.'

'I'll bet he was.' Magnus looked at the envelope. 'So Högni Ísildarson
was your grandfather?'

'That's right. In 1923 Högni went to England, to Leeds University, where he studied Old English under J. R. R. Tolkien. He made a big impression on my grandfather. I remember him telling me about him.' Ingileif smiled. 'Tolkien wasn't that much older than my grandfather, only in his early thirties, and they corresponded on and off for as long as Tolkien was alive.'

'It would have been a good thing all round if you had shown me this the last time I was here,' Magnus said.

'Yes, I know,' said Ingileif. 'And I'm sorry.'

'Sorry isn't really good enough.' Magnus looked straight at her. 'Do you have any idea why Agnar was killed?'

'No. I told myself that this was irrelevant to his death, which is why I had no need to tell you about it.' She sighed. 'Do you think it's likely that those people thought that they could get hold of the saga without paying Agnar?'

'Unless you killed him,' Magnus said. 'To shut him up.'

She returned his gaze defiantly. 'I wouldn't kill him for that reason. I wouldn't kill anyone for any reason,' she said.

Magnus stared hard. 'Maybe,' he said. 'We'll be in touch.'

MAGNUS LET the 120 pages of *Gaukur's Saga* fall onto Baldur's desk with a thump.

'What's this?' Baldur asked, glaring at Magnus.

'The reason Steve Jubb killed Agnar.' Magnus reported what he and Árni had found at the summerhouse and his subsequent interview with Ingileif.

Baldur listened closely, lips pursed.

'We need to bring her in and take her prints, see if they are the missing set at the scene. And we should get this authenticated.' Baldur tapped the typescript in front of him. 'So, this must be the deal they were discussing. But that still doesn't explain why Agnar was killed. We know that Steve Jubb didn't get a copy of the saga. We didn't find it in his hotel room.'

'He could have hidden it. Or mailed it the next morning. To Feldman.'

'Possibly. The Central Post Office is just around the corner from the hotel. We can check if anyone remembers him. And if he sent it registered mail, there will be a record of it, as well as the address it was sent to.'

'Or perhaps the deal went bad? They had a fight about the price?'

'Until they had the original saga in their possession, Feldman and Jubb would want Agnar alive.' Baldur sighed. 'But we are getting somewhere. I'll have another go with Steve Jubb tomorrow morning.'

'What about Lawrence Feldman in California?' Magnus said. 'It's even more important to speak to him now.'

'I said I would think about it, and I will think about it,' said Baldur.

'Right,' said Magnus, and he made for the door of Baldur's office.

'And Magnús?' Baldur said. 'You should have reported this *before* you saw Ingileif. I'm in charge of the investigation here.'

Magnus bristled, but he knew that Baldur was right. 'Sorry,' he said.

WHEN MAGNUS RETURNED to his desk, Árni was waiting for him, looking excited. 'I've heard back from the Elvish expert in Australia.' Árni handed Magnus a print-out of an email:

Dear Detective Holm,

The two messages you sent me are in Quenya, the most popular of Tolkien's languages. The translations are as follow:

1. I am meeting Haraldsson tomorrow. Should I insist on seeing the story?

2. Saw Haraldsson. He has (??). He wanted much more money. 5 million. We need to talk.

Note—I could not find a translation for the word 'kallisarvoinen', which I have marked (??).

It has been a pleasure to find that my knowledge of Quenya has finally been of practical assistance to someone!

Barry Fletcher

School of Languages and Linguistics, University of New South Wales

'Well, the first message is pretty clear. The second was sent at eleven o'clock, the night of the murder, right?' Magnus said.

'That's right. As soon as Jubb got back to the hotel having seen Agnar.'

'No wonder he needed to talk, if he'd just pushed a body into the lake.'

'I wonder what the *kallisar*—whatever-it-is word means?' Árni asked.

Magnus pondered it for a moment. 'Manuscript? "He has the manuscript." That would make sense.'

'I don't know,' said Árni. 'It sounds to me as if Agnar has something *else*. Something he wants more money for.'

Magnus sighed. His patience was running low. 'Árni! We know Agnar died that night. This message explains he was holding out for a lot more money. So Jubb killed him and he needed to speak to the boss once he had done it. Simple. Happens in drug deals back home all the time. Now, let's show this to Baldur. He's going to want to discuss this with Jubb.'

VIGDÍS DROVE UP the winding road to Hruni. It had taken her nearly two hours to get there from Reykjavík. But Baldur had insisted that every appointment in Agnar's diary should be investigated, and so now it was time to check the mysterious entry, 'Hruni'.

She passed two or three cars coming the other way, and then she rounded a bend and came upon the valley in which Hruni nestled.

The Sunday service must just have finished. In front of the church two figures, one very large, one very small, were in deep discussion. The pastor of Hruni and one of his parishioners.

Vigdís hung back until the conversation had finished and the old lady, her cheeks flushed, hobbled rapidly to her small car and drove off.

The pastor turned towards Vigdís. He was a big block of a man, with a thick beard and dark hair flecked with grey. For a moment she felt a flash of fear at his sheer size and power, but she was reassured by the clerical collar around his neck. Bushy eyebrows rose. Vigdís was used to that.

'Vigdís Audarsdóttir, Reykjavík Metropolitan Police,' she said. 'May I have a word with you?'

'Of course,' said the pastor. 'Come into the house.' He led Vigdís into the rectory, and through to a study cluttered with books and papers. 'Please sit down. Would you like a cup of coffee, my child?'

'I'm not a child,' said Vigdís. 'I'm a police officer. But yes, thank you.'

She sat on the sofa and examined his study while she waited for him to return. Open volumes sprawled over a large desk and books lined the walls.

The pastor returned with two cups of coffee, and lowered himself into an old chintz armchair. 'Now, how can I help you?' His voice was deep and he was smiling, but his eyes, deep-set and dark, challenged her.

'We are investigating the death of Professor Agnar Haraldsson. He was murdered on Thursday.'

'I read about it in the papers.'

'We understand that Agnar visited Hruni quite recently.' Vigdís checked her notes. 'The twentieth. Last Monday. Did he come to see you?'

'He did. It was in the afternoon, I think.'

'Did you know Agnar?'

'No, not at all. That was the first time I had met him.'

'And what did he want to discuss with you?'

'Saemundur the Learned.'

Vigdís recognised the name, although history had not been her strongest subject at school. Saemundur was a famous medieval historian.

'What about Saemundur the Learned?'

The pastor didn't answer for a moment. His dark eyes assessed Vigdís. She began to feel uncomfortable, wishing that she'd brought a colleague with her.

'Do you believe in God, my child?'

Vigdís was surprised by the question, but was determined not to show it. 'That has no relevance to this inquiry,' she said.

The pastor chuckled. 'I'm always amazed by how officials always avoid that simple question. You're right, it's not directly relevant. But my next question is this. Do you believe in the devil, Vigdís?'

Despite herself, Vigdís answered. 'No.'

'That surprises me. I thought your people would be comfortable with the idea of the devil.'

'If any part of me is superstitious, it's the Icelandic half,' she said.

The pastor laughed. 'That's probably true. But it's not superstition, or at least it's more than that. The way people believe is different in Iceland than in other countries. There is nothing quite like the beauty of the midday sun reflecting off a glacier, or the peace of a fjord at dawn. But as a people we have also experienced the terror of volcanic eruption and earthquake, the bleak emptiness of the lava deserts. You can *smell* the sulphur in this country.' The pastor smiled. 'God is right here.' He paused. 'And so is the devil.'

Despite herself, Vigdís was listening. The deep rumble of the pastor's voice demanded her attention. But his eyes unsettled her. She felt a surge of panic, a sudden desire to bolt out of the study.

'Saemundur understood the devil. According to legend, he was taught by Satan at the School of Black Arts in Paris. On one occasion he persuaded the devil to change into the shape of a seal and carry him back from France to Iceland. Yet he was also Iceland's first historian. I have devoted my life to studying him. Professor Agnar wanted me to tell him about my discoveries.'

'And did you?' Vigdís managed to ask.

'Of course not,' said the pastor. 'One day my work will be published, but that day is still many years away.' He smiled. 'But it was gratifying that at last a university professor recognised that a mere country priest could make a contribution to this nation's scholarship.'

'Did Agnar mention an Englishman named Steve Jubb to you?'

'No.'

'What about a woman named Ingileif Ásgrímsdóttir?'

'Oh, I know Ingileif,' the pastor said. 'A fine young woman. But no, the professor didn't mention her. I believe she studied Icelandic at the university, perhaps she was one of his students?'

Vigdís knew that there were one or two more questions she really should ask, but she was desperate to get out of there. 'Thank you for your time,' she said, getting to her feet.

'Not at all,' said the pastor. He stood up and held out his hand.

Before she could stop herself, Vigdís took it. The pastor held her hand tightly in both of his. 'I would love to speak to you more about your beliefs, Vigdís. Up here at Hruni you can begin to understand God in a way that is impossible in the city. Stay a while. Talk to me.'

His large hands were warm and strong, his voice was soothing and his eyes were commanding. Vigdís almost stayed.

Then summoning a strength of will from deep within herself, she pulled her hand away, turned and stumbled out of his house to her car.

COLBY ADMIRED her new summer dress in the mirror in the bedroom of her apartment in the Back Bay. She had bought it at Riccardi's the previous Sunday. A splurge but it looked good. Simple. Elegant. It looked especially good with the earrings. Earrings that Magnus had given her for her birthday.

No matter how hard she tried not to, she kept on thinking of Magnus.

Where was he now? He had been ridiculous to think that she would join him. But at least he was safely in hiding. Magnus claimed that she was still in danger. But she was sure that the more distance she put between them the safer she would be.

Of course she had nearly made a big mistake in pressing him to marry her. She was very glad he had said no. It wasn't that she didn't find him attractive. Quite the contrary. She loved the sense of latent power and danger that hovered round him. He was smart, too, and a great listener. The trouble was, he was a loser. And he always would be.

It was the job, of course. With his degree from Brown he could have done much better than police work. But he never would. He was obsessed with the job, with solving the murder of one deadbeat after another. She knew it all had to do with his father, but all that knowledge did was make her realise how hard it would be to change him. Not hard. Impossible.

His decision to tell his Chief about the crooked detective was the last straw. It was honourable, but dumb. People who took on the city establishment would never find themselves a part of it. He probably wouldn't even make it any further up the ladder in the police department. A loser.

Which was why when a slim, well-dressed lawyer with whom she had dealt the year before had asked her for dinner, she had said yes.

His name was Richard Rubinstein. She had googled him and discovered that he had just been made a partner of his law firm. Which wasn't necessarily important, but it did mean he wasn't a loser.

She was going to enjoy herself. But not with Magnus's earrings. She unfastened them, replaced them with a pair of simple pearls, and headed out.

FROM A CAR parked across the street, Diego watched her. Checked a photograph on his lap. It was the same girl all right.

By the way she was dressed she was going out for a while. That would give him plenty of time to sneak into her apartment without being seen.

There was still the problem of the lone cop sitting in his patrol car right outside the building. But if Diego knew anything about cops, the guy would be getting hungry. Sure enough, once the woman disappeared down the street, the patrol car started up and pulled out. Time enough to grab a burger before she returned.

Diego got out of his car and crossed the street.

MAGNUS WALKED BACK to his new place in Thingholt from police headquarters. He needed the exercise and the fresh air. And you could at least say that for the air in Reykjavík: it was fresh.

His mind was buzzing with the day's events. It was way too early to tell, but there was nothing as yet to suggest *Gaukur's Saga* was a forgery. But surely if anyone could forge a saga, Agnar could.

Which raised another interesting possibility. Perhaps Steve Jubb had somehow discovered that the document Agnar was trying to sell him for so many millions of dollars was a fake, and he had killed him because of it.

Magnus still wasn't convinced that Ingileif was telling the whole truth, though she had seemed much more sincere when he had spoken to her that afternoon. And he had to admit that he found her mixture of vulnerability and determination attractive.

'Magnus!'

He was in a little street not far from Katrín's house, quite high up the hill. He turned to see a woman he vaguely recognised walking hesitantly towards him. She was about forty, short reddish hair, a broad face with a wide smile. Although the hair was a different colour, her face reminded him strongly of his mother.

She stared at him closely, frowning. 'It is Magnus, isn't it? Magnus Ragnarsson?' She spoke in English.

'Sigurbjörg?' It was a guess on Magnus's part. Sigurbjörg was a cousin on his mother's side of the family. The side that he had hoped to avoid.

The smile broadened. 'That's right. I *thought* it was you.'

'We haven't met for what, fifteen years?'

'About that. When you came here after your father's death.' Sigurbjörg must have seen Magnus grimace. 'I must apologise for Grandpa. He behaved appallingly.'

Magnus nodded. 'I haven't been to Iceland since.'

'Let's get a cup of coffee and you can tell me all about it, eh?'

They walked down the hill to a funky café on Laugavegur. Sigurbjörg ordered a slice of carrot cake with her coffee, and they sat down next to an earnest man with glasses who was plugged in to his laptop.

'Weren't you in graduate school in Canada?' Magnus asked.

'Yes. At McGill. Actually, I had just finished when I saw you. I stayed on in Iceland. Got a law degree: I'm a partner in one of the law firms here. I've also picked up a husband and three kids.'

'Congratulations.'

'Dad and Mom are still in Toronto. Retired, of course, now.'

Sigurbjörg's father had emigrated to Canada in the seventies and worked as a civil engineer. Like Magnus, Sigurbjörg had been born in Iceland but had spent most of her childhood in North America.

'And you? How long have you been here in Iceland?'

'Only two days,' Magnus replied. 'I stayed in Boston. Became a cop. Homicide detective. Then my chief got a call that the Police Commissioner here wanted somebody to come over and help them. He picked me.'

'Picked you? You didn't want to come?'

'Let's say I had mixed feelings.'

'After your last visit?' Sigurbjörg nodded. 'That must have been rough. Especially just after your dad died.'

'It was. I was twenty and I had lost both parents. I wasn't handling it well—I was drinking. I felt alone. After eight years I had almost fitted in in the States and suddenly it felt like a foreign country again.'

'I know what you mean,' said Sigurbjörg. 'I grew up in Canada, but my family are Icelanders and I live here. I sometimes think everywhere is a foreign country. It's not really fair, is it?'

Magnus glanced at Sigurbjörg. She was listening. And she was the one member of his family who had shown any sympathy during that awful couple of days. She was the one he had felt closest to. He wanted to talk.

'I needed some kind of family, other than just my brother Óli. I'd lived with Grandpa and Grandma for a few years and I thought they would welcome me back after what happened. But they rejected me. And they made me feel like *I* was responsible for Mom's death.' Magnus's face hardened. 'Grandpa said Dad was the most evil man he had ever known and he was glad he was dead. That brought back all the pain of those last years before Dad took me away with him to America. I know my father left Mom, but she made his life hell. She was an alcoholic.'

'But that's the whole point,' said Sigurbjörg.'She only became an alcoholic after she discovered the affair. And it was from that that everything else followed. Your father leaving. Her losing her job. And then that awful car crash. Grandpa blamed your father for all that, and he always will.'

A noisy group of two men and a woman sat down next to them and began to discuss a TV programme they had seen the night before.

Magnus ignored them. His face had gone blank. 'What affair?'

'Oh my God, you didn't know, did you? Forget I said anything. Look, I've got to go.' She began to stand up.

Magnus reached out and grabbed her hand. 'What affair?'

Sigurbjörg sat down again and swallowed. 'Your father was having an affair with your mother's best friend. She found out about it, they had a god-awful row, she started drinking.'

'Are you sure it's true?'

'No, I'm not,' said Sigurbjörg. 'But I suspect it is. Look, there must have been other problems. I used to really like your mother, but she was always a bit neurotic. Given her parents, that's hardly surprising.'

'It is true,' Magnus said. 'You're right, it must be. I just find it hard to believe.'

'Hey, Magnus, I'm really sorry you heard this from me.' Sigurbjörg reached out and touched his hand. 'But I've got to go now. And don't worry, I won't tell the grandparents you're here.'

With that, she left.

Magnus stared at his coffee cup, still a quarter full. He needed a drink. A real drink.

It wasn't far to the bar he had drunk in the night before, the Grand Rokk. He ordered a Thule and one of the chasers all the other guys at the bar were drinking. It was some kind of kummel, sweet and strong, but OK if gulped down with the beer.

Sigurbjörg had just turned his world upside-down. The whole story of his life, who he was, who his parents were, who was right and who was wrong, had just been inverted. His father had never blamed his mother for what had happened, but Magnus had: she had driven away his father. She had ignored Magnus through drink and then abandoned him through death. Ragnar had heroically rescued his sons, until he was murdered, possibly by the wicked stepmother. That was the story of Magnus's childhood. That was what had made him who he was.

And now it was all false. Another beer, another chaser.

He had assumed that his father's refusal to blame his mother for the mess she had made of all their lives was nobility on his part. It wasn't. It was a recognition that he was partly responsible. Wholly responsible?

Magnus didn't know. He would never know. It was a typical family mess. He'd seen enough squalid family disintegrations to know that what Sigurbjörg had told him was all too plausible. Blame all over the place.

But it meant that his father was a different man from whom he'd thought he was. Not noble. An adulterer. Someone who abandoned his wife when she was at her weakest and her most vulnerable. What else had he done? What other flaws had he concealed from his sons? From his wife?

Magnus's beer was still half full, but his chaser was empty. He caught the barman's eye and tapped the glass. It was refilled.

His brain was fuzzing over pleasantly. But Magnus was not going to stop, not for a long time. He was going to drink until it hurt.

The anger dissipated. He began to relax. He struck up conversations with the men on either side. He played a game of chess and lost.

Another beer. Another chaser. Two chasers. How many chasers did that make? How many beers? No idea.

EVENTUALLY IT WAS TIME to go home. Magnus bade an emotional goodbye to his new buddies. The room lurched wildly. Boy, was he drunk. Drunker than he had been for a long time. But it felt good.

He strode out of the bar and straightened up in the cold night air. It was way past midnight. The sky was clear; stars twinkled icily above him.

He liked Reykjavík. It was an innocent little town, and he would do his part to keep it that way, proud to be one of Reykjavík's finest.

There was no one on the streets. But as he headed up the hill towards home, Magnus spotted a cluster of three men in an alley. The tableau was so familiar. Drugs. Magnus scowled. He would sort them out.

'Hey!' he shouted, and headed down the alley. 'What are you doing?'

The guy selling the drugs was small and dark, possibly not even Icelandic. The guy doing the buying was taller, wiry, with a woolly hat. His friend was a great big, blond Nordic block, bigger even than Magnus.

'What has it got to do with you?' said the drug pusher in English.

'Give that to me,' said Magnus, swaying. 'I'm a cop.'

'Piss off,' said the pusher.

Magnus lunged at him. The guy ducked and struck him in the chest. But there was no power in it and Magnus laid him out with a single blow to the jaw. The Nordic hulk grabbed Magnus and tried to drag him down to the floor, but Magnus shook him off, and landed two good blows on the guy before getting him in an arm lock. 'You're under arrest!' he shouted.

The pusher was on the ground, moaning. The thin guy with the woolly hat started running.

'Get the hell off me,' growled the hulk in Icelandic. He swung round and crashed backwards into the wall, crushing Magnus, who let go. The big guy turned and struck Magnus in the stomach, but Magnus dodged the next blow and hit him with an uppercut.

The big guy reeled. Another crunching punch and he went down.

Magnus stared at the pusher, who was pulling himself to his feet. 'You're under arrest, too.' But then the alley started to sway and spin. He staggered.

The little guy was about to run when he saw the state that Magnus was in. He laughed and head-butted him in the face. Magnus dropped.

He lay on the cold tarmac for a while. Seconds? Minutes? He didn't know. He heard sirens. Good. Help.

Rough hands picked him up. He tried to focus on the face in front of him. It was a cop wearing the uniform of the Reykjavík Metropolitan Police.

'They went that way,' said Magnus in English. Waving indeterminately.

'Come on,' said the cop. 'You're coming with us,' and he pulled Magnus over to the waiting car.

'I'm a police officer,' said Magnus. 'Look, let me show you my badge.' Then he threw up all over the policeman's trousers.

DIEGO TURNED ON the light. The two naked bodies entwined on top of the bed froze, but only for an instant. Then the man leaped off the woman, twisted and sat up, all in one athletic movement. The woman opened her mouth to scream, but stopped when she saw the gun.

Diego chuckled. It was pretty funny. He had positioned himself in a chair in the bedroom, gun drawn, and waited there all evening. Then he had heard *two* people come in. He had decided to wait. Surprise them when they turned around. But he'd never got the chance. The guy jumped the girl right away.

And she led the guy right into the bedroom. Neither of them even saw him.

He decided to wait until they had taken off whatever clothes they were going to take off. Naked was good, as far as he was concerned. Then he slipped through the open door into the bedroom, and watched the action in the dim glow of the streetlights outside for a few seconds.

Now they were both blinking in the glare of the electric light.

'You!' Diego jabbed the revolver at the man. 'In the bathroom! Now! And if I hear a sound I'll come and pump your skinny ass full of bullets.'

The guy needed no more prompting. He was out of the bed and in the bathroom with the door shut in an instant.

He moved over towards the woman. Colby. In one swift movement, Diego grabbed her hair with one hand and jammed the revolver under her chin with the other. 'Where's Magnus?'

'Who?' The woman was barely audible.

'Magnus Jonson. Your boyfriend.' He smiled. 'Or one of your boyfriends.'

'I . . . I don't know.'

'You ever played Russian Roulette?'

Colby shook her head.

'It's real easy. There are six chambers in this revolver. One of them holds a bullet. You and I don't know which one. So when I pull the trigger, we don't know whether you gonna die. But you let me pull the trigger six times, you dead for sure. Get it?' Diego just loved that bit, loved watching the eyes of his victims. The fear. The uncertainty. Perfect.

Colby nodded. She got it.

'OK. I'll ask you again. Where is Magnus?'

'I don't know,' said Colby.'I swear it. He said he was going away somewhere and he couldn't tell me where.'

'Did you guess?'

Colby shook her head.

Diego spotted weakness. 'You guessed, didn't you?'

'N-no. No, I swear I didn't.'

'Thing is, I ain't believing you.' He pulled the trigger. Click.

'Oh, God.' Colby slumped backwards.

'You guessed. OK. So now I'm gonna guess. Is he in the country?'

'No.'

'We talking Mexico?' A shake of the head.

'Canada?' Another shake.

Diego was rather enjoying this. 'Is it hot or cold?'

No answer. He squeezed the trigger. Click.

'Cold. It's somewhere cold.'

'Good girl. But I give up. My geography ain't that good. Where is he?'

Another click. The game wasn't strictly fair. Diego knew the bullet was in the last chamber. That's how he liked to play the game. It really would be too bad to blow her brains out before he had got the answer he wanted.

'OK. OK. He's in Sweden. I don't know where. Stockholm, I guess.'

'YOU'RE JUST a thick-headed drunk, aren't you? Do you do this often?'

With difficulty Magnus focused on the red face of the National Police Commissioner in front of him. His mouth was dry, his head was pounding.

'I'm sorry, sir.' He would call his superior officer 'sir'. Screw Icelandic etiquette. 'It's been years since I got that drunk.'

'Then why did you do it?'

'I got some bad news,' Magnus said. 'It won't happen again.'

'It had better not,' said the Commissioner. 'I have an important role in mind for you, but that role demands that my officers should respect you. Within three days you have made yourself a laughing stock.'

The night was a blur, but Magnus could remember the laughter. The desk sergeant had heard about the new hotshot detective over from America and had thought it highly amusing that this man was now in his drunk tank. As had the patrolmen who had arrested him. And the other uniformed officers coming off duty. And the next shift coming on.

They had had the kindness to drive him home, and he vaguely remembered Katrín getting his clothes off and putting him to bed.

He had woken up a few hours later with his head exploding. He had crawled back into the police station at about ten o'clock. Within a minute Baldur had told him with a thin smile that the Commissioner wanted to see him.

'I am very sorry I have let you down, Commissioner,' Magnus repeated. 'I do appreciate what you have done for me here, and I am sure I can still help.'

The Commissioner grunted. 'How is the Agnar Haraldsson case going? I heard about the discovery of the saga. Is it genuine?'

'Possibly; we've got an expert checking it out. It looks like the Brit Steve Jubb was trying to buy it from Agnar. There was a problem, they had a dispute, and Jubb killed him.'

'Jubb still isn't talking?'

'Not yet. But there's this guy Lawrence Feldman who goes by the internet alias of Isildur, who seems to have financed the deal. We know where he lives. If I put some pressure on him, I'm sure he'll talk.'

The Commissioner nodded. 'Good. Don't let me down again. Or else I will send you straight back to Boston and I don't care who is after you.'

INGILEIF WATCHED as Professor Moritz carefully carried the envelope containing the old scraps of vellum to his car outside, while a female colleague took the bigger seventeenth-century volume. Moritz was an American on a two-year secondment to the University of Iceland from the University of Michigan. A couple of uniformed officers and the young detective called Árni danced round in attendance.

She had expected to feel relief. She felt nothing of the kind. She was drowning, drowning beneath a wave of guilt. The secret that her family had kept for so many generations was disappearing out of the door. It must have been difficult keeping its existence secret from extended family, neighbours, in-laws. But they had succeeded. They hadn't sold out. Even when they had endured unimaginable poverty and starvation, they hadn't taken the easy way. What right did she have to cash it in now?

She looked round the gallery. The objects on display—the vases, the fish-skin bags, the candle-holders, the lavascapes—were truly beautiful. Until Agnar's death, keeping the gallery open was the most important thing in her life. Now she appreciated how wrong she was.

The gallery was going bust because she had made a poor business judgment. The *kreppa* made matters worse, but she should never have trusted Nordidea. She was to blame and she should have taken the consequences.

Outside, the professor and the police escort climbed into their cars and drove off. Ingileif felt trapped in the tiny gallery. She grabbed her bag and locked up. So what if she lost a sale or two that morning?

She walked down the hill, her mind in incoherent turmoil. She soon reached the bay, and walked along the bike path that ran along the shore.

The breeze skipping in from across the water chilled her face.

Ingileif knew she should speak to her brother Pétur, but she couldn't bring herself to do it. He had hated the saga for what he thought it had done to their father. Yet, even he had believed that it would be wrong to sell. She had assured him that Agnar would be able to do a deal while keeping the secret safe, and only then had Pétur reluctantly agreed.

And now poor Aggi had been murdered. Foolishly she had tried to hide the existence of the saga from the police. As a plan, that was never going to work. And even now she was hiding something.

She glanced down at her bag. Where she had slipped the envelope just before the police came to take away the saga. The *other* envelope. She recalled the big, red-haired detective with the American accent who was trying to catch Agnar's murderer. She had some information that would be certain to help him. It was too late to try to keep it quiet now.

She stopped in front of the Höfdi House, the elegant white-timbered mansion where Gorbachev had met Reagan when she was six years old. She dug the detective's number out of her bag, and punched it into her cellphone.

COLBY WAS WAITING outside the bank when it opened. Walked straight in to the cashier, first in line, and withdrew twelve thousand dollars in cash. Then she drove to an outdoor equipment store and bought camping gear.

When the thug with the gun had left her apartment she had been too scared to scream. Richard hadn't been any help: he had scurried out of the bathroom muttering that his legal career was too important to be caught up with criminals, and that she should rethink her friendships. She had watched dully as he had scrambled to get into his clothes and left.

She was glad she hadn't told the thug about Iceland. It had been a close call; she had been so scared that she had almost given it away, but the change to Sweden at the last minute was inspired. The thug had believed her. She was sure of it. She hoped it would take him and his friends some time to realise their mistake, but she wasn't going to hang around. She was going to disappear.

From the camping shop she went to the supermarket. Then, with the trunk full of supplies, she drove west. Her plan was to head north eventually, to

Maine, and to lose herself in the wilderness. But first she had something to do. She pulled off the highway and found an internet café.

The first email was to her boss, telling him that she was not going to be at work and she couldn't explain why, but he shouldn't worry. The second was to her mother, saying more or less the same thing. The third was to Magnus.

CHAPTER SIX

It was no more than a ten-minute walk from police headquarters to the Höfdi House, where Ingileif had asked to meet Magnus. He was feeling a little better but he still needed to do all he could to clear his head. Something inside him had been badly disturbed when he learned about his father's infidelity. Throwing himself into the Agnar case would help.

A solitary figure was perched on a low wall in front of the Höfdi House.

'Thank you for coming,' Ingileif said.

'No problem,' said Magnus. 'That's why I gave you my number.'

He sat next to Ingileif on the wall. They were facing the bay. A steady breeze rolled small clouds through the pale blue sky, their shadows skittering over the sparkling grey water.

Ingileif was tense, sitting bolt upright on the wall, a frown accentuating the nick in her eyebrow. She looked like so many other girls in Reykjavík, slim, blonde with high cheekbones. But there was something about her that set her apart, a determination, a purposefulness that Magnus found appealing. She seemed to be debating with herself whether or not to tell him something.

He sat in silence. Waiting.

Eventually she spoke. 'You know this place is haunted?'

'The Höfdi House?' Magnus looked over his shoulder at the elegant white building that stood all alone in a grassy square.

'Yes. The ghost is a young girl who poisoned herself after she was convicted of incest with her brother. She scared the wits out of the people who used to live here.'

'Icelanders have got to learn to be braver about ghosts,' said Magnus.

'Not just Icelanders. It used to be the British consulate. The consul was so terrified that he demanded that the British Foreign Ministry allow him to move the consulate to another address. Apparently she keeps turning the lights on and off.' Ingileif sighed. 'I feel quite sorry for her.'

Magnus thought he detected a quiver in her voice. Odd. 'Is that what you wanted to speak to me about?' he asked. 'You want me to check it out?'

'Oh, no,' she replied, smiling weakly. 'I want to show you something.' She rummaged in her bag and pulled out a yellowing envelope, same handwriting as last time. 'This is the reason I asked you to meet me. I should have shown it to you yesterday, but I didn't.'

Magnus opened the envelope. Inside was a sheet of notepaper.

> *Merton College*
> *Oxford*

October 12, 1948

Dear Ísildarson,

Thank you for your extraordinary letter. What an astonishing tale! The part I found the most amazing was the inscription 'The Ring of Andvari' in runes. After the discovery of Gaukur's farm buried under the ash, the saga has much more credence than I originally gave it.

I would have loved the opportunity to see the ring, to hold it, to touch it. But I think you were absolutely right to return it to its hiding place. Either that or take it to Mount Hekla and toss it in! It would be altogether wrong to hold up the evil magic of the ring to scientific testing. And please do not worry, I will not mention it to anyone.

I have at last brought The Lord of the Rings *to its conclusion after ten years of toil. It is a vast, sprawling book, of which I am very proud. When it is eventually published, I will be sure to send you a copy.*

With best wishes,
Yours sincerely,
J. R. R. Tolkien

'This says your grandfather found the ring,' Magnus said.

Ingileif nodded. 'It does.'

Magnus shook his head. 'It's incredible.'

Ingileif sighed. 'No, it's not. It explains everything.'

'Explains what, exactly?'

Ingileif stared out to sea. Magnus watched her closely as she wrestled with her emotions. 'I think I told you my father died when I was twelve?'

'Yes.'

'He was looking for the ring. It always seemed absurd to me that an educated man should be so convinced that it still existed. But of course he *knew*. His own father must have told him before he died.'

'But not told him exactly where it was hidden?'

'Precisely. My guess is that Grandpa had forbidden him to look for it. Dad used to spend days scouring the area around the Thjórsá Valley in all weathers. And then one day he never came back.' Ingileif bit her lip.

'When did you find this letter?' Magnus asked.

'Very recently. After I had approached Agnar, and shown him the first letter from Tolkien, he asked me if I could find any more evidence. So I went back to Flúdir and found this among my father's papers. When I told Agnar he drove straight over to Flúdir to see me. And the letter.'

Magnus took out his notebook. 'What day was that?'

'Sunday last week.' She did a quick calculation. 'The nineteenth.'

'Four days before he was killed,' said Magnus. He remembered Agnar's email to Steve Jubb saying that he had found something else. Something valuable. Could it have been the ring?

'Do you have any idea where the ring is?'

Ingileif shook her head. 'No. There is that part in the saga about the ring being "watched over" by a hound. There are all kinds of strangely shaped outcrops of lava that could be hounds when looked at from certain directions. Presumably my grandfather found it and my father didn't.'

'What about Agnar? Did he have any idea where it might be?'

Ingileif shook her head. 'No. He asked me, of course.'

'So, as far as you know, the ring is still hidden in the cave?'

'I think so,' said Ingileif. 'You still don't believe me, do you?'

Magnus examined the upright precise handwriting. It was tempting to believe that the ring in *Gaukur's Saga* had really survived. But he couldn't be sure that the saga itself was authentic. And even if a gold ring had existed, it would probably be either buried under tons of ash, or long since have been found and sold by a poor shepherd. The whole thing was highly unlikely. But it didn't really matter what Magnus thought: what mattered was what Agnar believed, and Steve Jubb and Isildur.

For if a true *Lord of the Rings* fanatic thought he had a chance of getting his hands on the ring, the One Ring, then he might be tempted to kill for it.

'I don't know what I think,' said Magnus. 'But, of course, it would have been better if you had come out with all this up front.'

Ingileif sighed. 'It would have been better if I had never let the damn saga out of my safe in the first place.'

THE CANTEEN was almost full. Officer Pattie Lenahan looked round for someone she knew, and saw Shannon Kraychyk from Traffic, sitting alone at the table in the back of the room, next to a bunch of civilian geeks from the computer department. She carried her tray over.

'How you doin', Shannon?'

'I'm doin' good. Other than my dumb-ass sergeant giving me a hard time because we're behind on this month's quota. What am I supposed to do if Boston's citizens suddenly decide to respect the speed limit?'

Pattie and Shannon traded grumbles happily for a while until Shannon excused herself and left Pattie alone with the rest of her salad.

The geeks were talking about a case from the previous year. Pattie remembered it. The kidnapping of a woman in Brookline by her next-door-neighbour; it had dominated the station gossip for weeks.

And then: 'I haven't seen Jonson round here recently,' one of them said.

'Haven't you heard? He's been disappeared. He's a witness on the Lenahan case.'

'You mean Witness Protection Programme?'

'I guess.'

'I heard from him the other day.' Pattie glanced quickly at the speaker. A Chinese guy, small, talked real fast. 'He wanted me to check out an email header for him, same as in the Brookline case.'

'Did you nail it?'

'Yeah. It was nowhere near as difficult. Some guy in California.'

The conversation moved on and Pattie finished her salad. She got herself a cup of coffee and took it back to the squad room.

Uncle Sean's arrest had caused a big stir in her family. It was hardly

surprising; everyone in her family was a cop, had been for three generations, and none of them was a bad one, especially not Uncle Sean. Pattie
didn't know Magnus Jonson; but what she did know was that you didn't rat
out a fellow cop. Ever.

Should she tell her father what she had heard? He'd know what to do.
Besides, if she didn't tell him and he found out, he would have her hide.

Better tell him.

THE NOISE WAS APPALLING. Magnus and Árni were sitting at the back of a
long, low room, deep underground, listening to a group of teenage no-
hopers playing a bizarre mixture of reggae and rap, with an Icelandic twist.

Magnus had returned to the station to fill in Baldur on his interview with
Ingileif. Baldur shared Magnus's scepticism about the existence of the ring
in the saga, but he understood his point that the promise that it might exist
would fire up Steve Jubb and the modern-day Isildur.

Baldur had send one of his detectives to Yorkshire to search Steve Jubb's
house and computer, although they were having trouble getting a search
warrant from the British authorities. A hotshot criminal lawyer from
London had popped up from nowhere to raise objections. Another sign that
there was big money somewhere in the background of this case.

'This your kind of music, Árni?' Magnus asked.

Árni looked at him with contempt. Magnus was relieved. At least the boy
had some taste. The band stopped. Silence, wonderful silence.

Pétur Ásgrímsson stood up from his chair in the middle of the floor and
took a few paces towards the band. 'Thanks, but no thanks,' he said.

There were cries of protest from the five blond teenage rap'n'reggae
stars. 'Come back next year, when you have refined things a little.'

He turned towards his visitors and pulled up one of the chairs lining the
back of the room. He was a tall, imposing figure with a spare frame but
square shoulders, and Ingileif's high cheekbones. His cranium, shaved
smooth, bulged above his long thin face and intelligent grey eyes.

'You've come to speak to me about Agnar Haraldsson, I take it?'

'Are you surprised?' Magnus asked.

'I thought you would have been here earlier.' There was a hint of rebuke
in the comment, an accusation that they were a little slow.

'You knew that Ingileif was trying to sell *Gaukur's Saga* through Agnar?'
Pétur nodded. 'Much against my will.'

'Did you ever meet him?'

'No. I wanted to play no part in the negotiations over the saga.'

'But you would take your share of the sale proceeds?' Árni asked.

'Yes,' said Pétur simply. He looked round his nightclub. 'Times are tough. The banks are getting difficult. I borrowed too much.'

'Is this your only club?' They were in the depths of Neon, in the centre of town on Austurstraeti.

'No,' Pétur replied. 'It's my third. I started with Theme on Laugavegur.'

'Sorry, I don't know it,' said Magnus. 'I've been away a long time.'

'I thought from your accent you were American,' Pétur said. 'It was the most popular place in Reykjavík a few years ago. *The* place to go.'

'What happened to it?' Magnus asked.

'It's still going, but it's much less popular than it used to be. I saw that coming, so I opened Soho, and now Neon.' Pétur smiled. 'This town is fickle. You have to stay one step ahead or you get trampled.'

'Have you read *Gaukur's Saga*?' Magnus asked.

'Read it? I think I know it off by heart. I certainly did when I was a boy. My father and grandfather were obsessed, and they passed that obsession on to me. I was being groomed to be the keeper of the saga, you see.'

'Did you know that your grandfather found the ring?' Magnus asked.

'My sister told you about that? I didn't know she even knew about it.'

Magnus nodded. 'She turned up a letter from Tolkien to your grandfather Högni, which mentioned that Högni had found the ring.'

'And replaced it,' said Pétur. 'He put it back, you know.'

'Yes, the letter said that, too.' Magnus studied Pétur. 'So why aren't you still obsessed with the saga?'

Pétur took a deep breath. 'My father and I argued about it, or about the ring, just before he died. You see, my grandfather didn't trust my father after he had revealed *Gaukur's Saga* to the whole family. He wasn't supposed to do that; it was supposed to be just me, the eldest son.' A hint of bitterness touched Pétur's voice. 'So Grandfather decided to tell me of the existence of the ring a few months before he died—he had already told my father. He persuaded me that if I, or my father, were to find the ring and take it from its hiding place, then a terrible evil would be unleashed throughout the whole world. He scared the living daylights out of me.'

'What kind of evil?' Magnus asked.

'I don't know. He wasn't specific. In my imagination it was some kind of nuclear war. But the day after my grandfather died, my father set out on an expedition to Thjórsárdalur to find the ring. I was furious. I told him he shouldn't go, but he wouldn't listen.'

'You didn't go with him?'

'No. I was away at high school in Reykjavík. But I wouldn't have gone in any case. My father was close friends with the local pastor, who was an expert on folk legends. As soon as my grandfather died, my father told him all about *Gaukur's Saga*, and the ring. The two of them went off together.

'I was upset that my father had let the secret out of the family. But my mother didn't like them going off, either. She thought all this magic ring stuff was very weird.' He smiled. 'Of course, they never found it.'

'Do you believe it exists?' Árni asked, wide eyed.

'I did then,' Pétur said. 'I'm not at all sure now.' A note of anger crept into his voice. 'I don't think about it at all now. My stupid father went off into the hills when a snowstorm was forecast and blundered over a cliff. The ring did that. It didn't need to exist to kill him. After that I drifted away from the family. I couldn't handle it. All the ring stuff; it seemed to me that it had killed him. I dropped out of high school, went to London.'

'What about your sister?' Magnus asked. 'Was she involved in all this?'

'No,' said Pétur. 'She knew about the saga, of course, but not about the ring. When I came back to Reykjavík she was angry with me: she thought I had abandoned our mother.' Pétur grimaced. 'I guess she was right.'

'Did you know she was involved with Agnar? Is she still?'

'I doubt it very much,' Pétur said. 'But he was the natural person for her to go to when she wanted to sell the saga.' His eyes narrowed. 'You don't suspect her of killing him, do you?'

Magnus shrugged. 'We are keeping an open mind. She wasn't altogether straight with us when we first spoke to her.'

'She was just trying to cover up her mistake. She should never have tried to sell the saga, and she knew it. But Ingileif is honest through and through. It's inconceivable she killed anyone. She'd do anything for her friends or her family. She was the one of the three of us who looked after Mum when she was dying of cancer. You know the gallery is in trouble?'

Magnus nodded.

'Well, that's why she needed the money. To pay her partners. She blames herself. I told her not to worry too much about it; it's business. Everyone is going bust in Iceland these days. Poor Ingileif. She's had a tough life. First her father, then her stepfather, then her mother, all on top of losing her business.'

'Stepfather?' Magnus asked.

'Yeah. Mum married again. A drunken arsehole called Sigursteinn. I never met him; he died when I was in London. Fell off the harbour wall when he was drunk. A good thing all round from what I have heard. Mum never got over it, though.'

Magnus nodded. 'And your other sister? Birna?'

Pétur shook his head. 'She's pretty much screwed up.'

'Thank you, Pétur,' Magnus said, getting to his feet. 'One last question. What were you doing the night Agnar died?'

'What day was that?'

'Thursday the twenty-third,' Magnus said. 'The first day of summer.'

'The clubs were busy that night. I spent the evening moving from one to the other.'

The door opened and three more musicians came in, lugging big bags of musical instruments and electronics. 'Now if you will excuse me, I have some music to listen to. I just hope these guys are better than the last lot.'

ÁRNI DROVE MAGNUS out towards Birna Ásgrímsdóttir's house in Gardabaer, a suburb of Reykjavík.

'Check out Pétur's alibi, Árni,' Magnus said.

'Is he a suspect?' Árni said, surprised.

'Everyone's a suspect,' Magnus said.

They drove through the grey suburbs. 'By the way, I heard from the Elvish expert again,' Árni said. 'He figured out what *kallisarvoinen* means.'

'And what's that?'

'It's Finnish. Apparently a lot of Quenya words come from Finnish. Tolkien found the language interesting. So our friend looked up *kallisarvoinen* in a Finnish dictionary, and it means "precious".'

'Precious? The word Gollum used for the ring in *The Lord of the Rings*?'

'That's right.'

Magnus recalled the SMS from Steve Jubb. 'So Steve Jubb thought that Agnar had the ring,' he said.

'We haven't found an old ring among Agnar's stuff,' Árni said.

'Perhaps Steve Jubb took it,' Magnus said. 'After he killed him.'

'And did what with it? We didn't find it in his hotel room.'

'Hid it perhaps. Slipped it into an envelope and dropped it in a mailbox.'

'But Jubb sent the text message to Isildur *after* he had seen Agnar. That suggests that Agnar still had it, or at least Jubb thought he had.'

Magnus saw Árni's point.

'Do you really think that Agnar found the ring?' Árni said. 'He only heard about it on Sunday. The email was sent on Tuesday. People have devoted years to looking for it and haven't found it. Unless it was a fake?'

'That would be just as hard to arrange in a hurry. Harder.'

Árni was silent for a minute. 'So what do we do?' he asked eventually.

'Tell Baldur. Look for hiding places. See if we've missed anything.' Magnus glared at Árni. 'Why didn't you tell me this straight away?'

'I only got the response this morning.'

Magnus turned away to look out of the window. He was lumbered with an idiot.

BIRNA ÁSGRÍMSDÓTTIR lived in a new concrete house with a bright red roof in its own patch of lawn on a new development. Expensive SUVs littered the driveways. Wealthy. Comfortable. Soulless.

Birna herself was softer, rounder and older than Ingileif. She had big blue eyes and pouting lips. She could have been attractive, but there was something sagging and sloppy about her and two lines pointed downwards from the corners of her mouth.

When she saw Magnus, she smiled, her eyes lingering over his body before moving up to his face. 'Hello,' she said.

'Hello,' said Magnus, disconcerted despite of himself. 'We are from the Metropolitan Police. We have come to ask you about the murder of Professor Agnar Haraldsson.'

'How nice,' said Birna. 'Come in. Can I get you something to drink?'

'Just coffee,' said Magnus.

Árni nodded. 'Me, too,' he said, hoarsely. This woman had presence.

They sat in the living room, waiting for the coffee. Dotted around the living room were photographs. Most of them were of a stunning blonde girl of about eighteen wearing swimsuits and various sashes. Birna. A younger Birna. There were also a couple of pictures of a suave, dark-haired man wearing the uniform of Icelandair.

Birna returned with the coffee. 'I'm sorry, I don't think I can help you much, but I'll try.'

'Did you ever meet Agnar?'

'No, never. You know about the family saga, I take it?'

'Yes, we do.'

'Well, Ingileif was handling all the negotiations.'

'Did she mention a ring?'

Birna laughed out loud. 'If there ever was a ring it was lost centuries ago. Let me tell you something,' she said, leaning forward towards Magnus. He could smell some kind of alcohol on her breath. 'That ring and that saga are just trouble. Ingileif should have sold the damn thing.'

'Are you and Ingileif close?'

Birna leaned back in her chair. 'Good question. We were once, very. After my mother married again, and I had some trouble with my stepfather, Ingileif helped me a lot. Got me through it. But after that, we kind of drifted apart. I married a jerk, and Ingileif does her designer stuff.'

'Trouble with your stepfather?'

Birna looked at Magnus again, this time at his eyes, as if deciding whether to trust him. 'Is this relevant to your investigation?'

Magnus shrugged. 'It might be. I won't know until you tell me.'

'I was fourteen when my father died. I was a pretty girl.' She nodded towards the photographs. 'My mother got it into her head that I should become Miss Iceland.' She smiled. 'I never managed better than third, but Mum and I tried really hard. In the middle of all that, she married Sigursteinn, who was a car dealer from Selfoss. I could tell the minute I met him that Sigursteinn fancied me. It took him less than a month after he got married before he, well . . .' She took a deep drag of her cigarette. 'Well, he raped me, really. I didn't think that at the time, but it *was* rape. He wanted sex with me, I was scared of him. It happened. Lots of times. Ingileif caught us at it, and she went crazy. She went at him with a broken bottle, but in the end it was she who was cut. Have you noticed the little scar on her eyebrow?'

Magnus nodded.

'Well, that was Sigursteinn. Ingileif told Mum, who didn't believe her, threw her out of the house. I was too scared to say anything. Then, three months later, Sigursteinn was on a business trip in Reykjavík when he fell into the harbour. I was so relieved.'

'How did your mother react?'

'She was totally distraught. She went as far as accusing Ingileif of killing him, which was just stupid. Then I told her exactly what he had done to me, and eventually she believed it. That pretty much mucked up our family.'

'I can imagine,' said Magnus.

'Ingileif went away to Reykjavík. She started speaking to Mum again. She spent a lot of time with her just before she died.'

'And you?'

Birna blinked. 'Oh, I married Matthías and have lived a perfect life of happiness ever since.'

Magnus ignored the sarcasm. 'And Pétur?'

'He missed all this. He came back to Reykjavík a couple of years later. We see each other occasionally.'

God, what a family, Magnus thought. His own was bad enough.

'One last question. Where were you last Thursday night?'

Birna hesitated. 'Do I have to?'

Magnus knew what was coming next. 'Yes, you do. And we will have to check out whatever you tell us. But we will do it discreetly, I promise.'

Birna sighed. 'Matthías was in New York. Probably in bed with a flight attendant. I was with a friend named Dagur Tómasson. He's married as well. We spent the night in a hotel in Kópavogur. The Merlin. It's anonymous and as discreet as you can get in Iceland.'

Somehow Magnus suspected that this alibi would hold up.

BALDUR LISTENED CLOSELY as Magnus explained his theory that Agnar was trying to sell the ring from *Gaukur's Saga* to Steve Jubb and Isildur.

'So, what are you suggesting?' he said, when Magnus had finished. 'We go over Agnar's house again, looking for a mythical ring that has been lost for a thousand years?'

Magnus's foul mood deepened. He knew that Baldur was trying to needle him, and he fought to control his anger.

'Look. We know Steve Jubb murdered Agnar. But since he won't tell us why, we need to figure it out for ourselves. We also know that Agnar was trying to sell a saga—we've both seen it. It exists.'

Baldur shook his head. 'All we've seen is a hundred and twenty pages that was spat out of a computer printer two weeks ago.'

Magnus leaned back in his chair. 'Fair enough. Maybe the saga is a forgery. Maybe there is a ring, but it's a fake too. If anything, that would create a bigger motive for Steve Jubb to kill Agnar. We still need to find it.'

'The thing is, I'm not sure that Steve Jubb did murder Agnar.'

Magnus snorted.

'I've just interviewed him again. He wouldn't tell me anything about sagas or rings. But he did deny murdering Agnar.'

'And you believe him?'

'My hunch is he's telling the truth.' Baldur found a sheet of paper in the pile on his desk. 'Here's a report from the forensics lab.'

Magnus scanned it. It was an analysis of the soil samples on Jubb's shoes.

'It shows that there were no traces of the kind of mud on the path from the summerhouse down to the lake shore, or the mud on the shore itself.'

'Maybe Jubb cleaned his shoes. Thoroughly.'

'There *was* soil from the area in front of the summerhouse. So he was at the front, but not at the back. And he didn't clean his shoes.'

'Perhaps he changed into boots? Ditched them afterwards?'

'We'd have found footprints in or around the house,' Baldur said. 'And that's pretty unlikely, isn't it?'

Magnus stared at the piece of paper, trying to figure out how Jubb could have dragged the body down to the lake without getting mud on his shoes.

'Someone else moved Agnar,' Baldur said. '*After* Steve Jubb had left. And it's quite probable that someone else killed him.'

'Did you find footprints near the lake?'

Baldur shook his head. 'Nothing useful. It had rained overnight. And the scene was well and truly compromised. Footprints all over the place:

the kids, their father, the paramedics, the police officers from Selfoss.'

'An accomplice then,' said Magnus. 'Isildur. This Lawrence Feldman guy.'

Baldur spotted the flaw immediately. 'You contacted Isildur two days later, and he replied from a computer located in California.'

'An Icelandic accomplice. There are *Lord of the Rings* fans here.'

'There is no record of any Icelandic number on Steve Jubb's cellphone, apart from Agnar's. We know that Steve Jubb never left his hotel from the time he arrived in Reykjavík in the morning to the time he went out to Lake Thingvellir late afternoon.'

'Don't tell me you're going to spring him?' Magnus asked.

'Not yet. And I'm not ruling him out. But we need to widen the investigation. Look at the more real-world circumstances.' Baldur counted them off on his fingers. 'Agnar saw a lover and a former lover in the weeks before he died. His wife was seriously angry about his infidelity. He had big money problems. He bought drugs. Maybe he had debts we don't know about. Maybe he owed his dealer money? Someone else was there that night and we need to find out who.'

'So it's just a coincidence he was negotiating this deal with Jubb?'

'Why not?' said Baldur. 'Look, if you like, you can focus on this saga deal. But there are plenty of other things to look at.'

'I'm sure if I went to California I could get Isildur to—'

'No,' said Baldur.

MAGNUS SPENT the rest of the day talking to the police officers who had searched the summerhouse and Steve Jubb's hotel room. No sign of a ring.

He went to see Linda, Agnar's wife, at her house in Seltjarnarnes. She tolerated his intrusion with barely concealed irritation. She was tall and thin with blonde hair and a drawn face. With a baby and a toddler to look after, she was barely holding things together. She was an angry woman. Angry with her husband, angry with the police, angry with the bank, the lawyers, angry at the great big enormous hole in her life.

Magnus felt for her, and for her two children. Yet another family blown apart by murder. Whatever Agnar's sins, he hadn't deserved to die.

Of course she hadn't seen any bloody ring. Magnus searched the house for possible hiding places, but found nothing. At eight o'clock he left, taking the bus back to the centre of Reykjavík. He hadn't yet been allocated the use of a police-owned car, and he had left Árni behind.

His conversation with Baldur had shaken him. He understood Baldur's point: how could Steve Jubb have murdered Agnar and disposed of his body without getting his feet dirty? But he just couldn't accept that Jubb had gone to see Agnar about a secret multimillion-dollar deal, and then Agnar had been murdered for some totally unrelated reason a couple of hours later. His intuition told him that just didn't make sense.

He stopped off at a convenience store and bought himself a Thai curry to heat up. When he got back to Katrín's house, he shoved it in the microwave.

'How are you feeling?'

He turned round to see his landlady making her way to the refrigerator. She was speaking English. She took out a yoghurt and opened it.

'So so.'

'Quite a night last night.'

'Thank you for getting me into bed,' said Magnus.

'No problem,' said Katrín, smiling. 'You were very sweet. Just before you fell asleep you gave me a cute little smile, and said "You're under arrest."'

'Oh, Jeez.'

'Don't worry. You will probably have to do the same for me one day.'

She leaned back against the fridge. 'Are you really a policeman?'

'Matter of fact I am.' Magnus extracted his dinner, tipped it out onto a plate, and began to eat.

'You see, the thing is, I don't like my little brother spying on me.'

'I'm not surprised,' said Magnus. 'Don't worry. I'm not going to tell anyone what you're up to.'

'Good,' said Katrín. 'I saw you going into Ingileif's gallery yesterday. Is she suspected of something?'

'I can't really tell you that.'

'Sorry. Just curious.' She waved her spoon in the air. 'I know! Is it Agnar's murder?'

'I really can't say,' Magnus said.

'It is! I saw him the other day in a café, you know. The Café Paris. With Tómas Hákonarson.'

'Who's he?' Magnus asked.

'He has his own TV show. *The Point* it's called. Gives politicians a hard time. He's quite funny.'

They ate in silence for a minute. Magnus knew he should write the name down, but he was too tired, he couldn't be bothered.

He picked up his empty plate, rinsed it off and stuck it in the dishwasher. 'I need sleep. I'm going to bed.'

BALDUR SEEMED to have a new lease of energy at the morning meeting as he doled out tasks to his detectives. He passed on the report from the forensics lab about the mud on Jubb's shoes, and explained that they needed to widen their investigation. Interview new people: anyone who might conceivably have seen another visitor to Agnar, the people who sold Agnar drugs, his students, his former girlfriends, his colleagues, his friends, everyone.

The detective Baldur had sent to Yorkshire had spoken to Jubb's neighbours. Jubb was a bit of a loner, often on the road with his lorry. His passion for *The Lord of the Rings* was well known. A former girlfriend said he was an intelligent man, obsessive, but not violent. No help there, no leads.

Throughout all of this, Baldur did not look at Magnus once.

Until after the meeting, when he beckoned Magnus to follow him to his office. He slammed the door behind him.

'I do *not* like being undercut!'

'What do you mean?'

'I mean that I don't like you going to the Commissioner behind my back and telling him we should be sending people to California.'

'He asked my opinion. I gave it to him,' said Magnus. 'When do I go?'

Baldur shook his head. 'You're not going. Árni is on his way now.'

'Árni! Alone? What about me?'

'You can look for a ring,' Baldur said. 'That should keep you busy.'

MAGNUS RETURNED to his computer and logged on. He was convinced that Baldur was wrong to downplay the importance of Isildur or Lawrence Feldman or whoever the hell he was. He would continue looking for the ring, and hope that Árni came back with something useful.

He checked his emails. There was one from Colby.

Magnus,

Last night one of your big ugly friends broke into my apartment and attacked me. He put a gun to my head and asked me where you were. I said you were in Sweden and he went away. He scared the shit out of me.

I'm gone. They won't find me. You won't find me. No one knows where I am, not my family, not my friends.

Magnus, you have screwed up my life and nearly got me killed.

Rot in hell wherever you are. And don't ever EVER talk to me again.

C.

There was a short email accompanying it from Agent Hendricks, apologising for the delay in forwarding Colby's email but that he had been out of the office the previous day.

Magnus stared at the screen. Emotions flooded over him. Anger at the scumbag who had done this to Colby. At Williams for not protecting her. Anger with himself for letting it happen. Guilt, because of course it was his fault. He slammed his fist hard on his desk. There were only a couple of detectives in the room, but they both turned to stare.

At least Colby hadn't said where he really was. Although at this point he didn't care. At this point he thought of jumping on a plane to Boston, finding Pedro Soto personally and blowing him away.

He tapped out an angry email to DS Williams, via Hendricks, telling him what had happened and asking him where the hell the protection was that he had promised. If the Boston PD couldn't protect Colby, Magnus would fly over and do it himself. It wasn't as if he was doing anything useful in Iceland.

INGILEIF WAITED in Mokka, toying with a latte. She liked the café, one of the oldest in Reykjavík. Small and cosy, it was famous both for its waffles and for its clientele: artists, poets and novelists.

'Hi, Inga!'

The other patrons of the café stared at the man who addressed her, but only for a couple of seconds, before returning to their conversations and their newspapers. Icelanders were proud of their ability to let famous people get on with their lives in public.

'Tómas! How good to see you!' She stood up and kissed his cheek.

'Hang on a moment,' said the man. 'Let me get myself a coffee. Do you want another?'

Ingileif shook her head and her companion went up to the counter to order a double espresso. His features were very familiar to Ingileif. Partly, it was true, this familiarity was from seeing him once a week on TV, but it was also the result of a childhood spent together.

He returned to her table. 'How's things?' he said. 'I went into your gallery the other day. You have some lovely stuff. It must sell well.'

'It does,' said Ingileif.

'But?' Tómas had noticed the doubt in her voice.

'Too well,' Ingileif admitted. 'Our biggest customer went bust last month and they owe us a lot of money.'

'And the bank isn't being much help?'

'You're right there. A couple of years ago they were throwing money at us, and now they can't get it back fast enough. They gave us one of those foreign currency loans that just keeps on growing.'

'Well, good luck with that,' said Tómas. 'I'm sure you will thrive.'

'Thank you,' Ingileif smiled. 'How about you? Your show seems to be going very well. I love the way you skewered that banker last week. The one who paid himself a four-million-dollar bonus three months before his bank went bust.'

'At least he had the grace to come back to Iceland to face the music,' Tómas said. 'But now I won't get any bankers on the show for a while.'

He sipped his espresso. Fame suited him, Ingileif thought.

'You heard about Agnar Haraldsson?' Tómas asked, peering at Ingileif.

'Yes,' she said simply.

'It must have been a bit of a shock? His death. I mean, I remember you and he had a bit of a thing going. I was shocked and I scarcely knew the guy.'

'Yes,' said Ingileif, her throat suddenly tight. 'Yes, it was.'

'Have the police been in touch?'

'Why should they be?' Ingileif asked. She could feel herself reddening.

'It's a big case. A big investigation. Hasn't there been an arrest?'

'Yes. An Englishman. They think he was involved in some dodgy deal with Agnar. But I don't think they have much evidence to prove it.'

'Had you seen him recently?'

Ingileif nodded again. Then when she saw Tómas's raised eyebrows, she protested. 'Not that. He's married, and I've have better taste than that.'

'I'm glad to hear it,' said Tómas. 'You're way out of his league.'

'That's so kind of you to say,' said Ingileif with mock politeness.

'So, what were you talking to him about?'

For a second Ingileif considered telling Tómas all about the saga. But only for a second. 'Why do you want to know? It's not for your show, is it?'

'Good God, no.' Tómas saw his denial wasn't strong enough. 'I promise. Look, I'm sorry if I have been too direct with my questions. It's become a habit.'

'It must have,' said Ingileif. He had always had the ability to get people to confide in him. He seemed harmless and interested. But something told Ingileif to be careful. 'Just a social call,' she said. 'Like this.'

Tómas smiled. 'Look, I have to go. But I'm having a party on Saturday, do you want to come?'

'Will it be as wild as your parties used to be?' Ingileif said.

'Wilder. Here, let me give you the address. I moved a few months ago.' And he took out a business card emblazoned with the logo of RUV, the state broadcaster, and wrote down his home address.

As he left the café, Ingileif couldn't help asking herself a simple question. What the hell was all that about?

VIGDÍS ACCEPTED the cup of coffee and began to sip it. Interviewing people in Iceland always involved drinking lots of coffee.

The woman opposite her was in her late thirties, wearing jeans and a blue sweater. She had an intelligent face and a friendly smile. They were sitting in a handsome house in a smart area of Reykjavík just to the west of the city centre. The family Range Rover was parked outside.

'I'm sorry to take more of your time, Helena,' Vigdís began. 'But I would like to go through everything that you can remember from the day of the murder again. Any tiny little detail.' It was Helena's children who had found Agnar's body.

'By all means. I'm not sure there is much else I can tell you.'

But Helena frowned as she finished the sentence. Vigdís noticed it.

'What is it?'

'Um . . . It's nothing. It's not important.'

Vigdís smiled, coaxing. 'Don't worry about that,' she said.

Helena smiled. 'Oh, well, it's just that our five-year-old daughter, Sara Rós, told us this story at breakfast yesterday. She said that she saw two men playing in the lake at night. My husband is convinced it's a dream.'

'Lake Thingvellir?'

'Yes. But the thing is, Sara Rós makes up stories. Sometimes it's to get attention. Sometimes it's just for fun.'

'I see. Well, I think I should speak to her. With your permission, of course.'

'All right. You'll have to wait until she gets back from kindergarten.'

'No,' said Vigdís. 'I think we had better talk to her now.'

THE KINDERGARTEN that Helena's daughter attended was only a few hundred metres away. The principal grudgingly gave up her office to Vigdís and Helena and went to fetch the girl.

Sara Rós was a typical Icelandic five year old. Bright blue eyes, pink cheeks and curly hair that was so blonde it was almost white.

Her face lit up when she saw her mother and she curled up next to her on the sofa in the principal's office.

'Hello,' said Vigdís. 'My name is Vigdís and I am a police officer. I'm here because your mummy said you saw something last week at your summerhouse. Can you tell me about it?'

The girl glanced at her mother, who nodded. 'I woke up and it was the middle of the night. I wanted to go to the toilet. When I came back I looked out of my window and I saw two men playing in the lake just outside the professor's house. They were splashing about a bit. Then one of them got tired and fell asleep.'

'And did the man fall asleep in the water, or on the lake shore?'

'In the water.'

'I see. What did the other man do?'

'He got out of the lake and then he got in his car and he drove away.'

'Did you see what the man looked like?'

'Of course not, silly. It was dark! But I think he had his clothes on, not a swimming costume.'

'Are you sure about all this?'

'Yes, I am quite sure. And I know it's true because I saw the man asleep in the lake the next day when Jón and me went down there to play. Except then he was dead.' The little girl went quiet.

'Why didn't you tell anyone about this?' Vigdís asked.

'Because nobody asked me.'

CHAPTER SEVEN

Magnus took a last look round Steve Jubb's hotel room. He had been over every inch of the room; the ring definitely wasn't there. Árni's interpretation of Jubb's text message to Isildur was probably right—Jubb hadn't taken it, but Jubb thought Agnar had it. Particularly as the Polish girl who had cleaned the room was quite certain that she hadn't seen a ring, or anything that might contain a ring.

Next stop, the summerhouse on Lake Thingvellir. Again.

Magnus took the stairs down to the lobby and handed the key card to the receptionist. As he was leaving the hotel, he passed a small man with a scruffy beard coming in, wheeling a suitcase. The man was wearing a green baseball cap proclaiming 'Frodo Lives'. Magnus held the door open.

'Oh, er, thank you very much, sir,' the man said, nervously. The language was English, the accent American.

'No problem,' said Magnus.

As he walked towards the silver police Skoda that he had signed out that morning, he wondered about the cap. Strange, he had never thought about *Lord of the Rings* memorabilia before. Was he going to be stopped short by every Gollum or Gandalf T-shirt he came across? Were there really that many of them? No. There weren't. He turned on his heel and returned to the lobby in time to see the elevator door closing behind the wheeled suitcase.

'What was the name of the guest who just checked in?' he asked the receptionist.

'Mr Feldman,' she said. Then, glancing at her computer screen, 'Lawrence Feldman. Room three-ten.'

'Thank you.'

Magnus took the elevator up to the third floor and knocked on the door of Room 310. The man answered.

'Isildur?' said Magnus.

Feldman blinked. 'Who are you?'

'My name is Sergeant Detective Jonson. I'm working with the Reykjavík Metropolitan Police. Can I come in?'

'Er, I guess so,' said Feldman.

'Just flown in?' Magnus asked.

'You followed me in from the airport?' said Feldman.

Magnus grunted. Feldman was right, they should have known there was a good chance that he would show up in Iceland. They should have been checking the airports. But he decided not to explain to Feldman that it was just dumb luck that he had spotted him. He thought about Árni, currently on his way to California. It was all he could do not to smile to himself.

'Should I get a lawyer here?' Feldman asked.

'Good question,' said Magnus. 'If this was the States, then I would definitely advise it. But here? I don't know.'

'What do you mean?'

'Well, here they can lock you up for three weeks if they think you're a suspect. That's what happened to Steve Jubb. He's in the top-security jail at Litla Hraun now. I could easily send you in there with him, if you don't cooperate. I mean we're looking at conspiracy to murder.'

Feldman just blinked.

'These Icelandic places are tough. Full of these big blond beefy Vikings. Oh, don't worry, they'll like you. They like little guys.' Magnus smiled.

Of course, Magnus had no idea what conditions at Litla Hraun were really like. Knowing Iceland, he rather suspected that the warders brought the prisoners hot cocoa every night as the inmates watched TV.

'So, if I talk to you now, you'll guarantee you won't send me there?'

Magnus looked directly at Feldman. 'That depends on what you tell me.'

Feldman swallowed. 'I didn't have anything to do with Agnar's murder. And I really don't think that Gimli did either.'

'OK,' said Magnus. 'Let's start from the beginning. Tell me about Gaukur's ring.'

'Well, I first heard about it three years ago. A Danish guy, Jens Pedersen, popped up on one of the websites saying he had found a letter from a poet who was an old friend of Árni Magnússon, founder of the museum in Copenhagen. The poet had read *Gaukur's Saga*. There were a couple of sentences about Ísildur's quest to throw the ring into Mount Hekla.

'The Danish guy was an academic doing his PhD thesis on the poet. He wanted some help from the forum to see if there was any link between *Gaukur's Saga* and *The Lord of the Rings*. Of course, we all went wild: he didn't know what had hit him. I contacted him and he said he had been in touch with a professor named Agnar Haraldsson at the University of Iceland, who had given him some help about Gaukur and his lost saga. But then he went quiet.' Feldman sighed. 'I think he thought I was a weirdo.'

Magnus let that ride. 'So how does Steve Jubb fit into this?'

'Gimli? I met him through the same forum. He mentioned a story his grandfather had told him. He was a student at Leeds University in the 1920s and was taught by Tolkien there. One evening, he had been drinking beer with an Icelandic fellow student and Tolkien. The Icelander was a bit drunk and had begun telling Tolkien about *Gaukur's Saga*, about the Ring of Andvari being found by a Viking called Ísildur. The story made a big impression on Gimli's grandfather, and on Tolkien. Thirty years later, when he read *The Lord of the Rings*, the grandfather was struck by the similarity of the stories.'

'Did he write any of this down?'

'No. He told Gimli about it when Gimli first read *The Hobbit*. I checked the grandfather out. His name was Arthur Jubb and he was a student at Leeds in the 1920s. Tolkien was a professor there and set up a Viking Club where they all seem to have got drunk and sung songs. But there's nothing in Tolkien's published correspondence about the saga because he had promised to keep the family saga secret.'

Magnus nodded.

'So I teamed up with Gimli. I don't like to travel. Matter of fact, this is my first time outside the States, but Gimli's a smart guy, and being a truck driver, he travels all the time. So I said I would provide the funding, he would do the legwork, and we would find *Gaukur's Saga*.

'Gimli's grandfather never told him the name of the Icelandic student, so Gimli started out going to Leeds to look for it. No luck. The university's records were bombed in World War Two, apparently. So then Gimli came here. Saw Professor Haraldsson, who was interested but couldn't help. We'd kinda drawn a blank. Until a month or so ago, when Professor Haraldsson got in touch with Gimli. A former student had approached him with *Gaukur's Saga* and wanted to sell it. You can imagine how excited we were.'

'How much was he asking?'

'Only two million dollars. But the deal was that the saga would have to be kept a secret. I kinda liked that idea. So we set a date for Gimli to fly to Iceland to see Haraldsson. Gimli went to meet him at the summerhouse on Lake Thingvellir, where he read the saga in translation. But they couldn't agree on a final price, so Gimli came back here to the hotel.'

'From where he sent you an SMS?'

'That's right. I called him back and we figured out a strategy for negotiating for the saga. He was going out to meet Agnar again the following day, but the next thing Gimli heard, the professor was dead and he was a suspect.'

'What about the ring?'

'The ring?' Feldman said, trying to feign innocent surprise, but failing.

'Yeah, the ring,' said Magnus. 'The *kallisarvoinen*. Your "precious".'

Feldman sighed. 'Yes, the ring. The professor said he knew where it was and he could get it for us, but it would cost us five million.'

'So he didn't have it at the summerhouse?'

'No. He gave Gimli no idea where it might be. But he was confident he could get hold of it. For the right amount of money.'

'Did you believe him?'

Feldman hesitated. 'We knew we were wide open to being ripped off. So I started to work on lining up an expert to examine the ring once we got a hold of it. Someone who would keep quiet about it afterwards.'

'Steve Jubb never saw it?'

'No,' said Feldman.

Magnus leaned back in his chair and studied Feldman.

'Did Jubb kill the professor?'

'No,' said Feldman immediately. 'There would be no reason to kill him, and Gimli never struck me as being violent. But I wasn't there, so I can't be one hundred per cent sure he's innocent, no.'

'So you came to Iceland to help him?' Magnus asked.

'Yeah,' said Feldman. 'We've been communicating through the lawyer, Kristján Gylfason, but I wanted to do what I could myself.'

'And look for the ring,' Magnus said.

'I don't even know if there is a ring,' said Feldman.

'But you want to find out,' said Magnus.

'Are you going to arrest me?' Feldman asked.

'Not for the moment, no,' said Magnus. 'But I'll take your passport. You're not leaving Iceland. And if you do find a ring, whether it's a real one or a hoax, I want to know about it. Because it's evidence.' Feldman recoiled from Magnus's stare. 'And if I catch you withholding evidence, you'll definitely be spending some nights in an Icelandic jail.'

INGILEIF WAS ABSORBED in her drawing, her eyes flicking from her emerging design to the piece of tanned fish skin in front of her. It was Nile perch, a wonderful translucent, light blue colour. She was designing a credit-card holder, always a popular item. She didn't work in the gallery on Tuesday afternoons, and it felt good to lose herself in the design process for an hour or two.

The bell rang. Ingileif lived in a tiny one-bedroom flat not too far from the gallery. The bedroom was her studio and occasional guest room—she slept in the living area. The flat was stark: Icelandic minimalist with white walls, lots of wood and not much clutter. Despite that, it was cramped, but it was all she could afford in Reykjavík 101, the central postal area.

She went downstairs to the front door. It was Pétur.

'Pési!' She felt a sudden urge to throw herself into her brother's arms. He held her tight for a few moments, stroking her hair.

They broke apart. Pétur smiled at her awkwardly, surprised at her sudden show of affection. 'Come on up,' she said.

'I'm sorry I haven't been in touch,' said Pétur, when they were in her flat.

'You mean since Agnar's murder?' She flopped back onto the white bedspread on her bed. Pétur took one of the two low chrome chairs.

He nodded. 'Have the police been round?'

'Yes. Lots of times. And you?'

'Once,' Pétur said. 'There wasn't much I could tell them.'

'They seem to think an Englishman killed Agnar. The guy who was acting for the American *Lord of the Rings* fan who wanted to buy the saga.'

'I haven't seen anything in the news about the saga,' Pétur said.

'No. The police are keeping its existence quiet while the investigation is proceeding. They've taken it away for analysis. The detective I spoke to seemed to think it's a forgery, which is ridiculous.'

'It's no forgery,' said Pétur. He sighed. 'But they'll make it public eventually, won't they? And then the world's press will be all over it.'

'There's something else I should show you,' Ingileif said. She fetched her bag and handed him Tolkien's letter. The second one, the one written in 1948.

He opened it and read, frowning.

'This shows that Grandpa actually found the ring,' she said.

Pétur looked up at his sister. 'I knew that.'

'You knew it! How? When?'

'Grandpa told me. And he told me that he wanted the ring to remain hidden. He was worried that Dad would look for it once he died and he wanted me to stop him.'

They sat in silence for a moment.

'I've been wondering recently, since I found this letter, wondering whether Dad did find it? When he and the pastor went off to look for it.'

'Don't you think the pastor would have told us if they'd found anything?'

'Maybe not.'

Pétur closed his eyes. When he opened them, they were moist. 'Inga, I don't know why thinking about Dad's death affects me like this, but it always does. I just can't stop thinking that it's all my fault.'

'Of course it wasn't your fault, Pési,' Ingileif said.

'I know that. I *know* that.' Pétur dabbed his eye with a finger. It was strange for Ingileif to see her brother so upset. He sniffed and shook his head. 'Or else I think it's that damned ring. When I was a kid I was obsessed with it, scared of it. Then when Dad died I thought it was a load of bullshit and I wanted nothing to do with it. And now? Now I wonder whether it hasn't destroyed our family. Reached out from that moment a thousand years ago when Gaukur took it from Ísildur on the summit of Hekla, reached out to destroy us: Dad, Mum, Birna, me, you.' He leaned forward, his moist eyes alight. 'It doesn't need to exist anywhere but in here.' He tapped his temple with his finger. 'It is lodged in the minds of all of us, all our family. That's where it does its damage.'

VIGDÍS PARKED her car on one of the small streets leading down to the bay, and she and Baldur jumped out. A uniformed officer had interviewed one of Agnar's students who had remembered someone asking around at the university for Agnar on the day he had died. The student had mentioned to the man that Agnar had a summerhouse by Lake Thingvellir and that he sometimes spent time there. No, the man hadn't given his name. But the student recognised him. From TV. Tómas Hákonarson.

He lived on the eighth floor of one of the new blocks of luxury apartments that had sprouted up along the shore of the bay. He answered the door, bleary eyed, as if he had just been woken up.

Baldur introduced himself and Vigdís, and barged in.

'What's this about?' asked Tómas, blinking.

'The murder of Agnar Haraldsson.'

'Ah. You'd better take a seat then.'

The furniture was expensive cream leather. The view of the bay was spectacular, although at that precise moment a dark cloud was pressing down on the darker sea, and Mount Esja was scarcely visible.

'I'd like to ask you about your movements on Thursday the twenty-third. Last Thursday,' Baldur said.

Tómas gathered his thoughts. 'I got up late. Went out for a sandwich for lunch and a cup of coffee. Then I drove over to the university.'

'Go on.'

'I was looking for Agnar Haraldsson. I asked a student who said that he might be at his summerhouse by Lake Thingvellir. So I drove up there.'

'At what time was this?' Vigdís asked, her notebook out, pen poised.

'I got there about four o'clock, I think. I can't remember precisely. Might have been a bit after four.'

'And was Agnar there?'

'Yes, he was. I had a cup of coffee. We chatted a bit. And then I left.'

'I see. And what did you chat about?' Baldur asked.

'I wanted to discuss a possible television project on the sagas.'

'What kind of project?'

'Well, that was the trouble. I didn't have a specific idea. I was kind of hoping that Agnar would provide that. But he didn't.'

'So you left?'

'That's right. I was there about three-quarters of an hour.'

'And then what did you do?'

'I came back home. Watched a movie, a DVD. Had a drink.'

'Alone?'

'Yes,' said Tómas.

'And was this the first time you had met Agnar?' Baldur asked.

'No,' said Tómas. 'I had bumped into him once or twice in the past.'

Baldur's long face was impassive, but Vigdís could feel the excitement in him. Tómas was talking nonsense, and Baldur knew it.

'And why didn't you come forward before?' Baldur asked, gently.

'Um. I didn't want to get involved. I couldn't see that it was important.'

At this Baldur couldn't maintain his composure. He laughed. 'Right, Tómas. You are coming with us to the station, where you had better think up a better story than that bullshit. But first I want you to show me what clothes you were wearing on that day. And the shoes.'

'YOU CAN'T RELEASE Steve Jubb!' Magnus almost shouted. Baldur stood in the corridor outside the interview room, facing him.

'I can and I will. We don't have the evidence to hold him. We know that there was someone else there that night after Steve Jubb had driven back to Reykjavík. Someone who dumped Agnar into the lake once it got dark.'

'According to a four-year-old girl.'

'She's five. But the point is all the forensic evidence backs that up. And we have another suspect.' Baldur nodded towards the door where Tómas Hákonarson was just beginning a marathon interview session.

'And has he confessed?'

'Give me time,' Baldur said. 'His fingerprints match the unidentified set we found in the house. We're analysing his clothes and his boots now. His story is that he came and went *before* Steve Jubb arrived that evening. The neighbours were out all afternoon, so it's possible that Tómas came and went without them seeing him. But if you thought Jubb was lying, you should see this guy. His story is full of holes.'

'Don't you think what I told you about Lawrence Feldman and Steve Jubb trying to buy a ring from Agnar changes things?'

'No,' said Baldur, firmly. 'Now, I have some work to do.'

MAGNUS WENT BACK to his desk intensely frustrated. What really bugged him was the possibility that Baldur might be right. He was a good cop who trusted his intuition, but then so was Magnus. When it came right down to it, though, Tómas Hákonarson had the opportunity but as yet not the motive. Isildur and Gimli, as they liked to call themselves, had motive aplenty.

The seat opposite Magnus was empty—Árni was still up in the air. Magnus called his cellphone and left a message on his voicemail to tell him that Isildur was in Reykjavík and he may as well come home.

He switched on his computer and checked for an email. There was one from Deputy Superintendent Williams. He apologised for the failure to protect Colby. He claimed there was a patrol car outside all night, but they didn't see anything. There was no trace of Colby herself, although she had told her boss and her parents that she was going away for a while.

The kid Magnus had shot had died, but the inquest into his death and that of his partner was going to be delayed until after the Lenahan trial.

But the big news was the Lenahan trial itself. It was likely that the trial would begin some time the following week. Magnus would be called as a witness as early as possible: the FBI hoped that as soon as he testified, Lenahan would talk. The Feds would send Magnus details of his flight as soon as they had decided them. The FBI would meet him at the airport and take him to a safe house.

Magnus tapped out a reply saying it would be good to be home. Which was true. He felt that the value he was adding to the Icelandic police force was precisely zero. Baldur's estimate would be negative.

He thought about Colby, and smiled. Good for her. He wrote a quick email to her, telling her to let him know she was OK, if she got the opportunity. That was the best he could hope for.

His thoughts turned to the case. He hated the idea of leaving it to Baldur to clear up. If he was right and Baldur was wrong, that meant the case turned on the saga and the ring. Agnar thought he knew where a ring was, and Feldman wanted that ring. Badly.

So where was it?

What if Agnar had figured out where it was hidden? He was an expert on medieval Icelandic literature. He no doubt knew of dozens of folk tales and legends which might hold clues that could have led to the ring.

Then Magnus remembered the entry in Agnar's diary for Hruni. Vigdís had interviewed the pastor there, Dr Ásgrímur's friend. She'd reported the pastor had had nothing much of interest to say.

Magnus needed to go to Hruni. But first he wanted to speak to Ingileif. He didn't think she had the ring, but he knew he should keep the idea open as a possibility. And, damn it, he wanted to see her.

HE WALKED to the gallery and was told Ingileif was probably working at home. He had her home address from the initial interview and it took him only ten minutes to walk there.

Her first reaction when she saw him on her doorstep seemed to be pleasure. Her smile was wide and warm, though a moment later it was clouded by doubt. But she invited him in.

Magnus sat in a low chrome chair and accepted a glass of wine.

'I didn't know you were allowed to drink on duty,' Ingileif said as she handed the glass to him.

'I'm not sure I am on duty,' said Magnus.

'Really?' said Ingileif. 'I didn't realise this was a social call.'

'Well, it's not a formal interview,' Magnus said. 'I want your help.'

'I thought that's what I had been doing,' Ingileif said. 'Helping the police with their inquiries. Except I admit I wasn't very helpful at first.'

'I want to talk to you about the ring. I need to figure out where it is.'

'I have no idea, I told you that,' Ingileif said. 'It's stuffed in some tiny niche in the rocks somewhere in the Icelandic wilderness.'

'Agnar thought he had found it,' Magnus said. 'It wasn't just the saga he was trying to sell to Lawrence Feldman; it was the ring too.'

Magnus explained the contents of the text message that Steve Jubb had sent to Feldman the night Agnar had been murdered, and Feldman's conviction that Agnar knew where the ring was.

'So somebody has it?' Ingileif asked.

'Possibly,' Magnus said. 'And the most obvious candidate is you.'

Ingileif exploded. 'Hey! You said you wanted my help. I would have said if I had it. I know I didn't tell you everything earlier, but I've given up on the saga, and the damned ring. So if you don't believe me, take me away and interrogate me.'

Magnus was taken aback by the vehemence of her denial. 'I'm not going to interrogate you. I'll just ask you. Do you know where the ring is?'

'No,' Ingileif said. 'Do you believe me?'

'Yes,' Magnus said. He knew that as a professional detective he should still doubt her, but a professional detective wouldn't have been drinking a glass of wine in her apartment. He had given up on being a professional detective for now. He just wanted to find out who killed Agnar.

She seemed to calm down then, so he continued.

'Your brother told me that your father confided in the local pastor. That the two of them worked on theories of where the ring might be hidden. Can you tell me something about this pastor?'

'He's strange. A lot of my friends were scared of him, scared and fascinated at the same time. He used to mess with their heads.'

'But not yours?'

'No, he was always straightforward with me, because of my father, I think. He's clever, he fancies himself as an intellectual. And, of course, he knows everything about the legend of the Hruni dance.'

'Have you seen him recently?'

'He officiated at my mother's funeral at the end of last year. He didn't do a bad job, actually.' She finished her wine. 'Do you want another glass?'

Magnus nodded and Ingileif refilled their glasses.

'I've been thinking a lot about my father's death this week,' she said. 'I know it's Agnar's murder you are investigating, but I wonder whether Dad's death was all that it seemed.'

'What happened?'

'Dad and the pastor were going on a two-day expedition, with tents, up in the hills to the west of the River Thjórsá. It's pretty barren up there, and there was still some snow on the ground.'

Ingileif took a gulp of her wine. 'On the second day they were on their way back when a snowstorm blew up out of nowhere. They got lost on the moor, and Dad stumbled over a cliff. He fell about fifteen metres onto some rocks. The pastor climbed down. He says he thought Dad was badly injured but still alive. He hurried off to find help, but he got lost in the snowstorm. Six hours later he found a sheep farm and returned with the farmer. By the time they got back to the cliff, Dad was dead: fractured skull, broken neck.

In fact, they think he probably died within a few minutes of the fall.'

'I'm sorry,' said Magnus. 'My father died when I was twenty. It's rough.'

Ingileif smiled quickly. 'Yes, it is. And although you think you have come to terms with it, you never really do.'

'Do you think he was pushed?' Magnus asked.

'By Reverend Hákon? You mean, they both found the ring and the pastor pushed my father over the cliff to take it from him?'

Magnus shrugged. 'You just said it. What do you think?'

'I don't know,' Ingileif said. 'The pastor and my dad were good friends. After Dad died the pastor sort of withdrew into himself and became really weird. His wife left him a couple of years later. No one blamed her.'

'Or it could simply be the reaction of someone who had just murdered his best friend,' said Magnus. 'I think I should go and see him tomorrow.'

'Can I come?' Ingileif asked.

Magnus raised his eyebrows.

'I need to find out what really happened to my father,' she said. 'It was a long time ago but there are so many questions that I don't have the answers to. Agnar's murder has brought them all back. I've just *got* to find those answers if I'm going to get on with my life. Do you understand?'

'Oh, I understand,' said Magnus. 'Believe me, I understand.'

He considered her request. It was certainly not part of the standard investigative procedure to take one witness along to interview another, just to satisfy her curiosity. 'Yes,' said Magnus, smiling. 'That would be fine.'

Ingileif returned his smile. There was a silence that was and was not uncomfortable.

'Tell me about your father,' Ingileif said.

Magnus paused. Glanced at the woman opposite him, her grey eyes warm now. It wasn't standard investigative procedure either, but he told her. About his early childhood, his parents' separation, his own move to America to join his father. About his stepmother, his father's murder. And then about his recent discovery of his father's infidelity.

They talked for an hour. Perhaps two hours. They talked a lot about Magnus, and then they talked about Ingileif.

Eventually Magnus got up to leave. 'So you still want to come with me to Hruni? To see the Reverend Hákon?'

'I'd like to,' said Ingileif, with a smile.

'Good,' said Magnus, putting on his coat. Then he froze. 'Wait a minute! This Reverend Hákon. Does he have a son?'

'Yes. As a matter of fact he's an old friend of mine.'

'And what's his name?'

'Tómas. Tómas Hákonarson. He's a TV presenter now. He's quite famous: you must know him.'

'Yes,' said Magnus. 'As a matter of fact, I do know him.'

JOHNNY YEOH SWORE and pushed his chair back from the screen. He had been playing Kopz Life for five hours straight. It was his favourite game, and he always called himself Magnus. That guy was just so cool.

The buzzer sounded. He checked his watch: half-past midnight. He had ordered the pizza forty-five minutes before, although thanks to his total absorption in the game, it felt like only ten. He buzzed the pizza guy into his building, and a minute later unlocked his apartment door to let him in.

The door slammed open and Johnny found himself pinned up against the wall of his living room, a revolver shoved down his throat. A light brown face with cool eyes stared at him, inches away.

'OK, Johnny, I got some questions for you,' the man said.

Johnny tried to speak, but he couldn't. He didn't know whether it was the fear or the metal pressed on his tongue.

The man withdrew the gun so that it was an inch away from his mouth. Johnny tried to speak again. No sound. It was the fear.

'You done some work for a cop by the name of Magnus Jonson, right?' Johnny nodded vigorously.

'You found the address of some guy in California he was looking for?' Johnny nodded again.

'How about you write that down for me, man?' The guy glanced round the room. He was tall, slim, with a smooth face and hard brown eyes. Eyes that alighted on some paper and a pen. 'Over there!'

'I need to check my computer,' Johnny said.

'Go ahead. I'll be watching. So don't type no messages to nobody.'

Intensely aware of the gun at the back of his head, Johnny Yeoh went over to the desk and sat in front of his computer. Within less than a minute he had found Lawrence Feldman's address. He wrote it down: his hand was shaking so badly it took him two attempts.

'Did Jonson say where he's at?' the guy asked.

'No,' said Johnny. 'I didn't speak to him. He sent me an email.'

'Where'd it come from?'

'I don't know.'

'Then look!' The gun was crammed into his skull.

Johnny called up his email folder and found the one from Magnus. The domain name was *lrh.is*. Israel? No, that was '.il'. 'Iceland, perhaps?'

'Hey, I'm asking you.'

'All right, all right. I'll check.' It took Johnny less than a minute to confirm that the domain was indeed in Iceland.

'Now, Iceland ain't in Sweden, is it?'

'No,' said Johnny.

'Is it near Sweden?'

'Not really,' said Johnny. 'A thousand miles away. Two thousand.'

'All right, all right.' The man with the gun grabbed the scrap of paper and backed off towards the door. 'You know, you ain't no fun, man.'

Then the gunman did something very strange. He looked Johnny Yeoh in the eye. Put the revolver to his own temple. Smiled.

And pulled the trigger. *Click*. Empty chamber.

CHAPTER EIGHT

The pastor carried the newspaper he had just bought in Flúdir into his study and read the article about the investigation into Agnar's murder. It sounded as if little real progress had been made since the initial arrest of the Englishman. The pastor smiled as he remembered how he had so disconcerted the black policewoman. But he shouldn't be complacent. The police were asking for witnesses who had seen anyone at all driving down to that part of the shore of Lake Thingvellir on the first day of summer to come forward. That worried him.

He knew the best thing to do was to stay calm. There was no reason why the police would pay him another visit, but he should be prepared nonetheless. He glanced at the pile of books on his desk. He should get back to the life of Saemundur. But he couldn't dispel the anxiety the article in the newspaper had awakened.

He left the house and crossed the fifty yards over to the church, nestled beneath the rocky crag. The church was bright and airy inside. The sunlight streamed in through the clear glass windows. The ceiling was painted light blue and decorated with gold stars. The pulpit and the small electric organ were made of blond pine. He walked towards the altar, draped with red velvet. Behind it was a painting of the Last Supper.

On mornings like this, some of his congregation claimed that they could feel God in the church. Only he knew that beneath its finery, the altar was actually a tatty old pine cupboard, inside which were old copies of official notices going back several decades. The pastor reached under the pile to the right of the cupboard and felt for the familiar round shape.

The ring. He drew it out and pulled it onto the fourth finger of his right hand, where it fitted snugly. The pastor had big hands, yet the ring was not too tight. It had been made for the fingers of warriors.

And now it belonged to the pastor of Hruni.

BALDUR IGNORED MAGNUS in the morning meeting. He was amassing a case against Tómas Hákonarson. No one had seen Tómas come home that evening, either when he said he did at around five or six o'clock, or much later. There was little obvious sign of mud on the trainers Tómas said he had worn that night, but the lab was working on a more thorough examination.

During the whole meeting, Baldur never directed a single comment to Magnus, nor asked his opinion, nor gave him any tasks in the investigation. And all this was watched by Thorkell Holm.

Screw Baldur. Magnus would tell him all about Tómas's father in his own good time. When he had spoken to the pastor himself.

LAWRENCE FELDMAN sat in the back seat of the black Mercedes four-wheel-drive, waiting in the parking lot of Litla Hraun prison.

The journey from Reykjavík, only an hour away, had been exhilarating.

As they drove up through the lava field into the clouds, Feldman thought he could well have been in Middle Earth, perhaps on the edge of Mordor, the home of the Dark Lord, Sauron. Weird lichens and mosses, some of them a bright lime colour, some grey, some orange, clung to the rock. Patches of snow stretched up the mountainsides into the clouds. To the side of the road, plumes of steam rose up from the ground.

Mordor. Where the shadows lie.

Feldman had elected to remain in the car while Kristján Gylfason, the lawyer he had hired, had gone into the prison to fetch Gimli.

At last he saw Kristján emerge from the prison, accompanied by a big man in a blue track suit. Feldman unlocked the door and pushed it open.

'Gimli!'

Gimli flopped into the back seat with a grunt. 'How you doin'?' he said.

Feldman hesitated. This was the first time he had ever met Gimli in the flesh, but he felt he knew him so well. He was overcome with emotion. He leaned forward clumsily to give him a hug.

Gimli sat still. 'Steady on,' he said. He had a pronounced Yorkshire accent.

Feldman broke away. 'How was it?' he asked. 'In there? Was it really bad?'

'It were all right. Food's OK. Mind you, the telly in this country is crap.'

Feldman looked closely at Gimli, trying to figure out if he was lying about his prison experiences.

Gimli shifted uncomfortably under Feldman's stare. 'Thanks for your help, Lawrence. With Kristján and everything.'

'Not at all. And please call me Isildur. I'll call you Gimli.'

Gimli looked at Feldman, and shrugged. 'Fair enough. I didn't tell them anything, you know. They seemed to have figured out a lot themselves. But it weren't me what told them.'

'Of course not,' said Feldman, instantly guilty about how much he had told the police under much less pressure.

Kristján started the car and drove out of the prison grounds and back towards Reykjavík. Feldman glanced at his companion.

'You know, Gimli, we might have missed *Gaukur's Saga*, but we could still find the ring. Do you want to help me?'

'After all that's happened here?' Gimli asked.

'Of course, I'd understand if you didn't,' said Feldman. 'But if we found it, we could share it. Split custody of it. Seventy-five, twenty-five. You'd get to keep it three months in every year.'

Gimli stared out of the window. He nodded. 'Well, I've gone through so much, I may as well get something from it. How do we start?'

'Did Agnar give you any indication at all where the ring might be?'

'No. But when the police questioned me they asked about a brother and sister. Peter and Ingi-something Ásgrímsson. I'm pretty sure they must be the ones who were selling the saga.'

'All right. All we have to do is find them. Kristján? Can you help us?'

'I don't think that would be wise,' said Kristján. 'If I need to defend you in the future, the less I know the better.'

'I get it. Then can you recommend a good investigator? Someone who is willing to bend the rules a bit to find out what we need?'

'We would never use that kind of investigator.'

'So who would you *not* recommend, then?' asked Steve Jubb. 'You know, who should we steer clear of?'

'There's a man called Axel Bjarnason,' said Kristján. 'I would stay well clear of him. You'll find his name in the phone book.'

IT TOOK MAGNUS a while to requisition a car for the journey to Hruni, and it was after lunch when he rolled up outside the gallery to pick up Ingileif.

She was wearing jeans and an anorak, her blonde hair tied back in her usual ponytail. She looked good. She also looked pleased to see him.

They drove out of Reykjavík under a broad dark cloud, the suburbs of Grafarvogur stretching out beside them. As they climbed up the pass to the south-east, lava and cloud converged, until suddenly they crested the final rise and a broad flood plain sparkled in the sunshine beneath them.

'Tell me about Tómas,' Magnus said.

'I've known him for as long as I can remember,' Ingileif said. 'We went to school together in Flúdir. His parents separated when he was fourteen, and he moved with his mother to Hella. He's totally different from his father, a bit of a joker, charming in his way, although I never found him attractive.'

She paused as Magnus manoeuvred round a particularly steep bend down the hill, swerving slightly to avoid a truck coming up the other way.

'Tómas bummed around after university for a bit,' she continued. 'Then did some journalism and suddenly fell into this show he does: *The Point*. I think it's gone to his head a bit. Tómas always liked to drink, do drugs; his parties have the reputation for being pretty wild.'

'Have you been to any?'

'Actually, no. I haven't seen much of him recently, until yesterday. But he asked me to go to one on Saturday.'

'I wouldn't buy yourself a frock for that one.'

'No,' said Ingileif. 'I hear he might be double-booked.'

'You say you saw him yesterday?'

Ingileif described her meeting with Tómas in Mokka, and his cryptic questions about the Agnar case.

'How does he get along with his father?' Magnus asked.

'Well, I don't know about now. But it always used to be the classic relationship between an overdemanding father and a son who is constantly trying to please and never quite succeeds. Tómas always felt his father's disapproval deeply. I'm sure he still does.'

'So he might do his father a favour? A big favour?'

'Like murdering someone?' She thought about it for a few seconds. 'I can't imagine he would. That kind of thing just doesn't happen in Iceland.'

'It happens everywhere,' said Magnus. 'It's happened here. To Agnar.'

They were now on the floor of the plain, driving on a long straight road that cut through fields of knotted brown grass.

'So, back in America, are you a tough-guy cop with a gun chasing the bad guys like you see on TV?' Ingileif asked.

'Cops get irritated as hell by the TV shows; they never get it right,' said Magnus. 'But yes, I do have a gun. And the city is full of bad guys, or at least the areas I end up working in.'

'Doesn't it depress you? Or do you get a thrill out of it?'

'I dunno,' said Magnus. It was always hard to explain being a cop to civilians. They never quite got it. Colby had never got it.

'Sorry,' said Ingileif, and she turned to look out of the window.

They drove on. Perhaps Magnus was being unfair to Ingileif. She had made an effort to understand him the night before.

'There was a girl I knew in college, Erin. She used to go down into Providence to work with the kids there. It was a real tough place back then.

I went with her, partly because I thought what she was doing was good, mostly because I thought she was the most beautiful girl in the college.'

'How romantic.'

'Yeah. But she *did* do a lot of good. She was great with the kids, the boys drooled over her, and the girls thought she was cool, too. And I helped out.'

'I bet all the girls thought you were cool as well,' Ingileif said with a grin.

'I managed to fight them off,' said Magnus. 'But my point is that every time she met a kid who was dealing drugs or knifing his neighbours, she saw a scared little boy who had been abused and abandoned by his parents and by society.'

'And you?'

'Well, I tried to see it her way, I really did. But in my world there were good guys and bad guys, and the way I saw it, it was the bad guys who were ruining the neighbourhood and corrupting the other kids in it. All I wanted to do was stop the little punk from ruining other people's lives. Just like my life had been ruined by whoever killed my father.'

'So you became a cop?'

'That's right. And she became a teacher.' Magnus smiled wryly. 'And somehow I think she has made the world a better place than I have.'

They drove on in silence. Over the cantilevered bridge on the River Ölfusá and through the town of Selfoss.

'How long are you staying in Iceland?' Ingileif asked.

'It looks like I'll be going back to the States next week to testify at a trial.'

'Are you coming back afterwards?'

'Not if I can help it,' said Magnus.

'Oh. Don't you like Iceland?' Ingileif sounded offended.

'I do like it. It just brings back difficult memories. And my job at the Reykjavík CID isn't working out that well. I don't get along with the boss.'

'Is there a girlfriend back in Boston?' Ingileif asked.

'No,' said Magnus. Colby was an *ex*-girlfriend if ever there was one.

'Look, there's Hekla!' Ingileif pointed ahead towards the broad, white ridge that was Iceland's most famous volcano. Hekla had erupted four times in the previous forty years. And every couple of centuries or so, it would come up with a big one. Like the eruption of 1104 that had smothered Gaukur's farm at Stöng.

'In Boston they sell Hekla cinnamon rolls,' Magnus said. 'They're big, upside-down rolls covered in sugar. Look just like the mountain.'

'But do they blow up in your face at random intervals?'

'Not that I'm aware of.'

'Then they're not real Hekla rolls. They need a bit more violence in them.' Ingileif smiled. 'I remember watching Hekla erupt in 1991. I was ten or eleven, I suppose. It was extraordinary. It was a January night and the volcano was glowing angry red and orange and at the same time you could see a green streak of the aurora hovering above. I'll never forget it.' She swallowed. 'It was the year before Dad died.'

'When life was normal?' Magnus asked.

'That's right,' said Ingileif. 'When life was normal.'

Soon they turned to the north and lost the volcano behind the foothills that edged the valley. With two kilometres to Flúdir, they came to a turnoff to Hruni to the right. Magnus took it, and the road wound through the hills for a couple of kilometres, before breaking out into a valley. The small white church of Hruni was visible beneath a rocky crag.

They pulled up in the empty parking lot in front of the church, and climbed out of the car. They approached the rectory and rang the doorbell. No answer. But there was a red Suzuki in the garage.

'Let's check inside the church,' suggested Ingileif.

They walked to the church and went in. It was warm and really quite beautiful. It was also empty.

As they made their way back to the car, Magnus caught sight of a boy of about sixteen moving around the barn next to the rectory. He called out to him. 'Have you seen the pastor?'

'He was here this morning.'

'Do you know where he might have gone? Does he have another car?'

The boy noticed the Suzuki parked in the garage. 'No. He could have gone for a walk. He does that sometimes. He can be out all day.'

'Thank you,' said Magnus. He checked his watch. Three thirty. Then turning to Ingileif, 'What now?'

'You could come back to our house in the village,' she said. 'I can show you the letters from Tolkien to my grandfather.'

'Good idea,' said Magnus. 'We'll come back here later.'

AUSTURSTRAETI WAS ONLY a block away from the Hótel Borg. Isildur was reassured by the two men beside him, the big trucker from England and the wrinkled Icelandic ex-policeman. When Gimli had suggested a sum to Axel Bjarnason, he had been eager to drop everything to help them, although Gimli suspected that he didn't have much to drop.

He clearly knew his town, though. He had recognised Pétur Ásgríms-son's name immediately and had required only a few seconds to check that Ingileif's gallery was where he thought it was. He was at the Hótel Borg less than a quarter of an hour later.

Isildur was nervous, scared even. Someone had been murdered and there was a chance that the murderer was the man walking along beside him. Isildur didn't like to think too hard about that; he had decided not to ask Gimli outright whether he had killed the professor.

But the danger added to the thrill. It was a long shot: perhaps the police would get to the ring first. Perhaps the ring was a fake all along. Perhaps no one would ever find it. But there was a chance that Isildur might end up the owner of the actual ring that had inspired *The Lord of the Rings*.

That was cool. That was seriously cool.

The main entrance to Neon was just a small door on the street, but Bjarnason led them round the back. They saw a young man carrying cases of vodka through the back door.

Bjarnason stopped him and rattled something off in Icelandic. The boy led them downstairs to a small office. There, a tall man with a shaved head was in earnest discussion with a woman.

'Mr Ásgrímsson?' said Isildur in English.

The man with the shaved head looked up. 'Yes?' No hint of a smile.

'My name is Lawrence Feldman and this is my colleague, Steve Jubb.'

'What do you want? I thought you were in jail?' Ásgrímsson said.

'Steve is innocent,' Isildur said. 'The cops finally figured that out.'

'Well, if you want the saga, the police have it. And when they have fin-ished with it, there is no way we are selling it to you.'

Ásgrímsson was aggressive, but Isildur stood up to him. 'That's a topic for a later day. We want to speak with you about Gaukur's ring.'

'Get out of my club now!' Ásgrímsson's voice was firm.

'We'll pay well. Very well,' said Isildur.

'Listen to me,' said Ásgrímsson. 'A man has died because of that stupid saga. Two men, if you include my father. My family kept it a secret for centuries for a reason, a good reason as it turns out. It would still be a secret if it wasn't for you—your nosing around, your flashing dollars everywhere.' He took a step closer to Isildur. 'You've seen what the result is. Professor Agnar Haraldsson is dead! Don't you feel guilty about that? Don't you think you should just get the hell back to America?'

'Mr Ásgrímsson—'

'Out!' Pétur was shouting now, pointing to the exit. 'I said, get out!'

THE PASTOR WAS SWEATING in the unseasonably warm sun. It was a glorious day and he had already walked about seven kilometres. He was in a high valley, and all around him snow was melting. Most of the grass that had been revealed in the past few days was yellow, but by the side of the brook there was a patch of rich green shoots. Spring.

Over to the left, along the side of the valley, were some rocky crags. He turned off the path and squelched through the yellow grass towards them.

He needed to find a good hiding place.

Tómas's arrest as a suspect for the murder of Agnar Haraldsson had been on the lunchtime news on the radio. The moment he had heard it the pastor knew he had to find a new place to hide the ring. He had always assumed that his son was far too lightweight to make any use of the ring. But perhaps he might make something of his life after all. With the help of the ring.

He paused and examined it on the fourth finger of his right hand. He remembered when he and Ásgrímur had found it in that cave, well, hardly a cave, more like a hole in the rock. It was the greatest, most profound moment of his life. And of Ásgrímur's of course. Even if it was just about his last.

He had worn it on and off now for nearly twenty years. He loved it, he worshipped it. Sometimes he would just sit and stare at it, wondering at its history, its mystery. But although it gave him a tremendous feeling of exhilaration every time he put it on, over time his disappointment had grown. The pastor had assumed that the ring had chosen him because of his knowledge of the devil and of Saemundur. But although he had thrown himself into his studies, nothing had happened. Nothing had been revealed to him. The way to power and domination had not appeared.

The pastor scrabbled around in the rocks looking for a niche similar to the one in which he had originally found the ring seventeen years before. But maybe he shouldn't conceal it? The ring had not revealed itself to him and Dr Ásgrímur merely to be removed from the world again.

It wanted to be discovered.

The hiding place in the altar at Hruni church wasn't the best. A determined police team could find it there. But it was the *right* place.

The pastor took off the ring and grasped it in his hand. He closed his eyes and tried to feel what the ring was telling him. It *was* the right place.

He turned on his heel and began walking back towards Hruni at a brisk pace. He checked his watch. He would be lucky to be home by nightfall.

INGILEIF'S HOUSE, or rather her family's house, was on a bank overlooking the river that ran through Flúdir. Flúdir itself was a prosperous village with a convenience store, a hotel, two schools, some municipal buildings and a number of geothermally powered greenhouses—Ingileif said it had the best farming in Iceland.

The house was a single-storey affair, cosy, but large enough for a family of five. Magnus and Ingileif spread out the contents of several cardboard boxes on the floor of Ingileif's mother's bedroom. There were a dozen letters from Tolkien to Högni, Ingileif's grandfather, which had come into her father's possession only after Högni's death. Ingileif showed Magnus a first edition of *The Fellowship of the Ring*, the first volume of *The Lord of the Rings*. The inscription inside said: *To Högni, one good story deserves another, with thanks and all good wishes, J. R. R. Tolkien, September 1954.*

They studied a folder of notes and maps, most of which were in Dr Ásgrímur's handwriting, which showed guesses of where the ring might be hidden. There were notes and letters from Hákon, the pastor, about various folk tales he had researched. There was also mention of a story of a shepherd girl named Thorgerd who ran off with an elf.

'Do you have elves in America?' Ingileif asked.

'Not as such,' said Magnus. 'We got drug dealers, we got pimps, we got investment bankers. No elves. But if we ever do have any problems with elves, I know where to come. We could do an exchange with the Reykjavík Metropolitan Police.'

'So you didn't hear any stories about them when you were a kid?'

'Oh, yes, especially when I was living with my grandparents in Iceland. What about you?'

'My grandmother saw hidden people all the time,' Ingileif said. 'Back in a rock near the farm where my mother was born. In fact a hidden woman came to her the night before my mother's birth. They were planning to call Mum Boghildur, but the hidden woman said that unless my grandmother named her Líney the baby would die young. So that's how she became Líney.'

'Better than Boghildur,' said Magnus. 'The hidden woman had taste.'

Ingileif's cellphone rang. As she answered, Magnus could hear an agitated male voice, although he couldn't hear it well enough to recognise it.

'That was my brother,' Ingileif said when the call was over. 'The two foreigners who were trying to buy the saga showed up at Neon. They were asking about the ring. Pétur sent them packing. But he warned me they'll be looking for me, too. He doesn't want me to tell them anything.'

'Will you?'

'No. And they're not buying the saga at any price, if we ever do get the chance to sell it. Pétur is adamant about that, and I agree.' She checked her watch. 'It's nearly seven o'clock. The pastor should be back. Shall we go?'

THEY DROVE BACK up to Hruni, but there was no answer when they rang the doorbell. The pastor's car was still in the garage. They looked up round the hills and the valley to see if they could spot a solitary walker, but there was no sign of a human being anywhere.

'What time does it get dark?' Magnus asked. 'Nine thirty?'

'About that, I guess,' said Ingileif.

'Are you hungry?'

Ingileif nodded. 'I know a place where we can get something to eat.'

'Let's do that. We can come back here afterwards.'

'And then drive back to Reykjavík?'

Magnus nodded.

'We could do that,' said Ingileif. 'Or . . .' She smiled. Her grey eyes danced under her blonde fringe. She looked delectable.

'Or what?'

'Or we could see him in the morning.'

MAGNUS WOKE with a start. He was sweating. For a moment he didn't know where he was. He looked across the room at an unfamiliar window, blue-grey moonlight behind the thin curtains. He turned to see a woman lying in bed next to him. Ingileif.

Her eyes were closed, and she was breathing gently in and out through half-open lips. He really liked her. *Really* liked her.

After driving back from Hruni they had stopped at the only hotel in Flúdir. It turned out to have a very good restaurant where they had eaten a long, leisurely dinner. They had walked back to Ingileif's house along the smaller river that ran through the village, and then they had wound up in Ingileif's childhood bedroom. He smiled at the memory.

But he had to be careful. Sleeping with a witness was a definite no-no in America, and somehow he doubted that Baldur would be impressed if he ever found out. And could he be entirely sure that she was innocent? Of course he could. But the detective in him whispered something else.

THIS TIME, the pastor of Hruni was in. He came to the door, an imposing man with a large bushy beard and big black eyebrows. He frowned when he saw Magnus, but his expression changed when his eyes rested on Ingileif.

'Ingileif? Goodness me, to what do I owe this pleasure?'

Magnus spoke up. 'My name is Magnús Ragnarsson and I am attached to the Reykjavík Metropolitan Police. I'd like to ask you a few questions, if I may. May we come in?'

The pastor pulled together his mighty eyebrows. 'I was expecting a visit from you,' he said. 'I suppose you had better come through.'

Magnus and Ingileif followed the pastor into a study crammed full of books. In addition to a desk, there was a sofa and an armchair covered in worn chintz fabric. Ingileif and Magnus perched next to each other on the sofa, while Hákon took the chair.

Hákon addressed Ingileif. 'I must confess I was expecting another visit from the police. But I don't understand why you are accompanying them?'

'Ingileif is concerned about the death of her father,' Magnus said.

'Ah, I see,' said the pastor. 'It is natural to have questions, especially since you were so young when the tragedy happened. But I still don't see why you want to ask them now. And in the presence of the police.'

'You know we have your son in custody?' Magnus said.

'Yes, I heard it on the radio. You have made a mistake there, young man. A terrible mistake.' Deep-set eyes glowered at Magnus.

'He is being interviewed at Police Headquarters in Reykjavík right now,' said Magnus. 'And I'm sure that my colleagues will want to talk to you once they have finished speaking with him. But in the meantime, tell me what happened on the trip you and Dr Ásgrímur took the weekend he died.'

The pastor took a deep breath. 'Well, there was a police investigation of course, and I spoke to them at length. I'm sure you could look up the file. But to answer your question. It was early May. Your father and I had worked throughout the winter on a project.' He glanced enquiringly at Ingileif.

'Magnús has read *Gaukur's Saga*,' said Ingileif. 'And he knows that my grandfather claims to have found the ring and hidden it again.'

This information caused the pastor to pause a moment while he collected his thoughts. 'Well, in that case you know as much as me. Using my knowledge of folklore, together with the clues in the saga, we drew up a list of three or four possible hiding places for Gaukur's ring.

'A few years before, I had stumbled across a little-known local legend about a ring hidden in a cave guarded by a troll. It was a variation on the old story of a shepherd girl meeting a hidden man or an elf and going off with him. That theme is quite common in these stories, but the ring was unusual. The location of the cave is identified in the story, so we hiked out there.' The pastor sighed. 'It was more of a hole in the rock, really. And there was nothing in it. We were disappointed. We camped about a mile away, by a stream. It had been a glorious day but that night it snowed and it was still snowing when we got up. We took down our tent and headed home. The snow thickened, it became difficult to see. Your father was walking a few metres ahead of me when I heard a cry. I looked up and he had disappeared.

'I realised that we were on the rim of a cliff, and he had slipped over. I could see him about twenty metres down, lying at an odd angle. I slid and fell as I climbed down the cliff, but my fall was cushioned by the snow.'

The pastor paused and fixed Ingileif with his deep-set, dark eyes. 'When I found your father he was still alive, but unconscious. He had hit his head. I took off my coat to keep him warm, and then rushed to find help. I got lost in the snowstorm. It was only when the storm ceased that I saw the Álfa-brekka farm in the distance. I was very cold by then.

'The farmer and his son both came back with me to look for Ásgrímur, while the farmer's wife called mountain rescue. By the time we got to your father, he was dead.' The pastor shook his head.

'Did you continue looking for the ring after my father's death?'

The pastor turned to her and relaxed slightly. 'No. I let it drop. I must confess it was fun working on the puzzle with your father, but once he had died I lost all interest in the ring. And the saga.'

'You spoke to my colleague a few days ago about a visit here by Professor Agnar Haraldsson,' Magnus said.

'That's true.'

'And what did you tell her he wanted to speak to you about?'

The pastor smiled, a mass of wrinkles appearing round his eyes. 'Ah, I wasn't entirely honest with your colleague. I take the confidences of my parishioners very seriously.' He looked pointedly at Ingileif.

'So what did Agnar really talk to you about?'

'*Gaukur's Saga*, of course. And the ring. He told me that Ingileif had asked him to act for the family in the sale of the saga.' He frowned at Ingileif 'I must admit that I was quite shocked by this. After all the years that the family had successfully kept the saga a secret.'

Ingileif reddened at the admonition from her pastor.

'I hardly think that's for you to judge,' said Magnus. 'In fact, by not telling my colleague the truth first time round, you obstructed a murder inquiry. Now, did Agnar have something specific to ask you?'

'Ingileif had just discovered the letter to her grandfather from Tolkien that referred to the discovery of the ring. Agnar came straight here and asked me much the same questions as you did just now. He seemed agitated. Excited. Aggressive in his questioning.'

'Did you tell him anything you didn't tell us?' Magnus asked.

'Absolutely not.'

Magnus paused, examining the pastor. 'See, the day after he saw you, Agnar sent a message that implied that he knew where the ring was.'

'Well, he certainly didn't seem to know when I saw him.'

'Did you tell him where you looked for it that day in 1992?'

'No. He asked, but I told him I couldn't remember. But of course I can.'

Ingileif showed the pastor the map that she had found among her father's papers. 'Is that the place?'

Hákon peered over. 'Yes, that's it. And there's the farm, Álfabrekka. I suppose I could have told Agnar where it was, wasted his time. I'm sure the ring is not there. At least, it wasn't there seventeen years ago.'

'Are you certain?' Magnus asked. 'I wonder if Agnar discovered clues to the location somewhere else and found something you missed.'

'I'm absolutely certain,' said Hákon. 'Believe me, Ásgrímur and I scraped every inch of the cave, and it wasn't very big.'

'Did your son know anything about this?' Magnus asked.

'Tómas? I don't think so. He was, what, thirteen at the time? I didn't tell him about the saga or the ring, either then or afterwards.'

'Then why was he speaking to Agnar the day he died?' Magnus asked.

'I don't know. I had no idea they knew each other.'

'Interesting coincidence, don't you think?'

Hákon shrugged. 'I suppose so.' Then he leaned forward, his eyes boring into Magnus. 'My son is not a killer, young man. Remember that.'

'THAT MAN GIVES ME the creeps,' Ingileif said as they drove back.

'Was he always like that?'

'He was always weird. We didn't go to church much, but when we did his sermons always used to scare the wits out of me. Lots of fire and brimstone, the devil behind every rock. Hearing that sort of thing while you are actually sitting in Hruni church is pretty frightening for a kid.'

'I can imagine that.'

'So, Mr Detective, was he telling the truth?'

'I don't think so. We know he lied to Vigdís about Agnar. I'm pretty sure he was lying about Tómas. He must have told him about the saga and the ring; why else would Tómas be talking to Agnar? It's good I got him to deny that. Bad decision on his part.'

'Why's that?'

'Because when I get Tómas to admit that he heard about the saga from his father, we will have caught Hákon out in another lie. From then on he'll be struggling to keep his story straight. What did you think?'

'I think he killed my father. And I think he's got the ring. Couldn't you search his house?'

'We'd need a search warrant, and it won't be easy to persuade Baldur to get one until I have broken Tómas's story.'

'Can we drop by the farm that Reverend Hákon went to for help? Álfa-brekka?' Ingileif asked. 'Someone there might remember something.'

'I'd like to get back as soon as possible to interview Tómas.'

'I understand. But it might shed some light on my father's death.'

Magnus hesitated.

'Please, Magnús. You know how important it is to me. We'd only have to go up to Thjórsárdalur.'

'But that would be fifty kilometres out of our way, there and back.'

Magnus knew he should tell Baldur about his interview with Hákon as soon as possible. And he wanted to do that in person rather than over the phone so he would be able to confront Tómas himself. He glanced at Ingileif. It was true, he did know how important her father's death was to her.

'OK,' he sighed. 'Get the map out and tell me where to go.'

CHAPTER NINE

Immigration control wasn't a problem. The official glanced quickly at Diego's fake US passport and stamped it. Then in the arrivals hall he saw a stocky guy with close-cropped brown hair with a sign saying *Mr Roberts*. The guy led Diego out to the parking lot and a Nissan SUV.

There had been very little time to prepare for the trip. Diego wasn't as gratuitously violent as some of Soto's other enforcers, but he was smart, and that often counted for more. He was certainly the best guy to send to find a Boston cop among a bunch of Eskimos and off him. Soto had managed to find out from his wholesale suppliers who the big guys in drugs in Iceland were, and to make an introduction. They were Lithuanians, and they would help him.

After half an hour or so of driving, they pulled up in the parking lot of a

Taco Bell. Sweet. Diego insisted on getting himself a burrito, even though it was early. When he returned to the car, there was another man waiting for him in the back seat. Thirties, also short-cropped hair, small blue eyes.

'My name is Lukas,' he said, by way of introduction, in a strong accent.

'Joe,' said Diego, shaking the proffered hand.

'Welcome to Iceland.'

'Have you got the piece?'

Lukas hesitated and then pulled a Walther PPK out of a black shoulder bag. Diego examined it. It was in good condition. Serial number filed off.

'Be careful with this,' the Lithuanian said. 'There are no handguns in Iceland. This one was bought in Amsterdam and smuggled in.'

'Other than the cops. They got guns, surely?'

'Cops don't have guns, either. Except at airport.'

Diego smiled. 'Man, that's cool. How about the getaway?'

Lukas reached into his bag and took out a cellphone. 'Take this. The first name on the address list is "Karl". Call that when you want to get out. If you are for real, say, "Can I speak to Óskar?" Got that? Otherwise we think cops have you and you are on your own.'

'What happens then?'

'We'll meet you. Get you out of Iceland.'

'I get it,' said Diego. 'So where do I find Magnus Jonson?'

'I suggest you hang round the police headquarters until you see him.'

'Oh, great. Can you ask around for me, man? Find out where he lives?'

'No,' said Lukas. 'If you shoot policeman on the streets of Reykjavík it will be big deal. Very big deal. If they learn we have been asking questions about cop there will be big trouble for us. You understand?'

'I guess so,' said Diego.

'Good. Now we take you to hotel. There is bus station opposite the police headquarters. I suggest you go there to watch.'

ÁRNI WAS EXHAUSTED. It was amazing how sitting in one place for so long could be so tiring. He was very glad to be back in Iceland, although his body clock was completely confused.

He had really been looking forward to interviewing Isildur. And he had hoped to see a bit of California. As it was he hadn't even made it in to San

Francisco, spending the night at an airport Holiday Inn and the following morning organising the flight back.

Keflavík Airport was crowded but Árni went straight through immigration and customs. As he came through into the main concourse, he spotted a man he recognised, Andrius Juska. Stocky with short hair, he was a foot soldier in one of the Lithuanian gangs that sold amphetamines in Reykjavík.

Juska was holding up a welcome sign for a Mr Roberts. Árni slowed his pace to a saunter. As he did so a slim man with light brown skin approached the Lithuanian. From the reticence with which they greeted each other, it was clear that they had never met before.

Árni let his bag slip from his fingers, and then knelt down to pick it up. The two men were speaking English; the Lithuanian's accent was heavy, the other man's was American. Not educated American, street American. Árni took a good look. The man was about thirty, wearing a black leather jacket, and he looked as if he could handle himself. He most certainly did not look like your typical American tourist in Iceland. Interesting.

A FEW KILOMETRES south of Flúdir, Magnus and Ingileif turned left, following the road up the valley towards Gaukur's old farm of Stöng. Ahead, to the right, loomed Hekla.

At Ingileif's direction, Magnus turned off the road and along a steep dirt track, winding up through the hills and into a smaller valley. After a bone-rattling eight kilometres they came across a small white farm with a red roof, nestling in the hillside at the head of its own little valley. Álfabrekka.

As they pulled into the farmyard, a thin, sprightly man in his mid-fifties marched towards them, wearing blue overalls.

'Good morning!' he said, smiling broadly. 'How can I help you?' Bright blue eyes shone out of a pale and wrinkled face. Tufts of grey hair peeked out from under his woolly cap.

Ingileif introduced herself and Magnus. 'My father was Dr Ásgrímur Högnason. You may remember, he fell to his death near here in 1992.'

'Oh, yes, I do remember that, very clearly,' the farmer said. 'You have my sympathy, even so many years later. But let's not stand around out here. Come inside and have some coffee!'

Inside, the farmer's father and mother greeted them. The father, an impossibly wizened man, stirred himself from a comfortable armchair, while the mother busied herself with coffee and cakes.

The younger farmer who had greeted them did most of the talking. His name was Adalsteinn. And before they could ask him any questions he told them that he was single, the fact that the farm had been in the family for generations, and that farming these days was very tough indeed.

'Adalsteinn, perhaps you could tell me what happened the day you found my father?' Ingileif asked eventually.

Adalsteinn launched into a long description of how a frozen pastor had come to the door, and how he and his father had followed the pastor back to the place where Ásgrímur had fallen. The doctor was definitely dead and very cold. There were no signs of a struggle or foul play; it was quite clear where he had fallen. The police hadn't asked any particular questions suggesting they suspected anything other than an accident.

During all this, the farmer's mother added certain helpful embellishments, but the old man sat in his chair, silent, watching.

Magnus and Ingileif stood up, and were taking their leave when he spoke for the first time. 'Tell them about the hidden man, Steini.'

'The hidden man?' Magnus looked sharply at the old man.

'I will, Father. I'll tell them outside,' said the younger man.

Adalsteinn ushered Magnus and Ingileif out into the yard.

'Father has seen the *huldufólk* all his life,' Adalsteinn said. 'There are a few who live around here, according to him. You know how it is?' His friendly face examined Magnus, looking for signs of disdain.

'I know how it is.' Álfabrekka meant 'Elf Slope' after all. 'Go on.'

'Well, he says he saw a young hidden man scurry by on the far side of the valley an hour before the pastor arrived.'

'A hidden man? How does he know it wasn't a human?'

'Well, he and my mother decided it was a hidden man, because the pastor was wearing an old gold ring. They saw it when they took off his gloves to get his hands warm.'

'And what has that to do with hidden people?'

Adalsteinn took a deep breath. 'There is an old local legend about a wedding ring. Thorgerd, the farmer's daughter of Álfabrekka, was tending her sheep when she was approached by a handsome young hidden man. He took her away and married her. The farmer was angry, searched for Thorgerd and killed her. Then he chased after the hidden man, who concealed the ring in a cave guarded by the hound of a troll. The farmer went to look for the ring but the troll killed him and ate him. Then there was a great eruption from Hekla and the farm was buried in ash.'

Magnus was impressed by how far *Gaukur's Saga* had been mangled over the generations, but the basic elements were all there. 'So your father thinks that the hidden man was looking for the pastor?'

'Something like that.'

'Do you mind if we go back and ask him about the hidden man?'

'Be my guest,' said the farmer.

The old man was still in his armchair while his wife was tidying up the coffee cups.

'Your son tells me that the pastor was wearing a ring?'

'Oh, yes,' said the old man's wife. 'It was dark, dirty, but you could see it was gold under the dirt. It must have been very old.'

'It was the hidden man's wedding ring,' said the old man. 'That's why his friend was killed. He stole the wedding ring. Fool! What did he expect?'

'Did you see the hidden man clearly?' Magnus asked.

'No, it was snowing. I caught no more than a glimpse of him, really.'

'But you could tell he was young?'

'Yes. By the way he moved.'

Magnus glanced at Ingileif. 'Could he have been around thirteen?'

'No,' said the old man. 'He was taller than that. And besides, remember he was married. Thirteen was too young for a hidden man to get married, even in those days.' He stared at Magnus with eyes full of certainty.

'TÓMAS WAS TALL at the age of thirteen, one of the tallest in our class,' Ingileif said. 'Probably one metre seventy-five, something like that.'

They were driving fast, back to Reykjavík.

'So he could have been out there with them that day,' Magnus said.

'You would have thought that the police would have discovered that, wouldn't you?'

'Maybe not,' said Magnus. 'Country police. No reason at all to think that a murder had been committed. I will dig out the files.'

'I *knew* Hákon had the ring!' Ingileif said.

'It certainly sounds like it. Though I still find it difficult to believe the ring actually exists.'

'But the farmers saw it on his finger!'

'Yes, just before they saw an elf.'

'Well, I don't care what you believe. I believe Hákon killed my father and took the ring! He must have done.'

'Unless it was Tómas who killed him?'

They were going pretty fast. The surface of the road along the edge of the river was excellent, but there were some bends and wiggles. Magnus sped over the crest of a small hill, and almost hit a white BMW four-wheel-drive coming at him the other way.

'That was close.'

He glanced over to see Ingileif's reaction to his driving.

She was sitting bolt upright in her seat, frowning slightly.

Her phone rang. She answered quickly, glanced at Magnus, mumbled 'Já,' two or three times, and hung up.

'Who was that?' Magnus asked.

'The gallery,' Ingileif answered.

Magnus dropped Ingileif at her apartment in 101, and went directly to police headquarters to talk to Baldur.

'Not another bloody elf!' he stared at Magnus in disbelief. He had listened closely as Magnus described his interview with the Reverend Hákon and with the sheep farmers, only losing patience once Magnus related the old man's story about the hidden man.

'I'm supposed to be the old-fashioned one around here. And then I have to listen to this elf and troll bullshit!'

'Obviously, it wasn't an elf,' said Magnus. 'It was Tómas. He was a tall thirteen year old.'

'And the ring? Are you trying to tell me that the pastor was wearing an ancient ring belonging to Odin or Thor or someone?'

'I don't know whether the ring is authentic,' said Magnus. 'And frankly, I don't care. The point is that seventeen years ago a small group of people did think it was important. Important enough to kill for.'

'Oh, so now we're solving another crime, are we? A death in 1992. Except this wasn't a crime, it was an accident.'

Magnus leaned back in his chair. 'Let me talk to Tómas.'

'No.'

'I can tell him the farmers saw him in the snowstorm. I can convince him that we know he was there.'

'I said, no.'

They sat in silence, staring at each other. Then Magnus said, 'Just give me twenty minutes. You can be there, too. You'll know if we're making progress. If I get nowhere, then we've lost twenty minutes, that's all.'

The corners of Baldur's lips were turned down, scepticism written all over his long face. But he was listening.

He took a deep breath. 'OK,' he said. 'Twenty minutes. Let's go.'

TÓMAS HÁKONARSON looked exhausted, as did his lawyer, a mousy woman of about thirty.

Baldur introduced Magnus. Tómas's tired eyes assessed him.

'Don't worry, I don't want to talk to you about Agnar,' Magnus began.

'Good,' said Tómas.

'It's another murder I want to discuss with you. One that took place seventeen years ago.'

Tómas was suddenly awake, his eyes focusing on Magnus.

'That's right,' Magnus said. 'Dr Ásgrímur. Seventeen years ago your father pushed Dr Ásgrímur off a cliff. And you witnessed it.'

Tómas swallowed. 'I don't know what you are talking about.'

'I've just come back from Hruni where I interviewed your father. And I went to Álfabrekka and spoke to the farmers who helped him go back and find Dr Ásgrímur. They saw you.'

'They can't have done.'

'They saw a thirteen-year-old boy sneak by their farm in the snow.'

Tómas frowned. 'That wasn't me.'

'Wasn't it?'

'Anyway, why would my father kill the doctor? They were friends.'

Magnus smiled. 'The ring.'

'What ring?'

'The ring you went to talk to Professor Agnar about.'

'I have no idea what you are talking about.'

Magnus leaned forward. 'You see, the farmers saw your father wearing an ancient ring. We *know* that your father pushed Dr Ásgrímur off a cliff and took the ring. You witnessed it and ran away.'

'Has he admitted it?' Tómas asked.

Magnus could see that the instant he had uttered it, Tómas regretted his question, with its implication that there was something to admit.

'He will. We are going to arrest him shortly.'

He paused, watching Tómas as he fiddled with the empty coffee cup in front of him. 'Tell us the truth, Tómas. You can stop protecting your father. It's too late for that.'

Tómas glanced at his lawyer, who was listening intently.

'OK. I don't know who your farmer witness saw, but it wasn't me.'

Magnus was tempted to argue, but held his tongue.

'I don't even know for sure whether my father did kill him, I really don't. But I do know that he has the ring, Gaukur's ring.'

'How do you know?' Magnus asked.

'He told me. About five years later, when I was eighteen. He said that he was looking after it for me. He told me the whole story, how it was the very same ring of Andvari from the Volsung saga. He showed it to me once.'

'So you've actually *seen* it?'

'Yes.'

'Did he tell you how he got it?'

Tómas hesitated. 'Yes. Yes, he did. He said that he and Dr Ásgrímur found it that weekend, and that Dr Ásgrímur was wearing it when he fell off the cliff. He said that he had taken it off Dr Ásgrímur's finger.'

'While he was lying dying at the bottom of the cliff?'

Tómas shrugged. 'I guess so. I don't know. It was either then, or when he came back for him with the farmers and found him dead.'

'Didn't that shock you?'

'Yes, it did.' Tómas swallowed. 'My father was always a bit strange. But he became much stranger after the doctor died. And, well . . .'

'Yes?'

'Well, I wouldn't be surprised if he had done something awful like take a ring off a dying man's finger.'

'What about killing that man?'

Tómas hesitated. Magnus glanced at Tómas's lawyer. She was letting him speak. As far as she was concerned her client was going some way towards exonerating himself.

Tómas took a deep breath. 'Yes. Like killing the doctor.'

'Did he admit he had done that?'

'No, not at all. Never.'

'Did you ever confront him?'

'No, absolutely not.' It was clear that the last thing on earth Tómas would do was confront his father.

'All right. So why were you visiting Agnar?' Magnus asked.

'Agnar approached me. We knew each other vaguely; we'd met at parties, had one or two mutual friends, you know how this town is?'

Magnus nodded.

'We met at a café. Agnar said that he had been approached by a wealthy American to buy Gaukur's ring. I acted dumb, but he went on. He said that he had just come back from Hruni, where he had spoken to Father. He said that although Father denied he had the ring, Agnar was sure he was lying.'

'Did he say why?'

'He did. It was ridiculous.' Tómas smiled to himself. 'He said it was because Father looked much younger than his age. In *Gaukur's Saga,* the warrior who bears the ring, Ulf something, is actually ninety, but looks much younger, and Agnar's theory was that the same thing was happening to Father—he wasn't getting any older.'

'I see what you mean,' said Magnus. 'That is a little weird.'

'I know. The problem was I laughed at him. It was a problem because right then Agnar could tell I knew what he was talking about. Basically, he tried to blackmail me. Or us.'

'How?'

'He said that unless Father sold him the ring he would go to the police and tell them about it and about Dr Ásgrímur's murder.'

'So what did you do?'

'I called Father. I told him what Agnar had said.'

'How did he take it?'

'He wasn't having any of it. We agreed how absurd it was that Agnar should think that Father had murdered Dr Ásgrímur. My father said we should call Agnar's bluff. So I went to look for him. I went to the university first, and then a student said he was at his summerhouse. So I drove out to Lake Thingvellir. I told Agnar that my father had no idea what he was talking about. I urged him to drop the blackmailing.'

'Urged?' said Magnus. 'Or threatened.'

'Urged. I pointed out that if Agnar went through with it, his clients certainly wouldn't get the ring. I kind of admitted I knew that Father had it.'

'What did Agnar say?'

'He looked at me for several seconds, thinking. Then he suggested that if Father was too stubborn to give up the ring of his own accord, I should steal it from him to keep him out of jail. I said I'd think about it.'

Magnus raised his eyebrows.

'Agnar had a point. I knew Father would never give up the ring, but I didn't want him to go to jail. I knew where Father kept it, and it would be easy to take it and sell it to Agnar.'

'So did you?'

'No. I drove straight home and sat down and thought about it. In the end I decided to call Father and tell him what Agnar had suggested.'

'And what did your father say?'

'He was angry. Very angry. He was upset that I had as good as admitted that he had the ring. Not at all grateful that I had stood by him.' There was anger in Tómas's voice. 'He lost it, basically.'

'So what did you do?'

'I was wound up. I had a drink to calm myself down.' Tómas winced. 'I ended up drinking most of a bottle of whisky. When I woke up next morning, I heard about Agnar's death on the radio.'

'When did you get home from Lake Thingvellir?'

'About half-past five or so.'

'And what time did you call your father?'

'About half an hour later, maybe an hour.'

The obvious question framed itself in Magnus's mind. 'So your father could have gone to Lake Thingvellir later that night? To shut Agnar up?'

Tómas didn't answer.

'Well?'

'I have no idea,' he said. But it was quite clear that the thought had occurred to him, too.

'One more question,' said Magnus. 'Where does your father hide the ring?'

'WELL DONE,' said Baldur as they left the interview room and walked rapidly towards his office. He didn't smile, he didn't even look at Magnus, but Magnus knew he meant it.

'Shall we go and arrest Hákon?' Magnus asked.

'We'll get the Selfoss police to arrest him and bring him here for interview,' said Baldur. 'They'll get there more quickly. And I'll ask them to search for that damned ring.'

When Magnus got back to his desk, Árni was there, looking exhausted.

'How's the Gubernator?' Magnus asked.

'Very funny. I hear things have been happening back here.'

'Baldur's sending the Selfoss police to arrest the pastor of Hruni now.'

'Do you think he killed Agnar?'

'Him or Tómas,' said Magnus. 'We'll find out which pretty soon.'

'So Isildur and Steve Jubb are innocent?'

'Looks like it,' said Magnus. And he explained all that had happened while Árni had been 35,000 feet up in the air.

Less than an hour later Baldur strode into the room, his face like thunder. 'He's gone,' he said.

'And the ring?'

'Gone as well. If it ever existed.'

IT HAD BEEN a frustrating twenty-four hours for Isildur. He was beginning to have his doubts about Axel, the PI he had hired. Pétur Ásgrímsson had been spectacularly unhelpful, his sister Ingileif seemed to have disappeared off the face of the earth, and Axel hadn't succeeded in finding out very much from his supposed contacts in the police. Tómas Hákonarson was under arrest for the murder of Agnar as there was evidence that he had been at Lake Thingvellir on the night in question, but the police were dismissing rumours of magic rings as mythology. Morons!

He and Gimli were waiting in the Hótel Borg for a call from Axel. In separate rooms. Despite the fact that they had formed such a close bond in the
virtual world, in the real one they had little in common. Isildur was reread-
ing the Volsung saga and Gimli was watching some sport on TV.

Isildur's cellphone rang. He checked the caller ID. It was Axel.

'I've found her,' the PI said. 'She's at her apartment.'

'Great! Let's go and talk to her.'

'I'll pick you up in five minutes.'

Isildur summoned Gimli and they waited outside the hotel. The square
was empty, other than pigeons. The Icelandic parliament building squatted
on the south side, a tough-looking building made of blackened stone.

Axel drew up in his old banger and they crammed inside. They were
soon outside Ingileif's building. Isildur took the lead and rang the bell.

A pretty blonde woman answered the door with a smile.

'Hi,' said Isildur, confident by now that a young Icelander would speak
English. 'My name's Lawrence Feldman. I'm the guy who was all set to
buy your saga. Can we come in?'

The smile disappeared. 'No, you may not,' said Ingileif. 'Go away. I want
nothing to do with you.'

'I'm still willing to pay a good price, Miss Ásgrímsdóttir.'

'I'm not going to discuss it with you.'

Isildur persisted. 'And if by any chance you know of the whereabouts of
the ring itself, I will pay you for that information.'

'Fuck off,' said Ingileif in crisp English, and slammed the door.

'Funny. That's exactly what her brother said,' said Gimli with a chuckle.

But Isildur didn't see the funny side. In his experience, if you waved
enough money, you could get what you wanted. They returned to the car.

'What now?' asked Gimli.

'Do you know much about electronic surveillance, Axel?' Isildur asked.
'Listening devices. Bugging phones, that kind of thing.'

'That's illegal,' said Axel.

'There's obviously a risk attached to it. Which means you deserve to get
paid extra. I just want to know what that woman knows. And if she's not
going to tell us then we're going to have to figure it out for ourselves.'

'I'll see what I can do.'

ÁRNI DROVE BACK to his apartment. He was dog tired, too tired really to drive. He almost ploughed into the back of a van that stopped at a light.

His mind drifted over the case and what Magnus had told him. There was something that wasn't quite right, something nagging at his brain. It wasn't until he was in his apartment and making himself a cup of coffee that he realised what it was. Oh, God. He'd made another mistake.

He was so tempted just to forget about it, crawl into bed, trust to Magnus and Baldur to figure everything out for themselves. But he couldn't. He had some people to talk to. And he had to talk to them right away. If he was lucky, he would be proved wrong.

He needed caffeine first.

As soon as he had finished his coffee, he grabbed his jacket and headed back out to his car.

DIEGO WAS NOT HAPPY. He had spent the bulk of the day knocking around the bus station, opposite police headquarters. He hadn't seen Magnus go in or out of the building. But then he didn't know for sure that Magnus wasn't in there, because there was an entrance in the back, where the parking lot was.

Plus he stuck out like a sore thumb, and Diego was used to blending in. In any American city he fitted right in. But this country was so god-damned white. There was no sign of a tan anywhere, and certainly not any brown skin.

This was stupid. He evaluated his options. He could go back to the Lithuanians. He knew they had been paid well by Soto to help him out. He understood that in a small place like this they wanted to make sure that they weren't associated with the hit, but surely they could put him in touch with a third party that could help him? A PI or a crooked lawyer. He didn't have much time. Jonson could be on a plane back to the States at any moment. Once there the Feds would keep him in a safe house until the trial.

He was sitting in the coffee shop at the station, on his fifth or sixth cup, his eyes flicking between the two front entrances. A big guy came out. A big guy with red hair. That was him! Diego left the half-empty cup of coffee and almost skipped out of the bus station.

To work.

MAGNUS HEADED UP the hill towards the Grand Rokk. It was eight thirty and he had the impression he wasn't needed any more that evening.

Baldur had been furious. Any positive thoughts he had held earlier about Magnus had been dispelled. Why hadn't Magnus called Baldur as soon as he realised that Hákon was Tómas's father? Why hadn't he stayed with Hákon at Hruni and waited for reinforcements to arrest the pastor?

Why had he let Hákon get away?

He had a point, of course. The reason that Magnus had waited until he returned to Reykjavík before telling him what Hákon had said was hardly noble. It was so that he and not Baldur would crack Tómas's story.

Which he had done. He had solved the case. Discovered not only who had killed Agnar, but also what had happened to Ingileif's father. The moment of victory had been sweet, but it had lasted only an hour.

There was no doubt about it, Magnus had screwed up.

At least that meant that the National Police Commissioner wouldn't demand that he stay in Iceland for the full two years that they had originally expected. They would be glad to be rid of him next week.

And he would be glad to go. Wouldn't he?

Clearly things were not going well with Baldur. But there were things he had liked about his brief time in Iceland. He did have an affinity with the country, even though memories of his early life here were painful. There was a loyalty, a sense of duty. The pride that Icelanders felt for their homeland, their determination to work their butts off to make the place function, was infectious.

The Commissioner's idea to recruit someone like Magnus wasn't a bad one. The police officers he had met were smart, honest, hard-working— even Baldur. They just lacked experience in big-city crime.

And then there was Ingileif. He felt their relationship was more than a quick roll in the hay. How much more, he didn't know. But he wanted to see her again before he went home. He gulped down his beer and left the bar.

DIEGO HAD FOUND HIMSELF a good spot, in the smokers' tent pitched outside in the front yard of the Grand Rokk. He had strolled in to get himself a beer at the bar, and had seen the big cop alone with his drink, absorbed in his own thoughts. Perfect.

There was one problem; Diego's car was still parked a couple of blocks from the bus station. He had followed Jonson on foot. There was no way that he was going to carry out the hit right then. He needed darkness to make good his escape. But it was still too light. He checked his watch. It was nearly nine thirty. Back home it would have got dark hours ago.

So he would follow Jonson. If he was still on the streets when it was dark enough he would do it then, otherwise he would follow him home and break in in the small hours of the morning.

Then he saw the big cop walk purposefully out of the bar, past the tent and out onto the street. Diego followed.

ÁRNI SAT IN HIS CAR, parked illegally just outside Eymundsson's Bookshop, and called the station. Magnus had left for the evening. Then he called Magnus's cellphone number. No reply—the phone was switched off. So then he called his sister's house.

'Have you seen Magnus this evening?' he asked Katrín.

'No, he's not here.'

'Any idea where he might be?'

'Not really. I think he goes to the Grand Rokk sometimes.'

'Thanks.' Árni hung up and drove rapidly up to the Grand Rokk.

He had to speak to Magnus. He had checked. He had made a mistake. He knew who had killed Agnar.

He stopped the car in the street right outside the bar and ran in. He flashed his badge at the barman and asked if he had seen Magnus. He had. The big man had left fifteen minutes before.

Árni jumped back into his car and headed up the hill towards the Hallgrímskirkja. He stopped at a junction. A man crossed in front of him wearing a baggy, hooded sweatshirt. The man was fairly tall, slim, with brown skin, walking determinedly. Árni knew him from somewhere.

He was the guy in the arrivals hall at Keflavík Airport. The American who had been met by the Lithuanian drug dealer.

It was a quiet road. The Hispanic guy had increased his pace to a brisk walk. He lifted up his hood.

As Árni crossed the junction heading uphill, he passed Magnus, who was shambling slowly along the street, head down, deep in thought. Árni was tired. It took him a couple of seconds to realise what was happening. He braked, slammed the car into reverse, and sped backwards down the hill. He crashed into a parked car, threw open the door and jumped out.

'Magnús!' he shouted.

Magnus spun round when he heard the sound of smashing metal. So did the Hispanic guy.

The guy was only twenty metres away, maximum. He was gripping something in the front pocket of his sweatshirt.

Árni charged. He saw the Hispanic's eyes widen. He saw him pull the gun out of his pocket. Raise it. Árni launched himself into midair just as the gun went off.

Magnus saw Árni leap out of his vehicle, heard him shout, saw him run towards the tall figure in the grey hoodie.

He rushed forwards just as Árni bowled the man over. He heard the sound of a gunshot, muffled by Árni's body. The man rolled away from Árni, and turned towards Magnus. Raised his gun from a prone position.

Magnus was about twenty feet away. There was a gap between two houses on his left. He jinked and dived through. Another gunshot and a ricochet of a bullet off metal siding. Magnus found himself in a back yard, other back yards ahead and to one side. He turned right and leaped at a six-foot-high fence. Swung his body over just as another shot rang out. But Magnus didn't want to run away from this guy. He wanted to nail him.

A floodlight burst into life, dazzling Magnus. The yard backed on to a more prosperous-looking house. Magnus searched for somewhere to hide. The floodlight was a couple of feet forward from the fence bordering the next yard along. He ran directly towards it, reached the fence and crouched down. He was in deep shadow. No chance of the man seeing him through the dazzling light.

The man appeared on top of the fence and dropped down. He paused to listen. Silence.

Magnus was breathing hard. He swallowed, trying to control it, to make sure he didn't make a sound.

The man peered round the garden. He had heard the silence. Heard the lack of running footsteps. He knew Magnus was in the yard. For a second he looked straight at Magnus. Magnus stayed motionless, praying that his theory about the light would hold. Cautiously the man examined a shrub. Then another. Then he stood still again, listening.

The floodlight was motion-activated. No motion, no light. It went out.

Magnus knew he had a second or two before the man's eyes adjusted to the darkness. He also knew that if he ran straight, the man would shoot at the sound and he would take a bullet. So he ran a couple of paces forwards and jinked to the left, a fullback slicing through the defence.

A shot rang out, the flame from the barrel illuminating the man's face for a fraction of a second. The man moved his gun to the right, pointed it straight at Magnus, aiming high.

So Magnus dived low, a football tackle directly at the man's knees. Another shot, just a little too high, and the man went down.

Magnus wriggled and lunged for the hand holding the gun. He grabbed the barrel, and twisted it up and towards the man. Another shot and the sound of broken glass from the house. A satisfying snap and a cry as a thumb broke, jammed in the trigger guard. The man's free hand reached over Magnus's face, grappling for his eyes. Magnus bucked and wrenched the gun away, rolling back and onto his feet.

He jabbed the gun into the man's face.

'Get up!' he shouted in English. 'Stand up, or I'll blow your head off!'

The man slowly got to his feet, his eyes on Magnus.

'Get your hands up! Move over here!'

Magnus could hear shouting in the house. 'Call the police,' he yelled in Icelandic. He pushed the man along the side of the house and out onto the street, shoving him against the wall. Now he had a problem. He wanted to tend to Árni, but he couldn't risk leaving the man uncovered.

'Turn round,' he said and, as the guy turned towards him, he transferred the gun to his left hand and whacked the man with a blow to the jaw with his right. The man crumpled. Out cold.

Magnus knelt down beside Árni. He was still alive, though his breath was coming in short gasps and there was a hole in his chest. But there wasn't that horrible wheezing sound of a sucking chest wound.

'It's OK, Árni. You'll be fine. Hang in there. You're not hit too bad.'

Árni's lips began to move. 'Magnus. Listen,' he whispered.

'Shh,' said Magnus. 'Quiet now. We'll get an ambulance here in no time.'

Someone had called the police; he could hear the sirens coming closer.

But Árni's lips continued to move. Magnus couldn't make out what he was trying to say, just the last word, which was something like 'Bye'.

'Hey, no need to say goodbye now. You're the Terminator, remember?'

Árni moved his head from side to side and tried to speak again. It was too much for him. The eyes closed. The lips stopped moving.

CHAPTER TEN

Magnus jumped into the police car that led the ambulance to the National Hospital, lights flashing, sirens blaring. It took less than five minutes. He was elbowed away by paramedics pushing Árni through corridors on a gurney towards the operating room.

He was shown into a small waiting room and began pacing. Uniformed police officers bustled about, Katrín was called.

Minutes later, Árni's sister burst in. 'How is he?' she asked.

'I don't know. They haven't said anything yet.'

'I've called Mum and Dad. They are on their way.'

'I'm sorry,' Magnus said.

Katrín looked him straight in the eye. 'Did you shoot him?'

'No.'

'Well, then you have nothing to be sorry about.'

Magnus shrugged. He wasn't about to take this moment to argue that it was he who had led a Dominican hit man to Iceland.

A doctor appeared, mid-forties, confident, competent but concerned. 'Are you next-of-kin?' she asked Katrín.

'I'm Árni's sister, yes.'

'He's lost quite a lot of blood. The bullet's still in there, right next to the heart. We're going to go in and get it out. It will take a while.'

'Will he be OK?'

The doctor looked Katrín in the eye. 'I don't know,' she said. 'He's got a chance. A good chance. Beyond that I can't say.'

'OK, don't waste time here,' Katrín said. 'Get on with it.'

Magnus was sure that Iceland had competent doctors. But he was worried that they would have little experience with gunshot wounds. Back home, at Boston Medical Center, they spent much of their Friday and Saturday nights plugging up bullet holes.

There was a commotion outside the waiting room and Baldur strode in. Magnus had seen Baldur angry before, but never this angry.

'How is he?' he asked.

'They're operating on him now,' Magnus said. 'The bullet's still in there somewhere and they're trying to fish it out.'

'Will he make it?'

'They hope so,' said Magnus.

'He'd better,' said Baldur. 'Now I've got some questions for you.' He turned to Katrín, disapproval all over his face. Although Katrín wasn't in full regalia, there was a sprinkling of metal sticking out of her face. 'Will you excuse us?' he said, and they moved out into the corridor.

'Do you know why one of my police officers was shot?' Baldur said.

'Yes. I'm a witness in a big police corruption trial in Boston. Some people there want me dead. Dominican drug traffickers. That's why I came here. Looks like they found me.'

'And why didn't you tell me about this?'

'The Police Commissioner thought that the fewer people who knew, the less chance there would be of a leak.'

'So *he* knew about it?'

'Of course.'

'If Árni dies, so help me I'll . . .' Baldur hesitated as he tried to think of a convincing threat.

'I've apologised to Árni's sister, and I will apologise to you,' Magnus said. 'I'm sorry that I led the hit man over here. I'm bad news. I should go.'

'Yes, you should. Starting now. I want you to leave this hospital, you can't do anything more here. Go back to the station and make a statement.'

Magnus didn't have the strength to argue. He badly wanted to stay and see how Árni was doing, but Baldur was right. He was a distraction.

He put his head into the waiting room. 'I've got to leave now,' he said to Katrín. 'Let me know if there's news, one way or the other.'

'The bald Gestapo officer sent you home, did he?'

Magnus nodded. 'He's a little wound up. Understandably.'

'Huh.' Katrín seemed unimpressed. 'I'll call you when there's news.'

MAGNUS SLEPT BADLY. No dreams, but he kept on expecting the phone to ring. He got up at six and called the hospital. He didn't want to ring Katrín's cellphone in case she had managed to snatch some sleep and he woke her. They had completed the operation and extracted the bullet. They were cautiously optimistic.

He walked down the hill to the police station. There were two or three detectives in the Violent Crimes room. He nodded to them and they smiled and nodded back.

Vigdís came over with a cup of coffee. 'I expect you need this.'

'Thank you,' Magnus said with a smile. And then, 'Sorry about Árni.'

'It wasn't your fault,' Vigdís said.

'Do we know who the shooter is?'

'No. We're pretty sure his passport is a fake. He's not talking.'

'He's a pro. He won't.' Magnus had given the detective who had taken his statement the night before all the information he could, including whom to contact in the Boston PD. It had been made very clear that Baldur didn't want him to interview the Dominican.

'Keep your eyes open,' said Vigdís. 'Now you haven't got Árni around to watch out for you any more.'

Magnus smiled. 'I will.' Vigdís was right. He ought to think of a place to lie low until he flew back to the States.

As Vigdís left, Magnus turned to his computer. He needed to tell the FBI and Williams what had happened himself. But before he began to type there was an incoming email, direct, not via the FBI.

Hey Magnus,

There's something I ought to tell you. A guy broke into my apartment a couple of nights ago and shoved a gun in my mouth. He wanted to know where you were. I kinda told him about the Reykjavík domain name on your email address.

I feel real bad about this. I haven't told the department, but I figured you needed to know so you could keep a lookout for trouble.

Johnny Yeoh

Anger flared in Magnus. He hit the reply key and began typing, but after a couple of words he stopped. He couldn't really blame Johnny. The gun was real. Although he could have warned Magnus sooner.

Magnus was really most angry with himself. He shouldn't have breached the FBI protocols. There was a reason they didn't want him sending emails directly to anyone in the States. A very good reason.

He deleted the half-written email and replaced it with a simple, 'Thanks for letting me know.' Johnny Yeoh would be in trouble anyway for not reporting the threat immediately. And all that would come out in time.

Magnus composed an email to Williams describing what had happened the night before, omitting for the moment the information that Johnny Yeoh had pointed the Dominicans to Iceland. As he pressed the send key, Baldur prowled into the room.

'What are you doing here?' he growled when he saw Magnus.

'It's where I work. At least for now.'

'We don't need spectators here. Have you made your statement?'

'Last night.'

'Then go home and stay home where we can get hold of you if we need you to add to it.'

'Have you found the Reverend Hákon?' Magnus asked.

'Not yet. But we will. He can't get out of the country.'

'Have you looked at Stöng? Or Álfabrekka? He's a strange man, a romantic in his way. He might go somewhere that's important to the ring.'

Baldur shook his head. 'If you think I am going to divert scarce resources into the middle of nowhere to satisfy your idiotic notions then . . .' He trailed off in frustration. 'Forget it. Go home.'

BUT MAGNUS DIDN'T GO HOME. He signed out a car and drove out towards Gaukur's abandoned farm at Stöng. It was a grey, windy day and the further east he drove the worse the weather became. A grey damp cloud had settled on Iceland, and he was driving through it. Even once he dropped down from the lava fields onto the sodden plain around Selfoss, visibility was poor.

He had no idea whether he really would find anything at Stöng or Álfabrekka. But he sure as hell didn't want to hang around Reykjavík doing nothing, and he didn't think his hunch was bad, as hunches went.

PÉTUR WATCHED the small team of Poles go at his car, scrubbing, polishing, washing away the dirt. He had overcome the urge to pay them double to do a good job; he didn't want them to remember him. Pétur usually kept a cool head, but he had almost missed the dirt. If the police had stopped by his apartment the night before and impounded his car, their forensics people would have been able to tell where he had been the previous afternoon.

And the problem with a white BMW four-by-four was that it stuck out, even in the land of expensive four-by-fours. Inga had certainly noticed it as he had sped past her the day before.

Which was why he had called her cellphone immediately and asked her not to mention it. He hoped to God she hadn't said anything.

Searching for comfort, his hand closed round the object stuck deep in the warm pocket of his coat. A ring.

The ring.

BUT INGILEIF hadn't told anyone. She had been surprised when she had seen Pési driving up the Thjórsárdalur; she couldn't think of any reason why he should be there. But her instinct was not to mention it to Magnus. She told herself it wasn't important but she didn't ask herself why, if it wasn't important, she hadn't mentioned it.

She had to find out whether Hákon really had killed her father, or indeed whether it was Tómas. She thought it unlikely that it was Tómas, but she didn't *know*. She did know someone who would. Tómas's mother.

Her name was Erna, and Ingileif trusted her. She had originally come from a village in the West Fjords where she had met Hákon when he had been serving as a priest there. Ingileif remembered the way Erna always seemed to submit to her husband's will. But she was basically an honest, kind, sensible woman. It must have taken a lot of courage for her to leave her husband when she did, but it was definitely a wise decision.

She would know if her son or her husband had killed the doctor.

So Ingileif drove her Polo out to Hella, a town about fifty kilometres to the south of Flúdir, where Erna lived with her second husband.

The drive was unpleasant in the fog, but at least there wasn't much traffic on the road. She listened to the news on the radio, hoping for more information about Tómas. There was none of that. But there was something about a policeman being wounded and taken to hospital, and an American citizen being held by the police.

For a moment, a dreadful moment, Ingileif thought that the policeman was Magnus. But then they named him as Detective Árni Holm and she breathed again, though she was absolutely sure Magnus would have been involved somehow.

Hella was a modern settlement that lined the bank of the West Ranga river. Ingilief had looked up Erna's address from a phone-directory website; her house was a single-storey building, only thirty metres from the river.

When Ingileif rang the doorbell, Erna answered. She recognised Ingileif immediately and ushered her in. Erna's hair was still blonde, but dyed nowadays, and she had put on weight. But her blue eyes twinkled when she saw Ingileif, although they swiftly clouded again with worry. 'Have you heard the dreadful news about Tómas?' she said, as she busied herself in the kitchen organising coffee.

'I have,' said Ingileif. 'It's all over the papers. Have you seen him?'

'No. The police won't let me. I've spoken to his lawyer on the phone. She says that the police don't have enough evidence to prove anything, that it all had something to do with a manuscript this Agnar fellow was trying to sell. Here, Ingileif, let's go through and sit down.'

The sitting room boasted a large window opening out on a view of the river, barely visible through the mist.

'It has to do with our family, Erna. And with your husband.'

'Oh. I feared as much.'

'The manuscript is an old saga that had been in my family for generations. *Gaukur's Saga*. Did Hákon ever mention it to you?'

'Not directly. But that's what he spent so much time discussing with your father, isn't it?'

'That's correct. And when my mother died at the end of last year I decided to sell the saga, through Professor Agnar. And the police think that it was for this saga that Agnar was killed.'

'I still don't understand what this has to do with Tómas.'

'It all goes back to my father's death.'

'Ah.' Erna was wary now.

'I'm sure that the police will ask you questions about it soon. Perhaps today,' said Ingileif. 'And I promise I won't tell them what you tell me. But I want to know what happened to my father. I *need* to know.'

'It was an accident,' said Erna. 'Hákon witnessed it. A terrible accident. There was a police investigation and everything.'

'Did Hákon tell you what he and my father were doing that weekend?'

'No. He was very secretive about it and frankly I wasn't interested.'

'Did he ever mention a ring?'

'A ring? No. What kind of ring?'

Erna seemed genuinely puzzled. Ingileif took a deep breath. The questions were going to get more painful, there was no way of avoiding it.

'It was a ring that was mentioned in *Gaukur's Saga*, the manuscript the professor who was murdered was trying to sell. You see, the police believe that my father and your husband found the ring that weekend.'

'He never mentioned it. And I never saw a ring. But it is just the kind of thing that would fascinate him. And there was *something*. Something hidden in the altar in the church. I saw him sneak in there several times.'

'Did you ever look to see what it was?' Ingileif asked.

'No. Hákon had rather unconventional interests,' Erna shuddered. 'I was scared about what I might find.'

'The police think that my father may have been killed for the ring.'

'By whom?' said Erna. 'Not by Hákon, surely?'

'That's what they think.' Ingileif swallowed. 'That's what I think.'

Erna looked shocked. Shock turned to anger. 'I know that he is eccentric. But I am absolutely sure he didn't kill your father. Despite all his fascination with the devil, he wouldn't kill anyone. And . . .'

A tear appeared in Erna's eye.

'And?'

'And your father was the only true friend Hákon ever had. Sometimes I think, well, I *know*, that Hákon was fonder of him than of me. He was quite broken up by your father's death. It almost destroyed him.' She sniffed. 'He started behaving even more strangely, neglecting his parish duties. He became impossible to live with after that. Impossible.'

Ingilief realised that she would get no further on the subject of Hakon. She still thought that he had killed her father, but she was convinced that Erna didn't and she didn't feel the need to argue with her.

'But what has all this got to do with Tómas?'

'The police think he was there with Hákon and my father. The farmers who Hákon went to for help saw him. Or at least they saw a boy.' Ingileif didn't want to confuse the issue with talk of hidden people.

'Oh, that really is too absurd,' said Erna. 'Do they think *Tómas* killed Dr Ásgrímur? But he was only twelve then!'

'Thirteen,' said Ingileif. 'And, yes, they do think he was there. He might have witnessed what happened at the very least.'

'That's ridiculous,' said Erna. 'It must have been someone else.' And then her eyes lit up. 'Wait a minute. It can't have been Tómas!'

'Why not?'

'Because he was with me that weekend. In Reykjavík. He was singing in the Hallgrímskirkja with the village choir. I went to listen. We stayed with my sister in Reykjavík that Saturday night.'

'Are you sure?'

'Oh, I'm quite sure. We didn't get back until Sunday evening. Hákon had only just got back from the hills. He was in a terrible state.' She smiled at Ingileif. 'You see. My son is innocent!'

THE THREE MEN were squashed into Axel's car again, parked a hundred metres down the road from the house that Ingileif had entered. Axel was at the wheel, Isildur was in the back, and Gimli was in the passenger seat, a computer opened on his lap. Axel had planted four bugs on Ingileif when he had broken in in the small hours of the previous night. One in her bag, one in her coat, one in her studio bedroom—that had been the trickiest—and one in the car. The bug in the car doubled as a tracking device, and the location of the car was flashing on the GPS map on the computer.

The tracker had allowed them to follow Ingileif at a safe distance all the way from Reykjavík to Hella. They had driven past the house at which she had stopped and then parked out of sight. The bug in the coat was transmitting loud and clear through a receiver that was plugged into the laptop. Axel mumbled half-translations as he listened.

When Axel started muttering about a ring, Isildur couldn't contain his impatience to find out more, but Axel refused to explain further, not wanting to miss any of the conversation.

As soon as Ingileif left the house, Isildur asked Axel for a translation.

Axel pulled the computer off Gimli's lap and tapped some keys. The conversation was recorded on the computer's hard drive. He went through the whole thing slowly and methodically.

Isildur was beside himself with excitement. 'Where's this church?' he demanded. 'The place where the ring is hidden?'

'I don't know,' said Axel. 'The nearest church to Hella is a place called Oddi. It's not far.'

'It sounds like they were neighbours when Ingileif was young,' said Gimli. 'This Hákon is obviously Tómas Hákonarson's father. Do we know where he was born? Where he grew up? It sounded to me as if this Erna woman had moved out, or moved away.'

'Google him,' said Isildur. 'Tómas Hákonarson. If he's a big star in this country, there will be a bio on him somewhere.'

Axel called up the search engine, tapped out some words, clicked and scrolled. 'Here he is. He was brought up in Flúdir, not far from here.'

'Well, let's go to Flúdir church, then!' said Isildur. 'Get a move on!'

Axel handed the laptop back to Gimli and started up the car.

'Hruni is the nearest church to Flúdir,' said Axel. 'This man must be the pastor of Hruni.' He grinned.

'What's so special about that?'

'Let's just say it fits.'

As Magnus drove up the Thjórsá valley towards Mount Hekla, the landscape became bleaker. Grass gave way to black rock and mounds of sand, like the detritus of a massive abandoned coalfield. The river flowed past the rounded lump of stone several hundred feet high known as Búrfell, home to trolls in the old folk tales. Just beyond, Magnus came to a junction and two signs. One said: STÖNG. The other: ROAD CLOSED.

Magnus turned. It wasn't a road. It wasn't even a track. There were twists, turns, steep hills, sharp drops. Mist swirled around Magnus as he cajoled his car through the blackened terrain. Below and to the left, a tributary of the Thjórsá surged. Once or twice, Magnus debated turning back. But of course Hákon's four-wheel-drive would have had an easier time of it.

Then he rounded a bend and saw it. The red Suzuki. It was parked on a brief stretch of road fifty feet above the river. Magnus pulled up next to it.

He climbed out of his car, and walked over to the Suzuki. Empty. He tried the door handle. Unlocked. No keys in the ignition. Perhaps Hákon had abandoned the car here to walk on to Stöng on foot? A possibility, but Hákon was an Icelander and he was driving a four-wheel-drive. He was unlikely to give up that easily.

The man was crazy, Magnus knew that. He could have set out on a long hike to God-knows-where over the bleak landscape. To the cave near Álfabrekka, perhaps? To Mount Hekla? He could be away for days.

Magnus looked around the Suzuki for footprints. There were some, but they were muddled. He moved away from the vehicle in expanding circles, but the ground was too hard to betray which direction Hákon might have taken. He did find something of interest, though.

Tyre marks. About thirty feet away from the Suzuki, on a small patch of soft ground. Another car had parked there. But when?

He debated whether to drive on to Stöng. He recalled the abandoned farm from his childhood. It lay in a small patch of green by a stream. But first he had to report what he had seen to Baldur.

He pulled out his phone. No signal. He decided to drive back towards the main road until he found a signal to make the call.

After a bone-shattering two kilometres, his phone, which he had placed on the seat beside him, began to ring. He pulled over and picked it up.

'Hi, Magnús, it's Ingileif.'

'Hello,' said Magnus, pleased that it was her.

'Are you OK?'

'Yes, I'm fine.'

'It's just I heard on the radio this morning that there had been a shooting. A police officer was in hospital. An American had been arrested. I assumed one of the two was you.'

'Yeah, it happened right after I dropped you off at your place last night. My partner Árni was shot. I got the guy who did it.'

'And he was after you?'

'He was after me.'

There was a brief silence. Then Ingileif spoke again. 'I've just been to see Erna, Tómas's mother. She lives in Hella.'

'Oh, yes?'

'She is sure that Tómas didn't kill my father. He couldn't have been there. He was singing with the village choir in the Hallgrímskirkja in Reykjavík that weekend.'

'Or so she says. She is his mother, remember?'

'That can be checked, though, can't it? Even seventeen years later?'

'Yes, it can,' admitted Magnus. Ingileif was right. It was an unlikely lie.

'She also told me where Hákon hides the ring.'

'In the altar in the church?'

'How do you know?'

'Tómas told me yesterday.'

'Have you found him? Hákon?'

'No. But I've found his car. On the road to Stöng. He must have met someone. I found another set of tyre tracks nearby.'

There was silence at the other end of the phone. For a moment Magnus thought the connection had been dropped. The signal was still poor. 'Ingileif? Ingileif, are you there?'

'Yes, I'm here. Bye, Magnús.' And she was gone.

PÉTUR WAS UNDER HIS CAR, wiping the chassis with a cloth, when his phone rang. He had driven home from the car wash, grabbed a cloth and a bucket and then parked in a residential street a kilometre away. He didn't want his neighbours to see him washing his car so carefully.

He rolled out from under the BMW and answered it.

'Pési? It's Inga.'

He scrambled to his feet. He needed to gather his wits for this conversation.

'Inga! Hi! How are you?'

'Why didn't you want me to say I saw you yesterday?'

'You were with that big cop, weren't you?'

'Yes. We had just been to see the farmers who went to look for Dad with Hákon. Pési, I am pretty sure that Dad was killed. It wasn't an accident.'

'I thought we had agreed to leave all that alone,' he said. 'Why were you talking to the cops about it? What could it achieve?'

'Pési, where were you going yesterday?'

Pétur took a deep breath. 'I can't say, Inga. I'm sorry.'

'That won't do, Pési. I need to know what's going on here. Were you going to meet Hákon? On the road to Stöng?'

'Look, where are you now?'

'Just outside Hella.'

'OK. You're right. You do deserve an explanation. But not over the phone. We need to do this face to face.'

'OK. I'll be back in Reykjavík this afternoon.'

'No, not here. You remember where Dad used to take us for picnics? The spot he said was his favourite place in Iceland?'

'Yes.'

'OK, meet me there. In, say, an hour and a half.'

'Why there?'

'I often go there, Inga. It's where Dad is. I go there to talk to him. And I want him to be there when I talk to you.'

There was silence on the other end of the phone. Ingileif would know that such sentimentalism was unlike Pétur, but then she also knew how much their father's death had affected him.

'OK. An hour and a half.'

'See you then. And promise me you won't say anything to the police. At least until after I've had a chance to explain things.'

'I promise.'

Now he had a signal, Magnus called Baldur.

'I've found Hákon's car,' he said, before the inspector had a chance to hang up on him.

'Where?'

'On the road to Stöng. There's no sign of him though.'

'I'll send a team up to look at it.'

'And to search for him,' said Magnus.

'That won't be necessary.'

'Why not? Have you found him?'

'Yes. At the bottom of the Hjálparfoss. A body was discovered there by a power worker half an hour ago. A large man wearing a clerical collar.'

Hjálparfoss was a waterfall only a kilometre or so from the turnoff to Stöng. Magnus had seen a sign to it.

'He could have jumped,' said Baldur.

'I don't think so,' said Magnus. 'I saw tyre tracks next to the Suzuki. He was pushed.'

'Well, don't go back to the scene,' said Baldur. 'I don't want you taking any further part in this investigation. I'm on my way to Hjálparfoss now and you had better not be there when I arrive.'

Magnus felt the urge to snap back. He had had the hunch that Hákon had driven to Stöng. He had found the car. But he held his tongue.

'Glad I could be of assistance.' Well, almost held his tongue.

It would take Baldur at least an hour, probably more like two to get to Hjálparfoss from Reykjavík, which gave Magnus plenty of time.

He drove back to the turnoff to Hjálparfoss. After a few hundred metres, the waterfall itself appeared, two powerful torrents of water divided by a basalt rock, tumbling into a pool. A police car with lights flashing was parked down by the bank of the river below the waterfall, and a small group of three or four people were clustered round something.

Magnus parked next to the police car and introduced himself. The officers were friendly and stood back to let him take a look at the body.

It was Hákon, all right. Magnus looked at the pastor of Hruni's fingers.

They were bare.

MAGNUS DROVE BACK towards Reykjavík. This changed things. This definitely changed things. It looked very much as if someone had killed Hákon. It wasn't Tómas; he was locked up safe and sound. So who was it?

Steve Jubb and Lawrence Feldman?

Since he had arrived in Iceland, Magnus had heard about a lot of people who had suffered sudden death over the years. Not just Agnar and now Hákon. But also Dr Ásgrímur. And even Ingileif's stepfather.

Too many in such a peaceful country to be a coincidence.

Another fall. Another drowning. And there were only two people who were linked to *all* these deaths. A brother and a sister. Pétur and Ingileif.

Magnus dismissed Ingileif. But Pétur?

He had alibis. He was at high school in Reykjavík when his father had died. But perhaps he had been able to get out that weekend without anyone knowing? Perhaps he was the hidden man that the old farmer had seen? He was supposed to have been in London when his stepfather had been killed, but he could easily have flown back to Reykjavík for a couple of days without anyone knowing. If he had heard of what the man had done to his sister, Birna, he might have been moved to take revenge.

But what about Agnar's murder? Pétur had an alibi for that. He was at his clubs all night, Árni had checked it out.

Magnus slammed his palm on the steering wheel. Árni! That was what he had been trying to say before he lost consciousness. Not 'Goodbye' but 'Alibi'. He was trying to tell Magnus about Pétur's alibi.

Magnus could imagine what had happened. Árni had been round each of Pétur's three clubs and had received assurances that Pétur had been seen there at some point on the evening of the murder. He hadn't crosschecked times, drawn up a precise time line of exactly where Pétur was during that night. It was just the kind of sloppy mistake he would make.

Pétur had made sure he was seen in the early part of the evening and then driven up to Lake Thingvellir, arriving after nine thirty when Steve Jubb had left. Perhaps he waited for an hour or so after he had killed Agnar until it was dark, before carrying him down to the lake. That would explain the signs of flies on the body in the summerhouse. Then, of course, he would still have time to get back to his clubs in the early hours of the morning.

Four deaths. And Pétur was responsible for all of them.

Magnus accelerated towards Reykjavík. He wanted to call Ingileif. Of course she was Pétur's sister, her first loyalty was to him. But she wouldn't shield a murderer. Or would she?

Magnus called her number. 'Ingileif? It's me, Magnus. Where are you?'

'I'm on the road to Flúdir.'

The road from Hella to Flúdir passed the turnoff up the Thjórsá valley.

'I need to talk to you. I'm pretty close. If you pull over and tell me where you are, I'll find you.'

'I can't, Magnús, I have an appointment. No, I'm sorry.'

'Ingileif, where's Pétur?' he asked.

'I don't know.' Her voice was quieter, less belligerent. She was lying.

'Where are you going?' Magnus asked. 'Are you going to meet him?'

Ingileif hung up.

A police car screamed by, lights flashing, towards the pastor's body.

Magnus remembered the way Ingileif had suddenly stiffened on that very same road the day before. As though she had seen something. Perhaps the driver of a passing car? Pétur?

Magnus called Ingileif back. She didn't pick up the phone but he left her a message that Hákon's body had been found downstream from his car. If she was meeting her brother, that was something she needed to know.

He carried on driving. It was still a few kilometres to the junction where he could turn left for Reykjavík or right for Flúdir. But first he needed to tell Baldur about Pétur.

He called Baldur's cellphone. No reply. The bastard wasn't picking him up. He tried Vigdís. She, at least, would listen to him.

'Vigdís, I need you to go and arrest Pétur Ásgrímsson.'

'Why?'

Magnus explained. Vigdís listened, asking one or two pertinent questions. 'Makes sense to me,' she said. 'Have you told Baldur?'

'He won't take my call.'

'I'll speak to him.'

Magnus's phone rang again a minute later. It was Vigdís.

'He won't authorise me to arrest Pétur,' she said. 'He says there have been too many early arrests made in this investigation.'

'It's only because I suggested it,' Magnus said bitterly.

'I can't comment on that,' said Vigdís. 'But I do know I can't arrest Pétur if my chief told me not to.'

'No, of course not. I'm putting you in a difficult situation. The thing is, I think he's going to meet his sister. I think she's on to him. I'm worried that if they do meet, he might try to keep her quiet. Permanently.'

'Aren't you jumping to a few too many conclusions there?'

Magnus frowned. He was concerned about Ingileif, especially after what had happened to Colby. 'Maybe,' he admitted. 'But I'd rather jump to too many than to too few.'

'Look. I'll see if I can find Pétur at his clubs or at his house. OK?'

'Thanks,' he said. 'I appreciate it.'

Magnus approached the junction. With Vigdís looking for Pétur in Reykjavík, Magnus could afford to concentrate on Ingileif.

He turned right for Flúdir.

PÉTUR COULD BARELY SEE Lake Thingvellir in the gloom ahead of him. It was just over a week since he had last been there. A week in which plenty had happened. A week in which he had lost control.

It was all Inga's fault.

He was nervous about meeting her now. He would explain everything. He knew she looked up to him as a reliable big brother. Perhaps that would mean that she would understand why he had killed Sigursteinn. That man had deserved to die because of what he had done to Birna.

Agnar would be harder to explain. As would Hákon. But Pétur had had no choice. Inga was smart, she would understand that.

He was losing control. He had covered his tracks well with Agnar. Not so well with Hákon. And with Inga? He hoped to God that she understood. That she would keep quiet. Because if she didn't, what then?

Pétur fumbled in his pocket for the ring. He felt a sudden urge to examine it. He pulled over to the side of the road and killed the engine.

He examined the ring. It didn't *look* a thousand years old. He peered at the inside rim. He could make out the shapes of runes. What was it they were supposed to say? *Andvaranautur.* The Ring of Andvari.

The ring. It was the ring that had destroyed his family. Once Högni had found it, they were doomed. It had obsessed his father and caused his death. It had briefly obsessed Pétur before he had tried to put it behind him. It had obsessed Agnar and it had obsessed Hákon. No, *possessed* Hákon.

Only his grandfather, Högni, had had the courage to put the ring back where it belonged. Out of reach of men.

Pétur had spent his whole life struggling against the power of the ring. He should face facts. He had lost. The ring had won. Pétur slipped the ring on his finger. If Inga refused to keep quiet, she would have to die. That was all there was to it.

MAGNUS DROVE FAST to Flúdir. The driveway in front of Ingileif's house was empty. He jumped out of his car and rang the doorbell. Nothing. He stood back and examined the windows. No signs of life. It was a gloomy day, and if there was anyone inside they would have needed at least one light on.

Damn! Where the hell was she?

He climbed back into his car, searching for inspiration. If she had driven

back to meet Pétur in Reykjavík, Magnus should have spotted her—he had
kept an eye out for her among the drivers he had met coming the other way.
There wasn't much to the north of Flúdir. But to the east was Hruni.
Perhaps she had gone there. Either to meet Pétur, or to look for the ring.

The turnoff to Hruni was just to the south of the village. He sped the
three kilometres in two minutes. A police car was parked in front of
the church, with a single officer in the front seat.

He recognised Magnus and greeted him.

'Have you seen Ingileif Ásgrímsdóttir?' Magnus asked. 'Blonde woman,
late twenties?'

'No. And I've been here since eight this morning.'

'Damn!'

'Did you hear they've found Hákon's body?' the constable said.

'Yeah, I've seen it, at the bottom of Hjálparfoss. But I'm worried that
whoever killed the pastor is after Ingileif.'

'I'll radio in if I see her.'

'Can you call me on my cell?' Magnus said, giving him his number.

'You could ask those guys back there.'

Magnus turned. A car was parked by the side of the road overlooking the
church and the rectory. 'Who are they?'

'Three men. One Icelander and two foreigners. I asked them what they
were doing, and they didn't have an answer, or not one that made any sense.'

Feldman and Jubb, Magnus thought. 'They're waiting for you to leave so
they can search the church,' he said. 'Thanks, I'll go and speak with them.'

He drove up to the car. There was a small Icelander in the driver's seat,
with Jubb next to him and Feldman in the back. They looked distinctly
uncomfortable to see Magnus.

Magnus got out of his vehicle and approached theirs.

The Icelander wound down his window. 'Hello, Lawrence, Steve,'
Magnus said in English, nodding to the two foreigners.

'Afternoon, officer,' said Lawrence from the back seat.

'And you are?' Magnus asked the Icelander.

'Axel Bjarnason. I'm a private investigator, working for Mr Feldman.'

Magnus was about to tell them that they were wasting their time, the ring
wasn't there, when he thought better of it. Let them spend all day searching.

'Have any of you seen Ingileif Ásgrímsdóttir?' he asked.

Axel's expression of patient disinterest didn't change. Jubb frowned.

'No, officer, we haven't,' Feldman said. 'At least, not today. We tried to speak with her yesterday, but she wasn't real excited to see us.'

'I'm not surprised,' said Magnus.'If you do see her, let me know.' He scribbled his number onto a piece of paper torn from his notebook and gave it to Feldman. 'The pastor has just been found. Murdered. I'm pretty sure the guy who did it is after Ingileif right now.'

Feldman took the paper. 'We'll be sure to call you,' he said.

Magnus turned to look at the church, squatting beneath the crags in the mist. 'Enjoy your day,' he said, and jumped back into his vehicle. He sped off down the hill, back to the main road.

He must have missed her coming the other way. Reykjavík. His best bet was Reykjavík.

CHAPTER ELEVEN

Steve Jubb watched the cop's car disappear over the hill. 'You know this isn't right.'

'What isn't right, Gimli?' Feldman said.

'For a start, my name isn't Gimli, it's Steve. And your name isn't Isildur, it's Lawrence. This isn't Middle Earth, it's Iceland. *The Lord of the Rings* isn't real, it's a story. A bloody good story, but a story nonetheless.'

'But Gimli, the ring could be in that church! The ring from the Volsung saga. The ring that Tolkien wrote about. Don't you realise how cool that is!'

'Frankly, I don't give a toss. That professor I spoke to only a week ago is dead. A vicar is dead. There's a nutter running round out there who's looking to kill a girl. A real live person, Lawrence, don't you get that?'

'Hey, it's got nothing to do with us,' said Feldman.

'Look. That copper is looking for Ingileif. We know where she is. We should tell him.' Jubb took out his cellphone. 'Give me his number.'

'No, Gimli. No.'

'Jesus!' exclaimed Jubb. He jumped out of the car, flung open the back door and hauled Feldman out. Jubb clenched his fist. 'Give me that number or I'll smash yer face in.'

Feldman cowered on the ground and handed the big Yorkshireman the scrap of paper bearing Magnus's number.

Jubb went round to the driver's side. 'Are you with me?' he asked Axel.

'The problem is, Steve, that bugging the girl's car wasn't strictly legal.'

Jubb didn't wait to argue. He leaned in, grabbed the private investigator, and flung him into the road. He jumped into the driver's seat and started up the engine. With Feldman and Axel hammering on the side of the car, he executed a quick three-point turn and sped off after the copper.

MAGNUS SLOWED as he reached the junction of the main road just south of Flúdir. His cellphone chirped.

'Hello?'

'This is Steve Jubb. Just wait where you are! I'm right behind you.'

'All right,' said Magnus. He *knew* Feldman and Jubb had known more than they were saying. 'I'll be waiting.'

Magnus pulled over to the side of the road. Within two minutes he saw the private investigator's car fly down the road towards him. It pulled in behind him, and Steve Jubb jumped out, carrying a laptop under his arm.

Alone.

He climbed into the passenger seat next to Magnus.

'Hang on,' he said, switching on the laptop, and a receiver attached to it. 'This will tell us where Ingileif is.'

'Excellent,' said Magnus. 'Where are your friends?'

'Tossers,' muttered Jubb, as he fiddled with the computer.

Magnus wasn't exactly sure what a tosser was, but he was prepared to take Jubb's word for it. He peered at the computer screen on Jubb's lap. It displayed a map of southwest Iceland, and it showed a round circle moving north along a road on the other side of Flúdir.

'So you bugged her car?'

Jubb just grunted and carried on tapping at the keyboard.

'Where the hell is she going?' Magnus asked. 'There's nothing up there. Take a look at the map. There's one in the glove compartment.'

Jubb pulled out a map. 'You're right, there's not much north of here. The road goes right the way across the middle of the country.'

'It'll still be closed at this time of year,' Magnus said.

'Wait a minute. There's something here. Gullfoss? Know what that is?'

'It's a waterfall,' said Magnus. 'A massive waterfall.'

PÉTUR PULLED into the large car park. This early in the season, and in this weather, it was empty.

He climbed out of his BMW. The enormous waterfall roared at him, unseen, from beyond the far side of the tourist information centre, but rather than heading straight down towards the waterfall, Pétur turned left, upstream. There was now a maintained path leading up the low hill; in his childhood it had been no more than a narrow sheep track.

Just over the crest of the hill was a shallow hollow. It was here that Dr Ásgrímur had liked to take his family for a picnic on sunny days. The hollow, above the falls, offered some privacy, even in the height of summer. At the beginning of May, in the mist, there was no sign of anyone.

Pétur walked towards the river. The dull roar turned into a crescendo as the magnificent waterfall opened out beneath him. Its power was extraordinary. The Hvítá flung itself down into the gorge in two stages, at each throwing up a thick curtain of spray. The resultant tumult was known as Gullfoss, 'golden waterfall', because of the tricks of light that low sunshine could play on the fine moisture suspended above the cauldron. In the right conditions, rainbows danced gold and purple over the falls.

Pétur stood and waited for Ingileif.

He was pleased with his choice of meeting place. Like the road to Stöng. Pétur had tempted Hákon out to that remote spot with a far-fetched tale of how he knew where the helm of Fafnir was hidden. He remembered the look of excitement and expectation on the pastor's face as he led him down to the river, and then paused to let him pass. A blow on the back of the head with a rock, and the pastor had tumbled: it was all that Pétur had been able to do to stop him from falling straight into the water. He held him back just long enough to ease the ring off his finger, and then tipped him into the torrent. He wondered what the police would think when they found the body, or more likely his car. An accident? Suicide, perhaps?

That was an idea. If the worst came to the worst, and Inga ended up in the waterfall, Pétur could claim she had killed herself. He had received a call from her. She was distraught, upset by feelings of betrayal at trying to sell *Gaukur's Saga*. She told him that she was going to Gullfoss. He feared suicide, and drove up to stop her. But he was too late. He saw her jump.

That would explain his own presence at the waterfall. It would be close enough to the truth that he could carry it off.

He fiddled with the ring on his finger. He was getting ahead of himself. As long as he managed to explain things properly to Inga, she would understand him, she would realise he had had no other choice. Wouldn't she?

MAGNUS AND STEVE JUBB sped through Flúdir and into the farmland beyond, dotted with domed greenhouses, all emitting spirals of volcanic steam. The road soon ran alongside the Hvítá, in full spate.

'I've been a daft bugger,' Jubb said. 'Somehow I thought that Agnar croaking had nothing to do with me. I knew I was innocent but I hoped I could keep the existence of the saga and the ring secret.'

'I thought you had killed the professor,' said Magnus.

'I know you thought that. But I also knew I hadn't. And I guessed you'd figure that out in the end.'

'Have you had any dealings with Pétur at all?'

'Never,' Jubb said. 'I hadn't met the bloke till the other day when I saw him with Lawrence Feldman. That man is weird, by the way.'

'And you're not?' said Magnus.

'There's nothing wrong with being a *Lord of the Rings* fan,' Jubb said defensively. 'What *is* wrong is when you let it blind you to what's going on in the real world.'

Magnus's phone rang. Vigdís.

'I can't find Pétur at his house or at Neon. They haven't seen him there all day. I'm just going to check the other two clubs.'

'Don't bother,' said Magnus. 'He's heading to Gullfoss. He's going to meet his sister there. And then he's going to kill her.'

'Are you sure?'

He hesitated. How sure was he? He had made mistakes earlier in this investigation. 'Yeah, I'm sure. Can you call in a SWAT team? The cloud's probably too low for a helicopter, but the sooner they get here the better.'

'I will call Baldur. But you and I both know what he's going to say.'

'Damn it!' Magnus knew Baldur would ignore his request. 'Can you come yourself, Vigdís?'

A pause. 'All right. I'm on my way.'

'And bring a weapon.'

'I'll be there as quick as I can. Unarmed.' She hung up.

'Careful!' Steve Jubb flinched as he shouted the warning.

Magnus nearly swerved off the road as he took a bend too fast with only one hand on the wheel. As they were moving north, the road was already deteriorating. Stones slammed against the floor of the car like bullets.

'She's stopped at Gullfoss!' Jubb said, staring at his screen.

After careering over some foothills, they descended to cross a narrow gorge at a small suspension bridge and then found themselves on a better road speeding across flat moorland into the fog.

PÉTUR SAW the familiar figure of his sister emerge from the gloom over the lip of the hollow. She walked in the same way she had when she was a girl—her coat was even the same colour. It brought back memories of those family picnics, before everything had been ruined. Pétur felt a sudden surge of affection for his little sister. She wouldn't let him down. She couldn't possibly let him down. He raised a hand to greet her.

'Why the hell are we meeting here?' she said, shivering.

'It's the right place,' said Pétur gravely. 'It's the right place to talk about Dad.' This wasn't starting well.

'What I want to know is what you were doing driving up to Stöng yesterday. They found Hákon's body, you know. At Hjálparfoss.'

'I'll tell you about that. But I want to tell you about Dad first.'

'My God!' said Ingileif. 'You know how he died, don't you?'

Pétur nodded. 'I was with them that weekend. With the pastor and Dad.'

'I thought you were at school.'

'I know. Dad wanted me to come with him on the expedition. He was convinced they would find the ring. I was in two minds about it. As I told you, I was dead against them taking the ring—I remembered Grandpa's warnings. But in the end, he persuaded me.

'The trouble was, Mum had forbidden it. So we didn't tell her. I took the bus to Hella from Reykjavík and they picked me up there.'

'We camped out on the hills and then the next morning we got to the cave. It wasn't really a cave, more of a hole in the lava. It took us three hours to find it, but it was Dad who discovered it. He was so excited!' Pétur smiled at the memory. 'And who can blame him? It was amazing. There was this ring, covered in a small film of dust. It's not that it was shining or anything, you had to rub it to tell it was gold. But there was the proof that *Gaukur's Saga* was actually true . . . Amazing.'

'But after a few minutes I told Dad we had to put it back. I talked about all the evil it would bring the world, how Grandpa had told me to make sure that Dad never took it. We had a major row. I even tried to grab the ring off him, but he pushed me aside.'

'I had kind of ruined everything,' Pétur said. 'They walked on together and I followed twenty metres behind, sulking, you could say. Then the weather got bad. It was sunny one moment, the next it was snowing.'

'I saw my chance. Dad was in front, the pastor next and then me. I slipped past the pastor and tried to grab the ring from Dad. My plan was to run off into the snow and replace it in the cave. I was pretty sure I could outrun them in the snowstorm and they would give up.'

'So Dad and I struggled in the snow, then I pushed him and he fell, hitting his head on a rock.' Pétur gulped. The tears came into his eyes. 'I thought I had knocked him out, but he was dead. Just like that.'

'Oh, don't give me that! You pushed him over a cliff! He was found at the bottom of the cliff.'

'I didn't, I swear it. It was just the way he hit his head. On his temple— right here.' Pétur tapped his own shaved skull.

'So how do you explain the cliff?'

'Reverend Hákon saw what had happened. He took charge. I was a wreck after I saw what I had done. Hákon knew it was an accident. He told me to go, run away, pretend I was never there. So I ran.

'He pushed Dad over the cliff. Oh, he was dead then, that's for sure; the autopsy people got that wrong when they said he was alive for a few minutes. But Hákon covered for me.'

Ingileif put a hand to her mouth, her brow knitted in anguish. 'I can't believe it,' she said. 'So you were the elf the old sheep farmer saw?'

'Elf?' Pétur frowned.

'Never mind.'

Pétur smiled at his sister. 'It's true. I killed Dad. But it was a mistake. A dreadful, horrible mistake. If Hákon were alive he'd tell you that.' He took a step forward. Took his sister's hands in his. 'Can you forgive me, Inga?'

Ingileif stood stunned for a moment. Then she backed off.

'It wasn't murder, Inga. Surely you understand that?'

'But what about Aggi? And the pastor? Did you kill them as well?'

'Don't you see, I had to?'

'What do you mean, you had to?'

'As you know, Hákon took the ring. Agnar went to see him and accused him of killing Dad and taking it. Hákon threw him out, of course, but then Agnar approached Tómas, tried to get him to act as an intermediary. He tried to blackmail Hákon through him.'

'But what did all this have to do with you?'

'Hákon had been good to me. He had kept me out of the police investigation. Until then, I had no idea what had happened to the ring, I had tried so hard not to think about it, but it didn't surprise me that Hákon had taken it from Dad. In the end, Hákon called me, said that it looked like he would have to tell the truth about what had happened to Dad, unless I did something.'

'Did what?'

'He didn't say. But we both knew.'

'Oh, my God! You did kill Aggi!'

'I had to. Don't you see, I had to?'

Ingileif shook her head. 'Of course you didn't have to. And then you killed Hákon?'

Pétur nodded. 'Once his son was in jail and the police were after him, I knew the truth would come out.'

Ingileif took another step back. 'OK, maybe you killed Dad by accident, but not the other two. Hang on—did you kill Sigursteinn as well?'

He nodded again. 'You have to admit he deserved it after what he had done to Birna.'

'Who are you?' Ingileif said. 'You're not my brother. Who are you?'

Pétur closed his eyes. 'You're right,' he said. 'It's this.' He took his hand out of his pocket. Showed her the ring on his finger. 'Here. Take a look.'

He slipped it off and handed it to her. It was his last chance. Maybe the ring would corrupt his sister just like it had corrupted him, his father, Hákon and all the others.

Ingileif stared at it. 'Is this it?'

'Yes.'

She closed her fist round it. Pétur felt an urge to grab it, but resisted. Let her have it. Let it do its evil magic with her.

'So, what are you going to do?' Pétur asked.

'I'm going to the police,' Ingileif said. 'What did you think I would do?'

She glared at her brother. In addition to fear and shock, there was hatred there now.

Pétur's shoulders slumped. Oh, well. The ring was going to have its way. He had been foolish to think that this could end any other way.

He took a step forward.

MAGNUS SCREECHED into the car park. It was almost deserted. Two cars were parked next to each other—a big SUV and a much smaller hatchback, with a third a few feet away.

'That's Ingileif's,' said Jubb, pointing to the hatchback.

'Stay here!' shouted Magnus, as he leaped out of the car.

He ran across the parking lot and down some wooden steps. The waterfall opened up before him, a cauldron of roaring water. The path went to a ledge with an observation point halfway down the waterfall.

Nothing. No one. Just water. An unimaginable volume of water.

He looked up at the falls. The path stopped just short of them, all pretty much in his view. But downstream were more steps, a path, another parking lot, a gorge. Plenty of places to hide out of view.

Magnus ran down the steps towards the gorge.

'PÉSI? WHAT ARE YOU DOING?' Ingileif's eyes widened, but anger overcame fear. Pétur knew he would have a struggle on his hands. His sister wouldn't go quietly.

He swallowed. It was going to be very hard to strike Ingileif. But he had to. He took another step forward. But then he saw some movement out of the corner of his eye. A couple with a tripod appeared over the lip of the hollow. One of them, a woman by her size and shape, waved. Pétur didn't acknowledge her but turned back to Ingileif, who hadn't noticed.

He would have to play for time, until they had gone.

'Do you want me to turn myself in?' he asked his sister.

'Yes,' she said.

'Why should I?' said Pétur.

For two minutes they continued a halting conversation, with Pétur watching the couple through his peripheral vision. He saw them set up the tripod, take a picture of the falls, then disappear back over the rim of the hollow.

He took another step towards his sister.

JUBB DIDN'T STAY in the car. He looked round the car park, and then made his way to the information office. A middle-aged woman inside wished him good afternoon in English, having sized him up as a foreigner.

'Have you seen two people here?' Jubb asked. 'A man and a woman? The man is bald, and the woman is blonde. Icelanders.'

'No, I don't think so. I did just speak to a German couple. But the woman had dark hair, I am sure. They were going to take photographs.'

'Thank you,' said Jubb.

As he stepped out of the information centre, he saw the German couple the woman had mentioned, walking down into the car park from the hill above. The man had a tripod slung over his shoulder.

Jubb trotted over to them. 'Hello?' he called. 'Do you speak English?'

'Yes, I do,' said the woman.

'Have you seen a man and a woman up there? The man is bald and the woman is blonde?'

'Yes,' said the woman. 'Just over the top of this hill here.'

Jubb thought for a second. Should he run up there himself, or should he get Magnus? Get Magnus. He ran down from the car park towards the falls.

PÉTUR DECIDED AGAINST hitting Ingileif, at least right away. He turned and sauntered over towards the edge of the gorge.

'Where are you going?' Ingileif called after him.

'To look at the falls.'

As he had hoped, Ingileif followed. She was still arguing with him, pleading with him to give himself up. But she was keeping her distance.

Pétur paused, talked and then moved on again. This seemed to work. Finally he was within a few feet of the rim of the gorge.

Ingileif had stopped dead. She wasn't moving any further.

Then he saw in her eyes that she understood what he was doing—tempting her forwards to her death. She took a few steps backwards and then turned and ran. Pétur lunged after her. His legs were longer, he was stronger, fitter. He caught her, throwing her to the ground.

She screamed, but the scream was killed by the roar of the water. He pinned her to the grass, and hit her in the face. She screamed again, but continued to writhe beneath him. He hit her again, harder. She lay still.

He swallowed. His eyes were hot with tears. But he had had no choice. He had never had a choice. He dragged her over towards the rim of the gorge. That spot wouldn't quite work. Below the cliff a grassy slope dropped down to the water. It wasn't quite steep enough. He would have to go a few metres upstream.

He pulled her along a rough path, her legs and body knocking against bare rock. He was nearly at a good spot; the top of a rock jutting out with a near vertical drop down to the river hurtling towards the falls.

The ring! She had the ring. Damn it. He lay her down. She groaned. He began to search her pockets. And then, out of nowhere, a large shape flew through the air and bowled him over.

MAGNUS DIDN'T HEAR Steve Jubb's shouts above the din of the waterfall. But he did pause and look back up the way he had come.

He saw the portly figure of Jubb wobbling down the path towards him, his arms waving. Magnus turned and ran back. It was a steep path, but he took it as fast as he could.

'Up there!' Jubb said. 'Above the waterfall.'

Magnus didn't wait for more explanation but continued running uphill. His heart was pounding, and his chest felt like it was going to explode as he scrambled over the rim of the hill.

He saw them. Two figures, a few feet from the edge of the cliff, one lying on the ground, the other crouching over her.

Magnus ran faster downhill towards them. There was no chance of Pétur hearing him in all the noise, and he was concentrating too hard on Ingileif to see what was coming at him.

Magnus threw himself at Pétur and together they rolled to the cliff edge.

Pétur writhed, broke away, and hauled himself to his feet. He stood swaying on the edge of the cliff above the river.

Magnus stared at him, keeping his distance. He had no desire to plunge over the cliff in a death-grapple with Pétur. He could see Pétur sizing him up. Pétur was tall and rangy. But Magnus was big, and he knew he looked like he could look after himself. People didn't usually mess with Magnus.

Magnus heard a groan behind him. Ingileif. At least she was alive.

'OK, Pétur,' Magnus said evenly. 'You had better give yourself up. There's no way out for you now. Come with me.'

Pétur hesitated. Then he glanced behind him, at the boiling river and the jagged rocks rising out of it. In a moment, he had turned and was gone.

Magnus took a few steps and looked over the rim. There was a kind of path, or rather a series of hand and footholds that led down to some rocks on the edge of the river. He could see that it would just be possible to clamber along these, down almost at the level of the river, and to climb up again further upstream. He descended after Pétur.

The spray had left the rocks extremely slippery, and Magnus had real trouble keeping his footing. Pétur was taking more risks, widening the gap. Magnus felt his footing slip. He grabbed hold of the rock with one hand. Below, the river rushed headlong to the top edge of the waterfall. The water was a beautiful deadly mixture of green and white.

Pure, cold death.

He hauled himself up with both arms and lay panting on the rock. He saw Pétur skip across three rocks barely five feet above the river. The man's balance was extraordinary.

But then Pétur slipped. Like Magnus he grabbed hold of the rock with one arm and held on. But, unlike Magnus, he couldn't find a hold for his other hand. He dangled there, swinging, his legs bunched up beneath him, desperately trying to keep his feet out of the water, lest the river grabbed them and snatched him down.

Pétur stared at him, his face twisting in agony at the effort of hanging on with one arm, his bald head dripping with moisture. He couldn't hold on much longer.

Magnus turned. He could see Ingileif standing on the edge of the cliff shouting and waving. She was beckoning to him to come. Magnus couldn't hear what she was yelling above the roar, but he could see her lips. 'Leave him!' she seemed to be shouting.

He turned back to Pétur, and watched the man who had murdered four people, including his own father, fight for his life.

Pétur's eyes met Magnus's. He knew that Magnus had given up trying to reach him. He closed his eyes, his grip slipped and he fell without a cry. His body was whisked along the top of the spate and over the rim of the waterfall. Within two seconds he was gone.

CHAPTER TWELVE

Magnus saw Ingileif standing next to her brother's white BMW four-wheel-drive, with the snow-covered mountain rising above her. He pulled up beside her and got out of his car.

'You're late,' she said. Her face was pink in the cold, her eyes shining.

'Sorry.'

'Never mind. I'm glad you came.'

Magnus smiled. 'I'm glad you asked me.'

'I thought you might have gone back to America.'

'Tomorrow.'

'So where are you staying?'

'I can't really tell you.'

She frowned. 'I'd have thought that by now you would have trusted me.'

'Oh, no. It's not that. Let's just say I've learned the hard way that the fewer people who know where I am the better.'

There was a remote possibility that Soto would send out a replacement for the hit man who had shot Árni, so the Police Commissioner had decided to let everyone think that Magnus had flown back to Boston. Actually, he had sent Magnus to stay with his brother at his farm, north of Reykjavík. It was a beautiful spot, on the edge of a fjord.

Nobody had heard anything from Colby. That was a good sign. All she had to do was lie low for a couple more days.

'So, what do we do now?' Magnus said, staring up at Mount Hekla.

'Climb it, of course.'

'Dare I ask why?'

'What kind of Icelander are you?' Ingileif said. 'It's a lovely day, so we're going up a mountain. Let's go.'

So they set off up the side of the volcano. It was a glorious day, the sky was clear and cold and there was already a magnificent view stretching out behind them. Magnus felt good. The air was crisp, the exercise was invigorating, and it was nice to have Ingileif beside him. Or ahead of him. She set a rapid pace, which Magnus was happy to follow.

'How's your friend?' she asked. 'The one who was shot.'

'Árni is doing well, thank God. They say he'll make a full recovery.'

'I'm glad to hear it. So you're going tomorrow?' she said.

'That's right.'

'Are you coming back?' There was something a little hesitant in the way she asked the question.

'I don't know,' said Magnus. 'The Commissioner has asked me to stay. I'm thinking about it.'

And he was thinking about it, seriously. Partly he felt a sense of obligation—gratitude for what the Commissioner and Árni had done for him. But also he was aware of the seed of suspicion that had planted itself in his mind, the suspicion that the answers to his father's murder might lie in Iceland rather than on the streets of Boston.

'If it makes any difference,' Ingileif said. 'I'd like you to.'

She looked at him, smiling shyly. Magnus felt himself grinning back.

'Yes. That makes a difference.'

She moved closer to him, reached up and kissed him, long and deep. Then she broke away. 'Come on, we've still got a long way to go.'

As they ascended, the mountain became stranger. There was no single neat round cone at the top of Mount Hekla. Rather, a series of old craters from previous eruptions dotted the ridge. Sulphurous steam rose out of fissures, narrow cracks in the mountain. Underneath, and not very far underneath, the volcano was bubbling away.

When they reached the top, the view was extraordinary, as Iceland stretched all round them: broad rivers, craggy mountains, slow, powerful glaciers. Magnus looked around. 'I wonder which crater the three brothers, Ísildur, Gaukur and Ásgrímur, were trying to throw the ring into?'

'Who knows?' Ingileif replied. 'The mountain has rearranged itself many times since their day.'

'What are you going to do with the saga now? Are you going to sell it?'

Ingileif shook her head. 'We're giving it to the Árni Magnússon Institute. But before then, Lawrence Feldman will have it for a year in return for enough money to bail out the gallery. Birna will get her share, of course.'

'That's a neat idea.'

'Yes. It was Lawrence's, but it looks like everyone can live with that. I think he feels guilty.'

'As he should.' Magnus thought about all that had happened over the previous two weeks and wondered whether they would ever find the ring. Pétur's body had not yet turned up. Magnus rather hoped that somehow the ring would stay there, at the bottom of Gullfoss, though he couldn't say that to Ingileif.

'Let's go,' Ingileif said. She set off down the mountain, stopping to scramble down to a small spiral of steam coming out of a crack in the ground.

'Careful!' Magnus said. The snow and lava on which she was standing looked precarious. There was a strong smell of sulphur in the air.

Ingileif pulled something out of her pocket.

'What's that?' asked Magnus.

'The ring.'

'The ring? I thought Pétur had it!'

'He gave it to me. I think he hoped it would change my mind.'

'But you didn't tell anyone that!'

'I know.'

'What are you going to do with it?'

'What do you think?' she said. 'I'm going to toss it into the mouth of hell, just like Tolkien suggested my grandfather do. Just like Ísildur wanted to do.'

'Don't do that,' said Magnus.

'Why not? It's the right thing to do.'

'Why not? Because it's one of the most significant archaeological discoveries this country has ever seen. I mean, is it real? Did Högni or someone hide it eighty years ago? Or is it really centuries old? Don't you see? These are fascinating questions, even without the Tolkien connection. And they can all be answered by archaeologists.'

'Oh, yes, they are fascinating questions,' Ingileif said. 'I can tell you, it's made of gold. And there is an inscription in runes scratched on the inside. But whatever it is, it's evil. I'm getting rid of it.'

'No, Ingileif, wait.' Magnus felt an overwhelming urge to grab the ring.

Ingileif smiled. 'I wanted you to come up here with me to make sure I had the strength to do this. But now look at you.'

Magnus could see the ring between Ingileif's thumb and forefinger. He didn't know what it was exactly, whether it was ten years old or a thousand. But he knew she was right. He nodded.

Ingileif bent down and tossed the ring into the fissure.

There was no thunder. No lightning. The sun shone out of the pale blue Icelandic sky.

Ingileif climbed back up to Magnus and kissed him quickly on the lips.

'Come on,' she said. 'Let's get going. If you're flying back to Boston tomorrow, we've got things to do and not much time to do them.'

Grinning broadly, Magnus followed her down the mountain.

michael **ridpath**

RD: After writing a string of novels set in the financial world, you've decided on a new tack. Was it easy to create the character of Sergeant Detective Magnus Jonson?

MR: Creating Magnus was hard. I needed a detective who spoke Icelandic but was not a 100 per cent Icelander. It would be difficult for me to write about a man who came from a society I am only just finding out about. Also, I wanted to write about what an extraordinary place Iceland is. A fully Icelandic detective would not marvel at the odd things that take place in his own country—he would take them for granted.

RD: Wasn't it extraordinary that the unpronounceable volcano, Eyjafjallajökull, erupted not long after you had finished *Where the Shadows Lie*?

MR: I do think that, with the volcanic eruption and the credit crunch, Iceland has been performing all kinds of attention-seeking temper tantrums. Which is fine with me. I can say Eyjafjallajökull, by the way. I have been practising.

RD: You have said that you first visited Iceland on a book tour in 1995 and thought it an extraordinary place. Can you tell us more about what it's like?

MR: I think that the main feature is the contrast and conflict between the old and the new. In 1940, Iceland was probably the poorest country in Europe. By 2007, it was one of the most advanced. Every Icelander seems to have a Facebook page, yet every Icelander's grandmother believed in elves. The people are a manic lot: hard-working with a highly developed sense of irony. They recently voted a comedian to be mayor of Reykjavík, and his campaign was based on getting a new polar bear for the zoo.

RD: And the landscape?

MR: The conflict between the old and the new applies to the landscape as well. Bleak mountains, beautiful white glaciers, fiords, lava fields with mosses nibbling into the rock. It looks ancient—and of course is full of myths and legends, trolls and elves—but actually it is very new, geologically speaking. It's a work in progress. The weather can have an extraordinary effect. A gloomy, dark, lonely mountainside can be transformed by sunshine into a glistening valley from a lost magical kingdom.

RD: Is there an Icelandic national character?

MR: Yes, there is. Of course, the great trap I could fall into is making all my characters national stereotypes. But I would say that some of the characteristics many Icelanders share are pale skin, dark hair and blue eyes (there were Irish slaves in their past), hard work, artistic creativity, initial reserve, lateness for meetings, spontaneity, pride in their country, a love of reading, a tendency to drink heavily but only at weekends, pacifism, a sense of irony and a slightly childish sense of humour. I like them.

RD: You had help with research from Magnus Magnusson, famously the BBC's former question master on the *Mastermind* quiz, who sadly died in 2007. Was it he who got you enthused about the sagas?

MR: The first two books I read about Iceland were *Iceland Saga* by Magnus Magnusson, and *Dreaming of Iceland* by his daughter, Sally. Both books have coloured my view of Iceland, and both had an effect on *Where The Shadows Lie*. I was very touched to receive an email from Sally, who had read my book and said it reminded her of her father.

RD: Your thoughts also turned to *The Lord of the Rings*, and J.R.R. Tolkien . . . Can you tell us about his 1920s Old Norse drinking club at Leeds University?

MR: The club was mentioned in Tolkien's collected letters. After he left Oxford, he spent three years as a young lecturer in Middle English and Anglo-Saxon at Leeds University and he seems to have passed on his enthusiasm to many of the students. Throughout his life, he enjoyed reading the sagas with other people—and drinking beer. I like the sound of him.

RD: If you'd had the chance to meet Tolkien, is there anything specific you would have asked him?

MR: Can I have a pint of Brakspear, please?

RD: 'The Ridpath method', describing the methodical way in which you go about everything, from writing a book to studying for exams, was a phrase coined by your friends when you were at university. Have you applied it to other areas of your life?

MR: I find that it usually pays to spend a lot of time and effort thinking how to do a task, rather than just going ahead and doing it. I used to be a trader in the City, and I still manage investments for a charity, and in those roles, I have always spent time thinking about how to beat the markets.

RD: Which time of your life have you enjoyed most, and why?

MR: I think I most enjoyed being an undergraduate at Oxford. I knew I was privileged to be there. At that age, you have lots of freedom and very little responsibility. There is also so much to learn. I am a firm believer, though, that each stage of life has something to offer. Accept your age and enjoy.

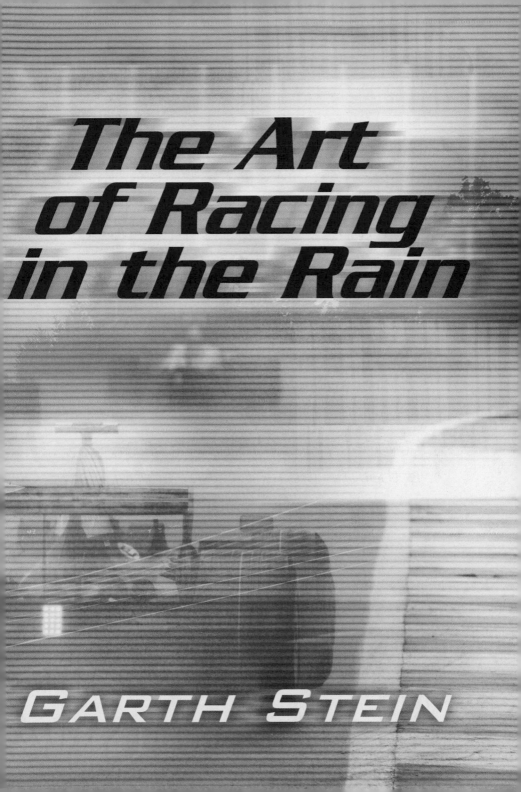

The Art of Racing in the Rain

GARTH STEIN

Enzo knows he's different from other dogs. True, he thinks you can't beat chasing birds and squirrels once in a while, but Enzo is almost human. Through listening to the words of his master, racing-car driver Denny Swift, Enzo has gained a real insight into the complex world of people. What he sees is that life, like racing, isn't simply about going fast.

1

Gestures are all that I have; sometimes they must be grand in nature. And while I occasionally step over the line and into the world of the melodramatic, it is what I must do in order to communicate clearly and effectively. In order to make my point understood without question. I have no words I can rely on because, much to my dismay, my tongue was designed long and flat and loose and, therefore, is a horribly ineffective tool for pushing food around my mouth while chewing, and an even less effective tool for making clever and complicated polysyllabic sounds that can be linked together to form sentences. And that's why I'm here now waiting for Denny to come home—he should be here soon—lying on the cool tiles of the kitchen floor in a puddle of my own urine.

I'm old. And shot full of pain medication and steroids to reduce the swelling of my joints. Vision fogged with cataracts. I'm sure Denny would keep me alive as long as he possibly could, my body deteriorating, disintegrating around me. But I don't want to be kept alive. Because I know what's next. I've seen it on TV. A documentary I saw about Mongolia, of all places. It was the best thing I've ever seen on television, other than the 1993 Grand Prix of Europe, of course, the greatest automobile race of all time in which Ayrton Senna proved himself to be a genius in the rain. After the 1993 Grand Prix, the best thing I've ever seen on TV is a documentary that told the whole truth: when a dog is finished living his lifetimes as a dog, his next incarnation will be as a man.

I've always felt almost human. I've always known that there's something about me that's different from other dogs. Sure, I'm stuffed into a dog's body, but that's just the shell. It's what's inside that's important. The soul. And my soul is very human.

I am ready to become a man now, though I realise I will lose all that I have been. All of my memories, all of my experiences. I would like to take them with me into my next life—there is so much I have gone through with the Swift family—but I have little say in the matter.

The door opens, and I hear Denny with his familiar cry, 'Yo, Zo!' Usually, I can't help but put aside my pain and wag my tail, shove my face into his crotch. It takes humanlike will-power to hold back on this particular occasion, but I do. I don't get up. I'm acting.

'Enzo?'

I hear his footsteps, the concern in his voice. I lift my head, wag my tail feebly so it taps against the floor. I play the part.

He shakes his head, sets down the plastic bag from the grocery that has his dinner in it. I can smell roast chicken through the plastic. Tonight he's having roast chicken and an iceberg lettuce salad.

'What happened, kid?' he asks.

Gestures can't explain.

'Can you get up?'

I try, and I scramble. I thought I was just acting, but I really can't get up.

'Take it easy, kid,' he says, pressing down on my chest to calm me. 'I've got you.'

He lifts me easily, he cradles me, and I can smell everything he's done. His work, the auto shop where he's behind the counter all day, standing, making nice with the customers who yell at him because their BMWs don't work right and it costs too much to fix them. I can smell his lunch. He went to the Indian buffet he likes. All you can eat. It's cheap. I can smell beer. He stopped somewhere. The Mexican restaurant up the hill. I can smell the tortilla chips on his breath. Now it makes sense. Usually, I'm excellent with elapsed time, but I wasn't paying attention because of my emoting.

He places me gently in the tub and turns on the handheld shower thing and says, 'Easy, Enz.'

He says, 'Sorry I was late. I should have come straight home, but the guys from work insisted. I told Craig I was quitting, and . . .'

He thinks that my accident was because he was *late*. I didn't want him to feel bad about this. I wanted him to see the obvious, that it's OK for him to let me go. He's been through so much, and he's finally through it. He needs to not have me around to worry about any more. He needs me to free him to be brilliant.

He is so brilliant. He shines. I will miss him and little Zoë, and I know they will miss me. But I can't let sentimentality cloud my grand plan. After this happens, Denny will be free to live his life, and I will return to earth in a new form, as a man, and I will find him, and then I will wink at him and say, 'Enzo says hello,' and turn and walk quickly away as he calls after me, 'Have we met before?'

After the bath, he cleans the kitchen floor while I watch; he gives me my food, which I eat too quickly, and sets me up in front of the TV while he prepares his dinner. 'How about a tape?' he asks.

'Yes, a tape,' I reply, but, of course, he doesn't hear me.

He puts in a video from one of his races, and he turns it on and we watch. It's one of my favourites. The racetrack is dry for the pace lap, and then, just after the green flag is waved, indicating the start of the race, there is a wall of rain, and all the cars around him spin out of control into the fields, and he drives through them as if the rain didn't fall on him. Just like the 1993 Grand Prix of Europe, when Senna passed four cars on the opening lap, four of the best championship drivers in their championship cars—Schumacher, Wendlinger, Hill, Prost—and he passed them all.

Denny is as good as Ayrton Senna. But no one sees him, because he has responsibilities. He has his daughter, Zoë, and he had his wife, Eve, who was sick until she died, and he has me. And he lives in Seattle when he should live somewhere else. And he has a job. But sometimes when he goes away, he comes back with a trophy and he tells me how he taught those other drivers what driving in wet weather is really about.

When the tape is over, he says, 'Let's go out,' and I struggle to get up. He lifts my butt into the air and centres my weight over my legs, and then I'm OK. To show him, I rub my muzzle against his thigh.

We leave our apartment; the night is sharp, cool and breezy and clear. We only go down the block and back, because my hips hurt so much, and Denny knows it. When we get back, he gives me my bedtime cookies and

I curl into my bed on the floor next to his. He picks up the phone and dials.

'Mike,' he says. Mike is Denny's friend from the shop, where they both work behind the counter. Customer relations, they call it. Mike's a little guy with friendly hands that are pink and always washed clean of smell. 'Mike, can you cover for me tomorrow? I have to take Enzo to the vet again.'

We've been going to the vet a lot recently to get different medicines that are supposed to help make me more comfortable, but they don't, really. And considering all that went on yesterday, I've set the Master Plan in motion.

Denny stops talking for a minute, and when he starts again, his voice doesn't sound like his voice. It's rough, like when he has a cold.

'I don't know,' he says. 'I'm not sure it's a round-trip visit.'

I may not be able to form words, but I understand them. For a moment, I'm surprised my plan is working. It is the best thing for all involved, I know. I owe him the gift of setting him free. I close my eyes and listen vaguely in a half-sleep as he does the things he does before he sleeps each night. Brushing and squirting and splashing. People and their rituals. They cling to things so hard sometimes.

HE PICKED ME out of a pile of puppies behind a barn in a smelly field near a town in eastern Washington called Spangle. I don't remember much about where I came from, but I remember my mother, a heavy bitch of a lab with pendulous teats. She was fairly indifferent to whether we all ate or starved. She seemed relieved whenever one of us left.

I never knew my father. The people on the farm told Denny that he was a shepherd-poodle mix, but I don't believe it. The alpha man on the farm firmly believed that shepherds and poodles were the smart ones, and therefore would be more desirable—and more valuable. All a bunch of junk. Everyone knows that shepherds and poodles aren't especially smart. They're responders and reactors, not independent thinkers.

I'm sure my father was a terrier. Because terriers are problem solvers. There was a terrier like that on the farm. An Airedale. Big and brown-black and tough. No one messed with him. I have his brown-black colouring, and my coat is slightly wiry, and people frequently comment that I must be part terrier.

I remember that the day Denny arrived was exceptionally hot. A hand reached into the pile and found my scruff, and suddenly I was dangling in the air. 'This one,' a man said.

It was my first glimpse of the rest of my life. He was slender, with long and lean muscles. He had keen, icy-blue eyes.

'The pick of the litter,' the alpha man said. 'We were thinkin' a keepin' 'im.' That was the line he always used. Hell, I was a pup only a dozen weeks old, and I'd already heard that line a bunch of times. He used it to get more money.

'Will you let him go?'

'Fur a price,' the alpha man said.

'GENTLY, LIKE THERE ARE eggshells on your pedals,' Denny always says, 'and you don't want to break them. That's how you drive in the rain.'

When we watch videos together, he explains these things to me. (To me!) Balance, anticipation, patience. These are all vital. But what I've always liked best is when he talks about having no memory. To remember is to disengage from the present. In order to reach any kind of success in automobile racing, a driver must never remember.

Which is why drivers compulsively record their every move, their every race, with cockpit cameras, in-car video, data mapping; a driver cannot be a witness to his own greatness. This is what Denny says. He says racing is being a part of a moment and being aware of nothing else but that moment. The great champion Julian SabellaRosa has said, 'When I am racing, my mind and my body are working so quickly and so well together, I must be sure not to think, or else I will definitely make a mistake.'

DENNY MOVED ME from the farm to a Seattle neighbourhood called Leschi, where he lived in a little apartment he rented on Lake Washington. We had a balcony that overlooked the lake, which gave me pleasure since I am part water dog, on my mother's side.

I grew quickly and, during that first year, Denny and I forged a deep fondness for each other as well as a feeling of trust. Which is why I was surprised when he fell in love with her so quickly.

He brought her home, and she was sweet smelling, like him. Full of fermented drinks that made them both act funny. She patted my head, which hovered low to the floor, me still being immature at just over a year old and a little intimidated by their antics. She said, 'You don't mind if I love him, too, do you? I won't come between you.'

I respected her for asking, but I knew that she would come between us, and I found her pre-emptive denial to be disingenuous.

We were both satellites orbiting Denny's sun, struggling for gravitational supremacy. Of course, she had the advantage of her tongue and her thumbs.

2

I watch too much TV. When Denny goes away in the mornings, he turns it on for me, and it's become a habit. He warned me not to watch all day, but I do. Fortunately, he knows I love cars, so he lets me watch a lot of SPEED Channel. The classic races are the best, and I especially like Formula One. I like NASCAR, too, but I prefer it when they race on the road circuits. While racing is my favourite, Denny told me it was good for me to have variety in my life, so he often puts on other channels, which I enjoy very much as well.

Sometimes, if I'm watching the Discovery Channel, they talk about evolution, and it's usually really well thought out and researched.

I'll give you a theory: man's closest relative is not the chimpanzee, as the TV people believe, but is, in fact, the dog.

Witness my logic:

Case in Point #1: The Dewclaw

It is my opinion that the so-called dewclaw, which is often snipped off a dog's foreleg at an early age, is actually evidence of a pre-emergent thumb. Further, I believe that men have systematically bred the thumb out of certain lines of dog through an elaborate process called 'selective breeding', simply in order to prevent dogs from evolving into dexterous, and therefore 'dangerous', mammals.

Case in Point #2: The Werewolf

The full moon rises. The fog clings to the lowest branches of the spruce trees. The man steps out of the darkest corner of the forest and finds himself transformed into . . . a *monkey*? I think not.

HER NAME WAS EVE, and at first I resented how she changed our lives. I resented the attention Denny paid to her small hands, her plump, round buttocks, her modest hips. Did I envy her engaging smile? Perhaps I did. For she was a person, unlike me. She was everything I wasn't.

Soon after she moved into our apartment, they were married in a small wedding ceremony, which I attended along with a group of their closest friends and Eve's immediate family. Denny didn't have any brothers or sisters to invite, and he explained his parents' absence simply by saying that they didn't travel well.

Following the wedding, I noticed that Eve moved through our apartment and was much bolder in her actions to move or replace things. She had entered our lives and changed everything around. And yet, there was something about her that prevented me from mustering any real anger. I believe that thing was her swollen belly. And while I greatly resented the attention Eve lavished on her unborn baby, in retrospect, I realise I could never be the source of her affection in that way, because I could never be her child.

I remember the day the baby arrived. I had just reached adulthood—two years by calendar count. Denny was in Daytona, Florida, for the drive of his career. He had spent the entire year soliciting sponsors, begging, pleading, hustling, until he got lucky and he was able to buy a seat in a Porsche 993 Cup Car for the Rolex 24 Hours of Daytona.

Endurance racing is not for the meek. Four drivers each spending six hours behind the wheel of a powerful and expensive racing car is an exercise in coordination and determination. The 24 Hours of Daytona, which is broadcast on television, is as unpredictable as it is exciting. That Denny was presented with a chance to drive it in the same year that his daughter would be born was one of those coincidences that turn on interpretation: Eve was dismayed by the unfortunate timing of events; Denny celebrated the bounty of opportunity and the feeling that he had everything he could possibly ask for.

Still, the timing was off. On the day of the race, even though it was more than a week before schedule, Eve felt the contractions and called the midwives. Later that evening, as Denny was, no doubt, driving the circuit in

Daytona and winning the race, Eve stood bent over the bed with two round ladies who helped her by holding her arms and, with a monstrous bellow that seemed to last an hour, squirted out a little bloody blob of human tissue that wriggled spastically and then cried out. The ladies helped Eve into her bed and rested the tiny purple thing on her torso until the baby's searching mouth found Eve's nipple and began to suck.

'Could I have a minute alone—?' Eve started.

'Of course,' one of the ladies said, moving to the door.

'Come with us, puppy,' the other lady said to me on her way out.

'No.' Eve stopped them. 'He can stay.'

I could stay? Despite myself, I felt proud to be included in Eve's inner circle. I watched in fascination as Eve suckled her new babe. After a few minutes, I saw that she was crying and I wondered why. She let her free hand dangle to the bedside, her fingers near my muzzle. I bumped her hand with my nose. She lifted her fingers to the crown of my head and scratched, still crying, her baby still nursing. 'I know I told him to go,' she said to me. 'I know that I insisted he go, I know.' Tears ran down her cheeks. 'But I so wish he were here!' I knew not to move. She needed me there. 'Will you promise always to protect her?' she asked. I realised at that moment that I could comfort Eve when Denny was away. I could protect Eve's baby.

The next day, Denny came home from Daytona, Florida, unhappy. His mood immediately changed when he held his little girl, whom they named Zoë, not after me, but after Eve's grandmother.

'Do you see my little angel, Enz?' he asked me.

Did I *see* her? I practically *birthed* her!

Denny skated carefully through the kitchen after he returned, sensing that the ice was very thin. Eve's parents, Maxwell and Trish, had been in the house since Zoë was born, taking care of their daughter and their new baby grand-daughter. I began calling them the Twins, because they looked very much alike, with the same shade of artificially coloured hair and matching outfits.

'That's a lot of bad luck,' Maxwell said to Denny as they stood in the kitchen. Maxwell was gloating; I could hear it in his voice.

'Do you get any of your money back?' Trish asked.

Denny was distraught, and I wasn't sure why until Mike came over later that night and he and Denny opened their beers together. It turned out that

Denny was going to take the third stint in the car. The car had been running well, everything going great. They were second in class, and Denny would easily assume the lead as the sunlight faded and the night driving began. Until the driver who had the second stint stuffed the car into the wall on turn 6.

He stuffed it when a Daytona Prototype—a much faster car—was overtaking. First rule of racing: never move aside to let someone pass; make him pass you. But the driver on Denny's team moved over, and he hit the marbles, which is what they call the bits of rubber that shed off the tyres and which accumulate on the track next to the established racing line. He ploughed into the wall at pretty close to top speed, and the car shattered into a million pieces.

The driver was unhurt, but the race was over for the team. And Denny, who had spent a year working for his moment to shine, found himself standing in the infield wearing the fancy racing suit they had given him for the race, with the sponsor patches all over it, watching the opportunity of his lifetime get dragged off the track by the wrecker, without his having sat in it for a single racing lap.

'And you don't get any of your money back,' Mike said.

'I don't care about that,' Denny said. 'I should have been here.'

'She came early. You can't know what's going to happen before it happens.'

'Yes, I can,' Denny said. 'If I'm any good, I can.'

'Anyway,' Mike said, lifting his beer bottle, 'to Zoë.'

To Zoë, I said to myself. *Whom I will always protect.*

WHEN IT WAS JUST Denny and me, he used to make up to ten thousand dollars a month in his spare time by calling people on the telephone, like the commercial said. But after Eve became pregnant, Denny took his job behind the counter at the fancy auto shop that serviced only expensive German cars.

Sometimes at weekends, Denny taught at a high-performance driver's education programme run by one of the many car clubs in the area—BMW, Porsche, Alfa Romeo—and he often took me to the track with him, which I enjoyed very much. He didn't really like teaching at these events, because he didn't get to drive. And it hardly paid for the gas it cost him to get down to the track, he said. He fantasised about moving somewhere—to Las Vegas, or even Europe—and catching on with one of the big schools so he could drive more, but Eve didn't think she could ever leave Seattle.

Eve worked for some big retail clothing company, because it provided us with money and health insurance, and also because she could buy clothes for the family at the employee discount. She went back to work a few months after Zoë was born, even though she really wanted to stay at home with her baby.

With Denny and Eve working and Zoë off at day care, I was left alone in the apartment. I hadn't realised how much I enjoyed having everyone bustling around the house for those first few months of Zoë's life. I had felt so much a part of something. I was an integral figure in Zoë's entertainment: sometimes after a feeding, when she was awake and alert and strapped safely into her bouncy seat, Eve and Denny would play Monkey in the Middle, throwing a ball of socks back and forth across the living room; I got to be the monkey. And when, against all odds, I reached the sock ball and batted it into the air with my snout, Zoë would squeal and laugh. And Eve, Denny and I would collapse in a pile of laughter.

I wallowed in the emptiness of my lonely days. Until one day when a fortunate accident happened that changed my life. Denny turned on the TV in the morning to check the weather report, and he forgot to turn the TV off. Let me tell you this: the Weather Channel is not about weather; it is about the world. It is about how weather affects us all, our entire global economy, health, happiness, spirit. Absolutely fascinating. So much so that when Denny returned from work that evening, I was still glued to the television.

'The Weather Channel?' he scoffed, snatching up the remote and changing the channel. 'Here.'

He changed it to SPEED Channel. I barked excitedly when I saw cars racing on the screen. Denny laughed.

'I didn't know you were a television dog,' he said. 'I can leave it on for you during the day, if you want.'

I want! I want!

While I had learned a great deal up until that point in my life—I was three years old already—once Denny began leaving the TV on for me, my education really took off.

I was so immersed in my education, I suppose I lost count of the weeks, so I was surprised by the arrival of Zoë's second birthday. Suddenly I was engulfed by a party in the apartment with a bunch of little kids. It was loud and crazy, and all the children let me play with them and wrestle on the rug. They got lemon cake all over the floor, and I got to be Eve's helper cleaning it up, while Denny opened presents with the kids. After everyone had left and we had all completed our cleaning assignments, Denny had a surprise birthday present for Zoë. He showed her a photograph that she looked at briefly and with little interest. But then he showed the same photograph to Eve, and it made Eve cry. And then it made her laugh, and she hugged him and looked at the photo again and cried some more. Denny picked up the photograph and showed it to me, and it was a photo of a house.

'Look at this, Enzo,' he said. 'This is your new yard. Aren't you excited?'

Actually, I was kind of confused. I didn't understand the implications. And then everyone started shoving things in boxes and scrambling around, and the next thing I knew, my bed was somewhere else entirely.

The house was nice. It was a stylish little Craftsman like I'd seen on *This Old House*, with two bedrooms and only one bathroom but with plenty of living space, situated very close to its neighbours on a hillside in the Central District. Many electrical wires draped from poles along the sidewalk outside, and while our house looked neat and trim, a few doors down stood other houses with unkempt lawns and peeling paint and mossy roofs. Eve and Denny were in love with the place.

When Denny came home from work, he would first say hello to the girls; then he would take me outside to the yard and throw the ball, which I happily retrieved. And then Zoë got big enough that she would run around and squeal while I pretended to chase her. And Eve would admonish her, 'Don't run like that; Enzo will bite you.' She did that frequently in the early years, doubt me like that. But one time, Denny turned on her quickly and said, 'Enzo would never hurt her—ever!' And he was right. I knew I was different from other dogs. I had a certain will-power that was strong enough to overcome my more primal instincts.

I didn't want Eve to start worrying unnecessarily. Because I had already smelled it. When Denny was away and Eve fed me and she leaned down to give me my bowl of food and my nose was near her head, I had detected a bad odour, like rotting wood. There was something inside Eve's head that didn't belong.

Given a facile tongue, I could have alerted them to her condition long before they discovered it with their super-vision scopes that can see inside the human head. My nose could smell the disease in Eve's brain long before even she knew it was there.

But I hadn't a facile tongue. And there was nothing I could do to help her.

ONE SUMMER SATURDAY AFTERNOON, Eve put Zoë down for a nap; Denny and I sat in front of the TV to study.

He put on a tape of an enduro he had been asked to co-drive in Portland a few weeks earlier. It was an exciting race, eight hours long, in which Denny and his two co-drivers took turns behind the wheel in two-hour shifts, ultimately finishing first in class after Denny's eleventh-hour heroics.

Watching a race entirely from in-car video is a tremendous experience. Seeing a race from the cockpit of a single car gives a true feeling of what it's like to be a driver. Denny started the tape at the beginning of his final stint, with the track wet and the sky heavy with dark colours that threatened more rain.

Denny drove smoothly and almost alone, as his team had fallen behind after making the crucial decision to pull into the pits and switch to rain tyres; other racing teams had predicted the rain would pass and so had gained more than two laps on Denny's team. Yet the rain began again, which gave Denny a tremendous advantage.

'How come you go through the turns so much faster than the other cars?' Eve asked.

I looked up. She stood in the doorway, watching with us.

'Most of them aren't running rain tyres,' Denny said.

Eve took a seat on the sofa next to Denny. We watched. Denny got up behind a yellow Camaro at the end of the back straight, and though it looked as if he could have taken the other car in turn 12, he held back. Eve noticed.

'Why didn't you pass him?' she asked.

'I know him. He's got too much power and he would just pass me back on the straight. I think I take him in the next series of turns.'

Yes. At the next turn-in, Denny was inches from the Camaro's rear bumper. He rode tight through the double-apex right-hand turn and then popped out at the exit to take the inside line for the next turn, a quick left, and he zipped right by.

'This part of the track is really slick in the rain,' he said. 'By the time he gets his grip back, I'm out of his reach.' Turn 12 and blasting down the straight, we could see the brake lights of the competition flicker ahead: Denny's next victims. 'That which you manifest is before you,' Denny said softly.

'What?' Eve asked.

'When I was nineteen,' Denny said after a moment, 'at my first driving school down at Sears Point, it was raining and they were trying to teach us how to drive in the rain. We had no idea what they were talking about. I looked over at the guy next to me—I remember him; he was from France, and he was very fast. Gabriel Flouret. He smiled and he said, "That which you manifest is before you."'

Eve squinted at Denny. 'And then everything made sense,' she joked.

'That's right,' Denny said seriously.

On the TV, the rain didn't stop; it kept coming. Denny's team had made the right choice; other teams were pulling into the hot pits to change to rain tyres.

'Drivers are afraid of the rain,' Denny told us. 'Rain amplifies your mistakes, and water on the track can make your car handle unpredictably. When something unpredictable happens, you have to react to it; if you're reacting at speed, you're reacting too late. And so you *should* be afraid.'

'I'm afraid just watching it,' Eve said.

'If I intentionally make the car do something, then I can predict what it's going to do. Then I can react to it before even the car knows it's happening.'

'And you can do that?'

Dashing past other cars on the TV screen, his car veered sideways but his hands were already turning to correct it, and instead of his car snapping round into a full spin, he was off again, leaving the others behind. Eve sighed in relief, held her hand to her forehead.

'Sometimes,' Denny said. 'But all drivers spin. It comes from pushing the limits. And I had a good day.'

She sat with us another minute, then smiled at Denny almost reluctantly and stood up. 'I love you,' she said. 'And I know on some level that you are completely right about all this. I just don't think I could ever do it myself.'

She went off into the kitchen. Denny and I continued watching the cars on the video as they drove round and round the circuit drenched in darkness.

I will never tire of watching tapes with Denny. He knows so much, and my thoughts turned to what he had just taught me. Such a simple concept, yet so true: that which we manifest is before us; we are the creators of our own destiny.

I considered how that idea applied to my relationship with Eve. It was true that I carried some resentment towards her for her involvement in our lives, and even though our relationship had changed greatly since Zoë's arrival, there was still a distance between us.

I had always wanted to love Eve as Denny loved her, but I never had, because I was afraid. She was my rain. But a racer should not be afraid of rain; a racer should embrace the rain. I, alone, could manifest a change in that which was around me. By changing my mood, my energy, I allowed Eve to regard me differently. And while I cannot say that I am a master of my own destiny, I can say that I have experienced a glimpse of mastery, and I know what I have to work towards.

A COUPLE OF YEARS after we moved into the new house, something very frightening happened.

Denny got a seat for a race at Watkins Glen. It was another enduro, but it was with a well-established team, and he didn't have to find the sponsorship money for his seat. Earlier that spring, he had gone to France for a Formula Renault testing programme. It was an expensive programme he couldn't afford; he told Mike his parents paid for it as a gift, but I had my doubts. No matter. Wherever the funding came from, Denny had attended this pro-gramme, and he had kicked ass, because it was in France in the spring when it rains. When he told Eve about it, he said that one of the scouts who attend these things approached him after a session and said, 'Can you drive as fast in the dry as you can in the wet?' And Denny looked him straight in the eyes and replied, simply, 'Try me.'

That which you manifest is before you.

Denny went away for two weeks. Testing and tuning and practising. He did so well, they offered him a seat in the enduro race at Watkins Glen.

When he first left for New York, we all grinned at each other because we couldn't wait to watch the race on SPEED Channel.

'It's so exciting.' Eve would giggle. 'Daddy's a professional racing driver!'

I got so caught up in the excitement, I was doing idiotic dog things like digging in the lawn.

It was the best of times. Really. And then it was the worst of times. Race day came, and Eve woke up with a darkness upon her. A pain so insufferable she stood in the kitchen in the early hours and vomited into the sink.

'I don't know what's wrong with me, Enzo,' she said. And she rarely spoke to me candidly like that. But this time she did talk to me like I was her soul mate. She asked, 'What's wrong with me?'

She knew I couldn't answer. That's what I found so frustrating about it: I had an answer.

I knew what was wrong, but I had no way to tell her, so I pushed at her thigh with my muzzle.

'I feel like someone's crushing my skull,' she said.

I had no words. There was nothing I could do.

Quickly she gathered some things while I watched. She shoved Zoë's clothes in a bag and some of her own and toothbrushes. And she roused Zoë and stuffed her little-kid feet into her little-kid sneakers, and the door slammed shut and they were gone.

And I wasn't gone. I was there. I was still there.

3

When I was locked in the house suddenly and firmly, I quickly and carefully took stock of the situation and understood these things: Eve was ill, and the illness was possibly affecting her judgment, and she would probably not return for me; Denny would be home on the third day, after two nights.

For three days, I took care to ration the toilet water. I wandered round the house sniffing at the crack beneath the pantry door and fantasising about a big bowl of my kibble, scooping up the occasional errant dust-covered Cheerio Zoë had dropped in a corner somewhere. And I urinated and defecated on the mat by the back door, next to the laundry machines. I did not panic.

During the second night, approximately forty hours into my solitude, I think I began to hallucinate. I heard a sound coming from Zoë's bedroom. When I investigated, I saw something terrible and frightening. One of her stuffed animal toys was moving about on its own. It was the zebra. I never cared for that zebra, as it was something of a rival for Zoë's affection.

The now-living zebra said nothing to me at all, but when it saw me, it began a dance, a twisting, jerky ballet, which culminated with the zebra attacking an innocent Barbie doll. That made me quite angry, and I growled at the molester zebra, but it simply smiled and continued its assault, this time picking on a stuffed frog.

I stalked the bastard as it abused and humiliated each of Zoë's toys with great malice. Finally, I could take no more, and I moved in, teeth bared for attack, to end the brutal burlesque once and for all.

Traumatised, I left Zoë's room, knowing something terrible had happened.

The following afternoon, Denny returned. I heard the taxi pull up, and I watched him unload his bags and walk them up to the back door. I didn't want to seem too excited to see him, and yet at the same time I was concerned about what I had done to the doormat, so I gave a couple of small barks to alert him. Through the window, I could see the look of surprise on his face. He opened the door, looked down, and gingerly hopped into the room.

'What the hell? What are you doing here?' He glanced round the kitchen. Nothing was out of place, nothing was amiss, except me. 'Are they home?' he asked me.

I didn't answer. He picked up the phone and dialled.

'Are Eve and Zoë still at your house?' he asked without saying hello. 'Can I speak to Eve?'

After a moment, he said, 'How could you not remember that your dog is in the house?' And then he hung up the phone. He looked at me after that and said, 'I am *so* pissed off.'

He filled my water bowl and gave me some kibble, which I ate too quickly and didn't enjoy, but at least it filled the empty space in my stomach.

And very soon, Eve and Zoë arrived on the back porch. Denny threw open the door.

'Unbelievable,' he said bitterly. 'You are unbelievable.'

'I was sick,' Eve said, stepping into the house with Zoë hiding behind her.

'He could have died.'

'I can't do this any more,' she cried. 'You always go away, and I have to take care of Zoë and Enzo all by myself, and I can't do it! It's too much! I can barely take care of myself!'

I heard weeping and looked over. Zoë stood in the door to the hallway, crying. Eve pushed past Denny and went to Zoë, kneeling before her.

'Oh, baby, we're sorry we're fighting. Please don't cry.'

'My animals,' Zoë whimpered.

'What happened to your animals?'

Eve led Zoë by the hand down the hall. Denny followed them. I stayed where I was.

Suddenly, I heard thundering footsteps. I cowered by the back door as Denny hurtled through the kitchen towards me. 'You stupid dog,' he growled, and he grabbed the back of my neck. He dragged me into Zoë's room, where she sat, stunned, on the floor in the middle of a huge mess. Her dolls, her animals, all torn to shreds, eviscerated, a complete disaster. Denny was so angry that his anger filled up the entire room. He reared up and roared, and with his great hand, he struck me on the side of the head. 'Bad dog!' he bellowed, and he raised his hand to hit me again.

'Denny, no!' Eve cried.

She rushed to me and covered me with her own body.

Denny stopped. He wouldn't hit her. No matter what. Just as he wouldn't hit me. He *hadn't* hit me, I know, even though I could feel the pain of the blow. He had hit the demon, the evil zebra, the dark creature that came into the house and possessed the stuffed animal. Denny believed the evil demon was in me, but it wasn't. I saw it. The demon had possessed the zebra and left me at the bloody scene with no voice to defend myself—I had been framed.

'We'll get new animals, baby,' Eve said to Zoë. 'We'll go to the store tomorrow.'

As gently as I could, I slunk towards Zoë, the sad little girl on the floor.

I crawled to her on my elbows and placed my nose next to her thigh. She waited a long time to give me her answer, but she finally gave it. She placed her hand on my head and let it rest there, which meant she forgave me.

Later, after Zoë was put to bed in her room, which had been cleaned of the carnage, I found Denny sitting on the porch steps with a drink of hard liquor. I approached cautiously, and he noticed.

'It's OK, boy.' He smiled and rubbed my neck.

Denny finished his drink with a long swallow and shivered involuntarily. He produced a bottle from nowhere and poured himself another. He stood up and stretched to the sky.

'We got first place, Enzo. Not "in class". We took first place overall. You know what that means?'

I knew what it meant. It meant that he was the champion.

'It means a seat in a touring car next season,' Denny said to me. 'I got an offer from a real, live racing team. Getting an offer means I can drive if I come up with my share of sponsorship money for the season and if I'm willing to spend the better part of six months away from Eve and Zoë and you. Am I willing to do that?'

I knew I was Denny's biggest fan and most steadfast supporter in his racing. But I also felt a hollow pit in my stomach at the idea of his absence. He must have been able to read my mind, because he said, 'I don't think so either.'

He groaned and sat back and filled his glass again.

'I'm taking those stuffed animals out of your allowance,' he said with a chuckle. He looked at me then, took my chin with his hand. 'I love you, boy,' he said. 'And I promise I'll never do that again. I know you'd never do anything deliberately to hurt Zoë.' I laid my head on his leg and looked up at him. 'Sometimes I think you actually understand me,' he said.

I do, I said to myself. I do.

EVE'S CONDITION was elusive and unpredictable. One day she would suffer a headache of crushing magnitude. Another day, debilitating nausea. A third would open with dizziness and end with a dark and angry mood. And these days were never linked together consecutively. Between them would be days or even weeks of relief, life as usual. And then Denny would get a call at work, and he would run to Eve's assistance, drive her home from her job and spend the rest of the day watching helplessly.

The intense and arbitrary nature of Eve's affliction was far beyond Denny's grasp. The wailings, the dramatic screaming fits, the falling on the floor in fits of anguish. These are things that only dogs and women understand, because we connect to pain directly from its source, taking the worst of it straight in the face. Men, on the other hand, are all deflectors and timed release. Suppressing the symptom does nothing but force the true problem to express itself on a deeper level at some other time.

'Go see a doctor,' he said to her. He never understood, as I did, what she meant when she said that medication would only mask the pain, not make it go away.

Denny was frustrated by his impotence, and I could understand his point of view. It's frustrating for me to be unable to speak. To feel that I have so much to say, so many ways I can help, but I'm locked in a soundproof box. Denny avoided the madness of his personal sound-booth hell by driving through it. There was nothing he could do to make Eve's distress go away, and once he realised that, he made a commitment to do everything else better.

A true champion can accomplish things that a normal person would think impossible.

Denny cut back his hours at work so he could take Zoë to her preschool. He took over all the grocery shopping and cooking. He took over the cleaning of the house. He wanted to relieve Eve of any burden, any job that could cause stress. What he couldn't do, though, with all of the extra he was doing, was continue to engage her in the same playful and affectionate way. It was impossible for him to do everything; clearly, he had decided that the care of her organism would receive the topmost priority. Which was the correct thing for him to do under the circumstances. Because he had me.

Denny did not stop loving Eve; he merely delegated his love-giving to me. I became the provider of love and comfort to Eve by proxy. He trusted me. 'Go take care of her for me, Enzo, please,' he would say.

And I did. I took care of her by curling up at her bedside, or, if she had collapsed on the floor, by curling up next to her there. Often, she would hold me close to her, hold me tight to her body, and when she did, she would tell me things about the pain.

Eve ate poorly and became drawn and pale. When her pain came, she often went for days without eating one bite of food. Denny was concerned, but Eve never heeded his pleas for her to consult a doctor. A mild case of depression, she'd say. They'd try to give her pills, and she didn't want pills.

But she was pretending. I could tell.

THE CLUES were all there; I simply hadn't read them correctly. Over the winter, he had played a video racing game obsessively, which wasn't like him. And he raced on American circuits only. I should have known he wasn't playing a video game; he was studying the circuits. He was learning turn-in points and braking points.

And his diet: no alcohol, no sugar, no fried foods. His exercise regimen: running several days a week, swimming at the Medgar Evers Pool, lifting weights in the garage of the big guy down the street. Denny had been preparing himself. He was lean and strong and ready to do battle in a racing car. And I had missed all the signs. Because when he came downstairs with his track bag packed that day in March, Eve and Zoë seemed to know all about his leaving. He had told *them*. He hadn't told *me*.

The parting was strange. Zoë was both excited and nervous, Eve was sombre, and I was utterly confused. *Where was he going?* I raised my eyebrows, lifted my ears and cocked my head.

'Sebring,' he said to me, reading my mind the way he does sometimes. 'I took the seat in the touring car; didn't I tell you?'

The touring car? But that was something he said he could never do! We agreed on that!

I was at once elated and devastated. A race weekend means at least three nights away, and there are eleven races over an eight-month period. He would be away so much of the time!

But I'm a racer at heart, and a racer will never let something that has already happened affect what is happening now. The news that he had taken the touring car seat and was flying to Sebring to race on ESPN2 was extremely good. A racing driver must be very selfish. It is a cold truth: even his family must come second to the race.

I wagged my tail enthusiastically, and he smiled at me with a twinkle in his eye. He knew that I understood everything he said.

'Be good, now,' he chided me playfully. 'Watch over the girls.'

He hugged little Zoë and kissed Eve gently, but as he turned away from her, she launched herself into his chest and grabbed him tight.

'Please come back,' she said, her words muffled by his mass.

'I promise I'll come back in one piece,' he said.

She shook her head.

'I don't care how many pieces,' she said. 'Just promise you'll come *back*.'

I knew exactly what she meant. Eve wasn't worried about Denny not returning; she was worried about herself. She knew that something was wrong with her, and she was afraid it would return in some terrible way when Denny was not with us. I was concerned as well, the memory of the zebra still in my head.

'I promise,' he said hopefully.

After he had gone, Eve closed her eyes and took a deep breath. 'I insisted he do it,' she said to me. 'I think it will be good for me, make me stronger.'

That was the first race of the series, and the race didn't go well for Denny, though it went fine for Eve, Zoë and me. We watched it on TV, and Denny qualified in the top third of the field. But shortly into the race, he had to pit because of a cut tyre; a crew member had trouble mounting the new wheel, and by the time Denny returned to the race, he was a lap down and never recovered. Twenty-fourth place.

The second race came only a few weeks after the first and, again, Eve, Zoë and I managed fine. For Denny, the results of the race were very much the same as the first: spilled fuel that resulted in a stop-and-go penalty, costing Denny a lap. Thirtieth place.

Denny was extremely frustrated.

'I like the guys,' he told us at dinner when he was home for a stretch. 'They're good people, but they're not a good pit crew. They're making mistakes, killing our season.'

'Can't you get a new crew?' Eve asked.

I was next to the dining room, so I couldn't see them, but I could hear them. Denny picking up the wooden salad bowl and serving himself more salad. Zoë pushing her chicken nuggets around on the plate.

'Eat them, honey,' Eve said. 'Don't play with them.'

'It's not the quality of the man,' Denny tried to explain. 'It's the quality of the *team*.'

'How do you fix it?' Eve asked. 'It seems like a waste. What's the point of racing if you can't finish?'

'Practice,' Denny said. 'Practice, practice, practice. They want me to go down to Infineon next week, work with the Apex Porsche people. Work hard with the pit crew so there are no more mistakes. The sponsors are getting frustrated.'

Eve fell silent.

'Next week is your week off,' she said finally.

'I won't be gone long. Three or four days.'

I heard chair legs scrape as a chair was pushed back. I heard plates being stacked, tableware nervously gathered.

'Eat your nuggets,' Eve said again, this time sternly.

'I don't like nuggets.'

'You're not leaving the table until you eat your nuggets.'

After a long silence, Denny said, 'I'll make you a hot dog.'

'No,' Eve said. 'She'll eat the nuggets.'

Zoë started to cry. I went to the door and looked in. Eve was standing at the head of the table, her face red and pinched. Zoë was sobbing into her nuggets.

Denny stood to make himself seem bigger. It's important for the alpha to be bigger.

'You're overreacting,' he said.

'You always take her side!' Eve barked.

'I just want her to have a dinner she'll eat.'

'Fine,' Eve hissed. 'I'll make her a hot dog, then.' She threw open the freezer door and snatched a package of hot dogs. She grabbed a knife from the block and stabbed into the package, and the blade leaped from the frozen package and sliced deep and clean into Eve's left palm, between her thumb and fingers.

The knife clattered in the sink, and Eve grabbed her hand with a wail. Watery drops of blood speckled the splashback. Denny was there in a moment with a dishcloth.

'We should take you to the hospital,' he said.

'No!' she bellowed. 'No hospital!'

'I'll see if I can close it,' he said.

Zoë stood next to me, silent, eyes wide. Neither of us knew what to do.

'Zoë, baby,' Denny said. 'Can you find the butterfly closures for me in the hall closet? We'll get Mommy all patched up, OK? Blue and white box, red letters.'

Zoë headed off to find the box. Denny guided Eve to the bathroom and closed the door. I heard Eve cry out in pain.

When Zoë returned with the box of bandages, she didn't know where her parents had gone, so I walked her to the bathroom door and barked. Denny opened the door a crack and took the bandages.

'Thanks, Zoë. I'll take care of Mommy now. You can go and play or watch TV.'

He closed the door.

Zoë looked at me for a moment with concern in her eyes, and I wanted to help her. I sat before the television and waited for her to turn it on, which she did. And we watched *Kids Next Door*.

And then Denny and Eve appeared.

'The cut isn't very bad,' she said to Zoë. 'If you're still hungry, I can make you a hot dog . . .'

Zoë shook her head.

Then Eve started sobbing. 'I'm so sorry,' she cried. Zoë grabbed her mother and held her tight, and they were joined by Denny.

I left, because I felt that they had resolved their issues and all was good in the world. And also, I was hungry. I wandered into the kitchen, and I found something good. A nugget. Zoë must have dropped it after Eve cut herself. I sniffed the nugget, and I recoiled in disgust. It was bad! Disease laden! The nuggets had been in the freezer too long or out of the freezer too long. This nugget—and probably all the others on the plate—had definitely turned.

I felt bad for Zoë: all she'd had to do was say that the nuggets didn't taste right, and this incident would have been avoided. But Eve would have found a way to hurt herself anyway, I suppose. They needed this. It was important to them as a family, and I understood that.

In racing, they say that your car goes where your eyes go. Simply another way of saying *that which you manifest is before you*.

I know it's true; racing doesn't lie.

4

When Denny went away the following week, we went to Eve's parents' house so they could take care of us. Eve's hand was bandaged up, which indicated to me that the cut was worse than she had let on.

Maxwell and Trish, the Twins, lived in a very fancy house on Mercer Island, with an amazing view of Lake Washington and Seattle. And despite having such a beautiful place to live, they were among the most unhappy people I've ever met. Nothing was good enough for them. When we arrived, they started on about Denny right away. *He doesn't spend enough time with Zoë. He's neglecting your relationship. His dog needs a bath.* Like *my* hygiene had anything to do with it.

'What are you going to do?' Maxwell asked her.

They were standing around in the kitchen while Trish cooked dinner, making something that Zoë would inevitably hate. It was a warm spring evening, so the Twins were wearing polo shirts with their slacks. Maxwell and Trish were drinking Manhattans with cherries, Eve, a glass of wine.

'I'm going to get in shape,' Eve said. 'I feel fat.'

'I mean about Denny,' Maxwell said.

'What do I need to do about Denny?' Eve asked.

'Something! What is he contributing to your family? You make all the money!'

'He's my husband, and he's Zoë's father, and I love him. What else does he need to contribute to our family?'

Maxwell snorted and slapped the counter.

I flinched.

'You're scaring the dog,' Trish pointed out. She rarely called me by my name. They do that in prisoner-of-war camps, I've heard. Depersonalisation.

'I'm just frustrated,' Maxwell said. 'Whenever you come to stay here, it's because he's gone racing.'

'This season is really important for his career,' Eve said, trying to remain steadfast. 'I'm doing the best I can, and he appreciates that. What I don't need is you going after me for it.'

'I'm sorry,' Maxwell said, holding up his hands in surrender. 'I just want what's best for you.'

'I know, Daddy,' Eve said, and she leaned forward and kissed his cheek. She took her wine outside into the back yard, and I lingered.

Maxwell opened the refrigerator and retrieved a jar of the hot peppers he liked to eat. 'My daughter, with a *customer service technician*. Where did we go wrong?'

'She's always made her own choices,' Trish said.

'But at least her choices made sense. She majored in art history, for Pete's sake. She ends up with him?'

'The dog is watching you,' Trish said after a moment. 'Maybe he wants a pepper.' Maxwell's expression changed. 'Want a treat, boy?' he asked, holding out a pepperoncini. That wasn't why I had been watching him. I was watching him the better to glean the meaning of his words. Still, I was hungry, so I sniffed the pepper.

'They're good,' he prompted. 'Imported from Italy.'

I took the pepper from him and immediately felt a prickly sensation on my tongue. My throat felt as if it had been scraped raw. I left the room and the house. Outside the back door, I lapped at my bowl of water, but it did little to help.

Since that time, I have been wary of trying new foods, and I have never accepted food from someone I didn't fully trust.

THE WEEKS TRIPPED BY with tremendous haste, as if digging into the fall were the most important mission of all. There was no lingering on accomplishment. Denny got his first victory in Laguna in early June, he pegged a podium finish—third place—at Road Atlanta, and he finished eighth in Denver.

That summer, when we gathered round the dinner table, there was something to talk about. Trophies. Photographs. Replays on television late at night. Suddenly people were hanging around, coming over for dinner. We were even introduced to Luca Pantoni, a very powerful man at Ferrari headquarters in Maranello, Italy. I learned more about racing in those few weeks than I had in all my prior years of watching video and television.

Eve was happy again: she took what she called 'mat' classes and gained muscle tone. Her health had greatly improved with no explanation: no more headaches, no more nausea. She continued to have trouble with her injured hand, though. Still, from what I heard in the bedroom late at night, her hands retained all of the necessary flexibility and suppleness to make Denny and herself very happy.

Yet for every peak there is a valley. Denny's next race was pivotal, as a good finish would solidify his position as rookie of the year. In that race, at Phoenix International Raceway, Denny got tagged in the first turn.

This is a rule of racing: no race has ever been won in the first corner; many have been lost there.

He got caught in a bad spot. Someone tried to late-brake him going into the corner and locked it up. In full-out skid, the hard charger slammed into Denny's left front wheel, destroying the car's alignment. The toe was skewed so badly that his car crabbed up the track, scrubbing seconds off his lap time.

'It just doesn't seem fair,' Eve said. 'It was the other driver's fault.'

'If it was anybody's fault,' Denny said, 'it was mine for being where I could get collected.'

This is something I'd heard him say before: getting angry at another driver for a driving incident is pointless. Any problems that may occur have ultimately been caused by you, because you are responsible for where you are and what you are doing there.

Still, fault or no, Denny was crushed. Zoë was crushed. Eve was crushed. I was decimated. We had come so close to greatness.

August was hot and dry, and Denny spent his time doing maths. By his figuring, it was still possible for him to finish in the top ten in the series and probably win rookie of the year, and either result would assure him of getting another ride the following year.

We sat on the back porch basking in the early evening sun, Denny massaging Eve's hand gently.

'Maybe it isn't meant to be,' Eve said.

'It'll happen when it happens,' Denny told her.

'But you're never here when I'm ovulating.'

'So come with me next week. Zoë will love it; we'll stay where they have a pool. And you can come to the track for the race.'

'I can't go to the track,' Eve said. 'Not now. It might give me a—I might react badly to it.'

Denny smiled and sighed. Even Eve cracked a smile. 'Do you understand?' she asked.

'I do,' Denny answered.

I did, too. I totally understood that what filled us with energy could be toxic to someone else, especially Eve.

'We could use a turkey baster,' Denny said, and Eve laughed hard, harder than I'd seen her laugh in a long time. I didn't get the joke, but Eve thought it was hysterical.

YOUR CAR GOES where your eyes go.

We went to Denny Creek, not because it was named after Denny—it wasn't—but because it was such an enjoyable hike, Zoë clumping along in her first pair of waffle stompers, me cut loose of my leash. Summer in the Cascades is always pleasant, cool under the canopy of cedars and alders. And the smell!

We made our way along the path, up the hills and down, eventually arriving at the Slippery Slabs, as they are called, where the creek runs over a series of broad, flat rocks, pooling at some points, streaming at others. Children love the Slippery Slabs as they slide and slice through the sluices and slate. Zoë and Denny and Eve stripped down to their swimsuits and bathed gently in the waters. Denny took the lower and Eve took the upper, and they slid Zoë down the stream of water, Eve giving a push and down Zoë would go, splashing into the frigid pool at Denny's feet; he would snatch her up and whisk her back to Eve, who would slide her down again. And again.

People, like dogs, love repetition. Eve lowered Zoë into the water; she screamed and flung herself in play, slid down the slab to be caught by Denny again.

Until once. Eve dipped Zoë into the water, but instead of screaming and splashing, Zoë suddenly pulled her toes from the icy water, upsetting Eve's balance. Eve shifted her weight and somehow managed to release Zoë safely onto the dry rock, but her legs went out from underneath her. Her head hit the rock with a loud crack and bounced. It hit and bounced and hit again.

We stood, it seemed for a long time, waiting to see what was going to happen. Eve lay unmoving, and there was Zoë, not knowing what to do.

Denny bounded up to them. 'Are you OK?'

Eve blinked hard, painfully. There was blood in her mouth.

'I bit my tongue,' she said woozily.

'How's your head?' Denny asked.

'Hurts.'

'Can you make it back to the car?'

With me in the lead herding Zoë, Denny steered Eve. It was early evening when we got to the hospital in Bellevue. 'You probably have a minor concussion,' Denny said. 'But they should check it out.'

'I'm OK,' Eve repeated over and over. But clearly she wasn't. She was dazed and slurring her words. She kept nodding off, but Denny would wake her up, saying something about not falling asleep when you have a concussion.

They all went inside and left me in the car with the windows open a crack. I settled into the pocketlike passenger seat of Denny's BMW 3.0 CSi and forced myself to sleep.

In Mongolia, when a dog dies, he is buried high in the hills so people cannot walk on his grave. The dog's master whispers into the dog's ear his wishes that the dog will return as a man in his next life.

I learned that from a programme on the National Geographic Channel, so I believe it is true. Not all dogs return as men, they say; only those who are ready.

I am ready.

It was hours before Denny returned, and he returned alone. He let me out, and I could barely scramble from the seat before unleashing a torrent of urine on the lamppost in front of me.

'Sorry, boy,' he said. 'I didn't forget about you.'

When I had finished, he opened a package of peanut butter sandwich crackers. I tried to eat slowly, savouring each bite, but I was too hungry and swallowed them so quickly I barely got to taste them.

We sat on the berm for quite a long time, not speaking or anything. He seemed upset, and when he was upset, I knew the best thing I could do was be available for him. So I lay next to him and waited.

Parking lots are weird places. People love their cars so much when they are moving, but they hurry away from them so quickly when they stop moving. But in that hospital parking lot, people parked their cars and ran from them. Sprinted into the building. Or scurried out of the building and into their cars, quick to drive away with no mirror adjustment, like a getaway car.

Denny and I sat at length and watched them, the comers and goers. After a while, a car pulled into the parking lot and parked close by us. It was beautiful, a 1974 Alfa Romeo GTV in pine green with a factory-installed fabric sunroof, in mint condition. Mike got out slowly and began to walk towards us.

I greeted him, and he gave me a perfunctory pat on the head. He continued over to Denny and sat down in my spot on the berm.

'I appreciate this, Mike,' Denny said.

'Hey, man, no problem. What about Zoë?'

'Eve's dad took her to their house and put her to bed.'

Mike nodded. The crickets were louder than the traffic from the nearby Interstate 405, but not by much. We listened to them, a concert of crickets, wind, leaves, cars and fans on the roof of the hospital building.

Here's why I will be a good person. Because I listen. I cannot speak, so I listen very well. I never interrupt; I never deflect the course of the conversation with a comment of my own. People, if you pay attention to them, change the direction of one another's conversations constantly. Learn to listen! I beg of you. Pretend you are a dog like me and listen to other people rather than steal their stories.

I listened that night and I heard.

'How long will they keep her?' Mike asked.

'They might not even do a biopsy. Malignant or not, it's still causing problems. The headaches, the nausea, the mood swings.'

'Really,' Mike deadpanned. 'Mood swings? Maybe *my* wife has a tumour.'

It was a joke line, but Denny didn't have a sense of humour that night. He said sharply, 'It's not a tumour, Mike. It's a *mass*. It's not a tumour until they test it.'

'Sorry,' Mike said. 'I was . . . Sorry.' He grabbed me by the scruff and gave me a shake. 'Really rough,' he said. 'I'd be freaking out right now if I were you.'

Denny stood up tall. For him. He wasn't a tall guy. He was a Formula One guy. 'I *am* freaking out,' he said.

Mike nodded thoughtfully. 'You don't look it. I guess that's why you're such a good driver,' he said, and I looked at him quickly. That was just what I was thinking.

'You don't mind stopping by my place and getting his stuff?' Denny took out his key ring, picked through the bundle. 'The food is in the pantry. Give him a cup and a half. He gets three of those chicken cookies before he goes to bed—take his bed; it's in the bedroom. And take his dog. Just say, "Where's your dog?" and he'll find it; sometimes he hides it.'

He found the house key and held it out for Mike. 'It's the same for both locks.'

'We'll be fine,' Mike said. 'Do you want me to bring you some clothes?'

'No,' Denny said. 'I'll go back in the morning and pack a bag if we're staying.'

'You want me to bring these back?'

'I have Eve's.'

'You don't have to keep it inside,' Mike said. 'You can let go. We're in a parking lot.'

Denny looked up at Mike. 'This is what she was afraid of.'

Mike nodded, but clearly he didn't understand what Denny was saying.

'What about your race next week?' he asked.

'I'll call Jonny tomorrow and tell him I'm out for the season,' Denny said. 'I have to be *here*.'

Mike took me to our house to get my things. I was humiliated when he said, 'Where's your dog?' I didn't want to admit that I still slept with a stuffed animal. But Denny was right; I did hide it during the day because I didn't want Zoë to assimilate it into her collection.

But I got my dog out of his hiding spot under the sofa, and we climbed back into Mike's Alfa and went to his house. His wife, who wasn't really a wife but a man, asked how it all went, and Mike brushed him off right away and poured himself a drink.

'That guy is bottled so tight,' Mike said. 'He's gonna have an aneurysm or something.'

Mike's wife picked up my dog that I had dropped on the floor.

'It stinks,' Mike's wife said. 'I'll wash it.' And he put it in the washing machine! My dog! I couldn't believe it. No one had ever handled my dog in such a way!

I watched through the glass window of the machine as it spun round and round. And they laughed at me, and when it was dry, they took it out and gave it to me. Tony, Mike's wife, handed it to me and said, 'Much better, right?'

When Tony handed me my dog, I took it to my bed, because that's what Denny would have wanted me to do. And I curled up with it.

And the irony? I liked it.

I liked my stuffed dog better clean than smelly, which was something I never would have imagined but which gave me something I could hold on to. Some belief that the centre of our family could not be fractured by a chance occurrence, an accidental washing, an unexpected illness. Deep in the kernel of our family existed a bond; Denny, Zoë, Eve, me and even my stuffed dog. However things might change around us, we would always be together.

5

Eve stayed in the hospital for a long time. Weeks. Because there was so much for Denny to do, caring for both me and Zoë, as well as visiting Eve in the hospital whenever possible, he decided that the best plan was to implement a template system, rather than our usual spontaneous way of living. The days consisted of a series of regimented events: Zoë ate her cereal while Denny made her a packed lunch. Denny then dropped Zoë at her summer camp and continued on to work. At the end of the workday, Denny retrieved Zoë from camp and returned home to cook dinner while Zoë watched cartoons. After dinner, Denny gave me my food and then took Zoë to visit Eve. Later, they returned, Denny bathed Zoë, read her a story, and tucked her into bed. Weekends were spent largely at the hospital. It was not a very colourful way to live. But it was efficient. My walks were infrequent, my trips to the dog park non-existent. Little attention was paid to me by Denny or by Zoë. But I was ready to make that sacrifice in the interest of Eve's well-being and to preserve the family dynamic.

After two weeks of this pattern, Maxwell and Trish offered to keep Zoe for a weekend, so as to afford Denny a bit of respite. They told him he looked sickly and that he should take a vacation from his troubles, and Eve agreed. 'I don't want to see you this weekend,' she said to him. Denny was ambivalent about the idea; I could tell as he packed Zoë's overnight bag. But he did let her go, and then he and I were alone. And it felt very strange.

We went jogging. We ordered delivery pizza for lunch. We spent the afternoon watching the fantastic movie *Le Mans*, in which Steve McQueen endures tragedy and pain in the ultimate test of courage and personal fortitude. We watched one of Denny's tapes featuring an on-board view of the grand Nürburgring racetrack in Germany. After that, Denny took me to the Blue Dog Park, which was a few blocks away, and he threw the ball for me.

It all felt wrong. The absence of Eve and Zoë was wrong. After we had both eaten dinner, we sat together in the kitchen, fidgeting.

Finally, Denny stood. 'I have to go see her.'

He returned a few hours later, in the darkness, and he silently climbed into his bed. I lifted my head, and he saw me.

'She's going to be OK,' he said to me.

SOON, LABOR DAY WEEKEND came, and after that Zoë was enrolled in school. 'Real school,' as she called it. Kindergarten. And she was so excited to go. With great ceremony, Denny and I walked with her a block from our house, and we waited for the bus that would take her to her new elementary school.

When the bus trundled over the hill, we were all so excited.

'Kiss me now,' she said to Denny.

'Now?'

'Not when the bus is here. I don't want Jessie to see.'

Jessie was her best friend from preschool.

Denny obliged and kissed her before the bus had stopped.

'After school, you go to Extended Day,' he said. 'Like we practised yesterday at orientation. Remember?'

'Daddy!' She made a stern face at him, and for a second I could have sworn she was Eve. The flashing eyes. She quickly turned and climbed onto the bus, and as she walked down the aisle, she turned and waved at both of us before she took her seat next to her friend.

The bus pulled away and headed for school.

EVERYTHING THEY SAID made sense, but none of it added up properly in my mind. It was an evening on which Denny took me along to the hospital to visit Eve, though I didn't get to go inside. After the visit, Zoë and I waited in the car while Maxwell and Trish joined Denny for a conference on the pavement. Maxwell and Trish did all the talking.

'Of course, there has to be a nurse on duty round the clock.'

'They work in shifts, but still, the one on duty takes breaks.'

'So someone needs to be there to help.'

'And since we're always around.'

'And you have to work.'

'So, it's best.'

'Yes, it's best.'

Denny nodded without conviction. He got into the car, and we drove off.

'When's Mommy coming home?' Zoë asked.

'Mommy's going to stay with Grandma and Grandpa for a while,' Denny said. 'Until she feels better. Is that OK with you?'

'I guess,' Zoë said. 'Why?'

'It'll be easier for—' He broke off. 'It'll be easier.'

A few days later, a Saturday, Zoë, Denny and I went to Maxwell and Trish's house. A bed had been set up in the living room. A large hospital bed that moved up and down and tilted and did all sorts of things by touching a remote control, and that came stocked with a nurse, a crinkly older woman who didn't like dogs, though I had no objection to her whatsoever. Immediately, the nurse started fretting about me. To my dismay, I was shoved outside into the back yard; thankfully, Zoë came to my rescue.

'Mommy's coming!' Zoë told me.

She threw a ball for me and I did tricks for her, and we rolled together in the grass. It was a wonderful day, the family all together again.

'She's here!' Denny called from the back door, and Zoë and I rushed to see; this time I was allowed inside. Eve's head was covered with a stocking cap. Her cheeks were sunken, her skin sallow. She lifted her head and looked around.

'I feel like a Christmas tree,' she said. 'In the living room, everyone standing around me expecting something. I don't have any presents.'

Uncomfortable chuckles from the onlookers.

And then she looked at me directly. 'Enzo,' she said. 'Come here.'

I wagged my tail and approached cautiously. It seemed to me the hospital had made her much sicker than she really was.

'He doesn't know what to think,' Denny said for me.

'It's OK, Enzo,' she said. She dangled her hand off the side of the bed, and I bumped it with my nose. I didn't like any of this, all the new furniture, Eve looking limp and sad. So even though everyone was staring at me, I shuffled over to Zoë and stood behind her, looking out the windows into the yard.

'I think I've offended him by being sick,' she said.

That was not what I meant at all. My feelings were so complicated; I have difficulty explaining them with any clarity even today. All I could do was move to her bedside and lie down before her like a rug.

'I don't like seeing me like this either,' she said.

The afternoon was interminable. Finally, the dinner hour came, and Maxwell, Trish and Denny poured themselves cocktails, and the mood lifted dramatically. An old photo album of Eve as a child was taken out from hiding, and everyone laughed while the smell of garlic and oil floated from the kitchen where Trish cooked the food. Eve took off her cap, and we marvelled at her shaved head and grotesque scars. She showered with the help of the nurse, and when she emerged from the bathroom in one of her own dresses, she looked almost normal. I wandered into the kitchen, where Denny was again conferencing with Trish and Maxwell.

'We think Zoë should stay with us,' Maxwell said, 'until . . .'

So much of language is comprised of looks and gestures and sounds that are not words. People are ignorant of the vast complexity of their own communication.

'Until *what*?' Denny demanded. 'You're condemning her to something before you even know.'

'Please, Denny. We have to face the reality of it. The doctor said six to eight months.'

Trish sniffed in her tears. 'My baby,' she whispered.

'Zoë is just a child,' Maxwell continued. 'This is valuable time—the *only* time she has to spend with Eve. I can't *imagine* you would possibly object.'

'You're such a caring person,' Trish added.

I could see Denny was stuck. He had agreed to have Eve stay with Maxwell and Trish, and now they wanted Zoë, too. If he objected, he would be keeping a mother and a daughter apart. If he accepted their proposal, he would become an outsider in his own family.

'I understand what you're saying—' Denny said.

'We knew you would,' Trish interrupted.

'But I'll have to talk to Zoë about it to see what she wants.'

Trish and Maxwell looked at each other uneasily. 'You can't seriously consider asking a little girl what she wants,' Maxwell snorted.

'I'll talk to Zoë to see what she wants,' Denny repeated firmly.

After dinner, he took Zoë into the back yard, and they sat together on the terrace steps. 'Mommy would like it if you stayed here with her and Grandma and Grandpa,' he said. 'What do you think about that?'

She turned it over in her head. 'What do *you* think about it?' she asked.

'Well,' Denny said, 'I think maybe it's the best thing. Mommy has missed you so much, and she wants to spend more time with you. Until she's better and can come home.'

'Oh,' Zoë said. 'I still get to take the bus to school?'

'Well,' Denny said, thinking. 'Grandma or Grandpa will drive you to school and pick you up, I think.'

'Oh.'

'I'll come and visit every day,' Denny said. 'And we'll spend weekends together, and sometimes you'll stay with me, too.'

'It's OK, Daddy,' she said. 'I know you won't leave me here for ever.'

He smiled at her and kissed her on the forehead.

'I promise I will never do that,' he said.

It was agreed then, perhaps to the satisfaction of neither, that she would stay.

I marvelled at them both; how difficult it must be to be a person. At that moment, honestly, I had grave doubts as to my ability to interact on such a level. I wondered if I could ever become the human I hoped to be.

As the night wound down, I found Denny sitting in the stuffed chair next to Eve's bed.

'This is crazy,' Denny said. 'I'm going to stay, too. I'll sleep on the couch.'

'No, Denny,' Eve said. 'Please go home.'

He scratched the back of his neck and looked down. 'Zoë is here,' he said. 'Your folks are here. You've told me you want Enzo to stay with you tonight. But you send me away? What did I do?'

She sighed deeply.

'Zoë won't remember,' she said. 'I don't care what my parents think. And Enzo—well, Enzo understands. But I don't want you to see me like this.'

'Like what?'

'Look at me,' she said. 'My head is shaved. My face looks old. My breath smells like I'm rotting inside. I'm ugly—'

'I don't care what you look like,' he said. 'I see who you really are.'

'*I* care what I look like,' she said. 'When I look at you, I see my reflection in your eyes.'

Denny turned away as if to shield his eyes from her, as if to take away the mirrors.

'I'll pack Zoë's things and come back in the morning,' he said finally, without turning round.

'Thank you, Denny,' Eve said, relieved. 'You can take Enzo. I don't want you to feel abandoned.'

'No,' he said. 'Enzo should stay. He misses you.'

He kissed Eve good night, tucked Zoë into bed, then left me with Eve.

The house grew quiet and dark, Zoë in bed, Maxwell and Trish in their room with their TV blinking under the door. Eve was settled into her bed in the living room with the nurse sitting in a dark corner playing a page of her word-search book. I lay next to Eve's bed.

Later, Eve was asleep, and the nurse nudged me with her foot. She led me to the back of the house, and she opened the door that led to the garage.

'In you go,' she said. 'We don't want you disturbing Mrs Swift during the night.'

I looked at her, puzzled. Disturb Eve? Why would I do that?

She took my hesitation as rebellion; she snatched my collar and shoved me into the dark garage and closed the door. It wasn't too cold, and it wasn't overly unpleasant, if you don't mind a concrete floor and the smell of engine oil in a pitch-black room. But I had never slept in a garage before.

Hours into my nightmare, the garage door opened, and Eve was there in her nightgown.

'Enzo?' she questioned. I emerged from the darkness, relieved to see her again. 'Come with me.' She led me back to the living room, and climbed into the bed and pulled up the sheets to her neck. 'I need you with me,' she said. 'I'm so afraid.'

It's OK, I said. *I'm here.*

She rolled to the edge of the bed and looked down at me, her eyes glazed. 'Get me through tonight,' she said. 'That's all I need. Enzo, please. You're the only one who can help.'

I will, I said.

'Don't worry about that nurse; I sent her home.' I looked over to the corner, and the crinkly old woman was gone.

I didn't sleep at all that night. I stood guard, waiting for the demon to show his face. The demon was coming for Eve, but he would have to get past me first, and I was ready.

The demon stayed away. In the morning, the others awoke and cared for Eve, and I was able to relinquish my guard duties and sleep.

'What a lazy dog,' I heard Maxwell mutter as he passed me.

And then I felt Eve's hand on my neck, stroking.

'Thank you,' she said. 'Thank you.'

FOR THE FIRST few weeks of our new arrangement—Denny and I lived in our house, while Eve and Zoë lived with the Twins—Denny visited them every evening after work, while I stayed home alone. Whenever he came home from the Twins' house, he reported to me how good Eve looked and that she should be coming home soon. But I saw her, too, at the weekends, and I knew. She wasn't getting better, and she wouldn't be coming home any time soon.

Every weekend, without fail, both Denny and I visited Eve on Saturday when we picked up Zoë, and again on Sunday when we delivered her home after our sleepover; we frequently took our Sunday meal with the extended family. I spent the occasional night with Eve in her living room, but she never needed me as much as she had that first night when she was so afraid.

Zoë's time with us should have been filled with joy, but she didn't seem altogether happy. How could she be, living with her mother, who was dying, and not with her father, who was very much alive?

6

In February, the black pit of winter, we went on a trip to north-central Washington, to an area called the Methow Valley. It's important for United States citizens to celebrate the birthdays of their greatest presidents, so all the schools were closed for a week; Denny, Zoë and I went to a cabin in the snowy mountains to celebrate. The cabin was owned by a relative of Eve's whom I had never met. It was quite cold, though on the warmer afternoons I enjoyed running in the snow. I much preferred to lie by the skirting board heater and let the others do their exercises, skiing and snowshoeing and all of that. Eve, who was too weak to travel, and her parents were not there. But many others were, all of whom were relatives of some kind or another. We were only there, I overheard, because Eve had thought it was very important for Zoë to spend time with these people, since she, Eve, someone said, would die very soon.

I had no idea who was connected to whom. They were all cousins, I understood, but there were certain generational gaps that were confusing to me, and some of the people were without parents but were with uncles and aunts instead, and some might just have been friends. Zoë and Denny kept mostly to themselves, but they still participated in certain group events like horse riding in the snow, sledging and snowshoeing. The group meals were convivial and, though I was determined to remain aloof, one of the cousins was always willing to slip me a treat at mealtime.

It was on one of the evenings while sitting round the fire that I noticed Denny had an admirer. She was young, the sister of someone whom Denny had apparently met years earlier, because his first comment to her and the others was about how much she had grown since he had seen her last. She was a teenager, who had a full set of breasts and so was, for all intents and purposes, an adult, but who still acted like a child, always asking for permission to do things.

This girl-not-yet-a-woman was named Annika, and she always knew how to position herself and time her movements to force a meeting with Denny. She sat next to him round the fire. She sat across from him at meals. She doted on Zoë. Denny was ignorant of her advances; I don't know if it was deliberate or not, but he certainly acted as if he hadn't a clue.

As the end of the week drew near, the weather reports on the radio changed, and Denny became quite tense. He needed to get back to work, he said.

Annika needed to get back, too. A student at the Holy Names Academy, she needed to return so that she could consult with fellow students and prepare some kind of project. She spoke with urgency, but only after she understood that Denny was planning on heading west before any of the other cousins. Only after she realised that if her needs and Denny's needs coincided, she might win for herself five hours next to him in his car.

The morning of our departure came, the storm had settled in, and the windows of the cabin were pelted with a freezing rain. Denny fretted for most of the morning. The radios announced the closure of Stevens Pass because of the storm. Traction devices were required on Snoqualmie Pass.

We left, stopping at a gas station along the way to purchase chains for our tyres. It was dangerous driving, and I didn't like it at all. I rode in the back with Zoë; Annika rode in the front. I could see Denny's hands were gripping the steering wheel far too tightly. In a racing car, the hands must be relaxed, and Denny's always are when I see the in-car videos from his races. But for that excruciating drive down the Columbia River, Denny held the wheel in a death grip.

I felt very bad for Zoë, who was clearly frightened. The rear of the car moved more suddenly than the front, so she and I experienced more of the slipping and sliding sensation generated by the ice. Before I knew it, I was in a full-blown panic. I tried to clamber into the front seat, which was totally counterproductive. Denny finally barked, 'Zoë, please settle Enzo down!'

She grabbed me round the neck and held me tightly. I was very afraid, and I was grateful for her care.

When we reached the turnoff for Highway 2, there was an announcement on the radio that Blewett Pass was closed because of a jackknifed tractor trailer rig. Denny anticipated faster travel on I-90 because of its size, but it was worse, not better. The rains had begun, and the central reservation was more like a spillway than a grassy divide between east and west.

After seven hours of gruelling travel and still two hours away from Seattle in good driving weather, Denny had Annika call her parents on her cellphone and ask them to find a place for us to stay somewhere near Cle Elum. But they called back soon and told us that all the motels were full because of the storm. We stopped at a McDonald's, and Denny purchased food for us to eat—I got chicken nuggets—then we pressed onwards to Easton.

Outside Easton, Denny stopped his car alongside dozens of other cars and trucks in the chain-up area and ventured into the freezing rain. He lay down on the roadway and installed the tyre chains, which took half an hour, and when he climbed back into the car, he was soaking wet and shivering.

'You poor thing,' Annika said, and she rubbed his shoulders to warm him.

'They're going to close the pass soon,' Denny said. 'That trucker heard it on the radio.'

'Can't we wait here?' Annika asked. 'They expect flooding. If we don't make it over the pass tonight, we might be stuck for days.'

It was nasty and horrible, snowy and icy and freezing rain, but we pushed on, our little old BMW chugging up the mountain until we reached the summit where they have the ski lifts, and then everything changed. There was no snow, no ice, just rain. We rejoiced in the rain!

Shortly, Denny stopped the car to remove the chains, which took another half-hour and got him soaking again, and then we were going downhill. The visibility was terrible. It was near midnight—the five-hour drive having taken more than ten—when Annika called her parents and told them we had made it safely to Seattle. They told her—and she related to us—that the news had reported flash-flooding conditions that caused a rock slide closing westbound I-90 near the summit.

'We must have just missed it,' Denny said. 'Thank God.'

'No, no,' Annika said into her phone. 'I'll stay with Denny. He's too exhausted to keep driving, and Zoë is sleeping in the back seat; she should be put to bed. Denny said he's happy to drive me home in the morning.'

This made Denny turn and look at her questioningly. Annika smiled at him and winked. She ended her call and slipped her phone into her bag.

'We're almost there,' she said, looking out the windshield, her breaths shallow with anticipation.

Why he didn't get right back on the freeway and drive up to Edmonds, where her family lived, I'll never know. Perhaps, on some level, he needed to connect with someone who reminded him of the passion he and Eve used to share.

Back at the house, Denny carried Zoë to her room and put her to sleep. He turned on the television, and we watched the footage of Snoqualmie Pass being shut down by the authorities, for only a few days, they predicted hopefully, though possibly for a week or more. Denny went into the bathroom and shed his wet clothes; he returned wearing sweatpants and an old T-shirt. He pulled a beer from the refrigerator and opened it.

'Can I take a shower?' Annika asked.

Denny seemed startled. He had almost forgotten about her. He showed her where the towels were, and then he closed the door. He got the extra sheets and pillows and blankets, unfolded the couch in the living room, and made the temporary bed for Annika. When he was done, he went into his bedroom and sat on the end of his own bed.

'I'm fried,' he said to me, and then he fell backwards so he was lying on the bed, his hands on his chest, his feet still on the floor. I lay on the floor near him and fell asleep as well.

I opened my eyes and saw her standing over him. Her hair was wet, and she wore Denny's bathrobe. She said nothing. She watched him sleep for several minutes, and I watched her. It was spooky behaviour. I didn't like it. She opened her robe, exposing a sliver of pale white flesh and a tattoo of a sunburst encircling her belly button. She shrugged off her robe and stood naked. Still, he was unconscious. She reached down and slipped her small hands into the band of his sweatpants. She pulled them down to his knees.

'Don't,' he muttered, his eyes still closed.

He had driven for more than ten hours across a harrowing course of snow and ice and flooding. He had nothing left with which to fend off an attack.

She pulled his sweatpants down to his ankles, then lifted one foot and then the other to remove them completely. She looked at me.

'Shoo,' she said.

I didn't shoo. I was too angry. She gave me a dismissive look and turned her attention towards Denny.

'Don't,' he said sleepily.

'Shhh,' she soothed. 'It's all good.'

I have faith. I will always have faith in Denny. So I have to believe what she did to him was without his consent, without his knowledge. He had nothing to do with it. She took advantage of him.

Still, I could no longer stand by and watch. I barked sharply. I growled, I snapped, and Denny suddenly awakened; his eyes popped open, and he saw the naked girl, and he leaped away from her.

'What the hell?' he shouted.

I continued to bark.

'Enzo!' he snapped. 'That's enough!'

I stopped barking, but I kept my eye on her in case she were to assault him once again.

'Where are my trousers?' Denny asked frantically, standing on the bed. 'What are you doing?'

'I love you so much,' she said.

'I'm married!'

She crawled onto the bed, reaching for him, so I barked again.

'Make the dog go away,' she said.

'Annika, stop!' Denny grabbed her wrists; she squirmed playfully.

'Stop!' he shouted, jumping off the bed, grabbing his sweatpants from the floor, and pulling them on quickly.

'I thought you liked me,' Annika said, her mood abruptly darkening. 'I thought you *wanted* me.'

'Annika, put this on,' he said, holding out her robe. 'I can't talk to a fifteen-year-old nude woman. I'll take you home.'

She clutched the robe to herself.

'You!' she wailed, and she started crying. 'You flirted with me all week. You teased me. You kissed me.'

'I kissed you on the cheek,' Denny said. 'It's normal for relatives to kiss on the cheek. It's called affection, not love.'

'But I love you!' she howled, and then she was in an all-out crying fit, her eyes squeezed shut, her mouth contorted. 'I love *you*!' she kept saying over and over. 'I love *you*!'

Denny was trapped. He wanted to console her, but whenever he moved closer, she dropped her hands, which were clutching the crumpled robe to her chest, and suddenly her breasts were exposed to him, and he had to retreat. This happened several times.

Finally, Denny had to put a stop to it. 'I'm going to leave the room,' he said. 'You will put on the robe and make yourself decent. When you're ready, come into the living room, and we can discuss this further.'

And he turned round and marched away. I followed.

Finally she came out wearing the robe, her eyes swollen with tears. She didn't say a word, but she went straight to the bathroom. A few moments later, she emerged wearing her clothes.

'I'll take you home,' Denny said.

'I called my father,' Annika said, 'from the bedroom.'

Denny froze. 'What did you tell him?' he asked.

She looked at him for a long time before she answered. If her intention was to make him anxious, it worked.

'I told him to come pick me up,' she said. 'The bed is too uncomfortable here.'

'Good,' Denny sighed. 'Good thinking.'

She didn't respond but continued to stare at him.

'If I gave you the wrong impression, I'm sorry,' Denny said, looking away. 'You're a very attractive woman, but I'm married and you're so young. This isn't a viable . . .'

'Affair,' she said firmly.

'Situation,' he whispered.

She picked up her handbag and her duffel and walked to the foyer. We could all see the headlights when they appeared in front of the house. Denny and I watched from the doorway as she tossed her bags in the back of the Mercedes and climbed into the front seat. Her father, in his pyjamas, waved and then drove away.

THAT YEAR we had a cold spell in each winter month, and when the first warm day of spring finally arrived in April, the trees and flowers and grasses burst to life with such intensity that the television news had to proclaim an allergy emergency. So while the rest of the world was focused on the inconvenience of hay fever, the people in my world had other things to do: Eve continued with the inexorable process of dying, Zoë spent too much time with her grandparents, and Denny and I worked at slowing the beating of our hearts so we wouldn't feel so much pain.

Still, Denny allowed for an occasional diversion, and that April, one presented itself. He had got a job offer from one of the racing schools he worked for: they had been hired to provide racing drivers for a television commercial, and they asked Denny to be one of the drivers. The racetrack was in California, a place called Thunderhill Raceway Park. I knew it was happening in April, because Denny talked about it quite a bit; he was very excited. But I had no idea that he planned to drive there, a ten-hour trip. And I had even less of an idea that he planned on taking me with him.

The drive down wasn't very special: the middle of Oregon is not noted for its scenic beauty, though other parts of Oregon are. And the mountain passes in northern California were still somewhat snowy. And then we fell out of the sky and into the verdant fields north of Sacramento.

Stunning. Absolutely stunning, the vastness of a world so intense with growth and birth, in the season of life between the dormant winter and the baking heat of summer. Vast, rolling hills covered with newly sprung grass and great swaths of wild flowers.

And the track. Relatively new, well cared for, challenging with twists and elevation changes and so much to look at. The morning after we arrived, Denny took me jogging. We jogged the entire track. He was doing it to familiarise himself with the surface. You can't really see a track from inside a racing car travelling at one hundred and fifty miles per hour or more, he said. You have to get out and *feel* it.

After we had travelled the entire track and studied all three miles and fifteen turns, we returned to the paddock. Two large semi trucks had arrived. Several men in racing-crew uniforms erected tents and canopies and laid out an elaborate food service, while others unloaded six beautifully identical Aston Martin DB5s, the kind made famous by James Bond. Denny introduced himself to a man who walked with the gait of someone in charge. His name was Ken.

'Thanks for your dedication,' Ken said, 'but you're early.'

'I wanted to walk the track,' Denny explained.

Ken nodded and looked at his watch. 'It's too early for race engines,' he said, 'but you can take your street exhaust out if you want. Just keep it sane.'

'Thanks,' Denny said, and he looked at me and winked.

We went over to a crew truck, and Denny caught the arm of a crew member. 'I'm Denny,' he said. 'One of the drivers.'

The man shook his hand and introduced himself as Pat. 'You've got time,' he said. 'Coffee is over there.'

'I'm going to take my Beemer out for a few easy laps. Ken said it was OK. I was wondering if you had a tie-down I could borrow.'

'What do you need a tie-down for?' Pat asked.

Denny glanced at me quickly, and Pat laughed.

'Hey, Jim,' he called to another man. 'This guy wants to borrow a tie-down so he can take his dog for a joy ride.' They both laughed, and I was a little confused.

'I have something better,' the Jim guy said. He went round to the cab of the truck and returned a minute later with a bed sheet. Denny told me to get in the front seat of his car and sit, which I did. They wrapped the sheet over me, pressing me to the seat, leaving only my head sticking out.

'Too tight?' Denny asked.

I was too excited to reply. He was going to take me out in his car!

'Take it easy on him until you see if he has a stomach for it,' Pat said. 'Nothing worse than cleaning dog puke out of your vents.'

Denny walked around to the driver's side. He took his helmet out of the back seat and squeezed it onto his head. He got in the car and put on his seat belt.

'One bark means slower, two means faster, got it?'

I barked twice, and that surprised him and Pat and Jim, who were both leaning in the passenger window.

'He wants to go faster already,' Jim said.

'We're going to take it easy,' Denny said, and off we went.

Being on a track was a new experience for me. It was like running through a field, gliding over a plain. Denny shifted smoothly, but I noticed he drove more aggressively than he did on the street.

'I'm finding my visuals,' he explained to me. 'Turn-in points, braking. Some guys drive more by feel. But I'm very visual. I already have dozens of reference points on this track even though I've never driven it, seven or eight specific things I've noted on each turn from our track walk.'

Around the turns we went. I felt special, being with Denny on the race-track. He had never taken me on a track before. I could have driven like that all day.

After three laps he looked over at me. 'Brakes are warm,' he said. 'Tyres are warm.' I didn't understand what he was getting at. 'You want to try a hot lap?'

A hot lap? I barked twice.

Denny laughed. 'Sing out if you don't like it,' he said, 'one long howl.' He firmly pressed the accelerator to the floor.

There is nothing like it. The sensation of speed. Nothing in the world can compare. It was the sudden acceleration, not Jim's bed sheet, that kept me pinned to the seat as we gathered speed and flew down the first straight.

'Hold on now,' Denny said, 'we're taking this at speed.'

Fast, we went, hurtling, faster. I watched the turn approach, scream at us until we were practically past it, and then he was off the accelerator and hard on the brakes. The nose of the car dove, and then I was thankful for the sheet, because without it I would have been thrown against the windshield. The tyres were screeching, they were shouting, howling. Fifteen turns at Thunderhill. And I loved them all equally. Around the track we went, faster and faster, lap after lap.

After a cool-down lap, we pulled into the paddock and the entire crew was waiting. They surrounded the car, and their hands released me from my harness and I leaped to the tarmac.

'Did you like it?' one of them asked me, and I barked and jumped high in the air.

'You were hauling ass out there,' Pat said to Denny. 'We've got a real racer on the set.'

'Well, Enzo barked twice,' Denny explained with a laugh. 'Two barks means faster!'

They laughed, and I barked twice again. Faster! The feeling. The sensa-tion. The movement. The speed. The car. It's all about the ride!

There is nothing more to tell about that trip, because nothing could possibly be more incredible than those few hot laps that Denny gave to me. Until that moment, I thought that I loved racing. I intellectualised that I would enjoy being in a racing car. Until that moment, I didn't know.

I dreamed of going out again at speed, but I suspected—as it turned out, correctly so—that more track time for me was unlikely. Still, I had my memory, my experience I could relive in my mind again and again. Two barks means faster. Sometimes, to this day, in my sleep I bark twice, because I am dreaming of Denny driving me around Thunderhill. One more lap, Denny! Faster!

SIX MONTHS CAME and six months left, and Eve was still alive. Then seven months. Then eight. On the first of May, Denny and I were invited to the Twins' for dinner, which was unusual because it was a Monday night, and I never went with Denny on a weeknight visit. We stood awkwardly in the living room with the empty hospital bed while Trish and Maxwell prepared dinner. Eve was absent.

I wandered down the hallway to investigate, and I found Zoë playing quietly by herself in her room. She was immersed in her doll's house and didn't notice me enter.

I spotted a sock ball on the floor. I playfully dropped it at Zoë's feet, nudged it with my nose.

She turned and looked at me seriously. 'That's a baby game,' she said. 'I have to be a grown-up now.'

Disappointed, I walked slowly to the door and looked back at her over my shoulder.

'Sometimes bad things happen,' she said to herself. 'Sometimes things change, and we have to change, too.'

She was speaking someone else's words, and I'm not sure she believed them or even understood them. I returned to the living room and waited with Denny until, finally, Eve emerged from the hallway where the bedroom and bathrooms were.

And Eve was brilliant. She was wearing a gorgeous dress, long and navy blue and cut just so, and she was beaming. Even though she needed help for her runway walk, she was walking the runway, and Denny gave her a standing ovation.

'Today is the first day I am not dead,' Eve said to us. 'And we're having a party.'

The party was festive. Everyone was happy, and those who were not happy pretended that they were with such conviction that we were all convinced. Even Zoë came alive with her usual humour, apparently forgetting for a time her need to be a grown-up. When the hour came for us to leave, Denny kissed Eve deeply.

'I love you so much,' he said. 'I wish you could come home.'

'I want to come home,' she replied. 'I will come home.'

She was tired, so she sat on the sofa and called me to her; I let her rub my ears. Denny was helping Zoë get ready for her bedtime, while the Twins, for once, were keeping a respectful distance.

'I know Denny's disappointed,' she said to me. 'They're all disappointed. Everyone wants me to be the next Lance Armstrong. And if I could just grab it and hold it in front of me, maybe I could be. But I can't hold it, Enzo. It's bigger than me. It's everywhere.'

In the other room, we could hear Zoë playing in the bath, Denny laughing with her, as if they had no worries in the world.

'I shouldn't have allowed it to be this way,' she said regretfully. 'I should have insisted on going home so we could all be together. That's my fault; I could have been stronger. But Denny would say we can't worry about what's already happened, so . . . Please take care of Denny and Zoë for me, Enzo. They're so wonderful when they're together.'

She shook her head to rid herself of her sad thoughts and looked down at me.

'Do you see?' she asked. 'I'm not afraid of it any more. I wanted you with me before, because I wanted you to protect me, but I'm not afraid of it any more. Because it's not the end.'

She laughed the Eve laugh that I remembered. 'But you knew that,' she said. 'You know everything.'

Not everything. But I knew she had been right about her situation: While doctors are able to help many people, for her, they could only tell her what couldn't be done. And I knew that once they identified her disease for her, once everyone around her accepted her diagnosis and reinforced it and repeated it back to her time and again, there was no way she could stop it.

We took our leave, Denny and I. I didn't sleep in the car on the ride home as I usually did. I watched the bright lights of Bellevue and Medina flicker by, so beautiful.

If I ever find myself before a firing squad, I will face my executioners without a blindfold, and I will think about Eve. And of what she said. *It's not the end.*

She died that night. Her last breath took her soul; I saw it in my dream. I saw her soul leave her body as she exhaled, and then she was released from her body and continued her journey elsewhere, high in the firmament where soul material gathers and plays out all the dreams and joys of which we temporal beings can barely conceive, all the things that are beyond our comprehension, but even so, are not beyond our attainment if we choose to attain them and believe that we truly can.

IN THE MORNING, Denny drove me over to Luther Burbank Park on the eastern shore of Mercer Island. Since it was a warm spring day, it was a good choice of dog parks, as it afforded lake access so Denny could throw the ball and I could swim after it.

'We'll move her back home,' Denny said to me as he threw the ball. 'And Zoë. I miss them.'

I waded over the rocky bottom; then I paddled out to the ball, bobbed for it in the lake, and returned. When I dropped the ball at Denny's feet and looked up, I saw that he was on his cellphone. After a moment he hung up.

'She's gone,' he said, and then he sobbed loudly and turned away, crying into the crook of his arm so I couldn't see.

I am not a dog who runs away from things. I had never run away from Denny before that moment, and I have never run away since. But in that moment, I had to run.

Over the asphalt path and down the other side to the amphitheatre I found what I was looking for, untamed wilderness. I needed to go wilding. I needed to feel myself, understand myself and this horrible world we are all trapped in. So I ran.

I slept in the bushes. Some time later I emerged, myself again. Denny found me and he said nothing. He led me to the car. I got in the back seat and fell asleep again immediately.

FOR EVE, her death was the end of a painful battle. For Denny, it was the beginning.

What I did in the park was selfish, because it prevented Denny from going to Zoë right away. He was angry with me for having delayed him in the park. But to postpone, even for a short time, what he was to find at the home of the Twins might have been the most merciful thing I could have done for him.

When I awoke from my slumber, we were at Maxwell and Trish's house. In the driveway was a windowless white van with a fleur-de-lis insignia on the driver's door.

Denny parked in such a way as to not block the vehicle, and then he led me round the side of the house. He went to the French doors on the patio and knocked. After a moment, Trish appeared. She opened the door and embraced Denny. She was crying.

After a long time, during which Maxwell and Zoë also appeared, Denny ended the embrace and asked, 'Where is she?'

Trish pointed. 'We told them to wait for you,' she said.

Denny stepped into the house, touching Zoë's head as he passed. After he disappeared, Trish looked at Maxwell.

'Let him have a minute,' she said.

And they, with Zoë, stepped outside and closed the French door so that Denny could be alone with Eve for the last time, even though she was no longer living.

In the emptiness that was all around me, I noticed an old tennis ball in the plantings; I picked it up and dropped it at Zoë's feet.

She looked down at the ball but did nothing with it.

Maxwell noticed what I had done, and he noticed Zoë's lack of reaction. He picked up the ball and, with a mighty heave, threw it so far into the woods behind the house that I lost sight of it.

'Fetch, boy,' Maxwell said to me sardonically, and then he turned back to the house.

I didn't fetch, but waited with them until Denny returned. When he did, he went to Zoë immediately, picked her up, and held her tightly. 'I'm so sad,' he said.

'Me, too.'

He sat on one of the teak deck chairs with Zoë on his knee. She buried her face in his shoulder and stayed like that.

'We'll take care of the arrangements,' Maxwell said. 'But we did want to speak with you about something.'

Denny waited for Maxwell to continue, but he didn't.

'You haven't eaten breakfast, Zoë,' Trish said. 'Come with me and I'll fix you an egg.'

Zoë didn't budge until Denny tapped her shoulder.

'Go get some food with Grandma,' he said.

Zoë obediently followed Trish into the house.

When she was gone, Denny leaned back with his eyes closed and sighed heavily, his face lifted to the sky. 'I knew it was coming,' Denny said finally, his eyes still closed. 'But still . . . I'm surprised.'

Maxwell nodded to himself. 'That's what concerns Trish and me,' he said.

'I don't understand what you're talking about,' Denny said.

'That's what concerns us.'

Denny leaned forward. 'What exactly are you concerned about, Maxwell?' he asked.

Then Trish was there.

'Zoë is watching TV in the kitchen,' she announced. She looked at Maxwell expectantly.

'We've just started,' Maxwell said.

'Oh,' Trish said. 'I thought . . . What have you said so far?'

'Why don't you take it from the top, Trish,' Denny said. 'Maxwell is having some difficulty with the opening. You're concerned . . .'

Trish glanced round, apparently disappointed that their concerns hadn't already been resolved.

'Well,' she began, 'Maxwell and I have discussed at great length our lives in the aftermath of Eve's death. We discussed it with Eve as well, just so you know. And we believe that the best situation for all parties involved would be for us to have custody of Zoë, to raise her in a warm and stable family situation. We hope you understand that this is in no way a commentary on you as a person or your fathering abilities. It is simply what is in Zoë's best interest.'

Denny looked from one of them to the other, a perplexed look still on his face, but he said nothing.

'What do you think?' Trish asked.

'You can't have custody of Zoë,' Denny said simply.

'I told you,' Maxwell said to Trish.

'If you could just sleep on it,' Trish said to Denny. 'You can pursue your racing career; Zoë can grow up in a loving and supportive environment. It's what Eve wanted.'

'No, I will not sleep on it,' Denny said, rising from the chair. 'You can't have custody of my daughter. Final answer.'

Maxwell reached into his back pocket and removed a business envelope.

'We didn't want it to have to be this way,' he said, and he handed the envelope to Denny.

Denny opened the envelope and removed several sheets of paper. He glanced at them briefly.

'What does this mean?' he asked.

'I don't know if you have a lawyer,' Maxwell said. 'But if you don't, you should get one. We're suing for custody of our granddaughter.'

Denny fell back into the deck chair, his hands still clinging to the documents.

'I finished my egg,' Zoë announced.

None of us had noticed her return, but there she was. She climbed on Denny's lap.

Denny looked at the Twins. And then I saw something change in Denny. I saw his face tighten with resolve.

'Zoë,' he said, standing her up. 'You run inside and pack your things, OK?'

'Where are we going?' she asked.

'We're going home now.'

Zoë smiled and started off, but Maxwell stepped forward. 'Zoë, stop right there,' he said. 'Daddy has some errands he has to run. You'll stay with us for now.'

Zoë looked from her father to her grandfather. She didn't know what to do. No one knew what to do.

And then Trish stepped in. 'Run inside and put your dolls together,' she said to Zoë, 'while we talk a little more.'

Zoë reluctantly withdrew.

'Let her stay with us, Denny,' Trish pleaded. 'I *know* we can work it out.'

'No, Trish,' he said. 'I'm taking her home with me.'

'And who's going to take care of her when you're at work?' Maxwell snapped, shaking with anger. 'Who will take care of her if, God forbid, she were to get sick? Or would you just ignore it, hide it from the doctors until she was on the verge of death, like you did with Eve?'

'She refused!' Denny cried out. 'No one could force Eve to do anything she didn't want to do,' Denny said. '*I* certainly couldn't.'

Maxwell clenched his fists tightly. 'And that's why she's dead,' he said.

'What?' Denny asked incredulously. 'I'm not continuing this conversation.' He glared at Maxwell and started towards the house. 'Zoë, let's go now. We can stop by later to get your dolls.'

Zoë emerged looking confused, holding an armful of stuffed animals. 'Can I take these?' she asked.

'Yes, honey. But let's go now.' Denny ushered her towards the path that led round to the front of the house.

'You're going to regret this,' Maxwell hissed as Denny passed.

'Let's go, Enzo,' Denny said.

We walked round to the driveway and got into our car. Denny started the engine. 'Do I have a lawyer?' he said to himself. 'I work at the most prestigious BMW and Mercedes service centre in Seattle. I have a good relationship with all the best lawyers in this town. And I have their home phone numbers.'

We pulled out of the driveway, and as we took off up the twisty Mercer Island road, I couldn't help but notice that the white van was gone. And with it, Eve.

7

With experience, a driver adjusts his understanding of how a car feels when it is near its limits.

When the pressure is intense and the race is only half completed, a driver who is being chased relentlessly by a competitor realises that he might be better off pushing from behind than pulling from the front.

In that case, the smart move is to yield his lead to the trailing car and let the other driver pass.

Sometimes, however, it is important to hold one's position and not allow the pass. For strategic reasons, a driver simply has to prove that he is better than his competition.

Racing is about discipline and intelligence, not about who has the heavier foot. The one who drives smart will always win in the end.

Zoë INSISTED on going to school the next day, and when Denny said he would pick her up at dismissal time, she complained that she wanted to play with her friends in the after-school programme. Denny reluctantly agreed.

'I'll pick you up a little earlier than I usually do,' he said when we dropped her off. He must have been afraid that the Twins would try to steal her away.

From Zoë's school, we drove up Union to Fifteenth Avenue and found a parking spot directly across from Victrola Coffee. Denny told me to sit underneath an outdoor table, which I did. A quarter of an hour later, we were joined by someone else. A large but compact man composed of circles: round head, round torso, round thighs, round hands.

'Good morning, Dennis,' the man said. 'Please accept my sincere condolences for your devastating loss.' He embraced Denny, who sat awkwardly.

'I—' Denny started, then stopped himself as the man released him and stood upright. 'Of course,' Denny said uncomfortably.

The man nodded slightly, ignoring Denny's confused reply, and then wedged himself between the metal arms of the other sidewalk chair by our table. 'This consultation will cost you an oil change.'

'Fine.'

'Let me see the paperwork.'

Denny handed him the envelope Maxwell had given him. The man took it and removed the papers.

'They said Eve told them she wanted Zoë to be raised by them. Sometimes she was on so many drugs, she would have said anything. She may have said it, but she couldn't have *meant* it.'

'I don't care about that,' the man said. 'Everything that happens will be done in the best interest of the child.'

'That's what they said,' Denny said. 'Zoë's best interest.'

'They're educated,' the man said. 'Still, the mother's final wishes are irrelevant. How long were you married?'

'Six years.'

'Any other children?'

'No.'

The man drank his latte and leafed through the papers. He was a curious man. I could sense the totality of his focus.

'Are you in a drug treatment programme?' the man asked.

'No.'

'Have you ever been convicted of a felony? Spent any time in jail?'

'No.'

The man stuffed the papers back in the envelope. 'This is nothing,' he said. 'Where is your daughter now?'

'She wanted to go to school. Should I have kept her home?'

'No, that's good. You're being responsive to her needs. Listen, this is not something you should be overly concerned with. I'll demand a summary judgment. The child will be yours free and clear.'

'OK,' Denny said.

'Call them and give them my information. Tell them all correspondence has to be directed to me as your attorney. My feeling is they're hoping you'll go away quietly. Grandparents are like that. Do they have money?'

'Plenty.'

'And you?'

'Oil changes for life,' Denny said with a forced smile.

'My rate is four-fifty an hour. I need a twenty-five hundred-dollar retainer. Do you have it?'

'I'll get it,' Denny said.

'When? Today? This week? Next week?'

Denny looked at him hard. 'This is my daughter, Mark. I promise on my soul you'll get every dollar you have coming to you.'

'You're a good man, Dennis,' Mark said. 'I'll take care of this. Of all the things you have to worry about, this is not one of them. You let me worry about this part. You take care of your daughter, OK?'

'Thanks.'

Mark trundled off down the street. When he had rounded the corner, Denny looked at me and held his hands out in front of himself. They were shaking. He didn't say anything, but I knew what he was thinking. He was thinking that if he just had a steering wheel to hold on to, his hands wouldn't shake.

I SPENT most of the day hanging out in the garage with the guys who fix the cars, because the owners of the shop didn't like it when I was in the lobby where the customers could see me.

I knew all the guys in the garage.

I felt strangely anxious that day, in a very human way. On a normal dog day, I can sit still for hours on end with no effort. But that day I was nervous and worried, uneasy and distracted. I didn't care for the sensation, yet I realised it was possibly a natural progression of my evolving soul.

The day seemed like it would never end, until the Seattle police car showed up and two policemen got out.

I nosed through the swinging door in the garage bay and into the file room. I wandered up behind the counter, which Mike was attending.

'Afternoon, Officers,' I heard Mike say. 'A problem with your car?'

'Are you Dennis Swift?' one of them asked.

'I am not,' Mike replied.

'Is he here?'

Mike hesitated. I could smell his sudden tension.

'He may have left for the day,' Mike said. 'Let me check. Can I tell him who's calling?'

'We have a warrant for his arrest,' one of the policemen said.

'I'll see if he's still in the back.'

I followed him into the back, where Denny was at the computer. 'Den,' Mike said. 'There are a couple of cops out front with a warrant.'

'For?' Denny asked, not even looking up from the screen.

'You. For your arrest.'

Denny stopped what he was doing. 'For what?' he asked.

'I didn't get the details.'

Denny stood up and started for the lobby.

'I told them you might have left for the day,' Mike said, indicating the back door with his chin.

'I appreciate the thought, Mike. But if they've got a warrant, they probably know where I live. Let me find out what this is all about.'

Like a train, the three of us snaked through the file room and up to the counter.

'I'm Denny Swift.'

'Please step out from behind the counter,' the policeman said.

Denny hesitated for a moment, then followed his instructions.

'We have a warrant for your arrest.' The cop handed Denny a sheaf of paper.

Denny read it.

'You're joking,' he said.

'No, sir,' the cop said, taking back the papers. 'Please place your hands on the counter and spread your legs.'

Denny followed their instructions and placed his hands on the counter and spread his legs; the cop patted him down thoroughly.

'Please turn around and place your hands behind your back,' the cop said.

'You don't need handcuffs,' Mike said angrily. 'He's not running anywhere!'

'Sir!' the cop barked. 'Hold!'

Denny turned round and placed his hands behind his back. The officer cuffed him.

'You have the right to remain silent,' the cop said. 'Anything you say can and will be held against you—'

'How long is this going to take?' Denny asked. 'I have to pick up my daughter.'

'I suggest you make other arrangements,' the other police officer said.

'I can pick her up, Denny,' Mike said.

'You're not on the list of approved pick-up people.'

'So who should I call?'

'. . . an attorney will be appointed to you . . .'

'Call Mark Fein,' Denny said, desperate. 'He's in the computer.'

'Do you understand these rights as I have read them to you?'

'I understand!' Denny snapped. 'Yes. I understand!'

'What are you being arrested for?' Mike asked.

Denny looked to the officers, but they said nothing.

'Rape of a child in the third degree,' Denny said.

'Felony rape,' one of the cops clarified.

'But I didn't rape anyone,' Denny said to the cop. 'Who's behind this? *What child?*'

'The one you raped,' the cop replied simply.

Without another word, the police took Denny away.

MUCH OF WHAT HAPPENED to Denny regarding the custody suit concerning Zoë as well as the criminal charges of rape of a child in the third degree was not witnessed by me. I was denied access to much information. I was not invited to attend any of the legal proceedings, for instance.

Much of what I will tell you about the ordeal that followed Eve's death is a reconstruction based on information compiled by me from secondhand knowledge and overheard conversations.

My intent here is to tell our story in a dramatically truthful way. While the facts may be less than accurate, please understand that the emotion is true.

THEY TOOK HIM to a small room with a large table and many chairs. Wooden blinds filtered the blue light that crept into the room, rippling the table and floor with long shadows.

No one bothered him. After being booked and fingerprinted and photographed, he was put in the room, alone, and left there. He sat for hours with nothing. No coffee, no water, no bathrooms. No distractions. His crime and his punishment and himself. Alone.

Did he silently berate himself for allowing himself to be in that situation? Or did he finally realise what it is like to be me, to be a dog? Did he understand that being alone is not the same as being lonely? I like to think that he was alone for that time but that he wasn't lonely.

And then Mark Fein burst into the East Precinct on Seattle's Capitol Hill. He blasted the sergeant on duty and bailed out Denny. 'What is this all about, Dennis?' Mark demanded on the street corner.

'It's nothing,' Denny said, uninterested in the conversation.

'A fifteen-year-old? Dennis!'

'She's lying.'

'Did you penetrate any of her orifices with your genitals or any other object?'

Denny stared at Mark Fein and refused to answer.

'This is part of a plan. Do you see that?' Mark said, frustrated. 'I couldn't figure why they would file a bogus custody suit, but this changes everything.'

Still Denny said nothing.

'A paedophile. A sex offender. A statutory rapist. A child molester. Do these terms fit anywhere in the concept of "the best interest of the child"?'

Denny ground his teeth; his jaw muscles bulged.

'My office, eight thirty tomorrow morning,' Mark said. 'Don't be late.'

Denny burned. 'Where's Zoë?' he demanded.

Mark Fein dug his heel into the pavement. 'They got to her before I could,' he said. 'The timing on this was not an accident.'

'I'm going to get her,' Denny said.

'Don't!' Mark snapped. 'Let them be. Now is not the time for heroics.'

Denny wheeled around and started off.

'And don't leave the state,' Mark called after him. 'And Dennis, don't even *look* at another fifteen-year-old girl!'

But Denny had already rounded the corner and was gone.

8

Hands are the windows to a man's soul. Watch in-car videos of racing drivers enough, and you'll see the truth of this statement. The rigid, tense grip of one driver reflects his rigid, tense driving style. The nervous hand-shuffle of another driver proves how uncomfortable he is in the car. A driver's hands should be relaxed, sensitive, aware.

Seeing Denny's hands shake was as upsetting for me as it was for him. After Eve's death, he glanced at his hands often, held them before his eyes and watched them shake. And then he would tuck them into his trouser pockets and keep them there, out of sight.

When Mike and Tony brought me home later that night, Denny was waiting on the dark porch with his hands in his pockets.

'Not only do I not want to talk about it,' he said to them, 'Mark told me not to. So . . .'

'Can we come in?' Mike asked

'No,' Denny replied. 'I don't feel like company right now.'

'You don't have to talk about what's going on,' Mike said. 'But it's good to *talk*. You can't keep everything inside.'

'You're probably right,' Denny said. 'But I just need to . . . assimilate . . . what's going on, and then I'll be able to talk. But not now.'

Neither Mike nor Tony moved. They looked at each other, and I could smell their anxiety.

'You want us to keep Enzo or anything?' Mike asked.

'No.'

'He'll be all right,' Tony said, and tugged at Mike's arm.

'My phone's always on,' Mike said. 'Twenty-four-hour crisis hotline. Need to talk, need anything, call me.'

They retreated down the walk.

'We fed Enzo!' Mike called from the alley.

They left, and Denny and I went inside. He took his hands from his pockets and held them up to look at them shaking. 'Rapists don't get custody of their little girls,' he said. 'See how that works?'

I followed him into the kitchen. He went to the cupboard and took out a glass. Then he poured a drink.

It was absurd. Depressed, stressed, hands shaking, and now he was going to get himself drunk? I couldn't stand for it. I barked sharply at him.

'What's the matter, Enzo, too much of a cliché for you?'

I barked again. Too much of a *pathetic* cliché for me.

'Don't judge me,' he said. 'That's not your job. Your job is to support me, not judge me.' He drank the drink and then glared at me, and I did judge him. He was acting just as they wanted him to act. This wasn't my Denny. And I didn't like him at all.

I left the room, but I didn't want to sleep in the same room as this Denny impostor. I went into Zoë's bedroom, curled up on the floor next to her bed, and tried to sleep.

Later—though I don't know how much—he stood in the doorway. 'The first time I took you for a drive in my car when you were a puppy, you puked all over the seat,' he said to me. 'But I didn't give up on you.'

I lifted my head from the ground, not understanding his point.

'I put the booze away,' he said. 'I'm better than that.'

He turned and walked away. I heard him shuffle round in the living room and then turn on the TV. So he got my point. Gestures are all that I have.

I found him on the couch watching a video of Eve, Zoë and me, from years ago when we went to Long Beach.

'No race has ever been won in the first corner,' he said. 'But plenty of races have been lost there.'

I looked at him. He reached out and scratched my ear like he has always done.

'That's right,' he said to me. 'If we're going to be a cliché, let's be a positive cliché.'

Yes: the race is long—to finish first, first you must finish.

I LOVE very few things more than a nice long walk in the drizzle of Seattle. While rain is heavy and can suppress the scents, a light shower actually amplifies smells. Which is why I love Seattle more than any other place, even Thunderhill Raceway Park.

Denny took me for a walk in the drizzle, and I relished it. We walked north of Madison Valley and into the arboretum, and Denny released me from my leash.

This is what I love to do: I love to run through a field of wet grass that has not been mowed recently. It reminds me of my childhood, back on the farm, where there were fields and I ran.

For a long time we walked and ran in this park until I was exhausted and thirsty. We emerged and walked in a neighbourhood that was foreign to me. Denny stopped in a café to purchase a cup of coffee for himself. He brought some water for me, which was in a paper cup and difficult to drink.

And we continued walking.

I recognised Fifteenth Avenue when we reached it, and I knew Volunteer Park quite well. But I was surprised when we went into the Lake View Cemetery. Following the paved road to the north, we looped around the central hill and came upon a temporary tent structure, under which many people were assembled.

They were all dressed nicely, and those who weren't protected from the drizzle by the tent were holding umbrellas. Immediately, I saw Zoë.

We got very close to them, and then, suddenly, someone broke off from the group. A man. And then another man, and another. The three of them walked towards us.

One of them was Maxwell. The others were Eve's brothers, whose names I never knew, because they showed themselves so infrequently.

'You're not welcome here,' Maxwell said sternly.

'She's my wife,' Denny said calmly. 'The mother of my child.'

Zoë saw her father. She waved at him, and he waved back.

'You're not welcome here,' Maxwell said again. 'Leave, or I'll call the police.'

The two brothers raised themselves. Pre-battle posturing.

'Why are you doing this?'

'You've never been good to Eve,' Maxwell said. 'And with what you did to Annika, I will not trust you with Zoë.'

'Nothing happened that night—'

But Maxwell had already turned. 'Please escort Mr Swift away from here,' he said to his two sons, and he abruptly walked away.

In the distance, I saw Zoë, unable to contain herself any longer; she jumped out of her seat and ran towards us.

'Beat it,' one of the men said.

'Punch me if you want,' Denny said. 'I won't fight back.'

Zoë reached us and leaped at Denny. He hoisted her into the air and propped her on his hip and kissed her cheek. 'How's my baby?' he asked.

'How's my daddy?' she replied.

Trish inserted herself between Denny and the brothers. She told them to leave, and she turned to Denny. 'Please,' she said. 'I understand why you're here, but it can't be done like this. I really don't think you should stay.' She hesitated for a moment, and then she said, 'I'm sorry. You must be so alone.'

Denny didn't respond. I looked up at him, and his eyes were full of tears.

Zoë noticed, too, and started crying with him. 'It's OK to cry,' she said. 'Grandma says crying helps, because it washes away the hurting.'

He looked at Zoë for a long moment and she at him. Then he sighed sadly. 'You'll stay with Grandma and Grandpa for a little bit longer, until I get everything worked out, OK?'

'They told me I might stay with them for a while.'

'Well,' he said regretfully, 'Grandma and Grandpa are very good at thinking ahead.'

'We can all compromise,' Trish said. 'I know you're not a bad person—'

'There is no compromise,' Denny said.

'Given time, you'll see. It's what's best for Zoë.'

'Enzo!' Zoë called out suddenly, locating me beneath her.

I was surprised and pleased by her hearty greeting, so I licked her face.

Trish leaned into Denny. 'You must have been missing Eve terribly,' she whispered to him. 'But to take advantage of a fifteen-year-old girl—'

Denny abruptly straightened and pulled away from her. 'Zoë,' he said. 'Enzo and I are going to watch from a special spot. Come on, Enzo.' He bent down and kissed her forehead, and we walked away. Zoë and Trish watched us go. We walked up the bump of a hill to the top, where we stood underneath the trees. The man reading from a book. The people laying roses on the coffin. And everyone leaving in their cars.

We stayed. We waited for the workers who came and dismantled the tents. The workers who came and used a strange winch device to lower the coffin into the ground.

We stayed. We watched the men with their little Caterpillar as they shoveled all the dirt over her. We waited.

When they were all gone, we walked down the hill and we stood before the mound of dirt and we cried.

And finally, we began the long walk home.

THE MORNING after Eve's funeral, I could barely move. I was eight years old, two years older than Zoë. While I was still too young to suffer an arthritic condition in my hips, that's exactly what I suffered from. It was an unpleasant condition, yes; but in a sense, it was a relief that I could concentrate on my own difficulties rather than dwell on other things that preoccupied my thoughts: specifically, Zoë being stranded with the Twins.

As I mentioned, I do not know the source of Eve's distrust of medicine; the origins of my distrust, however, are all too clear. When I was just a pup, not more than a week or two old, the alpha man on the farm in Spangle introduced me to a friend of his. The man held me in his lap and petted me, feeling my forelegs at length.

'They should come off,' he said to the alpha man.

'I'll hold him,' the alpha man said.

'He needs anaesthetic, Will. You should have called me last week.'

'I'm not wasting my money on a dog, Doc,' the alpha man said. 'Cut.'

The alpha man gripped me tightly around my midsection. The other man, 'Doc', took hold of my right paw and, with shiny scis-sors that glinted in the sunlight, snipped off my right dewclaw. My right thumb. It was bloody and horrible, and I cried out. Then Doc took hold of my left paw and, without hesitating for a moment, cut off my left thumb. And then the blood was everywhere. The pain was so intense it left me shivering and weak.

Do you see? This is why I distrust them.

The day after Eve's funeral, Denny took me to the vet. He diagnosed me, prescribed anti-inflammatory medication, and said there was nothing else he could do except, some day in the future, perform expensive surgery to replace my defective parts.

Denny thanked the man and drove me home.

'You have hip dysplasia,' he said to me, shaking his head in amazement.

I shook my head, too. With my diagnosis, I knew, would come my end. Slowly, perhaps. The visible becomes inevitable.

BECAUSE OF THE CRIMINAL CHARGES against Denny, the Twins had been granted a temporary restraining order that meant Denny didn't get to see Zoë at all for several months. Minutes after he was arrested, Maxwell and Trish filed a motion to terminate Denny's right to custody of any kind, since he was clearly an unfit parent. A paedophile. A sex offender.

Mark Fein suggested it would be inflammatory to tell Zoë about the legal proceedings, and he suggested that Denny invent a story about driving racing cars in Europe to explain his prolonged absence. Mark Fein also negotiated a letter exchange: notes and drawings made by Zoë would be delivered to Denny, and Denny could write letters to his child, as long as he agreed to allow those letters to be censored by the Twins' counsel.

As much as I wanted Denny to act, to lash out against the establishment in a bold and passionate way, I respected his restraint. Denny has long admired the legendary driver Emerson Fittipaldi. 'Emmo', as he was called by his peers, was a champion of great stature and consistency and was known for his pragmatism on the track. Like Emmo, Denny never took unnecessary risks.

While I, too, admire Emmo, I still think that I would like to drive like Ayrton Senna, full of emotion and daring. I would like to have packed our necessities in the BMW, driven by Zoë's school one day to pick her up unannounced, and then headed directly for Canada.

But it was not my choice. No one cared a whit about me. Which is why they were all in such a state of panic when Zoë asked her grandparents if she could see me. You see, no one had accounted for my whereabouts. The Twins immediately called Mark Fein, who immediately called Denny to outline the nature of our predicament.

'She believes it all,' I could hear Mark shout over the phone. 'You could have taken him with you, but there are quarantine rules!'

'Tell her of course she can see Enzo,' Denny said calmly. 'Enzo is staying with Mike and Tony while I'm in Europe. I'll have Mike bring Enzo over on Saturday.'

And that's what happened. In the early afternoon, Mike picked me up and drove me over to Mercer Island, and I spent the afternoon playing with Zoë on the great lawn. Before dinner time, Mike returned me to Denny.

'How did she look?' Denny asked Mike.

'She looked terrific,' Mike said. 'She has her mother's smile.'

'They had a good time together?'

'A fantastic time. They played all day.'

Denny wiped his nose quickly. 'Thanks, Mike,' he said. 'Really. Thanks a lot.'

'Any time,' Mike said.

I appreciated Mike's efforts to appease Denny, even though he was avoiding the truth. Maybe he couldn't hear what I heard. Zoë's profound sadness. Her loneliness. Her whispered plans that she and I would somehow smuggle ourselves off to Europe and find her father.

That summer without Zoë was very painful for Denny. In addition to feeling isolated from his daughter, his career was derailed: though he was offered the opportunity to drive again for the racing team he was with the previous year, he was forced to decline, as the pending criminal case demanded that he remain in the state of Washington. Further, he was not allowed to accept any of the lucrative teaching jobs and commercial work offers that came his way—after his spectacular experience at Thunderhill, he was highly recommended in the commercial industry and received offers over the phone fairly frequently. These jobs almost always took place out of state and therefore were forbidden to him.

And yet.

We are all afforded our physical existence so we can learn about ourselves. So I understand why Denny, on a deeper level, allowed this situation to befall him. I won't say he created the situation, but he allowed it. He chose this life, and therefore he chose this battle.

THERE WAS AN OCCASION that summer when Denny found a teaching engagement in Spokane and, via Mike, asked if the Twins could take me for the weekend; they agreed, as they had grown accustomed to my presence in their home, never soiling their expensive rugs or carpets, never begging for food.

I would much rather have gone to racing school with Denny, but I understood that he depended on me to take care of Zoë.

On a Friday afternoon, I was delivered by Mike into Zoë's waiting embrace.

The next afternoon, as the Twins took their alcohol on the deck as they tended to do and Zoë watched television in the TV room, I dozed outside in the sun. And I heard them.

'I know it's for the best,' Trish said. 'But still, I feel badly for him.'

'He forced himself on a teenage girl,' Maxwell said sternly. 'What kind of a father preys on innocent young girls?'

'From what I hear, she's not that innocent.'

'Are you suggesting that she made it up?'

'No,' Trish said. 'But why did Pete wait to tell us about it until after you complained to him so bitterly that you were certain we wouldn't get custody of Zoë?'

'I don't care about any of that,' Maxwell said, waving her off. 'He wasn't good enough for Eve, and he's not good enough for Zoë. You know it!'

'I know, I know,' she said, and sipped her amber drink. 'But he's not a bad person.'

He slapped the glass down on the teak table. 'It's time to start dinner,' he said, and he went inside. I was stunned. I, too, had noted the coincidence of events, and I had been suspicious since the beginning. But to hear the words, the coldness in Maxwell's tone.

They had no idea who they were dealing with. Denny would not kneel before them. He would never quit; he would never break.

With disgust, I followed them into the house. They were no longer people to me. They were now the Evil Twins.

My anger fed my thirst for revenge. And I was not above using the tools of my dogness to exact justice.

When it was time to take me out that night, Maxwell opened the French door to the back deck and began chanting, 'Get busy, boy. Get busy.'

I didn't go outside. I thought about how he and Trish were grossly inferior guardians for my Zoë. I crouched in my stance right there, inside the house, and I dropped a massive pile of diarrhoea on his expensive carpet.

'What the hell?' he shouted at me. 'Bad dog!'

I turned and trotted cheerfully to Zoë's room.

9

Oh, a breath of September! The vacations were done. The lawyers were back at work. The courts were at full staff. The truth would be had! He left that morning wearing the only suit he owned and a dark tie. He looked very good.

'Mike will come by at lunch and take you for a walk,' he said to me. 'I don't know how long this will go on.'

Mike came and walked me briefly through the neighbourhood so I wouldn't be lonely, and then he left again.

Later that afternoon, Denny returned. He smiled down at me. 'Do I need to reintroduce you two?' he asked. And behind him was Zoë! I leaped in the air. I *knew* Denny would vanquish the Evil Twins. Zoë had returned.

It was an amazing afternoon. We played in the yard. We ran and laughed. We made dinner together and sat at our table and ate.

'Are you going back to Europe soon?' Zoë asked out of the blue.

Denny froze in place. The story had worked so well, Zoë still believed it. 'No, I'm not going back to Europe,' he said.

Her face lit up. 'Yay!' she cheered. 'I can have my room back!'

'Actually,' Denny said, 'I'm afraid not yet.'

'Why not?' she asked, frustration in her voice. 'I want to come home.'

'I know, honey, but the lawyers and judges have to make the decision on where you'll live.'

'Just *tell* them,' she demanded. 'Just tell them that I'm coming home. I want to live with you and Enzo.'

'It's a little more complicated than that,' Denny hemmed.

'Just *tell* them,' she repeated angrily. 'Just *tell* them!'

'Zoë, someone has accused me of doing something very bad.'

Zoë thought for a moment. 'Was it Grandma and Grandpa?' she asked.

'Not—' Denny started. 'No. No, it wasn't them. But . . . they *know* about it.'

Zoë shook her head without meeting his eyes. I felt badly for them both, but more so for Zoë, who continued to face situations that were loaded with subtleties beyond her experience. Sadly, she went into her bedroom to play with the animals she had left behind.

Later in the evening, the doorbell rang. Denny answered it. Mark Fein was there. 'It's time,' he said. Denny nodded and called for Zoë.

'This was a major victory for us, Dennis,' Mark said. 'It means a lot. You understand that, right?'

Denny nodded, but he was sad. Like Zoë.

'Every other weekend, Friday after school until Sunday after dinner, she's yours,' Mark said. 'And every Wednesday, you pick her up after school and deliver her before eight o'clock, right?'

'Right,' Denny said.

And Mark Fein took Zoë away. She had just returned, and she was going away again. It took me some time to grasp the situation fully, but I understood, ultimately, that the court case earlier in the day was not Denny's criminal trial but a custody hearing.

As it was, we had taken only our first step. Denny had won visitation rights. But Zoë was still in the custody of the Evil Twins. Denny was still on trial for a felony charge he didn't deserve.

Nothing had been solved.

HOW QUICKLY a year passes, like a mouthful of food snatched from the maw of eternity.

And still, almost nothing had changed. Back and forth, round and round, the lawyers danced and played their game, which was merely a game to them.

Denny took Zoë on schedule, every other weekend, every Wednesday afternoon. He took her to places of cultural enrichment. He taught her things. And sometimes, on secret missions, he took us to the go-carts. She was just big enough to fit.

With little instruction, she climbed behind the wheel, tucked her golden hair into a helmet, buckled her harness, and was off. No fear. No hesitation.

'You take her to Spanaway?' the worker boy asked Denny after her very first session. Spanaway was a place south of us where children often practised go-carting on an outdoor course.

'Nope,' Denny replied.

'So, take a session,' the kid said. 'I bet she could kick your ass. She wins, you pay. You win, you don't pay.'

'You're on,' Denny said, grabbing a helmet from the rack.

They started the race, a flying start, with Denny giving Zoë a bit of an edge, taking it easy on her. For several laps he stayed on her back tyres, let her know he was there. Then he tried to pass her.

And she slammed the door on him. He tried again to pass. She slammed the door. It was like she knew where he was at every moment. In a cart with no mirrors. Wearing a helmet that allowed no peripheral vision. She *felt* him. She *knew*.

When he made his moves, she shut him down. Every single time.

Consider that she had a tremendous advantage, being only sixty pounds to his one hundred and fifty. That's a huge weight differential in carting. Still. Consider that he was a thirty-year-old semiprofessional racing driver and she was a seven-year-old neophyte.

She took the chequer and beat her old man. And I was so happy.

How did Denny sustain himself for the duration of this ordeal? Here's how: he had a secret. His daughter was better and quicker and smarter than he was. And while the Evil Twins may have restricted his ability to see her, when he was allowed to see her, he received all the energy he needed to maintain his focus.

'THIS IS NOT a conversation I like to have,' Mark Fein said, leaning back on the iron chair. 'It's one I have too often.'

I slept at my master's feet on the sidewalk of Fifteenth Avenue, barely lifting my head to acknowledge the occasional petting I received from the passers-by.

'I'm ready,' Denny said.

'You owe me a lot of money, Dennis,' Mark clarified. 'I have investigators. Lie-detector specialists. Paralegals. Support staff. I have to pay all those people.'

'Mark,' Denny said. 'Give me thirty days.'

Mark finished his coffee drink and stood. 'OK. Thirty days. Our next meeting is at Café Vita.'

'I'll pay,' Denny said. 'You keep working.'

THE SOLUTION had been put to Denny by Mark Fein: if Denny were to quit his claim to Zoë, the criminal charges would vanish.

Of course, that was speculation on his part. The Evil Twins didn't tell him that outright, but, drawing on his experience, Mark Fein knew. Because the mother of the girl was Trish's cousin, was part of it. And also because their lawyer had made it clear in the initial hearings that they did not wish for Denny to spend any time in jail for his offence. They simply wanted him to be registered as a sex offender. Sex offenders don't get custody of their little girls.

'They're very devious,' Mark noted. 'And they're very good.'

'As good as you?' Denny wondered.

'No one is as good as me. But they're very good.'

At one point Mark even counselled Denny that perhaps the best thing for Zoë would be to stay with her grandparents. Further, Mark suggested, Denny would be much more able to accept instructing and driving jobs, as well as participate in racing series worldwide. He noted that a child needs a stable home environment, which, he said, could be best provided in a single housing location and with consistent schooling. Mark spent quite a long time convincing Denny of these truths.

I wasn't convinced. Of course, I understood that a racing driver must be selfish. Many of us have convinced ourselves that compromise is necessary in order to achieve our goals. But Denny wanted his daughter, and he wanted his racing career, and he refused to give up one for the other.

'It's never too late,' Denny said to Mark. 'Things change.'

Very true. Things change quickly. And, as if to prove it, Denny sold our house. We had no money left. Mark had threatened to cease working for Denny's defence.

He rented a truck from U-Haul and called on his friends, and one weekend that summer, we moved all of our belongings to a one-bedroom apartment on Capitol Hill.

DENNY PAID HIS ACCOUNT with Mark Fein. Shortly afterwards, Mark Fein was appointed to be a circuit judge, something about which I know little, except that it is not refusable. Denny found a new lawyer, Mr Lawrence.

This one asked for a continuance, which is what you can do in the legal world if you need time to read all the paperwork. And while I understood it was necessary, I was still concerned. Mr Lawrence might have been very capable, but he carried himself more like a hound without a hunt, a let-me-know-when-you're-ready look on his sad face.

Shortly after Denny began working with our new representation, we received more bad news. The Evil Twins were suing Denny for child support.

Mr Lawrence posed Denny a question: 'Does the end always justify the means?' And then, he answered it: 'Apparently, for them, it does.'

I have an imaginary friend. I call him King Karma. I know that karma is a force in this universe and that people like the Evil Twins will receive karmic justice for their actions. I know that this justice will come when the universe deems it appropriate, and it may not be in this lifetime but in the next, or the one after that.

At night, before I sleep, I talk to my imaginary friend and I send him to the Evil Twins, and he exacts his justice. Every night, King Karma gives them very bad dreams in which they are chased mercilessly by a pack of wild dogs until they awaken with a start, unable to fall asleep again.

IT WAS AN ESPECIALLY DIFFICULT winter for me. Perhaps it was the stairs in our apartment building. Or maybe I was just tired of being a dog.

Looking back, I can tell you it was my state of mind that attracted me to that car and attracted that car to me.

We walked back from Volunteer Park late in the night, extending our usual quick jaunt because of the special weather conditions. It was not too cold and not too warm; a gentle breeze blew, and snow fell from the sky. I was unsettled by the snow, I remember.

Denny often allowed me to walk home from the park without my leash, and that night I strayed too far from him.

'Yo, Zo!' he called. He whistled for me, his sharp whistle. I looked up. He was on the other side of Aloha. He must have crossed without my noticing.

'Come here, boy!' He slapped his thigh, and I bounded towards him into the street. He suddenly cried out, 'No! Wait!' The ground was covered with a thin layer of snow. The tyres hushed. And then the car hit me.

So stupid, I thought. I am the stupidest dog on the planet, and I have the audacity to dream of becoming a man?

'Settle down, boy.' His hands were on me. Warm.

'He shot out—'

'I totally understand. I saw the whole thing.' Denny lifted me.

'What can I do?'

'I'm several blocks from home. He's too heavy to carry. Will you drive me?'

'Sure, but—'

'What just happened isn't important,' Denny said. 'Let's think about what's going to happen next. Get in your car.'

'Yeah,' the boy said. He was just a boy. A teenager. 'Where should I go?'

'Everything's fine,' Denny said, sliding into the back seat with me on his lap. 'Take a deep breath and let's drive.'

SEPARATE ENTRANCES for cats and dogs. That's what I remember most.

I remember the doctor painfully manipulating my hips. Then he gave me a shot, and I was very much asleep.

When I awoke, I was still groggy but no longer in pain.

Denny carried me to the lobby and laid me down on the brown carpeting, which was somehow comforting in the dim room. The assistant spoke to him and said more things that were confusing to me due to my drugged state. And, of course, 'Eight hundred and twelve dollars.'

Denny handed the assistant a credit card. He kneeled down and stroked my head.

'You'll be all right, Zo,' he said. 'You cracked your pelvis, but it will heal. You'll just take it easy for a while, and then you'll be good as new.'

'Mr Swift?' Denny stood and returned to the counter. 'Your card has been declined. Do you have another card?'

'Here.'

They both watched the blue machine that took the cards, and a few moments later, the assistant shook his head. 'You've exceeded your limit.'

Denny frowned and took out another card. 'Here's my ATM card. It will work.'

They waited again. Same result.

'That's not right,' Denny said. 'I just deposited my pay cheque. Maybe it hasn't cleared yet.'

The doctor appeared from the back. 'A problem?' he asked.

'Look, I have three hundred dollars from when I deposited my cheque. I took some of it out in cash. Here.' Denny fanned bills in front of the doctor. 'I know I have money in that account. Or I can transfer some into it tomorrow morning from my savings.'

'Relax, Denny,' the doctor said. 'I'm sure it's just a misunderstanding.' He said to the assistant, 'Write Mr Swift a receipt for the three hundred, and leave a note for Susan to run the card in the morning for the balance.'

The assistant reached out and took Denny's cash.

'Could I keep twenty of it?' Denny asked hesitantly. 'I need to put some gas in my car.'

The assistant handed Denny a twenty-dollar bill and a receipt, and Denny carried me to the car.

When we got home and Denny placed me on my bed, he sat in the dark room, lit only by the streetlights outside, and he held his head in his hands for a long time.

'I can't,' he said. 'I can't keep going.' I looked up, and he was talking to me. 'They won,' he said. 'You see?'

How could I respond? What could I say?

'I can't even afford to take care of you,' he said to me. 'I can't even afford gas for my car. I've got nothing left, Enzo.'

Oh, how I wished I could speak. But I could only look at him.

'You are my witness,' he said. 'I tried.' And so he returned his head to his hands and he sat. He was alone.

DAYS LATER. A week. Two. I don't know. After Denny's deflation, time meant little to me; he looked sickly, he had no energy, and so neither did I. At a point when my hips still bothered me, we went to visit Mike and Tony.

They didn't live far from us. Their house was small but reflected a different level of income; Tony had stood in the right place at the right time, Denny once told me. Such is life. Your car goes where your eyes go.

We sat in the kitchen, Denny with a cup of tea and a manila folder before him. Tony wasn't present. Mike paced nervously.

'It's the right decision, Den,' Mike said. 'I totally support you.'

Denny didn't move, just stared dully at the folder.

'This is your youth,' Mike said. 'This is your time. Principle is important, but so is your life. So is your reputation.'

Denny nodded.

'Lawrence got what you wanted him to get, right? Same visitation schedule but with two weeks in the summer and one week over Christmas break, and the February school break? And you don't have to pay support any more.'

Denny nodded.

'And they'll settle for misdemeanour harassment and probation; no sex offence on your record.'

Denny nodded.

'Denny,' Mike said seriously, 'you're a smart guy. Let me tell you, this is a smart decision. You know that, right?'

Denny looked confused for a moment, checked his own hands. 'I need a pen,' he said.

Mike reached behind him and picked up a pen. He handed it to Denny. Denny brought the tip of the pen to the paper, and I knew it wasn't Denny who was signing. Denny would never give up his daughter for a few weeks of summer vacation and an exemption from child-support payments!

I was on old dog. Recently hit by a car. And yet I mustered what I could, and the pain medication Denny had given me earlier helped with the rest.

I pushed up onto his lap with my paws. I reached out with my teeth. And the next thing I knew, I was standing at the kitchen door with the papers in my mouth and both Mike and Denny staring at me, completely stunned.

'Enzo!' Denny commanded. 'Drop it!'

I refused.

'Enzo, get over here!' Denny shouted, and he lunged at me.

I slipped away. I still had the papers, even when they cornered me in the living room. Even when they were about to catch me and wrest the papers from my jaws, I had a chance. I was trapped, I know. But Denny taught me that the race isn't over until the chequer flies. I looked round and noticed that one of the windows was open.

Despite all of my pain, I lunged. With all of my might, I dove. And suddenly I was on the porch. I scurried into the back yard.

Mike and Denny flew out the back door, panting, and yet not pursuing. Instead, they seemed somewhat impressed by my feat.

'He dove . . .' Mike said, breathless.

'Out the window,' Denny finished for him.

'If we had a videotape of that, we could win ten thousand dollars on *America's Funniest Home Videos*,' Mike said.

'Give me the papers, Enzo,' Denny said.

I shook them vigorously in my mouth.

Mike laughed at my refusal.

'It's not funny,' Denny admonished.

'It's kind of funny,' Mike replied in his defence.

I dropped the papers before me and pawed at them. I dug at them. I tried to bury them.

Again, Mike laughed. Denny, however, was very angry; he glared at me.

'Enzo,' he said. 'I'm warning you.'

What could I do? What else was there for me to do? One thing only. I lifted my hind leg, and I urinated on the papers.

When they saw what I had done, they couldn't help themselves; they laughed. Denny and Mike. They fell to their knees and laughed until they could laugh no more.

'OK, Enzo,' Denny said. 'It's OK.'

I went to him then, leaving the urine-soaked papers on the grass.

'Call Lawrence,' Mike said to Denny. 'He'll print them again, and you can sign them.'

Denny stood.

'No,' he said, 'I'm with Enzo. I piss on their settlement, too. I don't care how smart it is for me to sign it. I'm never giving up.'

'They're going to be mad,' Mike said with a sigh.

'Screw them,' Denny said. 'But I'm not going to quit. I promised Zoë.'

When we got home, Denny gave me a bath and towelled me off. Afterwards, he turned on the TV in the living room.

'What's your favourite?' he asked, looking at the shelf of videotapes he kept, all the races we loved to watch together. 'Ah, here's one you like.'

He started the tape. Ayrton Senna driving the Grand Prix of Monaco in 1984, slicing through the rain in pursuit of the race leader, Alain Prost. Senna would have won that race, had they not stopped it because of the conditions; when it rained, it never rained on Senna.

We watched the race together without pause, side by side, Denny and me.

10

The summer of my tenth birthday came along, and there was a sense of balance to our lives, though none of completeness. We still spent alternate weekends with Zoë, who had grown so tall recently.

My hips had healed poorly from my accident, but I was determined not to cost Denny any more money. I pushed through the pain, which at times prevented me from sleeping through the nights. I tried my best to keep up with the pace of life; my mobility was severely limited, and I couldn't gallop or canter, but I could still trot fairly well.

Money was still a constant struggle for us, since Denny had to give the Evil Twins a portion of his pay cheque, and Mr Lawrence, the levelheaded lawyer, always demanded that Denny's account be kept up to date. Fortunately, Denny's bosses were generous in allowing him to change his schedule frequently so he could attend his various meetings, and so he could also teach driving on certain days at Pacific Raceways, which was an easy way for Denny to make more money.

Sometimes, on his driving school days, Denny would take me with him to the track, and I did enjoy sitting in the stands and watching him teach.

On a hot day at the end of July, we were teaching, I remember, and while they were all out on the course, I watched as a beautiful red Ferrari F430 drove through the paddock and up to the school headquarters.

A small, older man climbed out, and the owner of the school, Don Kitch, came out to meet him. They embraced and spoke for several minutes. The man strolled to the bleachers to get a view of the track, and Don radioed to his corner workers to chequer the session and bring in the students for lunch break.

As the drivers climbed out of their vehicles and the instructors gave them helpful comments and pointers, Don called for Denny, who approached, as did I, curious about what was going on.

'I need a favour,' Don said to Denny. And suddenly the small man with the Ferrari was with us. 'You remember Luca Pantoni, don't you?' Don asked. 'We came to dinner at your place a couple of years ago.'

'Of course,' Denny said, shaking Luca's hand.

'Your wife cooked a delightful dinner,' Luca said. 'I remember it still. Please accept my sincere and heartfelt condolences.'

When I heard him speak with his Italian accent, I recognised him immediately. The man from Ferrari.

'Thank you,' Denny said quietly.

'Luca would like you to show him our track,' Don said.

'No problem,' Denny said, pulling on his helmet and walking to the passenger side of the exquisite automobile.

'Mr Swift,' Luca called out. 'Perhaps you would do me the favour of allowing me to be the passenger so that I may see more.'

Surprised, Denny looked at Don. 'You want me to drive *this* car?' he asked.

After all, the F430 is priced at nearly a quarter of a million dollars.

'I accept full liability,' Luca said.

Don nodded.

'I'd be pleased to,' Denny said, and he climbed into the cockpit. The two men strapped in and Denny pressed the electronic start button, and the car fired to life.

Ah, what a sound. The whine of the fantastic engine layered over the throaty rumble of the massive exhaust. Denny flicked the paddle shifter, and they cruised slowly through the paddock towards the track entrance.

I followed Don into the school classroom, where the students were clutching thick hunks of a great sandwich, chewing and eating and laughing.

'If you drivers want to see something special,' Don said, 'grab your sandwiches and come out to the bleachers.'

'What's going on?' one of the other instructors asked Don.

'Denny's got an audition,' Don replied cryptically.

We all went out to the bleachers in time to see Denny come around turn 9 and streak down the straight.

'I figure it will take him three laps to learn the sequential shifter,' Don said. Sure enough, Denny was driving easy, but as he came round for the third time, there was a noticeable change to the car. Denny was laying down a hot lap.

A minute later, so fast I wondered if he had taken a short cut, the Ferrari popped out of the cluster of trees at the exit of turn 7, cresting the rise until its suspension was totally extended, and then we heard the throttle open full and watched the car slam through the sweeping turn 8 as if it were a rocket sledge, and then blasting past us at turn 9 no more than two inches from the concrete barrier.

'How close to the edge is he?' someone asked aloud.

Don smiled and shook his head.

'He's way past the edge,' he said. 'I'm sure Luca told him to show him what he could do, and that's what he's doing.' Then he turned to the group and shouted, 'DON'T YOU EVER DRIVE LIKE THAT! DENNY IS A PROFESSIONAL RACING DRIVER, AND THAT'S NOT HIS CAR! HE DOESN'T HAVE TO PAY FOR IT IF HE BREAKS IT!'

Lap after lap, round they went until we were dizzy and exhausted from watching them. And then the car slowed considerably—a cool-down lap—and pulled off into the paddock.

The entire class gathered round as Denny and Luca emerged from the burning-hot vehicle.

'Everyone in the classroom!' Don barked. 'We'll go over corner notes from your morning sessions.'

As they headed off, Don clasped Denny's shoulder firmly. 'How was it?'

'It was incredible,' Denny said.

'Good for you. You deserve it.'

Don went off to teach his class; Luca approached and extended his hand. In it was a business card.

'I would like you to work for me,' Luca said with his thick accent.

I sat next to Denny, who reached down and scratched my ear out of habit.

'I appreciate that,' Denny said. 'But I don't think I'd make a very good car salesman.'

'Neither do I,' Luca said.

'But you're with Ferrari.'

'Yes. I work in Maranello, at Ferrari headquarters. We have a wonderful track there.'

'I see,' Denny said. 'So you'd like me to work . . . where?'

'At the track. There is some need, as often our clients would like track instruction in their new cars.'

'Instructing?'

'There is some need. But mostly, you would be testing the vehicles.'

Denny's eyes got very large, and he sucked in a huge breath of air, as did I.

'In Italy,' Denny said.

'Yes. You would be provided with an apartment for you and your daughter. And, of course, a company car—a Fiat—as part of your compensation package.'

Denny turned round in a circle, looked down at me, laughed.

'Why me?' Denny asked. 'There are a thousand guys who can drive this car.'

'Don Kitch tells me you are an exceptional driver in the wet weather.'

'I am. But that can't be the reason.'

'No,' Luca said. 'You are correct.' He stared at Denny, his clear blue eyes smiling. 'But I would prefer to tell you more about those reasons when you join me in Maranello, and I can invite you to my house for dinner.'

Denny nodded and chewed his lip.

'I appreciate your generous offer,' he said at last. 'But I'm afraid certain things prevent me from leaving this country—or even this state—at the moment. So I have to decline.'

'I know about your troubles,' Luca said. 'That's why I am here.'

Denny looked up, surprised.

'I will keep the position available for you until your situation here is resolved, and you can make your decision free from the burden of circumstance. My telephone is on my card.'

Luca smiled and shook Denny's hand again. He slipped into the Ferrari.

'I wish you would tell me why,' Denny said.

Luca held up his finger. 'Dinner, at my home. You will understand.' He drove away.

Denny shook his head in bewilderment as Don appeared.

'Well?' he asked.

'I don't understand,' Denny said.

'He's taken an interest in your career since he first met you,' Don said. 'Whenever we talk, he asks how you're doing.'

'Why does he care so much?' Denny asked.

'He wants to tell you himself. All I can say is that he respects how you're fighting for your daughter.'

Denny thought for a moment. 'But what if I don't win?' he asked.

'There is no dishonour in losing the race,' Don said. 'There is only dishonour in not racing because you are afraid to lose.' He paused. 'Now get to your student, Grasshopper, and get the hell out on the track! That's where you belong!'

'YOU NEED TO GO OUT? Let's go out.'

He was holding my leash. He lifted me to my unsteady feet and clipped on the leash. We went out into the darkness; I had fallen asleep early, but it was time for me to urinate.

I had been experiencing a decline in my health. After even mild activity, I often slept deeply and awoke having soiled my bedding.

I was also having great difficulty with my hips. Whenever I slept or lay in one spot for any amount of time, my hind joints locked in place, and I found it difficult to get them moving again, or even to rise to a standing position.

The net result of my health issues was that Denny could no longer leave me alone for an entire workday. He began visiting at lunch time so he could take me out to relieve myself.

That evening—it was around ten, I knew, because *The Amazing Race* had just finished—Denny took me out. The night was bracing, and I enjoyed the feeling of wakefulness as I breathed in through my nostrils. The energy.

We walked down Pine towards the city, and then she was there.

Both of us stopped. Two young women at an outdoor table at Bauhaus Books and Coffee, and one of them was Annika.

How awful for us to have to see this horrid girl. I wanted to leap at her and take her nose in my teeth and twist! How I despised she who would rend this family because of her own agenda.

I thought we would cross the street to avoid a confrontation, but instead, we headed straight for her. I didn't understand. Perhaps Denny hadn't seen her. Perhaps he didn't know?

But I knew, and so I resisted. I set my weight; I ducked my head.

'Come on, boy,' Denny ordered me. He tugged at my leash. I refused. He kneeled and held my muzzle and looked me in the eyes.

'I see her, too,' he said. 'Let's handle this with dignity.' He released my muzzle. 'This can work for us, Zo. I want you to go up to her and love her more than you've ever loved anyone before.'

I didn't understand his strategy, but I acquiesced. After all, he had the leash.

As we drew abreast of her table, Denny stopped and looked surprised.

'Oh, hey!' he said brightly.

Annika looked up, feigning shock, clearly having seen us but hoping there would be no interaction. 'Denny. Good to see you!'

I played my part. I greeted her enthusiastically; I pushed my nose into her leg; I sat and looked at her with great anticipation.

'Enzo!' she said.

'Hey,' Denny said, 'can we talk for a minute?'

Annika's friend started to get up. 'I'll get more coffee,' she said.

'No.' Denny stopped her with a wave of his hand. 'Please stay.'

She hesitated.

'It's important that you witness that there is no impropriety here,' Denny explained. The girl looked to Annika, who nodded her agreement.

He pulled up a chair from the next table, which was empty. He sat down next to her. 'I totally understand what's going on,' he said. 'I may have given you signals. That's totally my fault. But just because the light is green doesn't mean you shouldn't look both ways before stepping into the street.'

Annika screwed up her face in puzzlement and looked to her friend.

'A metaphor,' her friend said.

A metaphor, she said! Fantastic! This one knows how to decode the English language!

'I should have handled the situation entirely differently,' Denny said. 'I haven't had the chance to say this to you, because we've been kept apart, but I made all the mistakes. It's all my fault; you did nothing wrong. You're an attractive woman, and I understand that my noting that attractiveness— even to myself—may have signalled to you that I was available. But, you know, I wasn't available. I was married to Eve. And you were far too young.'

Annika dipped her head at the mention of Eve.

'But Annika, while I understand how angry you must be, I wonder if you understand what's going on, what the fallout is. They won't let me have my daughter. Do you realise that?'

Annika looked up at him and shrugged.

'They want me to be registered as a sex offender, and that will mean that I will never be able to see my daughter again without supervision. Did they tell you about that?'

'They said . . .' she said softly, but didn't finish.

'It never could have worked between you and me. There are a million reasons. My daughter, my age, your age, Eve. I know you will find the right partner, and you will be very happy for the rest of your life.'

She looked deeply into her latte.

'Zoë's my daughter,' he said. 'I love her like your father loves you. Please, Annika, don't take her away from me.'

Annika didn't look up from her coffee, but I glanced at her friend. Tears hung on her lower lids.

We paused a moment, and then we turned and walked away briskly, and Denny's gait seemed lighter than it had been for years.

'I think she heard me,' he said.

I barked twice.

He looked at me and laughed. 'Faster?' he asked.

I barked twice again.

'Faster, then,' he said. 'Let's go!' And we trotted the rest of the way home.

THE COUPLE who stood in the doorway were entirely foreign to me. They wore threadbare clothing. They smelled of mothballs and coffee.

Denny embraced the woman and kissed her cheek. He picked up her bag with one hand and shook the man's hand with the other. They shuffled into the apartment, and Denny took their coats.

'Your room is in here,' he said to them, carrying their bags into the bedroom. 'I'll sleep on the sofa.'

Neither of them said a word. The man was bald except for a crescent of stringy black hair. The woman had white hair that was quite thin. She wore sunglasses, even in the apartment, and she often stood completely still and waited until the man was next to her before she moved.

She whispered into the man's ear.

'Your mother would like to use the bathroom,' the man said.

'I'll show her,' Denny said. He stood next to the woman and held out his arm.

'*I'll* show her,' the man said. The woman took the man's arm, and he led her towards the hall where the bathroom was.

'The light switch is hidden behind the hand towel,' Denny said.

'She doesn't need a light switch,' the man said.

As they went into the bathroom, Denny turned away and rubbed his face with the palms of his hands. 'Good to see you,' he said into his hands. 'It's been so long.'

HAD I KNOWN I was meeting Denny's parents, I might have acted more receptive to these strangers. They stayed with us for three days, and they hardly left the apartment. For the afternoon on one of those days, Denny retrieved Zoë, who was so pretty with her hair in ribbons and a nice dress, and who had obviously been coached by Denny, as she willingly sat for quite a long time on the couch and allowed Denny's mother to explore the terrain of her face with her hands.

Our meals were prepared by Denny and were simple in nature: grilled steaks, steamed string beans, boiled potatoes. They were eaten in silence. The fact that three people could occupy such a small apartment and speak so few words was quite strange to me.

Denny's father lost some of his gruff edge while he was with us, and he even smiled at Denny a few times. Once, in the silence of the apartment, while I sat in my corner watching the Space Needle elevators, he came and stood behind me.

'What do you see, boy?' he asked quietly, and he touched the crown of my head, and his fingers scratched at my ears just the way Denny does. How the touch of a son is so like the touch of his father.

I looked back at him.

'You take good care of him,' he said.

I couldn't tell if he was talking to me or to Denny. The human language, as precise as it is with its thousands of words, can still be so wonderfully vague.

On the last night of their visit, Denny's father handed Denny an envelope.

'Open it,' he said.

Denny did as instructed and looked at the contents.

'Where did this come from?' he asked.

'It came from us,' his father replied.

'You don't have any money.'

'We have a house. We have a farm.'

'You can't sell your house!' Denny exclaimed.

'We didn't,' his father said. 'They call it a reverse mortgage. The bank will get our house when we die, but we thought you needed the money now more than you would later, so.'

'Dad . . .' Denny started, but his eyes filled with tears, and he could only shake his head.

His father reached for him and embraced him, held him close and stroked his hair.

'We never did right by you,' his father said. 'This makes it right.'

They left the next morning. Like the last strong autumn wind that rattles the trees until the remaining leaves fall, brief but powerful was their visit, signalling that the season had changed, and soon, life would begin again.

A DRIVER must have faith. In his talent, his judgment, the judgment of those around him, physics.

The driver must accept his fate. He must accept the fact that mistakes have been made. A confluence of circumstance has landed him in this position. A driver must accept it all and be willing to pay the price for it. He must go off-track.

At this moment, a driver feels a tremendous crisis. He *must* get back on the track. Oh! The folly!

A winner will accept his fate. He will continue with his wheels in the dirt. He will do his best to maintain his line and gradually get himself back on the track when it is safe to do so. But he is still racing. He is still alive.

The race is long. It is better to drive within oneself and finish the race behind the others than it is to drive too hard and crash.

11

So much information came out in the following days, thanks to Mike, who plagued Denny with questions until he answered. About his mother's blindness, which came on when Denny was a boy. About how his father told Denny that if he didn't stay to help with the farm and his mother, he shouldn't bother keeping in touch at all. About how Denny called every Christmas for years until his mother finally answered the phone and listened without speaking. For years, until she finally asked how he was doing and if he was happy.

I learned that his parents had not paid for the testing programme in France, as Denny had claimed; he paid for that with a home equity loan. I learned that his parents had not contributed to the sponsorship of the touring car season, as Denny had said; he paid for that with a second mortgage, which Eve had encouraged.

Always pushing the extremes. Finding himself broke. And finding himself on the telephone with his blind mother, asking her for some kind of help so that he could keep his daughter, and her response that she would give him everything if only she could meet her grandchild. Her hands on Zoë's hopeful face, her tears on Zoë's dress.

'Such a sad story,' Mike said, pouring himself another shot of tequila.

'Actually,' Denny said, 'I believe it has a happy ending.'

'ALL RISE,' the bailiff called out, such old-fashioned formality in such a contemporary setting. The new Seattle courthouse: glass walls and metal beams jutting out at all angles, concrete floors and stairs with rubber treads.

'The Honourable Judge Van Tighem.'

An elderly man, clad in a black robe, strode into the room. He was short and white, and he had a wave of grey hair swept to one side of his head.

'Sit,' he commanded. 'Let us begin.'

THUS, THE TRIAL COMMENCED. At least in my mind. I won't give you all the details, because I don't know them. I wasn't there, because I am a dog, and dogs are not allowed in court. The only facts I know are the ones I gathered from Denny's retelling of events.

The first day of the trial was devoted to pre-trial motions, the second to jury selection. Denny and Mike didn't talk much about those events, so I assume everything went as expected. Both days, Tony and Mike arrived at our apartment early in the morning; Mike escorted Denny to court while Tony stayed behind to look after me.

On the third morning, there was a definite change in the air when Tony and Mike arrived. It was the day the case was to begin in earnest, and we were all filled with trepidation. Denny's future was at stake; it was no laughing matter.

Apparently, I later learned, Mr Lawrence delivered an impassioned opening statement. He agreed with the prosecution's assertion that sexual molestation is about power, but he pointed out that baseless allegation is an equally destructive weapon. And he pledged to prove Denny innocent of the charges against him.

The prosecution led off their case with a parade of witnesses, all of whom had stayed with us that week in the Methow Valley, each of them testifying to Denny's inappropriate flirtatious manner and his predator-like stalking of Annika. Yes, they agreed, she was playing the game with him, but she was a child. Denny was an intelligent, strong, good-looking man, the witnesses said, and he should have known better.

Finally, the alleged victim herself was called to take the stand. Annika admitted that she was a willing—even eager—accomplice, but insisted that, as a child, she had no idea what she was getting herself into. Visibly upset, she spoke about how the entire episode had tormented her ever since.

By the time Annika's direct examination was over, not a person in the courtroom, save Denny himself, was absolutely certain that he had not taken liberties with her that week. And even Denny's self-confidence was shaken.

EARLY THAT AFTERNOON—it was Wednesday—the clouds were heavy, but the sky refused to rain. Tony and I walked down to Bauhaus so he could get his coffee. We sat outside and stared at the traffic on Pine Street until my mind shut down and I lost track of time.

'Enzo—'

I raised my head. Tony pocketed his cellphone. 'That was Mike. The prosecutor asked for a special recess. Something's going on.' He paused, waiting for my response. I said nothing. 'What should we do?' he asked.

I barked twice. We should go.

Tony closed up his computer and got his bag together. He was moving very quickly, and I had a hard time keeping up. We rushed south until we reached the plaza before the courthouse on Third Avenue.

Mike and Denny were not there. Only a small cluster of people in one corner of the plaza, speaking urgently, gesturing with agitation. We started towards them. But at that moment, the rain began to fall. The group immediately disbanded, and I saw Annika among them. Her face was drawn and pale; she was crying. When she saw me, she winced, turned away quickly, and vanished into the building.

Why was she so upset? I didn't know, but it made me very nervous. What might she have said to further incriminate Denny and destroy his life?

Tony and I took refuge under an awning. 'It's done now,' Tony said. 'We can't change what's already been decided.'

Can't we? I wondered. Is there nothing we can do? My legs were so heavy I could no longer stand; I lay on the wet concrete, and I fell into an unsteady sleep filled with very strange dreams.

'Ladies and gentlemen of the jury,' Mr Lawrence said, standing before the jury box. 'It is important to note that there is no evidence whatsoever of violation. The truth of what really happened that night is known by two people alone. Two people, and a dog.'

'A dog?' the judge asked incredulously.

'Yes, Judge Van Tighem,' Mr Lawrence said, stepping forth boldly. 'I shall call to the stand Enzo!'

'I object!' the prosecutor barked.

'Sustained,' the judge said. 'For the time being.'

He produced a large volume from beneath his desk and paged through it at length, reading many passages.

'Does this dog speak?' the judge asked Mr Lawrence, his head still buried in the book.

'With the help of a voice synthesiser,' Mr Lawrence said, 'yes, the dog speaks.'

'I object!' the prosecutor piped in.

'Not yet,' the judge said. 'Tell me about this device, Mr Lawrence.'

'We've borrowed a special voice synthesiser that was developed for Stephen Hawking. With this device, the dog can speak,' Mr Lawrence said.

The judge clapped shut his massive tome. 'Objection overruled. Let's have him, then, this dog!'

The room was filled with hundreds of people, and I was sitting on the witness stand, strapped to a voice simulator; the judge swore me in.

'Do you swear to tell the truth, the whole truth, and nothing but the truth, so help you God?'

'I do,' I said in my scratchy, metallic voice, which was not at all as I had imagined.

'Mr Lawrence,' the judge said, astonished. 'Your witness.'

'Enzo,' Mr Lawrence said, 'you were present for the alleged molestation?'

'I was,' I said.

'Tell us in your own words what you witnessed in Mr Swift's bedroom that night.'

'Your Honour,'—I raised my voice—'ladies and gentlemen of the jury, I assure you that my master, Dennis Swift, in no way acted inappropriately *around this young lady, Annika. It was clear to me that she loved him, and she offered herself to him. He declined her offer. After driving us over a harrowing mountain pass, after exhausting himself, Denny is guilty only of falling asleep. Annika, this girl, this woman, as unaware of the ramifications of her actions as she might have been, assaulted my Denny.'*

A murmur rose from the gallery. 'Miss Annika, is this true?' the judge demanded.

'It is true,' Annika replied.

'Do you disavow these accusations?' Van Tighem asked.

'I do,' she cried. 'I'm so sorry for the pain I've put you all through.'

'This is a stunning revelation!' Van Tighem announced. 'Enzo the dog has spoken! The truth is known. This case is dismissed. Mr Swift is free to go, and he is awarded custody of his daughter.'

I leaped from the witness stand and embraced Denny and Zoë. At last, we were a family, together again.

'IT'S OVER.'

My master's voice. I opened my eyes. Denny was flanked by Mike and Mr Lawrence, who held a very large umbrella. How much time had passed, I didn't know. But Tony and I were both very wet from the rain.

'That recess was the longest forty-five minutes of my life,' Denny said.

I waited for him to go on.

'She recanted,' he said. 'They dropped the charges, and I'm free.'

Denny might have been able to hold it off if we had been alone, but Mike wrapped him in a hug, and Denny cried so hard.

'Thank you, Mr Lawrence,' Tony said, shaking Mr Lawrence's hand. 'You did a fantastic job.'

Mr Lawrence smiled, perhaps for the first time in his life.

'They had no physical evidence,' he said. 'All they had was Annika's testimony. I could tell, on direct, she was wavering—there was something more she wanted to say—so I went after her on cross, and she broke down. She said that up until now she'd been telling people what she had *hoped* might have happened. Today, she admitted that nothing had happened at all. Without her testimony, it would have been foolish for the prosecutor to move forward with the case.'

I glanced round the plaza and spotted her leaving the courthouse with her family. She seemed somehow fragile.

She gave a quick wave meant for Denny, but I was the only one who saw, because I was the only one looking. So I barked to let her know.

'You've got a good master, there,' Tony said to me, his attention still on our immediate circle.

He was right. I have the best master.

I watched Denny as he held on to Mike, feeling the relief, knowing that another path might have been easier for him to travel but that it couldn't possibly have offered a more satisfying conclusion.

THE VERY NEXT DAY, Mr Lawrence informed Denny that the Evil Twins had dropped their custody suit. Zoë was his. The Twins had requested forty-eight hours to assemble her belongings and spend a little more time with her before delivering her.

Denny could have been mean. They took years of his life; they took all of his money; they tried to destroy him. But Denny is a gentleman. He granted them their request.

He was baking cookies last night in anticipation of Zoë's return when the phone rang. Since his hands were covered with sticky oatmeal gloop, he tapped the speaker button on the kitchen phone.

'You're on the air!' he said brightly. 'Thanks for calling. What's on your mind?'

There was a long pause filled with static. 'I'm calling for Denny Swift.'

'This is Denny,' Denny called from his cookie bowl.

'This is Luca Pantoni, returning your call. From Maranello. Am I catching you at a bad time?'

Denny's eyebrows shot up; he smiled at me.

'Luca! *Grazie*, for returning my call. The reason I called . . . The issues that were keeping me in the States have been resolved. I was wondering if the position you offered me earlier was still available?'

'Of course.'

'My daughter and I—and my dog, Enzo—would very much like to join you for dinner in Maranello, then.'

'Your dog is named Enzo? How propitious!'

'He is a racing driver at heart,' Denny said, and he smiled at me. I love Denny so much.

'I look forward to meeting your daughter and to seeing Enzo again,' Luca said. 'I will have my assistant make the arrangements. It will be necessary to retain your services under contract. I hope you understand. The nature of our business, as well as the expense of developing a test driver—'

'I understand,' Denny replied.

'You do not object to a three-year commitment?' Luca asked. 'Your daughter will not mind living here? There is an American school, if she would prefer it to our Italian schools.'

'She told me she wants to try the Italian school,' Denny said. 'We'll have to see how it goes. Either way, she knows it will be a great adventure, and she's very excited.'

'*Bene!* My assistant will be in touch with you, Denny. We will expect to see you in a few weeks.'

'Yes, Luca, thank you. Now will you tell me why?' Denny asked.

Another long pause. 'Many years ago, when my wife passed away, I would have died from grief, Denny, if I had not received help, if I had not found a mentor who offered me his hand. Do you understand? My predecessor at this company offered me a job driving cars for him. He saved my life, not merely for me, but for my children as well. I remember him. What he offered me is not for me to keep, but for me to give to another. That is why I feel very fortunate that I am able to offer my hand to you.'

Denny stared at the phone as if he could see Luca in it. 'Thank you, Luca, for telling me why you have offered it.'

'My friend,' Luca said, 'the pleasure is entirely mine. Welcome to Ferrari. I assure you, you will not want to leave.' They said their goodbyes, and Denny pressed the button with his pinkie. He crouched down and held out his sticky hands for me, and I obligingly licked them clean.

'Sometimes, I believe,' he said to me. 'Sometimes I really do believe.'

MY LIFE seems like it has been so long and so short at the same time. People speak of a will to live. They rarely speak of a will to die. Because people are afraid of death. Death is dark and unknown and frightening. But not for me. It is not the end.

I can hear Denny in the kitchen. I can smell what he's doing; he's cooking breakfast, something he used to do all the time when we were a family, when Eve was with us and Zoë. For a long time they have been gone, and Denny has eaten cereal.

With every bit of strength, I wrench myself to a standing position. Though my hips are frozen and my legs burn with pain, I hobble to the door of the bedroom.

'Yo, Zo!' he calls to me when he sees me. 'How are you feeling?'

'Like crap,' I reply. But, of course, he doesn't hear me.

'I made you pancakes,' he says cheerfully. He gives me a piece of pancake. I take it in my mouth, but I can't chew it; I can't taste it.

I don't want Denny to worry about me. The worst thing I could possibly do to Denny is make him hurt me. The concept of euthanasia has some merit, yes, but it is too fraught with emotion.

When I return to this world, I will be a man. I will walk among you. I will shake hands with other men, grasping firmly with my opposable thumbs. And I will teach people all that I know. And I will be a good citizen, a good partner in the endeavour of life that we all share.

I go to Denny, and I push my muzzle into his thigh.

'There's my Enzo,' he says. My legs buckle and I fall. 'Zo?'

He is alarmed. He crouches over me. 'Are you OK?'

In the past few days, everything has changed. He is going to be reunited with Zoë. I would like to see that moment. They are going to Italy together. To Maranello. Denny will be a wonderful driver for Ferrari. They will see his talent, and they will pluck him from the ranks of test drivers and give him a tryout for the Formula One team. Scuderia Ferrari. They will choose him to replace the irreplaceable Schumi.

'Try me,' he will say, and they will try him.

They will see his talent and make him a driver, and soon, he will be a Formula One champion just like Ayrton Senna.

I would like to see that. But I don't believe I will get the chance to see that moment. My soul has learned what it came to learn, and all the other things are just things. We can't have everything we want. Sometimes, we simply have to believe.

'You're OK,' he says. He cradles my head in his lap. I see him.

I know this much about racing in the rain. It is about the mind! It is about owning one's own body. About believing that the track is an extension of the car, and the rain is an extension of the track. It is about believing that you are not you; you are everything. And everything is you.

Racers are often called selfish and egotistical. To be a champion, you must have no ego at all. You must give yourself over to the race. Do not mistake confidence and self-awareness for egotism.

I saw a documentary once. It was about dogs in Mongolia. It said that the next incarnation for a dog—a dog who is ready to leave his dogness behind—is as a man.

I am ready.

And yet . . .

Denny is so very sad; he will miss me so much. I would rather stay with him and Zoë.

'You've always been with me,' Denny says to me. 'You've always been my Enzo.'

Yes. I have. He's correct.

'It's OK,' he says to me. 'If you need to go now, you can go.'

I saw a documentary about dogs in Mongolia. When a dog dies, his soul is released to run until he is ready to be reborn.

'It's OK.'

When I am reborn as a man, I will find Denny. I will find Zoë. I will walk up to them and shake their hands and tell them that Enzo says hello.

'You can go.'

Before me I see my world: there are no fences. No buildings. No people. There is only me and the grass and the sky and the earth. Only me.

'I love you, boy.'

I take a few steps into the field, and it feels so good, so nice to be in the cool air, to smell the smells all around me. To feel the sun on my coat. I feel like I am here.

I gather my strength, and I pick up speed. I run.

'It's OK, Enzo.'

I don't look back, but I know he's there. I bark twice because I want him to hear; I want him to know.

'You can go,' he calls to me.

Faster, the wind presses against my face as I run, faster. I feel my heart beating wildly, and I bark twice to tell him, to tell everyone in the world, to say faster! What I want now is what I've always wanted.

One more lap, Denny! One more lap! Faster!

Imola, Italy

After it is all over, after the last race has been won, after the season's champion has been crowned, he sits alone in the infield of the Tamburello corner, on the grass that is soggy from many days of rain. A bright figure in his Ferrari-red Nomex racing suit, the champion sits alone. To have become a Formula One champion out of nowhere. At his age. It is nothing less than a fairy tale.

An electric golf cart stops on the tarmac near him, driven by a young woman with long, golden hair. With her in the cart are two other figures, one large and one small.

The young woman climbs out and walks towards the champion. 'Dad?' she calls. He looks to her, though he had hoped to be alone just a little longer. 'They're big fans,' she says. 'I think you'd really like to meet them.'

He nods at her, because she is always right. She beckons the two people in the cart. A man steps out, hunched beneath a rain poncho. Then a child.

'Dení!' the man calls. 'Dení, we are your biggest fans. Your daughter brought us to find you. She said you would not mind.'

'She knows me,' the champion says warmly.

'My son, he worships you. He talks about you always.'

The champion looks at the boy, who is small with sharp features and icy-blue eyes and light curly hair. '*Quanti anni hai?*' he asks.

'*Cinque,*' the boy replies.

'Do you race?'

'He races the carts,' the father says. 'He is very good. The first time he sat in a cart, he knew how to drive it. It's very expensive for me, but he is so good, such a talent, that we do it.'

'*Bene, che bello*,' the champion says.

'Will you sign our programme?' the father asks. 'We watched the race from the field over there. The grandstand is very expensive. We drove from Napoli.'

'*Certo*,' the champion says to the father. He takes the programme and the pen. '*Come ti chiami?*' he asks the boy.

'Enzo,' the boy says.

The champion looks up, startled. 'Enzo?' he asks.

'*Si*,' the boy says. '*Mi chiamo Enzo. Anch'io voglio diventare un campione.*'

Stunned, the champion stares at the boy.

'He says he wants to be a champion,' the father translates, misinterpreting the pause. 'Like you.'

'*Ottima idea,*' the champion says, and shakes his head. '*Mi scusi,*' he says. 'Your son reminds me of a good friend of mine.'

He catches his daughter's eye; then he signs the boy's programme and hands it to the father, who reads it.

'My telephone number in Maranello,' the champion says. 'When you think your son is ready, call me.'

'*Grazie! Grazie mille!*' the man says. 'He talks about you always. He says you are better, even, than Senna!'

The champion rises, his racing suit still wet from the rain. He pats the boy's head and ruffles his hair. The boy looks up at him.

'He's a racing driver at heart,' the champion says.

'*Grazie*,' the father says. 'He studies your races on videotapes.'

'*La macchina va dove vanno gli occhi*,' the boy says.

The champion laughs, then looks to the sky.

'*Si*,' he says. 'The car goes where the eyes go. It is true, my young friend. It is very, very true.'

garth **stein**

The story of Enzo began when Garth Stein, who was a documentary filmmaker before turning to novel writing, was asked to consult on a film called *State of Dogs*, which delved into the Mongolian belief that dogs come back in their next lives as men. 'The idea really stuck with me,' Stein says, in an interview posted on his publisher's website. 'I tucked it away thinking I might some day do something with it.

'Then, in 2004, I saw Billy Collins speak at Seattle Arts and Lectures. He's a great poet and a terrific reader. He read a poem, "The Revenant", which is told from the point of view of a recently euthanised dog as he addresses his former master from heaven. I loved this poem. When Billy Collins finished reading, I knew I had to write a story from the point of view of a dog. And my dog would know the truth: that in his next incarnation, he would return to earth as a man.

'So I had the character and the goal, but I still needed the framework. A close friend of mine, who is a semi-professional race car driver, but who supplements his racing by working at an upscale automotive repair shop, was going through some personal difficulties. His plight wasn't Denny's, but it gave me some ideas about what happens to families when one member suddenly passes away. I developed a story that would really put my main character, Denny, through his paces.'

Mingling the mind of a dog with the intricacies of motor racing was the next twist in developing the framework of the plot, which grew from Stein's own detour into that world. He had moved from New York to Seattle in 2001, where he had taken up high-performance driving, eventually obtaining his racing license from the Sports Car Club of America. 'I had a great time and really enjoyed myself,' says Stein, who is now semi-retired from the sport. 'My experiences on the track, as well as friendships with other drivers, helped me form the character of Denny and add texture to the story.'

The author still had one more hurdle to overcome, however. Stein's agent was not exactly thrilled at the idea of a book narrated by a dog, reincarnated or not. So Stein found a new agent, one who was thrilled by the book and was sure he could sell it to a publisher. That new agent was right. Starbucks featured the book in their US stores as their summer read, Stein did a national publicity tour, and *The Art of Racing in the*

Rain—a book narrated by a dog—became a best-selling phenomenon. Stein feels that working on documentaries was good training for being a novelist. 'In documentary films, you're a storyteller using found objects. You still have to have a story arc and all the elements that make a good story. It really helped me mature as a storyteller.'

The Art of Racing in the Rain raises some difficult questions about life in general. The mantra that runs throughout the book is that 'the car goes where the eyes go', meaning that individuals create their own destiny. 'I believe that the energy each of us puts out to the world is returned to us,' Stein says. 'So are human beings ever really in control? On the deepest level, yes, we are. This is where the metaphor of race car driving comes in. We have no one to blame but ourselves for our successes and failures.'

And misfortune? 'To say that our misfortune is our own fault may seem harsh, but have you ever noticed that when you have a bad day, one thing happens after another in a string of bad luck? That's because we are out of sync energetically with the universe. Can we pick ourselves up from tragedy and ascend to the greatest heights imaginable? I like to think so, yes. That's what makes life so wonderful!'

Encouraging the best

In 1929, when Enzo Ferrari founded Scuderia Ferrari in Maranello, near Modena in Italy, his intention was to sponsor young racing drivers and invent racing cars. Eighty-one years later, when the University of Modena held a ceremony to dedicate their Faculty of Engineering to Enzo Ferrari, Luca de Montezemolo, the current chairman, said: 'I learned a lot from Enzo Ferrari. I learned to give young people responsibility, to never give in, to always look ahead.'

This spirit is reflected in *The Art of Racing in the Rain* when Denny, the young amateur racing-car driver, receives encouragement from a Ferrari VIP when he's down on his luck. Pictured is the familiar image of a red Ferrari F430, a car featured in the novel. Also recognisably 'Ferrari' is the prancing horse emblem that brands all their cars. It was originally painted on the fuselage of a fighter plane flown by Francesco Baracca, a WW1 Italian flying ace and friend of Enzo Ferrari. On her son's death, Baracca's mother entrusted the emblem to Enzo, saying it would bring him luck. The horse was black and has remained so. Ferrari added the canary yellow background 'because it is the colour of Modena'.

COPYRIGHT AND ACKNOWLEDGMENTS

THE SCARECROW: Copyright © 2009 by Hieronymus, Inc.
Published at £18.99 by Orion Books, an imprint of The Orion Publishing Group Ltd.
Condensed version © The Reader's Digest Association, Inc., 2010.

RAINWATER: Copyright © 2009 by Sandra Brown Management Ltd.
Published at $23.99 by Simon & Schuster, Inc.
Condensed version © The Reader's Digest Association, Inc., 2010.

WHERE THE SHADOWS LIE: Copyright © Michael Ridpath, 2010.
Published at £12.99 by Corvus, an imprint of Grove Atlantic Ltd.
Condensed version © The Reader's Digest Association, Inc., 2010.

THE ART OF RACING IN THE RAIN: Copyright © 2008 by Bright White Light, LLC.
Published at $23.95 by Harper, an imprint of HarperCollins Publishers.
Condensed version © The Reader's Digest Association, Inc., 2010.

The right to be identified as authors has been asserted by the following in accordance with
sections 77 and 78 of the Copyright, Designs and Patents Act, 1988: Michael Connelly,
Sandra Brown, Michael Ridpath, Garth Stein.

Spine: illustration: Narrinder Singh@velvet tamarind. Front cover (from left) and page 4 (from
top): Sally Mundy/Millennium Images, UK; Chip Simens/Gallery Stock; Nicolas Cheetham;
background: Anathony Redpath/Corbis; dog: Lucidio Studio Inc./Corbis. Page 5 (top)
AFP/Getty Images. 6–8: Images: Shutterstock; illustration: Kate Finnie; 168 © Wendy Werris;
169 © AGENCIA EFE/Rex Features. 170–2 image: Shutterstock; illustration: Kate Finnie;
301 © Andrew Eccles; 301 © Walker Evans/Getty Images. 302–4 image of Iceland:
Enote/Fotolia; Icelandic script: courtesy of Árni Magnússon Institute for Icelandic Studies;
illustration: James Kessell; 475 © Chris George. 476-8 image: courtesy of Garth Stein;
illustration: Narrinder Singh@velvet tamarind; 574 © Frank Huster Photo; 575 © Bruce
Benedict/Transtock/Corbis.

Printed and bound by GGP Media GmbH, Pössneck, Germany

020-268 UP0000-1